Elu'aḫlū machini.
1918.

Frederick Farley.

THE WORLD'S ILLUSION

BY

JACOB WASSERMANN

AUTHORIZED TRANSLATION BY

LUDWIG LEWISOHN

LONDON

GEORGE ALLEN & UNWIN LTD

MUSEUM STREET

The title of this novel in the original is "Christian Wahnschaffe."
The title adopted for this translation has been approved by the author.

Two volumes in one
Published 1929

THE FIRST VOLUME:
EVA

CONTENTS OF THE FIRST VOLUME

THE WORLD'S ILLUSION

CRAMMON, THE STAINLESS KNIGHT

I

From the days of his earliest manhood, Crammon, a pilgrim upon the paths of pleasantness and delight, had been a constant wayfarer from capital to capital and from country-seat to country-seat. He came of an Austrian family whose landed estates lay in Moravia, and his full name was Bernard Gervasius Crammon von Weissenfels.

In Vienna he owned a small but beautifully furnished house. Two old, unmarried ladies were its guardians—the Misses Aglaia and Constantine. They were his distant kinswomen, but he was devoted to them as to sisters of his blood, and they returned his affection with an equal tenderness.

On an afternoon in May the two sat by an open window and gazed longingly down into the street. He had announced the date of his arrival by letter, but four days had passed and they were still waiting in vain. Whenever a carriage turned the corner, both ladies started and looked in the same direction.

When twilight came they closed the window and sighed. Constantine took Aglaia's arm, and together they went through the charming rooms, made gleamingly ready for their master. All the beautiful things in the house reminded them of him, just as every one of them was endeared to him because it united him to some experience or memory.

Here was the chiselled fifteenth century goblet which the Marquis d'Autichamps had given him, yonder the agate bowl bequeathed him by the Countess Ortenburg. There were the coloured etchings, part of the legacy of a Duchess of Gainsborough, the precious desk-set which he had received from the old Baron Regamey, the Tanagra figurines which Felix Imhof had brought him from Greece. There, above all, was his own portrait, which the English artist Lavery had painted on an order from Sir Charles MacNamara.

They knew these things and esteemed them at their true worth. They stopped before his picture, as they so often delighted to do. The well rounded face wore a stern, an almost sombre expression. But that expression seemed deceptive, for a tell-tale gleam of worldly delight, of irony and roguishness, played about the clean-shaven lips.

When night fell the two ladies received a telegram informing them that Crammon had been forced to put off his return home for a month. They lit no lights after that, and went sadly to bed.

II

Once it had happened that Crammon was dining with a few friends at Baden-Baden. He had just returned from Scotland where he had visited the famous trout streams of MacPherson, and had left the train at the end of a long journey. He felt very tired, and after the meal lay down on a sofa and fell asleep.

His friends chatted for a while, until his deep breathing drew their attention to him, and they decided to perpetrate a jest at his expense. One of them shook him by the shoulder, and when he opened his eyes asked: " Listen, Bernard, can't you tell us what is the matter with Lord Darlington? Where is he? Why is he never heard of any more? "

Crammon without a moment's hesitation answered in a clear voice and with an almost solemn seriousness: " Darlington is on his yacht in the Bay of Liguria between Leghorn and Nice. What time is it? Three o'clock? Then he is just about to take the sedative which his Italian physician, Magliano, prepares and gives him."

He turned on his other side and slept on.

One of the men, who knew Crammon only slightly, said: " That's a pure invention! " The others assured the doubter that Crammon's word was above suspicion, and they spoke softly so as not to disturb his sleep.

III

On another occasion Crammon was a guest on an estate in Hungary, and planned with a group of young men, who were visiting a neighbouring country-house, to attend a festivity in the next town. The dawn was breaking when the friends separated. Crammon, with senses slightly dulled, went on alone and longed for the bed from which half an hour's walk still separated him. By chance he came upon a cattle market crowded with peasants, who had brought in their cows and calves from the villages around.

The crowd brought him to a halt, and he stopped to listen while a bull was being offered for sale. The auctioneer cried: " I am offered fifty crowns! " There was no answer; the peasants were slowly turning the matter over in their minds.

Fifty crowns for a bull? To Crammon's mind, from which the wine fumes had not quite faded, it seemed remarkable, and without hesitation he offered five crowns more. The peasants drew aside respectfully. One of them offered fifty-six; Crammon bid fifty-eight. The auctioneer raised his three-fold cry; the hammer fell. Crammon owned the bull.

A magnificent beast, he said to himself, and felt quite satisfied with his bargain. But when the time came for him to pay, he discovered that the bidding had been so much per hundred weight, and since the bull weighed twelve hundred and fifty pounds, he was required to pay seven hundred and twenty-five crowns.

He refused angrily. A loud squabble followed; but his arguments were useless. The bull was his property. But he had

no such sum of money on his person, and had to hire a man
to accompany him with the animal to his friend's house.

He strode on wretchedly vexed. The man followed, dragging the unwilling bull by a rope.

His host helped Crammon out of his embarrassment by
purchasing the bull, but the incident furnished endless amusement to the whole countryside.

IV

Crammon loved the theatre and everything connected with
it. When the great Marian Wolter died, he locked himself in
his house for a week, and mourned as if for a personal
bereavement.

During a stay in Berlin he heard of the early fame of Edgar
Lorm. He saw him as Hamlet, and when he left the theatre
he embraced an utter stranger and cried out: " I am happy! "
A little crowd gathered.

He had meant to stay in Berlin three days but remained
three months. His connections made it easy for him to meet
Lorm. He overwhelmed the actor with gifts—costly bric-à-
brac, rare books, exquisite delicacies.

Every morning, when Edgar Lorm arose, Crammon was
there, and with a deep absorption watched the actor at his
morning tasks and his gymnastic exercises. He admired his
slender stature, his noble gestures, his eloquent mimicry, and
the perfection of his voice.

He took care of Lorm's correspondence for him, interviewed
agents, got rid of unwelcome admirers of either sex. He
called the dramatic reviewers to account, and in the theatre
looked his rage whenever he thought the applause too tepid.
" The beasts should roar," he said. During the scene in
Richard II in which the king addresses the lords from the
castle wall, his enthusiasm was so great that his friend, the
Princess Uchnina, who shared his box, covered her face with
her fan to escape the glances of the public.

To him Lorm was in very truth the royal Richard, the melancholy Hamlet, Romeo the lover, and Fiesko the rebel. His faith in the actor's art was boundless; his imagination was wholly convinced. He attributed to him the wit of Beaumarchais, the eloquence of Antony, the sarcasm of Mephistopheles, the dæmonic energy of Franz Moor. When it was necessary for him to part, he did not conceal his grief, and from afar wrote him at intervals a letter of adoration.

The actor accepted this worship as a tribute that differed fundamentally from the average praise and love with which he was beginning to be satiated.

V

Lola Hesekiel, the celebrated beauty, owed her good fortune wholly to Crammon. Crammon had educated her and given her her place in the world and its appreciation.

When she was but an undistinguished young girl Crammon took a trip with her to Sylt. There they met Crammon's friend, Franz Lothar von Westernach. Lola fell in love with the handsome young aristocrat, and one evening, after a tender hour, she confessed her love for the other to Crammon. Then Crammon arose from his couch, dressed himself, went to Franz Lothar's room and brought the shy lad in. "My children," he said in the kindliest way, "I give you to each other. Be happy and enjoy your youth." With these words he left the two alone. And for long neither of them quite knew how to take so unwonted a situation.

VI

A curious occurrence was that connected with the Countess Ortenburg and the agate bowl.

The countess was an old lady of seventy, who lived in retirement at her château near Bregenz. Crammon, who had a great liking for ancient ladies of dignity and worldly wisdom, visited her almost annually to cheer her and to chat with her about the past.

The countess was grateful to him for his devotion, and determined to reward it. One day she showed him an agate bowl mounted on gold, an heirloom of her house, and told him that this bowl would be his after her death, as she had provided in her will.

Crammon flushed with pleasure, and tenderly kissed her hand. At every visit he took occasion to see the precious bowl, revelled in the sight of it, and enjoyed the foretaste of complete possession.

The countess died, and Crammon was soon notified concerning her legacy. The bowl was sent him carefully packed in a box. When it was freed of its wrappings he saw with amazement and disgust that he had been cheated. What he held was an imitation—skilfully and exactly made. But the material was base; only the setting had been copied in real gold.

Bitterly he considered what to do. Whom dared he accuse? How could he prove the very existence of the genuine bowl?

The heirs of the countess were three nephews of her name. The eldest, Count Leopold, was in ill repute as a miser who grudged himself and others their very bread. If he had played the trick, the bowl had been sold long ago.

It was easy to find a pretext for visiting Count Leopold at Salzburg. He sought distinction in piety and stood in favour at the bishop's court. Crammon thought that there was a gleam of embarrassment in the man's eyes. He himself peered about like a lynx. In vain.

He happened, however, to know all the prominent dealers in antiquities on the Continent, and so he set out on a quest. For two months and a half he travelled from city to city, from one dealer to another, and asked questions, investigated, and kept a sharp look-out. He carried the imitation bowl with him and showed it to all. The dealers were quite familiar with the sight of a connoisseur with his heart set on some object of art; they answered his questions willingly and sent him hither and thither.

He was on the point of despairing, when in Aix he was told of a dealer in Brussels who was said to have acquired the bowl. It was true. He found the object of his search in Brussels. Crammon inquired after the name of the seller and discovered it to be that of one who had business relations with Count Leopold. The Belgian dealer demanded twenty thousand francs for the bowl. Crammon at once deposited one thousand, with the assurance that he would pay the rest within a week and then take the bowl. He made no attempt at bargaining, much to the astonishment of the dealer. But in his rage he thought: I have snared the thief. Why should his rascality come cheaply?

Two days later he entered the count's room. He was accompanied by a hotel porter, who placed a box containing the imitation bowl on a table and disappeared. The count was breakfasting alone. He arose and frowned.

Crammon silently opened the little box, lifted the bowl out, polished it carefully with a handkerchief, kept it in his hand, and assumed a care-worn look.

" What is it? " asked the count, turning pale.

Crammon told him how, by the merest chance, he had discovered in a Brussels shop this bowl which, as he knew, had been for centuries in the possession of the Ortenburgs. It had, therefore, scarcely required the mournful memory of his dear and honoured old friend to persuade him to restore the precious object to the family treasury whence it came. He esteemed it a great good fortune that it was he who had discovered this impious trade in precious things. Had it been any one else the danger of loose tongues causing an actual scandal was obvious enough. He had, he continued, paid twenty thousand francs for the bowl, which he had brought in order to restore it to the house of Ortenburg. The receipt was at the count's disposal. All he requested of the count was a cheque for the amount involved.

He breathed no word concerning a will or a legacy, and betrayed no suspicion of how he had been tricked. The count understood. He looked at the imitation bowl on the table and recognized it for what it was. But he lacked courage to object. He swallowed his rage, sat down and made out the cheque. His chin quivered with fury. Crammon was radiant. He left the imitation bowl where it stood, and at once set out for Brussels to fetch the other.

VII

There were three things that Crammon hated from the bottom of his heart: newspapers, universal education, and taxes. It was especially impossible for him to realize that he, like others, was subject to taxation.

He had been summoned on a certain occasion to give an accounting of his income. He declared that during the greater part of the year he lived as a guest in the châteaux and on the estates of his friends.

The examining official replied that since he was known to live a rather luxurious life, it was clear that he must have a fixed income from some source.

" Undoubtedly," Crammon lied with the utmost cynicism. " This income consists wholly of meagre winnings at the various international gambling resorts. Earnings of that sort are not subject to taxation."

The official was astonished and shook his head. He left the room in order to consult his superiors in regard to the case. Crammon was left alone. Trembling with rage he gazed about him, took a stack of legal documents from a shelf, and shoved them far behind a bookcase against the wall. There, so far as one could tell, they would moulder in the course of the years, and in their illegal hiding place save the owners of the names they recorded from taxation.

For years he would chuckle whenever he thought of this deviltry.

VIII

The Princess Uchnina had made Crammon's acquaintance in one of the castles of the Esterhazys in Hungary. Even at that time the free manner of her life had set tongues wagging; later on her family disowned her.

He met her again in a hotel at Cairo. Since she was wealthy there was no danger of his being exploited. He had little liking for the professional vampire, nor had he ever lost the mastery over his senses. There was no passion that could prevent him from going to bed at ten and sleeping soundly through a long night. The princess was fond of laughing and Crammon helped her to laugh, since it pleased him to see her amused. He did not care to be loved beyond measure; he valued considerate treatment and a comradely freedom of contact. He had no desire for love with its usual spices of romance and disquietude, jealousy and enslavement. He wanted the delight of love in as tangible and sensible a form as possible; he cared less for the flame than for the dainty on the spit.

On the ship that took him and the princess to Brindisi there appeared a Danish lady with hair the hue of wheat and eyes like cornflowers. She was lonely, and he sought her out and succeeded in charming her. The three travelled together to Naples, where the Danish lady and Crammon seemed to have become friendlier than ever; but the princess only laughed.

They arrived in Florence. In front of the Baptistery Crammon met a melancholy young woman, whom he recognized as an acquaintance made at Ostende. She was the daughter of a manufacturer of Mainz. She had married recently, but her husband had lost her dowry at Monte Carlo and had fled to America. Crammon introduced her to the other ladies, but, for the sake of the Dane, who was suspicious and exacting,

passed her off as his cousin. It was not long, however, before
a quarrel broke out between the two, and Crammon was very
busy preaching the spirit of reconciliation and peace.

The princess laughed.

Crammon said: " I should like to see how many women one
can gather together like this without their thirsting for one
another's blood." He made a wager with the princess for a
hundred marks that he could increase the number to five,
herself of course excepted.

In the station at Milan a charming creature ran into him,
and gave signs of unalloyed delight. She was an actress who
had been intimate with a friend of his years before. She had
just been engaged by a theatre in Petrograd and was now on
her way there. Crammon found her so amusing that he
neglected the others for her sake; and although he was not
lacking in subtlety, the signs of a coming revolution in his
palace increased. The revolution broke out in Munich. There
were hard words and tears; trunks were packed; and the ladies
scattered to all the points of the compass,—North to Denmark,
West to Mainz, East to Petrograd.

Crammon was mournful; he had lost his bet. The little
princess laughed. She remained with him until another lure
grew stronger. Then they celebrated a cheerful farewell.

IX

When Crammon was but a youth of twenty-three he had once
been a member of a large hunting party at Count Sinsheim's.
Among the guests there was a gentleman named von Febronius
who attracted his attention, first by his silence, and next by
frequently seeking his society while carefully avoiding the
others.

One day Febronius, with unusual urgency, begged Crammon
to visit him.

Febronius possessed an extensive entailed estate on the
boundary between Silesia and Poland. He was the last of his

race and name, and, as every one knew, deeply unhappy on this account. Nine years earlier he had married the daughter of a middle-class family of Breslau, and in spite of the difference in age the two were genuinely devoted to each other. The wife was thirty, the husband near fifty. The marriage had proved childless, and there seemed now no further hope.

Crammon promised to come, and some weeks later, on an evening in May, he arrived at the estate. Febronius was delighted to see him, but the lady, who was pretty and cultivated, was noticeably chill in her demeanour. Whenever she was forced to look at Crammon a perceptible change of colour overspread her face.

Next morning Febronius showed him the whole estate— the park, the fields and forests, the stables and dairies. It was a little kingdom, and Crammon expressed his admiration; but his host sighed. He said that his blessings had all been embittered, every beast of the field seemed to regard him with reproachful eyes, and the land and its fertility meant nothing to him who had brought death to his race, and whom the fertility of nature but put in mind of the sterile curse which had come upon his blood.

Then he became silent, and silently accompanied Crammon, whose head whirled with very bold and equivocal thoughts.

After dinner they were sitting on the terrace with Frau von Febronius. Suddenly the lord of the manor was called away and returned shortly with a telegram in his hand. He said that an urgent matter of business required him to set out on a journey at once. Crammon arose with a gesture, to show his consciousness of the propriety of his leaving too. But his host, almost frightened, begged him to stay and keep his wife company. It was, he said, only a matter of two days, and she would be grateful.

He stammered these words and grew pale. His wife kept her face bent closely over her embroidery frame, and Crammon saw her fingers tremble. He knew enough. He shook hands

with Febronius, and knew that they would not and dared not
meet again in life.

He found the lady, when they were alone together, shier
than he had anticipated. Her gestures expressed reluctance,
her glances fear. When his speech grew bolder, shame and
indignation flamed in her eyes. She fled from him, sought him
again, and when in the evening they strolled through the park
she implored him to leave next day, and went to the stables to
order the carriage for the morning. When he consented, her
behaviour altered, her torment and her harshness seemed to
melt. After midnight she suddenly appeared in his room, struggling with herself and on the defensive, defiant and deeply
humiliated, bitter in her yielding, and in her very tenderness
estranged.

Early next morning the carriage was ready and drove him to
the station.

That marvellous night faded from his memory as a thousand
others, less marvellous, had done. The spectral experience
blended with a host of others that were without its aroma of
spiritual pain.

X

Sixteen years later chance brought him into the same part of
the country.

He inquired after Febronius, and learned that that gentleman had been dead for ten years. He was told, furthermore,
that during his last years the character of Febronius had
changed radically. He had become a spendthrift; frightful
mismanagement had ruined his estate and shaken his fortune;
swindlers and false friends had ruled him exclusively, so that
his widow, who was still living on the estate with her only
daughter, could scarcely maintain herself there. She was beset
by usurious creditors and a growing burden of debt; she did
not know an easy hour, and complete ruin was but a matter of
time.

Crammon drove over to the estate, and had himself announced under an assumed name. When Frau von Febronius entered he saw that she was still charming. Her hair was still brown, her features curiously young. But there was something frightened and suspicious about her.

She asked where she had had the pleasure of his acquaintance. Crammon simply regarded her for a while, and she too looked at him attentively. Suddenly she uttered a cry and hid her face in her hands. When she had mastered her emotion, she gave him her hand. Then she left the room, and returned in a few minutes leading a young girl of great sweetness.

" Here she is."

The girl smiled. Her lips curved as though she were about to pout, and her teeth showed the glittering moisture of shells to which the water of the sea still clings.

She spoke of the beautiful day and of her having lain in the sun. The broken alto voice surprised one in so young a creature. In her wide, brown eyes there was a radiance of unbounded desires. Crammon was flattered, and thought: If God had made me a woman, perhaps I should have been such an one. He asked after her name. It was Letitia.

Frau von Febronius clung to the girl with every glance.

Letitia brought in a basket full of golden pears. She looked at the fruit with greed and with an ironic consciousness of her greed. She cut a pear in half and found a worm in it. That disgusted her and she complained bitterly.

Crammon asked her what she cared for most, and she answered: " Jewels."

Her mother reproached her with being careless of what she had. " Only the other day," said Frau von Febronius, " she lost a costly ring."

" Just give me something to love," Letitia replied and stroked a white kitten that purred and jumped on her lap, " and I'll hold on to it fast."

When he said farewell Crammon promised to write, and Letitia promised to send him her picture.

A few weeks later Frau von Febronius informed him that she had taken Letitia to Weimar, and placed her in the care of her sister, the Countess Brainitz.

XI

On Crammon's fortieth birthday he received from seven of his friends, whose names were signed to it, a document written in the elaborate script and manner of an official diploma. And the content of the document was this:

" O Crammon, friend of friends, admirer of women and contemner of their sex, enemy of marriage, glass of fashion, defender of descent, shield of high rank, guest of all noble spirits, finder of the genuine, tester of the exquisite, friend of the people and hater of mankind, long sleeper and rebel, Bernard Gervasius, hail to thee! "

Gleaming with pride and satisfaction Crammon hung up the beautifully framed parchment on the wall beside his bed. Then with the two ladies of his household he took a turn in the park.

Miss Aglaia walked at his right, Miss Constantine at his left. Both were festively arrayed, though in a somewhat antique fashion, and their faces were the happiest to be seen.

CHRISTIAN'S REST

I

CRAMMON found the forties to be a critical period in a man's life. It is then that in his mind he sits in judgment upon himself; he seeks the sum of his existence, and finds blunder after blunder in the reckoning.

But these moral difficulties did not very much influence either his attitude or the character of his activities. He found his appetite for life growing, but he found loneliness a heavier burden than before. When he was alone he was overcome by a feeling which he called the melancholy of the half-way house.

In Paris he was overtaken by this distemper of the soul. Felix Imhof and Franz Lothar von Westernach had agreed to meet him, and both had left him in the lurch. Imhof had been kept in Frankfort by his business on the exchange and his real estate interests, and had telegraphed a later date of arrival. Franz Lothar had remained in Switzerland with his brother and Count Prosper Madruzzi.

In his vexation Crammon spent his days largely in bed. He either read foolish novels or murmured his annoyances over to himself. Out of sheer boredom he ordered fourteen pairs of boots of those three or four masters of the craft who work only for the elect and accept a new customer only when recommended by a distinguished client.

He was to have spent the month of September with the Wahnschaffe family on their estate in the Odenwald. He had made the acquaintance of young Wolfgang Wahnschaffe the summer before at a tennis tournament in Homburg, and had accepted his invitation. In his exasperation over his truant friends he now wrote and excused himself.

One evening in Montmartre he met the painter Weikhardt,
whom he had known in Munich. They walked together for
a while, and Weikhardt encouraged Crammon to visit a
neighbouring music hall. A very young dancer had been
appearing there for the past week, the painter told him, and
many French colleagues had advised seeing her.

Crammon agreed.

Weikhardt led him through a maze of suspicious looking
alleys to a no less suspicious looking house. This was the
Théâtre Sapajou. A boy in fantastic costume opened the door
that led to a moderately large, half-darkened hall with scarlet
walls and a wooden gallery. About fifty people, mostly
painters and writers with their wives, sat facing a tiny stage.
The performance had begun.

Two fiddles and a clarionet furnished the music.

And Crammon saw Eva Sorel dance.

II

His anger against his friends was extinguished. He was glad
that they were not here.

He was afraid of meeting any of his many Parisian acquaintances and passed through the streets with lowered eyes. The
thought was repulsive to him that he would be forced to speak
to them of Eva Sorel, and then to see their indifferent or curious
faces, beneath which there could be no feeling akin to his
own.

He avoided the painter Weikhardt, for the latter would rob
him of the illusion that he, Crammon, had discovered Eva
Sorel, and that for the present she lived only in his consciousness as the miracle that he felt her to be.

He went about like an unrecognized rich man, or else as
troubled as a miser who knows that thieves lie in wait for
his treasure. All who carried their chatter of delight from the
Théâtre Sapajou out into the world he regarded as thieves.
They threatened to attract to the little playhouse the crowd

of the stupid and the banal who drag great things into the dust by making them fashionable.

He nursed the dream of kidnapping the dancer and of fleeing with her to a deserted island of the sea. He would have been satisfied to adore her there and would have asked nothing of her.

For Lorm he had demanded applause. But he hated the favour which the dancer gained. Not because she was a woman. It was not the jealousy of the male. He did not think of her under the aspect of sex. Her being was to him the fulfilment of dark presentiments and visions; she represented the spirit of lightness as opposed to the heaviness of life which weighed him and others down; she was flight that mocked the creeping of the earth-bound, the mystery that is beyond knowledge, form that is the denial of chaos.

He said: "This boasted twentieth century, young as it is, wearies my nerves. Humanity drags itself across the earth like an ugly clumsy worm. She desires freedom from this condition, and in her yearning to escape the chrysalis she finds the dance. It is a barbaric spirit of comedy at its highest point."

He knew well that the life he led was a challenge and a disturbance to his fellow men who earned their bread by the sweat of their toil. He was an enthusiastic admirer of those ages in which the ruling classes had really ruled, when a prince of the Church had had a capon stuffer amid the officials of his court, and an insignificant count of the Holy Roman Empire had paid an army that consisted of one general, six colonels, four drummers, and two privates. And he was grateful to the dancer because she lifted him out of his own age even more thoroughly than the actor had done.

He made an idol of her, for the years were coming in which he needed one—he who, satiated, still knew hunger with senses avid for the flight of birds.

III

Eva Sorel had a companion and guardian, Susan Rappard, a thorough scarecrow, clad in black, and absent-minded. She had emerged with Eva out of the unknown past, and she was still rubbing its darkness out of her eyes when Eva, at eighteen, saw the paths of light open to her. But she played the piano admirably, and thus accompanied Eva's practice.

Crammon had paid her some attentions, and the tone in which he spoke of her mistress gained her sympathy. She persuaded Eva to receive him. " Take her flowers," she whispered. " She's fond of them."

Eva and Susan Rappard lived in two rooms in a small hotel. Crammon brought such masses of roses that the close corridors held the fragrance for many hours.

As he entered he saw Eva in an armchair in front of a mirror. Susan was combing her hair, which was of the colour of honey.

On the carpet was kneeling a lad of seventeen who was very pale and whose face bore traces of tears. He had declared his love to Eva. Even when the stranger entered he had no impulse to get up; his luckless passion made him blind.

Crammon remained standing by the door.

" Susan, you're hurting me! " Eva cried. Susan was startled and dropped the comb.

Eva held out her hand to Crammon. He approached and bent over to kiss it.

" Poor chap," she said, smiling, and indicating the lad, " he torments himself cruelly. It's so foolish."

The boy pressed his forehead against the back of her chair. " I'll kill myself," he whimpered. Eva clapped her hands and brought her face with its arch mockery of sadness near to the boy's.

" What a gesture! " Crammon thought. " How perfect in its light completeness, how delicate, how new! And how she

raised her lids and showed the strong light of her starry eyes,
and dropped her chin a little in that inclination of the head,
and wore a smile that was unexpected in its blending of desire
and sweetness and cunning and childlikeness! "

"Where is my golden snood?" Eva asked and arose.

Susan said that she had left it on the table. She looked
there in vain. She fluttered hither and thither like a huge
black butterfly: she opened and closed drawers, shook her
head, thoughtfully pressed her hand against her forehead, and
finally found the snood under the piano lid next to a roll of
bank notes.

"It's always that way with us," Eva sighed. "We always
find things. But we have to hunt a long time." She fastened
the snood about her hair.

"I can't place your French accent," Crammon remarked.
His own pronunciation was Parisian.

"I don't know," she answered. "Perhaps it's Spanish. I
was in Spain a long time. Perhaps it's German. I was born
in Germany and lived there till I was twelve." Her eyes grew
a little sombre.

IV

The lovelorn boy had left. Eva seemed to have forgotten
him, and there was no shadow upon the brunette pallor of
her face. She sat down again, and after a brief exchange of
questions she told him of an experience that she had had.

The reason for her telling the story seemed to inhere in
thoughts which she did not express. Her glance rested calmly
in the illimitable. Her eyes knew no walls in their vision;
no one could assert that she looked at him. She merely
gazed.

Susan Rappard sat by the tile-oven, resting her chin upon
her arm, while her fingers, gliding past the furrowed cheeks,
clung amid her greyish hair.

At Arles in Provence a young monk named Brother Leotade

had often visited Eva. He was not over twenty-five, vigorous,
a typical Frenchman of the South, though rather taciturn.

He loved the land and knew the old castles. Once he spoke
to her of a tower that stood on a cliff, a mile from the city;
he described the view from the top of the tower in words that
made Eva long to enjoy it. He offered to be her guide, and
they agreed on the hour and the day.

The tower had an iron gate which was kept locked, and the
key was in the keeping of a certain vintner. It was late afternoon when they set out, but on the unshaded road it was still
hot. They meant to be back before night fall, and so they
walked quickly; but when they reached the tower the sun had
already disappeared behind the hills.

Brother Leotade opened the iron gate and they saw a
narrow spiral staircase of stone. They climbed a few stairs.
Then the monk turned suddenly, locked the door from within,
and slipped the key into the pocket of his cowl. Eva asked his
reason. He replied that it was safer so.

It was dim in the vaulted tower, and Eva saw a menacing
gleam in the monk's eyes. She let him precede her, but on a
landing he turned and grasped her. She was silent, although
she felt the pressure of his fingers. Still silent, she glided from
his grasp, and ran up as swiftly as she could. She heard no
steps behind her in the darkness, and the stairs seemed endless. Still she climbed until her breath gave out, and she
panted for the light. Suddenly the greenish bell of the sky
gleamed into the shaft; and as she mounted, the circle of her
vision widened to the scarlet of the West, and when she stood
on the last step and on the platform, having emerged from
the mustiness of the old walls into the balsamic coolness and
the multiform and tinted beauty of earth and air, the danger
seemed wholly past.

She waited and watched the dark hole from which she had
come. The monk did not appear. His treacherous conceal-
ment strained her nerves to the uttermost. The brief twilight

faded; evening turned into night; there was no sound, no tread. Not until late did it occur to her that she could call for help. She cried out into the land, but she saw that it was a desolate region in which no one dwelled. And when her feeble cry had died away, the shape of Brother Leotade appeared at the head of the stairs.

The expression on his face filled her now with an even greater horror. He murmured something and stretched out his arms after her. She bounded backward, groping behind her with her hands. He followed her, and she leaped upon the parapet, crouched near the pinnacle, hard by the outer rim of the wall, her head and shoulders over the abyss. The wind caught the veil that had been wound about her head and it streamed forth like a flag. The monk stood still, bound to the spot by her eyes. His own were fixed relentlessly upon her, but he dared not move, for he saw the determination in her face: if he moved toward her, she would leap to her death.

And yet a rage of desire kept flaring in his eyes.

The hours passed. The monk stood there as though cast of bronze, while she crouched on the parapet, motionless but for her fluttering veil, and held him with her eye as one holds a wolf. Stars gathered in the sky; from time to time she glanced for a second at the firmament. Never had she been so near to the eternal flame. She seemed to hear the melody of a million worlds singing in their orbits; her unmoving limbs seemed to vibrate; the hands with which she clung to the harsh wall seemed to upbear the adamantine roof of the cosmos, while below her was the created thing, blind and wracked by passion and sworn to a God whom it belied.

Gradually the rim of heaven grew bright and the birds began to flutter upward. Then Brother Leotade threw himself upon his face and began to pray aloud. And as the East grew brighter he lifted up more resonantly the voice of his prayer. He crept toward the stairs. Then he arose and disappeared.

She saw him issue from the gate below and disappear in the dawn among the vineyards. Eva lay long in the grass below, worn and dull, before she could walk back to the city.

"It may be," she said at the end of her story, "that some one looked on from Sirius, some one who will come soon and perhaps be my friend." She smiled.

"From Sirius?" The voice of Susan was heard. "Where will he get pearls and diadems? What crowns will he offer you, and what provinces? Let us have no dealings with beggars, even though they come from the sky."

"Keep quiet, you Sancho Panza!" Eva said. "All that I ask is that he can laugh, laugh marvellously—laugh like that young muleteer at Cordova! Do you remember him? I want him to laugh so that I can forget my ambitions."

Hers is a virtue that hardly begs for pennies, thought Crammon, and determined to be on his guard and seek security while there was time. For in his breast he felt a new, unknown, and melancholy burning, and he knew well that he could not laugh like that young Cordovan muleteer and make an ambitious woman forget her striving.

V

Felix Imhof arrived, and with him Wolfgang Wahnschaffe, a very tall young man of twenty-two. There was an elegance about the latter that suggested unlimited means. His father was one of the German steel kings.

Crammon's refusal of his invitation had annoyed Wahnschaffe, and he was anxious to secure the older man's friendship. It was characteristic of the Wahnschaffes to desire most strongly whatever seemed to withhold itself from their grasp.

They went to the Théâtre Sapajou, and Felix Imhof agreed that the dancer was incomparable. Plans at once flew from his mind like sparks from beaten iron in a smithy. He talked of founding an Academy of the Dance, of hiring an impresario for a tour through Europe, of inventing a pantomime. All this was to be done, so to speak, over night.

They sat together and drank a good deal—first wine, then champagne, then ale, then whiskey, then coffee, then wine once more. The excess had no effect on Imhof at all; in his soberest moments he was like others in the ecstasy of drunkenness.

He celebrated the praises of Gauguin, of Schiller, and of Balzac, and developed the plan for a great experiment in human eugenics. Faultless men and women were to be chosen and united and to beget an Arcadian race.

In the midst of it all he quoted passages of Keats and Rabelais, mixed drinks of ten kinds, and related a dozen succulent anecdotes from his wide experience with women. His mouth with its sensual lips poured forth superlatives, his protruding negroid eyes sparkled with whim and wit, and his spare, sinewy body seemed to suffer if it was forced to but a minute's immobility.

The other two nearly fell asleep through sheer weariness. He grew steadily more awake and noisy, waved his hands, beat on the table, inhaled the smoky air luxuriously, and laughed with his gigantic bass voice.

Five successive nights were spent in this way. That was enough for Crammon and he determined to leave. Wolfgang Wahnschaffe had invited him to a hunting party at Waldleiningen.

It was at eleven in the forenoon when Felix Imhof burst in on Crammon. In the middle of the room stood a huge open trunk. Linen, clothes, books, shoes, cravattes were scattered about like things hastily saved in a fire. Outside of the window swayed in flaming yellow the tree-tops of the Park Monceau.

Crammon sat in an armchair. He was naked but for a pair of long hose. He had breakfasted thus, and his expression was sombre. His square Gothic head and his broad, muscular torso seemed made of bronze.

The day before Felix Imhof had made the acquaintance of Cardillac, ruler of the Paris Bourse, and was on his way to him now. He was going to embark on some enterprise of Cardillac to the extent of two millions, and asked Crammon in passing whether the latter did not wish to risk something too. A trifle, say fifty thousand francs, would suffice. Cardillac was a magician who trebled one's money in three days. Then you had had the pleasure of the game and the suspense.

"This Cardillac," he said, "is a wonder. He began life as an errand boy in an hotel. Now he is chief shareholder in thirty-seven corporations, founder of the Franco-Hispanic Bank, owner of the zinc mines of Le Nère, ruler of a horde of newspapers, and master of a fortune running into the hundreds of millions."

Crammon arose, and from the heaps on the floor drew forth a violet dressing gown which he put over his shivering body. He looked in it like a cardinal.

"Do you happen to know," he asked, thoughtfully and sleepily, "or did you by chance ever observe how the young muleteers in Cordova laugh?"

Imhof's helpless astonishment made him look stupid. He was silent.

Crammon took a large peach from a plate and began to eat it. You could see drops of the amber juice.

"There's no way out," he said, and sighed sadly, "I shall have to go to Cordova myself."

VI

On their journey Wahnschaffe told Crammon about his family: his sister Judith, his older brother Christian, his mother, who had the most beautiful pearls in Europe. "When she wears them," he said, "she looks like an Indian goddess." His father he described as an amiable man with unseen backgrounds of the soul.

Crammon was anxious to get as much light as possible on the life and history of one of those great and rich bourgeois families which had won in the race against the old aristocracy. Here, it seemed to him, was a new world, an undiscovered country which was still in the blossoming stage and which was to be feared.

His cleverly put questions got him no farther. What he did learn was a story of silent, bitter rivalry between this brother and Christian, who seemed to Wolfgang to be preferred to himself to an incomprehensible degree. He heard a story of doubt and complaint and scorn, and of words that the mother of the two had uttered to a stranger: "You don't know my son Christian? He is the most precious thing God ever made."

It was cheap enough, Wolfgang asserted, to praise a horse in the stable, one that had never been sent to the Derby because it was thought to be too noble and precious. Crammon was amused by the sporting simile. Why was that cheap, he asked, and what was its exact meaning?

Wolfgang said that it applied to Christian, who had as yet proved himself in no way, nor accomplished anything despite his twenty-three years. He had passed his final examinations at college with difficulty; he was no luminary in any respect. No one could deny that he had an admirable figure, an elegant air, a complexion like milk and blood. He had also, it was not to be denied, a charm so exquisite that no man or woman could withstand him. But he was cold as a hound's nose and smooth as an eel, and as immeasurably spoiled and arrogant as though the whole world had been made for his sole benefit.

"You will succumb to him as every one does," Wolfgang said finally, and there was something almost like hatred in his voice.

They arrived in Waldleiningen on a rainy evening of October. The house was full of guests.

VII

Wolfgang's prediction came true sooner than he himself would perhaps have thought. As early as the third day Crammon and Christian Wahnschaffe were inseparable and utterly united. They conversed with an air of intimacy as though they had known each other for years. The difference of almost two decades in their ages seemed simply non-existent.

With a laugh Crammon reminded Wolfgang of his prophecy, and added, " I hope that nothing worse will ever be predicted to me, and that delightful things will always become realities so promptly." And he knocked wood, for he was as superstitious as an old wife.

Wolfgang's expression seemed to say: I was quite prepared for it. What else is one to expect?

Crammon had expected to find Christian spoiled and effeminate. Instead he saw a thoroughly healthy blond young athlete, a head and more taller than himself, conscious of his vigour and beauty, without a trace of vanity, and radiant in every mood. It was true, as he had heard, that all were at his beck and call, from his mother to the youngest of the grooms, and that he accepted everything as he did fair weather —simply, lightly, and graciously, but without binding himself to any reciprocal obligation.

Crammon loved young men who were as elastic as panthers and whose serenity transformed the moods of others as a precious aroma does the air of a sick room. Such youths seemed to him to be gifted with an especial grace. One should, he held, clear their path of anything that might hinder their beneficent mission. He did not strive to impress them but rather to learn of them.

It was in England and among the English that he had found this respect for youth and ripening manhood, which had long become a principle with him and a rule of life. The climate of a perfectly nurtured understanding he thought the fittest atmosphere for such a being, and made his plans in secret. He thought of the grand tour in the sense of the eighteenth century, with himself in the rôle of mentor and guide.

In the meantime he and Christian talked about hunting, trout-fishing, the various ways of preparing venison, the advantages of each season over the others, the numerous charms of the female sex, the amusing characteristics of common acquaintances. And of all these light things he spoke in a thoughtful manner and with exhausting thoroughness.

He could not see Christian without reflecting: What eyes and teeth and head and limbs! Nature has here used her choicest substance, meant for permanence as well as delight, and a master has fitted the parts into harmony. If one were a mean-spirited fellow one could burst with envy.

One incident charmed him so much that he felt impelled to communicate his delight to the others who had also witnessed it. It took place in the yard where early in the morning the hunting parties assembled. The dogs were to be leashed. Christian stood alone among twenty-three mastiffs who leaped around and at him with deafening barks and yells. He swung a short-handled whip which whirred above their heads. The beasts grew wilder; he had to ward off the fiercer ones with his elbow. The forester wanted to come to his help and called to the raging pack. Christian beckoned him to stay back. The man's assumed anger and all his gestures irritated the dogs. One of them, whose mouth was flecked with foam, snapped at Christian, and the sharp teeth clung to his shoulder. Then all cried out, especially Judith. But Christian gave a short sharp whistle from between his teeth, his arms dropped, his glance held the dogs nearest to him, and suddenly the noise stopped, and only those in front gave a humble whine.

Frau Wahnschaffe had grown pale. She approached her

son and asked him whether he was hurt. He was not, although
his jacket showed a long rent.

" He leads a charmed life," she said that night after dinner
to Crammon, with whom she had withdrawn to a quiet corner.
" And that is my one consolation. His utter recklessness often
frightens me. I have noticed with pleasure that you take an
interest in him. Do try to guide him a little along reasonable
ways."

Her voice was hollow and her face immobile. Her eyes stared
past one. She knew no cares and had never known any, nor
had she, apparently, ever reflected concerning those of others.
Yet no one had ever seen this woman smile. The utter absence
of friction in her life seemed to have reduced the motions of her
soul to a point of deadness. Only the thought of Christian gave
her whole being a shade of warmth; only when she could speak
of him did she grow eloquent.

Crammon answered: " My dear lady, it is better to leave a
fellow like Christian to his own fate. That is his best protection."

She nodded, although she disliked the colloquial carelessness
of his speech. She told him how in his boyhood Christian had
once gone to visit the lumbermen in the forest. The trunk of a
mighty pine had been almost cut through, and the men ran to
the end of the rope attached to the tree's top. The great tree
wavered when they first noticed the boy. They cried out in
horror, and tried to let the tree crash down in another direction.
It was too late. And while some tugged desperately at the
rope and were beside themselves with fright, a few headed by
the foreman ran with lifted and warning arms into the very
sphere of danger. The boy stood there quietly, and gazed
unsuspectingly upward. The tree fell and crushed the foreman to death. But the branches slipped gently over Christian
as if to caress him; and when the pine lay upon the earth, he
stood in the midst of its topmost twigs as though he had
been placed there, untouched and unastonished. And those who

were there said he had been saved literally but by the breadth of a hair.

Crammon could not get rid of the vision which he himself had seen: the proud young wielder of the whip amid the unleashed pack. He reflected deeply. "It is clear," he said to himself, "that I need no longer go to Cordova to find out how the young muleteers laugh."

VIII

At the castle of Waldleiningen there was a wine room in which one could drink comfortably. In it Crammon and Christian drank one evening to their deeper friendship. And when the bottle was emptied of its precious vintage Crammon proposed that, since it was a beautiful night, they should take a turn in the park. Christian agreed.

In the moonlight they walked over the pebbles of the paths. Trees and bushes swam in a silvery haze.

"Gossamers and the mist of autumn," said Crammon. "Quite as the poets describe it."

"What poet?" Christian asked innocently.

"Almost any," Crammon answered.

"Do you read poetry?" Christian was curious.

"Now and then," Crammon answered, "when prose gets stale. Thus I pay my debts to the world-spirit."

They sat down on a bench under a great plantain. Christian watched the scene silently for a while. Then he asked suddenly, "Tell me, Bernard, what is this seriousness of life that most people make such a fuss about?"

Crammon laughed softly to himself. "Patience, my dear boy, patience! You'll find out for yourself."

He laughed again and folded his hands comfortably over his abdomen. But over the lovely landscape and the lovely night there fell a veil of melancholy.

IX

Christian wanted Crammon to accompany him and Alfred
Meerholz, the general's son, to St. Moritz for the winter sports;
but Crammon had to attend Konrad von Westernach's wedding
in Vienna. So they agreed to meet in Wiesbaden, where Frau
Wahnschaffe and Judith would join them in the spring.

Frau Wahnschaffe usually spent January and February in
the family's ancestral home at Würzburg. She had many
guests there and so did not feel the boredom of the provincial
city. Wolfgang had been studying political science at the
university there; but at the end of the semester he was to go
to Berlin, pass his examination for the doctorate, and enter
the ministry of foreign affairs. Judith said to him sarcastically: " You are a born diplomatist of the new school. The
moment you enter a room no one dares to jest any more.
It's high time that you enlarge your sphere of activity." He
answered: " You are right. I know that I shall yield my
place to a worthier one who knows better how to amuse you."
" You are bitter," Judith replied, " but what you say is true."

When Christian arrived in Wiesbaden in April his mother
introduced him to the Countess Brainitz and to her niece,
Letitia von Febronius. The countess was ostensibly here to
drink the waters; but her purpose was commonly thought to
be the finding of a suitable match for her niece among the
young men of the country. She had succeeded, at all events,
in gaining the confidence of Frau Wahnschaffe, who was distrustful and inaccessible. Judith was charmed by Letitia's
loveliness.

Christian accompanied the young ladies on their walks and
rides, and the countess said to Letitia: " If I were you I'd fall
in love with that young man." Letitia answered with her most
soulful expression: " If I were you, aunt, I'd be afraid of
doing so myself."

Crammon arrived in an evil mood. Whenever one of his

friends so far forgot himself as to marry, there came over him an insidious hatred of mankind which darkened his soul for weeks.

He was surprised when Christian told him of these new friends, and wondered at the trick by which fate brought him into the circle of Letitia's life. He had a feeling that was uncanny.

He was anything but delighted over the Countess Brainitz. He was familiar with the genealogy and history of the dead and living members of all the noble families of Europe, and so was thoroughly informed concerning her. " In her youth," he reported, " she was an actress, one of those favourite in-génues who attune souls of a certain sort poetically by a stri-dent blondness and by pulling at their aprons with touching bashfulness. With these tricks she seduced in his time Count Brainitz, a gentleman who had weak brains and a vigorous case of gout. She thought he was rich. Later it turned out that he was hopelessly in debt and lived on a pension allowed him by the head of the house. On his death this pension passed to her."

She was blond no longer. Her hair was white and had a metallic shimmer like spun glass. Its hue was premature, no doubt, for she was scarcely over fifty. She was corpulent; her body had a curious sort of carved rotundity; her face was like an apple in its smooth roundness; it gleamed with a healthy reddish tinge; and each feature—nose, mouth, chin, forehead—was characterized by a certain harmless daintiness.

From the first moment she and Crammon found themselves hopelessly at odds. She clasped her hands in despair over everything he said, and all his doings enraged her. With her feminine instinct she scented in him the adversary of all her cunning plans; he saw in her another of those arch enemies that, from time to time, spun for one of his friends the net of marriage.

She asked him to dine merely because of Letitia's insistence.

The girl explained: "Even if you don't like him in other ways, aunt, you'll approve of him as a guest. He's very like you in one way." But Crammon's dislike of the countess robbed him of his usual appetite, so that the reconciliation even on that plane did not occur. She herself ate three eggs with mayonnaise, half of a duck, a large portion of roast beef, four pieces of pastry, a plate full of cherries, and additional trifles to pass the time. Crammon was overwhelmed.

After each course she washed her hands with meticulous care, and when the meal was over drew her snow-white gloves over her little, round fingers.

" All people are pigs," she declared. " Nothing they come in contact with remains clean. I guard myself as well as I can."

Letitia sat through it all smiling in her own arch and tender way, and her mere presence lent to the common things about her a breath of romance.

x

Her estate having finally been sold at auction, and she herself being quite without means, Frau von Febronius had gone to live with her younger sister at Stargard in Pomerania. In order to spare her daughter the spectacle of that final débâcle she had sent the girl to the countess in Weimar.

The three sisters were all widowed. The one in Stargard had been married to a circuit judge named Stojenthin. She lived on her government pension and the income of a small fortune that had been her dowry. She had two sons who strolled through the world like gipsies, wrapped their sloth in a loud philosophy, and turned to their aunt the countess whenever they were quite at the end of all their resources.

The countess yielded every time. Both young men knew the style of letter-writing that really appealed to her. " They will get over sowing their wild oats," said the countess. She had been awaiting that happy consummation for years, and in the meantime sent them food and money.

It was not so simple to help Letitia. When the girl arrived she possessed just three frocks which she had outgrown and a little linen. The countess ordered robes from Vienna, and fitted out her niece like an heiress.

Letitia permitted herself calmly to be adorned. The eyes of men told her that she was charming. The countess said: " You are destined for great things, my darling." She took the girl's head between her two gloved hands and kissed her audibly on the porcelain clearness of her forehead.

Nor was she satisfied with what she had done. She desired to create a solid foundation and help her niece in a permanent way. That desire brought to her mind the forest of Heiligen-kreuz.

On the northern slope of the Röhn mountains there was a piece of forest land having an area of from ten to twelve square kilometres. For more than two decades it had been the subject of litigation between her late husband and the head of his house. The litigation was still going on. It had swallowed huge sums and the countess' prospects of winning were slight. Nevertheless she felt herself to be the future owner of the forest, and was so certain of her title that she determined to present the forest to Letitia as a dowry and to record this gift in proper legal form.

One evening she entered Letitia's bedroom with a written document in her hand. Over her filmy night dress she wore a heavy coat of Russian sable and on her head she had a rubber cap which was to protect her from the bacilli which, in her opinion, whirred about in the darkness like bats.

" Take this and read it, my child," she said with emotion, and handed Letitia the document according to which, at the end of the pending lawsuit, the forest of Heiligenkreuz was to become the sole property of Letitia von Febronius.

Letitia knew the circumstances and the probable value of the piece of paper. But she also knew that the countess had no desire to deceive any one, but was honestly convinced of the

importance of the gift. So she exerted her mind and her tact
to exhibit a genuine delight. She leaned her cheek against
the mighty bosom of the countess and whispered entrancingly:
" You are inexpressibly kind, auntie. You really force a confession from me."

" What is it, darling? "

" I find life so wonderful and so lovely."

" Ah, my dear, that's what I want you to do," said the
countess. " When one is young each day should be like a
bunch of freshly picked violets. It was so in my case."

" I believe," Letitia answered, " that my life will always be
like that."

XI

In the vicinity of Königstein in the Taunus mountains the
Wahnschaffes owned a little château which Frau Wahnschaffe
called Christian's Rest and which was really the property of
her son. At first—he was still a boy—Christian had protested
against the name. " I don't need any rest," he had said.
And the mother had answered: " Some day the need of it will
come to you."

Frau Wahnschaffe invited the countess to pass the month of
May at Christian's Rest. It was a charming bit of country,
and the delight of the countess was uttered noisily.

Crammon, of course, came too. He observed the countess
with Argus eyes, and it annoyed him to watch the frequent
conversations between Christian and Letitia.

He sat by the fishpond holding his short, English pipe between his lips. " We must get to Paris. That was our agreement. You know that I promised you Eva Sorel. If you
don't hurry more than fame is doing, you'll be left out in the
cold."

" Time enough," Christian answered laughing and pulling a
reed from the water.

" Only sluggards say that," Crammon grunted, " and it's the

act of a sluggard to turn the head of a little goose of eighteen and finally to be taken in by her. These young girls of good family are fit for nothing in the world except for some poor devil whose debts they can pay after the obligatory walk to church. Their manipulations aren't nearly as harmless as they seem, especially when the girls have chaperones who are so damnably like procuresses that the difference is less than between my waistcoat buttons and my breeches buttons."

"Don't worry," Christian soothed his angry friend. "There's nothing to fear."

He threw himself in the grass and thought of Adda Castillo, the beautiful lion-tamer whom he had met in Frankfort. She had told him she would be in Paris in June, and he meant to stay here until then. He liked her. She was so wild and so cold.

But he liked Letitia too. She was so dewy and so tender. Dewy is what he called the liquidness of her eyes, the evasiveness of her being. Daily in the morning he heard her in her tower-room trilling like a lark.

He said: "To-morrow, Bernard, we'll take the car and drive over to see Adda Castillo and her lions."

"Splendid!" Crammon answered. "Lions, that's something for me!" And he gave Christian a comradely thwack on the shoulder.

XII

Judith took Letitia with her to Homburg, and they visited the fashionable shops. The rich girl bought whatever stirred her fancy, and from time to time she turned to her friend and said: "Would you like that? Do try it on! It suits you charmingly." Suddenly Letitia saw herself overwhelmed with presents; and if she made even a gesture of hesitation, Judith was hurt.

They crossed the market-place. Letitia loved cherries. But when they came to the booth of the huckstress, Judith pushed forward and began to chaffer with the woman because she thought the cherries too dear. The woman insisted on her price, and Judith drew Letitia commandingly away.

She asked her: "What do you think of my brother Christian? Is he very nice to you?" She encouraged Letitia, who was frank, gave her advice and told her stories of the adventures that Christian had had with women. His friends had often entertained her with these romances.

But when Letitia, rocked into security by such sincere sympathy, blushed, and first in silence and with lowered eyes, later in sweet, low words, confessed something of her feeling for Christian, Judith's mouth showed an edge of scorn; she threw back her head and showed the arrogance of a family that deemed itself a race of kings.

Letitia felt that she had permitted herself to slip into a net. She guarded herself more closely, and Crammon's warnings would have been needed no longer.

He offered her many. He sought to inspire in her a wholesome fear of the bravery of youth, to attune her mood to the older vintages among men who alone could offer a woman protection and reliance. He was neither so clever nor so subtle as he thought.

With all his jesuitical cultivation, in the end he felt that something about this girl knocked at his heart. No posing to himself helped. His thought spun an annoying web. Was he to prove the truth of the foolish old legend concerning the voice of the blood? Then he must escape from this haunted place!

Letitia laughed at him. She said: "I'm only laughing because I feel that way, Crammon, and because the sky to-day is so blue. Do you understand?"

"O nymph," sighed Crammon. "I am a poor sinner." And he slunk away.

XIII

Frau Wahnschaffe had decided to arrange a spring festival. It was to illustrate all the splendour which was, on such occasions, traditional in the house of Wahnschaffe. Councils were held in which the major-domo, the housekeeper, the mistress' companion and the countess took part. Frau Wahnschaffe presided at the sessions with the severity of a judge. The countess was interested principally in the question of food and drink.

" My own darling," she said to Letitia, " seventy-five lobsters have been ordered, and two hundred bottles of champagne brought up from the cellar. I am completely overwhelmed. I haven't been so overwhelmed since my wedding."

Letitia stood there in her slenderness and smiled. The words of the countess were music to her. She wanted to lend wings to the days that still separated her from the festival. She trembled whenever a cloud floated across the sky.

Often she scarcely knew how to muffle the jubilation in her own heart. How wonderful, she thought, that one feels what one feels and that things really are as they are. No poet's verse, no painter's vision could vie with the power of her imagination, which made all happenings pure gold and was impenetrable to the shadow of disappointment. Her life was rich—a pure gift of fate.

She merged into one the boundaries of dream and reality. She made up her mind to dream as other people determine to take a walk, and the dim and lawless character of her dream world seemed utterly natural.

One day she spoke of a book that she had read. " It is beautiful beyond belief." She described the people, the scene, and the moving fortunes of the book with such intensity and enthusiasm that all who heard her were anxious to find the book. But she knew neither its title nor the name of the author. They asked her: " Where is the book? Where did

you get it? When did you read it? " " Yesterday," she replied. " It must be somewhere about." She hesitated. She
was begged to find it. And while she seemed to be reflecting
helplessly, Judith said to her: " Perhaps you only dreamed it
all." She cast down her eyes and crossed her arms over her
bosom with an inimitable gesture and answered with a sense
of guilt: " Yes, it seems to me that I did merely dream it all."

Christian asked Crammon: " Do you think that's mere
affection? "

" Not that," answered Crammon, " and yet a bit of feminine
trickery. God has provided this sex with many dazzling
weapons wherewith to overthrow us."

On the day of the festival Letitia wore a gown of white silk.
It was a little dancing frock with many delicate pleats in the
skirt and a dark blue sash about her hips. It looked like the
foam of fresh milk. When she looked into the mirror she
smiled excitedly as though she could not believe her eyes. The
countess ran about behind her and said: " Darling, be careful
of yourself! " But Letitia did not know what she meant.

There was a sense of intoxication in her when she spoke to
the men and women and girls. She had always been fond of
people; to-day they seemed irresistible to her. When she met
Judith in front of the pavillion, which was bathed in light, she
pressed her hands and whispered: " Could life be more beautiful? I am frightened to think this night must end."

XIV

On the meadow in front of the artificial water-fall Christian
and some young girls were playing hide and seek after the
manner of children. They all laughed as they played; young
men formed a circle about them, and watched them half
mockingly and half amused.

In the dark trees hung electric bulbs of green glass which
were so well concealed that the sward seemed to glow with a
light of its own.

Christian played the game with a carelessness that annoyed his partners. The girls wanted it to be taken more seriously, and it vexed them that, in spite of his inattention, he caught them with such ease. The young sister of Meerholz was among them, and Sidonie von Gröben, and the beautiful Fräulein von Einsiedel.

Letitia joined them. She went to the middle of the open space. She let Christian come quite near her. Then she eluded him more swiftly than he had thought possible. He turned to the others, but always Letitia fluttered in front of him. He sought to grasp her, but she was just beyond him. Once he drove her against the box-tree hedge, but she slipped into the foliage and was gone. Her movements, her running and turning, her merry passion had something fascinating; she called from the greenery with the little, laughing cries of a bird. Now he lay in wait for her, and the onlookers became curious.

When she reappeared he feigned not to see her, but suddenly he sped with incredible swiftness to the edge of the fountain's basin where she stood. But she was a shade swifter still and leapt upon the rock, since all the other ways were blocked, and jumped across the water lightly from stone to stone. Her frock with its delicate pleats and loose sleeves fluttered behind her, and when Christian started in pursuit those below applauded.

Above it was dark. Letitia's shoes became wet and her foot slipped. But before Christian could grasp her she swung herself upon a huge boulder between two tall pines as though to defend herself there or else climb still farther. But her footing failed her on the damp moss and she uttered a little cry, for she knew that he had caught her now.

He had caught her, caught her as she fell, and now held her in his arms. She was very quiet and tried to calm her fluttering breath. Christian was breathing heavily too, and he wondered why the girl was so still and silent. He felt her lovely form and drew her a little closer with that suppressed

or not. Nor did it please him to turn back upon a path. If ever it became necessary he soon grew weary.

He did not care for people whose faces showed the strain of intellectual labour, nor such as discoursed of books or of the sciences. Nor did he love the pale or the hectic or the over-eager or those who argued or insisted on the rightness of their opinions. If any one defended an opinion opposed to his own he smiled as courteously as though no difference existed. And it was painful to him to be asked concerning his opinion directly, and rather than bear the burden of a speech of explanation he did not hesitate to feign ignorance.

If in large cities he was forced to walk or ride through the quarters inhabited by the proletarian poor, he hastened as much as possible, compressed his lips, breathed sparingly, and his vexation would give his eyes a greenish glitter.

Once on the street a crippled beggar had caught hold of his great coat. He returned home and presented the coat to his valet. Even in his childhood he had refused to pass places where ragged people were to be seen, and if any one told of misery or need among men he had left the room, full of aversion for the speaker.

He hated to speak or to hear others speak of the functions or needs of the body—of sleep or hunger or thirst. The sight of a human being asleep was repulsive to him. He did not like emphatic leavetakings or the ceremonious greetings of those who had been absent long. He disliked church bells and people who prayed and all things that have to do with the exercise of piety. He was quite without understanding for even the very moderate Protestantism of his father.

He made no demand in words, but instinctively he chose to bear no company but that of well-clad, care-free, and clear-seeing people. Wherever he suspected secrets, hidden sorrows, a darkened soul, a brooding tendency, inner or outer conflicts, he became frosty and unapproachable and elusive. Therefore his mother said: " Christian is a child of the sun and can thrive only in the sunlight." She had made an early cult of keeping far from him all that is turbid, distorted, or touched with pain.

On her desk lay the marble copy of a plaster-cast of Christian's hand—a hand that was not small, but sinewy and delicately formed, capable of a strong grasp, but unused and quiet.

XVII

On the trip from Hanau to Frankfort the automobile accident occurred in which young Alfred Meerholz lost his life. Christian was driving, but, as in the old days when the great tree fell, he remained unharmed.

Crammon had accompanied Christian and Alfred as far as Hanau. There he wanted to visit Clementine von Westernach and then proceed to Frankfort by an evening train. Christian had sent the chauffeur ahead to Frankfort the day before in order to make certain purchases.

Christian at once drove at high speed, and toward evening, as the road stretched out before him empty and free of obstacles, he made the car fly. Alfred Meerholz urged him on, glowing in the intoxication of speed. Christian smiled and let the machine do its utmost.

The trees on both sides looked like leaping animals in a photograph; the white riband of the road rolled shimmering toward them and was devoured by the roaring car; the reddening sky and the hills on the horizon seemed to swing in circles; the air seethed in their ears; their bodies vibrated and yearned to be whirled still more swiftly over an earth that revealed all the allurement of its smoothness and rotundity.

Suddenly a black dot arose in the white glare of the road. Christian gave a signal with his horn. The dot quickly assumed human form. Again the signal shrieked. The figure did not yield. Christian grasped the steering wheel more firmly. Alfred Meerholz rose in his seat and shouted. It was too late for the brake. Christian reversed the wheel energetically; it went a trifle too far. There was a jolt, a concussion, a crash, the groan of a splintering tree, a hissing and crackling of flame, a clash and rattle of steel. It was over in a moment.

Christian lay stunned. Then he got up and felt his limbs and body. He could think and he could walk. " All's right," he said to himself.

Then he caught sight of the body of his friend. The young man lay under the twisted and misshapen chassis with a crushed skull. A little trickle of scarlet blood ran across the white dust of the road. A few paces to one side stood in surprised stupor the drunken man who had not made way.

People at once began gathering hurriedly from all directions. There was a hotel near by. Christian answered many questions briefly. The drunken man was taken in custody. A physician came and examined young Meerholz's body. It was placed on a stretcher and carried into the hotel. Christian telegraphed first to General Meerholz, then to Crammon.

His travelling bag had not been injured. While he was changing his clothes, police officers arrived, and took down his depositions concerning the accident. Then he went to the dining-room and ordered a meal and a bottle of wine.

He barely touched the food. The wine he gradually drank.

He saw himself standing in the dim hot-house awaiting Letitia. She had come animated by her excitement. Languishing and jesting she had whispered: " Well, my lord and master? " And he had said to her: " Have the image of a small toad made of gold, and wear the charm about your throat in order to avert the evil magic."

Her kiss seemed still to be burning on his lips.

At eleven o'clock that night came Crammon, the faithful. " I beg of you, my dear fellow, attend to all necessary arrangements for me," Christian said. " I don't want to pass the night here. Adda Castillo will be getting impatient." He handed Crammon his wallet.

Christian was thinking again of the romantic girl who, like all of her temper, gave without knowing what she gave or to whom, nor knew how long life is. But her kiss burned on his lips. He could not forget it.

Crammon returned. "Everything is settled," he said in a business like way. "The car will be ready in fifteen minutes. Now let us go and say farewell to our poor friend."

Christian followed him. A porter led them to a dim store-room in which the body had been placed until the morrow. A white cloth had been wrapped about the head. At the feet crouched a cat with spotted fur.

Silently Crammon folded his hands. Christian felt a cold breath on his cheeks, but there was no stirring in his breast. When they came out into the open he said: "We must buy a new car in Frankfort. We need not be back here before noon to-morrow. The general cannot possibly arrive until then."

Crammon nodded. But a surprised look sought the younger man, a look that seemed to ask: Of what stuff are you made?

About him, delicate, noble, proud, there was an icy air— the infinitely glassy clarity that rests on mountains before the dawn.

THE GLOBE ON THE FINGERTIPS OF
AN ELF

CRAMMON had been a true prophet. Ten months had sufficed to fix the eyes of the world upon the dancer, Eva Sorel. The great newspapers coupled her name with the celebrated ones of the earth; her art was regarded everywhere as the fine flower of its age.

All those to whose restless spiritual desires she had given form and body were at her feet. The leaders of sorely driven humanity drew a breath and looked up to her. The adorers of form and the proclaimers of new rhythms vied for a smile from her lips.

She remained calm and austere with herself. Sometimes the noise of plaudits wearied her. Hard beset by the vast promises of greedy managers, she felt not rarely a breath of horror. Her inner vision, fixed upon a far and ideal goal, grew dim at the stammered thanks of the easily contented. These, it seemed to her, would cheat her. Then she fled to Susan Rappard and was scolded for her pains.

" We wandered out to conquer the world," said Susan, " and the world has submitted almost without a struggle. Why don't you enjoy your triumph? "

" What my hands hold and my eyes grasp gives me no cause to feel very triumphant yet," Eva answered.

Susan lamented loudly. " You little fool, you've literally gone hungry. Take your fill now! "

" Be quiet," Eva replied, " what do you know of my hunger? "

People besieged her threshold, but she received only a few

and chose them carefully. She lived in a world of flowers. Jean Cardillac had furnished her an exquisite house, the garden terrace of which was like a tropical paradise. When she reclined or sat there in the evening under the softened light of the lamps, surrounded by her gently chatting friends, whose most casual glance was an act of homage, she seemed removed from the world of will and of the senses and to be present in this realm of space only as a beautiful form.

Yet even those who thought her capable of any metamorphosis were astonished when a sudden one came upon her and when its cause seemed to be an unknown and inconsiderable person. Prince Alexis Wiguniewski had introduced the man, and his name was Ivan Michailovitch Becker. He was short and homely, with deep-set Sarmatian eyes, lips that looked swollen, and a straggling beard about his chin and cheeks. Susan was afraid of him.

It was on a December night when the snow was banked up at the windows that Ivan Michailovitch Becker had talked with Eva Sorel for eight hours in the little room spread with Italian rugs. In the adjoining room Susan walked shivering up and down, wondering when her mistress would call for help. She had an old shawl about her shoulders. From time to time she took an almond from her pocket, cracked it with her teeth, and threw the shells into the fireplace.

But on this night Eva did not go to bed, not even when the Russian had left her. She entered her sleeping chamber and let her hair roll down unrestrained so that it hid her head and body, and she sat on a low stool holding her fevered cheeks in her hollow hands. Susan, who had come to help her undress, crouched near her on the floor and waited for a word.

At last her young mistress spoke. " Read me the thirty-third canto of the *Inferno*," she begged.

Susan brought two candles and the book. She placed the candles on the floor and the volume on Eva's lap. Then she read with a monotonous sound of lamentation. But toward the end, especially where the poet speaks of petrified and frozen tears, her clear voice grew firmer and more eloquent.

> " Lo pianto stesso lì pianger non lascia;
> E il duol, che trova in sugli occhi rintoppo,
> Si volve in entro a far crescer l'ambascia:
> Chè le lagrime prime fanno groppo,
> E, sì come visiere di cristallo,
> Riempion sotto il ciglio tutto il coppo." [1]

When she had finished she was frightened by the gleaming moisture in Eva's eyes.

Eva arose and bent her head far backward and closed her eyes and said: " I shall dance all that—damnation in hell and then redemption! "

Then Susan embraced Eva's knees and pressed her cheek against the bronze coloured silk of the girl's garment and murmured: " You can do anything you wish."

From that night on Eva was filled with a more urgent passion, and her dancing had lines in which beauty hovered on the edge of pain. Ecstatic prophets asserted that she was dancing the new century, the sunset of old ideas, the revolution that is to come.

II

When Crammon saw her again she showed the exquisitely cultivated firmness of a great lady and forced his silent admiration. And again there began that restless burning in his heart.

He talked to her about Christian Wahnschaffe and one evening he brought him to her. In Christian's face there was something radiant. Adda Castillo had drenched it with her passion. Eva felt about him the breath of another woman and her face showed a mocking curiosity. For several seconds

---

[1] " The very weeping there allows them not to weep; and the grief, which finds impediment upon their eyes, turns inward to increase the agony: for their first tears form a knot, and, like crystal vizors, fill up all the cavity beneath their eye-brows."

the young man and the dancer faced each other like two statues on their pedestals.

Crammon wondered whether Christian would ever thank him for this service. He gave his arm to Susan, and the two walked to and fro in the picture gallery.

" I hope your blond German friend is a prince," said Susan with her air of worry.

" He's a prince travelling incognito in this vale of tears," Crammon answered. " You've made some stunning changes here," he added, gazing about him. " I'm satisfied with you both. You are wise and know the ways of the world."

Susan stopped and told him of what weighed upon her mind. Ivan Machailovitch Becker came from time to time, and he and Eva would talk together for many hours. Always after that Eva would pass a sleepless night and answer no questions and have a fevered gleaming in her eyes. And how was one to forbid the marvellous child her indulgence in this mood? Yet it might hold a danger for her. No stray pessimist with awkward hands should be permitted to drag down as with weights the delicate vibrations of her soul. " What do you advise us to do? " she asked.

Crammon rubbed his smooth chin. " I must think it over," he said, " I must think it over." He sat down in a corner and rested his head on his hands and pondered.

Eva chatted with Christian. Sometimes she laughed at his remarks, sometimes they seemed strange and astonishing to her. Yet even where she thought her own judgment the better, she was willing to hear and learn. She regarded his figure with pleasure and asked him to get her, from a table in the room, an onyx box filled with semi-precious stones. She wanted to see how he would walk and move, how he would stretch out his arm and hand after the box and give it to her. She poured the stones into her lap and played with them. She let them glide through her fingers, and said to Christian with a smile that he should have become a dancer.

He answered naïvely that he was not fond of dancing in general, but that he would think it charming to dance with her. His speech amused her, but she promised to dance with him. The stones glittered in her hands; a quiver of her mouth betrayed vexation and pride but also compassion.

When she laughed it embarrassed Christian, and when she was silent he was afraid of her thoughts. He had promised to meet Adda Castillo at almost this hour. Yet he stayed although he knew that she would be jealous and make a scene. Eva seemed like an undiscovered country to him that lured him on. Her tone, her gestures, her expression, her words, all seemed utterly new. He could not tear himself away, and his dark blue eyes clung to her with a kind of balked penetration. Even when her friends came—Cardillac, Wiguniewski, d'Autichamps—he stayed on.

But Eva had found a name for him. She called him Eidolon. She uttered that name and played with its sound even as she played with the mani-coloured jewels in her lap.

III

One night Crammon entered a tavern in the outer boulevards. It was called " Le pauvre Job." He looked about him for a while and then sat down near a table at which several young men of foreign appearance were conversing softly in a strange tongue.

It was a group of Russian political refugees whose meeting place he had discovered. Their chief was Ivan Michailovitch Becker. Crammon pretended to be reading a paper while he observed his man, whom he recognized from a photograph which Prince Wiguniewski had shown him. He had never seen so fanatical a face. He compared it with a smouldering fire that filled the air with heat and fumes.

He had been told that Ivan Becker had suffered seven years of imprisonment and five of Siberian exile and that many thousands of the young men of his people were wholly devoted to him and would risk any danger or sacrifice at his bidding.

" Here they live in the most brilliant spot of the habitable earth," Crammon thought angrily, " and plan horrors."

Crammon was an enemy of violent overthrow. If it did not interfere with his own comfort, he was rather glad to see the poor get the better of the over-fed bourgeois. He was a friend of the poor. He took a condescending and friendly interest in the common people. But he respected high descent, opposed any breach of venerable law, and held his monarch in honour. Every innovation in the life of the state filled him with presentiments of evil, and he deprecated the weakness of the governments that had permitted the wretched parliaments to usurp their powers.

He knew that there was something threatening at the periphery of his world. A stormwind from beyond blew out lamps. What if they should all be blown out? Was not their light and radiance the condition of a calm life?

He sat there in his seriousness and dignity, conscious of his superiority and of his good deeds. As a representative of order he had determined to appeal to the conscience of these rebels if a suitable opportunity were to come. Yet what tormented him was less an anxiety over the throne of the Tsar than one over Eva Sorel. It was necessary to free the dancer from the snares of this man.

An accident favoured his enterprise. One man after another left the neighbouring table and at last Ivan Becker was left alone. Crammon took his glass of absinthe and went over. He introduced himself, referring to his friendship with Prince Wiguniewski.

Silently Becker pointed to a chair.

True to his kind and condescending impulses Crammon assumed the part of an amiable man who can comprehend every form of human aberration. He approached his aim with innocent turns of speech. He scarcely touched the poisonous undergrowth of political contentions. He merely pointed out with the utmost delicacy that, in the West of Europe, the private liberty of certain lofty personages would have to remain untouched unless force were to be used to oppose force. Gentle as his speech was, it was an admonition. Ivan smiled indulgently.

"Though the whole sky were to flare with the conflagrations that devastate your Holy Russia," Crammon said with conscious eloquence, and the corners of his mouth seemed to bend in right angles toward his square chin, "we will know how to defend what is sacred to us. Caliban is an impressive beast. But if he were to lay his hands on Ariel he might regret it."

Again Ivan Michailovitch smiled. His expression was strangely mild and gentle, and gave his homely, large face an almost feminine aspect. He listened as though desiring to be instructed.

Crammon was encouraged. "What has Ariel to do with your misery? He looks behind him to see if men kiss the print of his feet. He demands joy and glory, not blood and force."

"Ariel's feet are dancing over open graves," Ivan Michailovitch said softly.

"Your dead are safe at peace," Crammon answered. "With the living we shall know how to deal."

"We are coming," said Ivan Michailovitch still more softly. "We are coming." It sounded mysterious.

Half fearfully, half contemptuously Crammon looked at the man. After a long pause he said as though casually, "At twelve paces I can hit the ace of hearts four times out of five."

Ivan Michailovitch nodded. "I can't," he said almost humbly, and showed his right hand, which he usually concealed skilfully. It was mutilated.

"What happened to your hand?" Crammon asked in pained surprise.

"When I lay in the subterranean prison at Kazan a keeper

forged the chain about me too hard," Ivan Michailovitch murmured.

Crammon was silent, but the other went on: " Perhaps you've noticed too that it's difficult for me to speak. I lived alone too long in the desert of snow, in a wooden hut, in the icy cold. I became unused to words. I suffered. But that is only a single word: suffering. How can one make its content clear? My body was but a naked scaffolding, a ruin. But my heart grew and expanded. How can I tell it? It grew to be so great, so blood red, so heavy that it became a burden to me in the fearful attempt at flight which I finally risked. But God protected me." And he repeated softly, " God protected me."

In Crammon's mind all ideas became confused. Was this man with his gentle voice and the timid eyes of a girl the murderous revolutionary and hero of possible barricades whom he had expected to meet? In his surprise and embarrassment he became silent.

" Let us go," said Ivan Michailovitch. " It is late." He arose and threw a coin on the table and stepped out into the street at Crammon's side. There he began again, hesitatingly and shyly: " I don't want to presume to judge, but I don't understand these people here. They are so certain of themselves and so reasonable. Yet that reasonableness is the completest madness. A beast of the field that feels the tremor of an earthquake and flees is wiser. And another thing: Ariel, the being whom you strive so eloquently to protect, has no moral responsibility. No one thinks of blaming it. What is it but form, gesture, beauty? But don't you think that the darker hue and deeper power that are born of the knowledge of superhuman suffering might raise art above the interests of idle sybarites? We need heralds who stand above the idioms of the peoples; but those are possibilities that one can only dream of with despair in one's heart." He nodded a brief good-night and went.

Crammon felt like a man who had merrily gone out in a

light spring suit but had been overtaken by a rainstorm and returns drenched and angry. The clocks were striking two. A lady of the Opéra Comique had been waiting for him since midnight; the key to her apartment was in his pocket. But when he came to the bridge across the Seine he seized the key and, overcome by a violent fit of depression, flung it into the water.

"Sweet Ariel!" He spoke softly to himself. "I kiss the prints of your feet."

IV

Adda Castillo noticed that Christian was turning from her. She had not expected that, at least not so soon; and as she saw him grow cold, her love increased. But his indifference kept pace with her ardour, and so her passionate heart lost all repose.

She was accustomed to change and, in spite of her youth, had been greatly loved. She had never demanded fidelity before nor practised it. But this man was more to her than any other had been.

She knew who was robbing her of him; she had seen the dancer. When she called Christian to account he frankly admitted as a fact what she had mentioned only as a suspicion in the hope of having it denied. She instituted comparisons. She found that she was more beautiful than Eva Sorel, more harmoniously formed, racier and more impassioned. Her friends confirmed her in this opinion; and yet she felt that the other had some advantage to which she must yield. Neither she nor her flatterers could give it a name. But she felt herself the more deeply affronted.

She adorned her person, she practised all her arts, she unfolded all sides of her wild and entrancing temperament. It was in vain. Then she vowed vengeance and clenched her fists and stamped. Or else she begged and lay on her knees before him and sobbed. One method was as foolish as the other. He was surprised and asked calmly: " Why do you throw aside all dignity? "

One day he told her that they must separate. She turned very white and trembled. Suddenly she took a revolver from her pocket, aimed at him and fired twice. He heard the bullets whiz past his head, one on either side. They hit the mirror and smashed it, and the fragments clattered to the floor.

People rushed to the door. Christian went out and explained that the noise meant no harm and was due to mere carelessness. When he returned he found Adda Castillo lying on the sofa with her face buried in the pillows. He showed no fright and no sense of the danger that he had escaped. He thought merely how annoying such things were and how banal. He took his hat and stick and left the room.

It was long before Adda Castillo arose. She went to the mirror and shivered. There was but one fragment of it left in the frame. But by the help of this fragment she smoothed her coal-black hair.

A few days later she came to see Christian. On the card that she had sent in she begged for an interview of but five minutes. Her farewell performance in Paris was to take place that evening and she begged him to be present at the circus. He hesitated. The glowing eyes in the wax-white face were fixed on him in a mortal terror. It made him uncomfortable, but something like pity stirred within him and he agreed to come.

Crammon accompanied him. They entered just as Adda Castillo's act was about to begin. The cage with the lions was being drawn into the arena. Their seats were near the front. " They're getting to be a bit of a bore, these lions," Crammon grumbled and watched the audience through his glasses.

Adda Castillo in scarlet fleshings, her dark hair loose, her lips and cheeks heavily rouged, entered the cage of the lionness and her four cubs. Perhaps something in the woman's bearing irritated Teddy, the youngest lion. At all events he backed before her, roared and lifted his paw. Adda Castillo whistled and commanded him with a gesture to leave the mother animal. Teddy crouched and hissed.

At that moment Adda, instead of mastering the beast with her glance, turned to the public and searched the front rows with her sparkling eyes. Teddy leaped on her shoulder. She was down. One cry arose from many throats. The people jumped up. Many fled. Others grew pale but stared in evil fascination at the cage.

At that moment Trilby, the mother animal, came forward with a mighty leap, not to attack her mistress but to save her from the cubs. With powerful blows of her paw she thrust Teddy aside and stood protectingly over the girl who was bleeding from many wounds. But the cubs, greedy for blood, threw themselves on their mother and beat and bit her back and flanks, so that she retreated howling to a corner and left the girl to her fate.

The keepers had rushed up with long spears and hooks, but it was too late. The cubs had bitten their teeth deep into the body of Adda Castillo and torn her flesh to shreds. They did not let go until formaldehyde was sprinkled on her scattered remains.

The cries of pity and terror, the weeping and wringing of hands, the thronging at the gates and the noise of the circus men, the image of a clown who stood as though frozen on a drum, a horse that trotted in from the stables, the sight of the bloody, unspeakably mutilated body in its dripping shreds —none of all this penetrated in any connected or logical form the consciousness of Christian. It seemed to him mere confusion and ghostly whirl. He uttered no sound. Only his face was pale. His face was very pale.

In the motor car on their way to Jean Cardillac, with whom they were to dine, Crammon said: " By God, I wouldn't like to die between the jaws of a lion. It is a cruel death and an ignominious one." He sighed and surreptitiously looked at Christian.

Christian had the car stop and asked Crammon to present his excuses to Cardillac. "What are you going to do?" Crammon asked in his astonishment.

And Christian replied that he wanted to be alone, that he must be alone for a little.

Crammon could scarcely control himself. "Alone? You? What for?" But already Christian had disappeared in the crowd.

"He wants to be alone! What an insane notion!" Crammon growled. He shook his head and bade the chauffeur drive on. He drew up the collar of his greatcoat and dedicated a last thought to the unhappy Adda Castillo without assigning any guilt or blame to his friend.

V

"Eidolon is not as cheerful as usual," Eva said to Christian. "What has happened? Eidolon mustn't be sad."

He smiled and shook his head. But she had heard of the happening at the circus and also knew in what relation Adda Castillo had stood to Christian.

"I had a bad dream," he said and told her of it.

"I dreamed that I was in a railroad station and wanted to take a train. Many trains came in but roared and passed with indescribable swiftness. I wanted to ask after the meaning of this. But when I turned around I saw behind me in a semi-circle an innumerable throng. And all these people looked at me; but when I approached them, they all drew away slowly and silently with outstretched arms. All about in that monstrous circle they drew silently away from me. It was horrible."

She passed her hand over his forehead to chase the horror away. But she recognized the power of her touch and was frightened by her image in his eye.

When from the stage where she was bowing amid the flowers and the applause she perceived the touch of his glances she felt in them a threat of enslavement. When on his arm she approached a table and heard the delighted whisper of people at them both, she seemed to herself the victim of a conspiracy, and a hesitation crept into her bearing. When Crammon, practising a strange self-abnegation, spoke of Christian in extravagant terms, and Susan, even in their nocturnal talks, grew mythical concerning his high descent, when Cardillac grew restless and Cornelius Ermelang, the young German poet who adored her, asked questions with his timid eyes—when these things came to pass she feigned coldness and became unapproachable.

She scolded Susan, she made fun of Crammon, she laughed at Jean Cardillac, jestingly she bent her knee to the poet. She confused her entire court of painters, politicians, journalists, and dandies with her incomprehensible mimicry and flexibility, and said that Eidolon was only an illusion and a symbol.

Christian did not understand this—neither this nor her swift withdrawals from him, and then her turning back and luring him anew. A passionate gesture would arise and suddenly turn to reproof, and one of delight would turn into estrangement. It was useless to try to bind her by her own words. She would join the tips of her fingers and turn her head aside and look out of the corners of her eyes at the floor with a cool astuteness.

Once he had driven her into a corner, but she called Susan, leaned her head against the woman's shoulder and whispered in her ear.

Another time, in order to test her feeling, he spoke of his trip to England. With charmingly curved hands she gathered up her skirt and surveyed her feet.

Another time, in the light and cheerful tone they used to each other, he reproached her with making a fool of him. She crossed her arms and smiled mysteriously, wild and subdued at once. She looked as though she had stepped out of a Byzantine mosaic.

He knew the freedom of her life. But when he sought for the motives that guided her, he had no means of finding them.

He knew nothing of the intellectual fire of the dancer, but took her to be a woman like any other. He did not see that that which is, in other women, the highest stake and the highest form of life, needed to be in her life but a moment's inclination and a moment's gliding by. He did not grasp the form in her, but saw the contour melt in glimmering change. Coming from the sensual regions of one possessed like Adda Castillo, he breathed here an air purified of all sultriness, which intoxicated but also frightened him, which quickened the beat of the heart but sharpened the vision.

Everything was fraught with presages of fate: when she walked beside him; when they rode side by side in the Bois de Boulogne; when they sat in the twilight and he heard her clear and childlike voice; when in the palm garden she teased her little monkeys; when she listened to Susan at the piano and let the bright stones glide through her fingers.

One evening when he was leaving he met Jean Cardillac at the gate. They greeted each other. Then involuntarily Christian stopped and looked after the man, whose huge form threw a gigantic shadow on the steps. Invisible little slaves seemed to follow this shadow, all bearing treasures to be laid at Eva's feet.

An involuntary determination crystallized in him. It seemed important to measure his strength against this shadow's. He turned back and the servants let him pass. Cardillac and Eva were in the picture gallery. She was curled up on a sofa, rolled up almost like a snake. Not far from those two, on a low stool, sat Susan impassive but with burning eyes.

"You've promised to drive with me to the races at Longchamp, Eva," said Christian. He stood by the door to show that he desired nothing else.

"Yes, Eidolon. Why the reminder? " answered Eva without moving, but with a flush on her cheeks.

"Quite alone with me——? "

"Yes, Eidolon, quite alone."

"My dream suddenly came back to me, and I thought of that train that wouldn't stop."

She laughed at the naïve and amiable tone of his words. Her eyes grew gentle and she laid her head back on the pillows. Then she looked at Cardillac, who arose silently.

"Good-night," said Christian and went.

It was during these days that Denis Lay had arrived in Paris. Crammon had expected him and now welcomed him with ardour. "He is the one man living who is your equal and who competes with you in my heart," Crammon had said to Christian.

Denis was the second son of Lord Stainwood. He had had a brilliant career at Oxford, where his exploits had been the talk of the country. He had formed a new party amid the undergraduates, whose discussions and agitations had spared no time-honoured institutions. At twenty-two he was not only a marksman, hunter, fisherman, sailor, and boxer, but a learned philologist. He was handsome, wealthy, radiant with life, and surrounded by a legend of mad pranks and by a halo of distinction and elegance—the last and finest flower of his class and nation.

Christian recognized his qualities without envy and the two became friends at once. One evening he was entertaining Cardillac, Crammon, Wiguniewski, Denis Lay, the Duchess of Marivaux, and Eva Sorel. And it was on this occasion that Eva, in the presence of the whole company, lightly broke the promise that she had given him.

Denis had expressed the desire to take her to Longchamp in his car. Eva became aware of Christian's look. It was watchful, but still assured. She held a cluster of grapes in her hand. When she had placed the fruit back on the plate before her, she had betrayed him. Christian turned pale. He felt that she needed no reminder. She had chosen. It was for him to be quiet and withdraw.

Eva took up the cluster of grapes again. Lifting it on the palm of her hand she said with that smile of dreamy enthusiasm which seemed heartless to Christian now: "Beautiful fruit, I shall leave you until I am hungry for you."

Crammon raised his glass and cried: "Whoever wishes to do homage to the lady of our allegiance—drink! "

They all drank to Eva, but Christian did not lift his eyes.

VI

On the next night after her performance, Eva had invited several friends to her house. She had danced the chief rôle in the new pantomime called "The Dryads," and her triumph had been very great. She came home in a cloud of flowers. Later a footman brought in a basket heaped with cards and letters.

She sank into Susan's arms, happy and exhausted. Every pore of her glowed with life.

Crammon said: "There may be insensitive scoundrels in the world. But I think it's magnificent to watch a human being on the very heights of life."

For this saying Eva, with graceful reverence, gave him a red rose. And the burning in his breast became worse and worse.

It had been agreed that Christian and Denis were to have a fencing bout. Eva had begged for it. She hoped not only to enjoy the sight, but to learn something for her own art from the movements of the two young athletes.

The preparations had been completed. In the round hall hung with tapestries, Christian and Denis faced each other. Eva clapped her hands and they assumed their positions. For a while nothing was heard except their swift, muffled, and rhythmical steps and the clash of their foils. Eva stood erect, all eye, drinking in their gestures. Christian's body was slenderer and more elastic than the Englishman's. The latter had more strength and freedom. They were like brothers of whom one had grown up in a harsh, the other in a mild climate; the one self-disciplined and upheld by a long tradition of breeding, the other cradled in tenderness and somewhat uncertain within. The one was all marrow, the other all radiance. In virility and passion they were equals.

Crammon was in the seventh heaven of enthusiasm.

When the combat was nearly at an end, Cornelius Ermelang appeared, and with him Ivan Michailovitch Becker. Eva had asked Ermelang to read a poem. He and Becker had known each other long, and when he had found the Russian walking to and fro near the gate he had simply brought him up. It was the first time that Ivan showed himself to Eva's other friends.

Both were silent and sat down.

Christian and Denis had changed back to their usual garments, and now Ermelang was to read. Susan sat down near Becker and observed him attentively.

Cornelius Ermelang was a delicate creature and of a repulsive ugliness. He had a steep forehead, watery blue eyes with veiled glances, a pendulous nether lip, and a yellowish wisp of beard at the extreme end of his chin. His voice was extraordinarily gentle and soft, and had something of the sing-song rhythm of a preacher's.

The name of the poem was " Saint Francis and Why Men Followed Him," and its content was in harmony with the traditions and the writings.

Once upon a time Saint Francis was tarrying in the convent of Portiuncula with Brother Masseo of Marignano, who was himself a very holy man and could speak beautifully and wisely concerning God. And for this reason Saint Francis loved him greatly. Now one day Saint Francis returned from the forest where he had been praying, and just as he emerged from the trees Brother Masseo came to meet him and said: " Why thee rather than another? Why thee? "

Saint Francis asked: "What is the meaning of thy words?"
Brother Masseo replied: "I ask why all the world follows thee,
and why every man would see thee and listen to thee and obey
thee. Thou art not goodly to look upon, nor learned, nor of
noble blood. Why is it that all the world follows thee?"
When Saint Francis heard this he was glad in his heart, and he
raised his face to Heaven and stood without moving for a long
space, because his spirit was lifted up to God. But when
he came to himself again, he threw himself upon his knees
and praised and thanked God, and full of a devout passion
turned to Brother Masseo and spoke: "Wouldst thou know
why they follow me, and me always, and me rather than another? This grace has been lent to me by the glance of
Almighty God Himself which rests on the good and the evil
everywhere. For His holy eyes saw among the sinners on
earth none who was more wretched than I, none who was less
wise and able, nor any who was a greater sinner. For the
miraculous work that He had it in His heart to bring about He
found no creature on earth so mean as I. And therefore dio
He choose me to put to shame the world with its nobility and
its pride and its strength and its beauty and its wisdom, in
order that it might be known that all power and goodness
proceed from Him alone and from no created thing, and that no
one may boast before His face. But whoever boast, let him
boast in the Lord." And Brother Masseo was frightened at
this answer, which was so full of humility and spoken with
such fervour.

And the poem related how Brother Masseo went into the
forest out of which Saint Francis had come, and how tones as
of organ music came from the tops of the trees and formed
more and more clearly the question: Wouldst thou know why?
Wouldst thou know? And he cast himself upon the earth,
upon the roots and stones, and kissed the roots and stones and
cried out: "I know why! I know why!"

VII

The stanzas had a sweetness and an inner ecstasy; their music was muffled and infinitely fluid, with many but shy and half-hidden rimes.

"It is beautiful," said Denis Lay, who understood German perfectly.

And Crammon said: "It is like an old painting on glass."

"What I admire most," said Denis, "is that it brings the figure of Saint Francis very close to one with that magical quality of *cortesia* which he possessed above all other saints."

"*Cortesia?* What does it mean exactly?" Wiguniewski asked. "Does it mean a humble and devout courtesy?"

Eva arose. "That is it," she said, "just that." And she made an exquisite gesture with both hands. All looked at her, and she added: "To give what is mine, and only to appear to take what is another's, that is *cortesia.*"

During all this conversation Christian had withdrawn himself from the others. Aversion was written on his face. Even during the reading he had hardly been able to keep his seat. He did not know what it was that rebelled in him and irritated him supremely. A spirit of mockery and scorn was in him and fought for some expression. With assumed indifference he called out to Denis Lay, and began to talk to him about the stallion that Lay desired to sell and Christian to possess. He had offered forty thousand francs for it. Now he offered forty-five thousand, and his voice was so loud that all could hear him. Crammon stepped to his side as though to guard him.

"Eidolon!" Eva cried suddenly.

Christian looked at her with a consciousness of guilt. Their eyes met. The others became silent in surprise.

"The beast is worth that anywhere," Christian murmured, without taking his eyes from Eva.

"Come, Susan." Eva turned to the woman, and about her

mouth curled an expression of bitterness and scorn. "He knows how to fence and how to trade horses. Of *cortesia* he knows nothing. Good-night, gentlemen." She bowed and slipped through the green hangings.

In consternation the company scattered.

When she had reached her room Eva threw herself into a chair, and in bitterness of spirit hid her face in her hands. Susan crouched near her on the floor, waiting and wondering. When a quarter of an hour had passed she arose and took the clasps out of Eva's hair and began to comb it.

Eva was passive. She was thinking of her own master and of what he had taught her.

VIII

This is what her master had taught her: Train your body to fear and obey the spirit. What you grant the body beyond its necessity makes you its slave. Never be the one seduced. Seduce others, and your way will always be your own to see. Be a secret to others or you grow vulgar to yourself. Give yourself wholly only to your work. Passions of sense lay waste the heart. What one man truly receives of another is never the fullness of the hour or the soul, but lees and dregs that are fructified late and unconsciously.

She had been only twelve, when, persuaded by jugglers and answering the call of her fate, she had left her home in a remote little Franconian town. She was very far from her master then. But the way was pre-determined.

She never lost herself. She glided over difficulties and degradations as the chamois does over boulders and abysses. Whoever saw her amid the strolling jugglers held her to be the kidnapped child of distinguished parents. She was, as a matter of fact, the daughter of an obscure musician named Daniel Nothafft and of a servant girl. A dreamy feeling of pity and admiration united her to her father; her mother she had never known, and so discarded her ill-sounding name.

She was accustomed to pass the night in tents and barns. In towns by the sea she had often slept in the shelter of cliffs wrapped in a blanket. She knew the nocturnal sky with its clouds and stars. She had slept on straw amid the animals too, near asses and dogs, and on the rickety, over-burdened cart had ridden on the roadways through rain and snow. It was a romantic life that recalled another age.

She had had to sew her own costumes and to go through her daily and difficult exercises under the whip of the chief of the jugglers. But she learned the language of the country, and secretly bought at fairs in cities the books of the poets who had used it. Secretly she read, sometimes from pages torn out of the volumes and thus more easily concealed, Béranger, Musset, Victor Hugo, and Verlaine.

She walked the tight rope which, without any protective net below, was slung from gable to gable across the market-places of villages, and she walked as securely as on the ground. Or she acted as the partner of a dancing she-bear or with five poodles who turned somersaults. She was a trapeze artist too, and her greatest trick was to leap from one horse in full gallop to another. When she did that the hurdy-gurdy stopped its music so that the spectators might realize what a remarkable thing they were seeing. She carried the collection plate along the rope, and her glance persuaded many a one to dip into his pocket who had meant to slink away.

It was in villages and little towns lying along the Rhône that she first became aware among the spectators of a man who dragged himself about with difficulty on two crutches. He followed the troupe from place to place, and since his whole attention was fixed on Eva, it was evident that he did so for her sake.

It was after two years of this wandering life that in Lyons she was seized with typhoid fever. Her companions sent her to a hospital. They could not wait, but the chief juggler was to return after a period and fetch her. When he did return she was just beginning to convalesce. Suddenly by her bedside she also saw the man with the crutches. He took the juggler aside and one could see that they were talking about money. From the pressure of her old master's hand Eva knew that she saw him for the last time.

IX

The man with the crutches was named Lucas Anselmo Rappard. He saved Eva and awakened her. He taught her her art. He took her under his care, and this care was tyrannical enough. He did not set her free again until she had become all that he had desired to make of her.

He had long lived in retirement at Toledo, because there were three or four paintings in the Spanish city that rewarded him for his isolation from the busy world. Also he found that the sun of Spain warmed him through and through, and that he liked the folk.

In spite of his crippled state he journeyed northward once a year to be near the ocean. And like the men of old he went slowly from place to place. His sister Susan was his unfailing companion. It was on one of his return journeys that he had seen Eva quite by chance. The village fairs of this region had long attracted him. And there he found unexpectedly something that stimulated his creative impulse. It was a sculptor's inspiration. He saw the form in his mind's eye. Here was the material ready to his hand. The sight of Eva relit an idea in him to which he had long despaired of giving a creative embodiment.

First he called the whole matter a whim. Later, absorbed in his task, he knew the passion of a Pygmalion.

He was forty at that time or a little more. His beardless face was thick-boned, peasant-like, brutal. But on closer observation the intellect shone through the flesh. The greenish-grey eyes, very deep-set in their hollows, had so compelling a glance that they surprised and even frightened others.

This remarkable man had an origin and a fate no less remarkable. His father had been a Dutch singer, his mother a
Dalmatian. They had drifted to Courland, where an epidemic
killed both at almost the same time. The two children had
been taken into the ballet school of the theatre at Riga.
Lucas Anselmo justified the most brilliant hopes. His incomparable elasticity and lightness surpassed anything that had yet
been seen in a young dancer. At seventeen he danced at the
Scala in Milan, and roused the public to a rare exhibition of
enthusiasm. But his success was out of its due time—too late
or too early. His whole personality had something strange
and curiously transplanted; and soon he became estranged
from himself and from the inner forces of his life. At twenty
a morbid melancholy seized him.

He happened at that time to be dancing in Petrograd. A
young but lately married lady of the court fell in love with
him. She persuaded him to visit her on a certain night in a
villa beyond the city. But her husband had been warned.
He pleaded the necessity of going on a journey to make his
wife the more secure. Then with his servants he broke into
the lovers' chamber, had the lad beaten cruelly, then tied,
and thrown naked into the snow. Here in the bitter cold the
unhappy dancer lay for six hours.

A dangerous illness and a permanent crippling of his legs
were the result of this violent adventure. Susan nursed him
and never left him for an hour. She had always admired
and loved him. Now she worshipped him. He had already
earned a little fortune, and an inheritance from his mother's
side increased it, so he was enabled to live independ-
ently.

A new man developed in him. His deformity gave to his
mind the resilience and power that had been his body's. In
a curious way he penetrated all the regions of modern life;
and above pain, disappointment, and renunciation, he built a
road from the senses to the mind. In his transformation from

a dancer to a cripple he divined a deep significance. He now sought an idea and a law; and the harsh contrast between external calm and inner motion, of inner calm and outward restlessness, seemed to nim important in any interpretation of mankind and of his age.

At twenty-two he set himself to study Latin, Greek, and Sanskrit. He became a thorough student, and took courses at the German universities. And this strange student, who dragged himself along on crutches, was often an object of curiosity. At the age of thirty he travelled with Susan to India, and lived for four years at Delhi and Benares. He associated with learned Brahmins and received their mystic teachings. Once he had sight of an almost legendary Thibetan priest, who had lived in a cave of the mountains for eighty years, and whom the eternal darkness had blinded, but whom the eternal loneliness had made a saint. The sight of the centenarian moved him, for the first time in his life, to tears. He now understood saintliness and believed in it. And this saint danced: he danced at dawn, turning his blinded eyes to the sun.

He saw the religious festivals in the temple cities on the Ganges, and felt the nothingness of life and the indifference of death when he saw those who had died of pestilence float by hundreds down the stream. He had himself carried into primeval forests and jungles, and saw everywhere in the inextricable coil of life and death each taking the other's form and impulse—decay becoming birth and putrefaction giving life. He was told of the marble-built city of a certain king, in which dwelled only dancing girls taught by priests. When their flesh faded and their limbs lost their agility, they were slain. They had vowed chastity, and none was permitted to survive the breaking of that vow. He approached the fabled city but could not gain admission. At night he saw the fires on its roofs, and heard the songs of its virginal dancers. Now and then it seemed to him that he heard a cry of death.

This night, with its fires and songs, its unseen dancers and uncertain cries, stored up new energies within his soul.

X

He took Eva with him to Toledo. He had rented a house there in which, men said, the painter El Greco had once dwelled.

The building was a grey cube, rather desolate within. Cats shared the dwelling, and owls, bats, and mice.

Several rooms were filled with books, and these books became Eva's silent friends in the years that came now, and during which she saw almost no one but Rappard and Susan.

In this house she learned to know loneliness and work and utter dedication to a task.

She entered the house full of fear of him who had forced her into it. His speech and behaviour intimidated her so that she had terror-stricken visions when she thought of him. But Susan did all in her power to soothe the girl.

Susan would relate stories concerning her brother at morning or in the evening hours, when Eva lay with her body desperately exhausted, too exhausted often to sleep. She had not been spoiled. The life with the troupe of jugglers had accustomed her to severe exertions. But the ceaseless drill, the monotonous misery of the first few months, in which everything seemed empty and painful, without allurement or brightness or intelligible purpose, made her ill and made her hate her own limbs.

It was Susan's hollow voice that besought her to be patient; it was Susan who massaged her arms and legs, who carried her to bed and read to her. And she described her brother, who in her eyes was a magician and an uncrowned king, and on whose eyes and breath she hung, described him through his past, which she retold in its scenes and words, at times too fully and confusedly, at others so concretely and glowingly that Eva began to suspect something of the good fortune of the coincidence that had brought her to his attention.

Finally came a day on which he spoke to her openly: " Do you believe that you were born to be a dancer? " " I do believe it," she answered. Then he spoke to her concerning the dance, and her wavering feeling grew firmer. Gradually she felt her body growing lighter and lighter. When they parted on that day, ambition was beginning to flame in her eyes.

He had taught her to stand with outstretched arms and to let no muscle quiver; to stand on the tips of her toes so that her crown touched a sharp arrow; to dance definite figures outlined by needles on the floor with her naked feet, and, when each movement had passed into her very flesh, to brave the needles blindfolded. He taught her to whirl about a taut rope adjusted vertically, and to walk on high stilts without using her arms.

She had had to forget how she had walked hitherto, how she had stridden and run and stood, and she had to learn anew how to walk and stride and run and stand. Everything, as he said, had to become new. Her limbs and ankles and wrists had to adjust themselves to new functions, even as a man who has lain in the mire of the street puts on new garments. " To dance," he would say, " means to be new, to be fresh at every moment, as though one had just issued from the hand of God."

He inducted her into the meaning and law of every movement, into the inner structure and outer rhythm of every gesture.

He created gestures with her. And about every gesture he wove some experience. He showed her the nature of flight, of pursuit, of parting, of salutation, of expectancy and triumph and joy and terror; and there was no motion of a finger in which the whole body did not have a part. The play of the eyes and of facial expression entered this art so little that the swathing of the face would not have diminished the effect that was aimed at.

He drew the kernel from each husk; he demanded the quintessential only.

" Can you drink? Let me see you! " It was wrong. " Your gesture was a shopworn phrase. The man who had never seen another drink did not drink thus."

" Can you pray? Can you pluck flowers, swing a scythe, gather grain, bind a veil? Give me an image of each action! Represent it! " She could not. But he taught her.

Whenever she fell into a flat imitation of reality he foamed with rage. " Reality is a beast! " he roared, and hurled one of his crutches against the wall. " Reality is a murderer."

In the statues and paintings of great artists he pointed out to her the essential and noble lines, and illustrated how all that had been thus created and built merged harmoniously again with nature and her immediacy of truth.

He spoke of the help of music to her art. " You need no melody and scarcely tone. The only thing that matters is the division of time, the audibly created measure which leads and restrains the violence, wildness, and passion, or else the softness and sustained beauty of motion. A tambourine and a fife suffice. Everything beyond that is dishonesty and confusion. Beware of a poetry of effect that does not issue from your naked achievement."

At night he took her to wine rooms and taverns, where the girls of the people danced their artless and excited dances. He revealed to her the artistic kernel of each, and let her dance a bolero, a fandango, or a tarantella, which in this new embodiment had the effect of cut and polished jewels.

He reconstructed antique battle-dances for her, the Pyrrhic and the Karpaian; the dance of the Muses about the altar of Zeus on Helicon; the dance of Artemis and her companions; the dance of Delos, which imitated the path of Theseus through the labyrinth; the dance of the maidens in honour of Artemis during which they wore a short chiton and a structure of willow on their heads; the vintners' dance preserved on the cup of Hiero, which includes all the motions used by the gatherers of the vine and the workers at the winepress. He showed her pictures of the vase of François, of the geometrical vase of Dipylon, of many reliefs and terracotta pieces, and made her study the figures that had an entrancing charm and incomparable rhythm of motion. And he procured her music for these dances, which Susan copied from old manuscripts, and which he adapted.

And from these creative exercises he led her on to a higher freedom. He now stimulated her to invent for herself, to feel with originality and give that feeling a creative form. He vivified her glance, that was so often in thrall to the technical or merely beautiful, liberated her senses, and gave her a clear vision of that deaf, blind swarm and throng whom her art would have to affect. He inspired her with love for the immortal works of man, armoured her heart against seduction by the vulgar, against a game but for the loftiest stakes, against action without restraint, being without poise.

But it was not until she left him that she understood him wholly.

When he thought her ripe for the glances of the world he gave her recommendations to smooth the way, and also Susan. He was willing to be a solitary. Susan had trained a young Castilian to give him the care he needed. He did not say whether he intended to stay in Toledo or choose some other place. Since they had left him, neither Eva nor Susan had heard from him: he had forbidden both letters and messages.

XI

Often in the night Susan would sit in some dark corner, and out of her deep brooding name her brother's name. Her thoughts turned about a reunion with him. Her service to Eva was but a violent interruption of the accustomed life at his side.

She loved Eva, but she loved her as Lucas Anselmo's work

and projection. If Eva gained fame it was for him, if she gathered treasure it was for him, if she grew in power it was for him. Those who approached Eva and felt her sway were his creatures, his serfs, and his messengers.

After the incident with Christian Wahnschaffe, as Susan crouched at Eva's feet and, as so often, embraced the girl's knees, she thought: Ah, he has breathed into her an irresistible soul, and made her beautiful and radiant.

But always she harboured a superstitious fear. She trembled in secret lest the irresistible soul should some day flee from Eva's body, and the radiance of her beauty be dulled, and nothing remain but a dead and empty husk. For that would be a sign to her that Lucas Anselmo was no more.

For this reason it delighted her when ecstasy and glee, glow and tumult reigned in Eva's life, and she was cast down and plagued by evil presentiments when the girl withdrew into quietness and remained silent and alone. So long as Eva danced and loved and was mobile and adorned her body, Susan dismissed all care concerning her brother. Therefore she would sit and fan the flame from which his spirit seemed to speak to her.

" Just because you've chosen the Englishman, you needn't send the German away," she said. " You may take the one and let the other languish a while longer. You can never tell how things will change. There are many men: they rise and fall. Cardillac is going down-hill now. I hear all kinds of rumours."

Eva, hiding her face in her hands, whispered: " Eidolon."

It vexed Susan. " First you mock him, then you sigh for him! What folly is this? "

Eva sprang up suddenly. " You shan't speak of him to me or praise him, wretched woman." Her cheeks glowed, and the brightly mocking tone in which she often spoke to Susan became menacing.

" *Golpes para besos,*" Susan murmured in Spanish. " Blows

for kisses." She arose in order to comb Eva's hair and braid it for the night.

The next day Crammon appeared. " I found you one whose laughter puts to shame the laughter of the muleteer of Cordova," he said with mock solemnity. " Why is he rejected? "

His heart bled. Yet he wooed her for his friend. Much as he loved and admired Denis Lay, yet Christian was closer to him. Christian was his discovery, of which he was vain, and his hero.

Eva looked at him with eyes that glittered, and replied: " It is true that he knows how to laugh like that muleteer of Cordova, but he has no more culture of the heart than that same fellow. And that, my dear man, is not enough."

" And what is to become of us? " sighed Crammon.

" You may follow us to England," Eva said cheerfully. " I'm going to dance at His Majesty's Theatre. Eidolon can be my page. He can learn to practise reverence, and not to chaffer for horses when beautiful poems are being read to me. Tell him that."

Crammon sighed again. Then he took her hand, and devoutly kissed the tips of her fingers. " I shall deliver your message, sweet Ariel," he said.

XII

Cardillac and Eva fell out, and that robbed the man of his last support. The danger with which he was so rashly playing ensnared him; the abysses lured him on.

The external impetus to his downfall was furnished by a young engineer who had invented a hydraulic device. Cardillac had persuaded him with magnificent promises to let him engage in the practical exploitation of the invention. It was not long before the engineer discovered that he had been cheated of the profits of his labour. Quietly he accumulated evidence against the speculator, unveiled his dishonest dealings, and presented to the courts a series of annihilating charges. Although Cardillac finally offered him five hundred thousand francs if he would withdraw his charges, the outraged accuser remained firm.

Other untoward circumstances occurred. The catastrophe became inevitable. On a single forenoon the shares he had issued dropped to almost nothing. In forty-eight hours three hundred millions of francs had been lost. Innumerable well-established fortunes plunged like avalanches into nothingness, eighteen hundred mechanics and shop-keepers lost all they had in the world, twenty-seven great firms went into bankruptcy, senators and deputies of the Republic were sucked down in the whirlpool, and under the attacks of the opposition the very administration shook.

Felix Imhof hurried to Paris to save whatever was possible out of the crash. Although he had suffered painful losses, he was ecstatic over the grandiose spectacle which Cardillac's downfall presented to the world.

Crammon laughed and rubbed his hands in satisfaction, and pointed to Imhof. " He wanted to seduce me, but I was as chaste as Joseph."

On the following evening Imhof went with his friends to visit Eva Sorel. She had left the palace which Cardillac had furnished for her, and had rented a handsome house in the Chaussée d'Antin.

Imhof spoke of the curious tragedy of these modern careers. As an example he related how three days before his collapse Cardillac had appeared at the headquarters of his bitterest enemies, the Bank of Paris. The directors were having a meeting. None was absent. With folded hands and tear-stained face the sorely beset man begged for a loan of twelve millions. It was a drastic symptom of his naïveté that he asked help of those whom he had fleeced on the exchange year in and year out, whose losses had glutted his wealth, and whom he wanted to fight with the very loan for which he begged.

Christian scarcely listened. He stood with Crammon beside

a Chinese screen. Opposite them sat Eva in a curiously dreamy mood, and not far from her was Denis Lay. Others were present too, but Christian gave them no attention.

Suddenly there was a commotion near the door. " Cardillac," some one whispered. All glances sought him.

It was indeed Cardillac who had entered. His boots were muddy, his collar and cravat in disorder. He seemed not to have changed his garments for a week. His fists were clenched; his restless eyes wandered from face to face.

Eva and Denis remained calmly as they were. Eva pressed her foot against the edge of a copper jar filled with white lilies. No one moved. Only Christian, quite involuntarily, approached Cardillac by a few paces.

Cardillac became aware of him, and drew him by the sleeve toward the door of the adjoining room. They had scarcely crossed the threshold when Cardillac whispered in an intense but subdued tone: " I must have two thousand francs or I'm done for! Advance me that much, monsieur, and save me. I have a wife and a child."

Christian was astonished. No one dreamed that the man had a family. And why turn precisely to him? Wiguniewski, d'Autichamps, many others knew him far better.

" I must be at the station in half an hour," he heard the man say, and his hand sought his purse.

Wife and child! The words flitted through his head, and there arose in him the violent aversion he always felt in the presence of beggars. What had he to do with it all? He took out the bank notes. Two thousand francs, he thought, and remembered the huge sums which one was accustomed to name in connection with the man who stood before him begging.

" I thank you." Cardillac's voice came to him as through a wall.

Then Cardillac passed him with bent head. But two men had in the meantime appeared in the other room. At the open folding-door the lackeys stood behind them with an embarrassed expression, for the men were police officials who were seeking Cardillac and had followed him here.

Cardillac, seeing them and guessing their errand, recoiled with a gurgling noise in his throat. His right hand disappeared in his coat-pocket, but instantly the two men leaped on him and pinioned his arms. There was a brief, silent struggle. Suddenly he was made fast.

Eva had arisen. Her guests crowded about her. She leaned against Susan's shoulder and turned her head a little aside, as though a touch of uncanny terror brushed her. But she still smiled, though now with pallid cheeks.

" He's magnificent, magnificent, even at this moment," Imhof whispered to Crammon.

Christian stared at Cardillac's huge back. It was, he couldn't help thinking, like the back of an ox dragged to slaughter. The two men between whom he stood hand-cuffed had greasy necks, and the hair on the back of their heads was dirty and ill-trimmed.

An unpleasant taste on his palate tormented Christian. He asked a servant for a glass of champagne.

Cardillac's words, " I have a wife and a child," would not leave his mind. On the contrary, they sounded ever more stridently within him. And suddenly a second, foolish, curious voice in him asked: How do you suppose they look—this wife, this child? Where are they? What will become of them?

It was as annoying and as painful as a toothache.

XIII

In Devon, south of Exeter, Denis Lay had his country seat. The manor stood in a park of immemorial trees, velvety swards, small lakes that mirrored the sky, and flowerbeds beautiful in the mildest climate of such a latitude on earth.

" We're quite near the Gulf Stream here," Crammon explained to Christian and Eva, who, like himself, were Lay's guests. And he had an expression as though with his own hands he had brought the warm current to the English coast from the Gulf of Mexico simply for the benefit of his friends.

With a gesture of sisterly tenderness Eva walked for hours among the beds of blossoming violets. Large surfaces were mildly and radiantly blue. It was March.

A company of English friends was expected, but not until two days later.

The four friends, going for a walk, had been overtaken by showers and came home drenched. When they had changed their clothes, they met for tea in the library. It was a great room with wainscoting of dark oak and mighty cross-beams, Halfway up there ran along the walls a gallery with carved balustrades, and at one end, between the pointed windows, appeared the gilded pipes of an organ.

The light was dim and the rain swished without. Eva held an album of Holbein drawings, and turned the pages slowly. Christian and Crammon were playing at chess. Denis watched them for a while. Then he sat down at the organ and began to play.

Eva looked up from the pictures and listened.

" I've lost the game," Christian said. He arose and mounted the steps to the gallery. He leaned over the balustrade and looked down. In an outward curve of the balustrade there lay, like an egg in its cup, a globe on a metal stand.

" What were you playing? " Eva asked, as Denis paused.

He turned around. " I've been trying to compose a passage from the Song of Songs," he answered. He played again and sang in an agreeable voice: " Arise, thou lovely one, for the winter is past."

The sound of the organ stirred a feeling of hatred in Christian. He gazed upon Eva's form. In a gown of sea-green, slim, far, estranged, she sat there. And as he looked at her there blended with his hatred of the music another feeling—one of oppression and of poignant pain, and his heart began to throb violently.

"Arise, thou lovely one, and come with me," Denis sang again, and Crammon softly hummed the air too. Eva looked up, and her glance met Christian's. In her face there was a mysterious expression of loftiness and love.

Christian took the globe from its stand and played with it. He let it roll back and forth between his hands on the flat balustrade like a rubber ball. The sphere suddenly slipped from him, fell and rolled along the floor to Eva's feet.

Denis and Crammon gathered about it; Christian came down from the gallery.

Eva picked up the globe and went toward Christian. He took it from her, but she at once held out her hands again. Then she held it daintily poised upon the fingertips of her right hand. Her left hand, with fingers spread out, she held close to it; her head was gently inclined, her lips half open.

"So this is the world," she said, "your world! The blue bits are the seas, and that soiled yellow the countries. How ugly the countries are, and how jagged! They look like a cheese at which mice have nibbled. O world, the things that creep about on you! The things that happen on you! I hold you now, world, and carry you! I like that!"

The three men smiled, but a psychical shudder passed through them. For they could no longer stand in human erectness on this little round earth. A breath of the dancer could blow them down into the immeasurable depths of the cosmos.

And Christian saw that Denis, fighting with an impulse, regarded him. Suddenly the Englishman came up to him and held out his hand. And Christian took the hand of his victorious rival, and knew in his secretest mind that an ultimate advantage was his. For between Eva's face and the smudged globe he seemed to see a ghostly little figure which charmed her with its glance and which was a tiny image of himself— Eidolon.

They planned that summer to return to the manor and hunt

the deer, as was the custom of the gentlemen of that region. But when summer came all things had changed, and Denis had glided from the smooth sphere of earth into the depth.

XIV

One day in London Crammon came to Christian, sat down affectionately beside him, and said: " I am leaving."

" Where are you going? " Christian asked in surprise.

" North, to fish salmon," Crammon replied. " I'll join you later or you can join me."

" But why go at all? "

" Because I'll go straight to the dogs if I have to see this woman any longer without possessing her. That's all."

Christian looked at Crammon with a flame in his eyes, and checked a gesture of angry jealousy. Then his face assumed its expression of friendly mockery again.

So Crammon departed.

Eva Sorel became the undisputed queen of the London season. Her name was everywhere. The women wore hats à la Eva Sorel, the men cravats in her favourite colours. She threw into the shade the most sought-after celebrities of the day—including the Negro bruiser, Jackson. Fame came to her in full draughts, and gold by the pailfuls.

XV

May was very hot in London that year. Denis and Christian planned a night's pleasure on the Thames. They rented a steam yacht named " Aldebaran," ordered an exquisite meal on board, and Denis sent out invitations to his friends.

Fourteen members of his set joined the party. The yacht lay near the houses of Parliament, and shortly before midnight the guests appeared in evening dress. The son of the Russian ambassador was among them, the Honourable James Wheely, whose brother was in the ministry, Lord and Lady Westmoreland, Eva Sorel, Prince Wiguniewski, and others.

On the stroke of twelve the "Aldebaran" started out, and the small orchestra of well-chosen artists began to play.

When the yacht on its way upstream had reached the railway bridge of Battersea, there became visible on the left bank in the dim light of the street lamps an innumerable throng of men and women, close-packed, head by head, thousands upon thousands.

They were strikers from the docks. Why they stood here, so silent and so menacing in their silence, was known to no one on board. Perhaps it was a demonstration of some sort.

Denis, who had had a good deal of champagne, went to the railing, and in his recklessness shouted three cheers across the river. No sound answered him. The human mass stood like a wall, and in the sombre faces that turned toward the gleam of the yacht's light no muscle moved.

Then Denis said to Christian, who had joined him: " Let's swim across. Whoever reaches shore first is victor of the race, and must ask those people what they are waiting for and why they don't go home at this hour of the night."

" Swim over to *them?* " Christian shook his head. He was asked to touch slimy worms with his hands and pretend they were trophies.

" Then I'll do it alone! " Denis exclaimed, and threw his coat and waistcoat down on the deck.

He was known to be an admirable swimmer. The company therefore took his notion as one of the bizarre pranks for which he was known. Only Eva tried to restrain him. She approached him and laid her hand on his arm. In vain. He was quite ready to jump, when the captain grasped his shoulder and begged him to desist, since the river, despite its calm appearance, had a strong undercurrent. But Denis eluded him, ran to the promenade deck, and in another moment his slender body flew into the black water.

No one had a presentiment of disaster. The swimmer advanced with powerful strokes. The watchers on board were sure that he would easily reach the Chelsea shore. But suddenly, in the bright radiance of a searchlight from shore, they saw him throw up his arms above his head. At the same moment he cried piercingly for help. Without hesitation a member of the little orchestra, a cellist, sprang overboard in all his garments to help the drowning man. But the current caused by the ebbtide was very powerful, and both Denis and the musician were whirled onward by it, and disappeared in the inky waves.

Suddenly the confusion caused by these happenings lifted from Christian's mind, and before any could restrain him, he was in the water. He heard a cry, and knew that it came from Eva's lips. The ladies and gentlemen on board scurried helplessly to and fro.

Christian could no longer make out the forms of the other two. The water seemed to bank itself against him and hinder his movements. A sudden weakness took possession of him, but he felt no fear. Raising his head he saw the silent masses of the workers, men and women with such expressions as he had never seen. Although the glance which he directed toward them was but a momentary one, he felt almost sure that their sombre earnestness of gaze was fixed on him, and that these thousands and thousands were waiting for him, and for him alone. His weakness increased. It seemed to arise from his heart, which grew heavier and heavier. At that moment a life-boat reached him.

At three o'clock in the morning, in the earliest dawn, the bodies of Denis and the musician were found jammed between two beams near the arches of a bridge. Now they lay on deck and Christian could contemplate them. The guests had left the ship. Eva, too, had gone. She had been deeply shaken, and Prince Wiguniewski had accompanied her home.

The sailors had gone to their bunks. The deck was empty, and Christian sat alone with the two dead men.

The sun arose. The waters of the river began to glow. The

pavements of the desolate streets, the walls and the windows of the houses flushed with the red of dawn. Sea-gulls circled about the smokestack.

Christian sat alone with the dead men. He was huddled in an old coat which the captain had thrown around his shoulders. Steadily he gazed upon the faces of the dead. They were swollen and ugly.

XVI

North of Loch Lomond, Christian and Crammon wandered about shooting snipes and wild ducks. The land was rough and wild; always within their hearing thundered the sea; storm-harried masses of cloud raced across the sky.

"My father will be far from pleased," said Christian. "I've spent two hundred and eighty thousand marks in the last ten months."

"Your mother will persuade him to bear it," Crammon answered. "Anyhow, you're of age. You can use several times that much without any one hindering you."

Christian threw back his head, and drew the salty air deep into his lungs. "I wonder what little Letitia is doing," he said.

"I think of the child myself at times. She shouldn't be left entirely to that old schemer," Crammon replied.

Her kiss no longer burned on Christian's lips, for other flames had touched them since. Like laughing *putti* in a painting, the lovely faces fluttered about him. Many of them, to be sure, were laughing now no more.

In a dark gown, emerging from between two white columns, Eva had taken leave of him. He seemed to see her still—the brunette pallor of her face, her inexpressibly slender hand, the most eloquent hand in the world.

Jestingly and familiarly she had spoken to him in the language of her German homeland, which seemed more piercingly sweet and melodious in her mouth than in any other's.

"Where are you going, Eidolon?" she had asked carelessly.

He had answered with a gesture of uncertainty. He evidently thought that his going or coming was indifferent to her.

"It isn't nice of you to go without asking leave," she said, and put her hands on his shoulders. "But perhaps it is just as well. You confuse me. I am beginning to think of you, and I don't want to do that."

"Why not?"

"Because I don't. Why do you need reasons?"

The dead and swollen face of Denis Lay rose up before them, and they both saw it in the empty air.

After a little he had dared to ask: "When shall we meet again?"

"It depends on you," she had answered. "Always let me know where you are, so that I can send for you. Of course, it's nonsense, and I won't. But it might just happen that in some whim I may want you and none other. Only you must learn——" She stopped and smiled.

"What, what must I learn?"

"Ask your friend Crammon. He'll teach you." After these words she had left him.

The sea roared like a herd of steers. Christian stopped and turned to Crammon. "Listen, Bernard, there's a matter that comes back curiously into my mind. When I last talked to Eva she said there was something I was to learn before I could see her again. And when I asked after her meaning, she said that you could give me a hint. What is it? What am I to learn?"

Crammon answered seriously: "You see, my boy, these things are rather complicated. Some people like their steak overdone, others almost raw, most people medium. Well, if you don't know a certain person's taste and serve the steak the way you yourself prefer it, you risk making a blunder and looking like a fool. People are far from simple."

" I don't understand you, Bernard."

" Doesn't matter a bit, old chap! Don't bother your handsome head about it. Let's go on. This damned country makes me melancholy."

They went on. But there was an unknown sadness in Christian's heart.

AN OWL ON EVERY POST

I

LETITIA felt vague longings.

She accompanied her aunt, the countess, to the south of Switzerland, and loitered in wonder at the foot of blue glaciers; she lay on the shore of Lake Geneva, dreaming or reading poetry. When she appeared smiling on the promenade, admiring glances were all about her. Enthusiastically conscious of her youth and of her emotional wealth, she enjoyed the day and the evening as each came, pictures and books, fragrances and tones. But her longings did not cease.

Many came and spoke to her of love—some frankly and some by implication. And she too was full of love—not for him who spoke, but for his words, expressions, presages. If a delighted glance met hers, it delighted her. And she lent her ear with equal patience to wooers of twenty or of sixty.

But her yearnings were not assuaged.

Her aunt, the countess, said: "Have nothing to do with aristocrats, my dear. They are uncultivated and full of false pride. They don't know the difference between a woman and a horse. They would nail your young heart to a family tree, and if you don't appreciate that favour sufficiently, they stamp you as déclassée for life. If they have no money they are too stupid to earn any; if they have it they don't know how to spend it sensibly. Have no dealings with them. They're not quite human."

The countess' experiences with the aristocracy had been very bitter. "You can imagine, my dear," she said, " that I was hard pressed in my time to be forced to say these things now."

Letitia sat on the edge of her bed and regarded her silk stocking, which had a little hole in it, and still felt the same longing.

Judith wrote her: " We expect you and the countess so soon as we are settled in our new house near Frankfort. It's a kind of fairy palace that papa has built us, and it's to be the family seat hereafter. It's situated in the forest of Schwanheim, and is only ten minutes by motor from the city. Everybody who has seen it is mad about it. Felix Imhof says it reminds him of the palace of the Minotaur. There are thirty-four guest-rooms, a gallery fifty metres long with niches and columns, and a library that's been modelled after the cupola of St. Peter's at Rome. There are twenty thousand perfectly new books in it. Who's to read them all? "

" I love the thought of them," said Letitia, and pressed her hand against her heart.

She had had a golden charm made in the likeness of a tiny toad. She did not wear it about her neck, but kept it in a little leathern case, from which she often took it, and brooded over it lovingly.

In Schwetzingen she had met a young Argentinian of German descent. He was studying law at Heidelberg, but he confessed to her frankly that he had come to Europe to get him a German wife. He gave her this information at noon. At night he gave her to understand that in her he had met his goal.

His name was Stephen Gunderam. His skin was olive, his eyes glowing, his hair coal black and parted in the middle. Letitia was fascinated by his person, the countess by the rumours of his wealth. She made inquiries, and discovered that the rumours had not been exaggerated. The lands of the Gunderams on the Rio Plata were more extensive than the Duchy of Baden.

" Now, sweetheart, there's a husband for you!" said the countess. But when she considered that she would have to part with Letitia, she began to cry, and lost her appetite for a whole forenoon.

Stephen Gunderam told them about his far, strange country, about his parents, brothers, servants, herds, houses. He declared that the bride he brought home would be a queen. He was so strong that he could bend a horse-shoe. But he was afraid of spiders, believed in evil omens, and suffered from frequent headaches. At such times he would lie in bed, and drink warm beer mixed with milk and the yolk of eggs. This was a remedy which an old mulatto woman had once given him.

Letitia barely listened. She was reading:

> "And have you seen an inmost dream
> Fled from you and denied?
> Then gaze into the flowing stream,
> Where all things change and glide."

"You really must hurry, darling," the countess admonished her again.

But Letitia was so full of longing.

II

In a city on the Rhine, Christian and Crammon were delayed by an accident. Something had happened to the motor of their car, and the chauffeur needed a whole day for repairs.

It was a beautiful evening of September, so they left the city streets and wandered quietly along the bank of the river. When darkness fell, they drifted by chance into a beer-garden near the water. The tables and benches, rammed firmly into the earth, stood among trees full of foliage, and were occupied by several hundred people—tradesmen, workingmen, and students.

"Let us rest a while and watch the people," said Crammon. And near the entrance they found a table with two vacant seats. A bar-maid placed two pitchers of beer before them.

Under the trees the air had something subterranean about it, for it was filled with the odour of the exudations of so many people. The few lamps had iridescent rings of smoke about them. At the adjoining table sat students with their red caps and other fraternity insignia. They had fat, puffed-out faces and insolent voices. One of them hit the table three times with his stick. Then they began to sing.

Crammon opened his eyes very wide, and his lips twitched mockingly. He said: " That's my notion of the way wild Indians act—Sioux or Iroquois." Christian did not answer. He kept his arms quite close to his body, and his shoulders drawn up a little. There was a good deal of noise at all the tables, and, after a while, Christian said: " Do let us go. I'm not comfortable here."

" Ah, but my dear boy, this is the great common people!" Crammon instructed him with a mixture of arrogance and mockery. " Thus do they sing and drink and—smell. ' And calmly flows the Rhine.' Your health, your Highness! " He always called Christian that among strangers, and was delighted when those who overheard showed a respectful curiosity. As a matter of fact, several of the men at their table looked at them in some consternation, and then whispered among themselves.

A young girl with blond braids of hair wreathed about her head had entered the garden. She stopped near the entrance, and looked searchingly from table to table. The students laughed, and one called out to her. She hesitated shyly. Yet she went up to him. " Whom are you looking for, pretty maiden? " a freshman asked. The girl did not answer. " Hide in the pitcher for your forwardness," a senior cried. " It is for me to ask." The freshman grinned, and took a long draught of beer. " What do you desire, little maiden? " the senior asked in a beery voice. " Have you come to fetch your father, who clings too lovingly to his jug? " The girl blushed and nodded. She was asked to give her name, and said it was Katherine Zöllner. Her father, she said, was a boatman. She spoke softly, yet so that Christian and Crammon understood what she said. Her father was due to join his ship for Cologne at three o'clock in the morning. " For Cologne," the senior growled. " Give me a kiss, and I'll find your father for you."

The girl trembled and recoiled. But the fraternity approved of the demand, and roared applause. " Don't pretend! " the senior said. He got up, put his arms roughly about her waist, and, despite her resistance and fright, he kissed her.

" Me, too! Me, too! " The cries arose from the others. The girl had already been passed on to a second, a third snatched her, then a fourth, fifth, sixth. She could not cry out. She could scarcely breathe. Her resistance grew feebler, the roaring and the laughter louder. The fellows at the neighbouring table grew envious. A fat man with warts on his face called out: " Now you come to us! " His comrades brayed with laughter. When the last student let her go, it was this man who grasped her, kissed her and threw her toward his neighbour. More and more men arose, stretched out their arms, and demanded the defenceless victim. Nothing happened except that they kissed her. Yet there spread through the crowd a wildness of lust, so that even the women screeched and cried out. The students, in the meantime, proud of their little game, raised their rough voices and sang a foolish song.

The body of the girl, now an unresisting and almost lifeless thing, was whirled from arm to arm. Christian and Crammon had arisen. They gazed into the quivering throng under the trees, heard the shrieks, the cries, the laughter, saw the girl, now far away, and the hands stretched out after her, and her face with eyes that were now closed, now open again in horror. At last one was found who had compassion. He was a young workingman, and he hit the man who was just kissing the girl square between the eyes. Two others then attacked him, and there ensued a rough fight, while the girl with her little remaining strength reeled toward the fence where the ground was grassy. Her hair fell loose, her blue bodice was torn and showed her naked bosom, her face was covered with ugly bruises. She tried to keep erect, groped about, but fell. A few thoughtful people now came up, helped her, and asked each other what was to be done.

Christian and Crammon followed the shore of the river back to the city. The students had begun a new ditty, that sounded discordantly through the night, until the distance gradually silenced it.

III

In the middle of the night Christian left his couch, slipped into a silk dressing gown and entered Crammon's room. He lit a candle, sat down by the side of Crammon's bed, and shook his sleeping friend by the shoulder. Crammon battled with sleep itself, and Christian turned his head away in order not to see the struggling, primitive face.

At last, after much grunting and groaning, Crammon opened his eyes. "What do you want?" he asked angrily. "Are you practising to play a ghost?"

"I would like to ask you something, Bernard," Christian said.

This enraged Crammon all the more. "It is crazy to rob a man of his well-deserved rest. Are you moonstruck, or have you a bellyache? Ask what you want to ask, but hurry!"

"Do you believe I do right to live as I do?" asked Christian. "Be quite honest for once, and answer me."

"There is no doubt that he's moonstruck!" Crammon was truly horrified. "His mind is wandering. We must summon a physician." He half-rose, and fumbled for the electric button.

"Don't do that!" Christian restrained him mildly, and smiled a vexed smile. "Try to consider what I've said. Rub your eyes if you aren't quite awake yet. There's time enough for sleep. But I am asking you, Bernard, for your quite sincere opinion: Do you think I am right in living as I do? "

" My dear Christian Wahnschaffe, if you can tell me by what process this craze has——"

" Don't jest, Bernard," Christian interrupted him, frowning. " This is no time for a jest. Do you think that I should have remained with Eva? "

" Nonsense," said Crammon. " She would have betrayed you; she would have betrayed me. She would betray the emperor, and yet stand guiltless in the sight of God. You can't reckon with her, you can't really be yourself with her. She was fashioned for the eye alone. Even that little story of the muleteer of Cordova was a trick. Be content, and let me sleep."

Christian replied thoughtfully. " I don't understand what you say, and you don't understand what I mean. Since I left her I feel sometimes as though I had grown hunchbacked. Jesting aside, Bernard, I get up sometimes and a terror comes over me. I stretch myself out. I know that I'm straight, and yet I feel as though I were hunchbacked."

" Completely out of his head," Crammon murmured.

" And now tell me another thing, Bernard," Christian continued, undeflected by his friend, and his clear, open face assumed an icy expression. " Should we not have helped the boatman's daughter, you and I? Or should I not have done so, if you did not care to take the trouble? Tell me that! "

" The devil take it! What boatman's daughter? "

" Are you so forgetful? The girl in the beer-garden. She even gave her name—Katherine Zöllner. Don't you remember? And how those ruffians treated her? "

" Was I to risk my skin for a boatman's daughter? " Crammon asked, enraged. " People of that sort may take their pleasures in their own fashion. What is it to you or to me? Did you try to hold back the paws of the wild beasts that tore up Adda Castillo? And that was a good deal worse than being kissed by a hundred greasy snouts. Don't be an idiot, my dear fellow, and let me sleep! "

" I am curious," said Christian.

" Curious? What about? "

" I'm going to the house where she lives and see how she is. I want you to go along. Get up."

Crammon opened his mouth very wide in his astonishment. " Go now? " he stammered, " at night? Are you quite crazy? "

" I knew you'd scold," Christian said softly and with a dreamy smile. " But that curiosity torments me so that I've simply been turning from side to side in bed." And in truth his face had an expression of expectation and of subtle desire that was new to Crammon. He went on: " I want to see what she is doing, what her life is like, what her room looks like. One should know about all that. We are hopelessly ignorant about people of that kind. Do please come on, Bernard." His tone was almost cajoling.

Crammon sighed. He waxed indignant. He protested the frailty of his health and the necessity of sleep for his wearied mind. Since Christian, however, opposed to all these objections an insensitive silence, and since Crammon did not want to see him visit a dangerous and disreputable quarter of the city alone by night, he finally submitted, and, grumbling still, arose from his bed.

Christian bathed and dressed with his accustomed care. Before leaving the hotel they consulted a directory, and found the address of the boatman. They hired a cab. It was half-past four in the morning when their cab reached the hut beside the river bank. There was light in the windows.

Crammon was still at a loss to comprehend. With the rusty bell-pull in his hand, his confused and questioning eyes sought Christian once more. But the latter paid no attention to his friend. A care-worn, under-nourished woman appeared at the door. Crammon was forced to speak, and, with inner vexa⸗

tion, said that they had come to ask after her daughter. The woman, who immediately imagined that her daughter had had secret affairs with rich gentlemen, stepped aside and let the two pass her.

IV

What Crammon saw and what Christian saw was not the same thing.

Crammon saw a dimly lit room, with old chests of drawers that were smoke-stained, with a bed and the girl Katherine on it covered by the coarse, red-checked linen, with a cradle in which lay a whining baby. He saw clothes drying by the oven, the boatman sitting and eating potato soup, a bench on which a lad was sleeping, and many other unclean, ugly things.

To Christian it was like a strange dream of falling. He, too, saw the boatman and the poor woman and the girl, whose glassy eyes and convulsed features brought home to him at once the reason for his visit. But he saw these things as one sees pictures while gliding down a shaft, pictures that recur at intervals, but are displaced by others that slip in between them.

Thus he saw Eva Sorel feeding a walnut to one of her little monkeys.

The boatman got up and took off his cap. And suddenly Christian saw Denis Lay and Lord Westmoreland giving each other their white-gloved hands. It was an insignificant thing; but his vision of it was glaring and incisive.

Now the lad on the bench awakened, stretched himself, sat up with a start, and gave a sombre stare of astonishment at the strangers. The girl, ill from her horrible experience, turned her head away, and pulled the coverlet up to her chin. And suddenly Christian saw the charming vision of Letitia, playing at ball in the great room crossed by the gleams of lightning; and each thing that he saw had a relation to some other thing in that other world.

The curiosity that had brought him hither still kept that unwonted smile on his face. But he looked helplessly at Crammon now, and he was sensitive to the indecency of his silent, stupid presence there, the purposelessness and folly of the whole nocturnal excursion. It seemed almost intolerable to him now to stay longer in this low-ceiled room, amid the odour of ill-washed bodies, and clothing that had been worn for years.

Up to the last moment he had imagined that he would talk to the girl. But it was precisely this that he found it impossible to do. He did not even dare to turn his head to where she lay. Yet he was acutely conscious of her as he had seen her out there, reeling from the tables with loose hair and torn bodice.

When he thought over the words that he might say to her, each seemed strikingly superfluous and vulgar.

The boatman looked at him, the woman looked at him. The lad stared with malevolently squinting eyes, as though he planned a personal attack. And now there emerged also an old man from behind a partition where potatoes were stored, and regarded him with dim glances. In the embarrassment caused him by all these eyes, he advanced a few steps toward Katherine's bed. She had turned her face to the wall, and did not move. In his sudden angry despair he put his hands into pocket after pocket, found nothing, hardly knew indeed what he sought, felt the diamond ring on his finger which was a gift of his mother, hastily drew it off, and threw it on the bed, into the very hands of the girl. It was the act of one who desired to buy absolution.

Katherine moved her head, saw the magnificent ring, and contempt and astonishment, delight and fear, struggled in her face. She looked up, and then down again, and grew pale. Her face was not beautiful, and it was disfigured by the emotions she had experienced during the past hours. An impulse that was utterly mysterious to himself caused Christian suddenly to laugh cheerfully and heartily. At the same time he turned with a commanding gesture to Crammon, demanding that they go.

Crammon had meantime determined to ease the painfulness of the situation in a practical way. He addressed a few words to the boatman, who answered in the dialect of Cologne. Then he drew forth two bank notes and laid them on the table. The boatman looked at the money; the hands of the woman were stretched out after it. Crammon walked to the door.

Five minutes after they had entered the house, they left it again. And they left it swiftly, like men fleeing.

While the cab drove over the rough stones of the street, Crammon said peevishly: " You owe your paymaster a hundred marks. I won't charge you for anything except the money. You can't, I suppose, give me back my lost sleep."

" I shall give you for it the Chinese apple of amber-coloured ivory about which you were so enthusiastic at Amsterdam," Christian replied.

" Do that, my son," Crammon said, " and do it quickly, or my rage over this whole business will make me ill."

When he got up at noon thoroughly rested, Crammon reflected on the incident with that philosophic mildness of which, under the right circumstances, he was capable. After they had had a delightful breakfast, he filled his short pipe, and discoursed: " Such extravagances in the style of Haroun al Rashid get you nowhere, my dear boy. You can't fathom those sombre depths. Why hunt in unknown lands, when the familiar ones still have so many charms? Even your humble servant who sits opposite you is still a very treasure of riddles and mysteries. That is what a wise poet has strikingly expressed:

"What know we of the stars, of water or of wind?
What of the dead, to whom the earth is kind?
Of father and mother, or of child and wife?
Our hearts are hungry, but our eyes are blind."

Christian smiled coolly. Verses, he thought contemptuously, verses. . . .

V

When they reached the magnificent structure in the forest of Schwanheim, they found a great restlessness there and a crowd of guests. Letitia had not yet arrived; Felix Imhof was expected hourly; purveyors and postmen came and went uninterruptedly. The place hummed like a hive.

Frau Wahnschaffe greeted Christian with restraint and dignity, although her joy gave her eyes a phosphorescent gleam. Judith looked exhausted, and paid little attention to her brother. But one evening she suddenly rushed into his arms, with a strange wild cry that betrayed the impatience and the hidden desires that had so long preyed on the cold and ambitious girl.

Christian felt the cry like a discord, and disengaged himself.

He and Crammon went hunting or took trips to the neighbouring cities. Nothing held Christian anywhere. He wanted always to go farther or elsewhere. His very eyes became restless. When they walked through the streets, he glanced surreptitiously into the windows of apartments and into the halls of houses.

One night they sat in a wine cellar at Mainz, drinking a vintage that was thirty years old and had a rare bouquet. Crammon, who was a connoisseur through and through, kept filling his glass with an enchanted air. "It's sublime," he said, and began eating his caviare sandwich, "simply sublime. These are the realities of life. Here are my altars, my books of devotion, my relics, the scenes of my silent prayers. The immortal soul is at rest, and the lofty and unapproachable lies in the dust behind me."

"Talk like a decent man," said Christian.

But Crammon, who felt the ecstasy of wine, was not to be deflected. "I have drunk the draught of earthly delight. I have done it, O friend and brother, in huts and palaces, North

and South, on sea and land. Only the final fulfilment was
denied me. O Ariel, why did you cast me forth? "

He sighed, and drew from his inner pocket a tiny album
in a precious binding. He always had it with him, for it
contained twelve exquisite photographs of the dancer, Eva
Sorel. " She is like a boy," he said, wholly absorbed in the
pictures, " a slender, swift, unapproachable boy. She stands
on the mystic boundary line of the sexes; she is that equivocal
and twofold thing that maddens men if they but think of flesh
and blood. Elusive she is as a lizard, and chill in love as an
Amazon. Do you not feel a touch of horror, Christian? Does
not a cold ichor trickle through your veins, when you imagine
her in your arms, breast to breast? I feel that horror! For
there would be something of the perverse in it—something
of an unnatural violation. He who has touched her lips is lost.
We saw that for ourselves."

Christian suddenly felt a yearning to be alone in a forest,
in a dark and silent forest. He did feel a sense of horror, but
in a way utterly alien to Crammon's thought. He looked
at the older man, and it was hard for him to comprehend
that there, opposite him, sat his familiar friend, whose face
and form he had seen a thousand times unreflectively.

Crammon, contemplating the photograph on which Eva
appeared dancing with a basket of grapes, began again:
" Sweetest Ariel, they are all harlots, all, all, all, whether
shameless and wild or fearful and secretive: you alone are
pure—a vestal, a half-ghost, a weaver of silk, like the spider,
who conquers the air upon her half-spun web. Let us drink,
O friend! We are made of dirt, and must be medicined by
fire! "

He drained his glass, rested his head upon his hand, and
sank into melancholy contemplation.

Suddenly Christian said: " Bernard, I believe that we must
part."

Crammon stared at him, as though he had not heard right.

" I believe that we must part," Christian repeated softly and with an indistinct smile. " I fear that we are no longer suited to each other. You must go your ways, and I shall go mine."

Crammon's face became dark red with astonishment and rage. He brought his fist down on the table and gritted his teeth. " What do you mean? Do you think you can send me packing as though I were a servant? Me? " He arose, took his hat and coat, and went.

Christian sat there for long with his thoughts. The indistinct smile remained on his lips.

When Christian, on awakening next day, rang for his valet, Crammon entered the room in the man's stead and made a deep bow. Over his left arm he had Christian's garments, in his right hand his boots. He said good-morning quite in the valet's tone, laid the clothes on a chair, set the boots on the floor, asked whether the bath was to be prepared at once, and what Herr Wahnschaffe desired for breakfast. And he did all this with complete seriousness, with an almost melancholy seriousness, and with a certain charm within the rôle he was assuming that could not fail to be pleasing.

Christian was forced to laugh. He held out his hand to Crammon. But the latter, refusing to abandon his acting, drew back, and bowed in embarrassment. He pulled the curtains aside, opened the windows, spread the fresh shirt, the socks, the cravat, and went, only to return a little later with the breakfast tray. After he had set the table and put the plates and cups in order, he stood with heels touching and head gently inclined forward. Finally, when Christian laughed again, the expression of his features altered, and he asked half-mockingly, half-defiantly: " Are you still prepared to assert that you can get along without me? "

" It's impossible to close accounts with you, dear Bernard," Christian answered.

" It is not one of my habits to leave the table when only

the soup has been served," Crammon said. " When my time
comes I trundle myself off without urging. But I don't permit
myself to be sent away."

" Stay, Bernard," Christian answered. He was shamed by
his friend. " Only stay! " And their hands clasped.

But it almost seemed to Christian that his friend had really
in a sense become a servant, that he was one now, at all events,
toward whom one no longer had the duty of intimate openness,
with whom no inner bond united one—a companion merely.

From that time on, jests and superficial persiflage were
dominant in their conversations, and Crammon either did not
see or failed very intentionally to observe that his relations
with Christian had undergone a fundamental change.

VI

The arrival of the Argentinian caused a commotion among
the guests of the house of Wahnschaffe. He had exotic habits.
He pressed the hands of the ladies to whom he was presented
with such vigour that they suppressed a cry of pain. Whenever he came down the stairs he stopped a few steps from
the bottom, swung himself over the balustrade like an acrobat,
and went on as though this were the most natural thing in the
world. He had presented the countess with a Pekingese dog,
and whenever he met the animal he tweaked its ear so that it
howled horribly. And he did not do that merrily or with a
smile, but in a dry, businesslike manner.

Among the numerous trunks that he brought with him, one
was arranged in the form of a travelling pharmacy. Screwed
down tightly in neat compartments there were all possible
mixtures, powders, and medicaments; there were little boxes,
tubes, jars, and glasses. If any one complained of indisposition, he at once pointed out the appropriate remedy in his
trunk, and recommended it urgently.

Felix Imhof had taken an enthusiastic fancy to him. Whenever he could get hold of him, he took him aside, and ques-

tioned him regarding his country, his plans and undertakings, his outer and his inner life.

Judith, who was jealous, resented this bitterly. She made scenes for the benefit of Felix, and reproached Letitia for her failure to absorb Stephen Gunderam's attention.

Letitia was astonished, and her eyes grew large. With innocent coquetry she asked: "What can I do about it?"

Judith's answer was cynical. "One must study to please the men."

She hated the Argentinian. Yet when she was alone with him she sought to ensnare him. Had it been possible to alienate him from Letitia, she would have done so out of sheer insatiableness.

Her eyes glittered with a constant and secret desire. She went to the theatre with Imhof, Letitia, and Stephen to see Edgar Lorm in "The Jewess of Toledo." The applause which was so richly given to the actor stirred the very depth of her soul and filled it with more piercing desire. But whether she desired the man or the artist, his art or his fame, she was herself unable to tell.

She waited impatiently for Crammon, of whose friendship with Lorm she had heard. He was to bring the actor to the house with him. She was accustomed to have all men come after whom she cast her hook. They usually bit, were served up, and then enjoyed in proportion to their excellence of flavour. The household consumption of people was large.

But Crammon and Christian did not return until Lorm's visit to Frankfort was over. So Judith fell into an evil mood, and tormented all about her without reason. Had her wish been fulfilled, her flickering soul, that needed ever new nourishment, might have been calmed. Now she buried herself stubbornly in the thought of what had passed by her.

VII

Crammon and Christian had been spending a week with Clementine and Franz Lothar von Westernach in Styria. Clementine had summoned Crammon for the sake of her brother, who had recently returned from a stay in Hungary with a deeply shaken mind.

Crammon and Franz Lothar were very old friends. The latter's profession of diplomacy had made the frank and flexible man reserved and difficult. He took his profession seriously, although he did not love it. A hypochondriacal state of the nerves had developed in him, even in his youth.

Christian's sympathy went out to him in his present state. He felt tempted to question the man who sat so still and with a dim stare in his eyes. Clementine, in her empty chattering manner, gave Crammon directions for his behaviour, at which he shrugged his shoulders.

She said that she had written to her cousin, Baron Ebergeny, on whose estate in Syrmia Franz had been a guest. But the baron, who was half a peasant, had been able to give her no explanation of any real import. He had merely pointed out that he and Franz Lothar, on one of the last days of the latter's presence, had witnessed the burning of a barn at Orasje, a neighbouring village, during which many people had lost their lives.

No information was to be obtained from Franz Lothar himself. He was steadily silent. His sister redoubled her care, but his sombre reticence only increased. Perhaps Crammon was capable of some tone, some glance, that pierced and melted his petrified soul. One evening, at all events, the unexpected happened. Crammon learnt that the burning of the barn was the real cause of his morbid melancholy.

According to her custom, Clementine had gone to bed early. Christian, Crammon, and Franz Lothar sat silently together. Suddenly—without any external impetus—Franz covered his face with his hands, and deep sobs came from his breast. Crammon sought to soothe him. He stroked his hair and grasped his hands. In vain. The sobbing became a convulsion that shook the man's body violently.

Christian sat without moving. A bitterness rose in his throat, for there came to him with unexpected power a sense of the essential reality of the spiritual pain that was being uttered here.

The convulsion ceased as suddenly as it had begun. Franz Lothar arose, walked up and down with dragging footsteps, and said: "You shall hear how it was." Thereupon he sat down and told them.

In the village of Orasje a dance had been planned. No hall was available, and so the large, well-boarded barn of a peasant was prepared. Numerous lamps were hung up, and the wooden walls adorned with flowers and foliage. According to a local custom, the magnates on all the neighbouring estates and their families received invitations to attend the festivity. A mounted messenger delivered these solemnly by word of mouth.

Franz Lothar begged his brother to take him to the peasants' ball. He had long heard stories in praise of the picturesqueness of these feasts: the snow-white garments of the men, the strong and varied colours of the women's, the national dances, the primitive music. There was a promise in all these, both of pleasure and of a knowledge of new folk-ways.

They intended to drive over at a late hour when the dancing had already begun. Two young countesses and the latters' brother, all members of their circle, planned to join them. But in the end the others went first, for the young ladies did not want to miss any of the dancing. Franz Lothar had long and cordially admired the Countess Irene, who was the older of the two.

Several days before the ball, however, a quarrel had broken out between the youths and maidens of Orasje. On the way to chuch, a lad, whom a seventeen-year-old beauty had given too rude an evidence of her dislike, had put a live mouse on her naked shoulder. The girl ran crying to her companions, and they sent an envoy to the youths, demanding that the guilty one apologize.

The demand was refused. There was laughter and teasing. But they insisted on this punishment, although they were repeated their demand in a more drastic form. When it was refused a second time they determined to invite to their ball the young men of Gradiste, between whom and those of Orasje there was a feud of many years' standing. They knew the insult they were inflicting on the youths of their own village. But they insisited on this punishment, although they were warned even by their fathers and mothers, and by loud and silent threats which should have inspired them with fear.

The youths of Gradiste were, of course, loudly triumphant over their cheap victory. On the evening of the dance they appeared without exception, handsomely dressed, and accompanied by their own village band. Of the youths of Orasje not one was to be seen. In the twilight they passed in ghostly procession through the streets of the village, and were then seen no more.

The elders and the married folk of Orasje sat at tables in their yards and gardens, and chatted. But they were not as care-free as on other festive evenings, for they felt the vengeful mood of their sons, and feared it. They drank their wine and listened to the music. In the barn over three hundred young people were assembled. The air was sultry, and the dancers were bathed in sweat. Suddenly, while they were dancing a Czarda, the two great doors of the barn were simultaneously slammed to from without. Those who saw it and heard it ceased dancing. And now a powerful and disturbing noise broke in upon the loud and jubilant sound of the instruments. It was the sound of hammers, and a sharp and terror-shaken voice called out: " They are nailing up the doors."

The music stopped. In a moment the atmosphere had

become suffocating. As though turned to stone, they all stared at the doors. Their blood seemed to congeal under the terrible blows of the hammers. Loud and mingled voices came to them from without. The older people there raised their protesting voices. The voices grew loud and wild, and then rose to desperate shrieks and howls. Then it began to crackle and hiss. The blows of the hammers had shaken down a lamp. The petroleum had caught on fire, and the dry boarding of the floor flared like tinder that could no longer be extinguished.

All reason and all human restraints fled. In the twinkling of an eye the three hundred became like wild beasts. With the violence of mania the youths hurled themselves against the locked doors; but these had been built of heavy oak, and resisted all exertions. The girls shrieked madly; and since the smoke and the fumes did not all float out through the cracks in the walls and through the small, star-shaped window-holes, the girls drew up their skirts about their heads. Others threw themselves moaning to the floor; and when they were trodden on by the others, who surged so madly to and fro, they writhed convulsively, and stretched out their arms. Soon the dry woodwork had become a mass of flame. The heat was intolerable. Many tore off their garments, both youths and maidens, and in the terror and the torment of death, united in the wild embraces of a sombre ecstasy, and wrung from their doomed lives an ultimate sting of delight.

These embracing couples Franz Lothar saw later with his own eyes as lumps of cinders amid the smoking ruins. He arrived with his cousin, when the whole horror had already taken place. They had seen the reflection of the flames in the sky from afar, and whipped up their horses. From the neighbouring villages streamed masses of people. But they came too late to help. The barn had been burned down within five minutes, and all within, except five or six, had found their death.

Among the victims was also the Countess Irene, her sister

and brother. Terrible as this was, it added but little to the unspeakable horror of the whole catastrophe. The image of that place of ruins; the sight of the smouldering corpses; their odour and the odour of blood and burned hair and garments; the pied, short-haired village dogs, who crept with greedy growls about this vast hearth of cooked flesh; the distorted faces of the suffocated, whose bodies lay untouched amid the other burned and blackened ones; the loud or silent grief of mothers, fathers, brothers; the Syrmian night, fume-filled to the starry sky,—these things rained blow on blow upon the spirit of Franz Lothar, and caused a black despair to creep into the inmost convolutions of his brain.

It eased him that he had at last found the release of speech. He sat by the window, and looked out into the dark.

Crammon, a sinister cloud upon his lined forehead, said: " Only with a whip can the mob be held in leash. What I regret is the abolition of torture. The devil take all humanitarian twaddle! " Then he went out and put his arms about Lothar and kissed him.

But Christian felt a sense of icy chill and rigidness steal over him.

Their departure was set for the next morning. Crammon entered the room of Christian, who was so lost in thoughts that he did not reply to the greeting of his friend. " Look here, what's wrong with you? " Crammon exclaimed, as he examined him. " Have you looked in the glass? "

Christian had dispensed with his valet on this trip, or the slight accident could not have happened. The colours of his suit and his cravat presented an obvious discord.

" I'm rather absent-minded to-day," Christian said, half-smiling. He took off the cravat, and replaced it by another. It took him three times as long as usual. Crammon walked impatiently up and down.

VIII

Confusion seized upon Christian whenever he sought to think about the condition in which he found himself.

In his breast there was an emptiness which nothing could fill from without, and about him was a rigid armour that hindered all freedom of movement. He yearned to fill the emptiness and to burst the armour.

His mother became anxious, and said: " You look peaked, Christian. Is anything wrong with you? " He assured her that there was nothing. But she knew better, and inquired of Crammon: " What ails Christian? He is so still and pale."

Crammon answered: " Dear lady, that is his style of personality. Experiences carve his face. Has it not grown nobler and prouder? You need fear nothing. He follows his road firmly and unwaveringly. And so long as I am with him, nothing evil can happen to him."

Frau Wahnschaffe was moved in her faint way, though still in doubt, and gave him her hand.

Crammon said to Christian: " The countess has made a great catch—a person from overseas. Quite fitting."

" Do you like the man? " Christian asked, uncertainly.

" God forbid that I should think evil of him," Crammon replied, hypocritically. " He is from so far away, and will go so far away again, that I cannot but find him congenial. If he takes that child Letitia with him, he shall be accompanied by my blessings. Whether it will mean her happiness, that is a matter I refuse to be anxious about. Such remote distances have, at all events, something calming. The Argentine, the Rio de la Plata! Dear me, it might just as well be the moon! "

Christian laughed. Yet the figure of Crammon, as it stood there before him, seemed to dissolve into a mist, and he suppressed what he still had to say.

Twenty-three of the guest rooms were occupied. People

arrived and left. Scarcely did one begin to recognize a face, when it disappeared again. Men and women, who had met but yesterday, associated quite intimately to-day, and said an eternal farewell to-morrow. A certain Herr von Wedderkampf, a business associate of the elder Wahnschaffe, had brought his four daughters. Fräulein von Einsiedel arranged to settle down for the winter, for her parents were in process of being divorced. Wolfgang, who was spending his vacation at home, had brought with him three student friends. All these people were in a slightly exalted mood, made elaborate plans for their amusement, wrote letters and received them, dined, flirted, played music, were excited and curious, witty and avid for pleasure, continued to carry on their worldly affairs from here, and assumed an appearance of friendliness, innocence, and freedom from care.

Liveried servants ran up and down the stairs, electric bells trilled, motor car horns tooted, tables were laid, lamps shone, jewels glittered. Behind one door they flirted, behind another they brewed a scandal. In the hall with the fair marble columns sat smiling couples. It was a world thoroughly differentiated from those quite accidental modern groupings at places where one pays. It was full of a common will to oblige, of secret understandings, and of social charm.

Letitia had gone with her aunt to spend a week in Munich. She did not return until the third day after Christian's arrival. Christian was glad to see her. Yet he could not bring himself to enter into conversation with her.

IX

One morning he sat at breakfast with his father. He marvelled how strange to him was this gentleman with the white, parted hair, with the elegantly clipped and divided beard and the rosy complexion.

Herr Wahnschaffe treated him with very great courtesy. He inquired after the social relations that Christian had formed in England, and commented upon his son's frugal answers with instructive remarks concerning men and things. " It is well for Germans to gain ground there—useful and necessary."

He discussed the threatening clouds in the political sky, and expressed his disapproval of Germany's attitude during the Moroccan crisis. But Christian remained silent, through want of interest and through ignorance, and his father became visibly cooler, took up his paper, and began to read.

What a stranger he is to me, Christian thought, and searched for a pretext that would let him rise and leave. At that moment Wolfgang came to the table, and talked about the results of the races at Baden-Baden. His voice annoyed Christian, and he escaped.

It happened that Judith was sitting in the library and teased him about Letitia. Then Letitia herself and Crammon entered chatting. Felix Imhof soon joined them. Letitia took a book, and carefully avoided, as was clear, looking in Christian's direction. Then those three left the room again, and Judith listened with pallor to their retreating voices, for she had heard Felix pay Letitia a compliment. " Perhaps she is committing a great folly," she said. Then she turned to her brother. " Why are you so silent? " She wrinkled her forehead, and rested her folded hands on his shoulder. " We are all merry and light hearted here, and you are so changed. Don't you like to be among us? Isn't it lovely here at home? And if you don't like it, can't you go at any time? Why are you so moody? "

" I hardly know; I am not moody," Christian replied. " One cannot always be laughing."

" You'll stay until my wedding, won't you? " Judith continued, and raised her brows. " I'll never forgive you if you don't." Christian nodded, and then she said with a friendly urgency, " Why don't you ever talk to me, you bear? Ask me something! "

Christian smiled. " Very well, I'll ask you something," he said. " Are you contented, Judith? Is your heart at peace? "

Judith laughed. " That's asking too much at once! You used not to be so forthright." Then she leaned forward, with her elbows on her knees, and spread out her hands. " We Wahnschaffes can never be contented. All that we have is too little, for there is always so much that one has not. I'm afraid I shall be like the fisherman's wife in the fairy tale. Or, rather, I'm not afraid but glad at the thought that I'll send my fisherman back to the fish in the sea again and again. Then I shall know, at least, what he is willing to risk."

Christian regarded his beautiful sister, and heard the temerity of her words. There was an audacity about her gestures, her words, her bright, clear voice, and the glow of her eyes. He remembered how he had sat one evening with Eva Sorel; and she had been as near him as Judith was now. In silent ecstasy he had looked at Eva's hands, and she had raised her left hand and held it against the lamp, and though the radiance outlined only the more definitely the noble form of the rosy translucence of her flesh, the dark shadow of the bony structure had been plainly visible. And Eva had said: " Ah, Eidolon, the kernel knows nothing of beauty."

Christian arose and asked almost sadly: " You will know what he risks. But will that teach you to know what you gain? "

Judith looked up at him in surprise, and her face darkened.

x

One day he entered the sitting-room of his mother, but she was not there. He approached the door that led to her bed-room, and knocked. When he received no answer, he opened it. She was not in this room either. Looking about, he became aware of a brown silk dress trimmed with lace that belonged to his mother and that had been put on a form. And for a second he seemed to see her before him, but without a head. He fell to thinking, and the same thought came to him that he had had in his father's presence: What a stranger she is to me! And the dress, that hid only the wicker form, became an image of his mother, more recognizable to him than her living body.

For there was about her something impenetrable and inexplicable—the rigid attitude, the hopeless mien, the dull eye, the rough voice that had no resonance, her whole joyless character. She, in whose house all made merry, and whose whole activity and being seemed dedicated to give others the opportunity of delight, was herself utterly barren of joy.

But she had the most magnificent pearls in Europe. And all men knew this and esteemed her for it and boasted of it.

Christian's self-deception went so far, that he was about to talk to that hollow form more intimately than he would have done to his living mother. A question leaped to his lips, a tender and cheerful word. Then he heard her footsteps, and was startled. He turned around, and seemed to see her double.

She was not surprised at meeting him here. She was rarely surprised at anything. She sat down on a chair and her eyes were empty.

She discussed Imhof, who had introduced a Jewish friend of his to the house. She deprecated association with Jews as a practice. She added that Wahnschaffe—she always called her husband so—agreed with her.

She expressed her disapproval of Judith's engagement. "Wahnschaffe is really opposed to this marriage too," she said, "but it was difficult to find a pretext to refuse. If Judith sets her heart on anything! Well, you know her! I am afraid her chief ambition was to get ahead of her friend Letitia."

Christian looked up in amazement. His mother did not observe it, and continued: "With all his good qualities Imhof does not seem reliable. He is a plunger, and restless and changeable as a weather vane. Of the ten millions which his foster father left him, five or six are already lost through speculation and extravagance. What is your judgment of him? "

" I haven't really thought about it," Christian answered. This conversation was beginning to weary him.

" Then, too, his origin is obscure. He was a foundling. Old Martin Imhof, whom Wahnschaffe knew, by the way, and who belonged to one of the first patrician families of Düsseldorf, is said to have adopted him under peculiar circumstances. He was an old bachelor, and had a reputation for misanthropy. At last he was quite alone in the world, and absolutely adored this strange child. Hadn't you heard about that? "

" Some rumour, yes," Christian said.

" Well, now tell me something about yourself, my son," Frau Wahnschaffe asked, with a changed expression and with a smile of suffering.

But Christian had no answer. His world and his mother's world—he saw no bridge between the two. And as the knowledge came to him, another matter also became clear. And it was this, that there was likewise no bridge between the world of his conscious life and another that lay far behind it, misty and menacing, luring and terrible at once, which he did not understand, nor know, of which he had not even a definite presage, but which had come to him only as a vision through flashes of lightning, or as a dream or in a swift touch of horror.

He kissed his mother's hand, and hastened out.

XI

In spite of a gently persistent rain, he walked with Letitia through the twilit park. Many times they wandered up and down the path from the hot-houses to the pavillion, and heard the sound of a piano from the house. Fräulein von Einsiedel was playing.

At first their conversation was marked by long pauses. Something in Letitia was beseeching: Take me, take me!

Christian understood. He wore his arrogant smile, but he did not dare to look at her. " I love music heard from afar," Letitia said. " Don't you, Christian? "

He drew his raincoat tighter about him, and replied: " I care little about music."

" Then you have a bad heart, or at least a hard one."

" It may be that I have a bad heart; it is certainly hard."

Letitia flushed, and asked: " What do you love? I mean what things. What? " The archness of her expression did not entirely conceal the seriousness of her question.

" What things I love? " he repeated lingeringly, " I don't know. Does one have to love things? One uses them. That is all."

" Oh, no! " Letitia cried, and her deep voice brought a peculiar warmth to Christian. " Oh, no! Things exist to be loved. Flowers, for instance, and stars. One loves them. If I hear a beautiful song or see a beautiful picture, at once something cries within me: That is mine, mine! "

" And do you feel that too when a bird suddenly drops down and dies, as you have seen it happen? Or when a wounded deer dies before you when you are hunting? " Christian asked, hesitatingly.

Letitia was silent, and looked at him with a touch of fear. The glance of her eyes was inexpressibly grateful to him. Take me, take me, that silent voice pleaded with him again. " But those are not things," she said softly, " they are living beings."

His voice was gentler than hitherto when he spoke again: " All things that are fragrant and glowing, that serve adornment and delight are yours indeed, Letitia. But what are mine? " He stood still, and asked again with a look of inner distress which shook Letitia's soul. Never had she expected such words or such a tone of him.

Her glance reminded him: you kissed me once! Think of it—you kissed me once!

" When is your wedding going to be? " he asked, and his lids twitched a little.

" I don't know exactly. We're not even formally engaged at present," Letitia answered, laughing. " He has declared that I must be his wife and won't be contradicted. Christmas my mother is coming to Heidelberg, and then, I suppose, the wedding will take place. What I do look forward to is the voyage overseas and the strange country." And in her radiant eyes flamed up the impassioned plea: Oh, take me, take me! My yearning is so great! But with a coquettish turn of the head, she asked: " How do you like Stephen? "

He did not answer her question, but said softly: " Some one is watching us from the house."

Letitia whispered: " He is jealous of the very earth and air." It began to rain harder, and so they turned their steps toward the house. And Christian felt that he loved her.

An hour later he entered the smoking room. Imhof, Crammon, Wolfgang, and Stephen Gunderam sat about a round table, and played poker. The demeanour of each accorded with his character: Imhof was superior and talkative, Crammon absentminded and sombre, Wolfgang distrustful and excited. Stephen Gunderam's face was stonily impassive. He was as utterly dedicated to his occupation as a somnambulist. He has been winning uninterruptedly, and a little mountain of bank notes and gold was rising in front of him. Crammon and Imhof moved aside to make room for Christian. At that moment Stephen jumped up. Holding his cards in his hand, he stared at Christian with eyes full of hatred.

Christian regarded him with amazement. But when the other three, rather surprised, also moved to get up, Stephen Gunderam sank back into his chair, and said with sombre harshness: " Let us play on. May I ask for four cards? "

Christian left the neighbourhood of the table. He felt that he loved Letitia. His whole heart loved her, tenderly and with longing.

XII

A discharged workman had lain in wait one evening for the automobile of Herr Albrecht Wahnschaffe. When the car slowed up and approached the gate of the park, the assassin, hidden by the bushes, had stealthily shot at his former employer.

The bullet only grazed its victim's arms. The wound was slight, but Albrecht Wahnschaffe had to remain in bed for several days. After his deed the criminal had escaped under cover of darkness. It was not until next morning that the police succeeded in catching him.

This happening, inconsiderable as were its consequences, had disturbed for a little the merry life in the house of Wahnschaffe. Several persons left. Among these was Herr von Wedderkampf, who told his daughters that the ground here was getting too hot for his feet.

But on the third evening every one was dancing again.

It surprised Christian. He did not understand such swift forgetfulness. He was surprised at the equanimity of his mother, the care-free mood of his sister and brother.

He wished to learn the name of that workingman, but no one knew. He was told that the man's name was Müller. Also that it was Schmidt. He was surprised. Nor did any one seem to know exactly what motive impelled the man to his deed. One said that it had been mere vengefulness, the result of the flame of class hatred systematically fanned. Another said that only a lunatic could be capable of such a deed.

Whatever it was, this shot fired from ambush by an unknown man for an unknown cause was not quite the same to Christian as it was to all the others who lived about him and sought their pleasure in their various ways. It forced him to meditation. His meditation was aimless and fruitless enough. But it was serious, and caused him strange suffering.

He would have liked to see the man. He would have liked
to look into his face.

Crammon said: " Another case that makes it clear as day
that the discarding of torture has simply made the canaille
more insolent. What admirable inventions for furthering disci-
pline and humanity were the stocks and the pillory! "

Christian visited his father, who sat in an armchair with
his arm in a sling. A highly conservative newspaper was spread
out before him. Herr Wahnschaffe said: " I trust that you
and your friends are not practising any undue restraint. I
could not endure the thought of darkening the mood of my
guests by so much as a breath."

Christian was astonished at this courtesy, this distinction
and temperance, this amiable considerateness.

XIII

Deep in the woods, amid ruins, Stephen Gunderam demanded
of Letitia that she decide his fate.

A picnic in very grand style had been arranged; Letitia
and Stephen had remained behind here; and thus it had happened.

Around them arose the ancient tree-trunks and the immemorial walls. Above the tree-tops extended the pallid blue
of the autumnal sky. His knees upon the dry foliage, a man,
using sublime and unmeasured words, asserted his eternal love.
Letitia could not withstand the scene and him.

Stephen Gunderam said: " If you refuse me nothing is left
me but to put a bullet through my head. I have had it in
readiness for long. I swear to you by the life of my father
that I speak truly."

Could a girl as gentle and as easily persuaded as Letitia
assume the responsibility for such blood-guiltiness? And she
gave her consent. She did not think of any fetter, nor of the
finality of such a decision, nor of time nor of its consequences,
nor of him to whom her soul was to belong. She thought only

of this moment, and that there was one here who had spoken to her these sublime and unmeasured words.

Stephen Gunderam leaped up, folded her in his arms and cried: " From now on you belong to me through all eternity —every breath, every thought, every dream of yours is mine and mine only! Never forget that—never! "

" Let me go, you terrible man! " Letitia said, but with a shiver of delight. She felt herself carried voluptuously upon a wave of romance. Her nerves began to vibrate, her glance shimmered and broke. For the first time she felt the stir of the flesh. With a soft cry she glided from his grasp.

Even on the way home they received congratulations. Crammon slunk quietly away. When Christian came and gave Letitia his hand, there was in her eyes a restless expectation, a fantastic joy that he could not understand at all. He could not fathom what she hid behind this expression. He could not guess that even at this moment she was faithlessly withdrawing herself from him to whom she had just entrusted her life, its every breath and thought and dream, and that in her innocent but foolish way she desired to convey to Christian a sense of this fact.

He loved her. From hour to hour his love grew. He felt it to be almost an inner law that he must love her—a command which said to him: This is she to whom you must turn; a message whose burden was: In her shall you find yourself.

He seemed to be hearing the voice of Eva: Your path was from me to her. I taught you to feel. Now give that feeling to a waiting heart. You can shape it and mould it and yourself. Let it not be extinguished nor flicker out and die.

Thus the inner voice seemed to speak.

XIV

Crammon, the thrice hardened, had a dream wherein some one reproved him for standing by idly, while his flesh and blood was being sold to an Argentinian ranchman. So he

went to the countess, and asked her if she indeed intended
to send the tender child into a land of savages. "Don't you
feel any dread at the thought of her utter isolation in these
regions of the farthest South?" he asked her, and rolled his
hands in and out, which gave him the appearance of an elderly
usurer.

"What are you thinking of, Herr von Crammon?" The
countess was indignant. "What right have you to question
me? Or do you happen to know a better man for her, a
wealthier, more distinguished, more presentable one? Do you
imagine one can be happy only in Europe? I've had a look
at a good many people. They ran after us by the dozen at
Interlaken, Aix-les-Bains, at Geneva and Zürich and Baden-
Baden—old and young, Frenchmen and Russians, Germans
and Englishmen, counts and millionaires. We didn't start out
with any particular craze for the exotic. Your friend Christian
can bear witness to that! But he, I dare say, thought himself too good for us. It's bad enough that I have to let my
darling go across the ocean, without your coming to me and
making my heart heavier than ever!"

But Crammon was not to be talked down. "Consider the
matter very carefully once more," he said. "The responsibility is tremendous. Do you realize that venomous snakes
exist in those regions whose bite kills within five seconds?
I have read of storms that uproot the most powerful trees and
overturn houses nine stories high. So far as I have been
informed, certain tribes native to Terra del Fuego still practise cannibalism. Furthermore, there are species of ants
that attack human beings and devour them bodily. The heat
of summer is said to be insufferable, and equally so the cold
of winter. It is an inhospitable region, countess, and a dirty
one with dangerous inhabitants. I want you to consider the
whole matter carefully once more."

The countess was rather overcome. Delighted with the
effect of his words, Crammon left her with head erect.

That evening, when Letitia was already in bed, the countess, with arms crossed on her bosom, walked up and down in the girl's room. Her conscience was heavy, but she hardly knew how to begin a discussion. All afternoon she had been writing letters and addressing announcements of the engagement, and now she was tired. The little dog, Puck, meanwhile sat on a silken pillow in the adjoining room, and barked shrilly and without cause from time to time.

Letitia stared into the dim space above her with eyes that gleamed softly with the mystery of dreams. So rapt was she that if one had pressed a pin into her flesh she would not have noticed it.

At last the countess conquered herself sufficiently. She sat down near the bed, and took Letitia's hands into her own. " Is it true, sweetheart," she began, " and did Stephen tell you about all these things that Herr von Crammon speaks of— venomous snakes and cannibals and tornadoes and wild ants and frightful heat and cold in this terrible country that you're going to? If all this is true, I want to beseech you to recon- sider very thoroughly this step that you're about to take."

Letitia laughed a deep and hearty laugh. " Are you begin- ning to get frightened now, auntie? " she cried, " just as I've been dreaming about the future! Crammon has played an ill-timed prank. That is all. Stephen never lies, and accord- ing to his description the Argentine is a veritable earthly paradise. Do listen, auntie! " She said this with an air of mystery, moved to the edge of her bed, and regarded the countess full of confidence and delight. " The land is full of peaches as large as a child's head and of the most exquisite flavour. They are so plentiful that those that cannot be eaten or sold are piled up in great heaps and burned. They have game of all sorts, which they prepare in wonderful ways quite unknown in Europe, and fishes and fowl and honey, the rarest vegetables, and everything that the heart can desire."

The countess' face brightened. She petted Letitia's arm,

and said: " Well, of course, in that case, and if it is really
so . . ."

But Letitia went on: " When I've become thoroughly accli-
mated and familiar with everything, I'll ask you, dear aunt, to
come out to us. You'll have a house of your own, a charming
villa all overgrown with flowers. Your pantries shall be filled
afresh daily and you shall have a marble bath next to your
bedroom. You'll be able to get into it as often as you like, and
you will have Negro women to wait on you."

" That is right, my darling," the countess answered, and her
face was transfigured with delight. " Whether it's a paradise
or not, I am pretty sure that it will be dirty. And dirt, as you
know, is something I hate almost as much as poisonous serpents
or cannibals."

" Don't be afraid, auntie," said Letitia, " we'll lead a wonderful life there."

The countess was calmed, and embraced Letitia with overwhelming gratitude.

xv

In order to escape from the confusion at Wahnschaffe
Castle, as the new house was known, Christian and Crammon
retired for several days to Christian's Rest. Scarcely had
they settled down, when they were joined by Judith and her
companion, by Letitia and Fräulein von Einsiedel.

The countess and Stephen Gunderam had gone to Heidelberg, where they were expecting Frau von Febronius. Letitia
was to follow them a week later. Felix had been summoned
to Leipzig, where he was to join in the founding of a great
new publishing house. After his return to the castle, his and
Judith's wedding was to take place.

Judith announced that she intended to enjoy the last days of
her liberty. It had not needed much persuasion to bring
Letitia with her. The companion and Fräulein von Einsiedel
were regarded as chaperones, and so with laughter and merri-

ment these four surprised Christian and Crammon suddenly.

The weather was beautiful, though somewhat cold. They
passed most of their time out of doors, walking in the woods,
playing golf, arranging picnics. The evenings flew by in cheerful talk. Once Crammon read to them Goethe's "Torquato
Tasso," and imitated the intonation and the rhythms of Edgar
Lorm so deceptively that Judith grew excited and could not
hear enough. She was attracted by the very imitation that he
practised; to Letitia the verses were like wine; Fräulein von
Einsiedel, who had been mourning a lost love for years, struggled with her tears at many passages. Judith, on the other
hand, saw an adored image in a magic mirror, and when the
reading was over, turned the conversation to Lorm, and besought Crammon to tell her about him.

Crammon did as she desired. He told her of the actor's
romantic friendship with a king, of his first marriage to a
fair-haired Jewess. He had loved her madly, and she had left
him suddenly and fled to America. He had followed her
thither, and tracked her from place to place, but all his efforts
to win her back had been in vain. He had returned in grave
danger of losing himself and wasting his talent. Lonely and
divided in his soul, he had tried to settle in various places. He
had broken his contracts, been outlawed by the managers, and
barely tolerated by the public as a dangerous will o' the
wisp. At last, however, his genius had fought down all unfortunate circumstances as well as the weaknesses of his own
nature, and he was now the most radiant star in the heaven of
his art.

When Crammon had ended, Judith came up to him and
stroked his cheeks. "That was charming, Crammon. I want
you to be rewarded."

Crammon laughed in his deepest bass voice, and answered:
"Then I ask as my reward that you four ladies return to-
morrow morning to the castle, and leave my friend Christian

and me to each other's silence. Isn't it true, Christian, dear boy? We like to brood over the mysteries of the world."

"The brute!" they cried out, "the traitor! The base intriguer!" But it was only a jesting indignation. Their return had really been set for the next day.

Christian arose and said: "Bernard is not wrong when he says we desire silence. It is lovely to be surrounded by loveliness. But you girls are too restless and unquiet." He had spoken in jest. But as he passed his hand over his forehead, one could see the deep seriousness in his heart.

They all looked at him. There was something strangely proud about his appearance. Letitia's heart beat. When he looked at her, her eyes fell and she blushed deeply. She loved all that he was, all that lay behind him, all that he had experienced, all women he had loved, all men from whom he came or to whom he went.

Suddenly she remembered the little golden toad. She had brought it with her and she determined to give it to him to-day. But to do that she wanted to be alone with him.

XVI

It was her wish that their meeting be at night, and she gave him a sign. Unnoticed by the others, she succeeded in whispering to him that she would come to him that night with a gift. He was to wait for her.

He looked at her without a word. When she glided away, his lips throbbed.

After midnight, when all were asleep in the house, she left her chamber, and mounted to the upper floor where Christian had his rooms. She went softly but without especial fear. Bending her head forward, she held in her hands the folds of the white silken over-garment that she wore. Its transparent texture was more like a white shimmer, a pearly gleam upon her flesh than a garment. It was doubled only about her waist and bosom, and her steps were impeded by a satin riband about her knees. Thus, while her pulses throbbed, she had to trip, to her own amusement, like the Geisha girls she had seen in a theatre.

When Christian had locked the door behind her, she leaned against it in sudden weakness.

Gently he took her wrists, and breathed a kiss upon her forehead, smiled, and asked: "What did you want to bring to me, Letitia? I long to know."

Suddenly she was aware that she had forgotten the golden toy. Shortly before she had left her room, she had laid it in readiness; and yet she had forgotten it. "How stupid of me!" The words slipped out, and she gazed in shame at her little shoes of black velvet. "How stupid of me! There was a little toad made of gold that I meant to bring to you."

It startled him. Then he recalled the words that he had spoken so many months ago. The intervening time seemed thrice its natural length. He wondered now how he could ever have been frightened of a toad. He could, to be sure, hear his own words again: "Have a little toad made of gold, that the evil magic may disappear." But the monition had no validity to-day. The spell had been broken without a talisman.

And as he saw the girl stand before him, quivering and intoxicated, the trembling and the ecstasy seized him too. Many others had come to him—none so innocent and yet so guilty, none so determined and so deluded at once. He knew those gestures, that silent yearning, the eye that flamed and smouldered, the half-denial and the half-assent, the clinging and repulsing, the sighs and the magical tears that tasted like warm and salty dew. He knew! And his senses urged him with all their power to experience and to taste it all again.

But there were things that stood between him and his desire. There was a pallid brunette face whose eyes were upon him with unimaginable clearness. There was a blood-soaked face to which the black hair clung. There was a face that had once been beautiful, swollen by the waters of the

Thames. And there was a face full of hatred and shame against the coarse linen of a bed, and another in the storeroom of a hotel which was swathed in a white cloth. There were other faces—faces of men and women, thousands upon thousands, on the shore of a river, and still others that were stamped upon and charred, which he had seen as though they were concrete realities through the eyes of another. All these things stood between him and his desire.

And his heart opposed it too. And the love that he felt for Letitia.

He grew a little paler, and a chill crept into his finger-tips. He took Letitia by the hand, and led her to the middle of the room. She looked about her timidly, but every glance was his who filled her whole being. She asked him concerning the pictures that hung on the wall, and admired a picture of himself which was among them. She asked after the meaning of a little sculptured group which he had bought in Paris: a man and a woman emerging from the earth of which they were made, contending with primitive power.

Her deep voice had a more sensuous note than ever. And as he answered her, the temptation assailed him anew to touch with his lips the warm, rosy, throbbing curve of her shoulder, which was like a ripe fruit. But an inescapable voice within him cried: Resist once! Resist but this single time!

It was difficult, but he obeyed.

Letitia did not know what was happening to her. She shivered, and begged him to close the window. But when he had done so, her chill increased. She looked at him furtively. His face seemed arrogant and alien. They had sat down on a divan, and silence had fallen upon them. Why did I forget the little toad? Letitia thought. My folly is to blame for everything. And instinctively she moved away from him a little.

" Letitia," he said, and arose, " perhaps you will understand it all some day." Then he kneeled on the floor at her feet, and took her cool hands and laid them against his cheeks.

"No, I don't understand," Letitia whispered, and her eyes were wet, although she smiled, "and I shall never understand."

"You will! Some day you will!"

"Never," she asserted passionately, "never!" All things were confused within her. She thought of flowers and stars, of dreams and images. She thought of birds that fell dead out of the air, as he had described them once, and a deer dying at the hunter's feet. She thought of paths upon which she would go, of far sea-faring, and of jewels and costly garments. But none of these images held her. They were formed and dissolved. A chain broke in her soul, and she felt a need to lie down and weep for a while. Not for long. And it was possible that, when the weeping was over, she might look forward with delight once more to the coming day and to Stephen Gunderam and to their wedding.

"Good-night, Christian," she said, and gave him her hand as after a simple chat. And all the objects in the room had changed their appearance. On the table stood a cut-glass bowl full of meadow-saffron, and their white stalks were like the antennæ of a polypus. The night outside was no longer the same night. One seemed quite free now in a peculiar way— in a defiant and vengeful way.

Christian was amazed by her gesture and posture. He had not touched her; yet it was a girl who had come to him, and it was a woman who went. "I will think about it," she said, and nodded to him with a great, dark look. "I will learn to understand it."

So she went—went on into her rich, poverty-stricken, adventurous, difficult, trifling life.

Christian listened to the dying echo of her tread beyond the door. He stood without moving, and his head was bent. To him, too, the night had changed into another. Despite his obedience to the inner voice, a doubt gnawed at his soul whether what he had done was right or wrong, good or evil.

XVII

One day Christian received a letter that bore the signature of Ivan Michailovitch Becker. Becker informed him that he was staying for a short time in Frankfort, and that a woman, a mutual friend, had insisted that he should visit Christian Wahnschaffe. But this he would not do for well-considered reasons. If, however, Christian Wahnschaffe's state of mind was such as their friend seemed to assume, he would be glad to see him on some evening.

Eva's name was not mentioned. But twice he spoke of that woman who was their mutual friend—twice. And Becker had added the street where he lived and the number of the house.

Christian's first impulse was to ignore the invitation. He told himself that there was nothing in common between him and Becker. The Russian had not been congenial to him. He had disapproved and arrogantly overlooked the man's friendship with Eva. Whenever he thought of his ugly face, his dragging gait, his sombre, silent presence, a sense of discomfort seized upon him. What did the man want? Why this summons in which there was a shadow of menace?

After he had tried in vain to keep from brooding over this incident, he showed the letter to Crammon, in the secret hope that his friend would warn him against any response. Crammon read the letter, but shrugged his shoulders and said nothing. Crammon was in a bad humour; Crammon was hurt. He had felt for some time that Christian excluded him from his confidence. In addition he was thinking far more of Eva Sorel than was good for the peace of his soul. He paid ardent attention to Fräulein von Einsiedel, nor was that lady unresponsive. But this triumph could not restore the equilibrium of his mind, and Becker's letter opened his old wound anew.

Christian put an end to his vacillation by a sudden decision, and started out to find Becker. The house was in the suburbs.

and he had to climb the four flights of stairs of a common
tenement. He was careful to come in contact with neither the
walls nor the balustrades. When he had reached the door and
pulled the bell, he was pale with embarrassment and disgust.

When Christian had entered the shabbily furnished room
and sat opposite Becker, what impressed him most was the
stamp of suffering on the Russian's face. He asked himself
whether this was new or whether he had merely not perceived it before. When Becker spoke to him, his answers
were shy and awkward.

"Madame Sorel is going to Petrograd in the spring," Ivan
Michailovitch told him. "She has signed a three-months'
contract with the Imperial Theatre there."

Christian expressed his pleasure at this information. "Are
you going to stay here long?" he asked, courteously.

"I don't know," was the answer. "I'm waiting for a
message here. Afterwards I shall join my friends in Switzerland."

"My last conversation with Madame Sorel," he continued,
"was exclusively about you." He watched Christian attentively out of his deep-set eyes.

"About me? Ah . . ." Christian forced himself to a
conventional smile.

"She insisted on my remaining in communication with you.
She said that it meant much to her, but gave no reason. She
never does give reasons, though. She insisted likewise that
I send her a report. Yet she did not even give me a message
for you. But she kept repeating: 'It means something to
me, and it may mean very much to him.' So you see that I am
only her instrument. But I hope that you are not angry with
me for annoying you."

"Not in the least," Christian asserted, although he felt oppressed. "Only I can't imagine what is in her mind." He
sat there wondering, and added: "She has her very personal
ways!"

Ivan Becker smiled, and the moisture of his thick lips became unpleasantly visible. " It is very true. She is an enthusiastic creature, and a woman of great gifts. She has power over others, and is determined to use that power."

A pause ensued.

" Can I be of assistance to you? " Christian asked conventionally.

Becker regarded him coldly. " No," he said, " not of the least." He turned his eyes to the window, from which one could see the chimneys of the factories, the smoke, and the sinister snow-fraught air. Since the room was unheated, he had a travelling rug spread across his knees, and under it he hid his crippled hand. A movement of his limbs shifted the rug, and the hand became visible. Christian knew the story of it. Crammon had told him at the time in Paris of his meeting and his talk with Becker. He had heard it with indifference, and had avoided looking at the hand.

Now he regarded it. Then he got up, and with a gesture of freedom and assurance, which astonished even Becker, despite the Russian's superficial knowledge of him, he held out his own hand. Ivan Michailovitch gave him his left hand, which Christian held long and pressed cordially. Then he left without speaking another word.

XVIII

But on the following day he returned.

Ivan Michailovitch told him the story of his life. He offered him a simple hospitality, made tea, and even had the room heated. He spoke rather disconnectedly, with half-closed eyes and a morbid, suffering smile. Now he would relate episodes of his youth, now of his later years. The burden was always the same: oppression, need, persecution, suffering —suffering without measure. Wherever one went, one saw crushed hearts, happiness stamped out, and personalities destroyed. His parents had gone under in poverty, his brothers and sisters had drifted away and were lost, his friends had fallen in wars or died in exile. It was a life without centre or light or hope—a world of hate and malevolence, cruelty and darkness.

Christian sat there and listened until late into the night.

Next they met in a coffee house, an ugly place which Christian would once not have endured, and sat until far into the night. Often they sat in silence; and this silence tormented Christian, and kept him in a state of unbearable tension. But his expression was a gentle one.

They took walks along the river, or through the streets and parks in the snow. Ivan Michailovitch spoke of Pushkin and Byelinsky, of Bakunin and Herzen, of Alexander I and the legend of his translation to heaven, and of the peasants—the poor, dark folk. He spoke of the innumerable martyrs of forgotten names, men and women whose actions and sufferings beat at the heart of mankind, and whose blood, as he said, was the red dawn of the sunrise of a new and other age.

So Christian kept disappearing from his home, and no one knew where he went.

Once Ivan Michailovitch said: "I am told that a working-man made a murderous assault on your father. The man was condemned to seven years in the penitentiary yesterday."

"Yes, it is true," Christian replied. "What was his name? I have forgotten it."

It turned out that the man's name was neither Schmidt nor Müller, but Roderick Kroll. Ivan Michailovitch knew it. "There's a wife and five little children left in extreme distress," he said. "Have you ever tried for a moment to grasp imaginatively what that means—real distress? Is your imagination powerful enough to realize it? Have you ever seen the countenance of a human being that suffered hunger? There is this woman. She bore five children, and loves these children just as your mother loves hers. Very well. The drawers are empty, the hearth is cold, the bedding is in pawn, their clothes and

shoes are in rags. These children are human, each one, just
as you and I are. They have the same instinctive expectation
of content, bread, quiet sleep, and pure air, that you have or
Herr von Crammon or countless others, who never realize reflectively that all these things are theirs. Very well. Now
the world does not only feign to know nothing of all this, not
only resents being reminded of it, but actually demands of
these beings that they are to be silent, that they accept and
endure hunger, nakedness, cold, disease, the theft of their
natural rights, and the insolent injustice of it all, as something
quite natural and inevitable. Have you ever thought about
that? "

"It seems to me," Christian replied, softly, "that I have
never thought at all."

"This man," Ivan Michailovitch continued, "this Roderick
Kroll, so far as I have been able to learn, was systematically
exasperated to the very quick. He was an enthusiastic social-
ist, but somewhat of an annoyance even to his own party on
account of his extreme views and his violent propaganda.
The masters dug the ground from under his feet. They embittered him by the constant sting of small intrigues, and
drove him to despair. The intention was to render him harmless and to force him to silence. But tell me this: is there an
extreme on the side of the oppressed that is so unfair, so insolent, so damnable as the extreme on the other side—the arrogance, luxury, revelling, the hardness of heart, and the in-
sensate extravagance of every day and every hour? You did
not even know the name of that man! "

Christian stood still. The wind blew the snow into his
face, and wet his forehead and cheeks. "What shall I do,
Ivan Michailovitch? " he asked, slowly.   ,

Ivan Michailovitch stopped too. "What shall I do? " he
cried. "That is what they all ask. That is what Prince
Jakovlev Grusin asked, one of our chief magnates and marshal
of the nobility in the province of Novgorod. After he had

starved his peasants, plundered his tenants, sent his officials
to Siberia, violated girls, seduced women, driven his own sons
to despair, spent his life in gluttony, drunkenness, and whor-
ing, and heaped crime upon crime—he went into a monastery in
the seventy-fourth year of his age, and day after day kneeled in
his cell and cried: 'What shall I do? My Lord and Saviour,
what shall I do?' And no one, naturally, had an answer for
him. I have heard the question asked softly by another, whose
soul was clean and white. He was going to his death, and his
age was seventeen. Nine men with their rifles stood by the
trench of the fortress. He approached, reeling a little, and his
guiltless soul asked: 'Father in Heaven, what shall I do?
What shall I do?'"

Ivan Michailovitch walked on, and Christian followed him.
"And we poor men, we terribly poor men," Ivan Becker said,
"what shall *we* do?"

XIX

Judith's wedding was to be celebrated with great magnificence.

Even to the preliminary festival more than two hundred
guests had been invited. There was no end to the line of
motor cars and carriages.

The coal and iron barons of the whole province appeared,
military and civil officials of high rank with their ladies, the
chief patricians and financiers of Frankfort, members of the
Court circles of Darmstadt and Karlsruhe, and friends from
afar. A tenor from Berlin, a famous lyric singer, a Viennese
comedian, a magician, and a juggler had been engaged to
furnish the guests with amusement.

The great horse-shoe table in the dining-hall, radiant with
gold, silver, and cut glass, had three hundred and thirty covers.

The festive throng surged up and down in the marble gallery
and the adjoining rooms. Yellow and rose predominated in the
toilettes of the ladies; the young girls were mostly in white.

Bare shoulders were agleam with diamonds and pearls. The severe black and white of the men effectually softened the gorgeousness of the colour scheme.

Christian was walking up and down with Randolph von Stettner, a young lieutenant of hussars, stationed at Bonn. They had been friends since their boyhood, had not seen each other for several years, and were exchanging reminiscences. Randolph von Stettner said that he was not very happy in his profession; he would much rather have taken a university degree. He had a strong taste for the study of chemistry, and felt out of place as a soldier. " But it is futile to kick against the pricks," he ended, sighing; " a man must merely take the bit between his teeth and keep still."

Christian happened to observe Letitia, who stood in the centre of a circle of men. Upon her forehead was forgetfulness; she knew nothing of yesterday and nothing of to-morrow. There was no one else so absorbed by the passing hour as she.

A footman approached Christian and gave him a card. The footman frowned doubtfully, for the card was not quite clean. On it Christian read these pencilled words: " I. M. Becker must speak with you at once." Hurriedly he excused himself and went out.

Ivan Michailovitch stood perfectly still in the outer hall. Newly arrived guests, who gave the footmen their hats and coats, passed by without noticing him. The men took mincing steps, the ladies sought the mirror for a final look with their excited eyes.

Ivan Michailovitch wore a long grey coat, shabby and wet. The black-bearded face was pale as wax. Christian drew him into an empty corner of the hall, where they were undisturbed.

" I beg you to forgive me for throwing a shadow on all this festivity," Ivan Michailovitch began, " but I had no choice. I received a notification of expulsion from the police this afternoon. I must leave the city and the country within twelve hours. The simple favour I ask of you is to take this note-

book into your keeping, until I myself or some properly identified friend asks it back." He glanced swiftly about him, took
a thin, blue notebook out of his pocket, and gave it to
Christian, who slid it swiftly and unobtrusively into a pocket
of his evening coat.

" It contains memoranda in Russian," Ivan continued,
" which have no value to any one but myself, but which must
not be found on me. Since I am being expelled there is little
doubt but that my person and effects will be searched."

" Won't you come and rest in my room? " Christian asked,
timidly. " Won't you eat or drink something? "

Ivan Michailovitch shook his head. From the hall floated
the sound of the violins, playing an ingratiating air by Puccini.

" Won't you at least dry your coat? " Christian asked again.
The strains of the music, the splendour there within, the merriment and laughter, the fullness of beauty and happiness, all
this presented so sharp a contrast to the appearance of this
man in a wet coat, with wax-like face and morbidly flaming
eyes, that Christian could no longer endure his apparently unfeeling position between these two worlds, of whose utter and
terrible alienation from each other he was acutely aware.

Ivan Michailovitch smiled. " It is kind of you to think of
my coat. But you can't do any good. It will only get wet
again."

" I'd like to take you, just as you are," said Christian, and
he smiled too, " and go in there with you."

Ivan Michailovitch shrugged his shoulders, and his face grew
dark.

" I don't know why I should like to do that," Christian
murmured. " I don't know why it tempts me. I stand before
you, and you put me in the wrong. Whether I speak or am
silent does not matter. By merely being I am in the wrong.
We should not be conversing here in the servants' corner. You
are making some demand of me, Ivan Michailovitch, are you
not? What is it that you demand? "

The words bore witness to a confusion of the emotions that went to the very core of his being. They throbbed with the yearning to become and to be another man. Ivan Michailovitch, in a sudden flash of intuition, saw and understood. At first he had suspected that here was but a lordly whim, or that it was at best but the foolish and thoughtless defiance of a too swiftly ardent proselyte that urged this proud and handsome man to his words. He recognized his error now. He understood that he heard a cry for help, and that it came from the depth of one of those decisive moments of which life holds but few.

"What is it that I am to demand of you, Christian Wahnschaffe?" he asked, earnestly. "Surely not that you drag me in there to your friends, and ask me to regard that as a definite deed and as a triumph over yourself?"

"It would not be that," Christian said, with lowered eyes, "but a simple confession of my friendship and my faith."

"But consider what a figure I would cut in my blouse, taken so unwillingly and emphatically, to use the Russian proverb, into the realm of the spheres. You would be forgiven. You would be accused of an eccentricity, and laughed at; but it would be overlooked. But what would happen to me? You could guard me from obvious insult. The profound humiliation of my position would still be the same. And what purpose would such a boastful action serve? Do you see any promise of good in it—for myself, or you, or the others? I could accuse no one, persuade no one, convince no one. Nor would you yourself be convinced."

He was silent for a few seconds, and then regarded Christian with a kind and virile glance. Then he continued. "Had I appeared in evening clothes, this whole conversation would be without meaning. That shows how trivial it is. Why, Christian Wahnschaffe, should I exhibit my blouse and coat amid the garb of your friends? Do you go with me to a place where your coat is a blasphemy and a stain, and where my rough, wet one is a thing of pride and advantage. I know such a house. Go with me! "

Christian, without answering a word, summoned a footman, took his fur-coat, and followed Ivan Becker into the open. The lackey hurried to the garage. In a few minutes the car appeared. Christian permitted Ivan Michailovitch to precede him into it, asked for the address, and sat down beside him. The car started.

XX

Twice before this had Ivan Michailovitch visited the family of the imprisoned workman, Roderick Kroll. His interest in these people was not an immediate one. It had been evoked by the interest he took in Christian Wahnschaffe. There was something in Christian that moved him deeply. After their first conversation he had at once reflected long concerning his personality and his great charm, as well as concerning the circumstances of his life and the social soil from which he had sprung. And since the name of the industrial baron Wahnschaffe had been so closely connected with the trial of Roderick Kroll, and since that trial had made quite a stir in the world, his attention had naturally been drawn in this direction. It is possible that he had already weighed the step he was now taking. For he was immovably convinced that many men would be better, and deal more justly, if they could but be brought to see, or given an opportunity to see, the realities of the world.

Frau Kroll and her five children had found refuge in a mere hole of a garret at the top of a populous tenement on the extreme edge of the city. Before that she had inhabited one of the numerous cottages for workingmen that Albrecht Wahnschaffe had built near his factories. But she had been driven from this home, and had moved to the city.

The room she now had gave shelter not only to herself and

her children, the oldest of whom was twelve, but to three lodgers: a rag-picker, a hurdy-gurdy man, and a chronically drunken vagabond. The room had a floor-space of sixty square feet; the lodgers slept on dirty straw sacks, the children on two ragged mattresses pushed close together, Frau Kroll on a shawl and a bundle of old clothes in the corner where the slanting ceiling met the floor.

On this particular day the agent of the landlord had appeared three times to demand the rent. The third time, since no money was forthcoming, he had threatened to evict them all that night. Fifteen minutes before the arrival of Ivan Becker and Christian he had appeared with the janitor and another helper in the dim, evil-smelling room, and had proceeded to make good his threat. His face had an expression of good nature rather than of harshness. He was proud of the touch of humour which he brought to the execution of his duties. Cries and lamentations did not disturb him in the least. He said: " Hurry, children! Come on there! " Or else: " Shoulder your guns and march! Let's have no scenes! Don't get excited! No use getting on your knees! Time is money! Quick work is good work! "

As was usual on such occasions, a commotion stirred all the neighbours, and they assembled in the hall. There was a yellow-haired woman in her shift; there was one in a scarlet dressing gown; there was a cripple without legs, an old man with a long beard, children who were fighting one another, a painted woman with a hat as large as a cart-wheel, another with a burning candle in her hand, while a man who had just come in from the street in her company sought to hide in the darkness near the roof.

What one heard was the wailing of the Kroll children, and the hard beseeching voice of the woman, who looked on with desperate eyes as the agent and his men heaped up her poor possessions. The vagabond cursed, the hurdy-gurdy man dragged his straw sack toward the door, the agent snapped his fingers and said: " Hurry, good people, hurry! Let's have no tender scenes! My supper is getting cold! "

XXI

Christian and Ivan Becker entered. They forced their way through the staring crowd. Christian had on his costly fur-coat. The agent stood still and his jaw dropped. His men instinctively touched their caps. Ivan Michailovitch wanted to close the door, but the woman in the big hat stood on the threshold and would not stir. " The door should be closed," he said to the agent, who went forward and closed it, simply thrusting the woman roughly back. Ivan asked whether the woman and her children were to be evicted. The agent declared that she was unable to pay her rent, that one extension of time after another had been granted her, but that to continue would be to create disorder and institute a bad example. Ivan Michailovitch answered that he understood the situation. Then he turned to Christian, and repeated the words as though he needed to translate them into another tongue: " She cannot pay her rent." A whistle sounded from without, and a woman screeched. The agent opened the door, cried out a command, and slammed it again. Silence ensued.

Frau Kroll was crouching among her children, her elbows dug into her lap. She had a robust figure, and a bony face that was pale as dough and deeply furrowed. It looked like the head of a corpse. The children looked at her in terror: two were mother naked, and one of these had the itch. The agent, assuming a benevolent tone, asked Ivan Becker whether something was to be done for these people; he evidently did not dare to address Christian. " I think we shall be able to do something for them," Ivan answered, and turned to Christian.

Christian heard and saw. He nodded rapidly, and gave an impression of timidity and passionate zeal.

Christian's attention somehow became fixed on a water jug with a broken handle. The jug was stamped with a greenish pattern and the banal arabesques bit into his mind. The snow-edged, slanting window in the roof troubled him, and the sight of a single muddy boot. Next a sad fascination came to him from a rope that dangled from the roof, and from a little coal-oil lamp with a smoky chimney. His mere bodily vision clung to these things. But they passed into his soul, and he merged into oneness with them. He himself was that broken jug with its green figures, the snow-edged window, the muddy boot, the dangling rope, the smoky lamp. He was being transformed as in a melting furnace, shape glided into shape; and although he was objectively aware of what was taking place and also of the people—the beggar, the woman, the children, Ivan Michailovitch, the agent, and those who waited outside —yet it cost him a passionate effort to keep them outside of himself for yet a little while, until they should plunge down upon his soul with their torment, despair, cruelty, and madness, like wild dogs throwing themselves upon a bone.

A sigh escaped him; a disturbed and fleeting smile hovered about his lips. One of the children, a boy of four, clad in a shapeless rag, came to him, and gazed up at him as though he were a tower. At once the eyes of the others were fixed on him too. At least, he felt them. His breast seemed a fiery crucible upborne and held high by the boy's emaciated arms. In a moment he had filled his hand with gold pieces, and by a gesture encouraged the child to hold out its hands. He poured the gold into them. But they could grasp only a few. The coins rolled on the floor, and the people there watched them in dumb amazement.

He drew out his wallet, took from it with trembling fingers every bank note it held, looked about, and approached the cowering woman. Then suddenly there seized him a strange contempt for his own erectness while she crouched on the floor. And so he kneeled, kneeled down beside her, and let the notes slip into her lap. He did not know how much money there was. But it was found later that the sum was four thousand six hundred marks. He arose and took Ivan's arm, and the latter understood his glance.

There was a breathless silence when they left. The agent and his men, the lodgers, the children—all seemed turned to stone. The woman stared at the wealth in her lap. Then she uttered a loud cry and lost consciousness. The little boy played with the pieces of gold, and they clinked as only gold can, faintly sweet and without hardness.

Below, in the street, Ivan Michailovitch said to Christian: " That you kneeled down before her—that was it, and that alone! The gift—there was something fateful in it to me and something bitter! But that you kneeled down beside her— ah, that was it! " And with a sudden gesture he lifted himself on his toes, and took Christian's head between his hands, and kissed him with a kiss that was a breath upon the forehead. Then he murmured a word of farewell, and hurried down the street without looking at the waiting car.

Christian ordered the chauffeur to drive out to Christian's Rest. Two hours later he was there, in deep quietude, the quietude that he needed. He telephoned his family that unforeseen events had prevented him from staying to the end of the evening's festivities, but that he would be present at the ceremony of Judith's marriage without fail. Then he retired to the farthest room of his house, and held vigil all night.

XXII

Letitia married six weeks after Judith. At Stephen Gunderam's desire, however, the wedding was a quiet one. There was a simple meal in a hotel at Heidelberg, and those present were Frau von Febronius, the countess, their two nephews Ottomar and Reinhold, and an Argentinian friend of Stephen's —a raw-boned giant who had been sent to Germany for a year to acquire polish.

Ottomar recited an original poem in praise of his pretty

cousin, and Reinhold had composed an address in the style of Luther's table-talk. Stephen Gunderam showed small appreciation of the literary culture of his new kinsman.

Frau von Febronius was silent even at the moment of farewell. The countess wept very copiously. She provided Letitia with all manner of rules and admonitions, but the most difficult of all she had delayed, out of sheer cowardice to the very last. She drew Letitia into her own room and, blushing and paling by turns, attempted to give the girl some notion of the physiology of marriage. But her courage failed her even now, and whenever she approached the real crux of her subject, she began to stammer and grow confused. It amused Letitia immensely.

Stephen Gunderam wanted to depart in haste, like some one anxious to secure his booty.

Frau von Febronius said to her sister: " I have evil presentiments in regard to this marriage, even though the child seems quite happy. It is only her own nature that protects her against unhappiness. It is her only dowry, but a wonderful one." Then the countess folded her hands, and shed tears, and said: " If I have sinned, I pray God to forgive me."

The voyage proved Letitia to be an excellent sailor. For a few days she and her husband stopped in Buenos Ayres and met many people. Stephen's acquaintances regarded her with sympathetic curiosity; and everything was strange and fascinating to her—the people, the houses, animals, plants, the very earth and sky. But most fascinating and strange to her was still the jealous tyranny of the man she had married, although at times the fascination held a touch of fear. But when that assailed her, she jested even with herself, and drove it away.

Early one morning there drew up a firmly built, heavy little coach, with two small, swift horses, to carry them the thirty miles to the Gunderam estate. Generously provisioned they left the city. After a few hours the road ended as a brook

is lost in sands, and before them stretched to the very horizon
the pathless plain of the pampas.

Yet they were not unguided. On either side of the way
which the horses had to travel, poles had been driven into the
grassy earth. These poles were of about human height, and
stood at intervals of about twenty yards. Thus the horses
pursued their way calmly. The Negro on the box had no
need to urge them on. The safe and monotonous journey
permitted him to sleep.

There were no settlements at all. When the horses needed
food or came upon water, a halt was made under the open
sky. No house, no tree, no human being appeared from sun
to sun, and a dread stole upon Letitia. She had long given up
talking, and Stephen had long given up encouraging her. He
slept like his coachman.

When the sun had sunk behind a veil of whitish clouds,
Letitia stood up, and gazed searchingly over the endless plain
of grass. The high wooden posts still projected with unweary-
ing regularity at both sides of the uncut road.

But suddenly she saw on one of the posts a greyish-brown
bird, moveless and bent, with huge, round, glowing eyes.

"What kind of a bird is that?" she asked.

Stephen Gunderam started from his slumber. "It's an owl,"
he answered. "Have you never seen one? Every evening,
when darkness falls, they sit on the posts. Look, it is starting:
there is one on each."

Letitia looked and saw that it was true. On every post and
on either side, far as one's sight could reach, sat with its great,
circular, glowing eyes a heavy, slothful, solemn owl.

OR EVER THE SILVER CORD BE LOOSED

FRAULEIN VON EINSIEDEL took Crammon's tender trifling quite seriously. When Crammon observed this, he grew cold, and planned at once to rid himself of the threatened complication.

She sent him urgent little notes by her maid; he left them unanswered. She begged him for a meeting; he promised to come but did not. She reproached him and inquired after the reason. He cast down his eyes and answered sadly: " I was mistaken in the hour, dear friend. For some time my mind has been wandering. I sometimes wake in the morning and fancy that it is still evening. I sit down at table and forget to eat. I need treatment and shall consult a physician. You must be indulgent, Elise."

But Elise did not want to understand. According to Crammon's words of regretful deprecation, she belonged to the sort of woman who makes a kiss or a tender meeting an excuse for drawing all sorts of tiresome and impossible inferences.

He said to himself: " You must be robust of soul, Bernard, and not permit your innate delicacy to make a weakling of you. Here is a little trap for mice, and you can smell the cheese from afar. She is pretty and good, but alas, quite blind and deluded. As though a brief pleasure were not to be preferred to a long wretchedness! "

To be prepared for any event, he packed his belongings.

Crammon had discovered where and in whose company Christian had been on the night of the festival preceding

Judith's wedding. The chauffeur had been indiscreet. Then Crammon, in his brotherly concern, had made inquiries, and the rumours that had reached the castle had all been confirmed.

One morning, when they were both at Christian's Rest, Crammon entered his friend's room and said: "I can't hold in any longer. The sorrow of it gnaws at me. You ought to be ashamed, Christian, especially of your secretiveness. You join fugitive disturbers of the peace and hurlers of bombs, and then you confuse the innocent poor by your brainless generosity. What is it to lead to?"

Christian smiled, and did not answer.

"How can you expose yourself in that fashion," Crammon cried; "yourself and your family and your friends? I shall tell you this in confidence, dearest boy: If you imagine that you have really helped the woman to whom that Russian desperado dragged you, you are badly mistaken. Fortunately I can rob you of that illusion."

"Did you hear anything about her?" Christian asked, with a surprising indifference in his tone and expression.

Crammon seemed to expand, and told his tale with breadth and unction: "Certainly I have. I have even had dealings with the police and saved you annoyance. The woman was to have been arrested and the money confiscated. Luckily I was able to prevent that. I believe that the State should keep order, but I don't think it desirable that the government should interfere in our private affairs. Its duty is to safeguard us; there its function ends. So much for that! Concerning your protégée I have nothing pleasant to report. The rain of gold simply distracted the crowd in that house. They stuck to her and begged, and several of them stole. Naturally there was a fight, and some one plunged a knife into some one else's bowels, and the maddened woman beat them both with a coal shovel. The police had to interfere. Then the woman moved into other quarters, and bought all sorts of trash—

furniture, beds, clothing, kitchen utensils, and even a cuckoo clock. You have seen those little horrors. A cuckoo comes out of the clock and screams. I was once staying with people who had three of them. Whenever I went to sleep another cuckoo screeched; it was enough to drive one mad. In other respects my friends were charming.

" As for the Kroll woman—your gift robbed her of every vestige of common sense. She keeps the money in a little box, which she carries about and won't let out of her sight by night or day. She buys lottery tickets, penny dreadfuls; the children are as dirty as ever and the household as demoralized. Only that dreadful cuckoo clock roars. So what have you accomplished? Where is the blessing? Common people cannot endure sudden accessions of fortune. You do not know their nature in the slightest degree, and the best thing you can do is to leave them in peace."

Christian's eyes wandered out to the cloudy sky. Then he turned to Crammon. He saw, as though he had never seen it before, that Crammon's cheeks were rather fat, and that his chin was bedded in soft flesh and had a dimple. He could not make up his mind to answer. He smiled, and crossed his legs!

What shapely legs, Crammon thought and sighed, what superb legs!

III

A few days later Crammon appeared again with the intention of testing Christian.

" I don't like your condition, my dear boy," he began, " and I won't pretend to you that I do. It's just a week to-day that we've been perishing of boredom here. I grant you it's a delightful place in spring and summer with agreeable companions, when one can have picnics in the open and think of the dull and seething cities. But now in the midst of winter, without orgies or movement or women—what is the use of it?

Why do you hide yourself? Why do you act depressed? What
are you waiting for? What have you in mind? "

" You ask so many questions, Bernard," Christian replied.
" You should not do that. It is as well here as elsewhere.
Can you tell me any place where it is better? "

The last question aroused Crammon's hopes. In the
expectation of common pleasures his face grew cheerful.
" A better place? My dearest boy, any compartment in
a train is better. The greasy reception room of Madame
Simchowitz in Mannheim is better. However, we shall
be able to agree. Here is an admirable plan. Palermo,
Conca d'Oro, Monte Pellegrino, and Sicilian girls with
avid glances behind their virtuous veils. From there
we shall take a flying trip to Naples to see my sweet little
friend Yvonne. She has the blackest hair, the whitest teeth,
and the most exquisite little feet in Europe. The regions
between are—sublime. Then we can send a telegram to Prosper Madruzzi, who is nursing his spleen in his Venetian villa,
and let him introduce us into the most inaccessible circles of
Roman society. There one has dealings exclusively with
contessas, marchesas, and principessas. The striking characters of all five continents swarm there as in a fascinating mad-
house; cold-blooded American women commit indiscretions
with passionate lazzaroni, who have magical names and impossible silk socks; every kennel there can claim to be a curiosity,
every heap of stones adds to your culture, at every step you
stumble over some masterpiece of art."

Christian shook his head. " It doesn't tempt me," he said.

" Then I'll propose something else," Crammon said. " Go
with me to Vienna. It is a city worthy of your interest. Have
you ever heard of the Messiah? The Messiah is a person at
whose coming the Jews believe time will come to an end, and
whom they expect to welcome with the sound of shawms and
cymbals. It is thus that every distinguished stranger is greeted
in Vienna. If you cultivate an air of mystery, and are not

too stingy in the matter of tipping, and occasionally snub some one who is unduly familiar—all Viennese society will be at your feet. A pleasant moral slackness rules the city. Everything that is forbidden is permitted. The women are simply *hors concours;* the broiled meat at Sacher is incomparable; the waltzes which you hear whenever a musician takes up a fiddle are thrilling; a trip to the Little House of Delight—name to be taken literally, please—is a dream. I yearn for it all myself—the ingratiating air, the roast chicken, the apple-pudding with whipped cream, and my own little hut full of furniture of the age of Maria Theresa, and my two dear, old ladies. Pull yourself together, and come with me."

Christian shook his head. "It is nothing for me," he said.

A flush of indignation spread over Crammon's face. "Nothing for you? Very well. I cannot place the harem of the Sultan at your disposal, nor the gardens promised by the Prophet. I shall leave you to your fate, and wander out into the world."

Christian laughed, for he did not believe him. On the next day, however, Crammon said farewell with every sign of deep grief, and departed.

IV

Christian remained at his country house. A heavy snowfall came, and the year drew toward its end.

He received no visitors. He answered neither the letters nor the invitations of his friends. He was to have spent Christmas with his parents at the castle, but he begged them to excuse him.

Since he was of age, Christian's Rest had now passed fully into his possession, and all his objects of art were gathered here—statuary, pictures, miniatures, and his collection of snuff-boxes. He loved these little boxes very much.

The dealers sent him their catalogues. He had a trusted agent at every notable auction sale. To this man he would telegraph his orders, and the things would arrive—a beaker of mountain crystal, a set of Dresden porcelains, a charcoal sketch by Van Gogh. But when he looked at his purchases, he was disappointed. They seemed neither as rare nor as precious as he had hoped.

He bought a sixteenth century Bible, printed on parchment, with mani-coloured initials and a cover with silver clasps. It had cost him fourteen thousand marks, and contained the book-plate of the Elector Augustus of Saxony. Curiously he turned the pages without regarding the words, which were alien and meaningless to him. Nothing delighted him but his consciousness of the rarity and preciousness of the volume. But he desired other things even rarer and more precious.

Every morning he fed the birds. With a little basket of bread crumbs he would issue from the door, and the birds would fly to him from all directions, for they had come to know both him and the hour. They were hungry, and he watched them busy at their little meal. And doing this he forgot his desires.

Once he donned his shooting suit, and went out and shot a hare. When the animal lay before him, and he saw its dying eyes, he could not bear to touch it. He who had hunted and killed many animals could no longer endure this sport, and left his booty a prey to the ravens.

Most of his walks led him through the village, which was but fifteen minutes from his park. At the end of the village, on the high-road, stood the forester's house. Several times he had noticed at one of its windows the face of a young man, whose features he seemed to recall. He thought it must be Amadeus Voss, the forester's son. When he was but six he had often visited that house. Christian's Rest had not been built until later, and in those early years his father had rented the game preserve here and had often lodged for some days at the forester's. And Amadeus had been Christian's playmate.

The face, which recalled his childhood to him, was pallid and hollow-cheeked. The lips were thin and straight, and the head covered with simple very light blond hair. The reflection of the light's rays in the powerful lenses of spectacles made the face seem eyeless.

It amazed Christian that this young man should sit there for hours, day after day, without moving, and gaze through the window-panes into the street. The secret he felt here stirred him, and a power from some depth seemed to reach out for him.

One day Christian met the mayor of the village at the gate of his park. Christian stopped him. " Tell me," he said, " is the forester Voss still alive? "

" No, he died three years ago," the man answered. " But his widow still lives in the house. The present forester is unmarried, and lets her have a few rooms. I suppose you are asking on account of Amadeus, who has suddenly turned up for some strange reason—"

" Tell me about him," Christian asked.

" He was to have been a priest, and was sent to the seminary at Bamberg. One heard nothing but good of him there, and his teachers praised him to the sky. He got stipends and schol-arships, and every one expected him to do well for himself. Last winter his superiors got him a position as tutor to the boys of the bank president, Privy Councillor Ribbeck. You're familiar with the name. Very big man. The two boys whose education Voss was to supervise lived at Halbertsroda, an estate in Upper Franconia, and the parents didn't visit them very often. They say the marriage isn't a happy one. Well, everything seemed turning out well. Considering his gifts and the patron he had now, Amadeus couldn't have wanted for anything. Suddenly he drops down on us here, doesn't budge from the house, pays no attention to any one, becomes a burden to his poor old mother, and growls like a dog at any one who talks to him. There must have been crazy doings at Halbertsroda. No one knows any details, you know. But every now and then the pot seethes over, and then you get the rumour that there was something between him and the Privy Councillor's wife."

The man was very talkative, and Christian interrupted him at last. "Didn't the forester have another son?" A faint memory of some experience of his childhood arose in him.

"Quite right," said the mayor. "There was another son. His name was Dietrich, and he was a deaf-mute."

"Yes, I remember now," Christian said.

"He died at fourteen," the mayor went on. "His death was never properly explained. There was a celebration of the anniversary of the battle of Sedan, and he went out in the evening to look at the bonfires. Next morning they found his body in the fish-pond."

"Did he drown?"

"He must have," answered the mayor.

Christian nodded farewell, and went slowly through the gate toward his house.

v

Letitia and her husband were in the opera house at Buenos Ayres. The operetta of the evening was as shallow as a puddle left by the rain in the pampas.

In the box next to theirs sat a young man, and Letitia yielded now and then to the temptation of observing his glances of admiration. Suddenly she felt her arm roughly grasped. It was Stephen who commanded her silently to follow him.

In the dim corridor he brought his bluish-white face close to her ear, and hissed: "If you look at that fool once more, I'll plunge my dagger into your heart. I give you this warning. In this country one doesn't shilly-shally."

They returned to their box. Stephen smiled with a smile as glittering as a torero's, and put a piece of chocolate into his mouth. Letitia looked at him sidewise, and wondered whether he really had a dagger in his possession.

That night, when they drove home, he almost smothered her with his caresses. She repulsed him gently, and begged: " Show me the dagger, Stephen. Give it to me! I want so much to see it."

" What dagger, silly child? " he asked, in astonishment.

" The dagger you were going to plunge into my heart."

" Let that be," he answered, in hollow tones. " This is no time to speak of daggers and death."

But Letitia was stubborn. She insisted that she wanted to see it. He took his hands from her, and fell into sombre silence.

The incident taught Letitia that she could play with him. She no longer feared that sombre stillness of his, nor his great skull on his powerful neck, nor the thin mouth, nor the paling face, nor the great strength of his extraordinary small hands. She knew that she could play with him.

Great fire-flies flew through the air, and settled in the grass about them. When the carriage stopped at the villa, Letitia looked around with a cry of delight. Sparks seemed to be falling in a golden rain. The gleaming insects whirred about the windows, the roof, the flowery creepers on the walls. They penetrated into the hall.

Letitia stopped at the dark foot of the stairs, looked at the phosphorescent glimmer, and asked fearfully and with an almost imperceptible self-mockery in her deep voice: " Tell me, Stephen, couldn't they set the house on fire? "

The Negro Scipio, who appeared with a lamp at the door, heard her words and grinned.

VI

Around Twelfth Night Randolph von Stettner with several friends came to Christian's Rest. The young men had called up Christian by telephone, and he had been alone so long that he was glad to receive them and be their host. He was always glad to see Randolph. The latter brought with him two comrades, a Baron Forbach and a Captain von Griesingen, and also another friend, a young university teacher, who was fulfilling his required military service at Bonn and was therefore also in uniform. Christian had met him before at a celebration of the Borussia fraternity.

A delicious meal was served, followed by excellent cigars and liqueurs.

" It is consoling to see that you still don't despise the comforts of the flesh," Randolph von Stettner said to Christian.

Captain von Griesingen sighed: " How should one despise them? They torment us and they flit temptingly about us! Think of all that is desirable in the world—women, horses, wine, power, fame, money, love! There is a dealer of jewels in Frankfort, named David Markuse, who has a diamond that is said to be worth half a million. I have no desire for that special object. But the world is full of things that are possessed and give delight."

" It is the diamond known as Ignifer," Dr. Leonrod remarked, " a sort of adventurer among precious stones."

" Ignifer is an appropriate name for a diamond," said Randolph. " But why do you speak of it so gravely? What, except its price, makes it differ from other stones? Has it had so strange a fate? "

" Undoubtedly," said Dr. Leonrod, " most strange. I happen to know the details because, as a professional mineralogist, I take a certain interest in precious stones, too."

" Do tell us about it! " the young officers cried.

" Whoever buys Ignifer," Dr. Leonrod began, " will show no little courage. The jewel is a tragic thing. It has been proved that its first owner was Madame de Montespan. No sooner did it come into her possession than the king dismissed her. Marie Antoinette owned it next. It weighed ninety-five carats at that time. But during the Revolution it was stolen and divided, and did not reappear until fifty years later. The recovered stone weighed sixty carats. An Englishman, named Thomas Horst, bought it, and was soon murdered. The heirs sold it to an American. The lady who wore it, a Mrs. Malmcote, was throttled by a madman at a ball. Then Prince Alexander Tshernitsheff brought it to Russia, and gave it to an actress who was his mistress. Another lover shot and killed her on the stage. The prince was blown to pieces by a nihilist. Then the stone was brought to Paris, and purchased by the Sultan Abdul Hamid for his favourite wife. The woman was poisoned, and you all know what happened to the Sultan. After the Turkish Revolution Ignifer drifted West again, and then back to the Orient. For its new owner, Tavernier, took a voyage to India, and was shipwrecked and drowned. For a time it was thought that the diamond was lost. But that was an error; it had been deposited in a safety vault in a Calcutta bank. Now it is back in Europe, and for sale."

"The stone must harbour an evil spirit," said Randolph. "I confess that I have no desire for it. I am very little inclined to superstition; but when the facts are as compelling as in this case, the most enlightened scepticism seems rebuked."

"What does all that matter if the stone is beautiful, if it really is incomparably lovely?" Christian cried, with a defiant look, that yet seemed turned inward upon his soul. After this he said little, even when the conversation drifted to other subjects.

Next day at noon he ordered his car and drove in to Frankfort to the shop of the jeweller David Markuse.

VII

Herr Markuse knew Christian.

Ignifer was kept in the safe of a fire-proof and burglar-proof vault. Herr Markuse lifted the stone out of its case, laid it upon the green cloth of a table, stepped aside, and looked at Christian.

Christian looked silently at the concentrated radiance of the stone. His thought was: This is the rarest and costliest thing in the world; nothing can surpass it. And it was immediately clear to him that he must own the jewel.

The diamond had the faintest tinge of yellow. It had been cut so that it had many rich facets. A little groove had been cut into it near one end, so that a woman could wear it around her neck by a thin chain or a silken cord.

Herr Markuse lifted it upon a sheet of white paper and breathed upon it. "It is not of the first water," he said, "but it has neither rust nor knots. There is no trace of veins or cracks, no cloudiness or nodules. Not a flaw. The stone is one of nature's miracles."

The price was five hundred and fifty thousand marks. Christian offered the half million. Herr Markuse consulted his watch. "I promised a lady that I would hold it," he declared. "But the promised hour is past." They agreed upon five hundred and twenty thousand marks. Half was to be paid in cash, the other in two notes running for different periods. "The name of Wahnschaffe is sufficient guarantee," the merchant said.

Christian weighed the diamond in his hand, and laid it down again.

David Markuse smiled. "In my business one learns how to judge people," he said without any familiarity. "You are making this purchase with a deeper intention than you yourself are probably conscious of. The soul of the diamond has lured you on. For the diamond has a soul."

"Do you really mean that?" Christian was surprised.

"I know it. There are people who lose all shame when they see a beautiful jewel. Their nostrils quiver, their cheeks grow pale, their hands tremble uncertainly, their pupils expand, and they betray themselves by every motion. Others are intimidated, or bereft of their senses, or saddened. You gain curious insights into human nature. The masks drop. Diamonds make people transparent."

The indiscreet turn of the conversation irritated Christian. But he had often before become aware of the fact that something in him seemed to invite the communicativeness and confidence of others. He arose, and promised to return that evening.

" The lady of whom I was speaking," Markuse continued, as he accompanied him to the door, " and who was here yesterday, is a very wonderful lady. When she came in, I thought: is it possible for mere walking to be so beautiful? Well, I soon found out that she is a famous dancer. She is stopping at the Palace Hotel for a day, on her way from Paris to Russia, merely in order to see Ignifer. I showed her the stone. She stood looking at it for at least five minutes. She did not move, and the expression of her face! Well, if the jewel didn't represent a large part of all I have in the world, I would have begged her simply to keep it. Such moments are not exactly frequent in my business. She was to have returned to-day, but, as I have told you, she didn't keep her engagement."

" And you don't know her name? " Christian asked, shyly.

" Oh, yes. Her name is Eva Sorel. Did you ever hear of her? "

The blood came into Christian's face. He let go the knob of the door. " Eva Sorel is here? " he murmured. He pulled himself together, and opened the door to an empty room that was carpeted in red, and the walls of which were hidden by ebony cases. Almost at the same moment the opposite door was thrown open; and, followed by four gentlemen, Eva Sorel crossed the threshold.

Christian stood perfectly still.

" Eidolon! " Eva cried, and she folded her hands in that inimitably enthusiastic and happy gesture of hers.

VIII

Christian did not know the gentlemen who were with her. Their features and garments showed them to be foreigners. Accustomed to surprising events in Eva's daily life, they regarded Christian with cool curiosity.

Eva's whole form was wrapped in a grey mole-skin coat. Her fur cap was trimmed with an aigrette of herons' feathers, held by a marvellous ruby clasp. From under the cap her honey-coloured hair struggled forth. The wintry air had given her skin an exquisite delicate tinge of pink.

With a few steps she came stormily to Christian, and her white gloved hands sought both of his. Her great and flaming looks drove his conscious joy and his perceptions of her presence back upon his soul, and fear appeared upon his features. He found himself as defenceless as a ball flung by another's hand. He awaited his goal.

" Did you buy Ignifer? " That was her first question. Since he was silent, she turned with raised brows to David Markuse.

The merchant bowed and said: " I thought that I could no longer count on you, Madame. I am sorry with all my heart."

" You are right. I hesitated too long." Eva spoke her melodious German, with its slightly foreign intonation. Turning to Christian she went on: " Perhaps it makes no difference, Eidolon, whether you have it or I. It is like a heart that ambition has turned to crystal. But you are not ambitious. If you were, we should have met here like two birds swept by a storm into the same cave. The preciousness of the stone almost makes it ghostly to me, and I would permit no one to give it to me who was not conscious of its significance. And who is there? What do they give one? Wares from a shop, that is all."

David Markuse looked at her in admiration, and nodded.

" It is said to bring misfortune to its possessors," Christian almost whispered.

" Do you intend to test yourself, Eidolon, and put it to the proof? Will you challenge the demon to prevail against you? Ah, that is what allured me, too. Its name made me envious. As I held it, it seemed like the navel of Buddha, from which one cannot divert one's thought, if one has once seen it."

She noticed that the people about them seemed to make Christian hesitate, so she took his arm, and drew him behind the curtains of a window-niche.

" That it brings misfortune to people is certain," Christian repeated mechanically. " How can I keep it, Eva, since you desired it?"

" Keep it and break the evil spell," Eva answered, and laughed. But his seriousness remained unchanged; and she apologized for her laughter by a gesture, as though she were throwing aside the undue lightness of her mood. She watched him silently. In the sharp light reflected from the snow, her eyes were green as malachite. " What are you doing with yourself? " she asked. " Your eyes look lonesome."

" I have been living rather alone for some time," answered Christian. His utterances were dry and precise. " Crammon too has left me."

" Ivan Becker wrote me about you," Eva said in muffled tones. " I kissed the letter. I carried it in my bosom, and said the words of it over to myself. Is there such a thing as an awakening? Can the soul emerge from the darkness, as a flower does from the bulb? But there you stand in your pride, and do not move. Speak! Our time is short."

" Why speak at all? "

Although his eyes seemed so unseeing, it did not escape him that Eva's face had changed. A new severity was on it, and a heightened will controlled its nerves, even to the raising and lowering of her long lashes. Experience of men and things had lent it an austere radiance, and her unbounded mastery over them a breath of grandeur.

" I had not forgotten that this is the city where you dwell," she said, " but in these driven hours there was no place for you. They count my steps, and lie in wait for the end of my sleeping. What I should have is either a prison or a friend unselfish enough to force me to be more frugal of myself. In Lisbon the queen gave me a beautiful big dog, who was so devoted to me that I felt it in my very body. A week later he was found poisoned at the gate of the garden. I could have put on mourning for him. How silent and watchful he was, and how he could love! " She raised her shoulders with a little shiver, dropped them again, and continued with hurry in her voice. " I shall summon you some day. Will you come? Will you be ready? "

" I shall come," Christian answered very simply, but his heart throbbed.

" Is your feeling for me the same—changeless and unchangeable? " In her look there was an indescribably lyrical lift, and her body, moved by its spirit, seemed to emerge from veils.

He only bowed his head.

" And how is it in the matter of *cortesia?* " She came nearer to him, so that he felt her breath on his lips. " He smiles," she exclaimed, and her lips opened, showing her teeth, " instead of just once throwing himself on his knees in rage or jubilation —he smiles. Take care, you with your smile, that I am not tempted to extinguish your smiling some day." She stripped the glove from her right hand, and gave the naked hand to Christian, who touched it with his lips. " It is a compact, Eidolon," she said serenely now, and with an air of seduction, " and you will be ready." Emerging from the niche, she turned to the gentlemen who had come with her, and who had been holding whispered conversations: " Messieurs, nous sommes bien pressés."

She inclined her head to the jeweller, and the heron feathers trembled. The four gentlemen let her precede them swiftly, and followed her silently and reverently.

IX

When next Christian went through the village and saw Amadeus Voss at the window, he stopped.

Voss got up suddenly and opened the window, and thereupon Christian approached.

It was a time of thaw. The water dripped from the roofs and gutters. Christian felt the moist air swept by tepid winds as something that gives pain.

Behind the powerful lenses the eyes of Amadeus Voss had a yellowish glitter. "We must be old acquaintances," he said, "although it is very long ago since we hunted blackberries among the hedges. Very long." He laughed a little weakly.

Christian had determined to lead the conversation to the dead brother of Amadeus. There was that event in the mist of the past concerning which he could gain no clearness, much as he might reflect.

"I suppose everybody is wondering about me," Voss said, in the tone of one who would like to know what people are saying. "I seem to be a stumbling-block to them. Don't you think so?"

"I mustn't presume to judge," Christian said, guardedly.

"With what an expression you say that!" Voss murmured, and looked Christian all over. "How proud you are. Yet it must have been curiosity that made you stop."

Christian shrugged his shoulders. "Do you remember an incident that took place when I stayed here with my father?" he asked gently and courteously.

"What kind of an incident? I don't know. Or—but wait! Do you mean that affair of the pig? When they killed the pig over there in the inn, and I——"

"Quite right. That was it," Christian said with a faint smile. He had scarcely spoken when the scene and the incident appeared with unwonted clarity before his mind.

He and Amadeus and the deaf and dumb Dietrich had been

standing at the gate. And the pig had begun to scream. At that moment Amadeus had stretched out his arms, and held them convulsively trembling in the air. The long, loud, and piercing cry of the beast's death agony had been something new and dreadful to Christian too, and had drawn him running to the spot whence it came. He saw the gleaming knife, the uplifted and then descending arm of the butcher, the struggle of the short, bristly legs, and the quivering and writhing of the victim's body. The lips of Amadeus, who had reeled after him, had been flecked with foam, and he pointed and moaned: " Blood, blood! " And Christian had seen the blood on the earth, on the knife, on the white apron of the man. He did not know what happened next. But Amadeus knew.

He said: " When the pig screamed, a convulsive rigour fell upon me. For many hours I lay stiff as a log. My parents were badly frightened, for I had never had any such attacks before. What you remember is probably how they tried to cheer me or shame me out of my collapse. They walked into the puddle of blood and stamped about in it so that the blood spurted. My dumb brother noticed that this only increased my excitement. He made noises in his throat, and raised his hands beseechingly, while my mother was hastening from the house. At that moment you struck him in the face with your fist."

" It is true. I struck him," said Christian, and his face became very pale.

" And why? Why did you do that? We haven't met since that day, and we've only seen each other from afar. That is, I've seen you. You were far too proud and too busy with your friends to see me. But why did you strike Dietrich that day? He had a sort of silent adoration of you. He followed you about everywhere. Don't you remember? We often laughed about it. But from that day on he was changed—markedly so."

" I believe I hated him at that moment," Christian said,

reflectively. " I hated him because he could neither hear nor speak. It struck me as a sort of malevolent stubbornness."

" Strange! It's strange that you should have felt so."

They both became silent. Christian started to leave. Voss rested his arms on the window ledge and leaned far out. " There's a paragraph in the paper saying that you've bought a diamond for half a million. Is that true? "

" It is true," Christian replied.

" A single diamond for over half a million? I thought it was merely a newspaper yarn. Is the diamond to be seen? Would you show it to me? " In his face there was something of horrified revolt, of panting desire, but also of mockery. Christian was startled.

" With pleasure, if you'll come to see me," he answered, but determined to have himself denied to Voss if the latter really came.

For a secret stirred him again, a depth opened at his feet, an arm was stretched out after him.

X

On a certain night Letitia awoke and heard dragging, running steps, the breathing of pursuers and pursued, whispers and hoarse curses, now nearer, now farther. She sat up and listened. Her bed-chamber opened upon gardens. Its doors led to the verandah that surrounded the entire house.

Then the hurrying steps approached; she saw forms that detached themselves in black from the greenish night and flitted by: one, and then another, and then a third, and after a little while a fourth. She was frightened, but she hated to call for help. To rouse Stephen, who slept in the adjoining room, was a risk for her, as it was for every one. At such times he would roar like a steer, and strike out wildly.

Letitia laughed and shuddered at the thought.

She fought her fear, got up, threw on a dressing gown, and stepped determinedly on the verandah. At that moment thick

clouds parted and revealed the moon. Surprised by the unexpected light, the four forms stopped suddenly, collided against
each other, and stood panting and staring.

What Letitia saw was old Gottlieb Gunderam and his three
sons, Riccardo, Paolo, and Demetrios, the brothers of her husband. There was an unquenchable distrust between this
father and his sons. They watched and lay in wait for each
other. If there was cash in the house, the old man did not
dare go to bed, and each of the brothers accused the rest of
wanting to rob their father. Letitia knew that much. But it
was new to her that in their dumb rage and malice they went
so far as to chase each other at night, each pursuer and pursued
at once, each full of hatred of the one in front and full of terror
of the one behind him. She laughed and shuddered.

The old man was the first to slink away. He dragged himself to his room, and threw himself on the bed in his clothes.
Beside the bed stood two huge travelling boxes, packed and
locked. They had stood thus for twenty years. Daily, during
all that period, he had determined at least once to flee to the
house in Buenos Ayres, or even to the United States, whenever the conflict, first with his wife and later with his sons,
became too much for him. He had never started on that flight;
but the boxes stood in readiness.

Silently and secretively the brothers also disappeared. While
Letitia stood on the verandah and looked at the moon, she
heard the rattle of a phonograph. Riccardo had recently
bought it in the city, and it often happened that he set it to
playing at night.

Letitia stepped a little farther, and peered into the room
in which the three brothers sat with sombre faces and played
poker. The phonograph roared a vulgar waltz out of its brazen
throat.

Then Letitia laughed and shuddered.

XI

Christian wondered whether Amadeus would come. Two days passed in slightly depressing suspense.

He had really intended to go to Waldleiningen to look after his horses. Sometimes he could actually see their spirited yet gentle eyes, their velvet coats, and that fine nervousness that vibrated between dignity and restiveness. He recalled with pleasure the very odour of the stables.

The pure bred Scotch horse which he had bought of Denis Lay was to run in the spring races. His grooms told him that the beautiful animal had been in poor form for some weeks, and he thought that perhaps it missed his tender hand. Nevertheless he did not go to Waldleiningen.

On the third day Amadeus Voss sent a gardener to ask whether he might call that evening. Instead Christian went down to the forester's house that afternoon at four, and knocked at the door.

Voss looked at him suspiciously. With the instinct of the oppressed classes he divined the fact that Christian wanted to keep him from his house. But Christian was far from being as clear about his own motives as Amadeus suspected. He scented a danger. Some magic in it drew him on half-consciously to go forth to meet it.

Looking about in the plain but clean and orderly room Christian saw on the tinted wall above the bed white slips of paper on which verses of Scripture had been copied in a large hand. One was this: " He was led as a sheep to the slaughter; and like a lamb dumb before his shearer, so opened he not his mouth." And another was this: " For it is a day of trouble, and of treading down, and of perplexity by the Lord God of hosts in the valley of vision, breaking down the walls, and of crying to the mountains." And this other: "The Lord said unto me, Within a year, within the years of an hireling, and all the glory of Kedar shall fail." And finally there was this:

"I know thy works, that thou art neither cold nor hot; I would thou were cold or hot. So then because thou art lukewarm, and neither cold or hot, I will spue thee out of my mouth."

Christian looked at Amadeus Voss long and curiously. Then he asked, in a very careful voice, and yet not without an inevitable tinge of worldly mockery: "Are you very religious?"

Amadeus frowned and answered: "Whether I answer one way or the other it will mean equally little to you. Did you come to cross-question me? Have we anything in common that an answer to that question could reveal? Amadeus Voss and Christian Wahnschaffe—are those not the names of sundered poles? What image is there that could express the differences that divide us? Your faith and mine! And such things are possible on the same earth!"

"Was your youth especially hard?" Christian asked, innocently.

Voss gave a short laugh, and looked at Christian sidewise. "D'you know what meal days are? Of course you don't. Well, on such days you get your meals at strangers' houses who feed you out of charity. Each day of the week you're with another family. Each week repeats the last. Not to be thought ungrateful you must be obedient and modest. Even if your stomach revolts at some dish, you must pretend it's a delicacy. If the grandfather laughs, you must laugh too; if an uncle thinks he's a wit, you must grin. If the daughter of the house chooses to be insolent, you must be silent. If they respond to your greeting, it's a great favour; the worn overcoat with ragged lining they gave you when winter came binds you in eternal gratitude. You come to know all the black moods of all these people with whom you sit at table, all their shop-worn opinions, their phrases and hypocritical expressions; and for the necessary hour of each day you must learn to practise its special kind of dissembling. That is the meaning of meal days."

He got up, walked to and fro, and resumed his seat. "The devil appeared to me early," he said in a hollow voice. "Perhaps I took a certain experience of my childhood more grievously to heart than others, perhaps the poison of it filtered deeper into me. But you cannot forget. It is graven upon my soul that my drunken father beat my mother. He did it every Saturday night with religious regularity. That image is not to be obliterated."

Christian did not take his eyes from the face of Amadeus.

Softly, and with a rigid glance, Voss continued: "One night before Easter, when I was eight years old, he beat her again. I rushed into the yard, and cried out to the neighbours for help. Then I looked up at the window, and I saw my mother stand there wringing her hands in despair. And she was naked." And his voice almost died into silence as he added: "Who is it that dare see his own mother naked?"

Again he arose and wandered about the room. He was so full of himself that his speech seemed indeed addressed to himself alone. "Two things there are that made me reflect and wonder even in my childhood. First, the very many poor creatures, whom my father reported because they stole a little wood, and who were put in prison. I often heard some poor, little old woman or some ragged half-starved lad beg for mercy. There was no mercy here. My father was the forester, and had to do his duty. Secondly, there were the many rich people who live in this part of the country in their castles, on their estates, in their hunting-lodges, and to whom nothing is denied that their wildest impulses demand. Between the two one stands as between two great revolving cylinders of steel. One is sure to be crushed to bits in the end."

For a while he gazed into emptiness. "What is your opinion of an informer?" he asked, suddenly.

Christian answered with a forced smile: " It's not a good one."

" Listen to me. In the seminary I had a fellow-student named Dippel. His gifts were moderate, but he was a decent chap and a hard worker. His father was a signalman on the railroad—one of the very poor, and his son was his one hope and pride. Dippel happened to be acquainted with a painter in whose studio he came across an album of photographs displaying the female form in plastic poses. The adolescent boy gazed at them again and again, and finally begged the painter to lend him the album. Dippel slept in my dormitory. I was monitor, and I soon observed the crowding and the sensuous atmosphere about Dippel, who had shown the pictures to a few friends. It was like a spreading wound. I went into the matter and ruthlessly confiscated the pictures. I informed the faculty. Dippel was summoned, sternly examined, and expelled. Next day we found him swinging dead from the apple tree."

Christian's face flushed hotly. The tone of equanimity with which it was recited was more repulsive than the story itself.

Amadeus Voss continued: " You think that was a contemptible action. But according to the principles that had been impressed on us I was merely doing my duty. I was sixteen; and I seemed to be, and was, in a dark hole. I needed to get out to the air and light. I was like one squeezed in by a great throng, who cannot see what happens beyond. The fumes of impatience throttled me, and everything in me cried out for space and light. It was like living on the eternally dark side of the moon. I was afraid of the might of evil; and all that I heard of men was more or less evil. The scales rose and fell in my breast. There are hours in which one can either become a murderer or die on the cross. I yearned for the world. Yet I prayed much in those days, and read many books of devotion, and practised cruel penances. Late at night, when all others slept, a priest found me absorbed in prayer with the hair-shirt about my body. During mass or choral singing an incomparable and passionate devotion streamed through me. But then again I saw flags in the streets of the city, or well-dressed women, or I stood in the railway station, and a train of luxurious cars seemed to mock me. Or I saw a man who had hurled himself out of a window and whose brains spattered the pavement, and he seemed to cry out to me: Brother, brother! Then the evil one arose in bodily form and I desired to clutch him. Yes, evil has bodily form and only evil—injustice, stupidity, lying, all the things that are repulsive to one to the very core, but which one must embrace and be, if one has not been born with a silver spoon in one's mouth. To save a ray of light for myself, I learned to play the organ. It helped little. What does music matter, or poems or beautiful pictures, or noble buildings, or books of philosophy, or the whole magnificent world without? I cannot reach myself. Between me and that real self there is something—what is it? A wall of red-hot glass. Some are accursed from the beginning. If I ask: how could the curse be broken? there is but one answer: the monstrous would need to come to pass, the unimaginable! Thus it is with me."

Christian was shocked. "What do you mean by that?"

"One would have to gain a new experience," answered Amadeus Voss, "to know a being truly human—in the highest and deepest sense." In the gathering dusk his face had the hue of stone. It was a well-shaped face—long, narrow, intelligent, full of impassioned suffering. The lenses in front of his eyes sparkled in the last light of day, and on his fair hair was a glimmer as upon jewels.

"Are you going to stay in the village?" Christian inquired, not from a desire to know, but out of the distress which he felt in the heavy silence. "You were employed by Councillor Ribbeck. Will you return to him?"

Voss's nerves twitched. "Return? There is no return," he murmured. "Do you know Ribbeck? Well, I hardly know

him myself. I saw him just twice. The first time was when
he came to the seminary to engage a tutor for his sons. When
I think of him I have the image of something fat and frozen.
I was picked out at once. My superiors approved of me highly
and desired to smooth my path. Yes. And I saw him for the
second time one night in December, when he appeared at
Halbertsroda with a commissary of police to put me out. You
needn't look at me that way. There were no further consequences. It wouldn't have done to permit any."

He fell silent. Christian got up. Voss did not urge him to
stay longer, but accompanied him to the door. There he said
in a changed voice: "What kind of a man are you? One sits
before you and pours out one's soul, and you sit there in silence.
How does it happen?"

"If you regret it I shall forget all you have said," Christian
answered in his flexible, courteous way, that always had a
touch of the equivocal.

Voss let his head droop. "Come in again when you are passing," he begged gently. "Perhaps then I'll tell you about what
happened there!" He pointed with his thumb across his
shoulder.

"I shall come," said Christian.

XII

Albrecht Wahnschaffe came into his wife's bedroom. She
was in bed. It was a magnificent curtained bed with carved
posters. On both sides of the wall hung costly tapestries
representing mythological scenes. A coverlet of blue damask
concealed Frau Wahnschaffe's majestic form.

Gallantly he kissed the hand which she held out toward him
with a weary gesture, and glided into an armchair. "I want
to talk to you about Christian," he said. "For some time
his doings have worried me. He drifts and drifts. The latest
thing is his purchase of that diamond. There is a challenge
in such an action. It annoys me."

Frau Wahnschaffe wrinkled her forehead, and answered: " I see no need to worry. Many sons of wealthy houses pass their time as Christian does. They are like noble plants that need adornment. They seem to me to represent a high degree of human development. They regard themselves quite rightly as excellent within themselves. By birth and wealth they are freed from the necessity of effort. Their very being is in their aristocratic aloofness and inviolability."

Albrecht Wahnschaffe bowed. He played with his slender white fingers that bore no sign of age. He said: " I'm sorry that I cannot quite share your opinion. It seems to me that in the social organism each member should exercise a function that serves the whole. I was brought up with this view, and I cannot deny it in favour of Christian. I am not inclined to quarrel with his mere expenditure of money, though he has exceeded his budget considerably during the last few months. The house of Wahnschaffe cannot be touched even by such costly pranks. What annoys me is the aimlessness of such a life, its exceedingly obvious lack of any inner ambition."

From under her wearily half-closed lids Frau Wahnschaffe regarded her husband coolly. It angered her that he desired to draw Christian, who had been created for repose and play, delight and beauty, into his own turbid whirl. She answered with a touch of impatience: " You have always let him choose his own path, and you cannot change him now. All do not need to toil. Business is terribly unappetizing. I have borne two sons—one for you, one for myself. Demand of yours what you will and let him fulfil what he can. I like to think of mine and be happy in the thought that he is alive. If anything has worried me it is the fact that, since his trip to England, Christian has withdrawn himself more and more from us, and also, I am told, from his friends. I hope it means nothing. Perhaps there is a woman behind it. In that case it will pass; he does not indulge in tragic passions. But talking exhausts me, Albrecht. If you have other arguments, I beg you to postpone them."

She turned her head aside, and closed her eyes in exhaustion. Albrecht Wahnschaffe arose, kissed her hand with the same gallant gesture, and went out.

But her saying that she had borne one son for him and one for herself embittered him a little against his wife, whom he commonly regarded as an inviolable being of finer stuff. Why did I build all this? he asked himself, as he slowly passed through the magnificent halls.

It was more difficult for him to approach Christian than a member of the ministry or a distinguished foreigner. He vacillated between issuing a request and a command. He was not sure of his authority, and even less of any friendly understanding. But while he was spending a few days of rest and recreation in the family's ancestral house at Würzburg, he sent a message to Christian, and begged him for an interview.

XIII

Crammon wrote to Christian. It was his humour to affect an archaic manner of speech:

" Most Honoured and Worthy Friend: With deep satisfaction I learn that your Worship has ruefully returned to the god Dionysos, and as a sign thereof laid down upon his altar a jewel, whose price has caused the teeth of the Philistines in the land to rattle, and their lame digestions to work with unwelcome swiftness. Your servant, the undersigned, did, on the contrary, when the news of happy augury came to him, perform a dance in his lonely closet, which so shocked the ladies of his palace that they at once called up psychiatrists on the telephone. Thus the world, barren of understanding, is incapable of great reflections.

" Unlovely are my days. I am ensnared in amorous adventures which do not content me, and, in addition, disappoint those who are involved. At times I sit by the charming glow of my chimney fire, and, closing my eyes, peruse the book of memory. A bottle of golden-hued cognac is my sole companion, and while I nourish my heart upon its artificial warmth, the higher regions are wont to sink into the cold mystery of mere idiocy. My mental powers are moving, like the crab, backward; my virile powers decline. Years ago in Paris I knew a chess player, a purblind old German, who lost every game he played, and exclaimed each time: 'Where are the days in which I vanquished the great Zuckertort?' The latter, I must explain, was a great master of the royal game. The necessary application to myself embarrasses me. There was once a Roman emperor famous above all others for his power over women; Maxentius was, I believe, the man's name. But were I to exclaim: 'Where are the days in which I rivalled the great Maxentius?' it were but damnable boasting!

"It is a pity that you cannot be a beholder when I arise from my couch in the morning. Were this spectacle to be tested by connoisseurs and to be enjoyed by the laity, throngs would attend it, as whilom they did the rising of the kings of France. The gentry of the land would come to do me reverence, and lovely ladies would tickle me to elicit a beam of cheer upon my face. O blessed youth, friend and playmate of my dreams, I would have you know that the moments in which one leaves the linen well warmed by one's own body, and goes forth to twelve hours of the world's mischief, are to me moments of incomparable pitifulness. I sit on the bed's edge, and regard my underwear with a loud though inward rage. Sadly I gather the remnants of my ego, and reknot the thread of consciousness where Morpheus cut it yestereve. My soul is strewn about, and rolls in little globules, like mercury spilt from a broken thermometer. Only the sacrificial fumes of the tea kettle, the fragrance of ham and of an omelet like cowslips, and, above all, gentle words uttered by the soft lips of my considerate housekeepers, reconcile me to my fate.

"Dear old Regamey is dead. The Count Sinsheim has had a

paralytic stroke. My friend, Lady Constance Cuningham, a member of the highest aristocracy, has married a wealthy American bounder. The best are going, and the tree of life is growing bare. On my trip here I stopped over in Munich for three days as the guest of the young Imhofs. Your sister Judith is cutting a great figure. The painters paint her, the sculptors hew her in marble, the poets celebrate her. Yet her ambition is still vaulting. She desires passionately a little nine-pointed coronet upon her linen, her liveries, and her four motors, and flirts with everything that comes from the court or goes to it. Felix, on the contrary, being a democrat, surrounds himself with business men, speculators, explorers, and clever people of both sexes. Hence their house is a mixture of Guildhall, a grain exchange, a meeting of pettifoggers, and a jockey club. After watching the goings on for an evening, I retired to a corner with a pretty girl, and asked her to feel my pulse. She obeyed, and my suffering soul was soothed.

" Our sweet Ariel, I am told, intoxicates the Poles in Warsaw and the Muscovites in Moscow. In the latter city the students are said to have expressed their homage by a torchlight procession, and the officers to have covered the snowy streets from her dwelling to the theatre with roses. I am also told that the Grand Duke Cyril, commonly known as the human butcher, is half-mad with love of her, and is turning the world topsy-turvy to get her. It fills me with a piercing, depthless melancholy to think, O Ariel, that once I, too, felt thy breath. No more than that; but it suffices. *Le moulin n'y est plus, mais le vent y est encore.*

" With this final remark, dear brother of my heart and sorely missed friend, I commend you to God, and beseech you to give some sign to your affectionately longing Bernard Gervasius C. v. W."

When Christian had read the letter, he smiled, and laid it quietly aside.

XIV

On the slope of the hill behind the village Christian and Amadeus Voss met quite by chance.

"I have been waiting for you all week," said Voss.

"I was going to come to you to-day," said Christian. "Won't you walk a little with me?"

Amadeus Voss turned and accompanied Christian. They climbed the hill-top, and then turned toward the forest. Silently they walked side by side. The sun shone through the boughs and everything was watery. Remnants of snow rested on the dry foliage; the ground was slippery; on the road the water flowed in the deep ruts. When they left the forest the sun was just setting, the sky was greenish and pink, and when they reached the first houses of Heptrich, twilight had fallen. On the whole way they had not exchanged a syllable. At first Voss had deliberately not kept step with Christian. Later they walked in a rhythmic harmony that was like the prelude to their conversations.

"I'm hungry," said Amadeus Voss; "there is an inn yonder. Let us go."

They entered the guest room, which they found empty. They sat down at a table near the oven, for the cold air had chilled them. A bar-maid lit a lamp, and brought what they ordered. Christian, in an access of fear, which was less only than his curiosity, thought: What will happen now? and watched Voss attentively.

"The other day I read a moral tale in an old book," said Amadeus, and he used a sharpened match as a tooth-pick in a way that made Christian tremble with nervousness. "It tells about a king, who realized that men and things in his country were growing worse every day, and he asked four philosophers to find out the reason. The four wise men consulted, and then each went to one of the four gates of the city and inscribed thereon one of the chief reasons. The first wrote: ' Here might is right, and therefore this land has no law; day is night, and therefore this land has no road; conflict is flight, and therefore this land has no honour.' The second wrote: ' One is two here, and therefore this land has no truth; friend is enemy here, therefore this land has no troth; evil is good, therefore we see no piety.' The third wrote: ' The snail pretends to be an eagle, and thieves hold all power.' The fourth wrote: ' The will is our counsellor, and its counsel is evil; the penny pronounces judgment, therefore our rule is vile; God is dead, and therefore the land is filled with sins.' "

He threw the match away, and leaned his head upon his hand. " In the same book," he went on, " there is yet another story, and perhaps you will feel the connection between the two. Once upon a time the earth opened in the midst of Rome, and a yawning abyss was seen. The gods were questioned, and they made answer: ' This abyss will not close until some one has leaped into it of his own free will.' None could be persuaded to do that. At last a youth came and said: ' If you will let me live for one year according to my pleasure, then at the year's end I shall gladly and voluntarily plunge into the abyss.' It was decided that nothing should be forbidden him, and he used the women and possessions of the Romans freely and at his pleasure. All yearned for the moment to come when they could be rid of him. And when the year was gone, he rode up on a noble charger, and with it leaped into the abyss, which immediately closed behind him."

Christian shrugged his shoulders. " It is all dark to me," he said moodily. " Did you really want to tell me these old tales? They have no meaning."

Voss laughed hoarsely to himself. " You are not nimble," he said, " you have not a nimble mind. Have you never felt the need of seeking refuge in some metaphor? It is like a drug that stills pain."

" I don't know what you mean by that," Christian said, and again he heard the other's soft laughter.

"Let us go," said Christian and arose.

"Very well. Let us go." Voss spoke with a morose air. And they went.

XV

The night air was very still and the sky sown with stars that gleamed coldly. When the village lay behind them, they heard no sound.

"How long were you in Ribbeck's house?" Christian asked suddenly.

"Ten months," Amadeus Voss replied. "When I got to Halbertsroda, the land lay under ice and snow. When I left, the land lay under ice and snow. Between my coming and going, there was a spring, a summer, and an autumn."

He stopped for a moment, and gazed after an animal that in the darkness leaped across the road and disappeared in the furrows of a field. Then he began to talk, at first in a staccato manner and drily, then vividly and tempestuously, and at last gasping for breath. They wandered away from the road, but were not aware of it; the hour grew late, but they did not know it.

Voss told his story:

"I had never seen a house like that. The carpets, pictures, tapestries, the silver, the many servants—it was all new to me. I had never eaten of such dishes nor slept in such beds. I came from amid four bare walls, from a cot, an iron stove, a wash stand, a book shelf, and a crucifix.

"My two pupils were eleven and thirteen. The older was blond and spare, the younger brunette and stocky. Their hair hung down their shoulders like manes. From the very first hour they treated me with a jeering resistance. At first I did not see Frau Ribbeck at all. Not till a week had passed did she summon me. She made the impression of a young girl; she had rust-red hair and a pale, intimidated, undeveloped face. She treated me with a contempt that I had not expected, and that drove the blood into my temples. My meals were served to me alone. I was not permitted to eat at the master's table, and the servants treated me as their equal. That gnawed at me cruelly. When Frau Ribbeck appeared in the garden and I lifted my hat, she barely nodded, blind and shameless in her contempt for one whom she paid. I was no more to her than thin air!

"It is as old as the world, this sin that was sinned against my soul. Ye sinners against my soul, why did you let me famish? Why did I taste of renunciation while ye revelled? How shall a hungry man withstand the temptations which the living Tempter places before him? Do you think we are not aware of your gluttony? All action, whether good or evil, runs through all nature. When the grape blossoms in Madeira, the wine that has been pressed from it stirs in a thousand casks far over sea and land, and a new fermentation sets in.

"One morning the boys locked the door of their room and refused to come to their instruction. While I shook the knob they mocked me from within. In the halls the servants stood and laughed at my powerlessness. I went to the gardener, borrowed an axe, and crashed through the door with three blows. A minute later I was in the room. The boys looked at me in consternation, and realized at last that I would not endure their insolence. The noise had brought Frau Ribbeck to the scene. She looked at the broken door and then at me. I shall never forget that look. She did not turn her eyes from me even while she was speaking to the children, and that was at least ten minutes. Her eyes asked: How dare you? Who are you? When she went out, she saw the axe near the door and stopped a moment, and I saw her shiver. But I knew that the direction of the wind had changed. Also it came into my consciousness that a human woman had stood before me.

"The teasing of my pupils was by no means at an end. On the contrary, they annoyed me as much as possible. But they did it secretively now, and the blame was hard to fix. I found pebbles and needles in my bed, ink spilled over my books, a horrible rent in the best suit of clothes I had. They jeered at me before others, lied about me to their mother, and exchanged glances of shameless insolence when I held them responsible. What they did was not like the ordinary mischief of silly boys. They had been sophisticated by luxury. They were afraid of a draught, had the rooms so overheated that one grew faint, and thought of nothing but physical comforts. Once they fought, and the younger bit the older's finger. The boy went to bed for three days, and insisted that a physician be called. Nor was this merely a case of lazy malingering; bottomless malevolence and vengefulness entered into it. They considered me as far beneath them, and lost no chance to make me feel my dependent position. My mood was often bitter, but I determined to practise patience.

" One evening I entered the drawing-room. The hour which I had set as the boys' bed-time was past. Frau Ribbeck sat on the carpet, the boys snuggled on either side of her. She was showing them the pictures in a book. Her hair hung loose,— an unfitting thing, I thought—and its reddish splendour covered her as well as the boys like a mantle of brocade. The boys fixed green and evil eyes upon me. I ordered them to bed at once. There must have been something in my tone that frightened them and forced them to obey. Without contradiction they got up and retired.

" Adeline remained on the carpet. I shall simply call her Adeline, as, indeed, I did later during our intercourse. She looked at me exactly as she had done that day I had used the axe. One cannot well be paler than she was by nature, but her skin now became positively transparent. She arose, went to the table, lifted some indifferent object, and put it down again. At the same time a mocking smile hovered upon her lips. That smile went through and through me. And indeed the woman herself pierced me, body and soul. You'll misunderstand me. It doesn't matter. If you don't understand, no explanations will do any good. The sheet of ice above me cracked, and I had a glimpse of the upper world."

" I believe I do understand you," said Christian.

" To my question whether she desired me to leave the house, she replied that, since her husband had engaged me, it was for her to respect the arrangement. Her tone was frosty. I replied that the pressure of her dislike made it impossible for my activities to be fruitful. With an indirect glance at me, she answered that some method of decent co-operation could probably be found, and that she would think it over. Beginning with that evening, I was invited to table with her, and the boys and she treated me with respect, if not with kindness. Late one evening she sent for me and asked me to read to her. She gave me the book from which I was to read. It was a current fashionable novel, and, after I had read a few pages, I threw the volume on the table, and said that the stuff nauseated me. She nodded, and answered that that was quite her feeling, too, which she had not wanted to admit even to herself, and that she was grateful to me for my frankness. I went for my Bible, and read her the story of Samson from the Book of Judges. It must have seemed naïve to her, for when I had finished that mocking smile played again about her lips. Then she asked: ' It's hardly necessary, is it, to be a hero in Judah to share Samson's fate? And do you think that what Delilah accomplished was so remarkable? ' I replied that I had no experience of such matters, and she laughed.

" One word led to another, and I gathered the courage to reproach her with the morally neglected condition of her children, and with the wounding and vulgar quality of all I had so far seen and experienced in her house. I intentionally used the sharpest words, in order that she might flare up in wrath and show me the door. But she remained quite calm, and begged me to explain my ideas more fully. I did so, not without passion, and she heard me with pleasure. Several times I saw her breathe deeply and stretch herself and close her eyes. She contradicted me, then agreed, defended her position, and in the end admitted it to be indefensible. I told her that the love which she thought she felt for her sons was really a sort of hatred, based on a poisoning of her own soul, in which there was yet another life and another love, which it was wicked to condemn to withering and death. She must have misunderstood me at this point, for she looked at me with her large eyes suddenly, and bade me go. When I had closed her door behind me, I heard sobs. I opened the door again, and saw her sitting there with her face hidden in her hands. I had the impulse to return to her. But her gesture dismissed me.

" I had never before seen any woman cry except my mother. I cannot tell you of my feelings. If I had had a sister and grown up in her companionship, I might have acted and felt differently. But Adeline was the first woman whom, in any deeper sense, I truly saw.

" Several days later she asked me whether I had any hope of forming her boys into human beings in my sense. She said that she had reflected on all I had urged, and had come to the conclusion that things could not go on as they were. I answered that it was not yet too late. She begged me to save what was possible, and announced that, in order to leave me a free hand, she had determined to travel for a few months. Three days later she departed. She took no personal farewell of her sons, but wrote them a letter from Dresden.

" I took the boys with me to a hunting lodge, that lay isolated in the woods, at a distance of two hours from Halbertsroda. It belonged to the Ribbeck estate, and Adeline had assigned it to me as a refuge. There I settled down with the boys and took them sternly in hand. Sometimes dread overcame me, when I thought of the words of Scripture: Why do you seek constantly to change your way? Beware lest you be deceived by Egypt, as you were deceived by Assyria.

" A deaf, old man-servant cooked for us, and luxurious meals were a thing of the past. The boys had to pray, to fast once

a week, to sleep on hard mattresses, and to rise at five in the
morning. In every way I broke down their stubbornness, their
dull sloth, their furtive sensuality, their plots and tricks.
There was no play now, and the days were divided with iron
regularity. I shrank from no severity. I chastised them; at
the slightest disobedience I used a whip. I taught them the
meaning of pain. When they cowered naked before me, with
the bloody stripes on their bodies, I spoke to them of the mar-
tyrdom of the saints. I kept a diary, in order that Adeline
might know exactly what had happened. The boys started
when they heard me from afar; they trembled if I but raised
my head. Once I came upon them whispering to each other in
bed at night. I drove them out. They screamed and fled out
of the house from me. In their night shifts they ran into the
forest, and I, with two dogs following me, pursued them. Rain
began to pour, and at last they broke down and threw themselves on the ground and begged for mercy. Most difficult of
all it was to lead them to Confession. But I was stronger than
the Evil One within them, and forced them to cleanse their
souls. Bitter hours were the hours I endured. But I had
made a vow to Adeline in my heart.

" The boys became thoughtful, subdued, and silent. They
went into corners and wept. When Adeline returned I took
them to Halbertsroda, and she marvelled at the change in them.
They flung themselves into her arms, but they uttered no
complaint against me, either then or when they were left alone
with her. I had told them that if they were disobedient or
stubborn, we would return to the hunting lodge. One or two
days a week were spent there under any circumstances. Gradually they came to avoid their mother, and Adeline herself was
more indifferent to them. The softish, hectic, over-tender
element in their relations had disappeared.

" Adeline sought my companionship and conversation. She
watched me, and was condescending, weary, distracted in
mind, and restless. She adorned herself as though guests were

coming, and combed her hair thrice daily. In all respects she
submitted to my regulations. There are dulled, worm-eaten,
smouldering souls that kneel before the raised axe in another's
hand, and give only mockery to those who bend before them.
Often her loftiness and reserve overwhelmed me, and I thought
that she had no space for me in her mind. Then a look came
into her eyes that made me forget whence I came and what I
was in her house. Everything seemed possible with her. She
was capable of setting fire to the house by night, because she was
bored, and because the cancer that ate at her soul would cease
its gnawing for no nobler ecstasy: she was capable of standing
from noon to night before her mirror to watch a deepening
furrow on her brow. Everything seemed possible. For is it
not written: What man knoweth what is in man except only the
spirit of man that is in him?

" My deep temptations began on an evening when, in the
course of conversation, she carelessly laid her hand over mine,
and withdrew it hastily. That gesture snatched from my
sight the things about us. In the space between one thought
and the next I had become the slave of visions and desires.

" She asked me to tell her about my life. I fell into that
snare too, and told her.

" Once in the twilight I met her in the hall. She stood still,
and looked at me piercingly. Then she laughed softly and
moved away. I reeled, and the sweat stood in beads on my
forehead.

" My heart was heavy when I was alone. Visions appeared
that set my room in flames. My rosary and my missal were
hidden from me, and I could find neither. Always there rose
the cry in me: Once only! Let me taste that ecstasy but once!
Then demons came and tormented me. All the muscles and
nerves and sinews of my body seemed lacerated. Do with me
as God wills, I whispered to the demons, for my heart is prepared. During sleep a strange force hurled me from my bed,
and unconsciously I battered the walls with my head. One

whole week I fasted upon bread and water, but it did not avail. Once when I had sat down to read, a huge ape stood before me and turned the leaves of my book. Every night a seductive vision of Adeline came to my bed-side. She stood there and spoke: ' It is I, my beloved.' Then I would rise and run senselessly about. But she would follow me and whisper: ' You shall be my master and have all the good things of this world.' But when I sought to grasp that vision of her, it showed a sudden aversion, and she called fluttering shadows to her aid. One was a notary with a pen and an ink-well, another a locksmith with a red-hot hammer, there was a mason with his trowel, an officer with naked sword, a woman with a painted face.

" So terrible was my state, that I understood but slowly and gradually the dreadful realities that took place about me. One morning Adeline came into the room where I was teaching the boys, sat down, and listened. She drew from her finger a ring that had in it a great, lovely pearl, played with it thoughtfully, arose, went to the window to watch the falling of the snow, and then left the room to go into the garden. I could not breathe or see any longer. There was an intolerable pressure on my chest, and I had to leave the room for a little to catch my breath. When I returned I saw in the eyes of my pupils a look of unwonted malevolence. I paid no attention to it. From time to time the old rebelliousness flared up in them, but I let them be. They sat before me half-crouching, and recited their catechism softly and with glances full of fear.

" About ten minutes passed when Adeline returned. She said she had left her ring on the table, and asked me whether I had seen it. She began to search for it, and so did I. She called her maid and a footman, who examined everything in the room; but the ring was gone. Adeline and her servants looked at me strangely, for I stood there and could not move. I felt at once and in every fibre that I was exposed to their suspicion. They searched on the stairs and in the hall, in the new fallen snow of the garden, and again in the room, since Adeline insisted that she had taken the ring off there and forgotten it on the table. And I confirmed this statement, although I had not actually seen the ring on the table, since I had seen her and her gestures but as things in a dream. All the words that were exchanged between her and the servants seemed directed against me. I read suspicion in their looks and changed colour, and called the boys, who had stolen away as soon as they could, and questioned them. They suggested that their rooms be searched, and looked at me with malignity. I begged Adeline to have my room searched as well. She made a deprecating gesture, but said, as though in self-justification, that she attached a peculiar value to this ring and should hate to lose it.

" Meantime the manager of the estate, who happened to have spent that night at Halbertsroda, entered. He passed me by without greeting, but with a dark and hostile glance. Then it all came over me. I saw myself delivered over to their suspicions without defence, and I said to myself: Perhaps you have really stolen the ring. The fall from my previous spiritual condition to this vulgar and ugly one was so sudden, that I broke out into wild laughter, and insisted more urgently than ever that my room and effects and even my person be searched. The manager spoke softly to Adeline. She looked at me wanly and went out. I emptied my pockets in the man's presence. He followed me to my room. I sat down by the window while he opened drawer after drawer in my chest and opened my wardrobe. The footman, the maid, and the two boys stood by the door. Suddenly the manager uttered a hollow cry and held up the ring. I had known with the utmost certainty a moment before that he would find the ring. I had read it in the faces of the boys. Therefore I remained quietly seated while the others looked at one another and followed the manager out. I locked my door and walked up and down, up and down, for many, many hours.

"When the night was over, there was a solemn calm in my soul. I sent a servant to ask Adeline whether she would receive me. She refused. To justify myself in writing was a thing I scorned to do. I would but degrade myself by asserting my innocence thus. My soul felt pure and cold. I learned next day that the manager had long heard rumours of the frightful cruelties I was said to inflict on the boys, who had, moreover, accused their mother and myself of an adulterous intimacy. Hence he had visited Halbertsroda secretly on several occasions, had questioned the servants, and had, that very morning, caused the boys to strip in his presence and had seen on their bodies the marks of the stripes that they had received. Since, in addition, their entire state of mind made him anxious, he sent a telegram to the Councillor, who arrived during the night with an official of the police.

"I suspect that Adeline at once saw through the plot concerning the ring, for it was not mentioned. The commissary turned to me and spoke vaguely of serious consequences, but I made no attempt to explain or excuse anything I had done. I left Halbertsroda that same night. I did not see Adeline again. She was, I have been told, sent off to a sanatorium. Three weeks later a little package came to me by post. I opened it and found in it the ring with the pearl. In our yard is a very ancient well. I went to that well and cast the ring into its depths.

"And now you know what happened to me in that world of the higher classes, in the house of the Councillor Ribbeck."

XVI

They had to walk a while longer before they reached the gate of the park of Christian's Rest. As Voss was about to take his leave, Christian said: "You're probably tired. Why trouble to walk to the village? Be my guest over night."

"If it does not inconvenience you, I accept," Voss answered.

They entered the house and passed into the brightly lit hall.

Amadeus Voss gazed about him in astonishment. They went up the stairs and into the dining hall, which was furnished in the purest style of Louis XV. Christian led his guest through other rooms into the one that was to be his. And Amadeus Voss wondered more and more. " This is quite another thing from Halbertsroda," he murmured; " it is as a feast day compared to every day."

Silently they sat opposite each other at table. Then they went into the library. A footman served the coffee on a silver platter. Voss leaned against a column and looked upward. When the servant had gone, he said: " Have you ever heard of the Telchinian pestilence? It is a disease created by the envy of the Telchines, the hounds of Actæon who were changed into men, and it destroys everything within its reach. A youth named Euthilides saw with that eye of envy the reflection of his own beauty in a spring, and his beauty faded."

Christian looked silently at the floor.

" There is another legend of a Polish nobleman," Amadeus continued. " This nobleman lived alone in a white house by the Vistula river. All his neighbours avoided him, for his envious glance brought them nothing but misfortune. It killed their herds, set fire to their barns, and made their children leprous. Once a beautiful maiden was pursued by wolves and took refuge in the white house. He fell in love with her and married her. But because the evil that was in him passed into her also, he tore out the gleaming crystals of his eyes, and buried them near the garden wall. He had now recovered. But the buried eyes gained new power under the earth, and an old servitor who dug them up was slain by them."

Sitting on a low stool, Christian had folded his arms over his knee, and looked up at Voss.

" From time to time," said Amadeus Voss, " one must expiate the lust of the eye. Over in the village of Nettersheim a maid servant lies dying. The poor thing is deserted by all the world. She lies in a shed by the stables, and the peasants who think her merely lazy will not believe that she is about to die. I have visited her more than once, in order to expiate the lust of the eye."

A long silence fell upon them. When the clock in the tall Gothic case struck twelve, they went to their rooms.

XVII

In obedience to his father's summons, Christian travelled to Würzburg.

Their greeting was most courteous. " I hope I have not interfered with any plans of yours," said Albrecht Wahnschaffe.

" I am at your disposal," Christian said coolly.

They took a walk on the old ramparts but said little. The beautiful dog Freia, who was the constant companion of Albrecht Wahnschaffe, trotted along between them. It surprised the elder Wahnschaffe to observe on Christian's face the signs of inner change.

That evening, over their tea, he said with an admirably generous gesture. " You're to be congratulated, I understand, on a very unusual acquisition. A wreath of legends surrounds this diamond. The incident has caused quite a whirl of dust to fly and not a little amazement. Not unjustly so, it seems to me, since you are neither a British Duke nor an Indian Maharajah. Is the stone so very desirable? "

" It is marvellous," Christian said. And suddenly the words of Voss slipped into his mind: One must expiate the lust of the eye.

Albrecht Wahnschaffe nodded. " I don't doubt it, and I understand such passions, though, as a man of business, I must regret the tying up of so much capital. It is an eccentricity; and the world is endangered whenever the commoners grow eccentric. And so I should like to ask you to reflect on this aspect of things: all the privileges which you enjoy, all the easements of life, the possibility of satisfying

your whims and passions, the supremacy of your social station
—all these things rest on work. Need I add—on the work of
your father? "

The dog Freia had strolled out from a corner of the room,
and laid her head caressingly on Christian's knee. Albrecht
Wahnschaffe, slightly annoyed and jealous, gave her a smart
slap on one flank.

He continued. "An exploitation of one's capacity for work
which reaches the extent of mine involves, of course, the
broadest self-denial in all other matters. One becomes a
ploughshare that tears up the earth and rusts. Or one is like
a burning substance, luminiferous but self-consumed. Marriage, family, friendship, art, nature—these things scarcely
exist for me. I have lived like a miner in his shaft. And what
thanks do I get? Demagogues tell those whom they delude
that I am a vampire, who sucks the blood of the oppressed.
These poisoners of our public life either do not know or do
not wish to know the shocks and sufferings and renunciations
that have been mine, and of which their peaceful ' wage-slave '
has no conception."

Freia snuggled closer up to Christian, licked his hand, and
her eyes begged humbly for a look. The beast's dumb tenderness soothed him. He frowned, and said laconically: "If it is
so, and you feel it so keenly, why do you go on working? "

"There is such a thing as duty, my dear spoiled boy, such
a thing as loyalty to a cause," Albrecht Wahnschaffe answered,
and a gleam of anger showed in his pale-blue eyes. "Every
peasant clings to the bit of earth into which he has put his
toil. When I began to work, our country was still a poor
country; to-day it is rich. I shall not say that what I have
accomplished is considerable, when compared to the sum of
our national accomplishment, but it has counted. It is a symptom of our rise, of our young might, of our economic welfare.
We are one of the very great nations now, and have a body as
well as a countenance."

"What you say is doubtless most true," Christian answered. "Unhappily I have no instinct for such matters; my personality is defective in things of that kind."

"A quarter of a century ago your fate would have been that of a bread earner," Albrecht Wahnschaffe continued, without reacting to Christian's words. "To-day you are a descendant and an heir. Your generation looks upon a changed world and age. We older men have fastened wings upon your shoulders, and you have forgotten how painful it is to creep."

Christian, in a sombre longing for the warmth of some body, took the dog's head between his hands, and with a grunt of gratitude she raised herself up and laid her paws on his shoulders. With a smile, that included his petting of the dog, he said: "No one refuses the good things that fall into his lap. It is true I have never asked whence everything comes and whither it tends. To be sure, there are other ways of living; and I may yet embrace one of them some day. Then it will be apparent whether one becomes another man, and what kind, when the supports or the wings, as you put it, are gone." His face had grown serious.

Albrecht Wahnschaffe suddenly felt himself rather helpless before this handsome, proud stranger who was his son. To hide his embarrassment, he answered hastily: "A different way of living—that is just what I mean. It was the conviction that a life which is nothing but a chain of trifles must in the end become a burden, that made me suggest a career to you that is worthier of your powers and gifts. How would you like the profession of diplomacy? Wolfgang seems thoroughly satisfied with the possibilities that he sees opening up before him. It is not too late for you either. It will not be difficult to make up the time lost. Your name outweighs any title of nobility. You would stay in a suitable atmosphere; you have large means, the necessary personal qualities and relations. Everything will adjust itself automatically."

Christian shook his head. "You are mistaken, father," he

said, softly but firmly. " I have no capacity for anything like that, and no taste for it at all."

" I suspected as much," Albert Wahnschaffe said, in his liveliest manner. " Let us not speak of it any more. My second proposal is far more congenial to myself. I would encourage you to co-operate in the activities of our firm. My plan is to create a representative position for you in either our home or our foreign service. If you choose the latter you may select your own field of activity—Japan, let us say, or the United States. We would furnish you with credentials that would make your position very independent. You would assume responsibilities that are in no wise burdensome, and enjoy all the privileges of an ambassador. All that is needed is your consent. I shall arrange all details."

Christian arose from his chair. " I beg you very earnestly, father, to drop that subject," he said. His expression was cold and his eyes cast down.

Albrecht Wahnschaffe arose too. " Do not be rash, Christian," he admonished his son. " I shall not conceal the fact that a definitive refusal on your part would wound me deeply. I have counted on you." He looked at Christian with a firm glance. But Christian was silent.

After a while he asked: " How long ago is it since you were at the works? "

" It must be three or four years ago," Christian answered.

" It was three years ago on Whitsuntide, if I remember rightly," Albrecht Wahnschaffe said, with his habitual touch of pride in his memory, which was rarely at fault. " You had agreed on a pleasure trip in the Harz mountains with your cousin, Theo Friesen, and Theo was anxious to pay a flying visit to the factories. He had heard of our new welfare movement for workingmen, and was interested in it. But you scarcely stopped after all."

" No, I persuaded Theo to go on. We had a long way ahead of us, and I was anxious to get to our quarters."

Christian remembered the whole incident now. Evening had come before the car drove through the streets of the factory village. He had yielded to his cousin's wish, but suddenly his aversion for this world of smoke and dust and sweat and iron had awakened. He had not wanted to leave the car, and had ordered the driver to speed up.

Nevertheless he recalled the hellish music made up of beaten steel and whirring wheels. He could still hear the thundering, whistling, wheezing, screeching, hissing; he could still see the swift procession of forges, cylinders, pumps, steam-hammers, furnaces, of all kinds; the thousands of blackened faces, a race that seemed made of coal in the breath of the fierce glow of white and crimson fires; misty electric moons that quivered in space; vehicles like death barrows swallowed up in the violet darkness; the workingmen's homes, with their appearance of comfort, and their reality of a bottomless dreariness; the baths, libraries, club-houses, crêches, hospitals, infants' homes, warehouses, churches, and cinemas. The stamp of force and servitude, of all that is ugliest on earth, was bedizened and tinted in fair colours here, and all menaces were throttled and fettered.

Young Friesen had exhausted himself with admiration, but Christian had not breathed freely again until their car was out on the open road and had left the flaring horror in its panic flight.

"And you have not been there since?" Albrecht Wahnschaffe asked.

"No, not since that day."

For a while they stood opposite each other in silence. Albrecht Wahnschaffe took Freia by her collar, and said with notable self-control: "Take counsel with yourself. There is time. I shall not urge you unduly, but rather wait. When you come to weigh the circumstances, and test your own mind, you will realize that I have your welfare at heart. Do not answer me now. When you have made a clear decision— let me know what it is."

"Have I your permission to retire?" Christian asked. His father nodded, and he bowed and left the room.

Next morning he returned to Christian's Rest.

XVIII

In a side street of the busiest quarter of Buenos Ayres, there stood a house that belonged to the Gunderam family. The parents of Gottlieb Gunderam had bought it when they came to the Argentine in the middle of the nineteenth century. In those days its value had been small, but the development of the city had made it a considerable property. Gottfried Gunderam received tempting offers for it, not only from private dealers, but from the municipality. The rickety house was to be torn down, and to be replaced by a modern apartment house.

But Gottfried Gunderam turned a deaf ear to all offers. "The house in which my mother died," he declared, "shall not be sold to strangers so long as the breath is in my body."

This determination did not arise so much from filial piety, as from a superstition that was powerful enough to silence even his greed. He feared that his mother would arise from her grave and avenge herself on him, if he permitted the family's ancestral home to be sold and destroyed. Wealth, good harvests, a great age, and general well-being were, in his opinion, dependent on his action in this matter. He would not even allow strangers to enter the house.

His sons and kinsmen mockingly called it the Escurial. Gottfried Gunderam took no notice of their jeers, but he himself had, gradually and quite seriously, slipped into the habit of calling the house the Escurial.

One day, long before his voyage to Germany, Stephen had cleverly taken advantage of his father in an hour when the old man was tipsy and merry, and had extorted a promise that the Escurial was to be his upon his marriage. When he came home with Letitia he counted upon the fulfilment of this promise. He intended to establish himself as a lawyer in Buenos Ayres, and restore the neglected house.

He reminded his father of the compact. The old man denied it bluntly. He winked gravely. " Can you show me any record—black on white? Well, then, what do you want? A fine lawyer you are to think that you can enforce an agreement of which there is no record! "

Stephen did not reply. But from time to time—coldly, methodically, calmly—he reminded the old man of his promise.

The old man said: " The woman you have married is not to my taste. She doesn't fit into our life. She reads and reads. It's sickening. She's a milk-faced doll without sap. Let her be content with what she has. I shan't be such a fool as to plunge into expenditures on your account. It would cost a pretty penny to make the Escurial habitable. And I have no cash. Absolutely none."

Stephen estimated the available capital of his father as amounting to between four and five millions. " You owe me my patrimony," he answered.

" I owe you a damned good thrashing! " the old man replied grimly.

" Is that your last word? "

The old man answered: " Far from it. I won't speak my last word for a dozen years. But I like peace at home, and so I'll make a bargain with you. Whenever your wife gives birth to a man-child, you shall have the Escurial, and fifty thousand pesos to boot."

" Give me the promise in writing! Black on white counts —as you yourself said."

The old man laughed a dry laugh. " Good! " he cried, and winked with both eyes. " You're improving. Glad to see that the money spent on your legal studies wasn't quite wasted." With a sort of glee he sat down at his desk, and made out the required document.

A few weeks later Stephen said to Letitia: " Let us drive to the city. I want to show you the Escurial."

The only living creature in that house was a mulatto woman ninety years old. To rouse her one had to throw stones against the wooden shutters. Then she appeared, bent almost double, half-blind, clothed in rags, a yellow growth on her forehead.

The street, which had been laid out a century before, was a yard deeper than the more recent ones; and Stephen and Letitia had to use a short ladder to reach the door of the house. Within everything was mildewed and rotten, the furniture and the floors. In the corners the spiders' webs were like clouds, and fat hairy spiders sat in them peacefully. The wall-paper was in rags, the window-panes were broken, and the fire-places had caved in.

But in the room in which the mother of Gunderam had died, there stood a beautiful inlaid table, an antique piece from a convent of Siena. The mosaic showed two angels inclining palm-branches toward each other, and between the two sat an eagle. Upon the table lay the dead woman's jewels. Brooches and chains, rings and ear-rings and bracelets, had lain here dust-covered for many, many years. The reputation of the old house as being haunted had protected them more effectually than barred windows.

Letitia was frightened, and thought: " Am I to live here where ghosts may appear at night to don their old splendour? "

But when Stephen explained his plans for rebuilding and redecorating, she recovered her gaiety, and her imagination transformed these decayed rooms into inviting chambers and dainty boudoirs, cool halls with tall windows and airy, carpeted stairs.

" It depends quite simply on you whether we can have a happy and beautiful home very soon," Stephen declared. " I'm doing my share. I wish I could say the same of you."

Letitia looked away. She knew the condition which old Gunderam had made.

Again and again she had to disappoint Stephen. The Escurial lay in its deathlike sleep, and her husband's face grew more and more sombre. He sent her to church to pray; he strewed her bed with ground wall-nuts; he made her drink a powder of bones dissolved in wine. He sent for an old crone who was gifted in magic, and Letitia had to stand naked, surrounded by seven tapers, and let the woman murmur over her body. And she went to church and prayed, although she had no faith in her praying and felt no devotion and knew nothing of God. Yet she shuddered at the murmurs of the Italian witch, although when it was all over, she laughed and made light of the whole thing.

In spirit she conceived the image of the child which her body denied her. The image was of uncertain sex, but of flawless loveliness. It had the soft eyes of a deer, the features of one of Raphael's angels, and the exquisite soul of an ode by Hölderlin. It was destined to great things, and the dizzying curve of its fortune knew no decline. The thought of this dream child filled her with vaguely beautiful emotions, and she was amazed at Stephen's anger and growing impatience. She was amazed and was conscious of no guilt.

Stephen's mother, who was known as Doña Barbara to every one, said to her son: " I bore your father eight living creatures. Three are dead. Four are strong men. We need not even count your sister Esmeralda. Why is this woman barren? Chastise her, my son, beat her! "

Stephen gritted his teeth, and took up his ox-hide whip.

XIX

It was evening, and Christian went to the forester's house. The way was very familiar to him now. He did not analyze the inner compulsion that drew him thither.

Amadeus Voss sat by his lamp and read in an old book. Through the second door of the room the shadow of his mother slipped away.

After a while he asked: " Will you go with me to-morrow to Nettersheim? "

" What am I to do there? " Christian questioned in his turn.

Amadeus raised his face, and his spectacles glimmered. He murmured: " She may be dead by this time."

He drummed on his knees with his fingers. Since Christian said nothing, he began to tell him the story of the woman Walpurga, who was in the service of his uncle, the wealthy farmer Borsche.

" She was born in the village, a cottager's daughter. At fifteen she went to the city. She had heard of the fine life one leads there and had great ambitions. She was in service here and there. Last she was in the house of a merchant whose son seduced her; and of course, when it was discovered, she was driven out. So it comes to pass that those who are by nature the victims must bear a punishment in addition.

" She bore a child, but the child died. She fell deeper and deeper, until she became a street-walker. She practised this calling in Bochum and in Elberfeld. But the life wore on her, and she fell ill. One day a great home-sickness came upon her. She mustered her last strength, and returned to her native village. She was penniless and weak, but she was anxious to earn her bread, no matter at what wage or through what labour.

" But no one would hire her. Her parents were dead and she had no relatives, so she became a pubic charge. She was made to feel it grievously. One Sunday the minister inveighed against her from the pulpit. He did not mention her name, but he spoke of vile lives and sinks of iniquity, of visitations and punishments, and of how the anger of the Lord was visible in an example that was before the eyes of all. Thus she was branded and publicly delivered over to the scorn of all people, and she determined to put an end to her life. One evening, as Borsche was returning from his inn, he saw a woman lying in the road in dreadful convulsions. It was Walpurga. No man was near. Borsche lifted her on his broad back, and

carried her to his farm. She confessed that she had scraped
the phosphorus from many matches and eaten it. The farmer
gave her milk as an antidote. She recovered, and was permitted to stay on the farm.

" On some days she could work, and then she dragged herself
to the fields. On others she could not, and lay in a remote
corner. The men servants, of whom there were many, regarded her body as common property. Resistance was useless.
Not until Borsche learned this, and blazed out in anger, did
things get better. She was only twenty-three, and despite her
illness and the wretchedness of her life, she had preserved much
of her youthful good looks. Her cheeks had a natural glow
and her eyes were clear. So whenever she could not work,
the other maids fell upon her, and called her a malingering
bawd.

" Two weeks ago I happened to be wandering in the neighbourhood of Nettersheim, and stopped at Borsche's house. I
was well received there, for the family think highly of me as a
future priest. They talked about Walpurga. The farmer told
me her story, and asked me to have a look at her and give my
opinion as to whether she was really ill. I objected, and asked
why a physician had not seen her. He said that the doctor
from Heftrich had examined her and could find nothing
wrong. So I went to her. She lay in a shed, separated from
the cows only by a wooden partition. She was wrapped in an
old horse-blanket, and a little straw kept the chill of the
earth from her body. Her healthy colour and her normal
form did not deceive me. I said to the farmer: ' She's like
a guttering candle.' He and his wife seemed to believe me.
But when I demanded of them that they give the sick woman
decent lodging and care, they shrugged their shoulders, and
said that it was as warm in the stable as anywhere, and that
there was no sense in taking trouble or undergoing discomfort
on account of a creature who had fallen so low.

" On the third day I saw her again, and I have seen her on

every other day since then. My thoughts could not get rid
of her any more. In all my life no human creature has so
tugged at my heart. She could no longer get up; the most
malevolent had to admit that. I sat with her in the evil
smelling shed on a wooden bench near where she lay. Each
time I came she was happier to see me. I picked wild flowers
on the way, and she took them in her hands and held them
against her breast. They told her who I was, and gradually
she put many questions to me. She wanted to know whether
there really was an eternal life and eternal bliss. She wanted
to know whether Christ had died on the cross for her too.
She was afraid of the torments of purgatory, and said if they
were as bad as the torments men could inflict she was sorry
for the immortal part of her. She meant neither to re-
vile men nor to complain of them. She merely wanted to
know.

"And what answer could I give her? I assured her that
Christ had taken her cross upon Him too. Her other questions
left me silent. One is so dumb and desperate when a living
heart thirsts after truth, and the frozen Christ within would
melt into a new day and a new sun. They are even now in
purgatory and ask when it will begin. Hidden in blackness,
they do not see the dark; consumed by flames, they are unaware of the fire. Where is Satan's true kingdom—here or
elsewhere? And can that elsewhere be upon any star more
accursed than this? The poor man is thrust from the wayside,
the oppressed of the land creep into hiding; from the cities
come the moans of the dying, and the souls of those who are
wounded to death cry out. Yet God does not put an end to the
iniquity. And is it not written that the Lord said to Satan:
'From whence comest thou? And Satan answered the Lord,
and said, From going to and fro in the earth and from walking
up and down in it.'

"She confessed her sins to me, and begged me to grant her
absolution. But nothing that seemed sinful to her seemed so

to me. I saw the desolateness and loneliness of the world. I saw the bleak rooms and the barren walls, the streets by night with their flickering lamps, and the men with no compassion in their eyes. That is what I saw and what I thought of, and I took it upon my conscience to absolve her from all guilt. I set her free and promised her Paradise. She smiled at me and grasped my hand, and before I could prevent her she had kissed it. That was yesterday."

Amadeus was silent. "That was yesterday," he repeated, after a long and meditative pause. "I did not go to-day, out of fear of her dying. Perhaps she is dead even now."

"If you still want to go, I am ready," said Christian timidly. "I'll go with you. It's only an hour's walk.

"Then let us go," said Amadeus, with a sigh of relief, and arose.

XX

An hour later they were in Borsche's farm yard. The stable door was open. The men servants and the maid servants stood in front of it. An old man held a lantern high up, and they all stared into the shed. In the dim and wavering light, their faces showed a mixture of reverence and amazement. Within, on a pallet of straw, lay the body of Walpurga. Its cheeks were rosy. Nothing in that countenance recalled death, but only a peaceful sleep.

On the wooden bench a single candle was burning; but it was near extinction.

Amadeus Voss passed through that group of men and women, and kneeled at the dead woman's feet. The old man who held the lantern whispered something, and all the men and women kneeled down and folded their hands.

A cow lowed. After that there was no sound save from the bells of the unquiet cattle. The darkness of the stable, the face of the dead woman, which was like a face in a painting, the faces of the kneeling people, with their blunted foreheads and hard lips, in the yellow glimmer of the light—all these things Christian beheld, and something melted in his breast.

He himself watched it all from the darkness of the yard behind.

When Amadeus Voss joined Christian, the village carpenter came to measure the dead woman for her coffin. They started on their homeward way in silence.

Suddenly Christian stopped. It was near a tall mile-post. He grasped the post with both hands, and bent his head far back, and gazed with the utmost intensity into the drifting clouds of the night. Then he heard Amadeus Voss say: " Is it possible? Can such things be? "

Christian turned to him.

" I have a strange feeling in your presence, Christian Wahnschaffe," Voss said in a repressed and toneless voice. And then he murmured to himself: " Is it possible? Can the monstrous and incredible come to pass? "

Christian did not answer, and they wandered on.

XXI

Crammon gave a dinner. Not in his own house; meetings of a certain character were impossible there, on account of the innocent presence of the two old maiden ladies, Miss Aglaia and Miss Constantine. The disillusion would have been too saddening and final to the good ladies, who were as convinced of the virtue of their lord and protector as they were of the emperor's majesty.

In former years it had indeed sometimes seemed to them that their adored one did not always tread the paths of entire purity. They had closed an eye. Now, however, the dignity and intellectual resonance of his personality forbade any doubt.

Crammon had invited his guests to the private dining-room of a well-known hotel, in which he was familiar and esteemed. The company consisted of several young members of the nobility, to whom he was under social obligations, and, as for ladies, there were three beauties, entertaining, elegant, and yielding, in the precise degree which the occasion required. Crammon called them his friends, but in his treatment of them there was something languid and even vexed. He gave them clearly to understand that he was only the business manager of the feast, and that his heart was very far away.

No one, in fact, was present to whom he was not completely indifferent. Best of all he liked the old pianist with long, grey locks, who closed his eyes and smiled dreamily whenever he played a melancholy or languishing piece, just as he had done twenty years ago, when Crammon was still fired by the dreams and ambitions of youth. He gave the old man sweets and cigarettes, and sometimes patted his shoulder affectionately.

The table groaned under its burden of food and wine. Pepper was added to the champagne to heighten every one's thirst. There were cherries in the fruit bowls, and the gentlemen found it amusing to drop the pits down the semi-exposed bosoms of the ladies. The latter found it easier and easier, as the evening advanced, to resist the law of gravitation, and to display their charming shoes and the smooth silks and rustling laces of their legs in astonishingly horizontal attitudes. The most agile among them, a popular soubrette, climbed on the grand piano, and, accompanied by the grey-haired musician, sang the latest hit of the music halls.

The young men joined in the chorus.

Crammon applauded with just two fingers. "There is a sting in my soul," he whispered into the din. He got up and left the room.

In the corridor the head-waiter Ferdinand was leaning alone and somewhat wearily against the frame of a mirror. A tender intimacy of two decades bound Crammon to this man, who had never in his life been indiscreet, in spite of the innumerable secrets he had overheard.

"Bad times, Ferdinand," Crammon said. "The world is going to the deuce."

" One must take things as they are, Herr von Crammon,"
that dignified individual consoled him, and handed him the
bill.

Crammon sighed. He gave directions that if his guests
inquired after him, they were to be told that he was indisposed
and had gone home.

" There is a sting in my soul," he said, when he found himself on the street. He determined to travel again.

He yearned for his friend. It seemed to him that he had
had no friend but that one who had cast him off.

He yearned for Ariel. It seemed to him that he had possessed no woman, because she had not yielded to him who was
his very conception of genius and beauty.

At the door of his house stood Miss Aglaia. She had heard
him coming and had hastened to meet him. It frightened
Crammon, for the hour was late.

" There is a lady in the drawing-room," Miss Aglaia whispered. " She arrived at eight, and has been waiting since
then. She besought us so movingly to let her stay that we had
not the heart to refuse. She is a distinguished lady, and she
has a dear face——"

" Did she tell you her name? " Crammon asked, and the
thunder-clouds gathered on his brow.

" No, not exactly——"

" People who enter my dwelling are required to give their
names," Crammon roared. " Is this a railway station or a
public shelter? Go in and ask her who she is. I shall wait
here."

In a few minutes Miss Aglaia returned and said in a compassionate tone: " She's fallen asleep in an armchair. But
you can take a peep at her. I've left the door ajar."

On tip-toes Crammon passed through the hall, and peered
into the well-lit drawing-room. He recognized the sleeper at
once. It was Elise von Einsiedel. She slept with her head
leaned back and inclining a little to one side. Her face was

pale, with blue circles under her eyes, and her left arm hung
down limply.

Crammon stood there in his hat and overcoat, and gazed
at her with sombre eyes. " Unhappy child! " he murmured.

He closed the door with all possible precaution. Then he
drew Miss Aglaia toward the door and said: " The presence of
a strange lady makes it unseemly, of course, for me to pass the
night here. I shall find a bed elsewhere. I hope you appreciate my attitude."

Miss Aglaia was speechless over such purity and sternness.
Crammon continued: " As early as possible in the morning,
pack my bags and bring them to meet me in time to catch
the express to Ostende. And let Constantine come with you,
so that I may say good-bye to her as well. Let the strange
lady stay here as long as she desires. Entertain her courteously and fulfil all her wishes. She has a sorrow, and deserves
kindness. If she asks after me, tell her that urgent affairs
require my presence elsewhere."

He went out. Sadly, and quite astonished, Miss Aglaia looked
after him. " Good-night, Aglaia," he called out once more.
Then the door closed behind him.

XXII

During the last days of April Christian received a telegram
from Eva Sorel. The message read: " From the third to the
twentieth of May, Eva Sorel will be at the Hotel Adlon, Berlin,
and feels quite sure that Christian Wahnschaffe will meet her
there."

Christian read the message over and over. In his inner and
in his outer life all circumstances pointed to an approaching
crisis. He knew that this summons would be decisive in its
influence upon his fate. Its exact character and the extent of
its power he could not predict.

For weeks there had been a restlessness in him that robbed
him of sleep during many long hours of the night. On

certain days he had called for his motor in order to drive to some near-by city. When the car had covered half the distance, he ordered his chauffeur to turn back.

He had gone to Waldleiningen, and had patted his horses and played with his dogs. But he had suddenly felt like a schoolboy who lies and plays truant, and his pleasure in the animals had gone. At parting he had put his arms about his favourite dog, a magnificent Great Dane, and as he looked into the animal's eyes it had seemed to Christian, still in his character of a truant, that he wanted to say: "I must first go and pass my examination." And the dog seemed to answer: "I understand that. You must go."

Also the slender horse of Denis Lay had said, with a turn of its excessively graceful neck: "I understand that. You must go."

It was settled that the horse was to run in the races at Baden-Baden, and the Irish jockey was full of confidence. But on the day of his departure Christian was told that the animal had sickened again. He thought: "I have loved it too insistently. Now it wants the caressing hand, and is lonely without it."

With the coming of spring guests from the cities had appeared almost daily at Christian's Rest. But he had rarely received any one. A single guest he could not bear at all. If there were two they could address each other and make his silence easier.

One day came Conrad von Westernach and Count Prosper Madruzzi, bringing messages from Crammon. They were on their way to Holland. Christian asked them to dine with him, but he was very laconic. Conrad von Westernach remarked later, in his forthright fashion, to Madruzzi: "That fellow has a damned queer smile. You never know whether he's a born fool or whether he's laughing at you."

"It's true," the count agreed; "you never know where you are with him."

XXIII

Christian had given his valet orders to prepare for his journey. Then he had gone to the green-houses to interview the gardeners. In the meantime twilight had set in. It had rained all day, and the trees were still dripping. But now the fresh greenery gleamed against the afterglow, and the windows of the beautiful house were dipped in gold.

"Herr Voss is in the library," an old footman announced.

Christian had begged Amadeus Voss to use the library quite freely, whether he himself was at home or not. The servants had been instructed. Voss had offered to catalogue the library, but as yet he had made no beginning. He merely passed from book to book, and if one interested him he read it and forgot the passage of time.

The afterglow fell into the library too. Voss had taken fifty or sixty volumes from the shelves, and he was now arranging them in stacks on a large oak table.

"Why do you do that, Amadeus?" Christian asked carelessly.

"If you give me your permission, I'd like to burn these," Amadeus Voss answered.

Christian was surprised. "Why?" he asked.

"Because I lust after an *auto-da-fé*. It is worthless and corrupt stuff, the product of idle and slothful minds. Don't you scent the poison of it in the atmosphere?"

"No, I scent nothing," said Christian, more absent-mindedly than ever. "But burn them if it amuses you," he answered.

Amadeus had been in the library since three o'clock that afternoon, and he had had a remarkable experience there. In looking about among the shelves he had come upon a bundle of letters. By some accident it had probably fallen behind the books and been lost sight of. He had read a few lines of the topmost letter, and from the first words there breathed upon him the glow of an impassioned soul. Then he had yielded to the temptation of untying the package. He had taken the letters into a corner, and read them swiftly and with fevered eyes.

A few bore dates. The whole series had been written about two years before. They were signed merely by the initial F. But in every word, in every image, in every turn of speech there was such a fullness of love and devotion and adoration and self-abnegation, and so wild and at the same time so spiritual a stream of tenderness and pain, of happiness and yearning, that Amadeus Voss seemed to glide from a world of shadows and appearances into a far more real one. Yet in that, too, all was but feigned and represented to lure and madden him.

And F.—this unknown, eloquent, radiant, profoundly moved and nameless woman—where was she now? What had she done with her love? Pressed flowers lay between certain pages. Was the hand that plucked them withered as they? And what had he done with her love, he whom she had wooed so humbly and who was so riotous a spendthrift of great gifts? He had been only twenty. He had probably taken as a pastime all that was the fate of this full heart, and had used it and trampled it in a consciousness of wealth that neither counts nor reckons.

Deeper and deeper, as he read, a spear penetrated into the breast of Amadeus. The Telchines gained power over him. He turned pale and crimson. His fingers trembled, and his mouth shrivelled in dryness, and his head seemed to be full of needles. Had Christian entered then, he would have flung himself upon him in foaming hatred, to throttle or to stab him. Here was the unattainable, the eternally closed door. And a demon had hurled him down before it.

He sat long in dull brooding. Then he looked about furtively, and dropped the letters into his pocket. And then there arose in him the desire to destroy, to annihilate something. He chose books as sacrifices, and awaited Christian's coming with repressed excitement.

" It's practically all contemporary trash," he said drily, and pointed to the books. " Stories like tangled thread, utterly confused, without beginning or end. If you've read one page, you know a thousand. There are descriptions of manners with a delight in what is common and mean. The emotions riot like weeds, and the style is so noisy that you lose all perception. Love, love, love! That's one theme. And the other is wretchedness! There are histories and memoirs, too. Sheer gossip! The poems are empty rhymings by people with inflated egos. There's popular philosophy—self-righteous twaddle. A sincere parson's talk were more palatable. What is it for? Reading is a good thing, if a real spirit absorbs me, and I forget and lose myself in it. But the unspiritual has neither honesty nor imagination; he is a thief and a swindler."

" Burn it, burn it! " Christian repeated, and sat down at the other side of the room.

Amadeus went to the marble fire-place, which was so large that a man could easily have lain down in it, and opened the gates of brass. Then he carried the books there—one pile after another, and heaped them on the flat stones. When he had thrown them all in, he set fire to the pages of one book, and lowered his head and watched the flames spread.

" You know that I am going to leave Christian's Rest," Christian said, turning to him. It had grown quite dark now.

Voss nodded.

" I don't know for how long," Christian continued. " It may be very long before I return."

Amadeus Voss said nothing.

" What are you going to do, Amadeus? " Christian asked him.

Voss shrugged his shoulders. Involuntarily he pressed his hand against the inner pocket in which lay the letters of the unknown woman.

" It is dark and oppressive in the forester's house," said

Christian. "Won't you come and live here? I'll give the necessary orders at once."

"Don't make me a beggar with your alms, Christian Wahnschaffe," Voss answered. "If you were to give me the house, with all its forests and gardens, you would but rob me, and leave me poorer by so much."

"I don't understand that," said Christian.

Voss walked up and down. The carpet muffled his sturdy tread.

"You are far too passsionate, Amadeus," Christian said.

Amadeus stopped in front of a lectern that had been placed in a niche. Upon it lay the great Bible that Christian had bought. It was open. The flames of the burning books flared so brightly that he could read the words. For a space he read in silence. Then he took the book, and going nearer to the fire, sat down opposite Christian, and read aloud:

"Rejoice, O young man, in thy youth, and let thy heart cheer thee in the days of thy youth, and walk in the ways of thine heart and in the sight of thine eyes: but know thou that for all these things God will bring thee into judgment."

At the word, God, the almost unemphatic voice sounded like a bell.

"Remember now thy Creator in the days of thy youth, while the evil days come not, nor the years draw nigh, when thou shalt say, I have no pleasure in them; while the sun, or the light, or the moon, or the stars be not darkened, nor the clouds return after the rain: In the day when the keepers of the house shall tremble, and the strong men shall bow themselves, and the grinders cease because they are few, and those that look out of the windows be darkened, and the doors shall be shut in the streets; when the sound of the grinding is low, and he shall rise up at the voice of the bird, and all the daughters of music shall be brought low; also when they shall be afraid of that which is high, and fears shall be in the way, and the almond tree shall flourish, and the grasshopper shall be a

burden and desire shall fail: because man goeth to his long
home, and the mourners go about the street: or ever the silver
cord be loosed, or the golden bowl be broken, or the pitcher
be broken at the fountain, or the wheel broken at the
cistern." . . .

He stopped.   Christian, who had seemed scarcely to listen,
had arisen and come nearer to the fire.   Now he sat down on
the floor, with his legs crossed under him, and gazed with a
serene wonder into the flames.

" How beautiful is fire! " he said softly.

Speechlessly Amadeus Voss regarded him.   Then he spoke
quite suddenly. " Let me go with you, Christian Wahnschaffe."

Christian did not take his eyes from the fire.

" Let me go with you," Voss said more insistently.   " It is
possible that you may need me: it is certain that without you
I am lost.   Darkness is in me and a demon.   You alone break
the spell.   I do not know why it is thus, but it is.   Let me go
with you."

Christian replied: " Very well, Amadeus, you shall stay with
me. I want some one to stay with me."

Amadeus grew pale, and his lips quivered.

Christian said: " How beautiful is fire!"

And Amadeus murmured: " It devours uncleanness and
remains clean."

THE NAKED FEET

I

With her companion, Fräulein Stöhr, the Countess Brainitz travelled about the world.

She had been the guest of an incredibly aged Princess Neukirch at Berchtesgaden. But she grew to be immensely bored, and fled to Venice, Ravenna, and Florence. Armed with a Baedeker, and accompanied by a guide, she " did " the galleries, churches, basilicas, palaces, sarcophagi, and monuments, and her tirelessness reduced Fräulein Stöhr to despair.

She quarrelled with the gondoliers over their fare, with waiters over a tip, with shopkeepers over the price of their wares. She thought every coin a counterfeit, and in her terror of dirt and infection she touched no door-knob or chair, no newspaper and no one's hand. She washed herself repeatedly, screeched uninterruptedly, and by her appetite struck her companions at the table d'hôte with awe.

With rancour in her heart she left the land of miracles and of petty fraud. She visited her nephews, the brothers Stojenthin, in Berlin. They were charmed at her coming, and borrowed a thousand marks of her over the oysters and champagne. Then she proceeded to Stargard, to be with her sisters Hilde Stojenthin and Else von Febronius.

She was vastly amused at the middle-class ladies in Stargard, who curtsied to her as to a queen. At their teas she lorded it over them from the heights of a sofa covered with dotted calico. She entertained her devoutly attentive audience with stories of the great world. At times these anecdotes were of such a character that the judge's widow had to administer a warning pinch to the arm of her noble sister.

Frau von Febronius had been ailing since the beginning of winter. Careless exposure on a sleigh drive had brought on an attack of pneumonia. The consequences threatened to be grave. The countess, who not only feared illness for herself but hated it in others, grew restive and talked of leaving.

"When my dear husband saw his end approaching, he sent me to Mentone," she told Fräulein Stöhr. "Stupid and devoid of understanding as he was—though not more so than most men—in this respect he showed a praiseworthy delicacy of feeling. I was simply not made to bear the sight of suffering. Charity is not among my gifts."

Fräulein Stöhr assumed a pastoral expression and cast her eyes to heaven. She knew her mistress sufficiently to realize that the anecdote of the dying count and the expedition to Mentone was a product of the imagination. She said: "Man should prepare himself in time for his latter end, Madame."

The countess was indignant. "My dear Stöhr, spare me your spiritual wisdom! It suits only times of trouble. Pastoral consolations are not to my taste. It is not your proper task to preach truths to me, but to offer me agreeable illusions."

One evening Frau von Febronius asked to see the countess. The latter went. But terror made her pale. She put on a hat, swathed her face in a veil and her hands in gloves. Sighing she sat down beside her sister's bed, and carefully measured the distance, so as to be out of reach of the patient's breath.

Frau von Febronius smiled indulgently. Her illness had smoothed the lines of petty care and sorrow from her face, and, among her white pillows, she looked strikingly like her daughter Letitia. "I'm sorry to trouble you, Marion," she began, "but I must talk to you. There's something that weighs on my mind, and I must confide in some one. The fact in question should be told to one who knows me, and should not be buried with me."

"I beseech you, Elsie, my poor darling, don't talk of graves

and such things," the countess exclaimed in a whining voice.
" My appetite will be gone for a week. If you'll only fling the
medicine bottles out of the window, and tell all quacks to go
to the devil, you'll be well by day after to-morrow. And, for
heaven's sake, don't make a confession. It reminds one of
quite dreadful things."

But Frau von Febronius went on: " It's no use, Marion.
I must tell you this. The reason I turn to you is because
you've really been so very good and kind to Letitia, and
because Hilde, sensible and faithful as she is, wouldn't quite
understand. Her notions are too conventional."

In whispers she now related the story of Letitia's birth. An
illness of his earlier years had deprived her husband of the hope
of posterity; but he had yearned for a son, a child. This
yearning had finally silenced all scruples and all contradictory
emotions to such an extent that he had chosen a congenial
stranger to continue his race. He had persuaded her, his
wife, whom he loved above all things, after a long struggle.
Finally she had yielded to his unheard-of demand. But when
the child was born, a progressive melancholy had seized upon
her husband. It had become incurable, and under its control
he had ruined his estate and in the end himself. He had felt
nothing of the happiness he had expected. He had, on the
contrary, always shown a contemptuous dislike of Letitia, and
had avoided her as far as possible.

" It doesn't surprise me a bit," the countess remarked.
" You were uncommonly naïve to be astonished. A strange
child is a strange child, no matter how it got into the nest.
But it's really like a fairy tale. I confess I underestimated
you. Such delightful sophistication! And who is the child's
father? Who is responsible for the life of that darling angel?
He deserves great credit for his achievement."

Frau von Febronius mentioned the name. The countess
screamed, and leaped up as though she had been stung.
" Crammon? Bernard von Crammon? " She clasped her

hands in agony. "Is that true? Aren't you dreaming? Consider, my dear! It must be the fever. Oh, certainly, it's sheer delirium. Take a little water, I beg of you, and then think carefully, and stop talking nonsense."

Frau von Febronius gazed at her sister in utter amazement. "Do you know him?" she asked.

The countess' voice was bitter. "Do I know him? I do. And tell me one more thing: Does this—this—creature know? Has he always known?"

"He knows. Two years ago he saw Letitia at our old home. Since that time he has known. But you act as if he were the fiend incarnate, Marion. Did you have a quarrel with him or what? You always exaggerate so!"

Excitedly the countess walked up and down. "He knows it, the wretch! He has always known it, the rogue! And such dissembling as he has practised! Such hypocrisy! The wretched rogue, I'll bring it home to him! I'll seek him out!" She turned to her sister. "Forgive me, Elsie, for letting my temperament run away with me. You are right. His name awakened an anger of some years' standing. My blood boils, I confess. He may have been a man of honour and a gentleman in his youth. He must have been, or you would never have consented to such an adventure. But I hesitate to say what he is to-day. He is still perfectly discreet; you need have no anxiety on that score. But I assert that even discretion has its limits. Where these are passed, decent people shake their heads, and virtue looks like mere baseness. *Voilà*."

"All that you say is quite dark to me," Frau von Febronius replied wearily, "and I really haven't any desire to fathom it. I wanted to tell you this oppressive secret. Keep it to yourself. Never reveal it, except to prevent some misfortune, or to render Letitia a service. I don't quite see how either purpose will ever be served by a revelation. But it consoles me that one other human being, beside myself and that man, knows the truth."

The countess gazed thoughtfully at her sister. " Your life wasn't exactly a gay one, was it, Elsie? "

The sick woman answered: " No, hardly gay."

During the following days she rallied a little. Then came a relapse that left no room for hope. In the middle of March she died.

By this time the countess was already far away. Her goings and comings were as purposeless as ever. But she nursed a favourite vision now. Some day she would meet Crammon, confront him with her knowledge, avenge herself upon him, challenge him and annihilate him, in a word, enjoy a rich triumph. At times when she was alone, or even in the presence of Miss Stöhr, whom it astonished, she would suddenly wrinkle her childlike forehead, clench her little fists, and her shiny face would turn red as a lobster, and her violet-blue eyes blaze as for battle.

II

It was three o'clock in the morning when Felix Imhof left a party in the Leopoldstrasse, where there had been gaming for high stakes. He had won several thousand marks, and the gold coins clinked in the overcoat pocket into which he had carelessly stuffed them.

He had had a good deal to drink, too. His head was a bit heavy. At his first steps into the fresh air he reeled a little.

Nevertheless he was in no mood to go home. So he wandered into a coffee-house that was frequented by artists. He thought he might still find a few people with whom he could chat and argue. The day he had passed was not yet full enough of life for him. He wanted it brimming.

In the room, which was blue with smoke, there were only two men, the painter Weikhardt, who had recently returned from Paris, and another painter, who looked rather ragged and stared dejectedly at the table.

Felix Imhof joined the two. He ordered cognac and served

them, but, to his annoyance, the conversation would not get started. He got up and invited Weikhardt to walk with him. With contemptuous joviality he turned to the other: " Well, you old paint-slinger, your lamp seems about burned out! "

The man didn't stir. Weikhardt shrugged his shoulders, and said softly: " He has no money for bread and no place to sleep."

Felix Imhof plunged his hand into his pocket, and threw several gold coins on the table. The painter looked up. Then he gathered the gold. " Hundred and sixty marks," he said calmly. " Pay you back on the first."

Imhof laughed resoundingly.

When they were in the street, Weikhardt said good-naturedly: " He believes every word of it. If he didn't absolutely believe it, he wouldn't have taken the money. There are still eleven days before the first—time for a world of illusions."

" It may be that he believes it," Imhof replied, with an unsteady laugh, " it may be. He even believes that he exists, and yet he's nothing but a melancholy corpse. O you painters, you painters! " he cried out into the silent night. " You have no feeling for life. Paint life! You're still sitting by a spinning-wheel, instead of at some mighty wheel of steel, propelled by a force of sixteen thousand horse-power. Paint my age for me, my huge delight in being! Smell, taste, see, and grasp that colossus! Make me feel that great rhythm, create my grandiose dreams. Give me life—my life and its great affirmation!"

Weikhardt said drily: " I have heard that talk before—between midnight and dawn. When the cock crows we all calm down again, and every man pulls the cart to which fate has hitched him."

Imhof stopped, and somewhat theatrically laid his hand on Weikhardt's shoulder. He gazed at him with his intensely black, bloodshot eyes. " I give you a commission herewith, Weikhardt," he said. " You have talent. You're the only

one with a mind above your palette. Paint my portrait. I
don't care what it costs—twenty, fifty thousand. Doesn't
matter. Take your own time—two months or two years. But
show me—me—the innermost me. Take this vulture's nose,
this Hapsburg lip, these gorilla arms and spindle shanks, this
coat and this chapeau claque, and drag from it all the animat-
ing Idea. To hell with the accidents of my phiz, which looks
as though an unskilful potter had bungled it in the making.
Render my ambition, my restlessness, my inner tempo and
colourfulness, my great hunger and the time-spirit that is in
me. But you must hurry; for I am self-consumed. In a few
years I shall have burned out. My soul is tinder. Render this
process with the divine objectivity of art, and I'll reward you
like a Medici. But I must be able to see the flame, the flaring
up, the dying down, the quiver of it! I want to see it, even
if to make me see it you have to lash the whole tradition since
Raphael and Rubens into rags! "

" You are an audacious person," Weikhardt said, in his dry
way. " But have patience with us, and restrain your admiration for your particular century. I do not let the age overwhelm me to the point of folly. I do not share the reverential
awe of speed and machinery that has seized upon many young
men like a new form of epilepsy. I haven't any attitude
of adoration toward seven-league boots, express trains, dreadnoughts, and inflated impressionism. I seek my gods elsewhere. I don't believe I'm the painter you're looking for.
Where were you? You've been travelling again? "

" I'm always on some road," Felix Imhof replied. " It's a
crazy sort of life. Let me tell you how I spent the last five
days. Monday night I went to Leipzig. Tuesday morning
at nine I had a conference with some literary people in regard
to the founding of a new review. Splendid fellows—keen critics and intellectual Jacobins, every one of them. Then I went
to an exhibition of majolicas. Bought some charming things.
At noon I left for Hamburg. On the train I read two manu-

scripts and a drama, all by a young genius who'll startle the world. That evening attended a meeting of the directorate of the East African Development Corporation. Festivities till late that night. Slept two hours, then proceeded to Oldenburg to a reunion of the retired officers of my old regiment. Talked, drank, and even danced, though the party was stag. Six o'clock in the morning rushed to Quackenbruck, a shabby little country town on the moors, where the officers had arranged for a little horse race. My beast was beaten by a head. Drove to the station and took a train for Berlin. Attended to business next morning in the Ministry of Foreign Affairs, interviewed agents, witnessed a curious operation in the clinic, made a flying-trip to Johannisthal, where a new aeroplane was tried out; went to the Deutsches Theater that evening, and saw a marvellous performance of ' Peer Gynt.' Drank the night away with the actors. Next morning Dresden. Conference with two American friends. Home to-day. Next week won't be very different, nor the one after that. I ought to sleep more; that's the only thing." He waved his thick bamboo cane in air.

"It is enough to frighten any one," said Weikhardt, who took more comfort in the contrast between his own phlegm and his companion's excitement. "How about your wife? What does she say to your life? She was pointed out to me recently. She doesn't look as if she would let herself be pushed aside."

Imhof stopped again. He stood there, with his legs far apart and his trunk bent forward, and rested on his cane. "My wife! " he said. "What a sound that has! I have a wife. Ah, yes. I give you my word, my dear man, I should have clean forgotten it to-night, if you hadn't reminded me. It's not her fault, to be sure. She's a born Wahnschaffe; that means something! But somehow . . . God knows what it is—the damned rush and hurry, I suppose. You're quite right. She's not the sort to be neglected or pushed to the wall. She

creates her own spaces, and within these "—he described
great circles in the air with his cane—" she dwells, cool to her
fingertips, tense as a wire of steel. A magnificent character—
energetic, but with a strong sense for decorative effects. She's
to be respected, my dear man."

Weikhardt had no answer ready for this outburst. Its
mixture of boasting and irony, cynicism and ecstatic excitement disarmed and wearied him at once. They had reached
a side street, which led to the Englischer Garten, and in which
stood the painter's little house. He wanted to say good-night.
But Imhof, who seemed still unwilling to be alone, asked:
" Are you working at anything? "

Weikhardt hesitated before answering. That was enough
to make Imhof accompany him. The sky grew grey with dawn.
Felix Imhof recited softly to himself:

> " Where the knights repose, and streaming
> Banners fold at last their gleaming,
> Towers rise to the way-farers,
> And the wanderers seek a spring;
> And the lovely water-bearers
> Lift a goblet to the dreaming
> Shadow of the fleeing king."

Weikhardt, who would not yield to Imhof in a knowledge or
love of the poet Stefan George, continued the quotation in a
caressing voice:

> " With a smile serene he watches,
> Yet flits on with shyer seeming,
> For beneath him fades the height,
> And he fears all mortal touches,
> And he almost dreads the light."

They entered the studio. Weikhardt lit the lamp, and let
its glow fall upon a picture that was not quite completed. It
was a Descent from the Cross.

"Rather old-fashioned, isn't it?" Weikhardt asked, with a sly smile. He had grown pale.

Imhof looked. He was a connoisseur through and through. No other had his eye. The painters knew it.

The picture, which reminded one of the visionary power as well as of the brushwork of El Greco, was bizarre in composition, intense in movement, and filled with an ecstatic passion. The forms of an old master, through which the painter had expressed himself, were but an appearance. The vision had been flung upon the canvas with a burning splendour. The figures had nothing old-fashioned about them; there was no *cliché;* they were like clouds, and the clouds like architecture. There were no concrete things. There was a chaos, which drew meaning and order only from the concentrated perceptions of the beholder.

Felix Imhof folded his hands. "To have such power," he murmured. "Great God, to have the power to project such things!"

Weikhardt lowered his head. He attributed little significance to these words. A few days before he had stood in front of his canvas, and he had imagined that a peasant was standing beside him—an old peasant or any other simple man of the people. And it had seemed to him that this peasant, this humble man, who knew nothing of art, had kneeled down to pray. Not from piety, but because what he saw had in its own character overwhelmed him.

Almost rudely Imhof turned to the painter and said: "The picture is mine. Under all circumstances. Mine. I must have it. Good-night." With his top hat set at a crazy angle, and his sleepless, dissipated face, he was a vision to frighten one.

At last he went home.

Next day Crammon informed him of his arrival in Munich. He had come because Edgar Lorm was about to give a series of performances there.

III

Christian considered how he could convey money to Amadeus Voss without humiliating him. Since it was agreed that they travel together, it was necessary for Voss to have the proper outfit; and he possessed nothing but what he had on.

Amadeus Voss understood the situation. The social abyss yawned between them. Both men gazed helplessly into it, one on each shore.

In his own heart Voss mocked at the other's weakness, and at the same time loved him for his noble shame—loved him with that emotional self that had been humiliated, estranged from the world, stamped on and affronted from his youth on. He shuddered at the prospect of sitting in the forester's house again with perished hopes and empty hands, and letting his soul bleed to death from the wounds of unattainable lures. He brooded, regarding Christian almost with hatred. What will he do? How will he conquer the difficulty?

Time passed. The matter was urgent.

On the last afternoon Christian said: " The hours crawl. Let us play cards." He took a pack of French cards from a drawer.

" I haven't touched a card in my life," Voss said.

" That doesn't matter," Christian replied. " All you need do is to tell red from black. I'll keep the bank. Bet on a colour. If you've bet on red and I turn up red, you've won. How much will you risk? Let us start with one taler."

" Very well, here it is," said Voss, and put the silver coin on the table. Christian shuffled the cards and drew one. It was red.

" Risk your two talers now," Christian advised. " Novices have luck."

Voss won the two talers. The betting continued. Once or twice he lost. But finally he had won thirty talers.

"Now you take the bank," Christian proposed. He was secretly pleased that his ruse was working so well.

He bet ten talers and lost. Then fifteen, then twenty, then thirty, and lost again. He risked a hundred marks, two hundred, five hundred, more and more, and still lost. Voss's cheeks turned hectic red, then white as chalk: his hands trembled, his teeth rattled. He was seized by a terror that his luck would change, but he was incapable of speech or of asking for an end of the game. The bank notes were piled up in front of him. In half an hour he had won over four thousand marks.

Christian had previously marked the cards in a manner that no inexperienced eye could detect. He knew exactly which colour Voss would find. But the curious thing was that, though he forgot occasionally to watch the markings, Voss still won.

Christian got up. "We're in a hurry," he said. "You must get ready for our journey, Amadeus."

Voss was overwhelmed by the change which had come over his life within a few minutes. If a spark of suspicion glowed in his soul, he turned away from it, and plunged into rich dreams.

The motor took them to Wiesbaden, and there, with Christian's help, Amadeus bought garments and linen, boots, hats, gloves, cravats, a razor, a manicure set, and a trunk.

At ten o'clock that evening they sat in the sleeper. "Who am I now?" asked Amadeus Voss. He looked about him with a curious and violent glance, and pushed the blond hair from his forehead. "What do I represent now? Give me an office and a title, Christian Wahnschaffe, in order that I may know who I am."

Christian watched the other's excitement with quiet eyes. "Why should you think yourself another to-night or changed from yesterday?" he asked in surprise.

IV

Eva Sorel passed through the countries of Europe—a comet leaving radiance in its wake.

Her day was thickly peopled. It needed the flexibility of an experienced practitioner to test and grant the many-sided demands upon her. Monsieur Chinard, her impresario, served admirably in this capacity. Only Susan Rappard treated the man morosely. She called him a Figaro *pris à la retraite*.

In addition, the dancer employed a courier and a secretary. Several of her adorers had been following her from city to city for months. They were Prince Wiguniewski, a middle-aged American, named Bradshaw, the Marquis Vicente Tavera, of the Spanish legation at Petrograd, Herr Distelberg, a Jewish manufacturer of Vienna, and Botho von Thüngen, a very young Hanoverian, a student in his second year.

These, as well as others who drifted with the group from time to time, neglected their callings, friends, and families. They needed the air that Eva breathed in order to breathe themselves. They had the patience of petitioners and the optimism of children. They were envious of one another's advantage, knowledge, and witticisms. Each noted with malicious delight if another blundered. They vied zealously for the friendship of Susan, and made her costly presents, in order that she might tell them what her mistress had said and done, how she had slept, in what mood she had awakened, and when she would receive.

Since Count Maidanoff had joined Eva's circle they had all been profoundly depressed. They knew, everybody knew, who was concealed behind this pseudonym. Against him—mighty and greatly feared—no one hoped to prevail.

Eva consoled them with a smile. They counted for nothing in her eyes. " How are my chamberlains? " she asked Susan, " how do my time-killers kill their time? "

But she was not quite as light and serene of soul as she had once been.

v

She had made the acquaintance of Count Maidanoff in Trou-ville. She had been presented to him on the promenade, and a far-flung circle of fashionables had looked on. Careful murmurs had blended with the thunder of the sea.

She came home and grasped Susan by the shoulders. " Don't let me go out again," she said, pale and breathing heavily. " I don't want to look into those eyes again. I must not meet that man any more."

Susan exhausted herself promising this. She did not know who had awakened such horror in her mistress. " Elle est un peu folle," she said to M. Labourdemont, the secretary, " mais ce grain de folie est le meilleur de l'art."

The next day Count Maidanoff announced his formal call, and had to be received.

The conventional act of homage, to which he was entitled by his birth, he repaid with a personal and sincere one.

His speech was heavy and slow. He seemed to despise the words, the use of which caused him such exertion. Sometimes he stopped in the middle of a sentence and frowned in annoy-ance. Between his eyebrows there were two straight, deep lines that made his face permanently sombre. His smile began with an upward curl of the lips, and quivered down into his thin, colourless beard, like the effect of a muscular paralysis.

He went straight and without circumlocution toward his pur-pose. It was commonly the office of his creatures to clear the road toward his amatory adventures. By doing the wooing himself in this instance he desired to single out its object by an act of especial graciousness.

The cool timidity of the dancer had pleased him at first. Fear was to him the most appealing quality in men. But Eva's repressed chill in the face of his courteous proposals confused him. His eyes became empty, he looked bored, and asked for permission to light a cigarette.

He talked of Paris, of a singer at the Grand Opera there. Then he became silent, and sat there like some one who has all eternity ahead of him. When he arose and took his leave, he looked as though he were really asleep.

With arms crossed Eva walked about the room till evening. During the night she picked up books which she did not read, thought of things that were indifferent to her, called Susan only to torment her, wrote a letter to Ivan Becker and tore it up again. Finally, in spite of the driving rain, she wrapped herself in a cloak and went out on the terrace.

Maidanoff repeated his visit. At the inevitable point Eva conveyed to him with great delicacy that his expectations were doomed to disappointment. He looked at her with slothful, oblique glances, and condescended to smile. What nonsense, his morose frown seemed thereupon to say.

Suddenly he opened his eyes very wide. The effect was uncanny. Eva bent her head forward in expectation, and spread out her fingers.

He said: "You have the most beautiful hands I have ever seen. To have seen them is to desire to know their touch."

Three hours later she left Trouville, accompanied by Susan and by M. Labourdemont, and travelled to Brussels, where Ivan Becker was staying.

VI

Becker lived in the suburbs, in a lonely house that stood in a neglected garden. He received her in a tumbled room that was as big as a public hall. Two candles burned on the table.

He looked emaciated, and moved about restlessly, even after he had bidden Eva welcome.

She told him with some haste of her engagement in Russia, which she was about to fulfil, and asked whether he had any commissions to give her. He said that he had not.

"The Grand Duke was attentive to me," she said, and looked at him expectantly.

He nodded. After a little he sat down and said: "I must tell you a dream I had; or, rather, a hallucination, for I lay with my eyes wide open. Listen!

"About a richly laid board there sat five or six young women. They were in evening dress, with very deep décolletage, and laughed wildly and drank champagne. With frivolous plays on words and seductive gestures, they turned to one who sat at the head of the table. But that one had no form: he was like a lump of dough or clay. The footmen trembled when they approached him, and the women grew pale under their rouge when he addressed them. In the middle of the gleaming cloth there lay, unnoticed by any one, a corpse. It was covered with fruits, and from its breast, between the peaches and the grapes, projected the handle of a dagger. Blood trickled through the joints of the table and tapped in dull drops on the carpet.

"The meal came to an end. All were in a wildly exuberant mood. Then that formless one arose, grasped one of the women, drew her close to him, and demanded music. And while the thunderous music resounded, that lump expanded and grew, and a skull appeared on it, and eyes within that skull, and these eyes blazed in a measureless avidity. The woman that he held became paler and paler, and sought to free herself from his embrace. But long, thin arms grew out of his trunk. And with these he pressed her so silently and so cruelly that she began to moan and turn blue. And her body snapped in two in the middle. Lifeless she lay in his arms, and nothing seemed left of her but her dress. Then the corpse, that lay with pierced breast amid the fruit and sweets, raised its head, and said with closed eyes: 'Give her back to me.'

"Suddenly many people streamed into that room—peasants and factory workers, soldiers and ragged women, Jews and Jewesses. An old man with a white beard said to the formless

one: ' Give me back my daughter.' Others who stood behind
screamed frantically: ' Give us our daughters, our brides, our
sisters.' Then peasants pressed forward, and bent to the earth
their melancholy faces, and said: ' Give us our lands and our
forests.' Over all rose the piercing voices of mothers: ' Give
us our sons, our sons.' The formless one receded step by step
into empty space. But even as he receded he assumed a more
clearly defined shape. The face, the hands, and the garments
were brown as though encrusted with rust or dried slime.
The features of the face gave not the least notion of that
being's character, and precisely this circumstance heightened
the despair of all beyond endurance. They cried without ceas-
ing: ' Our brothers! Our sons! Our sisters! Our lands!
Our forests, O thou accursed unto all eternity! ' "

Eva said no word.

Ivan Becker rested his head upon his hand. " One thing is
certain. He has caused so many tears to be shed, that were
they gathered into one lake, that lake were deeper than the
Kremlin is tall; the blood that he has caused to flow would
be a sea in which all Moscow could be drowned."

He walked to and fro a few times. Then he sat down again
and continued: " He is the creator and instigator of an incomparable reign of terror. Our living souls are his victims. Wherever there is a living soul among us, it becomes his prey. Six
thousand intellectuals were deported during the past year.
Where he sets his foot, there is death. Ruins and fields full of
murdered men mark his path. These expressions are not to be
taken metaphorically but quite, quite literally. It was he who
created the organization of the united nobility, which holds
the country in subjection, and is a modern instrument of torture on the hugest scale. The pogroms, the murderous Finnish
expedition, the torturing of the imprisoned, the atrocities of the
Black Hundreds—all these are his work. He wastes untold
millions from the public treasury; he pardons the guilty and
condemns the innocent. He throttles the spirit of man and

extinguishes all light. He is all-powerful. He is God's living adversary. I bow before him."

Eva looked up in astonishment. But Becker did not observe her.

"There is no one who knows him. No one is able to see through him. I believe he is satiated. Nothing affects him any longer except some stimulus of the epidermis. The story is told that sometimes he has two beautiful naked women fight in his presence. They have daggers and must lacerate each other. One must bow down before that."

"I do not understand," Eva whispered wide-eyed. "Why bow?"

Becker shook his head warningly, and his monotonous voice filled the room once more. "He has found everything between heaven and earth to be for sale—friendship, love, the patience of a people, justice, the Church, peace and war. First he commands or uses force; that goes without saying. What these cannot conquer he buys. It seems, to be sure, that pressure and force can accomplish things that would defy and wreck ordinary mortals. While hunting bears in the Caucasus his greatest favourite, Prince Szilaghin, fell ill. His fever was high and he was carried into the hut of some Circassians. Szilaghin, by the way, is a creature of incredible corruption—only twenty years old and of astonishing though effeminate beauty. To win a bet he once disguised himself as a cocotte, and spent a night in the streets and amusement resorts of Petrograd. In the morning he brought back a handful of jewels, including a magnificent bracelet of emeralds, that had been given him as tributes to his mere beauty. It was he who fell ill in the mountains. A mounted messenger was sent to the nearest village, and dragged back with him an old, ignorant country doctor. The Grand Duke pointed to his favourite writhing in delirium, and said to the old man: 'If he dies, you die too.' Every hour the physician administered a draught to the sick man. In the intervals he kneeled trembling by the bed and prayed. As fate would have it, Szilaghin recovered consciousness toward morning, and gradually became well. The Grand Duke was convinced that the inexorable alternative which he had offered the old physician had released mysterious forces in him and worked something like a miracle. Thus he does not feel nature as a barrier to his power."

A swift vividness came into Eva's features. She got up and walked to the window and opened it. A storm was shaking the trees. The ragged clouds in the sky, feebly illuminated by moonlight and arching the darkness, were like a picture of Ruysdael. Without turning she said: " You say no one can penetrate him. There is nothing to penetrate. There is an abyss, dark and open."

" It may be that you are right and that he is like an abyss," Ivan Becker answered softly, " but who will have the courage to descend into it? "

Another silence fell upon them. " Speak, Ivan, speak out at last the thought in your mind! " Eva cried out into the night. And every fibre of her, from the tips of her hair to the hem of her gown, was tense with listening.

But Becker did not answer. Only a terrible pallor came over his face.

Eva turned around. " Shall I throw myself into his arms in order to create a new condition in the world? " she asked proudly and calmly. " Shall I increase his opinion of the things that can be bought among men by the measure of my worth? Or do you think that I could persuade him to exchange the scaffold for the confessional and the hangman's axe for a flute? "

" I have not spoken of such a thing; I shall not speak of it," said Ivan Michailovitch with solemnly raised hand.

" A woman can do many things," Eva continued. " She can give herself away, she can throw herself away, she can sell herself, she can conceal indifference and deny her hatred. But against horror she is powerless; that tears the heart in two.

Show me a way; make me insensitive to the horror of it; and I shall chain your tiger."

"I know of no way," answered Ivan Michailovitch. "I know none, for horror is upon me too. May God, the Eternal, enlighten you."

The loneliness of the room, of the house, of the storm-ploughed garden, became as the thunder of falling boulders.

VII

Her friends awaited developments in suspense. None expected her to offer Maidanoff any serious resistance. When she seemed to hold out, her subtlety was admired. Paris predicted a radiant future for her. Much public curiosity centred upon her, and many newspaper columns were devoted to her.

When she arrived in Russia it was clear that the authorities and officials had received special instructions. No queen could have been treated with more subtle courtesy. Palatial rooms in a hotel were in readiness and adorned. A slavish humility surrounded her.

When the Grand Duke called, she begged him to rescind the orders that made her his debtor. He devoured her words with a frosty and lurking expression, but remained inactive. She was indignant at this slothfulness of a rigid will, this deaf ear that listened so greedily.

His contempt of mankind had something devastating in it. His slow eyes seemed to say: Man, thou slimy worm, grovel and die!

In his presence Eva felt her thoughts to be so loud at times that she feared he would perceive them.

She ventured to oppose and judge him. A young girl, Vera Cheskov, had shot the governor of Petrograd. Eva had the courage to praise that deed. The Grand Duke's answer was smooth, and he left quite unruffled. She challenged him more vigorously. Her infinitely expressive body vibrated in rhythms of bitterness and outrage. She melted in grief, rage, and sympathy.

He watched her as one would watch a noble beast at its graceful antics and said: " You are extraordinary, Madame. I cannot tell what wish of yours I would leave ungranted for the reward of winning your love." He said that in a deep voice, which was hoarse. He had also a higher voice, which had a grinding sound like that of rusty hinges.

Eva's shoulders quivered. His iron self-sufficiency reflected no image of her or her influence. Against it all forces were shattered.

Twice she saw him change countenance and give a start. The first time was when she told him of her German descent. An inbred hatred against all Germans and everything German filled him. An evil mockery glared in his face. He determined not to believe her and dropped the subject.

And the second time was when she spoke of Ivan Michailo-vitch Becker. She could not help it; she had to bring that name to the light. It was her symbol and talisman.

A glance like a whip's lash leaped out of those slothful eyes. The two deep grooves between the eyebrows stretched like the antennæ of an insect. A diagonal groove appeared and formed with the others a menacing cross. The face became ashen.

Susan was impatient. She urged her on and lured her on. " Why do you hesitate? " she said to her mistress one evening. " So near the peak one cannot go back. Remember our dreams in Toledo! We thought they were insolent then. Reality puts us to shame. Take what is given you. Never will your sweet, little dancing feet win a greater prize."

Eva walked in a circle about the rug. " Be quiet," she said thoughtfully and threateningly, " You don't know what you are advising me to do."

Crouching near the fire-place, Susan's lightless, plum-like eyes followed her mistress. " Are you afraid? " she asked with a frown.

" I believe I am afraid," Eva replied.

" Do you remember the sculptor whom we visited in Meudon last winter? He showed us his work, and you two talked art. He said: ' I mustn't be afraid of the marble; the marble must be afraid of me.' You almost kissed him in gratitude for those words. Don't be afraid now. You are the stronger."

Eva stood still, and sighed: " Cette maladie, qu'on appelle la sagesse! "

Then Susan went to the piano-forte, and with her fluttering angularity of movement began to play a Polonaise of Chopin. Eva listened for a while. Then she went up to Susan from behind, tapped her shoulder, and said, as the playing ceased, with a dark, strange cooing in her voice:

" If it must be, I shall first live one summer of love, the like of which has not been seen on earth. Do not speak, Susan. Play on, and do not speak."

Susan looked up, and shook her puzzled head.

VIII

On the day of Eva's last appearance in Petrograd, a well laid high explosive mine blew up the central building of the Agricultural Exposition.

The plot had been aimed at the person of the Grand Duke. His visit had been expected, the order in which he would inspect the buildings had been carefully mapped out. A slight mal-adjustment in the machinery of his car delayed him and his train a few minutes beyond the precisely fixed hour.

At the very moment when he put his foot on the first step of the building, a terrific crash resounded. The sky dis-appeared behind fume and fragments. Several manufacturers and bureaucrats, who had officiously hurried ahead, as well as ten or twelve workingmen, were killed. The air pressure smashed the window panes in all the houses within a mile of the spot.

For a while the Grand Duke stood quite still. Without

curiosity or fear, but with an indescribably sombre look, he surveyed the devastation. When he turned to go, the great crowds who had streamed thither melted back silently at his approach. They left him a broad path through which his abnormally long legs, accompanied by the clinking of his sword, strode with the steps of a sower.

For her final performance Eva had selected the rôle of the fettered and then liberated Echo, in the pantomime called The Awakening of Pan. It had always created enthusiasm; but this time she celebrated an unparalleled triumph.

She danced a dance of freedom and redemption, that affected with complete immediacy the nerves of the thronging audiences, and released the tensions of the day of their lives. There was a present and significant eloquence in the barbaric defiance, the fiery terror of the pursued. Then came her sudden rallying, her heroic determination, her grief over a first defeat, her toying with the torch of vengeance, her jubilant welcome of a rising dawn.

The curtain dropped, and the twenty-five hundred people sat as though turned to stone. Innumerable glances sought the box of the Grand Duke and found those slothful, unseeing eyes of his. They saw the slightness and disproportionate length of his body, the sinewy, bird-like neck above the round collar of his uniform, the thin beard, the bumpy forehead, and felt the atmosphere that rolled silently out from him and dwelled in his track—the atmosphere of a million-atomed death. And in the midst of these were those slothful eyes.

Then the applause broke out. Distinguished ladies contorted their bodies, toothless old men yelled like boys, sophisticated experts of the theatre climbed on their seats and waved. When Eva appeared the noise died down. For ten seconds nothing was heard but the sound of breathing and the rustle of garments.

She looked into that gleaming sea of faces. The folds of her white Greek garment were still as marble. Then the storm of

applause burst out anew. Over the balustrade of the gallery
a girl bent and stretched out her arms, and cried with a sob in
her voice, that rose above all the plaudits: " You have understood us, little soul! "

Eva did not understand the Russian words. But it was not
necessary. She looked up, and their sense was clear to her.

IX

At midnight she appeared, as she had consented to do, in
the palace of Prince Fyodor Szilaghin.

So soon as she was seen, a respectful murmur and then a
silence surrounded her. Bearers of the most ancient names
were assembled, the most beautiful women of society and of the
court, and the representatives of foreign powers. Several
gentlemen had already formed a group about her, when Fyodor
Szilaghin approached, kissed her hand reverently, and drew her
skilfully from the group.

She passed through several rooms at his side. He did his
best to fascinate her and succeeded in holding her attention.

There was not a touch of banality about him. His gestures
and words were calculated to produce a desired effect with the
utmost coolness and subtlety. When he spoke he lowered his
eyes a little. The ease and fullness of speech that is characteristic of all Russians had something iridescent in his case.
An arrogant and almost cynical consciousness of the fact that
he was handsome, witty, aloof, mysterious, and much desired
never left him. His eyebrows had been touched with kohl,
his lips with rouge. The dull blackness of his hair threw into
striking relief the transparent pallor of his beardless face.

" I find it most remarkable, Madame," he said in a voice of
unfathomable falseness, " that your art has not to us Slavs the
oversophistication that is characteristic of most Western artists.
It is identical with nature. It would be instructive to know
the paths by which, from so different a direction, you reached
the very laws and forms on which our national dances as well

as our modern orchestral innovations are based. Undoubtedly
you are acquainted with both."

" I am," Eva answered, " and what I have seen is most uncommon. It has power and character and enthusiasm."

" Enthusiasm and perhaps something more—wild ecstasy,"
said the prince, with a significant smile. " Without that there
is no great creation in the world. Do you not believe that
Christ shared such ecstasy? As for me, I cannot be satisfied
with the commonly accepted figure of a gentle and gently
harmonious Christ."

" It is a new point of view. It is worth thinking about," Eva
said with kindly tolerance.

" However that may be," Szilaghin went on, " among us all
things are still in the process of becoming—the dance as well
as religion. I do not hesitate to name these two in one breath.
They are related as a red rose is to a white. When I say that
we are still becoming, I mean that we have yet discovered no
limits either of good or evil. A Russian is capable of committing the most cruel murder, and of shedding tears, within the
next hour, at the sound of a melancholy song. He is capable
of all wildness, excess, and horror, but also of magnanimity and
self-abnegation. No transformation is swifter or more terrible
than his, from hate to love, love to hate, happiness to despair,
faithfulness to treachery, fear to temerity. If you trust him
and yield yourself to him, you will find him pliant, high-souled,
and infinitely tender. Disappoint and maltreat him—he will
plunge into darkness and be lost in the darkness. He can
give, give, give, without end or reflection, to the point of
fanatical selflessness. Not until he is hurled to the uttermost
depths of hopelessness, does the beast in him awaken and
crash into destruction all that is about him." The prince
suddenly stood still. " Is it indiscreet to ask, Madame, where
you will pass the month of May? I am told you intend to go
to the sea-shore." He had said these words in a changed tone,
and regarded Eva expectantly.

The question came to her like an attack from ambush.

Insensibly they had left the rooms destined for the guests and passed into the extensive conservatories. Labyrinthine paths, threading innumerable flowers and shrubs, led in all directions. A dim light reigned, and where they stood in a somewhat theatrical isolation, thousands of ghostly orchids exhaled a breathless fragrance.

Skilfully and equivocally chosen as they were, the sense and purport of Szilaghin's words were very clear to Eva. Yet she was tempted to oppose her own flexibility to his eel-like smoothness of mind, despite the hidden threat of the situation. She assumed a smile, as impenetrable as Szilaghin's forehead and large pupils, and answered: " Yes; I am going to Heyst. I must rest. Life in this land of hidden madmen has wearied me. It is too bad that I must be deprived, dear Prince, of a mentor and sage like yourself."

Suddenly Szilaghin dropped on one knee, and said softly: " My master and friend beseeches you through me for the favour of being near you wherever you may elect to go. He insists on no exact time, but awaits your summons. I know neither the degree nor the cause of your hesitation, dear lady, but what pledge do you demand, what surety, for the sincerity of a feeling that avoids no test and stops at no sacrifice? "

" Please rise, prince," Eva commanded him. She stepped back a pace and stretched out her arms in a delicate gesture of unwilling intimacy. " You are a spendthrift of yourself at this moment. Please rise."

" Not until you assure me that I shall be the bearer of good news. Your decision is a grave one. Clouds are gathering and awaiting a wind that may disperse them. Processions are on the roads praying to avert an evil fate. I am but a single, but a chance messenger. May I rise now? "

Eva folded her arms across her bosom, and retreated to the very wall of hanging flowers. She became aware of the mighty and naked seriousness of fate. " Rise," she said, with lowered head, and twice did fire and pallor alternate on her cheeks.

Szilaghin arose and smiled, swiftly breathing. Again, in silent reverence, he carried her hand to his lips. Then he led her, subtly chatting as before, back among the other guests.

It was twelve hours after this that Christian received the telegram which called him to Berlin.

X

Edgar Lorm played to crowded houses in Munich. His popularity was such that he had to prolong his stay.

It pleased Crammon enormously and puffed him up. He walked about as though he were the sole nurse of all this glory.

One day he was at a tea given by a literary lady. In a corner arose laughter that was obviously directed at him. He was amused when he discovered that the whispering group gathered there believed firmly that he was copying Lorm's impersonation of the Misanthrope.

Felix Imhof writhed in laughter when he heard the story. " There's something very attractive in the notion to people who don't really know you," he said to Crammon. " It's far more likely that it's the other way around, and that Lorm created his impersonation by copying you."

This interpretation was very flattering. Crammon smiled in appreciation of it. Unconsciously he deepened the lines of misanthropy in his chubby ecclesiastical face. When Lorm had his picture taken as Alceste, Crammon took up his stand behind the camera, and gazed steadily at the ripe statuesqueness of the actor's appearance.

It was his intention to learn. The rôle which had been assigned him in the play of the actor's life—the play that lasted from nine o'clock every morning until eleven at night —began to arouse his dissatisfaction. He desired it to be less episodic. It seemed to him that Lorm, the director of this particular play, should be persuaded to change the cast. He told Lorm so quite frankly. For the actor was no longer to him, as in the days of his youth, the crown and glory of human existence and the vessel of noblest emotions, but a means to an end. Nowadays one was forced to learn of Lorm, to conceal one's true feelings impenetrably, to gather all one's energy for the moment of one's cue, to be thrifty of one's self, bravely to wear a credible mask, and thus to assure each situation of a happy ending.

So Crammon said: " I've always had rather pleasant relations with my partners. I can truly say that I'm an obliging colleague and have always stolen away into the background when it was their turn to have their monologues or great scenes in the centre of the stage. But two of them, the young lover and the heroine, have undoubtedly abused my good nature. They've gradually shoved me out of the play entirely. To their own hurt, too. The action promised to be splendid. Since I've been shoved into the wings, it threatens to be lost in the sand. It annoys me."

Edgar Lorm smiled. " It seems to me rather that the playwright is at fault than those two," he answered. " And no doubt it's a mistake in construction. No experienced man of the theatre would dispense with a character like yourself."

" Prosit," said Crammon, and lifted his glass. They were sitting late in the Ratskeller.

" One must await developments," Lorm continued. The whole charade amused him immensely. " In the works of good authors you sometimes find unexpected turns of the action. You mustn't scold till the final curtain."

Crammon murmured morosely. " It's taking a long time. Some day soon I'm going to mount the stage and find out in which act we are. I may make an extempore insertion."

" For what particular line have you been engaged anyhow? " Lorm inquired. " Man of the world, character parts, or heavy father? "

Crammon shrugged his shoulders. The two men looked seriously at each other. A pleasant mood gleamed about the actor's narrow lips. " How long is it since we've seen each other, old boy? " he said, and threw his arm affectionately over Crammon's shoulder. " It must be years. Until recently I had a secretary who, whenever a letter came from you, would lay it on my pillow at night. He meant that action to express something like this: Look, Lorm, people aren't the filthy scamps you always call them. Well, he was an idealist who had been brought up on chicory, potatoes, and herring. You find that sort once in a while. As for you, my dear Crammon, you've put on flesh. You're comfortable and compact in that nice tight skin of yours. I'm still lean and feed on my own blood."

" My fat is only a stage property," said Crammon sadly. " The inner me is untouched."

XI

Whenever Lorm played, Judith Imhof was in the theatre. But she went neither with her husband nor with Crammon. They broke in upon her mood. She cared very little for Crammon at any time. Unless he was very jocular, he seemed to her insufferable.

She sat in the stalls, and in the entr'actes waved graciously and calmly to Felix and Crammon in their box. She was careless of the amazement of her acquaintances. If any one had the temerity to ask why she sat alone, she answered, " Imhof is annoyed when another is not pleased with something that arouses his enthusiasm. So we go on different paths."

Inevitably the curious person would ask next: " Then you don't care for Lorm? " Whereupon she would reply: " Not greatly. He forces me to take a certain interest; but I resent that. I think he's terribly overrated."

One day a lady of her acquaintance asked her whether she was happy in her marriage. " I don't know," she answered, and laughed. " I haven't any exact conception of what people mean by happiness." Her friend then asked her why she had married. " Very simply," she replied, " because being a young girl got to be such an undelightful situation that I sought to escape from it as soon as possible." The lady wanted to know whether she didn't, then, love her husband. " My dear woman," Judith said, " love! There's nothing so mischievous as the loose way in which people use that word. Most people, I believe, pretend quite shamelessly when they talk about it, and defend it simply because they don't want to admit that they've been taken in. It's exactly like the king's new clothes in the old fable. Every one acts mightily important and enthusiastic, and won't admit that the poor king is naked to the winds."

Another time she was asked whether she didn't yearn to have a child. " A child! " she cried out. " Horrors! Shall I bring forth more food for the worms? "

Once, in company, the conversation turned to the question of one's sensitiveness to pain. Judith asserted that she could bear any bodily torment without moving a muscle. She was not believed. She procured a long, golden needle, and bade one of the gentlemen pierce her whole arm with it. When he refused in horror, she asked another of stronger nerves who obeyed her. And really she did not twitch a muscle. The blood gathered in a little pool. She smiled.

Felix Imhof could weep at the least excuse. When he had a sick headache he wept. She despised this in him.

The actor took hold of her. She resisted in vain. The spell he cast over her grew ever firmer, more indissoluble. She brooded over it. Was it his transformations that attracted her so?

Although he was forty, his body was as elegent and flexible as polished steel. And like the ringing of steel was his voice. The words were sparks. Under his tread the wooden stage became a palæstra. Nothing clung or whined or crept. Everything was tension, progression, verve, the rhythm of storms. There was no inner weight or weariness. Bugles soared. She agreed with Felix when he said: " There is more of the true content of our age in this man than in all the papers, editorials, pamphlets, and plethoric three-deckers that the press has spewed forth within the past twenty years. He has crowned the living word and made it our king."

She was impatient to make the personal aquaintance of Lorm. Crammon became the intermediary, and brought the actor to her house. She was amazed at the homeliness of the man's face. She resented his insignificant, tilted nose and his mediocre forehead. But the spell was not broken. She desired to overlook these details and succeeded. They represented but another transformation of that self which she believed to be so infinitely varied.

He revealed himself as an epicure, with remnants of that greed which marks the man who has risen from humble things. The delights of the table induced in him outbursts of noisy merriment. Over the oysters and the champagne he discussed his worst enemies with benevolence.

He was so changeable of mood that it was exhausting to associate with him. No one opposed him, and this lack of opposition had produced an empty space about him that had almost the guise of loneliness. He himself took it for the solitariness of the soul, and cherished it with a proud pain.

He discoursed only in monologues. He listened only to himself. But he did all that with the innocence of a savage. When others spoke he disappeared in an inner absorption, his eyes assumed a stony look. The part of him that remained conscious was undeviatingly courteous, but this courtesy often had an automatic air. When he came to speak again, he delighted his hearers by his wit, his paradoxes, and his masterly rendition of anecdotes.

He avoided conversation with women. Beauty and coquetry
made no impression on him. When women became enthusiastic
over him, his expression was one of merely courteous attention, and his thoughts were contemptuous. He had no adventures, and his name occurred in no racy stories. Once out of
the theatre, he lived the life of a private gentleman of simple
habits.

With cool but delicate perceptivity Judith examined the
conformation of his character. She who was utterly without
swift aspiration, whose dry nature perceived only the utili-
tarian, only the expedient, who had been stifled in mere forms
from her girlhood, and esteemed nothing in others but the
external, garments, jewels, display, title, name—she was like
one possessed and charged with an electric fluid within three
days. She was fascinated primarily by external things: his
eye, his voice, his fame. But there was one deeper thing: the
illusion of his art.

She knew what she was doing. Her steps were scrupulously
calculated.

One day Lorm complained of the disorganization in his life,
the frightful waste of his substance. It was at table, and he
was answered by empty phrases. But Judith, when she succeeded in having him to herself later, took up the subject
again. She persuaded him to describe the persons whom he
held responsible, and expressed doubts of their trustworthiness.
She disapproved of arrangements that he had made, gave him
advice that he found excellent, and reproached him with the
neglect of which he confessed himself guilty. "I wade in
money and suffocate in debt," he sighed. "In twenty years
I'll be an old man and a poor devil."

Her practical insight filled him with naïve admiration. He
said to her: "I've been told once in a while that there are such
women in the world as you, but I never believed in their existence. All I've ever seen were full of empty exactions and
florid emotions."

" You're unjust," she replied and smiled. " Every woman has some field in which she has character and firmness, but the world pays no attention. Then, too, our relation to the world is usually a false one."

" That is a wise remark," said Lorm in a satisfied voice. He was a miser of praise.

From now on he loved to have her draw him into talk concerning his little needs and worries. She examined him in detail, and he was glad to submit. He brought her the bills rendered him by his tradespeople. " They capitalize your inexperience, and cheat you," was Judith's judgment of the situation. It made him feel ashamed.

" Have you been lending money? " she asked. It appeared that he had. For years and years he had loaned considerable sums to numerous parasites. Judith shrugged her shoulders. " You might just as well have thrown the money away."

Lorm answered: " It's such a bother when they come and beg, and their faces are so unappetizing. I give them what they ask just to be rid of them."

In this wise their conversations moved wholly within the circle of the prosaic things of daily life. But it was precisely this that Edgar Lorm had missed and needed. It was as new and as moving to him, as the discovery of a rapt and ecstatic soul to a bourgeois becoming aware of poetry and passion.

Judith had a dream. She lay quite naked beside a slippery, icy fish. And she lay with it from choice, and snuggled close to its cold body. But suddenly she began to beat it, for its cool, damp, slippery scales, which had a gleam of silver and were opaline along its back, suddenly inspired in her a witch-like fury. She beat and beat the creature, until she lost consciousness and awoke exhausted.

An excursion int the valley of the Isar was arranged. Crammon went, and Felix, a young friend of the latter, Lorm and Judith. They took their coffee in the garden of an inn, and on the way back, which led through woods, they went in couples, Lorm and Judith being the last. "I've lost my gold cigarette case," Lorm announced suddenly, examining his pocket, "I've got to go back the last part of the way. I know I had it when we were in the village." It was an object precious in itself, and to which he attached a great value because it had been given him by a king who had been devoted to him in an enthusiastic friendship in his youth, and so it was irreplaceable.

Judith nodded. "I'll wait here," she said, "I'm afraid I'm too tired to cover the distance three times."

He walked back and left Judith standing there, leaning her head against a tree and reflecting. Her forehead wrinkled and her eyes assumed a piercing look. It was silent in the wood; no breeze stirred, no bird cried, no animal rustled in the bushes. Time passed. Driven not at all by impatience, but by her thoughts, which were both violent and decisive, she finally left her place, and walked in the direction from which Lorm would have to come. When she had been walking for a while, she saw something golden gleaming in the moss. It was the cigarette case, which she picked up calmly.

Lorm came back sorely vexed. He was silent, and as he walked beside her, she quietly presented the case on her flat hand. He made a gesture of joyous surprise, and she had to tell him how she had found it.

For a while he seemed to be struggling with himself. Suddenly he said: "How much easier life would be with you."

Judith answered with a smile: "You talk of it as of something unattainable."

"I believe it to be so," he murmured, with lowered head.

"If you're thinking of my marriage," Judith said, still smiling, "I consider your expression exaggerated. The way out would be simple."

"I wasn't thinking of your marriage, but of your wealth."

"Will you tell me your meaning more clearly."

"At once." He looked about him, and went up to a tree.

"Do you see that little beetle? Look how busily he works to climb the height before him. He has probably worked his way up a considerable distance to-day. No doubt he started before dawn. When he's on top, he will have accomplished something. But if I take him between my fingers now and place him at the top, then the very path which his own labour has dug becomes a thing of no value to him. That's the way it is with beetles and also with men."

Judith considered. " Comparisons must halt. That's their prerogative, you know." She spoke with gentle mockery. " I don't understand why one should reject another, simply because that other doesn't come with empty hands. It's a funny notion."

" Between a hand that is empty, and one that commands immeasurable treasures, there is a fatal difference," Lorm said with deep earnestness. " I have worked my way up from poverty. You have no faintest notion of the meaning of that word. All that I am and have, I owe to the immediate exertions of my body and my brains. By your birth you have been accustomed all your life to buy the bodies and the brains of others. And though you had a thousand times more instinct and vision for practical things and for the necessities of a sane life than you have, yet you do not and could not comprehend the profoundly moral and rightly revered relation of accomplishment to reward. Your adventitious advantages have constantly made it possible for you to ignore this relation, and to substitute for it an arbitrary will. To me your wealth would be paralysis, a mockery and a spectre."

He looked at her with head thrown back.

" And so you think our case hopeless? " Judith asked, pale and defiant.

" Since I cannot and dare not expect you to abandon your millions and share the fate of a play-actor, it does indeed seem hopeless."

Judith's face was quite colourless. " Let us go," she said;

" the others will remark our absence, and I dislike being gossiped about."

Swiftly and silently they walked on. They came to a clearing and saw beneath a black rampart of clouds the throbbing, crimson disc of the sun. Judith stared into it with raging fury. For the first time her will had encountered a still stronger will. It was rage that filled her eyes with tears, rage that wrung from her discordant laughter. When Lorm looked at her in pained surprise, she turned away and bit her lip.

" I'm capable of doing it," she said to herself in her rage. And the impulse hardened into a stubborn determination: " I will!   I will! "

XII

When Christian arrived in Berlin with Amadeus Voss he found, quite as he had expected, many people and a great tumult about Eva. He could scarcely get to her. " I am tired, Eidolon," she cried out, when she caught sight of him. " Take me away from everything."

And again, when she had escaped the oppressive host of admirers, she said: " How good it is that you are here, Eidolon. I have waited for you with an ache in my heart. We'll leave to-morrow."

But the journey was postponed from day to day. They planned to live alone and in retirement at the Dutch watering place that was their immediate goal, but Christian had already met a dozen people who had ordered accommodations there, and so he doubted the seriousness of Eva's intentions. People had become indispensable to her. When she was silent she wanted, at least, to hear the voices of others; when she was quiet she wanted movement about her.

When he stood before her the fragrance of her body penetrated him like a great fear. His blood flowed in such violent waves that his pulses lost the rhythm of their beating.

He had forgotten her face, the inimitable veracity of her

gestures, her power of feeling and inspiring ecstasy, her whole powerful, delicate, flowerlike, radiant being. Everything seemed to yield to her, even the elements. When she appeared in the street, the sun shone more purely and the air was more temperate; and thus the wild turmoil about her was transformed into a steady and obedient tide.

Susan said to Christian: "We are to dance here, and have offers. But we don't like the Prussians. They seem an arid folk, who save their money for soldiers and barracks. I haven't seen a real face. All men and all women look alike. They may be worthy, no doubt they are; but they seem machine-made."

"Eva herself is a German," Christian rebuked the woman's spiteful words.

"Bah, if a genius is cast forth from heaven and tumbles on the earth, it is blind and cannot choose its place. Where is Herr von Crammon?" she interrupted herself. "Why doesn't he come to see us? And whom have you brought in his stead?" She poked out her chin toward Amadeus Voss, who stood timidly in a corner, and whose large spectacles made him look like an owl. "Who is that?"

Who is that? The same question appeared in the astonished faces of Wiguniewski and of the Marquis of Tavera. Amadeus was new to the world with a vengeance. The fixed expression on his features had something so silly at times, that Christian was ashamed of him and the others laughed.

Voss wandered about the streets, pushed himself into crowds, surveyed the exhibits behind the plate-glass windows of shops, stared into coffee-houses, bought newspapers and pamphlets, but found no way of calming his soul. All he could see was the face of the dancer, and the gestures with which she cut a fruit or greeted a friend or bowed or sat down in a chair or arose or smelled a flower, or the motions of her lids and lips and neck and shoulders and hips and legs. And he found all these things in her provocative and affected, and yet they had bitten into his brain as acid bites into metal.

One evening he entered Christian's room, and his face was the colour of dust.

"Who really is Eva Sorel?" he asked, with a bitter rancour. "Where does she come from? To whom does she belong? What are we doing here with her? Tell me something about her. Enlighten me." He threw himself into a chair, and stared at Christian.

When Christian, unprepared for this tempest of questions, made no answer, he went on: "You've put me into a new skin, but the old Adam writhes in it still. Is this a masquerade? If so, tell me at least what the masks represent. I seem to be disguised too, but badly. I expect you to improve my disguise."

"You aren't disguised any worse than the others," Christian said, with a soothing smile.

Voss rested his head on his two hands. "So she's a dancer, a dancer," he murmured thoughtfully. "To my way of feeling there has always been something lewd about that word and what it means. How can it help arousing images that bring the blush to one's cheek?" Suddenly he looked up, and asked with a piercing glance: "Is she your mistress?"

The blood left Christian's face. "I think I understand what disturbs you so," he said. "But now that you've gone with me, you must bear with me. I don't know how long we shall stay with this crowd, and I can't myself tell exactly why we are here. But you must not ask me about Eva Sorel. We must not discuss her either for praise or blame."

Voss was silenced.

XIII

Christian, Amadeus, Bradshaw, Tavera, and Wiguniewski went by motor. Eva used the train.

But this way of travelling agreed with her as ill as any other. All night she lay sleepless in her crumpled silks, her head buried among pillows. Susan crouched by her, giving her perfume or a book or a glass of cold lemonade. There was a prickling in her limbs that would not let her rest, a weight on her bosom, an alternation of thought and fancy, of willing and the weariness of willing in her mind. The hum of the wheels on the rails cut into her nerves; the sable landscape, as it glided by, irritated her like a delusion that forever changed and melted. Malignity seemed to lurk in the fields; treacherous forests seemed to block the way; she saw haunted houses and terror-stricken men.

"What a torturer time is!" she whispered. "Oh, that it stood before me, and I could have it whipped."

Susan bent nearer, and gazed at her attentively.

Suddenly she whispered tenderly: "What do you expect of him? What is the purpose of this new game? He's the most banal of them all. I never heard him make a polished or a witty remark. Does he realize what you are? Not in his wildest dreams. His head is empty. Your art means about as much to him as the acrobatics of a circus dancer to some dreary shop-keeper. Nations are at your feet, and he grants you a supercilious smile. You have given the world a new kind of delight, and this German know-it-all is untouched and unchanged by it."

Eva said: "If the North Sea is too sinister, we must seek a coast in the South."

Susan grew excited: "One would like to yell into his ears: 'Get on your knees! Pray!' But he wouldn't be shaken any more than the pillar of Vendôme. Is he ever shaken by anything? I described to him how we were adored in Russia, the ecstasy, the festivities, the outbursts of enthusiasm. He acted as if he were hearing a moderately interesting bit of daily news. I told him about the Grand Duke. No, don't frown. I had to, or I would have choked. I described that chained barbarian, that iron soul dissolved! It's certainly uncommon; it would make any heart beat faster. I tried to make him visualize the situation: fifty millions of trembling slaves and all, through his power, at your bidding. No poet could have been more impressive than I was. If you had heard me trying to penetrate his mind, you would have been astonished at my talent for sewing golden threads on sack cloth. It was all in vain. His breath came as regularly as the ticking of a clock. Once or twice he seemed to be startled. But it was due to a breeze or a mosquito."

"I wonder whether the gowns from Paris have arrived at Heyst," Eva said. The long oval of her face seemed to grow a trifle longer; her lips curled a little, and her teeth showed like pallid, freshly peeled almonds.

"Why did you refuse yourself to him?" Susan went on. "What we possess is part of our past, but a joy put off is a burden. Men are to be the rungs of your ladder—no more. Let them give you magical nights, but send them packing when the cock crows. How has he deserved a higher office? You've yielded to a whim, and made a grinning idol of him. Why did you summon him? I'm afraid you're going to commit a folly."

Eva did not answer. The tip of her tongue appeared between her lips, and she closed her eyes cunningly. Susan thought she understood those gestures, and said: "It's true, he has the marvellous diamond for which you cried. But you have but to command, and they'll trim your very shoes with such baubles."

"When did you ever see me cry for a diamond?" Eva asked indifferently. She raised herself up, and in her transparent, wavering, blossomy wrappings seemed like a spirit emerging from the dimness. "When did you ever see me cry for a diamond?" she asked again, and touched Susan's shoulder.

"You told me so yourself."

"Have you no better proof?" Eva laughed, and her laughter was her most sensuous form of expression, as her smile was her most spiritual.

Susan folded her hands and said resignedly: "Volvedme del

otro lado, que de esto ya estoy tostado! " It is a Spanish
ejaculation, and means: Lay me on the other side, for I have
been toasted enough on this.

XIV

The house that Eva had taken was not very far from the
beach. It was an old manor, which William of Orange had
built, and which had belonged to the late Duchess of Leuchten-
berg until a few years ago.

The rooms, built of mighty blocks of stone, soothed Eva.
By day and night she heard the long-drawn thunder of the
waves. Whenever she picked up a book, she dropped it again
soon and listened.

She walked through those rooms, full of ancient furniture
and dark portraits, glad to possess herself, and to await without
torment him who came to her. She greeted him with half-
closed eyes, and with the smile of one who has yielded herself
wholly.

Susan practised on a piano with muted strings. When she
had finished her task, she slunk away and remained hidden.

Christian and Amadeus Voss had taken lodgings in a neighbouring villa—Voss on the ground floor, Christian above. Since
Christian neither asked questions nor detained him, Voss went
out in the morning and returned in the evening or even late
at night. He did not say where he had been, or what he had
seen or experienced.

At breakfast on the third morning, he said to Christian:
" It's a thankless task to unchain a fellow like me. I breathe
a different breath and sleep a different sleep. Somewhere my
soul is ranging about, and I'm chasing it. I've got to catch it
first, before I know how things are with me."

Christian did not look up. " We're invited to dine with Eva
Sorel to-night," he said.

Voss bowed ironically. " That invitation looks damnably
like charity," he said harshly. " I feel the resistance of those

people to me, and their strangeness, in my very bones. What a superfluous comedy! What shall I do there? Nearly all of them talk French. I'm a provincial, a villager, and ridiculous. And that's worse than being a murderer or thief. I may make up my mind to commit arson or murder, so as not to be ridiculous any more." He opened his mouth as though to laugh, but uttered no sound.

"I'm surprised, Amadeus, that your thoughts always cling to that one point," Christian said. "Do you really believe it to be of such decisive importance? No one cares whether you're poor or rich. Since you appear in my company, no one questions your equality, or would be so vulgar as to question it. The feelings that you express orginate in yourself, and you seem to take a kind of perverse joy in them. You like to torment yourself, and then revenge yourself on others. I hope you won't take my frankness amiss."

Amadeus Voss grinned. "Sometimes, Christian Wahnshaffe, I'd like to pat your head, as though I were your teacher, and say: You did that very well. Yes, it was wonderfully well done. And yet your little arrow went astray. To hit me, you must take better aim. It is true that the morbidness is deep in my soul, far too deep to be eradicated by a few inexpensive aphorisms. When this Russian prince or this Spanish legate shake hands with me, I feel as though I had forged cheques and would be discovered in a minute. When this lady passes by me, with her indescribable fragrance and the rustling of her garments, I grow dizzy, as though I dangled high over an abyss, and my whole soul writhes in its own humiliation and slavishness. It writhes and writhes, and I can't help it. I was born that way. This is not my world, and cannot become mine. The under dogs must bleed to death, for the upper dogs consider that the order of the world. I belong to that lower kind. My place is with those who have the odour of decayed flesh, whom all avoid, who go about with an eternally festering wound. The law of my being ranges me with them. I have no power to change that, nor has any pleasant agreement. This is not my world, Wahnschaffe; and if you don't want me to lose my reason and do some mischief, you had better take me out of it so soon as possible, or else send me away."

Christian passed the tips of his fingers over his forehead. "Have patience, Amadeus. I believe it is not my world any longer. Give me but a little more time in which to straighten out my own thoughts."

Voss's eyes clung to Christian's hands and lips. The words had been quietly, almost coolly uttered, yet there was a deep conflict in them and an expression that had power over Voss. "I cannot imagine a man leaving this woman, if once he has her favour," he said, with a hovering malice on his lips, "unless she withdraws her favour."

Christian could not restrain a gesture of aversion. "We'll meet to-night then," he said, and arose.

An hour later Amadeus Voss saw him and Eva on the beach. He was coming down the dunes, and saw them on the flat sands by the foam of the waves. He stopped, shaded his eyes with his hands, and gazed out over the ocean as though watching for a sail. The other two did not see him. They walked along in a rhythmic unity, as of bodies that have tested the harmony of their vibrations. After a while they, too, stopped and stood close together, and were defined like two dark, slender shafts against the iron grey of air and water.

Voss threw himself into the sparse, stiff grass, and buried his forehead in the moist sand. Thus he lay many hours.

Evening came. Its great event was to be the appearance of Eva with the diamond Ignifer in her hair. She wore it in an exquisitely wrought setting of platinum, and it shone above her head, radiant and solitary, like a ghostly flame.

She felt its presence in every throb of her heart. It was a part of her, at once her justification and her crown. It was no longer an adornment but a blazing and convincing symbol of herself.

For a while there was an almost awestruck silence. The lovely Beatrix Vanleer, a Belgian sculptress, cried out in her astonishment and admiration.

The smile of gentle intoxication faded from Eva's face, and her eyes turned far in their sockets, and she saw Amadeus Voss, whose face was of a bluish pallor.

His mouth was half open like an imbecile's, his head thrust brutally forward, his hanging arms twitched. He approached slowly, with eyes staring at the ineffable glow of the jewel. Those who stood on either side of him were frightened and made way. Eva turned her face aside, and stepped back two paces. Susan emerged beside her, and laid protective arms about her. At the same moment Christian went up to Voss, grasped his hand, and drew the quite obedient man aside.

Christian's attitude and expression had something that calmed every one. As though nothing had happened, a vivid and twittering conversation arose.

Voss and Christian stood on the balcony of stone. Voss drank the salt sea air deep into his lungs. He asked hoarsely: "Was that Ignifer?"

Christian nodded. He listened to the sea. The waves thundered like falling fragments of rock.

"I have grasped the whole secret of your race," Amadeus murmured, and the convulsion in his face melted under the influence of Christian's presence. "I have understood both man and woman. In this diamond are frozen your tears and your shudderings, your voluptuousness and your darkness too. It is a bribe and an accursed delusion, a terrible fetish! How keenly aware am I now of your days and nights, Wahnschaffe, of all that is between you and her, since I have seen the gleam of this mineral which the Lord created out of the slime, even as He created me and you and her. That stone is without pain—earthly, and utterly without pain, burned pure and merciless. My God, my God, and think of me, of me!"

Christian did not understand this outburst, but it shook

him to the soul. Its power swept aside the vexation which
Voss's shameless eloquence had aroused. He listened to
the sea.

Voss pulled himself together. He went up to the balustrade,
and said with unnatural self-control, " You counselled patience
to-day. What was your purpose? It sounded as equivocal
and as general as all you say to me. It is convenient to talk
of patience. It is a luxury like any other luxury at your command, only less costly. There is no word, however, worthier
of hatred or contempt. It is always false. Closely looked upon,
it means cowardice and sloth. What have you in mind? "

Christian did not answer. Or, rather, he assumed having
answered; and after a long while, and out of deep meditation,
he asked: " Do you believe that it is of any use? "

" I don't understand," said Voss, and looked at him helplessly. " Use? To what end or how? "

Christian, however, did not enlighten him further.

Voss wanted to go home, but Christian begged him to stay,
and so they went in and joined the others at dinner.

xv

When the dinner was over, the company returned to the
drawing-room. The conversation began in French, but in
deference to Mr. Bradshaw, who did not understand that
language, changed to German.

The American directed the conversation toward the dying
races of the New World, and the tragedy of their disappearance.
Eva encouraged him, and he told of an experience he had had
among the Navaho Indians.

The Navaho tribe had offered the longest resistance to
Christianity and to its civilization. To subdue them the
United States Government forbade the practice of the imme-
morial Yabe Chi dance, the most solemn ritual of their cult.
The commissioner who was to convey this order, and on whose

staff Mr. Bradshaw had been, yielded to the passionate en-
treaty of the tribal chief, and gave permission for a final celebration of the dance. At midnight, by the light of campfires
and of pine torches, the brilliantly feathered and tattooed
dancers and singers appeared. The singers sang songs which
told of the fates of three heroes, who had been captured by a
hostile tribe and freed by the god Ya. He taught them to ride
the lightning; they fled into the cave of the Grizzly Bear, and
thence into the realm of butterflies. The dances gave a plastic
representation of these adventures. While the craggy mountains re-echoed the songs, and the contorted dances in the
tawny glow rose to an ecstasy of despair, a terrific storm broke.
Cascades of water poured from the sky and filled the dried
river-beds with roaring torrents; the fires were extinguished;
the medicine men prayed with uplifted arms; the dancers and
singers, certain now that they had incurred the anger of their
god, whose sacred ceremony they had consented to betray,
hurled themselves in their wild pain into the turbulent waters,
which carried their bodies far down into the plain.

When Mr. Bradshaw had ended, Eva said: " The gods are
vengeful; even the gentlest will defend their seats."

" That is a heathen view," said Amadeus, in a sharp and
challenging voice. " There are no gods. There are idols, to be
sure, and these must be broken." He looked defiantly about
him, and added in a dragging tone: " For the Lord saith, no
man can look upon me and live."

Smiles met his outburst. Tavera had not understood, and
turned to Wiguniewski, who whispered an explanation in
French. Then the Spaniard smiled too, compassionately and
maliciously.

Voss arose with a tormented look on his face. The merriment in those faces was like a bodily chastisement to him.
From behind his glittering eye-glasses he directed a venomous
glance toward Eva, and said in troubled tones: " In the same
context of Scripture the Lord bids Israel hurl aside its adorn-

ments that He may see what He will do with them. The meaning is clear."

"He cannot expiate the lust of the eye," Christian thought,
and avoided Eva's glance.

Amadeus Voss left the company and the house. On the
street he ran as though pursued, clasping his hands to his
temples. He had pushed his derby hat far back. When he
reached his room, he opened his box and drew out a package
of letters. They were the stolen letters of the unknown woman
F. He sat down by his lamp, and read with tense absorption
and a burning forehead. It was not the first night that he
had passed thus.

When Eva was alone with Christian, she asked: "Why did
you bring that man with you? "

He laughed, and lifted her up in his arms, and carried her
through many flights of rooms and out of light into darkness.

"The sea cries! " her lips said at his ear.

He prayed that all sounds might die out of the world except
the thunder of the sea and that young voice at his ear. He
prayed that those two might silence the disquiet that overcame
him in her very embraces and made him, at the end of every
ecstasy, yearn for its renewal.

That slender, passionate body throbbed toward him. Yet
he heard the lamentation of an alien voice: What shall we do?

"Why did you bring this man? " Eva asked him far in the
night, between sleep and sleep. "I cannot bear him. There is
always sweat on his forehead. He comes from a sinister
world."

There was a bluish twilight in the room that came from the
blue flame of a blue lamp, and a bluish darkness lay beyond the
windows.

"Why don't you answer me? " she urged, and raised herself, showing the pale face amid its wilderness of brown hair.

He had no answer for her. He feared the insufficiency of
any explanation, as well as the replies that she would find.

"What is the meaning of it all? What ails you, dearest?"
Eva drew him toward her, and clung to him, and kissed his
eyes thirstily.

"I'll ask him to avoid your presence," said Christian. And
suddenly he saw himself and Voss in the farm yard of Nettersheim, saw the kneeling men and maid servants, the old rusty
lantern, the dead woman, and the carpenter who was measur-
ing her for her coffin.

"Tell me what he means to you," whispered Eva. "It seems
to me suddenly as though you were gone. Where are you
really? Tell me, dear friend."

"You should have let me love you in those old days in
Paris," said Christian gently, and softly rested his cheek
against her bosom, "in those days when Crammon and I came
to you."

"Speak, only speak," Eva breathed, seeking to hide the
fright in her heart.

Her eyes gleamed, and her skin was like luminous white
satin. In the darkness her face had a spiritualized thinness;
the restrained charm of her gestures mastered the hour, and
her smile was deep and intricate of meaning, and everything
about her was play and mirroring and raptness and unexpected
magic. Christian looked upon her.

"Do you remember words that you once spoke to me?" he
asked. "You said: 'Love is an art like poetry or music, and
he who does not understand that, finds no grace in love's
sight.' Were not those your words?"

"Yes, they were. Speak to me, my darling!"

He held her in his arms, and the life of her body, its warmth,
its blood that was conscious of him, and its vibration that was
toward him, made speech a little easier. "You see," he said
thoughtfully, and caressed her hand, "I have only enjoyed
women. Nothing more. I have been ignorant of that love
which is an art. It was so easy. They adored me, and I took
no pains. They put no hindrances on my path, and so my

foot passed over them. Not one demanded a fulfilment of me.
They were happy enough if I was but contented. But you,
Eva, you're not satisfied with me. You look at me searchingly
and watch me; and your vigil continues even at those moments
when one floats beyond thought and knowledge. And it is because you are not satisfied with me. Or is that an error, a
deception? "

" It is so very late," said Eva, and, leaning her head back
upon the pillows, she closed her eyes. She listened to the
perished echo of her own voice, and the oppression of her
heart almost robbed her of breath.

XVI

It was in another night. They had been jesting and telling
each other amusing stories, and at last they had grown
weary.

Suddenly in the darkness outside of the window Christian
had a vision of his father and of the dog Freia; and his father
had the tread of a lonely man. Never had Christian seen loneliness so visibly embodied. The dog was his only companion.
He had sought for another friend, but there had been none to
go with him.

" How is that possible? " Christian thought.

His senses were lost in a strange drowsiness, even while he
held Eva's beautiful body, which was as smooth and cool as
ivory. And in this drowsiness visions emerged of his brother,
his sister, his mother, and about each of them was that great
loneliness and desolation.

" How is that possible? " Christian thought. " Their lives
are thronged with people."

But he answered himself, and said: " Is not your own life
likewise thronged with people to suffocation, and do you not
also feel that same loneliness and desolateness? "

Now a dark object seemed to descend upon him. It was a
coat—a wet, dripping coat. And at the same moment some

one called out to him: "Arise, Christian, arise!" But he could not arise, for those ivory arms held him fast.

Suddenly he became aware of Letitia. She uttered but one word: "Why?" It seemed to him, while he slept, if indeed he slept, that he should have chosen Letitia, who lived but for her dreams, her yearnings and imaginings, and who had been sacrificed with her dreams to the vulgar world of reality. It seemed to him as though Letitia, pointing to Eva, were saying: "What do you seek of her? She knows nothing of you, but weaves at the web of her own life. She is ambitious, and can give you no help in your suffering; and it is only to forget and deaden the pain of your soul that you are wasting yourself upon her."

Christian was astonished to find Letitia so wise. He was almost inclined to smile at her wisdom. But he knew now clearly that he was suffering. It was a suffering of an unfathomable nature, which grew from hour to hour and from day to day, like the spreading of a gangrened wound.

His head rested on the shoulder of his beloved; her little breasts rose from the violet shadows and had trembling contours. He felt her beauty with every nerve, and her strangeness and exquisite lightness. He felt that he loved her with all his thoughts and with every fibre of his flesh, and that, despite it all, he could find no help in her.

And again a voice cried: "Arise, Christian, arise!" But he could not arise. For he loved this woman, and feared life without her.

The dawn was breaking when Eva turned her face to him again: "Where are you?" she asked. "What are you gazing at?"

He answered: "I am with you."

"To the last stirrings of your thought?"

"I don't know. Who knows the last recesses of his mind?"

"I want you wholly. With every breath. And something of you escapes."

" And you," Christian asked evasively, " are you utterly with me? "

She answered passionately, and with an imperious smile, as she drew closer to him: " You are more mine than I am yours."

" Why? "

" Does it frighten you? Are you miserly in your love? Yes, you are more mine. I have broken the spell that held you and melted your soul of stone."

" Melted my soul . . .? " Christian asked in amazement.

" I have, my darling. Don't you know that I'm a sorceress? I have power over the fish in the sea, the horse on the sod, the vulture in the air, and the invisible deities that are spoken of in the books of the Persians. I can make of you what I would, and you must yield."

" That is true," Christian admitted.

" But your soul does not look at me," Eva cried, and flung her arms about him, " it is an alien soul, dark, hostile, unknown."

" Perhaps you're misusing the power you have over me, and my soul resists."

" It is to obey—that is all."

" Perhaps it is not wholly sure of you."

" I can give your soul only the assurance of the hour that is."

" What are you planning? "

" Don't ask me! Hold me fast with your thoughts. Don't let me go for a moment, or we are lost to each other. Cling to me with all your might."

Christian answered: " It seems to me as though I ought to know what you mean. But I don't want to know it. Because you see, you . . . I . . . all this . . . it's too insignificant." He shook his head in a troubled way. " Too insignificant."

" What, what do you mean by that? " Eva cried in fright,

and clung to his right hand with both hers. Tensely she looked into his face.

" Too insignificant," Christian repeated stubbornly, as though he could find no other words.

Then he reflected on all he had said and heard with his accustomed scepticism and toughmindedness, and arose and bade his friend good-night.

XVII

Edgar Lorm was playing in Karlsruhe. On a certain evening he had increased the tempo of his playing, and given vent to his disgust with his rôle, the piece, his colleagues, and his audience so obviously that there had been hissing after the last act.

" I'm a poor imbecile," he said to his colleagues at their supper in a restaurant. " Every play actor is a poor imbecile." He looked at them all contemptuously, and smacked his lips.

" We must have had more inner harmony in the days when we were suspected of stealing shirts from the housewife's line and children were frightened at our name. Don't you think so? Or maybe you're quite comfortable in your stables."

His companions observed a respectful silence. Wasn't he the famous man who filled the houses, and whom both managers and critics flattered?

Dust was whirling in the streets, the dust of summer, as he returned to his hotel. How desolate I feel, he thought, and shook himself. Yet his step was free and firm as a young huntsman's.

When he had received his key and turned toward the lift, Judith Imhof suddenly stood before him. He started, and then drew back.

" I am ready to be poor," she said, almost without moving her lips.

" Are you here on business, dear lady? " Lorm asked in a

clear, cold voice. " Undoubtedly you are expecting your husband——? "

" I am expecting no one but you, and I am alone," answered Judith, and her eyes blazed.

He considered the situation with a wrinkled face that made him look old and homely. Then with a gesture he invited her to follow him, and they entered the empty reading room. A single electric lamp burned above the table covered with newspapers. They sat down in two leather armchairs. Judith toyed nervously with her gold mesh-bag. She wore a travelling frock, and her face was tired.

Lorm began the conversation. " First of all: Is there any folly in your mind that can still be prevented? "

" None," Judith answered in a frosty tone. " If the condition you made was only a trick to scare me off, and you are cowardly enough to repudiate it at the moment of its fulfilment, then, of course, I have been self-deceived, and my business here is at an end. Don't soothe me with well-meant speeches. The matter was too serious to me for that."

" That is sharply and bitterly said, Judith, but terribly impetuous," Lorm said, with quiet irony. " I'm an old hand at living, and far from young, and a good bit too experienced to fly into the passion of a Romeo at even the most precious offers and surprises of a woman. Suppose we discuss what you've done like two friends, and you postpone for a bit any final judgment of my behaviour."

Judith told him that she had written her father, and requested him to make some other disposition of the annual income which he had settled on her at the time of her marriage, since she had determined to get a divorce from Felix Imhof, and to marry a man who had made this step a definite condition of their union. At the same time she had made a legal declaration of her renunciation before a notary, which she had brought to show Lorm, and intended thereupon to send on to her father. All this she told him very calmly. Felix had known nothing of her intentions at the time of her departure. She had left a note for him in the care of his valet. "Explanations are vain under such circumstances," she said. "To tell a man whom one is leaving why one is leaving him is as foolish as turning back the hands of the clock in the hope of really bringing back hours that are dead. He knows where I am and what I want. That's enough. Anyhow, it's not the sort of thing he comprehends, and there are so many affairs in his busy life that one more or less will make little difference."

Lorm sat quietly, his head bent forward, his chin resting on the mother-of pearl handle of his stick. His carefully combed hair, which was brown and still rather thick, gleamed in the light. His brows were knit. In the lines about his nose, and his wearied actor's mouth, there was a deep joylessness.

A waiter appeared at the door and vanished again.

"You don't know what you're letting yourself in for, Judith," Lorm said, and tapped the floor lightly with his feet.

"Then tell me about it, so that I can adjust myself."

"I'm an actor," he said almost threateningly.

"I know it."

He laid his stick on the table, and folded his hands. "I'm an actor," he repeated, and his face assumed the appearance of a mask. "My profession involves my representing human nature at its moments of extreme expressiveness. The fascination of the process consists in the artificial concentration of passion, its immediate projection, and the assigning to it of consequences that reality rarely or never affords. And so it naturally happens—and this deception is the fatal law of the actor's life—that my person, this Edgar Lorm who faces you here, is surrounded by a frame that suits him about as well as a Gothic cathedral window would suit a miniature. A further consequence is that I lack all power of adjustment to any ordered social life, and all my attempts to bring myself in harmony with such a life have been pitiable failures. I struggle and dance in a social vacuum. My art is beaten foam.

" I've been told of people who have a divided personality. Well, mine is doubled, quadrupled. The real me is extinct. I detest the whole business; I practise my profession because I haven't any other. I'd like to be a librarian in the service of a king or a rich man who didn't bother me, or own a farm in some Swiss valley. I'm not talking about the accidental miseries of the theatre, disgusting and repulsive as they are—the masquerading, the lies and vanities. And I don't want you to believe either that I'm uttering the average lament of the spoiled mime, which is made up of inordinate self-esteem and of coquettish fishing for flattering contradiction.

" My suffering lies a little deeper. Its cause is, if you will try to understand me, the spoken word. It has caused a process within me that has poisoned my being and destroyed my soul. What word, you may ask? The words that pass between man and man, husband and wife, friend and friend, myself and others. Language, which you utter quite naturally, has in my case passed through all the gamuts of expression and all the temperatures of the mind. You use it as a peasant uses his scythe, the tailor his needle, the soldier his weapon. To me it is a property and a ghost, a mollusk and an echo, a thing of a thousand transformations, but lacking outline and kernel. I cry out words, whisper them, stammer them, moan, flute, distend them, and fill the meaningless with meaning, and am depressed to the earth by the sublime. And I've been doing that for five and twenty years. It has worn me thin; it has split my gums and hollowed out my chest.

" Hence all words, sincere as they may be on others' lips, are untrue on mine, untrue to me. They tyrannise over me and torment me, flicker through the walls, recall to me my powerlessness and unrewarded sacrifices, and change me into a helpless puppet. Can I ever, without being ashamed to the very marrow, say: I love? How many

meanings have not those words! How many have I been
forced to give them! If I utter them I practise merely the
old trick of my trade, and make the pasteboard device upon my
head look like a golden crown. Consider me closely and you
will see the meaning of literal despair. Words have been my
undoing. It sounds queer, I know; but it is true. It may be
that the actor is the absolute example of hopeless despair."

Judith looked at him rather emptily. " I don't suppose
that we'll torture each other much with words," she said, merely
to say something.

But Edgar Lorm gave to this saying a subtle interpretation,
and nodded gratefully. " What an infinitely desirable condition
that would be," he answered, in his stateliest manner; " because, you see, words and emotions are like brothers and
sisters. The thing that I detest saying is mouldy and flat to me
in the realm of feeling too. One should be silent as fate. It
may be that I am spoiled for any real experience—drained dry.
I have damned little confidence in myself, and nothing but
pity for any hand stretched out to save me. However that
may be," he ended, and arose with elastic swiftness, " I am
willing to try."

He held out his hand as to a comrade. Charmed by the
vividness and knightly grace of his gesture, Judith took his
hand and smiled.

" Where are you stopping? " he asked.

" In this hotel."

Chatting quite naturally he accompanied her to the door
of her room.

XVIII

On the next afternoon Felix Imhof suddenly appeared at
the hotel. He sent up his card to Judith, and waited in the
hall. He walked up and down, swinging his little cane, carelessly whistling through his thick lips, his brain burdened with
affairs, speculations, stock quotations, a hundred obligations

and appointments. But whenever he passed the tall windows, he threw a curious and merry glance out into the street, where two boys were having a fight.

But now and then his face grew dark, and a quiver passed over it.

The page returned, and bade him come up.

Judith was surprised to see him. He began to talk eagerly at once. " I have business in Liverpool, and wanted to see you once more before leaving. A crowd of people came, who all had some business with you. Invitations came for you, and telephone calls; your dressmaker turned up, and letters, and I was, of course, quite helpless. I can't very well receive people with the agreeable information that my wife has just taken French leave of me. There are a thousand things; you have to disentangle them, or the confusion will be endless."

They talked for a while of the indifferent things which, according to him, had brought him here. Then he added: " I had an audience with the Prince Regent this forenoon. He bestowed a knighthood on me yesterday."

Judith's face flushed, and she had the expression of one who, in a state of hypnosis, recalls his waking consciousness.

Felix tapped against his faultlessly creased trousers with his stick. " I beg your pardon for venturing any criticism," he said, " but I can't help observing that the whole matter might have been better managed. To run off with that degree of suddenness—well, it wasn't quite the proper thing, a little beneath us, not quite fair."

Judith shrugged her shoulders. " Things that are inevitable might as well be done quickly. And I don't see that your equanimity is at all impaired."

" Equanimity! Nonsense! Doesn't enter the question." He stood, as was his habit, with legs stretched far apart, rocking to and fro a little, and regarding his gleaming boots. " What has equanimity to do with it? We're cultivated people. I'm neither a tiger nor a Philistine. Nihil humanum a me alienum, et cetera. You simply don't know me. And it doesn't astonish me, for what chance have we ever had to cultivate each other's acquaintance? Marriage gave us no opportunity. We should retrieve our lost occasions. It is this wish that I should like to take with me into my renewed bachelorhood. You must promise not to avoid me as rigorously in the future as you did during the eight months of our married life."

" If it will give you any pleasure, I promise gladly," Judith answered good-humouredly.

With that they parted.

An hour later Felix Imhof sat in the train. With protruding eyes he stared at the passing landscape until darkness fell. He desired conversation, argument, the relief of some projection of his inner self. With wrinkled brow he watched the strangers about him who knew nothing of him or his inner wealth, of his great, rolling ideas, or his far-reaching plans.

At Düsseldorf he left the train. He had made up his mind to do so at the last possible moment. He checked his luggage, and huddled in his coat, walked, a tall, lean figure, through the midnight of the dark and ancient streets.

He stopped in front of one of the oldest houses. In this house he had passed his youth. All the windows were dark. " Hello, boy! " he shouted toward the window behind which he had once slept. The walls echoed his voice. " O nameless boy," he said, " where do you come from? " He was accustomed to say of himself often: " I am of obscure origin like Caspar Hauser."

But no secret weighed upon him, not even that of his own unknown descent. He was a man of his decade—stripped of mystery, open to all the winds.

He entered a house, which he remembered from his student days. In a large room, lined with greasy mirrors, there were fifteen or twenty half-dressed girls. In his hat and coat he sat down at the piano and played with the false energy of the dilettante.

"Girls," he said, "I've got a mad rage in me!" The girls played tricks on him as he sat there. They hung a crimson shawl over his shoulders and danced.

"I'm in a rage, girls," he repeated. "It's got to be drowned out." He ordered champagne by the pailful.

The doors were locked. The girls screeched with delight.

"Do something to relieve my misery, girls," he commanded, bade half a dozen stand in a row and open their mouths. Then he rolled up hundred mark notes like cigarettes, and stuck them between the girls' teeth. They almost smothered him with their caresses.

And he drank and drank until he lost consciousness.

XIX

Christian could not be without Eva. If he left her for the shortest period, the world about him grew dark.

Yet all their relations had the pathos of farewells. If he walked beside her, it seemed to be for the last time. Every touch of their hands, every meeting of their eyes had the dark glow and pain of the irrevocable.

His love for her was in harmony with this condition. It was clinging, giving, patient, at times even obedient.

It showed its nature in the way he held her cloak for her, gave her a glass that her lips were to touch, supported her when she was weary, waited for her if she was later than he at some appointed spot.

She felt that often and questioned him; but he had no answer. He might have conveyed his sensation of an eternal farewell, but he could not have told her what was to follow it. And it became very clear to him, that not a farewell from her alone was involved, but a farewell from everything in the world that had hitherto been dear and pleasant and indispensable to him. Beyond that fact he understood nothing; he had no plans and did not make any.

He was so void of any desire or demand that Eva yielded recklessly to a hundred wishes, and was angry when none remained unfulfilled. She wanted to see the real ocean. He rented a yacht, and they cruised on the Atlantic for two weeks. She had a longing for Paris, and he took her there in his car. They had dinner at Foyot in the Rue de Tournon, where they had invited friends—writers, painters, musicians. On the following day they returned. They heard of a castle in Normandy which was said to be like a dream of the early Middle Age. She desired to see it by moonlight; so they set out while the moon was full and cloudless nights were expected. Then the cathedral at Rouen lured her; next the famous roses of a certain Baron Zerkaulen near Ghent; then an excursion into the forest of Ardennes, or a sunset over the Zuyder Zee, or a ride in the park at Richmond, or a Rembrandt at The Hague, or a festive procession in Antwerp.

" Do you never get tired? " Christian asked one day, with that unquiet smile of his that seemed a trifle insincere.

Eva answered: " The world is big and youth is brief. Beauty yearns toward me, exists for me, and droops when I am gone. Since Ignifer is mine, my hunger seems insatiable. It is radiant over my earth, and makes all my paths easy. You see, dear, what you have done."

" Beware of Ignifer," said Christian, with that same, apparently secretive smile.

Eva's lids drooped heavily. " Fyodor Szilaghin has arrived," she said.

" There are so many," Christian answered, " I can't possibly know them all."

" You see none, but they all see you," said Eva. " They all wonder at you and ask: Who is that slender, distinguished man with very white teeth and blue eyes? Do you not hear their whispering? They make me vain of you."

" What do they know of me? Let them be."

" Women grow pale when you approach. Yesterday on the promenade there was a flower-seller, a Flemish girl. She looked after you, and then she began to sing. Did you not hear? "

" No. What was the song she sang? "

Eva covered her eyes with her hands, and sang softly and with an expression on her lips that was half pain and half archness:

> " ' Où sont nos amoureuses?
> Elles sont au tombeau,
> Dans un séjour plus beau
> Elles sont heureuses.
> Elles sont près des anges
> Au fond du ciel bleu,
> Où elles chantent les louanges
> De la Mère de Dieu.'

" It touched my very soul, and for a minute I hated you. Ah, how much beauty of feeling streams from human hearts, and finds no vessel to receive it! "

Suddenly she arose, and said with a burning glance: " Fyodor Szilaghin is here."

Christian went to the window. " It is raining," he said.

Thereupon Eva left the room, singing with a sob in her throat:

> " Où sont nos amoureuses?
> Elles sont au tombeau."

That evening they were walking down the beach. " I met Mlle. Gamaleja," Eva told him. " Fyodor Szilaghin introduced her to me. She is a Tartar and his mistress. Her beauty is like that of a venomous serpent, and as strange as the landscape of a wild dream. There was a silent challenge in her attitude to me, and a silent combat arose between us. We talked about the diary of Marie Bashkirtseff. She said that such creatures should be strangled at birth. But I see from your expression, dear man, that you have never heard of Marie Bashkirtseff. Well, she was one of those women who are born a century before their time and wither away like flowers in February."

Christian did not answer. He could not help thinking of the faces of the dead fishermen which he had seen the night before.

" Mlle. Gamaleja was in London recently and brought me a message from the Grand Duke," Eva continued; " he'll be here in another week."

Christian was still silent. Twelve women and nineteen children had stood about the dead men. They had all been scantily clad and absorbed in their icy grief.

They walked up the beach and moved farther away from the tumult of the waves. Eva said: " Why don't you laugh? Have you forgotten how? " The question was like a cry.

Christian said nothing. " To-morrow," she remarked swiftly, and caught her veil which was fluttering in the breeze, " to-morrow there's a village fair at Dudzeele. Come with me to Dudzeele. Pulcinello will be there. We will laugh, Christian, laugh! "

" Last night there was a storm here," Christian began at last. " You know that, for we were long among the dunes up there. Toward morning I walked toward the beach again, because I couldn't sleep. Just as I arrived they were carrying away the bloated corpses of the fishermen. Three boats went to pieces during the night; it was quite near Molo, but there was no chance for help. They carried seven men away to the morgue. Some people, all humble folk, went along, and so did I. There in that death chamber a single lantern was burning, and when they put down the drenched bodies, puddles gathered on the floor. Coats had been spread over the faces of the dead men; and of the women I saw but a single one shed tears. She was as ugly as a rotten tree-trunk; but when she wept all her ugliness was gone. Why should I laugh, Eva? Why should I laugh? I must think of the fishermen who earn their bread day after day out on the sea. Why should I laugh? And why to-day?"

With both hands Eva pressed her veil against her cheeks.

In that tone of his, which was never rudely emphatic, Christian continued: "Yesterday at the bar Wiguniewski and Botho Thüngen showed me a man of about fifty, a former star at the opera, who had been famous and made money in his day. The day before he had broken down on the street—from starvation. But in his pocket, they found twenty francs. When he was asked why, having the money, he had not satisfied his hunger, he answered that the money was an advance given him toward travelling expenses. He had been engaged to sing at a cabaret in Havre. It had taken him months to find this employment. But the fare to Havre is thirty-five francs, and for six days he had made frantic efforts to scrape together the additional fifteen francs. He had resisted every temptation to touch the twenty francs, for he knew that if he took but a single centime his life would be finally wrecked. But on this day the date of the beginning of his engagement had lapsed, and he returned the twenty francs to the agent. They pointed this man out to me. Leaning on his arms, he sat before an empty cup. I meant to sit down by him, but he went away. Why should I laugh, Eva, when there are such things to think about? Don't ask me to-day of all days that I should laugh."

Eva said nothing. But when they were at home, she flung herself in his arms, as though beside herself, and said: "I must kiss you."

And she kissed him and bit his lip so hard that drops of blood appeared.

"Go now," she said with a commanding gesture, "go! But don't forget that to-morrow we shall visit the fair at Dudzeele."

XX

They drove to the fair and made their way through the crowds to the little puppet-show. The benches were filled with children; the grown people stood in a semi-circle. From the harbour floated the odours of machine oil, leather, and salt herring; in the air resounded the discords of all kinds of music and of the criers' voices.

Christian made a path for Eva; half-surprised and half-morosely the people yielded. Eva followed the play with cheerful intensity. She had loved such scenes from childhood, and now they brought back to her with a poignant and melancholy glow the years of her obscure wanderings.

The Pulcinello, who played the rôle of an outwitted cheat, was forced to confess that no cunning could withstand the magic of the good fairies. His simplicity was too obvious, and his downfall too well deserved to awaken compassion. The rain of blows which were his final portion constituted a satisfying victory of good morals.

Eva applauded, and was as delighted as a child. " Doesn't it make you laugh, Christian? " she asked.

And Christian laughed, not at the follies of the rogue, but because Eva's laughter was so infectious.

When the curtain had fallen upon the tiny stage, they followed the stream of people from one amusement to another. A little line of followers was formed in their wake; a whispering passed from mouth to mouth and each pointed out Eva to the other. Several young girls seemed especially stubborn in their desire to follow the exquisitely dressed lady. Eva wore a hat adorned with small roses and a cloak of silk as blue as the sea in sunshine.

One of the maidens had gathered a bunch of lilacs, and in front of an inn she gave the flowers to Eva with a dainty courtesy. Eva thanked her, and held the flowers to her face. Five or six of the girls formed a circle about her, and took each others' hands and danced and trilled a melody of wild delight.

" Now I am caught," Eva cried merrily to Christian, who had remained outside of the circle and had to endure the mocking glances of the girls.

" Yes, now you are caught," he answered, and sought to put himself in tune with the mood of the merrymakers.

On the steps of the inn stood a drunken fellow, who watched the scene before him with inexplicable fury. First he exhausted himself in wild abuse, and when no one took notice of him, he seemed overcome by a sort of madness. He picked up a stone from the ground, and hurled it at the group. The girls cried out and dodged. The stone, as large as a man's fist, narrowly missed the arm of the girl who had presented the flowers, and in its fall hit both of Eva's feet.

She grew pale and compressed her lips. Several men rushed up to the drunken brute, who staggered into the inn. Christian had also run in that direction; but he turned back, thinking it more important to take care of Eva. The girls surrounded her, sympathized and questioned.

" Can you walk? " he asked. She said yes with a determined little air, but limped when she tried. He caught her up in his arms, and carried her to the car, which was waiting nearby. The girls followed and waved farewell with their kerchiefs. Hoarse cries sounded from the inn.

" Pulcinello grew quite mad," Eva said. She smiled and suppressed all signs of pain. " It is nothing, darling," she whispered after a while, " it will pass. Don't be alarmed." They drove with racing speed.

Half an hour later she was resting in an armchair in the villa. Christian was kneeling before her, and held her naked feet in his hands.

Susan had been quite terror stricken, when she had whisked off her mistress's shoes and stockings, and saw to her horror the red bruises made by the stone. She had stammered out contradictory counsels, had summoned the servants, and excitedly cried out for a physician. At last Eva had asked her to be quiet and to leave the room.

"The pain's almost gone," said Eva, and nestled her little feet luxuriously into Christian's cool hands. A maid brought in a ewer of water and linen cloths for cold bandages.

Christian held and regarded those two naked feet, exquisite organs that were comparable to the hands of a great painter or to the wings of a bird that soars far and high. And while he was taking delight in their form, the clearly defined net of muscles, the lyrical loveliness of the curves, the rosy toes with their translucent nails, an inner monitor arose in him and seemed to say: "You are kneeling, Christian, you are kneeling." Silently, and not without a certain consternation, he had whispered back: "Yes, I am kneeling, and why should I not?" His eyes met Eva's, and the gleam of delight in hers heightened his inner discomfort.

Eva said: "Your hands are dear physicians, and it is wonderful to have you kneel before me, sweet friend."

"What is there wonderful about it?" Christian asked hesitantly.

The twilight had fallen. Through the gently waving curtains the evening star shone in.

Eva shook her head. "I love it. That's all." Her hair fell open and rippled down her shoulders. "I love it," she repeated, and laid her hands on his head, pressing it toward her knees. "I love it."

"But you are kneeling!" Christian heard that voice again. And suddenly he saw a water jug with a broken handle, and a crooked window rimmed with snow, and a single boot crusted with mud, and a rope dangling from a beam, and an oil lamp with a sooty chimney. He saw these lowly, poverty-stricken things.

"Have you kneeled to many as though you adored them?" Eva asked.

He did not answer, but her naked feet grew heavy in his hands. The sensuous perception which they communicated to him through their warmth, their smoothness, their instinctive flexibility vanished suddenly, and gave way to a feeling in which fear and shame and mournfulness were blended. These human organs, these dancing feet, these limbs of the woman he loved, these rarest and most precious things on earth seemed suddenly ugly and repulsive to him, and those lowly and poverty-stricken objects—the jug with the broken handle, the crooked window with its rim of snow, the muddy boot, the dangling rope, the sooty lamp, these suddenly seemed to him beautiful and worthy of reverence.

" Tell me, have you kneeled to many? " he heard Eva's voice, with its almost frightened tenderness. And it seemed to him that Ivan Becker gave answer in his stead and said: " That you kneeled down before her—that was it, and that alone. All else was hateful and bitter; but that you kneeled down beside her —ah, that was it! "

He breathed deeply, with closed eyes, and became pale. And he relived, more closely and truly than ever, that hour of fate. He felt the breath of Becker's kiss upon his forehead, and understood its meaning. He understood the feverish transformations of an evil conscience that had caused him to identify himself with that jug, that window, that boot and rope and lamp, only to flee, only to gain time. And he understood now that despite his change from form to form, he had well seen and heard the beggar, the woman, Ivan Michailovitch, the sick, half-naked children, but that his whole soul had gathered itself together in the effort to guard himself against them for but a little while, before they would hurl themselves upon him with all their torment, despair, madness, cruelty, like wild dogs upon a piece of meat.

His respite had come to an end. With an expression of haste and firmness at once he arose. " Let me go, Eva," he said, " send me away. It is better that you send me away than that I wrench myself loose, nerve by nerve, inch by inch. I cannot stay with you nor live for you." Yet in this very moment his love for her gathered within him like a storm of flames, and he would have torn the heart from his breast to have unsaid the irrevocable words.

She sprang up swiftly as an arrow. Then she stood very still, with both hands in her hair.

He walked to the window. He saw the whole space of heaven before him, the evening star and the unresting sea. And he knew that it was all illusion, this great peace, this glittering star, this gently phosphorescent deep, that it was but a garment and a painted curtain by which the soul must not let itself be quieted. Behind it were terror and horror and unfathomable pain. He understood, he understood at last.

He understood those thousands and thousands on the shore of the Thames and their sombre silence. He understood the shipman's daughter, whose violated body had lain on coarse linen. He understood Adda Castillo and her will to destruction. He understood Jean Cardillac's melancholy seeking for help, and his sorrow over his wife and child. He understood that ancient rake who cried out behind the gates of his cloister: "What shall I do? My Lord and Saviour, what shall I do?" He understood Dietrich, the deaf and dumb lad who had drowned himself, and Becker's words concerning his dripping coat, and Franz Lothar's horror at the intertwined bodies of the Hungarian men and maids, and the panting hunger of Amadeus Voss and his saying concerning the silver cord and the pitcher broken at the fountain. He understood the stony grief of the fishermen's wives, and the opera singer who had twenty francs in his pocket.

He understood. He understood.

"Christian!" Eva cried out in a tone as though she were peering into the darkness.

"The night has come upon us," Christian said, and trembled.

"Christian!" she cried.

Suddenly he became aware of Amadeus Voss, who emerged out there from among the dark trees, and who seemed to have awaited him, for he made signs to him at the window. With a hasty good-night Christian left the room.

Eva looked after him and did not move.

A little later, forgetting the ache in her feet, she went into her dressing-room, opened her jewel case, took Ignifer out, and regarded the stone long and with brooding seriousness.

Then she put it into her hair, and went to the mirror—cool in body, pale of face, quiet-eyed. She folded her arms,.lost in this vision of herself.

XXI

Christian and Amadeus walked across the dam toward Duin-bergen.

" I have a confession to make to you, Wahnschaffe," Amadeus Voss began. " I've been gambling, playing roulette, over at Ostende."

" I've heard about it," said Christian absent-mindedly. " And, of course, you lost? "

" The devil appeared to me," said Amadeus, in hollow tones.

" How much did you lose? " Christian asked.

" Maybe you think it was some refined modern devil, a hallucination, or a product of the poetic fancy," Amadeus continued in his breathless and strangely hostile way. " Oh, no, it was a regular, old-fashioned devil with a goat's beard and great claws. And he spoke to me: ' Take of their super-fluity; clothe your sensitiveness in armour; let them not intimi-date you, nor the breath of their insolently beautiful world drive you into the cloudy closets of your torment.' And with his cunning fingers he guided the little, jumping ball for me. The light of the lamps seemed to cry, the rouge fell from the cheeks of the women, the spittle of poisonous greed ran down the beards of the men. I won, Christian Wahnschaffe, I won! Ten thousand, twelve thousand—I hardly remember how much.

The thousand franc notes looked like tatters of a faded flag. There were gleaming halls, stairs, gardens, white tables, champagne coolers, platters of oysters; and I breathed deep and lived and was like a lord. Strange men congratulated me, honoured me with their company, ate with me—experienced people, spick and span and respectable. In the Hotel de la Plage my goat-footed devil finally became transformed into a worthy symbol. He became a spider that had a huge egg between its feet and sucked insatiably."

"I believe you ought to go to bed and have a long sleep," said Christian drily. "How much did you lose in the end?"

"I have lost sleep," Amadeus admitted. "How much I lost? About fourteen thousand. Prince Wiguniewski advanced the money; he thought you'd return it. He's a very distinguished person, I must say. Not a muscle in his face moves when he's courteous; nothing betrays the fact that he scents the proletarian in me."

"I'll straighten out the affair with him," said Christian.

"It is not enough, Wahnschaffe," Amadeus answered, and his voice shook, "it is not enough!"

"Why isn't it enough?"

"Because I must go on gambling and win the money back. I can't remain your debtor."

"You will only increase your indebtedness, Amadeus. But I won't prevent you, if you'll make up your mind to name a limit."

Amadeus laughed hoarsely. "I knew you'd be magnanimous, Christian Wahnschaffe. Plunge the thorn deeper into my wound. Go on!"

"I don't understand you, Amadeus," Christian said calmly. "Ask as much money of me as you please. To be sure, I'd prefer to have you ask it for another purpose."

"How magnanimous again, how magnanimous!" Amadeus jeered. "But suppose that naming a limit is just what I won't do? Suppose I want to strip off my beggar's shame and become frankly a robber? Would you cast me off in that case? "

" I don't know what I should do," Christian answered. " Perhaps I should try to convince you that you are not acting justly."

These sober and simple words made a visible impression on Amadeus Voss. He lowered his head and, after a while, he said: " It crushes the heart—that interval between the hopping of the little ball and the decision of the judge. The faded bank notes rustle up, or a round roll of gold is driven up on a shovel. I invented a system. I divided eight letters into groups of three and five. Once I won seventeen hundred with my system, another time three thousand. You mustn't leave me in the lurch, Wahnschaffe. I have a soul, too. Three and five—that's my problem. I'll break the bank. I'll break the bank thrice—ten times! It is possible, and therefore it can be done. Can three and five withstand a cloudburst of gold? Would Danaë repel Perseus, or would she demand that he bring her first the head of the Gorgon Medusa? "

He fell silent very suddenly. Christian had laid an arm about his shoulder, and this familiar caress was so new and unexpected that Amadeus breathed deep as a child in its sleep. " Think of what has happened, Amadeus," said Christian. " Do think of the words you said to me: ' It is possible that you need me; it is certain that without you I am lost.' Have you forgotten so soon, dear friend? "

Amadeus started. He stood still and grasped Christian's hands: " For the love of God . . . no one has ever spoken to me thus . . . no one! "

" You will not forget it then, Amadeus? " Christian said softly.

A weakness overcame Amadeus Voss. He looked about him with unquiet eyes, and saw a low post to which the ships' hawsers were made fast. He sat down on it, and buried his face in his hands. Then he spoke through his hands: " Look you, dear brother, I am a beaten dog; that and nothing else. I feel as though I had leaned too long against a cold, hard, tinted church wall. The chill has remained in my very marrow, and I struggle because I don't want that feeling to enslave me. Often I think I should like to love a woman. I cannot live without love; and yet I live on without it, day after day. Always without love! The accursed wall is so cold. I cannot and would not and must not live without love. I am only human, and I must know woman's love, or I shall freeze to death or be turned to stone or utterly destroyed. Yet I am a Christian, and it is hard for a Christian who bears a certain image in his heart to give himself up to woman. Help me to find a woman, brother, I beseech you."

Christian looked out upon the dark sea. " How can I help him? " he thought, and felt all the coldness of the world and the confusion of mortal things.

While he stood and reflected he heard from afar across the dunes a cry, first dulled by the distance, then nearer and clearer, and then farther away again. It was such a cry as a man might utter, at his utmost need, in the very face of death. Amadeus Voss also lifted his head to listen. They looked at each other.

" We must go," said Christian.

They hurried in the direction of the cry, but the dunes and the beach were equally desolate. Thrice again they heard the cry in the same fashion, approaching and receding, but their seeking and listening and hurrying were in vain. When they were about to return Voss said: " It was not human. It came from something in nature. It was a spirit cry. Such things happen oftener than men believe. It summons us somewhere. One of us two has received a summons."

" It may be," said Christian, smiling. His sense for reality could accept such an interpretation of things only in jest.

XXII

On his way to Scotland Crammon stopped over for a day in Frankfort. He informed Christian's mother of his presence, and she begged him with friendly urgency to come to her.

It was the end of June. They had tea on a balcony wreathed in fresh green. Frau Wahnschaffe had ordered no other callers to be admitted. For a while the conversation trickled along indifferently, and there were long pauses. She wanted Crammon to give her some news of Christian, from whom she had not heard since he had left Christian's Rest. But first, since Crammon was a confidant and a witness in the suit, it was necessary to mention Judith's divorce and approaching remarriage to Edgar Lorm, and Frau Wahnschaffe's pride rebelled at touching on things that could, nevertheless, not be silently passed over.

She sought a starting point in vain. Crammon, outwardly smooth, but really in a malicious and woodenly stubborn mood, recognized her difficulty, but would do nothing to help her.

"Why do you stay at a hotel, Herr von Crammon?" she asked. "We have a right to you and it isn't nice of you to neglect us."

"Don't grudge an old tramp his freedom, dear lady," Crammon answered, "and anyhow it would give me a heartache to have to leave this magic castle after just a day."

Frau Wahnschaffe nibbled at a biscuit. "Anything is better than a hotel," she said. "It's always a bit depressing, and not least so when it's most luxurious. And it isn't really nice. You are next door to quite unknown people. And the noises! But, after all, what distinction in life is there left to-day? It's no longer in fashion." She sighed. Now she thought she had found the conversational bridge she needed, and gave herself a jolt. "What do you think of Judith?" she said in a dull, even voice. "A lamentable mistake. I thought her marriage to Imhof far from appropriate and regretted it. But this! I can hardly look my acquaintances in the face. I always feared the child's inordinate ambitions, her utter lack of restraint. Now she throws herself at the head of an actor. And to add to the painful complications, there is her bizarre renunciation of her fortune. Incomprehensible! There's some secret behind that, Herr von Crammon. Does she realize clearly what it will mean to live on a more or less limited salary? It's incomprehensible."

"You need have no anxiety," Crammon assured her. "Edgar Lorm has a princely income and is a great artist."

"Ah, artists!" Frau Wahnschaffe interrupted him, with a touch of impatience and a contemptuous gesture. "That means little. One pays them; occasionally one pays them well. But they are uncertain people, always on the knife's edge. It's customary now to make a great deal of them, even in our circles. I've never understood that. Judith will have to pay terribly for her folly, and Wahnschaffe and I are suffering a bitter disappointment." She sighed, and looked at Crammon surreptitiously before she asked with apparent indifference, "Did you hear from Christian recently?"

Crammon said that he had not.

"We have been without news of him for two months," Frau Wahnschaffe added. Another shy glance at Crammon told her that he could not give her the information she sought. He was not sufficiently master of himself at this moment to conceal the cause of his long and secret sorrow.

A peacock proudly passed the balcony, spread the gleaming magnificence of his feathers in the sunlight, and uttered a repulsive cry.

"I've been told that he's travelling with the son of the forester," said Crammon, and pulled up his eyebrows so high that his face looked like the gargoyle of a mediæval devil. "Where he has gone to, I can only suppose; but I have no right to express such suppositions. I hope our paths will cross,

We parted in perfect friendship. It is possible that we shall find each other again on the same basis."

" I have heard of the forester's son," Frau Wahnschaffe murmured. " It's strange, after all. Is it a very recent friendship? "

" Yes, most recent. I have no explanation to offer. There's nothing about a forester's son that should cause one any anxiety in itself; but one should like to know the character of the attraction."

" Sometimes hideous thoughts come to me," said Frau Wahnschaffe softly, and the skin about her nose turned grey. Abruptly she bent forward, and in her usually empty eyes there arose so sombre and frightened a glow, that Crammon suddenly changed his entire opinion of this woman's real nature.

" Herr von Crammon," she began, in a hoarse and almost croaking voice, " you are Christian's friend; at least, you caused me to believe so. Then act the part of a friend. Go to him; I expect it of you; don't delay."

" I shall do all that is in my power," Crammon answered. " It was my intention to look him up in any event. First I'm going to Dumbarton for ten days. Then I shall seek him out. I shall certainly find him, and I don't believe that there is any ground for real anxiety. I still believe that Christian is under the protection of some special deity; but I admit that it's just as well to see from time to time whether the angel in question is fulfilling his duties properly."

" You will write me whatever happens," Frau Wahnschaffe said, and Crammon gave his promise. She nodded to him when he took his leave. The glow in her eyes had died out, and when she was alone she sank into dull brooding.

Crammon spent the evening with acquaintances in the city. He returned to the hotel late, and sat awhile in the lobby, immovable, unapproachable, nourishing his misanthropy on the aspect of the passersby. Then he examined the little directory on which the names of the guests appeared. " What are these people doing here? " he asked himself. " How important that looks: ' Max Ostertag (retired banker) and wife.' Why Ostertag of all things? Why Max? Why: and wife? "

Embittered he went up to his room. Embittered and world-weary he wandered up and down the long corridor. In front of each door, both to the right and to the left, stood two pairs of boots—one pair of men's and one pair of women's. In this pairing of the boots he saw a boastful and shameless ex-hibitionism of marital intimacies; for the shape and make of the boots assured him of the legal and officially blameless status of their owners. He seemed to see in those boots a morose evidence of overlong, stale unions, a vulgar breadth of tread caused by the weight of money, a commonness of mind, a self-righteous Pharisaism.

He couldn't resist the foolish temptation of creating con-fusion among the boots of these Philistines. He looked about carefully, took a pair of men's boots, and joined them to a pair of women's boots at another door. And he continued until the original companionship of the boots was utterly de-stroyed. Then he went to bed with a pleasant sensation, com-parable to that of a writer of farces who has succeeded in creating an improbable and scarcely extricable confusion amid the puppets of his plot.

In the morning he was awakened by the noise of violent and angry disputes in the hall. He raised his head, listened with satisfaction, smiled slothfully, stretched himself, yawned, and enjoyed the quarrelling voices as devoutly as though they were music.

XXIII

When on the day after his nocturnal wandering Christian came to see Eva, he was astonished to find her surrounded by a crowd of Russians, Englishmen, Frenchmen, and Belgians. Until this day she had withdrawn herself from society entirely, or else had received only at hours previously agreed upon between Christian and herself. This unexpected change suddenly made a mere guest of him, and pushed him from the centre to the circumference of the circle.

The conversation turned on the arrival of Count Maidanoff, and there was a general exchange of speculation, both in regard to the duration and the purpose of his visit. A political setting of the stage had been feigned with conscious hypocrisy. There was to be a visit to the king, and ministerial conferences. He had first stopped at the Hotel Lettoral in Knocke, but had soon moved to the large and magnificent Villa Herzynia, which his favourite and friend, Prince Szilaghin, had rented.

Szilaghin appeared soon after Christian. Wiguniewski, obviously under orders, introduced the two men.

" I'm going to have a few friends with me to-morrow night," Szilaghin said, with the peculiar courtesy of a great comedian. " I trust you will do me the honour of joining us." Coldly he examined Christian, whose nerves grew painfully taut under that glance. He bowed and determined not to go.

Eva was in the room that gave on the balcony, and was posing for the sculptress, Beatrix Vanleer. The latter sat with a block of paper and made sketches. Meantime Eva chatted with several gentlemen. She held out her hand for Christian to kiss, and ignored his questioning gaze.

In her cinnamon dress, with her hair high on her head and a diadem of ivory, she seemed extraordinarily strange to him. Her face had the appearance of delicate enamel. About her chin there was a hostile air. Gentle vibrations about the muscles at her temples seemed to portend an inner storm. But these perceptions were fleeting. What Christian felt about her was primarily a paralyzing coldness.

When Mlle. Vanleer had finished for the day, Eva walked up and down talking to a certain young Princess Helfersdorff. She led her to the balcony, which was bathed in the sunlight, and then into her boudoir, where she liked to be when she read or rested from her exercises. Christian followed the two women, and felt, for the first time in his life, that he was being humiliated. But it did not depress him as profoundly as, an hour ago, the mere thought of such an experience would have done.

The Marquis Tavera joined him. Standing on the threshold of the boudoir, they talked of indifferent things. Christian heard Eva tell the young princess that she expected to go to Hamburg within a week. The North German Lloyd was planning a great festivity on the occasion of the launching of a magnificent ship, and she had been asked to dance. " I'm really delighted at the prospect," she added cheerfully. " I'm little more than a name to most Germans yet. Now they'll be able to see me and tell me what I amount to and where I belong."

The young lady looked at the dancer with enthusiasm. Christian thought: " I must speak to her at once." In every word of Eva's he felt an arrow of hostility or scorn aimed at him. He left Tavera, and entered the room. The decisiveness of his movement forced Eva to look at him. She smiled in surprise. A scarcely perceptible shrug marked her astonishment and censure.

Tavera had turned to the princess, and when these two moved toward the door, Eva seemed inclined to follow them. A gesture of Christian, which she saw on glancing back, determined her to wait. Christian closed the door, and Eva's expression of amazement became intense. But he felt that this was but acting. He slipped into a sudden embarrassment, and could find no words.

Eva walked up and down, touching some object here and there. " Well? " she asked, and looked at him coldly.

" This Szilaghin is an insufferable creature," Christian murmured, with lowered eyes. " I remember I once saw a mani-coloured marine animal in an aquarium. It was very beautiful and also extremely horrible. I couldn't get rid of its image.

I wanted constantly to go back to it, and yet felt constantly an ugly horror of it."

"O la, la!" said Eva. Nothing else. And in this soft exclamation there was contempt, impatience, and curiosity. Then she stood before him. "I am not fond of being caged," she said in a hard voice. "I am not fond of being caught and isolated from my guests to be told trivial things. You must forgive me, but it doesn't interest me what impression Prince Szilaghin makes on you. Or, to be quite truthful, it interests me no longer."

Christian looked at her dumbly. It seemed to him that he was being chastised, beaten, and he turned very pale. The feeling of humiliation grew like a fever. "He invited me to his house to-morrow," he stammered, "and I merely wanted to tell you that I'm not going."

"You must go," Eva replied swiftly. "I beg of you to go." Avoiding the astonished question in his eyes, she added: "Maidanoff will be there. I wish you to see him."

"For what reason?"

"You are to know what I grasp at, what I do, whither I go. Can you read faces? I dare say not. Nevertheless, come!"

"What have you determined on?" he asked, awkwardly and shyly.

She gave her body a little, impatient shake. "Nothing that was not settled long ago," she answered, with a glassy coolness in her voice. "Did you think that I would drag on our lovely, wild May into a melancholy November? You might have spared us both your frankness of last night. The dream was over no moment sooner for you than for me. You should have known that. And if you did not know it, you should have feigned that knowledge. A gentleman of faultless taste does not throw down his cards while his partner is preparing to make a last bet. You do not deserve the honourable farewell that I gave you. I should have led you about, chained, like those stupid little beasts who are always whining for permission to ruin themselves for my sake. They call this thing their passion. It is a fire like any other; but I would not use it to kindle a lamp, if I needed light to unlace my shoes."

She had crossed her arms and laughed softly, and moved toward the door.

"You have misunderstood me," said Christian overwhelmed. "You misunderstand me wholly." He raised his hands and barred her way. "Do you not understand? If I had words. . . . But I love you so! I cannot imagine life without you. And yet (how shall I put it into words?) I feel like a man who owes colossal sums and is constantly dunned and tormented, and does not know wherewith to pay nor whom. Do try to understand! I was hasty, foolish. But I thought that you might help me."

It was the cry of a soul in need. But Eva did not or would not heed it. She had built of her love a soaring arch. She thought it had fallen, and no abyss seemed deep enough for its ruins to be hurled. She had neither ears now nor eyes. She had decided her fate even now; and though it frightened her, to recede was contrary to her pride and her very blood. A sovereign gesture silenced Christian. "Enough!" she said. "Of all the ugly things between two people, nothing is uglier than an explanation that involves the emotions. I have no understanding for hypochondria, and epilogues bore me. As for your creditors, see that you seek them out and pay them. It is troublesome to keep house with unpaid bills."

She went from the room.

Christian stood very still. Slowly he lowered his head, and hid his face in his hands.

XXIV

Next day Christian received a telegram from Crammon, in which the latter announced his arrival for the middle of the following week. He gazed meditatively at the slip of paper, and had to reconstruct an image of Crammon from memory, feature by feature. But it escaped him again at once.

At Fyodor Szilaghin's he found about twenty people. There were eight or ten Russians, including Wiguniewski. Then there were the brothers Maelbeek, young Belgian aristocrats, a French naval captain, Tavera, Bradshaw, the Princess Helfersdorff and her mother (a very common looking person), Beatrix Vanleer, and Sinaide Gamaleja.

Christian arrived a little later than the others, and Szilaghin was half-sitting, half-lying on a *chaise-longue*. A young wolf crouched on his knees, and on the arm of the *chaise-longue* sat a green parrot. He smiled and excused himself for not arising, pointing to the animals as though they held him fast.

From Wiguniewski's anecdotes Christian knew of Szilaghin's fondness for such trickery. At Oxford he had once gone boating alone and at night with an eagle chained to his skiff; at Rome he had once rented a palace, and given a ball to the dregs of the city's life—beggars, cripples, prostitutes, and pimps. The boastfulness of such things was obvious. But as Christian stood there and saw him with those animals, the impression he received was not only one of frantic high spirits, but also one of despair. A retroactive oppression crept over him.

The lighting of the rooms was strikingly dim and scattered. A thunderstorm was approaching, and the windows were all open on account of the sultry heat; and every flicker of lightning flashed an unexpected brightness into the rooms.

At the invitation of several guests, Sinaide Gamaleja sat down with a lute under a cluster of long-stemmed roses, and began to sing a Russian song. Over her shoulders lay a gold-embroidered shawl, and her hair was held by a band of diamonds. Her figure was fragile. She had broad cheekbones, a wide mouth, and dully-glowing, heavy-lidded eyes.

The greyish-yellow wolf on Szilaghin's knees raised his head, and blinked sleepily at the singer. The melody had awakened in him a dream of his native steppes. But the parrot stirred too, and, croaking an unintelligible word, he preened himself and displayed the gorgeous plumage of his throat. Szilaghin raised a finger and bade the bird be silent; obediently it hid its beak in the feathers which a breeze lifted. A voluble old Russian kept talking to Szilaghin. The latter overheard him contemptuously, and joined in the singing of the song's second stanza.

His voice was melodious—a deep, dark baritone. But to Christian there seemed something corrupt in its music, as corrupt as the half-shut, angry, melancholy eyes with their contempt of mankind; as corrupt as the well-chiselled, waxen face, that could pass for eighteen, yet harboured all the experiences of an evil old age; as corrupt as the long, pale, sinuous, nerveless hand or the sweetish, weary, clever smile.

The Maalbeeks, Wiguniewski, the Captain, and Tavera had settled down to a game of baccarat in the adjoining room. In the pauses of the singing, one could hear the click of gold and the tap of the cards on the table. These strange noises excited the parrot; he forgot the command of his master, and uttered a discordant cry. Sinaide Gamaleja threw the animal a furious glance, and for a moment her hand twitched on the strings.

At that moment Szilaghin arose, grasped the bird's feet with one hand, its head with the other, and twisted the head of the screaming, agonizedly fluttering animal around and around as on an axis. Then he tossed the green, dead thing aside with an expression of disgust, and calmly intoned the third stanza of the song.

A flame of satisfaction appeared in Sinaide Gamaleja's eyes. The old Russian, who had visited his endless babble on the sculptress, fell suddenly silent. The wolf yawned, and, as though to confirm the fact of his own obedience, snuggled his chin against his master's arm.

Christian looked down at the dead bird, whose tattered

plumage gleamed in the lightning that flashed across the floor like a fantastic emerald. Suddenly the dead animal became to him the seal and symbol of all the corruption, vanity, unveracity, bedizenment, and danger of all he saw and felt. He looked at Szilaghin, at Sinaide, at the chattering dotard, at the gamesters, and turned away. There was an acridness in his throat and a burning in his eyes. He approached the window. The foliage rustled out there, and the thunder pealed. And the question arose within him: Whence does all this evil come? Whence does it come, and why is it so hard to separate oneself from it?

The night, the rain, and the storm drove him forth, lured him out. He ached to lose himself in the darkness, far from men. He was afraid for the first time in his life that he would shed tears. Never, in all his conscious memory, had he wept. His whole body was shaken by an emotional tumult such as he had never known, and he repressed it only by using his utmost energy. Just as he was about to touch the knob of the door, a lackey opened it, and Maidanoff and Eva appeared on the threshold. Christian stood quite still; but every vestige of colour left his face.

A vivid stir went through the company. Szilaghin jumped up to welcome these two. Maidanoff's weather-beaten leanness contrasted in a striking and sombre fashion with Eva's flower-like symmetry of form. She wore a garment diaphanous as breathing; it was held to her shoulders by ropes of pearls. Her skin had a faintly golden glow; her throat and arms and bosom pulsed with life.

The vision absorbed Christian. He stared at her. His name was spoken, with other names that were new to Maidanoff; and still he stared at that unfathomable and fatal image. His heart, in its sudden, monstrous loneliness, turned to ice; he felt both wild and stricken with dumbness; the tension of his soul became unendurable. Curious glances sought him out. He failed to move at the proper moment, and the moan that

arose from the confusion of his utter grief had made a thing
of mockery and scorn of him, before he fled past barren walls
and stupid lackeys into the open.

The rain came down in torrents. He did not call his car,
but walked along the road.

XXV

After losing twenty-eight thousand francs, the amount that
he had gradually borrowed from Mr. Bradshaw and Prince
Wiguniewski, Amadeus Voss got up from the gaming table, and
staggered into the open. He had a dim notion that he would
seek out Christian, to tell him that he would be able to settle
the debt within twenty-four hours.

He went to the telegraph office, and sent a message to
Christian. Then he stood beneath a chestnut tree in bloom,
and muttered: " Brother, brother."

A woman came along the road, and he joined her. But suddenly he burst out into wild laughter, turned down a side street,
and went on alone.

He walked and walked for six endless hours. At two o'clock
in the morning he was in Heyst. His brain seemed to have
become an insensitive lump, incapable of light or reason.

Masses of dark grey clouds that floated in the sky assumed
to him the aspect of women's bodies. The clouds, which the
hot night drove toward the north, were like cloaks over the
forms he desired. He felt an obscure yearning for all the love
in all the lands in which he had no part.

At the garden-gate of the villa he stopped and stared up at
Christian's windows. They were open and showed light.
" Brother," he muttered again, " brother! " Christian appeared at the window. The sight of him filled Voss with a
sudden, overwhelming hatred. " Take care, Wahnschaffe! "
he cried.

Christian left the window, and soon appeared at the gate.
Amadeus awaited him with clenched fists. But when Christian

approached, he turned and fled down the street, and Christian looked after him. Then his steps became slower, and Christian followed.

After Voss had wandered about aimlessly for a time, he felt a torturing thirst. He happened to pass a sailors' tavern, considered for a moment, and entered. He ordered grog, but did not touch the glass. Five or six men sat at various tables. Three slept; the eyes of the others had a drunken stare. The tavern keeper, an obese fellow with a criminal face, sat behind the bar, and watched this elegantly attired guest, whose face was so pale and so disturbed. He concluded that the late comer was in a mood of despair, and beckoned to the bar-maid, a dark-haired, dirty Walloon, to sit down by him.

Impudently she did so, and started to talk. He did not understand her. She gave a coarse laugh, and put a hand on his knee. Behind her thin and ragged bodice her breasts stirred like animals. She had a primitive, animal odour. He turned dizzy. Then a lust to murder stirred in him.

He drew from his pocket all the money he had left. There were seventy francs—three gold and five silver coins. " The magic numbers," he muttered, and grew a shade paler, " three and five! "

The Walloon woman turned greedy and caressing eyes upon the coins. The tavern keeper, scenting business, dragged his bulk forward.

" Strip off your clothes, and it's yours! " said Amadeus Voss.

She looked at him stupidly. The tavern keeper understood German and translated the words. She laughed shrilly, and pointed toward the door. Amadeus shook his head. " No; now; here! " He was stubborn. The girl turned to her employer, and the two consulted in whispers. Her gestures made it evident that she cared little for the presence of the drunken or snoring men. She disappeared behind a brown partition that had once been yellow. The tavern keeper gathered the money on the table, waddled from window to window to see that the red hangings covered all the panes, and then stood guard at the door.

Amadeus sat there as though steeped in seething water. A few minutes passed. Then the Walloon woman appeared from behind the partition. The sailors looked up. One arose and gesticulated; one uttered a wild laugh. The woman stood with lowered eyes—stubborn, careless, rubbing one foot with the other. She was rather fat, quite without charm, and the lines of her body had been destroyed.

But to Amadeus Voss she was like a supernatural vision, and he gazed upon her as though his whole soul was in that gaze. His arms reached out, and his fingers became claws, and his lips twitched. The fishermen and the tavern keeper no longer saw the woman. They saw him. They felt fear. So unwonted was the sight that they did not observe the opening of the door. The tavern keeper's whistled warning came too late. Christian, who entered, still saw the naked woman as she hurried toward the partition.

He approached Amadeus. But the latter took no notice of him. He stared spell-bound at the spot where the woman had stood.

Christian laid a hand upon his shoulder. Amadeus roused himself from his absorption, turned slow, questioning eyes upon his friend, and strangely uttered with his quivering lips these words: " Est Deus in nobis; agitante calescimus illo."

Then he broke down, his forehead dropped on the table, and a shudder shook his body.

The tavern keeper muttered morosely.

" Come, Amadeus," said Christian very quietly.

The drunken fishermen and sailors stared.

Amadeus arose, and groped like a blind man for Christian's hand.

" Come, Amadeus," Christian repeated, and his voice seemed to make a deep impression on Voss, for he followed him without hesitation. The tavern keeper and the sailors accompanied them into the street.

The tavern keeper said to the men with him: "Those are what you call gentlemen. Look how they behave! It shows you why the world is ruled so ill."

"The dawn is breaking," said one of the fishermen, and pointed to a purple streak in the eastern heaven.

Christian and Amadeus likewise stared at the purple seam of the east, and Amadeus spoke again: "Est Deus in nobis; agitante calescimus illo."

KAREN ENGELSCHALL

I

On the appointed hour of the appointed day Crammon arrived. He had prepared himself to stay and to be festive; but he was disappointed. Eva and her train were on the point of leaving. Maidanoff had proceeded to Paris, whither Eva was to follow him.

Crammon had been informed of this new friendship of his idol. All other news came to him too, and so he was aware that a quarrel had arisen between Christian and Eva. He was the more astonished to see Christian determined to follow Eva to Hamburg.

They had exchanged but a few words, when the transformation in Christian struck him. He laid his hand on the young man's shoulder, and asked sympathetically: " Have you nothing to confide? "

He spent the evening with Wiguniewski. " It isn't possible," he said; " you're mistaken. Or else the world is topsy-turvy and I can no longer tell a man from a woman."

" I had no special liking for Wahnschaffe from the start," Wiguniewski confessed. " He's too impenetrable, mysterious, spoiled, cold, and, if you will, too German. Nevertheless I knew from the first that he was the very man for Eva Sorel. You couldn't see the two together without a sense of delight —the sort of delight that a beautiful composition gives you, or anything that is spiritually fitting and harmonious."

Crammon nodded. " He has a strange power over women," he said. " I've just had another instance which is the more remarkable as it developed from a mere sight of his picture. At the Ashburnhams' in Yorkshire, where I've been staying, I made the acquaintance of a Viennese girl, a banker's daughter, rather ugly, to be frank, but with a peculiar little sting and charm and wit of her own. Not a bad figure, though rather—shall we say scanty? Yes. Her name is Johanna Schöntag, though that matters little. I called her nothing but Rumpelstilzkin. That fitted her like a glove. God knows how she got there. Her sister, a russet-haired person who looks as though she'd jumped out of a Rubens, is married to an attaché of some minor legation, Roumanian or Bulgarian or something like that. The big capitalists fit their daughters into society that way. Well, anyhow, this Rumpelstiezkin and I agreed to amuse each other in the murky boredom of Lord and Lady Ashburnham's house. So one day I showed the girl a miniature of Christian which Gaston Villiers painted for me in Paris. She looked at the picture and her merry face grew grave, absorbed, and she handed it back to me silently. A couple of days later she asked to see it again, and it had the same effect on her. She asked me about the man, and I, of course, became very eloquent, and happened to remark, too, that I expected to meet Christian here. She insisted at once that she must meet him, and that I must plan to have her do so. Remember she's rather unapproachable as a rule, fastidious, turning up her nose—her worst feature by the way—at things that please most people. The request was unexpected and rather a nuisance. One mustn't, as you know, bring the wrong people together and land one's self in difficulties. So I said at once: ' The Almighty forbid! ' I admonished her gently to change her mind, and painted the danger in its darkest hues. She laughed at me, and asked me whether I'd grown strait-laced; then she at once developed a most cunning plan. She had time enough. She wasn't expected home till the first of November, which gave her seven weeks. So she would announce her intention of studying the Dutch galleries, the pursuit of culture being always respectable. She had a companion and chaperone, as it was, and her sister, who was broad-minded in such matters, could be taken into her confidence. Her energy and astuteness made me feel weak, and forced me into the conspiracy. Well, she arrived yesterday. She's at the Hotel de la Plage, a little scared, like a bird that's dropped out of its nest, a little dissatisfied with herself, vexed by little attacks of morality; and I, for my part, don't know what to do with her. I bethought me too late that Christian isn't to be caught by such tricks, and now I've got to make it clear to the girl. All this is by the way, prince—a sort of footnote to your discourse, which I did not intend to interrupt."

Wiguniewski had listened with very slight sympathy. He began again: "These past months, as I've said, have given us all an unforgettable experience. We have seen two free personalities achieving a higher form of union than any of the legitimized ones. But suddenly this noble spectacle turns into a shabby farce; and it is his fault. For such a union has its organic and natural close. A man of subtle sensitiveness knows that, and adjusts himself accordingly. Instead of that, he actually lets it get to the point of painful scenes. He seeks meetings that humiliate him and make him absurd. When she is out he waits in her rooms for her return, and endures her passing him by with a careless nod. Once he sat waiting all night and stared into a book. He lets the Rappard woman treat him insolently, and doesn't seem to mind that the fruits and flowers he sends daily are regularly refused. What is it? What does it mean?"

"It points to some sorrow, and assuredly to a great sorrow for me," Crammon sighed. "It's incomprehensible."

"She entertained at dinner day before yesterday," Wiguniewski continued. "As though to mock him he was placed at the lower end of the table. I didn't even know the people who sat by him. It seems to arouse a strange cruelty in her that he doesn't refuse to bear these humiliations; he, on the other hand, seems to find some inexplicable lure in his suffering. He sat down that evening in silence. Afterwards a curious thing happened. Groups had been formed after dinner.

He stood a few feet from Eva and gazed at her steadily. His
face had a brooding look as he observed her. She wore Ignifer,
which is his gift, and looked like Diana with a burning star
above her forehead."

" That's excellently well put, prince," Crammon exclaimed.

" The conversation touched upon many subjects without
getting too shallow. You know her admirable way of checking
and disciplining talk. Finally there arose a discussion of
Flemish literature, and some one spoke of Verhaeren. She
quoted some verses of a poem of his called ' Joy.' The sense
was somewhat as follows: My being is in everything that lives
about me; meadows and roads and trees, springs and shadows,
you become me, since I have felt you wholly. There was a
murmur of appreciation. She went to a shelf and took down a
volume of Verhaeren's poems. She turned the pages, found the
poem she sought, and suddenly turned to Wahnschaffe. She
gave him the book with a gesture of command; he was to
read the poem. He hesitated for a moment, then he obeyed.
The effect of the reading was both absurd and painful. He
read like a schoolboy, low, stammering, and as though the
content were beyond his comprehension. He felt the absurdity
and painfulness of the incident himself, for his colour changed
as the ecstatic stanzas came from his lips like an indifferent
paragraph in a newspaper; and when he had finished the reading, he laid the book aside, and left without a glance at any
one. But Eva turned to us, and said as though nothing had
happened: ' The verses are wonderful, aren't they? ' Yet her
lips trembled with fury. But what was her purpose? Did she
want to prove to us his inability to feel things that are beautiful
and delicate? Did she want to put him to shame, to punish
him and publicly expose the poverty of his nature? Or was it
only an impatient whim, the annoyance at his dumb watchfulness and his searching glances? Mlle. Vanleer said later:
' If he had read the verses like a divine poet, she would have
forgiven him.' ' Forgiven him what? ' I asked. She smiled,

and answered: 'Her own faithlessness.' There may be something in that. At all events, you should get him out of this situation, Herr von Crammon."

" I shall do all in my power," said Crammon, and the lines of care about his mouth grew deeper. He wiped his forehead. " Of course I don't know how far my influence goes. It would be empty boastfulness to guarantee anything. I've been told too that he frequents all sorts of impossible dives with impossible people. I could weep when I think of it. He was the flower of modern manhood, the pride of my lengthening years, the salt of the earth! Unfortunately he had, even when I left him, certain attacks of mental confusion, but I put those down to the account of that suspicious fellow, Ivan Becker."

" Don't speak of him! Don't speak of Becker! " Wiguniewski interrupted sharply. " Not at least in that manner, I must beg and insist."

Crammon opened his eyes very wide, and the tip of his tongue became visible, like a red snail peering out of its shell. He choked down his discomfort and shrugged his shoulders.

Wiguniewski said: " At all events you've given me an indication. I never considered such a possibility. It throws a new light on many things. It's true, by the way, that Wahnschaffe associates with questionable people. The queerest of them all is Amadeus Voss, a hypocrite and a gambler. One must not couple such persons with Ivan Becker. Becker may have set him upon a certain road. If we assume that, a number of incidents become clear. But anything really baneful comes from Voss. Save your friend from him! "

" I haven't seen the fellow yet," Crammon murmured. " What you tell me, Prince, doesn't take me quite unawares. Nevertheless, I'm grateful. But let that scoundrel beware! May I never drink another drop of honest wine, if he escape me! Let me never again glance at a tempting bosom, if I don't grind this infamous cur to pulp. So help me! "

Wiguniewski arose, and left Crammon to plan his revenge.

II

The morning sun of late September was gilding sea and land, when Crammon entered Christian's room. Christian was sitting at his curved writing table. The bright blue tapestries on the walls gleamed; chairs and tables were covered by a hundred confused objects. Everything pointed to the occupant's departure.

" Don't let me disturb you, dear boy; I have time enough," said Crammon. He swept some things from a chair, sat down, and lit his pipe.

But Christian put down his pen. " I don't know what's the matter with me," he said angrily, without looking at Crammon, " I can't get two coherent sentences down on paper. However carefully I think it out, by the time it's written it sounds stiff and silly. Have you the same experience? "

Crammon answered: " There are those who have the trick. It takes, primarily, a certain impudence. You must never stop to ask: Is that correct? Is it true? Is it well-founded? Scribble ahead, that's all. Be effective, no matter at what cost. The cleverest writers are often the most stupid fellows. But to whom are you writing? Is the haste so great? Letters can usually be put off."

" Not this time. It is a question of haste," Christian answered. " I have a letter from Stettner and I can't make out his drift. He tells me that he's quitting the service and leaving for America. Before he goes he wants to see me once more. He takes ship at Hamburg on October 15. Now it fortunately happens that I'll be in Hamburg on that date, and I want to let him know."

" I don't see any difficulty there," Crammon said seriously. " All you need say is: I'll be at such a place on such a day, and expect or hope, et cetera. Yours faithfully or sincerely or cordially, et cetera. So he's going to quit? Why? And run off to America? Something rotten in the state of Denmark? "

"He was challenged to a duel, it appears, and refused the challenge. That's the only reason he gives. He adds that matters shaped themselves so that he is forced to seek a new life in the New World. It touches me closely; I was always fond of him. I must see him."

"I'd be curious too to know what really happened," said Crammon. "Stettner didn't strike me as a chap who'd lightly run away and risk his honour. He was an exemplary officer. I'm afraid it's a dreary business. But I observe that it gives you a pretext for going to Hamburg."

Christian started. "Why a pretext?" He was a little embarrassed. "I need no pretext."

Crammon bent his head far forward, and laid his chin on the ivory handle of his stick. His pipe remained artfully poised in one corner of his mouth, and did not move as he spoke. "You don't mean to assert, my dearest boy, that your conscience doesn't require some additional motive for the trip," he began, like a father confessor who is about to use subtle arguments to force a confession from a stubborn malefactor, "and you're not going to try to make a fool of an old boon-companion and brother of your soul. One owes something to a friend. You should not forget under whose auspices and promises you entered the great world, nor what securities *he* offered—securities of the heart and mind—who was the author and master of your radiant entry. Even Socrates, that rogue and revolutionary, recalled such obligations on his death bed. There was a story about a cock—some sort of a cock, I be-lieve. Maybe the story doesn't fit the case at all. No matter. I always thought the ancients rather odious. What does matter is that I don't like your condition, and that others who love you don't like it. It rends my very heart to see you pilloried, while people who can't tell a stud-horse from a donkey shrug their shoulders at you. It's not to be endured. I'd rather we'd quarrel and exchange shots at a distance of five paces. What has happened to you? What has come over you? Have you stopped gathering scalps to offer your own head? The hares and the hounds, I tell you, are diverse creatures. I understand all things human, but the divine order must be kept intact. It's flying in the face of providence that you should stand at the gate like a beggar. You used to be the one who showed others the door; they whined and moaned after you—and that was proper. I had an uncle who was something of a philosopher, and he used to say: when a woman, a lawyer, and a stove are at their hottest—turn your back to them. I've always done that, and kept my peace of mind and my reputation. There are extenuating circumstances in your case, I admit. There is but one such woman in a century, and whoever possesses her may well lose his reason. But even that should not apply to you, Christian. Splendour is your natural portion: it is for you to grant favours; at your board the honey should be fresh each day. And now tell me what you intend to do."

Christian had listened to this lengthy though wise and pregnant discourse with great patience. At times there was a glint of mockery or anger in his eyes. Then again he would lower them and seem embarrassed. Sometimes he grasped the sense of Crammon's words, sometimes he thought of other things. It cost him an effort to recall clearly by what right this apparently complete stranger interfered in his life and sought to influence his decisions. And then again he felt within himself a certain tenderness for Crammon in the memory of common experiences and intimate talks; but all that seemed so far away and so estranged from the present.

He looked out of the window, from which the view was free to the horizon where sea and sky touched. Far in the distance a little white cloud floated like a white, round pillow. The same tenderness that he felt for Crammon, he now felt for that little cloud.

And as Crammon sat before him and waited for an answer, there suddenly came into his mind the story of the ring which Amadeus had told him. He began: " A young candidate for

Holy Orders, who was tutor to the children of a banker, fell under the suspicion of having stolen a costly ring. He told me the story himself, and from his words I knew that the ring, when he saw it on the hand of his employer's wife, aroused his desire. In addition he loved this woman, and would have been happy to have had something by which to remember her. But he was utterly innocent of the disappearance of the ring, and some time after he had left that house, his innocence received the most striking confirmation. For the lady sent him the ring as a gift. He was wretchedly poor, and the ring would have meant much to him; but he went and threw it into a well, a deep old-fashioned well. The costliest thing he had ever possessed in life, he threw without hesitation or reflection into a well—that's what this man did."

"Oh, well, very well. Although . . . no, I don't quite see your meaning," said Crammon, discontentedly, and shifted his pipe from the right to the left corner of his mouth. "What good did the ring do the poor fool? How absurd to take something that reaches you in a manner so delicate and discreet, and throw it into a well? Would not a box have served, or a drawer? There at least it could have been found. It was a loutish trick."

Crammon's way of sitting there with his legs crossed, showing his grey silk socks, had something about it so secure and satiated, that it reminded one of an animal that basks in the sun and digests its food. Christian's disgust at his words quieted, and was replaced by a gentle, almost compassionate tenderness. He said: "It is so hard to renounce. You can talk about it and imagine it; you can will it and even believe yourself capable of it. But when the moment of renunciation comes, it is hard, it is almost impossible to give up even the humblest of things."

"Yes, but why do you want to renounce?" Crammon murmured in his vexation. "What do you mean exactly by renunciation? What is it to lead to?"

Christian said almost to himself: " I believe that one must cast one's ring into a well."

" If you mean by that that you intend to forget our wonderful Queen Mab, all I have to say is—the Lord help you in your purpose," Crammon answered.

" One holds fast and clings because one fears the step into the unknown," Christian said.

Crammon was silent for a few minutes and wrinkled his forehead. Then he cleared his throat and asked: " Did you ever hear about homœopathy? I'll explain to you what is meant by it. It means curing like with like. If for instance some food has disagreed with you violently, and I give you a drug that would, in a state of health, have sickened you even more violently than your food—that would be a homœopathic treatment."

" So you want to cure me? " Christian asked, and smiled. " From what and with what? "

Crammon moved his chair nearer to Christian's, laid a hand on his knees, and whispered astutely: " I've got something for you, dear boy. I've made an exquisite find. There's a woman in your horoscope, as the sooth-sayers put it. Some one is yearning for you, is immensely taken with you, and dying of impatience to know you. And it's something quite different, a new type, something prickling and comical, indeterminate, sensitive, a little graceless and small and not beautiful, but enormously charming. She comes from the bourgeoisie at its most obese, but she struggles with both hands and feet against the fate of being a pearl in a trough. There's your chance for employment, distraction, and refreshment. It won't be a long affair,—an interlude of her holidays, but instructive, and, in the homœopathic sense, sure to work a cure. For look you: Ariel, she is a miracle, a star, the food of the gods. You can't live on such nourishment; you need bread. Descend, my son, from the high tower where you still grasp after the *miraculum cœli* that once flamed on your bosom. Put it out of your mind;

descend, and be contented with mortality. To-night at seven in the dining-room of the Hotel de la Plage. Is it a bargain? "

Christian laughed, and got up. On the table stood a vase filled with white pinks. He took out one of the flowers, and fastened it into Crammon's button-hole.

" Is it a bargain or not? " Crammon asked severely.

" No, dear friend, there's nothing in that for me," Christian answered, laughing more heartily. " Keep your find to your-self."

The veins on Crammon's forehead swelled. " But I've prom-ised to bring you, and you mustn't leave me in the lurch." He was in a rage. " I don't deserve such treatment, after all the slights which you have put on me for months. You give rights to an obscure vagabond that astonish the whole world, and you cast aside heartlessly an old and proved friend. That does hurt and embitter and enrage one. I'm through."

" Calm yourself, Bernard," said Christian, and stooped to pick up some blossoms that had fallen on the floor. And as he put back the flowers into the vase, there came to him the vision of Amadeus Voss' white face, showing his bleeding soul and paralyzed by desire and renunciation, even as it was turned toward the fat, morose Walloon woman. " I don't comprehend your stubbornness," he continued. " Why won't you let me be? Don't you know that I bring misfortune to all who love me? "

Crammon was startled. Despite Christian's equivocal smile, he felt a sudden twinge of superstitious fear. " Idiotic! " he growled. He arose and took his hat, and still tried to wring from Christian a promise for the evening. At that moment a knock sounded at the door, and Amadeus Voss entered.

" I beg your pardon," he stammered, and looked shyly at Crammon, who had at once assumed an attitude of hostility. " I merely wanted to ask you, Christian, whether we are going to leave. Shall the packing be done? We must know what to do."

Crammon was furious. " Fancy the scoundrel taking such a tone," he thought. He could hardly force himself to assume the grimace of courtesy that became inevitable when Christian, quite hesitatingly, introduced them to each other.

Amadeus bowed like an applicant for some humble office. His eyes behind their lenses clung to Crammon, like the valves of an exhaust pump. He found Crammon repulsive at once; but he thought it advisable not only to hide this feeling but to play the part of obsequiousness. His hatred was so immediate and so violent, that he was afraid of showing it too soon, and stripping himself of some chance of translating it into action.

Crammon sought points of attack. He treated Voss with contempt, looked at him as though he were a wad of clothes against the wall, neither answered him nor listened to what he said, deliberately prolonged his stay, and paid no attention to Christian's nervousness. Voss continued to play the part he had selected. He agreed and bowed, rubbed the toe of one of his boots against the sole of the other, picked up Crammon's stick when the latter dropped it; but as he seemed determined not to be the first to yield, Crammon at last took pity on the silent wonder and torment in Christian's face. He waved his well-gloved left hand and withdrew. He seemed to swell up in his rage like a frog. " Softly, Bernard," he said to himself; " guard your dignity, and do not step into the ordure at your feet. Trust in the Lord who said: Vengeance is mine." He met a little dog on his path, and administered a kick to it, so that the beast howled and scurried into an open cellar.

Across the table Christian and Voss faced each other in silence. Voss pulled a flower from the vase, and shredded its calyx with his thin fingers. " So that was Herr von Crammon," he murmured. " I don't know why I feel like laughing. But I can't help it. I do." And he giggled softly to himself.

" We leave to-morrow," said Christian, held a handkerchief

to his mouth, and breathed the delicate perfume that aroused in him so many tender and slowly fading images.

Voss took a blossom, tore it in two, gazed tensely at the parts, and said: " Fibre by fibre, cell by cell. I am done with this life of sloth and parasitism. I want to cut up the bodies of men and anatomize corpses. Perhaps one can get at the seat of weakness and vulgarity. One must seek life at its source and death at its root. The talent of an anatomist stirs within me. Once I wanted to be a great preacher like Savonarola; but it's a reckless thing to try in these days. One had better stick to men's bodies; their souls would bring one to despair."

" I believe one must work," Christian answered softly. " It does not matter at what. But one must work." He turned toward the window. The round, white cloud had vanished; the silver sea had sucked it up.

" Have you come to that conclusion? " Voss jeered. " I've known it long. The way to hell is paved with work; and only hell can burn us clean. It is well that you have learned that much."

III

Crammon and Johanna Schöntag were sitting in a drawing-room of the hotel. They had had dinner together. Johanna's companion, Fräulein Grabmeier, had already retired.

" You must be patient, Rumpelstilzkin," said Crammon. " I'm sorry to say that he hasn't bitten yet. The bait is still in the water."

" I'll be patient, my lord," said Johanna, in her slightly rough, boyish voice, and a gleam of merriment, in which charm and ugliness were strangely blended, passed over her face. " I don't find it very hard either. Everything is sure to go wrong with me in the end. If ever unexpectedly a wish of mine is fulfilled, and something I looked forward to does happen, I'm as wretched as I can be, because it's never as nice as I thought it would be. The best thing for me, therefore, is to be disappointed."

" You're a problematic soul," said Crammon musingly.

Johanna gave a comical sigh. " I advise you, dear friend and protector, to get rid of me by return post." She stretched her thin little neck with an intentionally bizarre movement. " I simply interfere with the traffic. I'm a personified evil omen. At my birth a lady by the name of Cassandra appeared, and I needn't tell you the disagreeable things that have been said of her. You remember how when we were at target practice at Ashburnhill I hit the bull's-eye. Everybody was amazed, yourself included; but I more so than any one, because it was pure, unadulterated chance. The rifle had actually gone off before I had taken aim. Fate gives me such small and worthless gifts, in order to seem friendly and lull me into security. But I'm not to be deceived. Ugh! A nun, a nun! " she interrupted herself. Her eyes became very large, as she looked into the garden where an Ursuline nun was passing by. Then she crossed her arms over her bosom, and counted with extraordinary readiness: " Seven, six, five, four, three, two, one." Then she laughed, and showed two rows of marvellous teeth.

" Is it your custom to do that whenever a nun appears? " Crammon asked. His interest in superstitions was aroused.

" It's the proper ritual to follow. But she was gone before I came to one, and that augurs no good. By the way, dear baron, your sporting terminology sounds suspicious. What does that mean: ' he hasn't bitten yet; the bait is still in the water ' ? I beg you to restrain yourself. I'm an unprotected girl, and wholly dependent on your delicate chivalry. If you shake my tottering self-confidence by any more reminiscences of the sporting world, I'll have to telegraph for two berths on the Vienna train. For myself and Fräulein Grabmeier, of course."

She loved these daring little implications, from which she

could withdraw quite naïvely. Crammon burst into belated laughter, and that fact stirred her merriment too.

She was very watchful, and nothing escaped her attentive eyes. She took a burning interest in the characters and actions of people. She leaned toward Crammon and they whispered together, for he could tell a story about each form and face that emerged from the crowd. The chronicle of international biography and scandal of which he was master was inexhaustible. If ever his memory failed him, he invented or poetized a little. He had everything at his tongue's end—disputes concerning inheritances, family quarrels, illegitimate descent, adulteries, relationships of all sorts. Johanna listened to him with a smile. She peered at all the tables and carefully observed every uncommon detail. She picked up and pinned down, as an entomologist does his beetles, any chance remark or roguish expression, any silliness or peculiarity of any of these unconscious actors of the great world or the half world.

Suddenly the pupils of her greyish blue eyes grew very large, and her lips curved in a bow of childlike delight. "Who is that?" she whispered, and thrust her chin out a little in the direction of a door at Crammon's back. But she at once knew instinctively who it was. She would have known it without the general raising of heads and softening of voices, of which she became aware.

Crammon turned around and saw Eva amid a group of ladies and gentlemen. He arose, waited until Eva glanced in his direction, and then bowed very low. Eva drew back a little. She had not seen him since the days of Denis Lay. She thought a little, and nodded distantly. Then she recognized him, kicked back her train with an incomparable grace, and, speaking in every line before her lips moved, went up to him.

Johanna had arisen too. Eva remarked the little figure. She gave Crammon to understand that he had a duty toward his companion, and that she would not refuse an introduction to the unknown girl, on whose face enthusiasm and homage were so touchingly to be seen. Crammon introduced Johanna in his most ceremonious manner. Johanna grew pale and red and curtsied. She seemed to herself suddenly so negligible that she was overcome with shame. Then she tore off the three yellow roses at her corsage, and held them out to Eva with a sudden and yet timid gesture. Eva liked this impulse. She felt its uniqueness and veracity, and therefore knew its value.

IV

Christian and Amadeus wandered across the Quai Kokerill in Antwerp.

A great transatlantic liner lay, silent and empty, at the pier. The steerage passengers waited at its side for the hour of their admission. They were Polish peasants, Russian Jews, men and women, young ones and aged ones, children and sucklings. They crouched on the cold stones or on their dirty bundles. They were themselves dirty, neglected, weary, dully brooding—a melancholy and confused mass of rags and human bodies.

The mighty globe of the sun rolled blood-red and quivering over the waters.

Christian and Amadeus stopped. After a while they went on, but Christian desired to turn back, and they did so. At a crossing near the emigrants' camp, a line of ten or twenty donkey-carts cut off the road. The carts looked liked bisected kegs on wheels, and were filled with smoked mackerels.

"Buy mackerels!" the cart-drivers cried. "Buy mackerels!" And they cracked their whips.

A few of the emigrants approached and stared hungrily; they consulted with others, who were already looking for coins in their pockets, until finally a few determined ones proceeded to make a purchase.

Then Christian said to Voss: "Let us buy the fish and distribute them. What do you think?"

Amadeus was ill pleased. He answered. " Do as you wish. Great lords must have their little pleasures." He felt uncomfortable amid the gathering crowd.

Christian turned to one of the hucksters. It was difficult to make the man understand normal French, but gradually he succeeded. The huckster summoned the others, and there followed excited chatter and gesticulations. Various sums were named and considered and rejected. This process bored Christian; it threatened to be endless. He offered a sum that represented a considerable increase over the highest price named, and handed his wallet to Amadeus that the men might be paid. Then he said to the increasing throng of emigrants in German: " The fish are yours."

A few understood his words, and conveyed their meaning to the others. Timidly they ventured forward. A woman, whose skin was yellow as a lemon from jaundice, was the first to touch a fish. Soon hundreds came. From all sides they brought baskets, pots, nets, sacks. A few old men kept the crowd in order. One of these, who wore a flowing white beard and a long Jewish coat, bowed down thrice before Christian. His forehead almost touched the earth.

A sudden impulse compelled Christian to see in person to the just distribution of the fish. He turned up his sleeves, and with his delicate hands threw the greasy, malodourous fish into the vessels held out for them. He laughed as he soiled his fingers. The hucksters and some idle onlookers laughed too. They thought him a crazy, young Englishman out for a lark. Suddenly his gorge rose at the odour of the fish, and even more at the odour of these people. He smelled their clothes and their breath, and gagged at the thought of their teeth and fingers, their hair and shoes. A morbid compulsion forced him to think of their naked bodies, and he shuddered at the idea of their flesh. So he stopped, and slipped away into the twilight.

His hands still reeked of the smoked fish. He walked

through the streets that had had nothing to do with his adventure and the night seemed empty.

Amadeus Voss had escaped. He waited in front of the hotel. There the line of motor cars had gathered that was to accompany Eva on her journey to Germany. Among the travellers were Crammon and Johanna Schöntag.

v

In October the weather turned hot on the Rio de la Plata. All day one had to stay in the house. If one opened a window, living fire seemed to stream in. Once Letitia fainted, when she wanted to air her stuffy room, and opened one of the wooden shutters.

The only spot that offered some shade and coolness toward evening was an avenue of palms beside the river. Sometimes, during the brief twilight, Letitia and her young sister-in-law Esmeralda would steal away to that place. Their road passed the ranchos, the wretched cave-like huts in which the native workmen lived.

Once Letitia saw the people of the ranchos merrily feasting and in their best garments. She asked for the reason, and was told that a child had died. " They always celebrate when some one dies," Esmeralda told her. " How sad must their lives be to make them so in love with death."

The avenue of palms was forbidden ground. When darkness came, the bushes rustled, and furtive men slipped back and forth. Not long before the mounted police had caught a sailor here who was wanted for a murder in Galveston. Somehow Letitia dreamed of him. She was sure he had killed his man through jealousy and bore the marks of a beautiful tragedy.

One evening she had met in this spot a young naval officer, who was a guest on a neighbouring estate. Letitia exchanged glances with him, and from that time on he sought some way of approaching her. But she was like a prisoner, or

like a Turkish woman in a harem. So she determined to
outwit her guards; she really fell in love with the young
officer. Her imagination made an heroic figure of him, and
she began to long for him.

The heat increased. Letitia could not sleep at night. The
mosquitoes hummed sweetishly, and she cried like a little child.
By day she locked herself in her room, stripped off her
clothes, and lay down on the cold tiles.

Once she was lying thus with arms outstretched. "I'm
like an enchanted princess," she thought, "in an enchanted
castle."

Some one knocked at the door, and she heard Stephen's
voice calling her. Idly she raised her head, and from under
her heavy lids gazed down at her naked body. "What a
bore it is," she thought, "what a terrible bore always to be
with the same man. I want others too." She did not answer, and let her head droop, and rubbed her glowing cheek
against the warm skin of her upper arm. It pleased the master of the harem out there to beg for admission; but Letitia
did not open the door.

After a while she heard a tumult in the yard—laughter,
the cracking of whips, the report of rifles, and the cries of
beasts in torment. She jumped up, slipped into a silk dressing gown, opened the window that gave on the verandah, and
peered out.

Stephen had tied together the tails of two cats by means
of a long fuse. Along the fuse were fastened explosive bits
of firework. The hissing little rockets singed the cats' fur,
and the glowing cord burned into their flesh. The cats tumbled about in their agony and howled. Stephen goaded them
and followed them. His brothers, bent over the balustrade,
roared with delight. Two Indians, grave and silent, watched
from the gate.

Stephen had, of course, counted on Letitia's opening the
door in her curiosity. A few great leaps, and he was beside

her. Esmeralda, who was in the plot, had at once faced Letitia and prevented her from locking the door. White with rage, and with raised fist, he stormed across the threshold. She fell to her knees, and hid her face in her hands.

"Why do you beat me?" she moaned, in horror and surprise. But he did not touch her.

His teeth gnashed. "To teach you to obey."

She sobbed. "Be careful! It's not only me you're hurting now!"

"Damnation, what are you saying?" He stared at her crouching figure.

"You're hurting two now." Letitia enjoyed fooling him. Her tears were now tears of pity for herself.

"Woman, is that true?" he asked. Letitia peered furtively between her fingers, and thought mockingly: "It's like the last act of a cheap opera." She nodded with a gesture of pain, and determined to deceive him with the naval officer.

Stephen gave a howl of triumph, danced about, threw himself down beside her, and kissed her arms, her shoulders, and her neck. At the windows and doors appeared Doña Barbara, Esmeralda, Stephen's brothers, and the servants. He lifted Letitia on his strong shoulders, and carried her about on the verandah. He roared his orders: a feast was to be prepared, an ox slaughtered, champagne to be put on ice.

Letitia had no qualms of conscience. She was glad to have made a fool of him.

When old Gunderam learned the cause of the rejoicing in his house, he chuckled to himself. "Fooled all the same, my sly lawyer man. In spite of the written agreement, you won't get the Escurial, not for a good while, even if she has a whole litter." With an unappetizing, broken little comb he smoothed his iron grey beard, and poured eau de Cologne on his head, until his hair, which was still thick, dripped.

But, strangely enough, the lie that Letitia had told in her terror turned out to be the truth. In a few days she

was sure. Secretly she was amazed. Every morning she
stood before the mirror, and looked at herself with a strange
respect and a subtle horror. But she was unchanged. Her
mood became gently melancholy, and she threw a kiss to
her image in the glass.

Since they were now afraid of crossing her wishes, she was
permitted to attend a ball given by Señor and Señora Küchel-
bäcker, and it was there that she made the formal acquaintance of the naval lieutenant, Friedrich Pestel.

VI

Felix Imhof and the painter Weikhardt met at the exhibition of the " secessionists " in Munich. For a while they
strolled through the rooms, and looked at the paintings;
then they went out on the terrace, and sat down at a table
that commanded a view of the park.

It was in the early afternoon, and the odours of oil and
turpentine from within blended with the fragrance of the
sun-warmed plants.

Imhof crossed his long legs, and yawned affectedly. " I'm
going to leave this admirable home of art and letters for
some months," he declared. " I'm going to accompany the
minister of colonial affairs to South West Africa. I'm anxious to see how things are going there. Those people need
looking after. Then, too, it's a new experience, and there
will be hunting."

Weikhardt was utterly self-absorbed. He was full of his
own annoyances, his inner and outer conflicts, and therefore
spoke only of himself. " I am to copy a cycle by Luini for
the old Countess Matuschka," he said. " She has several
blank walls in her castle in Galicia, and she wants tapestries
for them. But the old creature is close as the bark on the
tree, and her bargaining is repulsive."

Imhof also pursued his own thoughts. " I've read a lot
about Stanhope recently," he said. " A tremendous fellow,

modern through and through, reporter and conquistador at the same time. The blacks called him the ' cliff-breaker.' It makes one's mouth water. Simply tremendous! "

Weikhardt continued: " But I dare say I'll have to accept the commission. I've come to the end of my tether. It'll be good to see the old Italians again, too. In Milan there's a Tintoretto that's adorable. I'm on the track of a secret. I'm doing things that will count. The other day I finished a picture, a simple landscape, and took it to an acquaintance of mine. He has a rather exquisite room, and there we hung it. The walls had grey hangings, and the furnishings were in black and gold. He's a rich man and wanted to buy the picture. But when I saw how much he liked it, and saw, too, the delicate, melancholy harmony of its colours with the tints of the room, I felt a sudden flash of encouragement. I couldn't bear to talk money, and I simply gave him the thing. He accepted it quietly enough, but he continued saying: ' How damned good it is! ' "

" It'll take my thoughts off myself, this little trip to the Southern Hemisphere," said Imhof. " I'm not exactly favoured of fortune just now. To be frank—everything's in the deuce of a mess. My best horse went to smash, my favourite dog died, my wife took French leave of me, and my friends avoid me—I don't know why. My business is progressing backward, and all my speculations end in losses. But, after all, what does it matter? I say to myself: Never say die, old boy! Here's the great, beautiful world, and all the splendour and variety of life. If you complain, you deserve no better. My sandwich has dropped into the mud. All right; I must get a fresh one. Whoever goes to war must expect wounds. The main thing is to stick to your flag. The main thing is faith—quite simple faith."

It was still a question which of the two would first turn his attention from himself, and hear his companion's voice. Weikhardt, whose eyes had grown sombre, spoke again: " O this dumb loneliness in a studio, with one's hundred failures, and the ghosts of one's thousand hours of despair! I have a chance to marry, and I'm going to take it, too. The girl has no money, to be sure, but she has a heart. She's not afraid of my poverty, and comprehends the necessary quixotism of an artist's life. She comes of a Protestant family of very liberal traditions, but two years ago she became a Catholic. When I first met her I was full of suspicion, and assumed all sorts of reasons for her step except the simple and human ones. It's very difficult to see the simple and the human things, and still more difficult to do them. Gradually I understood what it means—to believe! and I understood what is to be reverenced in such faith. It is faith itself that is sacred, not that in which the faith is placed. It doesn't matter what one has faith in—a book, a beast, a man, a star, a god. But it must be pure faith—immovable and unconquerable. Yes, I quite agree with you—we need simple faith."

So they had found each other through a word. "When do I get my picture, your Descent from the Cross?" Imhof inquired.

Weikhardt did not answer the question. As he talked on, his smooth, handsome, boyish face assumed the aspect of a quarrelsome old man's. Yet his voice remained gentle and slow, and his bearing phlegmatic. "Humanity to-day has lost its faith," he continued. "Faith has leaked out like water from a cracked glass. Our age is tyrannised by machinery: it is a mob rule without parallel. Who will save us from machinery and from business? The golden calf has gone mad. The spirit of man kowtows to a warehouse. Our watchword is to be up and doing. We manufacture Christianity, a renaissance, culture, et cetera. If it's not quite the real thing, yet it will serve. Everything tends toward the external—toward expression, line, arabesque, gesture, mask. Everything is stuck on a hoarding and lit by electric lamps.

Everything is the very latest, until something still later begins to function. Thus the soul flees, goodness ceases, the form breaks, and reverence dies. Do you feel no horror at the generation that is growing up? The air is like that before the flood."

"Create, O artist, and don't philosophize," Imhof said gently.

Weikhardt was shamed a little. "It's true," he said, "we have no means of knowing the goal of it all. But there are symptoms, typical cases that leave little room for hope. Did you hear the story of the suicide of the German-American Scharnitzer? He was pretty well known among artists. He used to go to the studios himself, and buy whatever took his fancy. He never bargained. Sometimes he would be accompanied by a daughter of eighteen, a girl of angelic beauty. Her name was Sybil, and he used to buy pictures for her. She was especially fond of still-life and flower pieces. The man had been in California and made millions in lumber. Then he returned to the fatherland to give the girl an atmosphere of calm and culture. Sybil was his one thought, his hope, his idol and his world. He had been married but a short time. His wife, it is said, ran away from him. All that a life of feverish activity had left him of deep feeling and of hope for the future was centred in this child. He saw in her one girl in a thousand, a little saint. And so indeed she seemed—extraordinarily dainty, proud and ethereal. One would not have dared to touch her with one's finger. When the two were together, a delightful sense of harmony radiated from them. The father, especially, seemed happy. His voluntary death caused all the more consternation. No one suspected the motive; it was assumed that he had suffered a moment of madness. But he left behind him a letter to an American friend which explained everything. He had been indisposed one day, and had had to stay in bed. Sybil had invited several girl friends to tea, and the little com-

pany was in a room at the other end of their suite. But
all the doors between were open, even the last was slightly
ajar, so that the murmur of the girls' voices came to him
inarticulately. A sudden curiosity seized him to know what
they were saying. He got up, slipped into a dressing gown,
went softly through the intervening rooms, and listened at
the door. The conversation was about the future of these
girls—the possibilities of love, happiness, and marriage. Each
gave her ideas. Finally it was Sybil's turn to speak her
thoughts. At first she refused; but they urged her again
and again. She said she took no interest in emotions of any
sort; she didn't yearn for love; she wasn't able to feel even
gratitude to any one. What she expected of marriage was
simply liberation from a galling yoke. She wanted a man
who could give her all that life held—boundless luxury and
high social position—and who, moreover, would be abjectly
at her feet. That, she said, was her program, and she
intended to carry it out too. The other girls fell silent.
None answered. But that hour poisoned the father's soul.
This cynicism, uttered by the pure and spiritual voice of
the child he adored and thought a miracle of depth and
sweetness, the child on whom he had wasted all he was and
had, plunged him into an incurable melancholy, and caused
him finally to end his life."

" My dear fellow," cried Imhof, and waved his arm, " that
man wasn't a lumber merchant, he was a minor poet."

" It's possible that he was," Weikhardt replied, and smiled;
" quite possible. What does it alter? I admire a man who
cannot survive the destruction of all his ideals. It's better
than to be a cliff-breaker, I assure you. Most people haven't
any ideals to be destroyed. They adapt themselves end-
lessly, and become vulgar and sterile." Again his eyes grew
sombre, and he added, half to himself: " Sometimes I dream
of one who neither rises nor falls, of one who walks on

earth whole and unchangeable, unswerving and unadaptable.
Perfectly unadaptable. It is of such an one that I
dream."

Imhof jumped up, and smoothed his coat. " Talk, talk! "
he rattled, in the disagreeable military tone that he assumed
in his moments of pseudo-virility. " Talk won't improve
things." He passed his arm through Weikhardt's, and as
they left the terrace, which had been gradually filling with
other guests, he recited, boldly, unashamed, and in the same
tone, the alcaic stanza of Hölderlin:

" Still man will take up arms against all who breathe;
　Compelled by pride and dread he consumes himself
　　in conflict, and destroys the lovely
　　　Flower of his peace that is brief of blooming."

VII

On their first evening in Hamburg, Crammon rented a
box in the playhouse, and invited Christian, Johanna Schöntag, and Herr Livholm, one of the directors of the Lloyd,
to be his guests. He had made the latter's acquaintance in
the hotel where he had gone to pay Eva a visit of welcome.
He had liked the man, who cut a good figure, and so he had
added him to the party in order, as he put it, to keep the
atmosphere normal by the presence of an entirely neutral
person.

" Social skill," he was accustomed to say, " is not unlike
skill in cookery and serving. Between two heavy, rich dishes
there must be one like foam that stimulates the palate quite
superficially. Otherwise the meal has no style."

The play was a mediocre comedy, and Christian was frankly
bored. Crammon thought it his duty to show a condescending and muffled amusement, and now and then he gave Christian a gentle poke, to persuade him also to show some appreciation of the performance. Johanna was the only one who
was genuinely amused. The source of her amusement was

an actor to whom a serious rôle had been assigned, but who talked with such silly affectation and false importance that every time he appeared she had to hold her lacy handkerchief to her lips to smother her laughter.

Occasionally Christian gave the girl a far and estranged glance. She wasn't either agreeable or the reverse; he did not know what to make of her. This feeling of his had not changed since he had first seen her during the journey in Eva's company.

She felt the coldness of his glance. Her merriment did not vanish; but on the lower part of her face appeared a scarcely perceptible shadow of disappointment.

As though seeking for help, she turned to Christian. "The man is terribly funny, don't you think so?" It was characteristic of her to end a question with a negative interrogation.

"He's certainly worth seeing," Christian agreed politely.

The door of the box opened, and Voss entered. He was faultlessly dressed for the occasion; but no one had expected or invited him. They looked at him in astonishment. He bowed calmly and without embarrassment, stood quite still, and gave his attention to the stage.

Crammon looked at Christian. The latter shrugged his shoulders. After a while Crammon arose, and with sarcastic courtesy pointed to his seat. Voss shook his head in friendly refusal, but immediately thereafter assumed once more his air of humility and abjectness. He stammered: "I was in the stalls and looked up. I thought there was no harm in paying a visit." Suddenly Crammon went out, and was heard quarrelling with the usher. Johanna had become serious, and looked down at the audience. Christian, as though to ward off disagreeable things, ducked his shoulders a little. The people in the near-by seats became indignant at the noise Crammon was making. Herr Livholm felt that the proper atmosphere had hardly been preserved.

Amadeus Voss alone showed himself insensitive to the situation.

He stood behind Johanna, and thought: " The hair of this woman has a fragrance that turns one dizzy." At the end of the act he withdrew, and did not return.

Late at night, when he had him alone, Crammon vented his rage on Christian. " I'll shoot him down like a mad dog, if he tries that sort of thing again! What does the fellow think? I'm not accustomed to such manners. Damned gallow's bird—where'd he grow up? Oh, my prophetic soul! I always distrusted people with spectacles. Why don't you tell him to go to hell? In the course of my sinful life, I've come in contact with all kinds of people; I know the best and I know the dregs; but this fellow is a new type. Quite new, by God! I'll have to take a bromide, or I won't be able to sleep."

" I believe you are unjust, Bernard," answered Christian, with lowered eyes. But his face was stern, reserved, and cold.

VIII

Amadeus Voss submitted the following plan to Christian: to go to Berlin, first as an unmatriculated student, and later to prepare himself for the state examination in medicine.

Christian nodded approvingly, and added that he intended to go to Berlin shortly too. Voss walked up and down in the room. Then he asked brusquely: " What am I to live on? Am I to address envelopes? Or apply for stipends? If you intend to withdraw your friendship and assistance, say so frankly. I've learned to wade through the mud. The new kind won't offer more resistance than the old."

Christian was thoroughly surprised. A week ago, in Holland, he had given Amadeus ten thousand francs. " How much will you need? " he asked.

"Board, lodging, clothes, books . . ." Voss went over the items, and his expression was that of one who formulates demands and uses the tone of request only as a matter of courtesy. "I'll be frugal."

"I shall order two thousand marks a month to be sent you," Christian said, with an air of aversion. The impudent demand for money pained him. Possession weighed upon him like a mountain. He could not get his arms free nor lift his chest, and the weight grew heavier and heavier.

In a bowl of chrysolite on the table lay a scarf-pin with one large, black pearl. Voss, whose hands always groped for some occupation, had taken it up, and held it between his thumb and index finger against the light. "Do you want the pin?" Christian asked. "Take it," he persuaded Amadeus, who was hesitating. "I really don't care about it."

Voss approached the mirror, and with a curious smile stuck the pin into his cravat.

When Christian was left alone, he stood for a while quite lost in thought. Then he sat down, and wrote to his manager at Christian's Rest. He wrote in his lanky script and his no less awkward style. "My dear Herr Borkowski:— I have determined to sell Christian's Rest, together with all furnishings and objects of art, as well as the park, woods, and farms. I herewith commission you to find a capable and honest real estate dealer, who might telegraph me any favourable offers. You know people of that sort, and need merely drive over to Frankfort. Have the kindness to settle the matter as quietly as possible. No advertisements are to appear in the press."

Then he wrote a second letter to the manager of his racing stable at Waldleiningen. To write this he had to do more violence to his heart than the first had cost him, for he saw constantly fixed upon him the gentle or spirited eyes of the noble animals. He wrote: "My dear Herr Schaller:—

I have determined to discontinue my racing stable. The horses are to be sold at auction or quietly to fanciers. I should prefer the latter method, and I suppose you share that feeling. Baron Deidinger of Deidingshausen was at one time much interested in Columbus and the mare Lovely. Inquire of him whether he wants them. Admirable and Bride o' the Wind could be offered either to Prince Pless or Herr von Strathmann. Have my friend Denis Lay's Excelsior sent to Baden-Baden, and boarded temporarily in the stables of Count Treuberg. I don't wish him to remain at Waldleiningen alone."

When he had sealed the letters, he sighed with relief. He rang, and gave the letters to his valet. The latter had turned to go, when Christian called him back. " I'm very sorry to have to give you notice, Wilhelm," he said. " I'm going to attend to myself hereafter."

The man could not trust his ears. He had been with Christian for three years, and was genuinely devoted to him.

" I'm sorry, but it's necessary," said Christian, looked past the man, and had almost the same strange smile with which he had watched Amadeus Voss at the mirror putting the black pearl pin into his cravat.

IX

Crammon asserted that Amadeus Voss was paying his attentions to Johanna Schöntag. Johanna was annoyed, and tapped him with her long gloves. " I congratulate you on your conquest, Rumpelstilzkin," Crammon teased her. " To have a monster like that in leash is no small achievement. I should advise muzzling the monster, however. What do you think, Christian, wouldn't you advise a muzzle, too? "

" A muzzle? " answered Christian. " Yes, if it would keep people from talking. So many talk too much."

Crammon bit his lips. The reproof struck him as harsh.

Somewhere beneath the downs of life on which he lay and
enjoyed himself, there was, evidently, a stone. The stone
hurt. He sought for it, but the softness of the down calmed
him again, and he forgot his pain.

" I was sitting in the breakfast room, and waiting for Madame Sorel," Johanna began in a voice whose every shading
and inflection sought to woo Christian's ear, " when Herr
Voss came in and marched straight up to me. ' What does
that bad man want of me? ' I asked myself. He asked me,
as though we'd been bosom friends for years, whether I didn't
want to go with him to St. Paul's to hear the famous itinerant
preacher Jacobsen. I couldn't help laughing, and he stalked
away insulted. But this afternoon, as I was leaving the hotel,
he seemed suddenly to spring from the earth, and invited
me to a trip around the harbour. He had rented a motor
launch, and was looking for a companion. He had the same
gruff familiarity, and when he left he was quite as insulted
as before. And you call that paying attentions? I felt much
more as though he were going to drag me off and murder
me. But perhaps that's only his manner." She laughed.

" You're the only person, at all events, whom he distin-
guishes by observing at all," Crammon said, with the same
mockery.

" Or the only one whom he considers his equal," Johanna
said, with a childlike frown.

Christian was wondering: " Why does she laugh so often?
Why are her hands so pudgy and so very pink? " Johanna
felt his disapproval, and was as though paralysed. And yet
Christian felt himself drawn toward her by some hidden
power.

Why should he resist? Why be so ceremonious? Such was
his thought, as Johanna arose, and he, with unobtrusive glances,
observed her graceful form that still possessed the flexibility
of immaturity. He saw the nape of her slender neck, in which
were expressed both the weakness of her will and the fineness

of her temper. He knew these signs; he had often been guided by them and used them.

Crammon, massive and magnificent in a great easy chair, spoke with some emphasis of Eva's appearance on the morrow. The whole city was in a state of expectancy. But Christian and Johanna had suddenly become truly aware of one another.

" Are you coming along? " Christian turned carelessly, and with a sense of boredom, to Crammon.

" Yes, my boy, let us eat! " Crammon cried. He called Hamburg the Paradise of Saint Bernard, concerning whom, as his patron saint and namesake, he had instituted especial investigations, and who, according to him, had been a mighty trencherman during his lifetime at Tours.

A frightened, subtle, and very feminine smile hovered about Johanna's lips. As she preceded the two men, the motions of her dainty body expressed a vague oppression of the spirit, and at the same time a humorous rebellion against her own un-freedom.

x

Amadeus Voss knew that he had no one's sympathy, no one's except Christian's. And him he suspected, watching him, weighing and analysing his words and actions. In his terror of hypocrisy and treachery, he practised both himself. Nothing healed or convinced or reconciled him. Least of all did he pardon Christian the fact that the latter's glance and presence had the effect of subduing him. His bitterness moaned from his very dreams.

He read in the Scriptures: " There was a certain house-holder, which planted a vineyard, and hedged it round about, and digged a winepress in it, and built a tower, and let it out to husbandmen, and went into a far country: and when the time of the fruit drew near, he sent his servants to the husbandmen that they might receive the fruits of it. And the husbandmen took his servants, and beat one, and killed another, and stoned another. Again he sent other servants, more than the first, and they did unto them likewise. But last of all, he sent unto them his son, saying, They will reverence my son. But when the husbandmen saw the son, they said among themselves, This is the heir; come, let us kill him, and let us seize on his inheritance. And they caught him, and cast him out of the vineyard, and slew him."

Sometimes he would not leave Christian's side for hours. He would study his gestures and the expressions of his counte-nance, and all these perceptions fed the corrosive fire in his brain. For this was the heir! Then he would flee and bruise and stamp upon his very soul, until his consciousness of guilt cast him down into the very dust. He would return, and his demeanour would be a silent confession: " I can thrive only in your presence." It seemed to him that this silence of his was like a cry; but it was not heard, and so his brother seemed again to become his foe. Thus he kept passing from darkness, through fires and fumes, back into the dark-ness.

He suffered from his own embarrassment and importunate-ness. In the midst of luxury and plenty, into which he had been transferred by a fabulous turn of fortune, he suffered from the memories of his former poverty, still felt how it had bound and throttled him, and still rebelled against what was gone. He could not freely take what was given him, but closed his eyes, and shuddered with both desire and a pang of conscience. He would not look upon the pattern of his web of life. He turned its texture around, and brooded over the significance of the intricately knotted threads. And there was no human relationship which did not rouse his suspicion, no harmless conversation in which he did not seek a sting directed toward himself, no face that did not feed his hatred, no beauty whose counter part of ugliness he did not see. To him everything turned to poison and decay, all blossoms became noxious weeds. all velvet a Nessus shirt. all light an evil smouldering, every stimulus a wound: on every wall he saw the flaming letters, *mene tekel upharsim.*

He could not yield himself or conquer the stubbornness of his heart. With the object of his desire in his very hands, his envy burned on. Whatever had once humiliated him spurred his vengefulness through retrospection. Chastisements which his father had inflicted distorted the old man's image beyond the grave; his fellow pupils in the seminary had once strewn pepper into his coffee, and he could not forget it; he could not forget the expression on the face of Adeline Ribbeck with which she had given him his first month's salary in a closed envelope; he remembered the contempt and contumely of hundreds, who had inflicted upon him their revenge for the oppression or degradation which they themselves had endured. He could not conquer these things nor forgive fate. The marks that had been burned into his flesh throbbed like new wounds.

But at other times he would cast himself into the dust in prayer and in great need of forgiveness. Religious scruples plagued him into remorse; he panted for an hour's release from consciousness, judged himself with cruel severity, and condemned himself to ascetic practices.

And these hurled him into the other extreme of a wild, undiscriminating, and senseless dissipation and a mad waste of money. He could no longer resist the excitement of gambling, and fell into the hands of sharpers, drifted into loathsome dives, where he acted the part of a wealthy man and an aristocrat in incognito, for he desired to test this human mask and prove its worthlessness to himself. Since his companions took him seriously in this rôle, which filled his own mind with shame and despair, he took his high losses with apparent calm, and overlooked the open cheating. One evening the den in which he happened to be was raided by the police, and he escaped by a hair's breadth. One creature clung to him, frightened him with possible dangers ahead, threatened exposure, and wrung from him a considerable sum of hush money.

He became the prey of cocottes. He bought them jewels and frocks and instituted nightly revels. In his eyes they were outcasts that he used as a famishing man might slake his thirst at a mud puddle with no clean water within reach. And he was brutally frank with them. He paid them to endure his contempt. They were surprised, resisted only his most infamous abuses, and laughed at his unconquerable traits of the churchly hypocrite. Once he remained alone with a girl who was young and pretty. He had blindfolded himself. But suddenly he fled as though the furies were at his heels.

Thrice he had set the date for his departure and as many times had put it off. The image of Johanna had joined that of Eva in his soul, and both raged in his brain. Both belonged to an unattainable world. Yet Johanna seemed less alien; she might conceivably hear his plea. Eva and her beauty were like a strident jeer at all he was. He had heard so much and read so much of her art that he determined to await her appearance, in order (as he told Christian) to form a judgment of his own, and be no longer at the mercy of those who fed her on mere adulation and brazen flattery.

The audience was in full evening dress. Amadeus sat next to Christian in the magnificent and radiant hall, in which had gathered royal and princely persons, the senators of the free city, the heads of the official and financial world, and representatives of every valley and city of Germany. Christian had bought seats near the stage. Crammon, who was an expert in matters of artistic perspective, had preferred the first row in the balcony. With him were Johanna and Botho von Thüngen, to whom he had emphatically explained that the play of the dancer's feet and legs was interfered with by the dark line of the stage below, while from their present position its full harmony would be visible.

Amadeus Voss had almost determined to remain rigid in mind. He hardly resisted actively, for he did not expect anything powerful enough to make resistance worth while.

He was cold, dull, unseeing. Suddenly there floated upon the stage a bird-like vision, a being miraculously eased of human heaviness, one who was all rhythm, and turned the rhythm of motion into music. She broke the chains of the soul, and made every emotion an image, every action a myth, every step a conquest over space and matter. But the face of Amadeus seemed to say: How can that serve me? How does that serve you? Filled by the fury of sex, he saw only a scabrous exhibition, and when the thunder of applause burst out, he showed his teeth.

Eva's last number was a little dramatic episode, a charming *jeu d'esprit,* which she had invented and worked out, to be accompanied by a composition of Delibes. It was very simple. She was Pierrot playing with a top. She regulated and guided the whimsical course of the toy. In ever new positions, turns, and rhythms, she finally drove the top toward a hole into which it disappeared. But this trivial action was so filled with life by the wealth and variety of her rhythmic gestures, so radiant with spirit and swiftest grace, so fresh in inspiration, so heightened in the perfection of its art, that the audience watched breathlessly, and released its own tensity in a fury of applause.

In the foyer Crammon rushed up to Christian, and drew him through the crowd along the dim passage way that led back of the stage. Amadeus Voss, unnoticed by Crammon, followed them unthinkingly and morosely. The sight of the wings, of cliffs and trees, of discarded drops, electrical apparatus and pulleys and of the hurrying stage-hands, stirred in him a dull and hostile curiosity.

An excited crowd thronged toward Eva's dressing-room. She sat in the silken Pierrot costume of black and white, the dainty silver whip still in her hand, amid a forest of flowers. Before her kneeled Johanna Schöntag with an adoring moisture in her eyes. Susan gave her mistress a glass of cool champagne. Then in a mixture of five or six languages she tried to make it clear to the unbidden guests that they were in the way. But each wanted a look, a word, a smile of Eva for himself.

Next to the room in which Eva sat, and separated from it by a thin partition with an open door, was a second dressing-room, which contained only her costumes and a tall mirror. Accidentally pushed in that direction, and not through any will of his own, Amadeus Voss suddenly found himself alone in this little chamber. Having entered it, his courage grew, and he ventured a little farther in.

He looked around and stared at the garments that lay and hung here—the shimmering silks, the red, green, blue, white, and yellow shawls and veils, the fragrant webs of gauze, batiste, and tulle. There were wholly transparent textures and the heaviest brocades. One frock glowed like pure gold, another gleamed like silver; one seemed made of rose-leaves, another knitted of spun glass, one of white foam and one of amethyst. And there stood dainty shoes—a long row of them, shoes of Morocco leather and of kid and silk; and there were hose of all colours, and laces and ribands and antique beads and brooches. The air was drenched with a fragrance that stung his senses—a fragrance of precious creams and unguents, of a woman's skin and hair. His pulses throbbed and his face turned grey. Involuntarily he stretched out his hand, and grasped a painted Spanish shawl. Angrily, greedily, beside himself, he crushed it in his hands, and buried his mouth and nose in it and trembled in every limb.

At that moment Susan Rappard saw him, and pointed to him with a gesture of astonishment. Eva saw him too, gently thrust Johanna aside, arose, and approached the threshold. When she saw the man in his strange and absorbed ecstasy, she felt as though she had been spattered with filth, and uttered a soft, brief cry. Amadeus Voss twitched and dropped the shawl. His eyes were wild and guilty. With a light laugh and an expression of transcendent contempt, which summed up a long dislike, Eva raised the little silver whip and struck him full in the face. His features grew very white, in a contortion of voluptuousness and terror.

In the tense silence Christian went up to Eva, took the silver whip from her hand, and said in a tone scarcely distinguishable from his habitual one: " Oh, no, Eva, I shall not let you do that." He held the handle of the whip firmly at both ends, and bent it until the fragile metal snapped. Then he threw the two pieces on the floor.

They gazed at each other. Disgust at Amadeus still flamed in Eva's face. It yielded to her astonishment at Christian's temerity. But Christian thought: " How beautiful she is! " And he loved her. He loved her in her black and white Pierrot's costume with the black velvet buttons, he loved her with that little cap and its impudent little tassel on her head; he loved her, and she seemed incomparable to him, and his blood cried out after her as in those nights from which she had driven him forth. But he also asked himself: " Why has she grown evil? " And a strange compassion for her stole over him, and a stranger sense of liberation. And he smiled. But to all who were watching, this smile of his seemed a little empty.

Again Amadeus Voss read in the Scripture: " What mean ye that ye beat my people to pieces, and grind the faces of the poor? Because the daughters of Zion are haughty, and walk with stretched forth necks and wanton eyes, walking and mincing as they go, and making a tinkling with their feet: Therefore the Lord will strike with a scab the crown of the head of the daughters of Zion, and the Lord will discover their secret parts. In that day will the Lord take away the bravery of their tinkling ornaments about their feet, and their cauls, and their round tires like the moon, the chains, and the bracelets, and the mufflers, the bonnets, and the ornaments of the legs, and the headbands, and the tablets, and the earrings, the rings, and nose jewels, the changeable suits of apparel, and the mantles, and the wimples, and the crisping pins, the glasses, and the fine linen, and the hoods and the veils. And it shall come to pass, that instead of sweet smell there shall be stink; and instead of a girdle a rent; and instead of well set hair baldness; and instead of a stomacher a girding of sackcloth; and burning instead of beauty. Thy men shall fall by the sword, and thy mighty in the war. And her gates shall lament and mourn; and she being desolate shall sit upon the ground."

On the same evening he left for Berlin.

XI

Lorm and Judith had a magnificent apartment near the Tiergarten in Berlin.

Edgar Lorm flourished. Order and regularity ruled his life. With childlike boastfulness he spoke of his home. His manager and friend, Dr. Emanuel Herbst, congratulated him on his visible rejuvenation.

He introduced to Judith the people whom he had long valued; but she judged most of them sharply and without sympathy. Her characteristic arrogance drove away many who meant well. But under the sway of his new comforts Lorm submitted to her opinions.

But he would not give up Emanuel Herbst. When Judith mocked at his waddling gait, his homeliness, his piping voice, his tactless jokes, Lorm grew serious. " I've known him for over twenty years. The things that annoy you endear him to me quite as much as those precious qualities in him which I know well, and which you've had no chance to discover."

" No doubt he's a monster of virtue," Judith replied, " but he bores me to extinction."

Lorm said: " One should get used to the idea that other people don't exist exclusively for our pleasure. Your point of view is too narrowly that of use and luxury. There are human qualities that I value more highly than a handsome face or polished manners. One of these is trustworthiness. People with whom one has professional dealings often refuse to honour

the demands of common decency—especially in regard to the
keeping of their given word—with a calm frivolity that makes
one's gorge rise. So I'm intensely grateful to Herbst, since it
means so infinitely much to me, for this—that our relations
have never been shadowed by distrust, and that our simplest
verbal agreements are as firm and as valid as a written contract."

Judith recognized that in this case she would have to change
her tactics. She was amiable, as though she were convinced
of his virtues, and sought to gain his favour. Dr. Herbst saw
through her, but showed no consciousness of his insight. He
treated her with an elaborate courtesy that seemed a trifle old-
fashioned, and effectually concealed his reservations.

Sometimes in the evening she would sit with the two men,
and join in their shop talk of playwrights and plays, actors and
actresses, successes and failures. And while she seemed attentive, and even asked an occasional question, she thought of
her dressmaker, of her cook, of her weekly account, or of her
old life, that was so different and had perished so utterly.
And her eyes would grow hard.

It would happen that she would pass through the rooms
with a bitter expression on her face and a hostile glance for
the things about her. She hated the many mirrors which Lorm
required, the rugs that had been recently bought, the pretentious furniture and paintings, the countless bibelots, photographs, ornaments, books, and piously guarded souvenirs.

She had never before lived in a house where other tenants
above and below reminded her of their repulsive and unfamiliar
lives. She listened to the slightest noises, and felt that she had
fallen into a slum.

It was hardly in harmony with her nature to wait each
morning until her husband happened to rise, to see that the
breakfast was complete, to stand aside while the barber, the
masseur, the chauffeur, the messenger of the theatre, and the
secretary had completed their tasks or received their instruc-

tions; to wait again until he returned from rehearsal, tired, annoyed, and hungry, and then to watch him at luncheon—a meal that he required to be both rich and exquisite—gobble his food; to guard him from noise and interruption when he memorized his lines; to answer strange voices on the telephone, to give information, refuse invitations, to send the troublesome away and to soothe the impatient. She was wholly out of her natural element, but she forced herself to endure even as she had endured bodily pain when the long needle had been thrust through her arm.

Emanuel Herbst, who was a keen observer and a learned student of human nature, quietly analysed the relations of this husband and this wife. He said to himself: " Lorm is not fulfilling her expectations; so much is clear. She fancied she could peel him the way one peels an onion, and that the removal of each layer would reveal something so new and surprising as to make up to her for all she has renounced. She will soon discover her miscalculation, for Lorm is always the same. He can't be stripped. He wears his costumes and puts on make-up. She will soon reproach him for this very ability to fill empty forms with a beautiful content, and to remain, in his own person, but a humble servitor of his art. And the more guilty he becomes in her eyes, the more power over him will she gain. For he is tired—tired to death of the affected, the flatterers and sentimentalists, of the sweets and easements of his daily life. Terribly spoiled as he is, he yearns unconsciously for chains and a keeper."

The result of his reflection filled Emanuel Herbst with anxious apprehension.

But Judith remembered her dream—how she had lain beside a fish because it pleased her, and then beaten it in sudden rage over its cool, moist, slippery, opalescent scales. And she lay beside the fish and struck it, and the fish became more and more subservient and her own.

Her constant terror was this thought: " I am poor, impoverished, dependent, without security." The thought tormented her to such a degree that she once expressed it to the house-keeper. The latter was astonished and replied: " But in addition to your pin money, the master gives you two thousand marks a month for the house. Why should you yield to morbid fancies? "

Judith looked at the woman suspiciously. She distrusted all whom she paid. The moment they mentioned money she fancied herself robbed.

One day the cook gave notice. She was the fourth since the establishment of the household. A quantity of sugar was missing. There was a quarrel, an ugly one, and Judith was told things that no one had ever dared to tell her before.

The secretary mislaid a key. When at last it was found Judith rushed to the drawer which it fitted to see whether the stationery, the pencils, and the pen-points were intact.

The housekeeper had bought twenty yards of linen. Judith thought the price paid too high. She drove to the shop herself. The taxi-fare amounted to more than she could possibly have saved on the purchase. Then she chaffered with the clerk for a reduction, until it was granted her through sheer weariness. She told Lorm the story with a triumphant air. He neglected to praise her. She jumped up from the table, locked herself in her room, and went to bed. Whenever she thought that she had some reason for anger, she went to bed.

Lorm came to her door, knocked softly, and asked her to open it. She let him stand long enough to regret his conduct, and then opened the door. She told her story all over, and he listened with a charming curiosity on his face. " You're a jewel," he said, and stroked her cheek and hand.

But it would also happen, if she really wanted something, that she would spend sums out of all proportion to her wretched little economies. She would see a hat, a frock, an ornament in a show window, and not be able to tear herself away. Then she would go into the shop, and pay the price asked at once.

One day she visited an auction sale, and happened to come in just as an old Viennese bon-bon dish was offered for sale. It was one of those objects that make little show, but which delight the collector's heart. At first the dish didn't tempt her at all. Then the high bidding for it excited her, and she her-self began to bid for it. It kindled something in her, and she made bid after bid, and drove all competitors from the field.

Hot and excited, she came home and rushed into Lorm's study. Emanuel Herbst was with him. The two men sat by the fire in familiar talk. Judith disregarded Herbst. She stood before her husband, unwrapped the dish, and said: " Look at this exquisite thing I bought, Edgar."

It was toward evening, but no lights had been lit. Lorm loved the twilight and the flicker of the fire in his chimney, which was, alas, only a metropolitan imitation of a log fire. In the rich, red, wavering reflection of the glow, Judith looked charming in her delight and mobility.

Lorm took the dish, regarded it with polite interest, drew up his lips a little, and said: " It's pretty." Herbst's face puckered into innumerable ironical little wrinkles.

Judith grew angry. " Pretty? Don't you see that it's magical, a perfect little dream, the sweetest and rarest thing imaginable? The connoisseurs were wild after it! Do you know what it cost? Eighteen hundred marks. And I had six or seven rabid competitors bidding against me. Pretty! " She gave a hard little laugh. " Give it to me. You handle it too clumsily."

" Calm yourself, sweetheart," said Lorm gently. " I suppose its virtues are subtle."

But Judith was hurt, more by Herbst's silent mockery than by Lorm's lack of appreciation. She threw back her head, rustled through the room, and slammed the door behind her. When she was angry, her own manners had, at times, a touch of commonness.

For a while the two men were silent. Then Lorm, embar-

rassed and with a deprecating smile, said: "A little dream
. . . for eighteen hundred marks. . . . Oh, well! There's
something childlike about her."

Emanuel Herbst rubbed his tongue up and down between his
teeth and his upper lip. It made him look like an ancient baby.
Then he ventured: "You ought to make it clear to her that
eighteen hundred marks are one thousand eight hundred times
one mark."

"She won't get that far," answered Lorm. "Somebody who
has always lived on the open sea, and is suddenly transported
to a little inland lake, finds it hard to get the new measure-
ments and perspectives. But women are queer creatures." He
sighed and smiled. "Have a nip of whiskey, old man?"

Sorrowfully Herbst rocked his Cæsarean head. "Why
queer? They are as they are, and one must treat them accordingly. Only one mustn't be under any mistaken impression
as to what one has. For instance: A horseshoe is not birch
wood. It looks like a bow, but you can't bend it—not with all
your might. If you string it, the string droops slackly and will
never propel your arrow. All right, let's have your whiskey."

"But occasionally," Lorm replied cheerfully, and filled the
tiny glasses, "you can turn a horseshoe into the finest
Damascene steel."

"Bravo! A good retort! You're as ready as Cardinal
Richelieu. Your health!"

"If you'll let me be Richelieu, I'll appoint you to be my
Father Joseph. A great rôle, by the way. Your health, old
man!"

XII

Crammon and Johanna Schöntag planned to drive to Stel-
lingen to see Hagenbeck's famous zoological gardens, and Crammon begged Christian to lend them his car. They were just
about to start when Christian issued from the hotel. "Why
don't you come along?" Crammon asked. "Have you any-

thing better to do? The three of us can have a very amusing time."

Christian was about to refuse, when he caught Johanna's urgent and beseeching look. She had the art of putting her wishes into her eyes in such a way that one was drawn by them and lost the power to resist. So he said: "Very well, I'll come along," and took the seat next to Johanna's. But he was silent on the whole drive.

It was a sunny day of October.

They wandered through the park, and Johanna made droll comments on the animals. She stopped in front of a seal, and exclaimed: "He looks quite like Herr Livholm, don't you think so?" She talked to a bear as though he were a simple sort of man, and fed him bits of sugar. She said that the camels were incredible, and only pretended to look that way to live up to the descriptions in the books of natural history. "They're almost as ugly as I am," she added; and then, with a crooked smile: "Only more useful. At least I was told at school that their stomachs are reservoirs of water. Isn't the world a queer place?"

Christian wondered why she spoke so contemptuously of herself. She bent over a stone balustrade, and the sight of her neck somehow touched him. She seemed to him a vessel of poor and hurt things.

Crammon discoursed. "It is very curious about animals. Scientists declare they have a great deal of instinct. But what is instinct? I've usually found them to be of an unlimited stupidity. On the estate where I passed my childhood, we had a horse, a fat, timid, gentle horse. It had but one vice: it was very ticklish. I and my playmates were strictly enjoined from tickling it. Naturally we were constantly tempted to tickle it. There were five of us little fellows—no higher than table legs. Each procured a little felt hat with a cock's feather in it. And as the horse stood dull-eyed in front of the stable, we marched in single file under the belly of the stupid beast, tickling it with our feathers as we passed. The feathers tickled so frightfully that he kicked with all fours like a mule. It's a riddle to me to this day how one of us, at least, failed to be killed. But it was amusing and grotesque, and there was no sign of instinct anywhere."

They went to the monkey house. A crowd stood about a little platform, on which a dainty little monkey was showing off its tricks under the guidance of a trainer. " I have a horror of monkeys," said Crammon. " They annoy me through memory. Science bids me feel a relationship with them; but after all one has one's pride. No, I don't acknowledge this devilish atavism." He turned around, and left the building in order to wait outside.

Alone with Christian, a wave of courage conquered Johanna's timidity. She took Christian's arm and drew him nearer to the platform. She was utterly charmed, and her delight was childlike. " How dear, how sweet, how humble! " she cried. A spiritual warmth came from her to Christian. He yielded himself to it, for he needed it. Her boyish voice, however, stirred his senses and aroused his fear. She stood very close by him; he felt her quiver, the response to the hidden erotic power that was in him, and the other voices of his soul were silenced.

He took her hand into his. She did not struggle, but a painful tension showed in her face.

Suddenly the little monkey stopped in its droll performance and turned its lightless little eyes in terror toward the spectators. Some shy perception had frightened it; it seemed, somehow, to think and to recollect itself. As it became aware of the many faces, the indistinctness of its vision seemed to take on outline and form. Perhaps for a second it had a sight of the world and of men, and that sight was to it a source of boundless horror. It trembled as in a fever; it uttered a piercing cry of lamentation; it fled, and when the trainer tried to grasp it, it leaped from the platform and frantically sought a hiding-place. Tears glittered in its eyes and its teeth chattered, and in spite of the animal characteritsics of these gestures and expressions, there was in them something so human and soulful that only a few very coarse people ventured to laugh.

To Christian there came from the little beast a breath from an alien region of earth and forests and loneliness. His heart seemed to expand and then to contract. "Let us go," he said, and his own voice sounded unpleasantly in his ears.

Johanna listened to his words. She was all willingness to listen, all tension and all sweet humility.

XIII

Randolph von Stettner had arrived. There were still several days before the date of his sailing, and he was on his way to Lübeck, where he wished to say good-bye to a married sister. Christian hesitated to promise to be in Hamburg on his friend's return. Only after much urging did he consent to stay.

They dined in Christian's room, discussed conditions in their native province, and exchanged reminiscences. Christian, laconic as usual, was silently amazed at the distance of all these things from his present self.

When the waiter had removed the dishes, Stettner gave an account of all that had driven him to the determination to expatriate himself. While he talked he stared with an un‚ changing look and expression at the table cover.

"You know that for some years I've not been comfortable in my uniform. I saw no aim ahead except the slow and distant moments of advancement. Some of my comrades hoped for war. Well, the life makes that hope natural. In war one can prove one's self in the only way that has any meaning to a professional soldier in any army. But personally I couldn't share that hope. Others marry money, still others go in for sports and gambling. None of these things attracted me. The service itself left me utterly dissatisfied. I seemed to myself in reality an idler who lives pretentiously on others.

" Imagine this: you stand in the barracks yard; it's raining, the water makes the sand gleam; the few wretched trees drip and drip; the men await some command with the watchfulness of well-trained dogs; the water pours from their packs, the sergeant roars, the corporals grit their teeth in zeal and rage; but you? With a monotony like that of the drops that trickle from your cap, you think: ' What will to-night be like? And to-morrow morning? And to-morrow night? ' And the whole year lies ahead of you like a soaked and muddy road. You think of your desolate room with its three dozen books, the meaningless pictures, and the carpet worn thin by many feet; you think of the report you've got to hand in, and the canteen accounts you've got to audit, and the stable inspection, and the next regimental ball, where the arrogant wives of your superior officers will bore you to the point of illness with their shallow talk; you think your way through the whole circle of your life, and find nothing but what is trivial and cheerless as a rainy day. Is that endurable?

" One day I put the question to myself: What was I really accomplishing, and what was the nature of my reward? The answer was that, from a human and intellectual point of view, my accomplishment was an absolute zero. My reward consisted of a number of privileges, the sum of which raised me very high in the social scale, but gave me this position only at the cost of surrendering my personality wholly. I had to obey my superiors and to command my inferiors. That was all. The power to command was conditioned in the duty to obey. And each man in the service, whatever his station, is bound in the identical way, and is simply a connective apparatus in a great electrical circuit. Only the humblest, the great mass of privates, were confined to obedience. The ultimate responsibility at the very top was lost in the vague. In spite of its ultimate primitiveness. the structure of every military organization has a mystery at its core. But between the arbitrary will of a very few and the touching and incomprehensible humility of the great mass, the parts function according to iron laws. Whoever refuses to function, or rebels, is crushed.

" There are those who assert that this compulsion has a moral effect and subserves a higher conception of freedom. I was myself of that opinion for a long time; but I did not find it permanently tenable. I felt myself weakening, and a rebellion seething in my blood. I pulled myself together, and fought against criticism and doubt. In vain. Something had gone out of me. I lost the readiness to obey and the security to command. It was torment. Above me I saw implacable idols, below me defenceless victims. I myself was both idol and victim, implacable and defenceless at once. It seemed to me that humanity ceased where the circle of my activity began. My life seemed to me no longer a part of the general life of mankind, but a fossilized petrefaction conditioned in certain formulæ of command and obedience.

" This condition could, of course, not remain hidden. My comrades withdrew their confidence from me. I was observed and distrusted. Before I had time to clarify either my mind or my affairs, an incident occurred which forced me to a decision. A fellow officer in my regiment, Captain von Otto, was engaged to the daughter of an eminent judge. The wedding, although the date had been set, could not take place. Otto had a slight attack of pulmonary trouble and had to go South for cure. About four weeks after his departure, there was a celebration in honour of the emperor's birthday, and among the ladies invited was the captain's betrothed. Everybody was rather gay and giddy that evening, especially a dear friend of mine, Georg Mattershausen, a sincere, kindly chap who had just received a promotion in rank. The captain's betrothed, who had been his neighbour at table, was infected by his merriment, and on the way home he begged her for a kiss. She refused, and he was going to steal one. She now grew very serious; he at once came to his senses, apologized with the utmost sincerity, and, at the very door of her paternal house, received her solemn promise to mention the incident to no one. When, however, seventeen weeks later, Captain von Otto returned, the girl was seized by some queer scruple, and thought it her duty to tell him of the incident between herself and Mattershausen. The result was a challenge. The conditions were extraordinarily severe: ten paces distance, drawn revolvers, half a minute to aim, exchange of shots to the disablement of either combatant. I was Mattershausen's second. Otto, who had held himself to be affronted and had sent the challenge, had the first shot. He aimed carefully at the head of his adversary. I saw that. But the bullet whistled past my friend's ear. Mattershausen aimed, but his revolver did not go off. This was counted a shot. New pistols were brought. Otto aimed as carefully as before and this time shot Mattershausen straight through the heart. Death was immediate.

" I wonder whether you, too, think that that was a harsh punishment for a moment of youthful thoughtlessness and impropriety. To me it seemed terribly harsh. I felt profoundly that a crime had been committed against my friend. Our fossilized caste had perpetrated a murder. Two days later, in the officers' mess, I expressed this opinion quite frankly. There was general astonishment. One or two sharp replies were made. Some one asked me what I would have done in such a situation. I answered that I would certainly not have sent a challenge, that I could never approve a notion of honour so morbid and self-centred as to demand a human life for a trifle. Even if the young girl's over-tender conscience had persuaded her to break her promise, I would have caused no further trouble, and let the little incident glide into forgetfulness. At that there was general indignation—a great shaking of heads, angry or troubled faces, an exchange of significant glances. But I kept on. Mattershausen's wretched end had hit me damned hard, and I relieved my whole mind. So I added that, if I had been in Mattershausen's place, I would have refused the challenge, quite regardless of consequences. That statement fell among them like a bomb, and a painful silence followed. ' I imagine you would have reconsidered,' said the ranking major, ' I don't think you would have disregarded all the consequences.' ' All,' I insisted, ' certainly, all! ' At that moment Captain von Otto, who had been sitting at another table, arose, and asked frostily: ' You would have risked the odium of cowardice? ' I too arose, and answered: ' Under such circumstances I would have risked that too.' Captain von Otto smiled a contorted smile, and said with an emphasis that could not be misinterpreted: ' Then I don't understand your sitting at the same table with officers of His Majesty.' He bowed stiffly, and went out.

" The die had been cast. No one was curious as to what I would do; no one doubted but that there was only one thing left for me to do. But I was determined to push the matter to its logical conclusion. That super-idol, known as the code of honour, had issued its decree; but I was determined to refuse obedience and take the consequences upon myself. That very evening, when I came home, two comrades were awaiting me to offer me their services. I refused courteously. They looked at me as though I had gone mad, and went off in absurd haste.

" The inevitable consequences followed. You can understand that I could no longer breathe in that air. You cannot outrage the fetishes of your social group and go unpunished. I had to avoid insult, and learned what it was to be an outcast. And that is bad. The imagination alone cannot quite grasp the full horror of it. I saw clearly that there was no place left for me in my fatherland. The way out was obvious."

Christian had listened to his friend's story with unmoved countenance. He got up, took a few turns through the room, and returned to his seat. Then he said: " I think you did the right thing. I am sorry you must leave us, but you did right."

Stettner looked up. How strange that sounded: You did right. A question hovered on his lips. But it was not uttered. For Christian feared that question, and silenced it by a sudden conventionality of demeanour.

XIV

Christian, the brothers Maelbeek, who had followed Eva from Holland, Botho von Thüngen, a Russian councillor of state named Koch, and Crammon sat at luncheon in the dining hall of the hotel.

They were talking about a woman of the streets who had been murdered. The police had already caught the murderer. He was a man who had once belonged to good society, but had gradually gone to the dogs. He had throttled the woman and robbed her in a sailor's tavern.

Now all the prostitutes in the city had unanimously determined to show their sister, who had sacrificed her life to her calling, a last and very public mark of respect, and to follow her coffin to the grave. The respectable citizens of Hamburg felt this to be a sort of challenge and protested. But there was no legal provision by which the demonstration could be stopped.

" We ought to see the spectacle," said Crammon, " even if we have to sacrifice our siesta."

" Then there's no time to be lost," the elder Maelbeek declared, and looked at his watch. " The friends will assemble at the house of mourning at three sharp." He smiled, and thought this way of putting the matter rather witty.

Christian said that he would go too. The motor took them to a crossing that had been closed by the police. Here they left the car, and Herr von Thüngen persuaded the police captain to let them pass.

They were at once surrounded by a great throng of humble folk—sailors. fishermen, workingmen, women, and children.

The windows of the houses were thronged with heads. The Maelbeeks and Koch stopped here, and called Thüngen to join them. Christian walked farther. Somehow the behaviour of his companions irritated him. He felt the kind of curiosity which filled them as something disagreeable. He was curious too, but in another way. Or, at least, it seemed different to him.

Crammon remained by his side. But the throng grew rowdy. "Where are you going?" Crammon asked peevishly. "There is no use in going farther. Let us wait here."

Christian shook his head.

"Very well. I take my stand here," Crammon decided, and separated from Christian.

The latter made his way up to the dirty, old house at the door of which the hearse was standing. It was a foggy day. The black wagon was like a dark hole punched into the grey. Christian wanted to go a little farther, but some young fellows purposely blocked his way. They turned their heads, looked him over, and suspected him of being a "toff." Their own garb was cheap and flashy; their faces and gestures made it clear what trade they drove. One of them was a young giant. He was half a head taller than Christian, and his brows joined over the bridge of his nose. On the index finger of his left hand he wore a huge carnelian ring.

Christian looked about him quite unintimidated. He saw hundreds of women, literally hundreds, ranging in age from sixteen to fifty, and in condition from bloom to utter decay, and from luxury to rags and filth.

They had all gathered—those who had passed the zenith of their troubled course, and those who had barely emerged from childhood, frivolous, sanguine, vain, and already tainted with the mire of the great city. They had come from all streets; they were recruited from all nations and all classes; some had escaped from a sheltered youth, others had risen from even direr depths; there were those who felt themselves pariahs and had the outcast's hatred in their eyes, and there were others who showed a certain pride in their calling and held themselves aloof. He saw cynical and careworn faces, lovely and hardened ones, indifferent and troubled, greedy and gentle faces. Some were painted and some pallid; and the latter seemed strangely naked.

He was familiar with them from the streets and houses of many cities, as every man is. He knew the type, the unfailing stamp, the acquired gesture and look—this hard, rigid, dull, clinging, lightless look. But he had never before seen them except when they were exercising their function behind the gates of their calling, dissembling their real selves and under the curse of sex. To see many hundreds of them separated from all that, to see them as human beings stripped of the stimulus and breath of a turbid sexuality—that was what seemed to sweep a cloud from his eyes.

Suddenly he thought: "I must order my hunting lodge to be sold, and the hounds too."

The coffin was being carried from the house. It was covered with flowers and wreaths; and from the wreaths fluttered ribands with gilt inscriptions. Christian tried to read the inscriptions, but it was impossible. The coffin had small, silver-plated feet that looked like the paws of a cat. By some accident one of these had been broken off, and that touched Christian, he hardly knew why, as unbearably pitiful. An old woman followed the coffin. She seemed more vexed and angry than grief-stricken. She wore a black dress, but the seam under one arm was ripped open. And that too seemed unbearably pitiful.

The hearse started off. Six men carrying lighted candles walked in front of it. The murmur of voices became silent. The women, walking by fours, followed the hearse. Christian stood still close pressed against a wall, and let the procession pass him by. In a quarter of an hour the street was quite desolate. The windows of the houses were closed. He remained alone in the street, in the fog.

As he walked away he reflected: "I've asked my father to take care of my collection of rings. There are over four thousand of them, and many are beautiful and costly. They could be sold too. I don't need them. I shall have them sold."

He wandered on and on, and lost all sense of the passing of time. Evening came, and the city lights glowed through the fog. Everything became moist, even to the gloves on his hands.

He thought of the missing foot on the coffin of the murdered harlot, and of the torn seam of the old woman's dress.

He passed over one of the great bridges of the Elbe, and then walked along the river bank. It was a desolate region. He stopped near the light of a street lamp, gazed into the water, drew forth his wallet, took out a bank note of a hundred marks, turned it about in his hands, shook his head, and then, with a gesture of disgust, threw it into the water. He took a second and did the same. There were twenty bank notes in his wallet. He took them out one by one, and with that expression half of disgust, half of dreaminess, he let them glide into the river.

The street lamps illuminated the inky water for a short distance, and he saw the bank notes drift away.

And he smiled and went on.

xv

When he reached the hotel he felt an urgent need of warmth. By turns he entered the library, the reception hall, the dining-room. All these places were well heated, but their warmth did not suffice him. He attributed his chill to walking so long in the damp.

He took the lift and rode up to his own rooms. He changed his clothes, wrapped himself warmly, and sat down beside the radiator, in which the steam hissed like a caged animal.

Yet he did not grow warm. At last he knew that his shivering was not due to the moisture and the fog, but to some inner cause.

Toward eleven o'clock he arose and went out into the corridor. The stuccoed walls were divided into great squares by gilt moulding; the floor was covered by pieces of carpet that had been joined together to appear continuous. Christian felt a revulsion against all this false splendour. He approached the wall, touched the stucco, and shrugged his shoulders in contempt.

At the end of the long corridor was Eva's suite. He had passed the door several times. As he passed it again he heard the sound of a piano. Only a few keys were being gently touched. After a moment's reflection he knocked, opened the door, and entered.

Susan Rappard was alone in the room. Wrapped in a fur coat, she sat at the piano. On the music rack was propped a book that she was reading. Her fingers passed with ghostly swiftness over the keys, but she struck one only quite rarely. She turned her head and asked rudely: " What do you want, Monsieur? "

Christian answered: " If it's possible, I should like to speak to Madame. I want to ask her a question."

" Now? At night? " Susan was amazed. " We're tired. We're always tired at night in this hyperborean climate, where the sun is a legend. The fog weighs on us. Thank God, in four days we have our last performance. Then we'll go where the sky is blue. We're longing for Paris."

" I should be very happy if I could see Madame," Christian said.

Susan shook her head. " You have a strange kind of patience," she said maliciously. " I hadn't suspected you of being so romantic. You're pursuing a very foolish policy, I assure you. Go in, if you want to, however. Ce petit laideron est chez elle, demoiselle Schöntag. She acts the part of a court fool. Everything in the world is amusing to her—herself not least. Well, that is coming to an end too."

Voices and clear laughter could be heard. The door of

Eva's rooms opened, and she and Johanna appeared on the threshold. Eva wore a simple white garment, unadorned but for one great chrysoprase that held it on the left shoulder. Her skin had an amber gleam, the quiver of her nostrils betrayed a secret irritation. The beautiful woman and the plain one stood there side by side, each with an acute feminine consciousness of her precise qualities: the one vital, alluring, pulsing with distinction and freedom; the other all adoration and yearning ambition for that vitality and that freedom.

Tenderly and delicately Johanna had put her arm about Eva and touched her friend's bare shoulder with her cheek. With her bizarre smile she said: " No one knows how it came that Rumpelstilzkin is my name."

They had not yet observed Christian. A gesture of Susan's called their attention to him. He stood in the shadow of the door. Johanna turned pale, and her shy glance passed from Eva to Christian. She released Eva, bowed swiftly to kiss Eva's hand, and with a whispered good-night slipped past Christian.

Although Christian's eyes were cast down, they grasped the vision of Eva wholly. He saw the feet that he had once held naked in his hands; under her diaphanous garment he saw the exquisite firmness of her little breasts; he saw the arms that had once embraced him and the perfect hands that had once caressed him. All his bodily being was still vibrantly conscious of the smoothness and delicacy of their touch. And he saw her before him, quite near and hopelessly unattainable, and felt a last lure and an ultimate renunciation.

" Monsieur has a request," said Susan Rappard mockingly, and preparing to leave them.

" Stay! " Eva commanded, and the look she gave Christian was like that she gave a lackey.

" I wanted to ask you," Christian said softly, " what is the meaning of the name Eidolon by which you used to call me. My question is belated, I know, and it may seem foolish to-day." He smiled an embarrassed smile. "But it torments me not to know when I think about it, and I determined to ask you."

Susan gave a soundless laugh. In its belated and unmotivated urgency, the question did, indeed, sound a little foolish. Eva seemed amused too, but she concealed the fact. She looked at her hands and said: "It is hard to tell you what it means —something that one sacrifices, or a god to whom one sacrifices, a lovely and serene spirit. It means either or perhaps both at once. Why remind ourselves of it? There is no Eidolon any more. Eidolon was shattered, and one should not exhibit the shards to me. Shards are ugly things."

She shivered a little, and her eyes shone. She turned to Susan. "Let me sleep to-morrow till I wake. I have such evil dreams nowadays, and find no rest till toward morning."

XVI

Passing back through the corridor Christian saw a figure standing very still in the semi-darkness. He recognized Johanna, and he felt that this thing was fated—that she should be standing here and waiting for him.

She did not look at him; she looked at the floor. Not until he came quite close to her did she raise her eyes, and then she looked timidly away. Her lips quivered. A question hovered on them. She knew all that had passed between Eva and Christian. That they had once been lovers only increased her enthusiastic admiration for them both. But what happened between them now—her brief presence made her sure of its character—seemed to her both shameful and incomprehensible.

She was imaginative and sensitive, and loved those who were nobly proud; and she suffered when such noble pride and dignity were humbled. Her whole heart was given over to her ideal of spiritual distinction. Sometimes she would misunderstand her own ideal, and take external forms and modes as expressions of it. And this division in her soul, to which she was not equal, sometimes delivered her into the power of mere frivolity. " It is late," she whispered timidly. It was not a statement; it was an attempt to save herself. Each time that Christian had been mentioned, three things had struck her mind: his elegance, his fine pride, his power over all hearts. That was the combination that called to her and stirred her and filled her days with longing.

Thus she had followed Crammon in search of the great adventure, although she had said of him but an hour after she had met him: " He is grandiosely and grotesquely comic." She had followed him like a slave to a market of slaves, hoping to catch the eye of the khalif.

But she had no faith in her own power. Voluntarily and intentionally she crumbled the passions of her being into small desires. She suffered from that very process and jeered at herself. She was too timid to take greatly what she wanted. She nibbled at life and had not the adventurousness of great enjoyments. And she mocked at her own unhappy nature, and suffered the more.

And now he stood before her. It frightened and surprised her, even though she had waited for him. Since he stayed, she wanted to think him bold and brave. But she could not, and at once she shrank into self-contempt. " It is late," she whispered again, nodded a good-night, and opened the door of her room.

But Christian begged silently with an expression that was irresistible. He crossed the threshold behind the trembling girl. Her face grew hard. But she was too fine to play a coquettish game. Before her blood was stirred her eyes had yielded. The pallor of her face lit it with a new charm. There was no hint of plainness any more. The stormy expectation of her heart harmonized the lines of her features and melted them into softness, gentleness, and delicacy.

Of her power over the senses of men she was secure. She had tested her magnetism on those whom one granted little and who gave less. Flirtations had been used as anodynes in her social group. One had played with false counters, and by a silent compact avoided serious moments. But her experience failed her to-night, for here there was not lightness but austerity. She yielded herself to this night, oblivious of the future and its responsibilities.

XVII

Stephen Gunderam had to go to Montevideo. In that city there was a German physician who had considerable skill in the treatment of nervous disorders; and the bull-necked giant suffered from insomnia and nocturnal hallucinations. Furthermore, there was to be a yacht race at Montevideo, on the results of which Stephen had bet heavily.

He appointed Demetrios and Esmeralda as Letitia's guardians. He said to them: " If anything happens to my wife or she does anything unseemly, I'll break every bone in your bodies." Demetrios grinned. Esmeralda demanded that he bring her a box of sweets on his return.

Their leave-taking was touching. Stephen bit Letitia's ear, and said: " Be true to me."

Letitia immediately began to play upon the mood of her guardians. She gave Demetrios a hundred pesos and Esmeralda a gold bracelet. She corresponded secretly with the naval lieutenant, Friedrich Pestel. An Indian lad, of whose secrecy and reliability she was sure, served as messenger. Within a week Pestel's ship was to proceed to Cape Town, so there was little time to be lost. He did not think he would be able to return to the Argentine until the following winter. And Letitia loved him dearly.

Two miles from the estate there was an observatory in the lonely pampas. A wealthy German cattle-man had built it, and now a German professor with his two assistants lived there and watched the firmament. Letitia had often asked to see the observatory. but Stephen had always refused to let her visit it. Now she intended to make it the scene of her meeting with Friedrich Pestel. She yearned for a long talk with him.

To use an observatory as a refuge for forlorn lovers—it was a notion that delighted Letitia and made her ready to run any risk. The day and the hour were set, and all circumstances were favourable. Riccardo and Paolo had gone hunting; Demetrios had been sent by his father to a farm far to the north; the old people slept. Esmeralda alone had to be deceived. Fortunately the girl had a headache, and Letitia persuaded her to go to bed. When twilight approached, Letitia put on a bright, airy frock in which she could ride. She did not hesitate in spite of her pregnancy. Then, as though taking a harmless walk, she left the house and proceeded to the avenue of palms, where the Indian boy awaited her with two ponies.

It was beautiful to ride out freely into the endless plain. In the west there still shone a reddish glow, into which projected in lacy outline the chain of mountains. The earth suffered from drought; it had not rained for long, and crooked fissures split the ground. Hundreds of grasshopper traps were set up in the fields, and the pits behind them, which were from two to three metres deep, were filled with the insects.

When she reached the observatory, it was dark. The building was like an oriental house of prayer. From a low structure of brick arose the mighty iron dome, the upper part of which rotated on a movable axis. The shutters of the windows were closed, and there was no light to be seen. Friedrich Pestel waited at the gate; he had tethered his horse to a post. He told her that the professor and his two assistants had been absent for a week. She and he, he added, could enter the building nevertheless. The caretaker, an old, fever-stricken mulatto, had given him the key.

The Indian boy lit the lantern that he had carried tied to his saddle. Pestel took it, and preceded Letitia through a desolate brick hallway, then up a wooden and finally up a spiral iron stairway. " Fortune is kind to us," he said. " Next week there's going to be an eclipse of the sun, and astronomers are arriving in Buenos Ayres from Europe. The professor and his assistants have gone to receive them."

Letitia's heart beat very fast. In the high vault of the observatory, the little light of the lantern made only the faintest impression. The great telescope was a terrifying shadow; the drawing instruments and the photographic apparatus on its stand looked like the skeletons of animals; the charts on the wall, with their strange dots and lines, reminded her of black magic. The whole room seemed to her like the cave of a wizard.

Yet there was a smile of childlike curiosity and satisfaction on Letitia's lips. Her famished imagination needed such an hour as this. She forgot Stephen and his jealousy, the eternally quarrelling brothers, the wicked old man, the shrewish Doña Barbara, the treacherous Esmeralda, the house in which she lived like a prisoner—she forgot all that completely in this room with its magic implements, in this darkness lit only by the dim flicker of the lantern, beside this charming young man who would soon kiss her. At least, she hoped he would.

But Pestel was timid. He went up to the telescope, unscrewed the gleaming brass cover, and said: " Let us take a look at the stars." He looked in. Then he asked Letitia to do the same. Letitia saw a milky mist and flashing, leaping fires. " Are those the stars? " she asked, with a coquettish melancholy in her voice.

Then Pestel told her about the stars. She listened with radiant eyes, although it didn't in the least interest her to know how many millions of miles distant from the earth either Sirius or Aldebaran happened to be, and what precisely was the mystery which puzzled scientists in regard to the southern heavens.

" Ah," she breathed, and there was indulgence and a dreamy scepticism in that sound.

The lieutenant, abandoning the cosmos and its infinities,

talked about himself and his life, of Letitia and of the impression she had made on him, and of the fact that he thought only of her by day and by night.

Letitia remained very, very still in order not to turn his thoughts in another direction and thus disturb the sweet suspense of her mood.

As befitted a man with a highly developed conscience, Pestel had definitely laid his plans for the future. When he returned at the end of six months, ways and means were to be found for Letitia's divorce from Stephen and her remarriage to him. He thought of flight only as an extreme measure.

He told her that he was poor. Only a very small capital was deposited in his name in Stuttgart. He was a Suabian—simple-hearted, sober, and accurate.

" Ah," Letitia sighed again, half-astonished and half-saddened. " It doesn't matter," she said with determination. " I'm rich. I own a great tract of forest land. My aunt, the Countess Brainitz, gave it to me as a wedding present."

" A forest? Where? " Pestel asked, and smiled.

" In Germany. Near Heiligenkreuz in the Rhön region. It's as big as a city, and when it's sold it will bring a lot of money. I've never been there, but I've been told that it contains large deposits of some ore. That would have to be found and exploited. Then I'd be even richer than if I sold the forest." These facts had grown in Letitia's imagination; they were the children of the dreams and wishes she had harboured since her slavery in this strange land. She was not lying; she had quite forgotten that she had invented it all. She wished this thing to be so, and it had taken on reality in her mind.

" It's too good, altogether too good to be true," Pestel commented thoughtfully.

His words moved Letitia. She began to sob and threw herself on his breast. Her young life seemed hard to her and ugly and surrounded by dangers. Nothing she had hoped for had become reality. All her pretty soap-bubbles had burst in the wind. Her tears sprang from her deep realization of this fact and out of her fear of men and of her fate. She yearned for a pair of strong arms to give her protection and security.

Pestel was also moved. He put his arms about her and ventured to kiss her forehead. She sobbed more pitifully, and so he kissed her mouth. Then she smiled. He said that he would love her until he died, that no woman had ever inspired such feelings in him.

She confessed to him that she was with child by the unloved husband to whom she was chained. Pestel pressed her to his bosom, and said: " The child is blood of your blood, and I shall regard it as my own."

The time was speeding dangerously. Holding each other's hands they went down the stairs. They parted with the promise to write each other daily.

" When he returns from Africa I'll flee with him on his ship," Letitia determined, as she rode home slowly across the dark plain. Everything else seemed ugly and a bore to her. " Oh, if only it were to be soon," she thought in her anxiety and heart-ache. And curiosity stirred in her to know how Pestel would behave and master the dangers and the difficulties involved. She believed in him, and gave herself up to tender and tempting dreams of the future.

In the house her absence had finally been noticed, and servants had been sent out to look for her. She slipped into the house by obscure paths, and then emerged from her room with an air of innocence.

XVIII

Stettner had returned to Hamburg. His ship was to sail on that very evening. He had several errands in the city, and Christian and Crammon waited for him in order to accompany him to the pier.

Crammon said: " A captain of Hussars who suddenly turns up in mufti—I can't help it, there's something desperate about

it to me. I feel as though I were on a perpetual visit of con-
dolence. After all, he's déclassé, and I don't like people in that
situation. Social classes are a divine institution; a man who
interferes with them wounds his own character. One doesn't
throw up one's profession the way one tosses aside a rotten
apple. These are delicate and difficult matters. Common
sense may disregard them; the higher intelligence reverences
them. What is he going to do among the Yankees? What
good can come of it? "

" He's a chemist by inclination, and scholarly in his line,"
Christian answered. " That will help."

" What do the Yankees care about that? He's more likely to
catch consumption and be trodden under. He'll be stripped of
pride and dignity It's a country for thieves, waiters, and
renegades. Did he have to go as far as all this? "

" Yes," Christian answered, " I believe he did."

An hour later they and Stettner arrived at the harbour.
Cargoes and luggage were still being stowed, and they strolled,
Stettner between Crammon and Christian, up and down a narrow alley lined with cotton-bales, boxes, barrels, and baskets.
The arc lamps cast radiant light from the tall masts, and a
tumult of carts and cranes, motors and bells, criers and whistles
rolled through the fog. The asphalt was wet; there was no
sky to be seen.

" Don't forget me wholly here in the old land," said Stettner.
A silence followed.

" I don't know whether we shall be as well off in the old
country in the future as we have been in the past," said Crammon, who occasionally had pessimistic attacks and forebod-
ings. " Hitherto we haven't suffered. Our larders and cellars
have been well-stocked, nor have the higher needs been neglected. But times are getting worse, and, unless I mistake,
clouds are gathering on the political horizon. So I can't call it
a bad idea, my dear Stettner, to slip away quietly and amiably.
I only hope that you'll find some secure position over there

from which you may calmly watch the spectacle of our débâcle. And when the waves rise very high, you might think of us and have a mass said for us, that is for me, because Christian has been expelled from the bosom of Holy Church."

Stettner smiled at this speech. But he became serious again at once. " It seems to me too that, in a sense, we're all trapped here. Yet I have never felt myself so deeply and devotedly a German as at this moment when I am probably leaving my fatherland forever. But in that feeling there is a stab of pain. It seems to me as though I should hurry from one to another and sound a warning. But what to warn them of, or why warn them at all—I don't know."

Crammon answered weightily. " My dear old Aglaia wrote me the other day that she had dreamed of black cats all night long. She is deep, she has a prophetic soul, and dreams like that are of evil presage. I may enter a monastery. It is actually within the realm of the possible. Don't laugh, Christian; don't laugh, my dearest boy! You don't know all my possibilities."

It had not occurred to Christian to laugh.

Stettner stopped and gave his hands to his friends. " Goodbye, Crammon," he said cordially. " I'm grateful that you accompanied me. Good-bye, dear Christian, good-bye." He pressed Christian's hand long and firmly. Then he tore himself away, hastened toward the gang-plank, and was lost in the crowd.

" A nice fellow," Crammon murmured. " A very nice fellow. What a pity! "

When the car met them Christian said: " I'd like to walk a bit, either back to the hotel or somewhere else. Will you come, Bernard? "

" If you want me, yes. Toddling along is my portion."

Christian dismissed his car. He had a strange foreboding, as though something fateful were lying in wait for him.

"Ariel's days here are numbered," said Crammon. "Duty calls me away. I must look after my two old ladies. Then I must join Franz Lothar in Styria. We'll hunt heath-cocks. After that I've agreed to meet young Sinsheim in St. Moritz. What are your plans, my dear boy?"

"I leave for Berlin to-morrow or the day after."

"And what in God's name are you going to do there?"

"I'm going to work."

Crammon stopped, and opened his mouth very wide. "Work?" he gasped, quite beside himself. "What at? What for, O misguided one?"

"I'm going to take courses at the university, under the faculty of medicine."

Horrified, Crammon shook his head. "Work . . . courses . . . medicine . . . Merciful Providence, what does this mean? Is there not enough sweat in the world, not enough bungling and half-wisdom and ugly ambition and useless turmoil? You're not serious."

"You exaggerate as usual, Bernard," Christian answered, with a smile. "Don't always be a Jeremiah. What I'm going to do is something quite simple and conventional. And I'm only going to try. I may not even succeed; but I must try it. So much is sure."

Crammon raised his hand, lifted a warning index finger, and said with great solemnity: "You are upon an evil path, Christian, upon a path of destruction. For many, many days I have had a presentiment of terrible things. The sleep of my nights has been embittered; a sorrow gnaws at me and my peace has flown. How am I to hunt in the mountains when I know you to be among the Pharisees? How shall I cast my line into clear streams when my inner eye sees you bending over greasy volumes or handling diseased bodies? No wine will glitter beautifully in my glass, no girl's eyes seem friendly any more, no pear yield me its delicate flavour!"

"Oh, yes, they will," Christian said, laughing. "More than

that: I hope you'll come to see me from time to time, to convince yourself that you needn't cast me off entirely."

Crammon sighed. "Indeed I shall come. I must come and
soon, else the spirit of evil will get entire control of you. Which
may God forbid! "

XIX

Johanna told Eva, whom she adored, about her life. Eva
thus received an unexpected insight into the grey depths of
middle-class existence. The account sounded repulsive. But
it was stimulating to offer a spiritual refuge to so much thirst
and flight.

She herself often seemed to her own soul like one in flight.
But she had her bulwarks. The wind of time seemed cold to
her, and when she felt a horror of the busy marionettes whose
strings were in her hands, she felt herself growing harder.
The friendship which she gave to this devoted girl seemed to
her a rest in the mad race of her fate.

They were so intimate that Susan Rappard complained.
The latter opened her eyes wide and her jealousy led her to
become a spy. She became aware of the relations that had
developed between Johanna and Christian.

At dinner there had been much merriment. Johanna had
bought a number of peaked, woollen caps. She had wrapped
them carefully in white paper, written some witty verses on
each bundle, and distributed them as favours to Eva's guests.
No one had been vexed. For despite her mockery and gentle
eccentricity, there was a charm about her that disarmed every
one.

"How gay you are to-day, Rumpelstilzkin," Eva said. She,
too, used that nickname. The word, which she pronounced
with some difficulty, had a peculiar charm upon her lips.

"It is the gaiety that precedes tears," Johanna answered,
and yielded as entirely to her superstitious terror as she had
to her jesting mood.

A wealthy ship-owner had invited Eva to view his private picture gallery. His house was in the suburbs. She drove there with Johanna.

Arm in arm they stood before the paintings. And in that absorbed union there was something purifying. Johanna loved it as she loved their common reading of poetry, when they would sit with their cheeks almost touching. Extinguished in her selfless adoration, she forgot what lay behind her—the anxious, sticky, unworthily ambitious life of her family of brokers; she forgot what lay before her—oppression and force, an inevitable and appointed way.

Her gestures revealed a gentle glow of tenderness.

On their way back she seemed pale. "You are cold," Eva said, and wrapped the robe more firmly about her friend.

Johanna squeezed Eva's hand gratefully. "How dear of you! I shall always need some one to tell me when I'm hot or cold."

This melancholy jest moved Eva deeply. "Why do you act so humble?" she cried. "Why do you shrink and hide and turn your vision away from yourself? Why do you not dare to be happy?"

Johanna answered: "Do you not know that I am a Jewess?"

"Well?" Eva asked in her turn. "I know some very extraordinary people who are Jews—some of the proudest, wisest, most impassioned in the world."

Johanna shook her head. "In the Middle Ages the Jews were forced to wear yellow badges on their garments," she said. "I wear the yellow badge upon my soul."

Eva was putting on a tea gown. Susan Rappard was helping her. "What's new with us, Susan?" Eva asked, and took the clasps out of her hair.

Susan answered: "What is good is not new, and what is new is not good. Your ugly little court fool is having an affair with M. Wahnschaffe. They are very secretive, but there are whispers. I don't understand him. He is easily and quickly consoled. I have always said that he has neither a mind nor a heart. Now it is plain that he has no eyes either."

Eva had flushed very dark. Now she became very pale. "It is a lie," she said.

Susan's voice was quite dry. "It is the truth. Ask her. I don't think she'll deny it."

Shortly thereafter Johanna slipped into the room. She had on a dress of simple, black velvet which set off her figure charmingly. Eva sat before the mirror. Susan was arranging her hair. She had a book in her hand and read without looking up.

On a chair near the dressing-table lay an open jewel case. Johanna stood before it, smiled timidly, and took out of it a beautifully cut cameo, which she playfully fastened to her bosom; she looked admiringly at a diadem and put it in her hair; she slipped on a few rings and a pearl bracelet over her sleeve. Thus adorned she went, half hesitatingly, half with an air of self-mockery, up to Eva.

Slowly Eva lifted her eyes from the book, looked at Johanna, and asked: "Is it true?" She let a few seconds pass, and then with wider open eyes she asked once more: "Is it true?"

Johanna drew back, and the colour left her cheeks. She suspected and knew and began to tremble.

Then Eva arose and went close up to her and stripped the cameo from the girl's bosom, the diadem from her hair, the rings from her fingers, the bracelet from her arm, and threw the things back into the case. Then she sat down again, took up her book, and said: "Hurry, Susan! I want to rest a little."

Johanna's breath failed her. She looked like one who has been struck. A tender blossom in her heart was crushed forever, and from its sudden withering arose a subtle miasma. Almost on the point of fainting she left the room.

As though to seal the end of a period in her life and warn her of evil things to come, she received within two hours a telegram from her mother which informed her of a catastrophe and urgently summoned her home. Fräulein Grabmeier began packing at once. They were to catch the train at five o'clock in the morning.

From midnight on Johanna sat waiting in Christian's room. She lit no light. In the darkness she sat beside a table, resting her head in her hands. She did not move, and her eyes were fixed on vacancy.

xx

In the course of their talk Christian and Crammon had wandered farther and farther into the tangled alleys around the harbour. "Let us turn back and seek a way out," Crammon suggested. "It isn't very nice here. A damnable neighbourhood, in fact."

He peered about, and Christian too looked around. When they had gone a few steps farther, they came upon a man lying flat on his belly on the pavement. He struggled convulsively, croaked obscene curses, and shook his fist threateningly toward a red-curtained, brightly lit door.

Suddenly the door opened, and a second man flew out. A paper box, an umbrella, and a derby hat were pitched out after him. He stumbled down the steps with outstretched arms, fell beside the first man, and remained sitting there with heavy eyes.

Christian and Crammon looked in through the open door. In the smoky light twenty or thirty people were crouching. The monotonous crying of a woman became audible. At times it became shriller.

The glass door was flung shut.

I shall see what goes on in there," said Christian, and mounted the steps to the door. Crammon had only time to utter a horrified warning. But he followed. The reek of cheap whiskey struck him as he entered the room behind Christian.

Beside tables and on the floor crouched men and women. In every corner lay people, sleeping or drunk. The eyes which were turned toward the newcomers were glassy. The faces here looked like lumps of earth. The room, with its dirty tables, glasses, and bottles had a colour-scheme of scarlet and yellow. Two sturdy fellows stood behind the bar.

The woman whose crying had penetrated to the street sat on a bench beside the wall. Blood was streaming down her face, and she continued to utter her monotonous and almost bestial whine. In front of her, trying hard to keep erect on legs stretched far apart, stood the huge fellow whom Christian had observed at the public funeral of the murdered harlot. In a hoarse voice, in the extreme jargon of the Berlin populace, he was shouting: "Yuh gonna git what's comin' to yuh! I'll show yuh what's what! I'll blow off yer dam' head-piece'n yuh cin go fetch it in the moon!"

On the threshold of an open door in the rear stood a stout man with innumerable watch-charms dangling across his checked waistcoat. A fat cigar was held between his yellow teeth. He regarded the scene with a superior calm. It was the proprietor of the place. When he saw the two strangers his brows went up. He first took them to be detectives, and hastened to meet them. Then he saw his mistake and was the more amazed. "Come into my office, gentlemen," he said in a greasy voice, and without removing the cigar. "Come back there, and I'll give you a drink of something good." He drew Christian along by the arm. A woman with a yellow head-kerchief arose from the floor, stretched out her arms toward Christian, and begged for ten pfennigs. Christian drew back as from a worm.

An old man tried to prevent the gigantic lout from maltreating the bleeding woman any more. He called him Mesecke and fawned upon him. But Mesecke gave him a blow under the

chin that sent him spinning and moaning. Murmurs of protest sounded, but no one dared to offend the giant. The proprietor whispered to Christian: "What he wants is brass;
wants her to go on the street again and earn a little. Nothing
to be done right now."

He grasped Crammon by the sleeve too, and drew them both
through the door into a dark hall. "I suppose you gentlemen
are interested in my establishment?" he asked anxiously. He
opened a door and forced them to enter. The room into which
they came showed a tasteless attempt at such luxury as is
represented by red plush and gilt frames. The place was
small, and the furniture stood huddled together. Crossed
swords hung above a bunch of peacock feathers, and above the
swords the gay cap of a student fraternity. Between two windows stood a slanting desk covered with ledgers. An emaciated
man with a yellowish face sat at the desk and made entries in
a book. He quivered when the proprietor entered the room,
and bent more zealously over his work.

The proprietor said: "I've got to take care of you gents
or something might happen. When that son of a gun is quiet
you can go back and look the place over. I guess you're
strangers here, eh?" From a shelf he took down a bottle.
"Brandy," he whispered. "Prime stuff. You must try it.
I sell it by the bottle and by the case. A number one! Here
you are!" Crammon regarded Christian, whose face was without any sign of disquiet. With a sombre expression he went
to the table and, as though unseeing, touched his lips to the
glass which the proprietor had filled. It was a momentary
refuge, at all events.

In the meantime a frightful noise penetrated from the outer
room. "Fighting again," said the proprietor, listened for a
moment, and then disappeared. The noise increased furiously
for a moment. Then silence fell. The book-keeper, without
raising his waxy face, said: "Nobody can stand that. It's
that way every night. And the books here show the profits.

That man Hillebohm is a millionaire, and he rakes in more
and more money without mercy, without compassion. Nobody
can stand that."

The words sounded like those of a madman.

"Are we going to permit ourselves to be locked up here?"
Crammon asked indignantly. "It's rank impudence."

Christian opened the door, and Crammon drew from his
back pocket the Browning revolver that was his constant companion. They passed through the hall and stopped on the
threshold of the outer room. Mesecke had vanished. Many
arms had finally expelled him. The woman from whom he had
been trying to get money was washing the blood from her
face. The old man who had been beaten when he had pleaded
for her said consolingly: "Don't yuh howl, Karen. Things'll
get better. Keep up, says I!" The woman hardly listened.
She looked treacherous and angry.

A tangle of yellow hair flamed on her head, high as a helmet
and unkempt. While she was bleeding she had wiped the
blood with her naked hand, and then stained her hair with it.

"You go home now," the proprietor commanded. "Wash
your paws and give our regards to God if you see him. Hurry
up, or your sweetheart'll be back and give you a little
more."

She did not move. "Well, how about it, Karen," a woman
shrilled. "Hurry. D'yuh want some more beating?"

But the woman did not stir. She breathed heavily, and
suddenly looked at Christian.

"Come with us," Christian said unexpectedly. The bar-
tenders roared with laughter. Crammon laid a hand of desperate warning on Christian's shoulder.

"Come with us," Christian repeated calmly. "We will take
you home."

A dozen glassy eyes stared their mockery. A voice brayed:
"Hell, hell, but you're gettin' somethin' elegant." Another
hummed as though scanning verses: "If that don't kill the

bedbugs dead, I dunno what'll do instead! Don't yuh be
scared, Karen. Hurry! Use your legs! "

Karen got up. She had not taken her shy and sombre eyes
from Christian. His beauty overwhelmed her. A crooked,
frightened, cynical smile glided over her full lips.

She was rather tall. She had fine shoulders and a well-
developed bosom. She was with child—perhaps five months;
it was obvious when she stood. She wore a dark green dress
with iridescent buttons, and at her neck a flaming red riband
fastened by a brooch that represented in silver, set with garnets,
a Venetian gondola, and bore the inscription: *Ricordo di Venezia*. Her shoes were clumsy and muddy. Her hat—made of
imitation kid and trimmed with cherries of rubber—lay beside
her on the bench. She grasped it with a strange ferocity.

Christian looked at the riband and at the silver brooch with
its inscription: *Ricordo di Venezia*.

Crammon sought to protect their backs. For new guests
were coming in—fellows with dangerous faces. He had simply
yielded to the inevitable and incomprehensible, and determined
to give a good account of himself. He gritted his teeth over the
absence of proper police protection, and said to himself: " We
won't get out of this hole alive, old boy." And he thought of
his comfortable hotel-bed, his delicious, fragrant bath, his excellent breakfast, and of the box of chocolates on his table.
He thought of young girls who exhaled the fresh sweetness of
linen, of all pleasant fragrances, of Ariel's smile and Rumpelstilzkin's gaiety, and of the express train that was to have
taken him to Vienna. He thought of all these things as though
his last hour had come.

Two sailors came in dragging between them a girl who was
pale and stiff with drunkenness. Roughly they threw her on
the floor. The creature moaned, and had an expression of
ghastly voluptuousness, of strange lasciviousness on her face.
She lay there stiff as a board. The sailors, with a challenge in
their voices, asked after Mesecke. He had evidently met them

and complained to them. They wanted to get even with the proprietor. One of them had a scarlet scratch across his forehead; the other's arms were naked up to his shoulders and tattooed until they were blue all over. The tattooing represented a snake, a winged wheel, an anchor, a skull, a phallus, a scale, a fish, and many other objects.

Both sailors measured Christian and Crammon with impudent glances. The one with the tattooed arms pointed to the revolver in Crammon's hand, and said: " If you don't put up that there pistol I'll make you, by God! "

The other went up to Christian and stood so close to him that he turned pale. Vulgarity had never yet touched him, nor had the obscene things of the gutter splashed his garments. Contempt and disgust arose hotly in him. These might force him to abandon his new road; for they were more terrible than the vision of evil he had had in the house of Szilaghin.

But when he looked into the man's eyes, he became aware of the fact that the latter could not endure his glance. Those eyes twitched and flickered and fled. And this perception gave Christian courage and a feeling of inner power, the full effectiveness of which was still uncertain.

" Quiet there! " the proprietor roared at the two sailors. " I want order. You want to get the police here, do you? That'd be fine for us all, eh? You're a bit crazy, eh? The girl can go with the gentlemen, if they'll pay her score. Two glasses champagne—that's one mark fifty. And that ends it."

Crammon laid a two-mark piece on the table. Karen Engelschall had put on her hat, and turned toward the door. Christian and Crammon followed her, and the proprietor followed them with sarcastic courtesy, while the two sturdy bar-tenders formed an additional bodyguard. A few half-drunken men sent the strains of a jeering song behind them.

The street was empty. Karen gazed up and down it, and seemed uncertain in which direction she should go. Crammon asked her where she lived. She answered harshly that she

didn't want to go home. "Then where shall we take you?"
Crammon asked, forcing himself to be patient and considerate.
She shrugged her shoulders. "It don't matter," she said.
Then, after a while, she added defiantly. "I don't need you."

They went toward the harbour, Karen between the two men.
For a moment she stopped and murmured with a shudder of
fear: "But I mustn't run into him. No, I mustn't."

"Will you suggest something then?" Crammon said to her.
His impulse was simply to decamp, but for Christian's sake,
and in the hope of saving him uninjured from this mesh of
adventures, he played the part of interest and compassion.

Karen Engelschall did not answer, but hurried more swiftly
as she caught sight of a figure in the light of a street lamp.
Until she was beyond its vision she gasped with terror.

"Shall we give you money?" Crammon asked again.

She answered furiously: "I don't need your money. I want
no money." Surreptitiously she gazed at Christian, and her
face grew malicious and stubborn.

Crammon went over beside Christian, and spoke to him in
French. "The best thing would be to take her to an inn where
she can get a room and a bed. We can deposit a sum of money
there, so that she is sheltered for a while. Then she can help
herself."

"Quite right. That will be best," Christian replied. And, as
though he could not bear to address her, he added: "Tell her
that."

Karen stopped. She lifted her shoulders as though she were
cold, and said in a hoarse voice: "Leave me alone. What are
you two talking about? I won't walk another step. I'm tired.
Don't pay no attention to me!" She leaned against the wall
of a house, and her hat was pushed forward over her forehead.
She was as sorry and dissipated a looking object as one could
possibly imagine.

"Isn't that the sign of an inn?" Crammon asked and pointed
to an illuminated sign at the far end of the street.

Christian, who had very keen eyes, looked and answered: " Yes. It says ' King of Greece.' Do go and inquire."

" A lovely neighbourhood and a lovely errand," Crammon said plaintively. " I am paying for my sins." But he went.

Christian remained with the woman, who looked down silently and angrily. Her fingers scratched at her riband. Christian listened to the beating of the tower-clock. It struck two. At last Crammon reappeared. He beckoned from a distance and cried: " Ready."

Christian addressed the girl for the first time. " We've found a shelter for you," he said, a little throatily, and, quite contrary to his wont, blinked his eyes. His own voice sounded disagreeably in his ears. " You can stay there for some days."

She looked at him with eyes that glowed with hatred. An indescribable but evil curiosity burned in her glance. Then she lowered her eyes again. Christian was forced to speak again: " I think you will be safe from that man there. Try to rest. Perhaps you are ill. We could summon a physician."

She laughed a soft, sarcastic laugh. Her breath smelt of whiskey.

Crammon called out again.

" Come on then," Christian said, mastering his aversion with difficulty.

His voice and his words made the same overwhelming impression on her that his appearance had done. She started to go as though she were being propelled from behind.

A sleepy porter in slippers stood at the door of the inn. His servile courtesy proved that Crammon had known how to treat him. " Number 14 on the second floor is vacant," he said.

" Send some one to your lodgings to-morrow for your things," Crammon advised the girl.

She did not seem to hear him. Without a word of thanks or greeting she followed the porter up the soiled red carpet of the stairs. The rubber cherries tapped audibly against the brim of her hat. Her clumsy form disappeared in the blackness.

Crammon breathed a sigh of relief. " My kingdom for a four-wheeler," he moaned. At a nearby corner they found a cab.

XXI

When Christian entered his room and switched on the electric light, he was surprised to find Johanna sitting at the table. She shaded her eyes from the sudden glare. He remained at the door. His frown disappeared when he saw the deadly pallor of the girl's face.

" I must leave," Johanna breathed. " I've received a telegram and I must start for Vienna at once."

" I am about to leave, too," Christian answered.

For a while there was silence. Then Johanna said: " Shall I see you again? Will you want me to? Dare I? " Her timid questions showed the old division of her soul. She smiled a smile of patience and renunciation.

" I shall be in Berlin," Christian answered. " I don't know yet where I shall live. But whenever you want to know, ask Crammon. He is easily reached. His two old ladies send him all letters."

" If you desire it, I can come to Berlin," Johanna said with the same patient and resigned smile. " I have relatives there But I don't think that you do desire it." Then, after a pause, during which her gentle eyes wandered aimlessly, she said: " Then is this to be the end? " She held her breath; she was taut as a bow-string.

Christian went up to the table and rested the index finger of one hand on its top. With lowered head he said slowly: " Don't demand a decision of me. I cannot make one. I should hate to hurt you. I don't want something to happen again that has happened so often before in my life. If you feel impelled to come—come! Don't consider me. Don't think, above all, that I would then leave you in the lurch. But just now is a critical time in my life. More I cannot say."

Johanna could gather nothing but what was hopeless for herself from these words. Yet through them there sounded a note that softened their merely selfish regretfulness. With a characteristically pliant gesture, she stretched out her arm to Christian. Her pose was formal and her smile faint, as she said: " Then, au revoir—perhaps! "

XXII

When the girl had gone, Christian lay down on the sofa and folded his hands beneath his head. Thus he lay until dawn. He neither switched off the light nor did he close his eyes.

He saw the paintless stairs that led to the den where he had been and the red carpet of the inn soiled by many feet; he saw the lamp in the desolate street and the watch charms on the proprietor's waistcoat; he saw the brandy bottle on the shelf, and the green shawl of one of the drunken women, and the tattooed symbols on the sailor's naked arm: the anchor, the winged wheel, the phallus, the fish, the snake; he saw the rubber cherries on the prostitute's hat and the silver brooch with the garnets and the foolish motto: *Ricordo di Venezia.*

And more and more as he thought of these things they awakened in him an ever surer feeling of freedom and of liberation, and seemed to release him from other things that he had hitherto loved, the rare and precious things that he had loved so exclusively and fruitlessly. And they seemed to release him likewise from men and women whose friendship or love had been sterile in the end.

As he lay there and gazed into space, he lived in these poor and mean things, and all fruitless occupations and human relationships lost their importance; and even the thought of Eva ceased to torment him and betray him into fruitless humiliation.

That radiant and regal creature allured him no more, when he thought of the blood-stained face of the harlot. For the latter aroused in him a feeling akin to curiosity that gradually filled his soul so entirely that it left room for nothing else.

Toward dawn he slumbered for an hour. Then he arose, and bathed his face in cold water, left the hotel, hired a cab, and drove to the inn called "The King of Greece."

The nightwatchman was still at his post. He recognized this early guest and guided him with disagreeable eagerness up two flights of stairs to the room of Karen Engelschall.

Christian knocked. There was no answer. "You just go in, sir," said the porter. "There ain't no key and the latch don't work. All kinds of things will happen, and it's better for us to have the doors unlocked."

Christian entered. It was a room with ugly brown furnishings, a dark-red plush sofa, a round mirror with a crack across its middle, an electric bulb at the end of a naked wire, and a chromo-lithograph of the emperor. Everything was dusty, worn, shabby, used-up, poor and mean.

Karen Engelschall lay in the bed asleep. She was on her back, and her dishevelled hair looked like a bundle of straw; her face was pale and a little puffy. Recent scars showed on her forehead and right cheek. Her full but flaccid breasts protruded above the coverings.

His old and violent dislike of sleeping people stirred in Christian, but he mastered it and regarded her face. He wondered from what social class she had come, whether she was a sailor's or a fisherman's daughter, a girl of the lower middle-classes, of the proletariat or the peasantry. Thus his curiosity employed his mind for a while until he became fully aware of the indescribable perturbation of that face. It was as void of evil as of good; but as it lay there it seemed distraught by the unheard of torment of its dreams. Then Christian thought of the carnelian on Mesecke's hand, and the repulsively red stone which was like a beetle or a piece of raw flesh became extraordinarily vivid to him.

He made a movement and knocked against a chair; the noise

awakened Karen Engelschall. She opened her lids, and fear
and horror burned in her eyes when she observed a figure in
her room; her features became distorted with fury, and her
mouth rounded itself for a cry. Then she saw who the intruder
was, and with a sigh of relief slid back among the pillows. Her
face reassumed its expression of stubbornness and of enforced
yielding. She watched, not knowing what to make of this
visit, and seemed to wonder and reflect. She drew the covers
up under her chin, and smiled a shallow, flattered smile.

Involuntarily Christian's eyes looked for the red riband and
the silver brooch. The girl's garments had been flung pell-mell
on a chair. The hat with the rubber cherries lay on the table.

"Why do you stand?" Karen Engelschall asked in a cheerful voice. "Sit down." Again, as in the night, his splendour
and distinction overwhelmed her. Smiling her empty smile, she
wondered whether he was a baron or a count. She had slept
soundly and felt refreshed.

"You cannot stay in this house very long," Christian said
courteously. "I have considered what had better be done for
you. Your condition requires care. You must not expose
yourself to the brutality of that man. It would be best if you
left the city."

Karen Engelschall laughed a harsh laugh. "Leave the city?
How's that going to be done? Girls like me have to stay where
they are."

"Has any one a special claim on you?" Christian asked.

"Claim? Why? How do you mean? Oh, I see. No, no.
It's the way things are in our business. The feller to whom you
give your money, he protects you, and the others mind him.
If he's strong and has many friends you're safe. They're all
rotten, but you got no choice. You get no rest day or night,
and your flesh gets tired, I can tell you."

"I can imagine that," Christian replied, and for a second
looked into Karen's round and lightless eyes, "and for that
reason I wanted to put myself at your disposal. I shall leave

Hamburg either to-day or to-morrow, and probably stay in Berlin for some months. I am ready to take you with me. But you must not delay your decision, because I have not yet any address in Berlin, I don't know yet where I shall live, and if a plan like this is delayed it is usually not carried out at all. At the moment you have eluded your pursuer, and so the opportunity to escape is good. You don't need to send for your things. I can get you whatever you need when we arrive."

Those words, spoken with real friendliness, did not have the effect which Christian expected. Karen Engelschall could not realize the simplicity and frankness of their intention. A mocking suspicion arose in her mind. She knew of Vice Crusaders and Preachers of Salvation; and these men her world as a rule fears as much as it does the emissaries of the police. But she looked at Christian more sharply, and an instinct told her that she was on the wrong track. Clumsily considering, she drifted to other suppositions that had a tinge of cheap romance. She thought of plots and kidnapping and a possible fate more terrible than that under the heel of her old tormentor. She brooded over these thoughts in haste and rage, with convulsed features and clenched fist, passing from fear to hope and from hope to distrust, and yet, even as on the day before, compelled by something irresistible, a force from which she could not withdraw and which made her struggles futile.

" What do you want to do with me? " she asked, and gave him a penetrating glance.

Christian considered in order to weigh his answer carefully. " Nothing but what I have told you."

She became silent and stared at her hands. " My mother lives in Berlin," she murmured. " Maybe you'd want me to go back to her. I don't want to."

" You are to go with me." Christian's tone was firm and almost hard. His chest filled with breath and exhaled the air painfully. The final word had been spoken.

Karen looked at him again. But now her eyes were serious

and awake to reality. " And what shall I do when I'm with you? "

Christian answered hesitatingly: " I've come to no decision about that. I must think it over."

Karen folded her hands. " But I've got to know who you are."

He spoke his name.

" I am a pregnant woman," she said with a sombre look, and for the first time her voice trembled, " a street-walker who's pregnant. Do you know that? I'm the lowest and vilest thing in the whole world! Do you know that? "

" I know it," said Christian, and cast down his eyes.

" Well, what does a fine gentleman like you want to do with me? Why do you take such an interest in me? "

" I can't explain that to you at the moment," Christian answered diffidently.

" What am I to do? Go with you? Right away? "

" If you are willing, I shall call for you at two, and we can drive to the station."

" And you won't be ashamed of me? "

" No, I shall not be ashamed."

" You know how I look? Suppose people point their fingers at the whore travelling with such an elegant gentleman? "

" It does not matter what people do."

" All right. I'll wait for you." She crossed her arms over her breast and stared at the ceiling and did not stir. Christian arose and nodded and went out. Nor did Karen move when he was gone. A deep furrow appeared on her forehead, the fresh scars gleamed like burns upon her earthy skin, a dull and primitive amazement turned her eyes to stone.

XXIII

When Christian crossed the reception room of the hotel he saw Crammon sitting sadly in a chair. Christian stopped and

smiled and held out his hand. " Did you sleep well, Bernard? "
he asked.

" If that were my only difficulty I should not complain,"
Crammon answered. " I always sleep well. The troubles begin
when I'm awake. Age with his stealing steps! The old pleasures no longer sting, the old delights are worn out. One counts
on gratitude and affection, and gets care and disappointment.
I think a monastery would be the best place for me. I must
look into that plan more closely."

Christian laughed. " Come now, Bernard, you would be a
very unsuitable person in a monastery. Drive the black
thoughts away and let us have breakfast."

" All right, let us have breakfast." Crammon arose. " Have
you any idea why poor Rumpelstilzkin suddenly fled by night?
She had bad news from home, I am told, but that's no reason
why she should have gone without a word. It was not nice or
considerate. And in a few hours Ariel too will be lost to us.
Her rooms are filled with cases and boxes, and M. Chinard is
bursting with self-importance. Black clouds are over us, and
all our lovely rainbows fade. This caviare, by the way, is
excellent. I shall withdraw into an utterly private life. Perhaps I shall hire a secretary, either a man or a fat, appetizing,
and discreet woman, and begin to dictate my memoirs. You,
my dear fellow, seem in more excellent spirits than for a long
time."

" Yes, excellent," Christian said, and his smile revealed his
beautiful teeth. " Excellent! " he repeated, and held out his
hand to his astonished friend.

" So you have finally become reconciled to your loss? "
he winked, and pointed upward with a significant gesture.

Christian guessed his meaning. " Entirely," he said cheerily.
" I'm completely recovered."

" Bravo! " said Crammon, and, comfortably eating, he phi-
losophized: " It would be saddening were it otherwise. I re-

peat what I have often said: Ariel was born for the stars.
There are blessed stars and fateful stars. Some are inhabited
by good spirits, others by demons. We have known that
from times immemorial. Let them wage their battles among
themselves. If it comes to collisions and catastrophes, it is a
cosmic matter in which we mortals have no share. When all
is said and done, you are but a mortal too, though one so
blessed that you were even granted a stay in the happy hunting grounds of the gods. But excesses are evil. You cannot
compete with Muscovite autocrats. Siegfried can conquer the
dragons in the end; were Lucifer to attack him with fire-
breathing steeds, the hero would but risk his skin in vain.
Your renunciation is as wise as it is delightful. I drink to
your pleasant future, dearest boy! "

Christian went to a buffet where magnificent fruit was exposed for sale. He knew Crammon's passionate delight in rare
and lovely fruit. He selected a woven basket and placed in the
middle a pine-apple cut open so that its golden inside showed.
He surrounded it with a wreath of flawless apples and of great,
amber-coloured peaches from the South of France. They were
elastic and yet firm. He added seven enormous clusters of
California grapes. He arranged the fruit artistically, carried
the basket to Crammon, and presented it to him with jesting
solemnity.

They separated. When, late that afternoon, Crammon returned to the hotel, he learned to his bitter amazement that
Christian had left.

He could not compose himself. It seemed to him that he
was the victim of some secret cabal. " They all leave me in the
lurch," he murmured angrily to himself; " they make a mock of
me. It's like an epidemic. You are through with life, Bernard
Gervasius, you are in every one's way. Go to your cell and
bemoan your fate."

He ordered his valet to pack, and to secure accommodations
on the train to Vienna. Then he placed the basket of fruit on

the table, and in his sad reflections plucked berry after berry of the grape.

XXIV

In his quiet little house, furnished in the style of the age of Maria Theresa, he forgot what he had suffered. He lived an idyl.

He accompanied the two pious ladies to church, and out of considerateness and kindness to them even prayed occasionally. His chief prayer was: Lord, forgive those who have trespassed against me and lead me not into temptation. On sunny afternoons the carriage appeared and took the three for a ride through the parks. In the evening the bill of fare for the following day was determined on, and the national and traditional dishes were given the preference. Then he read to the devoutly attentive Misses Aglaia and Constantine classical poems: a canto of Klopstock's " Messiah," Schiller's " Walk," or something by Rückert. And he still imitated the voice and intonation of Edgar Lorm. Also he related harmless anecdotes connected with his life; and he adorned and purified them so that they would have been worthy of a schoolgirl's library.

Not till the two ladies had retired did he light his short pipe or pour himself out a glass of cognac; he practised reminiscence or introspection, or became absorbed in his little museum of treasures, which he had gathered during many years.

Shortly before his proposed meeting with Franz Lothar von Westernach, he received an alarming letter from Christian's mother.

Frau Wahnschaffe informed him that Christian had ordered all his possessions to be sold—Christian's Rest, Waldleiningen, the hunting lodge, the stables and kennels, the motor cars, the collections, including the wonderful collection of rings. This incomprehensible plan was actually being carried out, and no one had an inkling of the motive. She herself was in the utmost despair, and begged Crammon for some explanation and, if possible, to come to the castle. She besought him in God's name for some hint in regard to Christian's actions and state of mind. No news of her son had reached her for weeks; he seemed lost, and they were groping in the dark. The family did not, of course, desire his possessions to pass into the hands of strangers, and would bid in everything, although it was both difficult and hateful to oppose the impudent offers and the tricky manœuvres which the auction ordered by Christian would entail. Above all, however, there was her personal anxiety about Christian. She expected Crammon to stand by her in her hour of need, and justify the high opinion she had formed both of his friendship for her son and of his attachment to her family.

Crammon re-read the lines that mentioned the sale of Christian's Rest and of the collections. He shook his head long and sadly, pressed his chin into his hands, and two large tears rolled down his cheeks.

END OF VOL. I

THE SECOND VOLUME:

RUTH

CONTENTS OF THE SECOND VOLUME

THE WORLD'S ILLUSION

CONVERSATIONS IN THE NIGHT

I

WHEN Wolfgang visited his home during the Christmas
vacation he congratulated his father on the latter's accession
to a new dignity; Albrecht Wahnschaffe had been made
a Privy Councillor.

He found the house changed—silent and dull. From a
brief conversation with his father he learned that Christian
was causing anxiety and excitement. He listened avidly, but
did not succeed in gathering any details. Strangers had told
him of Christian's sale of his properties; but he had no
notion of the meaning of this step.

He had but one long talk with his mother. She seemed
to him to be morbid and to treat him with an indifference
that wounded him.

Rumours of all kinds reached him. The major-domo informed him that Herr von Crammon had spent a couple of days
at the castle, almost constantly closeted with its mistress.
They had sent an enormously long telegram to Berlin, offer-
ing some one a bribe of forty or fifty thousand marks. The
telegram had not been addressed directly to the person in
question, but to an intermediary. The reply must have been
unfavourable, for on its receipt Herr von Crammon had announced that he himself would proceed to Berlin.

Wolfgang decided to write to Crammon, but his letter
remained unanswered.

Since, at bottom, he took very little interest in Christian's
doings, he refrained from any further investigation, and at

the beginning of January returned to Berlin. From the behaviour of his acquaintances it was evident that a secret in
which he was concerned weighed on their minds. In many
eyes there was an indefinite yet watchful curiosity. But he
was not particularly sensitive. His aim was to appear faultless in the worldly sense and not to alienate any who might
affect his career. He was so wholly indentified with the views
of his social group that he trembled at the very thought of
being accused of a mistake or an unconventionality. For this
reason his demeanour had an element of the nervously watchful
and restless. He was extremely careful to venture the expression of no opinion of his own, but always to be sure that whatever he said represented the opinion of the majority who set
the standards of his little world.

At a social gathering he observed near him several young
men engaged in eager but whispered conversation. He joined
them and they became silent at once. He could not but
remark the fact. He drew one of them aside and put the
question to him brusquely. It was a certain Sassheimer, the
son of an industrial magnate of Mainz. He could have made
no better choice, for Sassheimer envied him, and there was
an old jealousy between his family and the house of
Wahnschaffe.

"We were talking about your brother," he said. "What's
the matter with him? The wildest stories are floating around
both at home and here in Berlin. Is there anything to them?
You ought to know."

Wolfgang grew red. "What could be wrong?" he replied
with reserve and embarrassment. "I know of nothing.
Christian and I scarcely communicate with each other."

"They say that he's taken up with a loose woman," Sassheimer continued, "a common creature of the streets. You
ought to do something about that report. It isn't the sort
of thing your family can simply ignore."

"I haven't heard a syllable about it," said Wolfgang, and

became redder than ever. "It's most improbable too. Christian is the most exclusive person in the world. Who is responsible for such rot?"

"It is repeated everywhere," Sassheimer said maliciously; "it's queer that you're the only one who has heard nothing. Besides, he is said to have broken with all his friends. Why don't you go to him? He is in the city. Things like that can ordinarily be adjusted in a friendly way before the scandal spreads too far."

"I shall inquire at once," said Wolfgang, and drew himself very erect. "I'll probe the matter thoroughly, and if I find the report to be a slander I shall hold those who spread it strictly accountable."

"Yes, that would seem the correct thing to do," Sassheimer answered coolly.

Wolfgang went home. All his old hatred of his brother flamed up anew. First Christian had been the radiant one who threw all others in the shade; now he threatened to bring disgrace and danger into one's most intimate circles.

The hatred almost choked him.

II

The hours of consultations and interviews were drawing to an end. The features of Privy Councillor Wahnschaffe showed weariness. The last person who had left him had been a Japanese, a councillor of the ministry of war at Tokio. One of the directors had been present at the conference, which had been important and of far-reaching political implications. He was about to go when Wahnschaffe called him back by a gesture.

"Have you selected an engineer to go to Glasgow?" he asked. He avoided looking at the man's face. What annoyed him in the men around him was a certain expression of greed after power, possession, and success, which they wore like a

mental uniform. He saw almost no other expression any
more.

The director mentioned a name.

Herr Wahnschaffe nodded. " It is a curious thing about the
English," he said. " They are gradually becoming wholly dependent on us. Not only do they no longer manufacture
machines of this type, but we have to send an expert to set
them up and explain their workings. Who would have thought
that possible ten years ago? "

" They frankly admit their inferiority in this respect," the
director answered. " One of the gentlemen from Birmingham,
whom we took through the works recently, expressed his utter
amazement at out resistless progress. He said it was phenom-
enal. I gave him the most modest reason I could think of.
I explained that we didn't have the English institution of the
week-end, and this added five to six hours a week to our pro-
ductive activity."

" And did that explanation satisfy him? "

" He asked: ' Do you really think that accounts for your
getting ahead of us? ' I said that the time amounted to several
thousand hours a year in the activity of a whole nation. He
shook his head and said that we were extremely well-informed
and industrious, but that, closely looked upon, our competition
was unfair."

The Privy Councillor shrugged his shoulders. " It is always
their last word—unfair. I do not know their meaning. In
what way are they fairer than ourselves? But they use the
word as a last resort."

" They haven't much good-will toward us," said the director.

" No. I regret it; but it is true that they have not." He
nodded to the director, who bowed and left the room.

Herr Wahnschaffe leaned back in his chair, glanced wearily
at the documents scattered over his huge desk, and covered
his eyes with his pale hand. It was his way of resting and of
collecting his thoughts. Then he pressed one of the numerous

electric buttons on the edge of the desk. A clerk entered. " Is there any one else? "

The clerk handed him a card, and said: " This gentleman is from Berlin, and says he has an appointment with you, sir."

The card read: " Willibald Girke, Private Detective. The Girke and Graurock Private Detective Agency. Puttbuser Street 2, Berlin, C."

III

" Have you anything new to report? " the Privy Councillor asked.

A swift glance showed him in this face, too, that well-known and contemptible greed for power and possession and success that stopped in its hard determination at no degradation and no horror.

" Your written communications did not satisfy me, so I summoned you in order to have you define more closely the methods to be used in your investigations." The formal phraseology hid Herr Wahnschaffe's inner uncertainty and shame.

Girke sat down. His speech was tinged with the dialect of Berlin. " We have been very active. There is plenty of material. If you'll permit me, I can submit it at once." He took a note-book out of his pocket, and turned the leaves.

His ears were very large and stood off from his head. This fact impressed one as a curious adaptation of an organism to its activity and environment. His speech was hurried; he sputtered his sentences and swallowed portions of them. From time to time he looked at his watch with a nervous and uncertain stare. He gave an impression as of a man whom the life of a great city had made drunken, who neither slept nor ate in peace through lack of time, whose mind was shredded from a ceaseless waiting for telephone calls, letters, telegrams, and newspapers.

He spoke with hurried monotony. " The apartment on

Kronprinzenufer has been kept. But it is not clear whether your son may be regarded as still occupying it. During the past month he passed only four nights there. It seems that he turned the apartment over to the student of medicine, Amadeus Voss. We have been watching this gentleman right along as you directed. The style in which this young man lives is most unusual, in view of his origin and notorious poverty. It is obvious, of course, where he gets the money. He is matriculated at the university; and so is your son."

"Suppose we leave Voss out for the moment," Herr Wahn-schaffe interrupted, still burdened by his uncertainty and shame. "You wrote me that my son had rented in succession quite a series of dwellings. I should like an explanation of this, as well as the exact facts of his present whereabouts."

Girke turned the leaves of his note-book again. "Here we are, sir. Our investigations provide an unbroken chain. From Kronprinzenufer he moved with the woman concerning whom we have gathered full and reliable data to Bernauer Street, in the neighbourhood of the Stettiner Railroad Station. Next he moved to 16 Fehrbelliner Street; then to No. 3 Jablonski Street; then to Gaudy Street, quite near the Exerzier Square; finally to Stolpische Street at the corner of Driesener. The curious thing is not only this constant change of habitation, but the gradual decline in the character of the neighbourhoods selected, down to a hopelessly proletarian level. This fact seems to reveal a secret plan and a definite intention."

"And he stopped at Stolpische Street?"

"He's been there five weeks, since the twentieth of February. But he rented two flats in this place, one for the woman in question and one for himself."

"This place is far in the north of the city, isn't it?"

"As far as you can get. West and north of it there are empty lots. To the east the roads lead to the cemeteries of Weissensee. All around are factories. It's an unhealthy, un-safe, and hideous locality. The house itself was built about six years ago, but is already in a deplorable condition. There are forty-five flats with outside light, and fifty-nine with nothing but light from the court. The latter are inhabited by factory hands, hucksters, people of uncertain occupations, and characters that are clearly suspicious. Karen Engelschall, the woman in question, has an outside flat on the third floor, consisting of two rooms and a kitchen. The furnishings belong to a widow named Spindler. The monthly rent is eighty marks, payable in advance. She has a servant, a young girl named Isolde Schirmacher, who is the daughter of a tailor. Your son lodges on the ground-floor of the inside flats with a certain Gisevius, who is night watchman in the Borsig works. His accommodation consists of a barely furnished living-room and a half-dark sleeping chamber in which there is nothing but a cot."

Herr Wahnschaffe's eyes grew wide, under the influence of a fright which he could not quite control. " For heaven's sake," he said, " what can be the meaning of it? "

" It is a mystery indeed, sir. We have never had a similar case. There is plenty of room for supposition, of course. Then there's the hope that future events may throw light on everything."

Herr Wahnschaffe recovered his self-control, and coldly dismissed the other's attempts at consolation. " And what is your information concerning the woman? " he asked in his most official tone. " What results have you in that direction? "

" I was just about to come to that, sir. We have done our best, and have succeeded in uncovering the woman's antecedents. It was an extremely difficult task, and we had to send a number of agents to different parts of the country. The name and occupation of her father could not be discovered, since her birth was illegitimate. Her mother is a Frisian. She was housekeeper on a small estate near Oldenburg. After that she lived with a pensioned tax-gatherer. After his death she opened a small shop in Hanover, but the business failed. In 1895 she was convicted of fraud, and spent three months in prison at Cleve. We lost track of her after that, until she turned up in Berlin in 1900. First she lived in Rixdorf. Next she rented rooms—first in Brüsseler Street behind the Virchow Hospital, at present in Zionskirch Square. She has been accused of renting rooms for immoral purposes, but nothing could be proved against her. She pretends to be an art-embroiderer, but as a matter of fact she practises fortune-telling and clairvoyance. To judge by her way of living there is money in the business. She never had but two children, Karen, and a son, now twenty-six, named Niels Heinrich, who is known to the police as a worthless rogue and has come into conflict with the law on several occasions. Karen has had a shady career since her early girlhood. No doubt her mother put her up to everything. When she was seventeen her mother is reported to have sold her to a Dutch ship captain for five hundred gilders. She has given birth to two illegitimate children, at Kiel in 1897 and at Königsberg in 1901. Both died shortly after birth. In addition to the cities named, she has lived in Bremen, Schleswig, Hanover, Kuxhaven, Stettin, Aachen, Rotterdam, Elberfeld, and Hamburg. At nearly all these places she was a registered prostitute. We lost sight of her between 1898 and '99. Her circumstances seemed to have improved temporarily during that year. According to one informant she accompanied a Danish painter to Wassigny in the North of France. From Hamburg, where she gradually sank lower and lower, she was brought to Berlin in the manner concerning which we had the honour of rendering you an account in our report of February 14th."

Girke drew a long breath. His achievement in its architectonic structure somehow impressed him anew. He enjoyed the methodical arrangement of the material gleaned from so many sources, and threw a glance of triumph at the Privy Councillor. He did not observe the latter's stony expression, but continued on his victorious progress. " On her arrival in Berlin she sought out her mother, and they rapidly became very intimate again The mother came to visit both at Kronprinzenufer and at all the other places. The brother Niels Heinrich also came to see Karen—twice at Fehrbelliner Street, once on Gaudy, and five times on Stolpische. Quarrels arose among these three persons, which grew noisier on every occasion. On the eleventh inst., at five o'clock in the afternoon, Niels Heinrich left his sister's flat in a rage, uttered threats and boasted and created an uproar in a gin-shop. On the twelfth he came from the house in the company of your son. They went together as far as Lothringer Street; there your son gave the fellow money. On the sixteenth he walked up and down before the house on Kronprinzenufer till evening. When your son, accompanied by the student Voss, appeared in the street, he approachd them. After a brief exchange of words your son gave him money again, gold-pieces as well as a bank note. Your son and Voss walked on together as far as the Tiergarten, and during that time Voss seemed to be violently expostulating with your son. The subject of their conversation is unknown. Our agent did not succeed in getting close enough to them, and I had other engagements that day. We are credibly informed, however, by parties in the house on Kronprinzenufer, that Voss is often of an extreme insolence and bitter aggressiveness which are both directed again your son."

Albrecht Wahnschaffe was white to the very lips. To hide the tumult of his soul, he arose and went to the window.

The foundations were trembling. The peak of life on which he stood was being obscured by dark fumes, even as out there the smoke and soot which the wind blew down from the great smoke-stacks covered all things. The chaotic noises of toil and the whir of machines floated dully to him. On roofs and cornices lay soiled snow.

What was to be done? There were provisions in law for extreme cases; but to have Christian declared irresponsible would not destroy the disgrace. There was nothing to do but persuade, prevent, guard, hush up.

Words finally wrung themselves from his aching throat: " Does he associate with any other questionable people? "

" Not that I know of," Girke answered. " With plain people, yes; both in the house and on the street. But he goes to lectures regularly, and studies at home. He does not associate with his fellow students or, rather, did not until lately. We are told, however, that at the university his personality has aroused attention. Two days ago he received a visit from a Herr von Thüngen, who is stopping in the Hotel de Rome. Whether this event will have any consequences we cannot say yet."

With clouded brow the Privy Councillor said: " I have bought all of my son's possessions. The proceeds of the sale amounting to thirteen million five hundred thousand marks, have been deposited in the Deutsche Bank. There are un- happily no legal methods by means of which I can be informed concerning the use to which this money is put, and whether not only the income but the capital is being used. Some clear information on this point would be of importance."

The sum named filled Girke with a reverential shudder. He lowered his head, and saliva gathered in his mouth. " In addition to the thirteen millions, your son also receives his annual income, doesn't he? "

Herr Wahnschaffe nodded. " It is paid him by the firm in quarterly installments through a branch of the Bank of Dresden."

" I merely ask, of course, to have a clear view of the situa- tion. Considering such unlimited means, your son's way of life is mysterious, most mysterious. He usually takes his meals at very humble inns and restaurants; he never uses a motor or a cab, and even the tramway quite rarely. He walks long distances both morning and evening."

This bit of information stabbed the Privy Councillor. It

made a deeper impression on him than anything else the detective had told him.

"I shall have due regard to your wishes in every respect, sir," Girke said. "The information you last referred to will not be easy to obtain. But I shall see to it, sir, that you will be satisfied with the services of our firm."

That ended the interview.

IV

From the unconscious brooding of many days there arose in the mind of Albrecht Wahnschaffe the clear memory of an incident which had taken place at Aix-les-Bains when Christian was fourteen years old.

Albrecht Wahnschaffe had made the acquaintance of a Marchesa Barlotti, a witty old lady who had been a famous opera singer in her youth, and who was now of a positively fascinating ugliness. One day she had met Albrecht Wahnschaffe and Christian on the promenade, and had been so enchanted by the boy's beauty that she had cordially asked him, in her fine, free way, to visit her. Christian had turned pale; but his father had promised, and appointed an hour in his stead. But Christian, in whom the ugliness of the Marchesa had aroused an unconquerable aversion, calmly and coldly refused obedience to his father's wish. No persuasion or request or command had influenced the boy. Albrecht Wahnschaffe fell into one of those Berserker rages which made him drunk and dizzy; it didn't happen more than once in ten years, and when the attack had passed he felt like a man who had had a serious illness. In his rage he had approached Christian and struck him with his stick. But no second blow fell. The expression in the boy's face paralyzed his arm. For it was as of ice, yet as of flame: there was in it a loftiness and also a deadly scorn, against which anger broke as glass will break on granite. And that icy and infinitely astonished expression seemed to say: You hope to chastise me? To force me?

And the father, in his amazement and humiliation and shame, had recognized the fact that here was a human soul that could not and must not be forced, never, under no circumstances, unto no purpose in the world.

It was this incident that came into his mind now, and was the reason why he definitively gave up the intention of using force.

Months ago he had written to Christian, asking him to come home and explain himself, to rescue his parents from the pressure of anxiety and confusion, and especially his mother, who was suffering beyond her strength. To this letter Christian had replied laconically that there would be no purpose in his coming, and that there was no ground for anxiety, that he was very well and in excellent spirits, and that no one need suffer because he followed his own devices.

But what was the sense of his action? Was there any key to this mystery? Was it possible in this age of science and enlightenment to conceive of a mystic metamorphosis of personality?

He had a vision of Christian walking through the long streets, especially at night, going into humble inns and eating poor food. What was the meaning of it? And he could imagine meeting Christian on such an occasion, and could see his son's conventional courtesy, the proud, cool eyes, the firm, white teeth which that conventional smile revealed. And even to imagine such a meeting filled him with fear.

But perhaps that was necessary. Perhaps he would have to go to him. Perhaps all that had happened did not in reality have the deadly seriousness which it seemed to have at a distance. Perhaps there was some simple confusion that could be cleared and disentangled easily enough.

The thought of Christian burrowed deep into his brain, and his fear grew. If he sought release from that thought, it emerged to torment him the more, in dreams, in sleepless nights, amid the tumult of affairs, in conversation, in every place, at all times, through all the weeks and months.

V

The castle of the Wahnschaffes, built for delight and splendour, lay desolate. The great reception halls and the guest-rooms were empty. Some American friends had announced their arrival; but Frau Wahnschaffe had begged to be excused.

Her husband sent her delicacies and flowers from the hot-houses. She cared for neither. In a lethargy she sat in an armchair or lay in her bed of state. The curtains were drawn even by day. The electric lamps were veiled.

Memories of Christian's childhood were her refuge. She lived them over in imagination: how Christian as a child of five had lain in bed with her. Early in the morning the nurse had brought him in his loud delight, still with the rosy warmth of sleep upon him. She recalled the bird-like voice, the golden locks, the flexible hands, the radiant, deep-blue eyes. He had stretched out his little hands after her ropes of pearls, when she had come in evening dress into the nursery. Once little maidens had placed a wreath of sweet peas on his head and danced about him in innocent homage. He had raced through the park with two dogs, and stopped with an admirable gesture of astonishment before a statue of bronze. Later, when he was a youth, at the carnival in Mainz he had stood amid lovely women in a flowery chariot and raised a silver goblet toward the beholders.

Unforgettable to her were his gestures, his glances, his resilient walk, the dark tones of his voice. Equally unforgettable were the expectation of his coming, the delight of his presence, the admiration that met him from the eyes of men. The world contained him only.

She read the few letters that he had written her. She

guarded them like relics in a little ebony box. They were
sober, dry notes, but to her they were magical. There were
ten or twelve lines from Paris or San Sebastian, Rome, Viareg-
gio, Corfu, or the Isle of Wight. Once she had drunk all the
beauty of earth from these places. Now that he was no longer
there, they faded and died to her.

She had loved her womb because it had borne him; she
hated it now because she had lost him. But how or why she
had lost him—that was a thing unfathomable. She brooded
over it by day and night.

No one could guide her. No thought revealed a gleam of
light. She stood before a wall and stared at it in despair.
She listened, but no voice reached her ear from the other side.
All that people told her seemed absurd and false.

In her bedroom hung a portrait of Christian painted in his
twentieth year. It had been done three years before by a
Swedish painter. It was very like him, and she adored it. One
night she took it from the wall and placed it on a table and
lifted the shade from a lamp nearby. She crouched in a chair,
rested her head upon her hands, and gazed at the picture
steadily and with a questioning passion.

She asked the picture, but it gave no answer. She thrilled
with a desire to take that head into her hands. But the face
on the canvas smiled its equivocal and remote smile. If
only she could have wept! But tears were denied her: too
hard and unmoved had she passed through life.

When morning came her maid found her still sitting before
Christian's picture. The painted face beside the burning lamp
still smiled its alien smile.

VI

Johanna Schöntag wrote to Christian: " It is two months
now since I parted from you. In those two months misfortune
has been very busy with me and mine. My father committed

suicide; that was why I was summoned home so suddenly. Rash speculations complicated his affairs beyond his power; he saw no way to prevent his being reduced to beggary, and determined to leave the scene of his failure thus abruptly. All obligations have been decently satisfied, and his good name has been saved. We are also told, as if it were a consolation, that he lost his head too soon, that things might have turned out better than he feared. But we are in an unenviable situation, and life is not showing us an admirable aspect. Such sudden transformations should be confined to melodrama. I am still badly confused; I hardly know what is happening to me. I envy those who have an aim of some kind and also the vitality to pursue it. I wonder whether you will write to me. Or have you already forgotten me? Have I even the right to ask that? "

She sent this letter to Crammon with the request to forward it. Crammon replied: " My dear Rumpelstilzkin:—I hope that your voice will not die in the desert. Unhappy things have taken place. The man to whom you are writing has denied himself and his own past and all who love him. The Lord has darkened his soul; we are striving for his salvation. May your assistance bear rich fruit."

The words frightened her, and she did not know how to interpret them. She had time to reflect, for weeks passed before she received an answer to her letter; and this answer was worse than none at all. It came not from Christian himself but from Amadeus Voss, and was as follows:

" My dear Fräulein:—While arranging some documents which my friend Christian Wahnschaffe left in the apartment which I have taken off his hands, I found your letter among other things. Since he has failed for some months, with very rare exceptions, to answer any letters, I think I may take it for granted that you have not heard from him. I can hardly dare hope to make up for his negligence. Who am I? What am I to you? You may not even recall me. I, on the contrary, remember you very exactly, and regret most constantly that I did not succeed in making you more conscious of my devotion and sympathy. But I am diffident by nature, and the fear of being repulsed or having my feelings misunderstood has assumed morbid intensity in my mnid. Do not therefore, pray, regard it as a tactless importunity if I venture to write you in Christian's stead. The thought of your uncertainty and fruit-less waiting pained me, and I determined to put an end to it so far as it lies in my power to do.

"I believe I can give you the assurance that Christian Wahnschaffe is not as guilty, so far as you are concerned, as he may seem to be, unless we agree that his guilt toward all who knew and loved him is the same. To speak of his practising neglect or failing in a duty would be unbecoming in me as well as incorrect in fact. He has sloughed off his former skin, and the coin in which he pays to-day is of another mintage. Whether its value is higher or lower than formerly it is not my office to decide. He has, in the prover-bial expression, burned his bridges behind him. What he does may arouse the horror of the morally immature; I, too, I confess, find the motivation obscure and difficult. But one must have patience and faith in a benevolent providence; for we all eat the bread of some abyss and it is bitter on each man's lips.

"It is in view of the uncommon circumstances that I beg you to pardon my taking upon myself the part of an *alter ego* of our friend and making his affairs, as it were, my own. I have done it only after mature reflection; and what may at first seem to you sheer forwardness, and an indelicate intrusion into secrets that are not my own, has been prompted purely by a profound regard for your peace of mind. In closing may I express to you my deep and sincere sympathy? You have suffered from terrible visitations. God in His good-ness will assuredly brighten your path again."

Johanna read this letter innumerable times, and each time

with a pang of intolerable shame, each time on the verge of tears. It made her feel so exposed and affronted. And then she would burrow again and again into the artifice of those stilted sentences. Frightened and desperate, and yet with a stabbing curiosity, she asked: What could have happened to make Christian, him whom she trusted immeasurably, whom she knew to be the soul of delicacy and reserve—what could have happened to make him callously expose the most intimate things in life to the treachery and hypocrisy of this man?

In her excitement she went to Crammon's house, but he had left Vienna long ago. She asked where he was, but received no certain information. Aglaia named a Berlin hotel, Constantine the château of Count Vitztum in the mountains of Saxony. Johanna wrote letters, tore them up, reflected and brooded, was pursued by shame and doubt, and finally determined to write to Amadeus Voss. She wrote a brief note in her rigid, angular writing, her left hand clenched in rage, her forehead wrinkled, her little teeth gnawing at her lip. With a certain mockery of implication she thanked him for his trouble, contemptuously ignored his indiscretion, controlled her profoundly instinctive aversion, and finally, with an impatient turn of speech, demanded some clear information concerning Christian Wahnschaffe, since she had never been taught the reading of riddles or the solving of mysteries. She admitted that she had no right to make this demand, since her interest in Christian was merely a friend's. But as such it was strong and kind enough to justify her inquiries.

Four days later Voss's answer reached her. Her heart beat as she held the letter. Unopened she hid it in a drawer. Not till evening, when she had locked herself into her room, did she open and read it.

"My dear Fräulein Schöntag:—I am surprised that you are unaware of a rumour which the very sparrows twitter from the house-tops here. Everybody whispers and peers and is astonished, and dares not trust the evidence of his senses.

Hence to spare you unnecessary circumlocutions I shall proceed at once to the point. You may remember that I left Hamburg a week before Christian Wahnschaffe, and rented a comfortable apartment for us both in Berlin. Since we had both determined to study medicine there, I had every reason to suppose that as long as our relations were harmonious we would have a common household. So I waited for him, and he came at last; but he did not come alone. He brought a woman with him. Here words fail me. I use the word woman because my consideration for you forbids me the use of any other. And yet how shall I convey the true state of affairs, if I shrink back from the unchangeable facts? The truth cannot remain hidden. This person's name is Karen Engelschall. He rescued her in a state of hopeless degradation from some harlots' haunt near the harbour. She is a characteristic outcast. Her appearance is coarse and her manners repulsive. She expects to be confined shortly. She was in the power of a ruffian who maltreated her and beat her; whenever she thinks of him she shakes with terror and horror. She is between thirty and thirty-two years old, but she looks older. One look at her face suffices to convince one that she is familiar with every vice and with every crime.

" My dear young lady, pray do not stop here as you would stop listening were I saying these things to you. The words I have written down are brutally frank, and your imagination, unaccustomed to such images, may identify me with the horrors I am forced to evoke. But I shall be patient, if it be so, until your impressions become sufficiently clarified to do me justice. What I have said is only an introduction, and I must proceed.

" He came with his cases and boxes, but he had discharged his valet. Toward me he was of an extreme cordiality, and indeed he seemed far more cheerful than he had been when I left him. Two rooms were set aside for this woman—a bedroom and a sitting-room. There remained three rooms for him and two for me. But I had not been prepared for this additional companion and hardly knew what to say. He gave me a superficial explanation of her presence, but he withheld his real confidence. How repulsive is this smoothness of the mere worldling, how indistinguishable from downright falseness! To smile and be silent convinces no one, though it may serve to deceive. We who are lowly born do not know such gestures, and disdain to take refuge in polite irresponsibility. The woman appeared at our meals. She sat there like a clod, played with the cloth, asked foolish question, rattled the silver, and used her knife as a shovel. Whenever Wahnschaffe glanced at her, she looked like a thief who had been caught. I was confounded. He seemed to me out of his senses. His entire behaviour toward her was marked by a considerateness so exquisite that I was compelled to believe that her influence over him had been gained in some supernatural way. But what was its nature? I soon ascertained beyond a doubt that she was not his mistress. Nor was such a thing conceivable; it was a thought to be dismissed at once. What then was the source of her power? It was in some devilish magic. Do not think that my mind is wandering. In hours of spiritual insight I have looked deeply into the secrets of creation. The human soul, poor and rich at once, has endless capacities and powers of transformation. The stars gleam over us and we know them not, neither their influence nor their power. The fissures of the earth have been closed, and we know but as through the memory of a dream that there are demons seeking to rule us. I trust that in this matter we shall some day understand each other when we meet. Accept this prophecy in proof of the truth of my assertions.

"I must continue. I no longer felt at home in those handsome rooms. At night I often stood alone in the darkness, and listened for sounds from the rooms of the other two. I conquered my aversion, and sought out the woman when she was alone. She was talkative in a disagreeable way. I did

not conceal my contempt. In his presence she was dull. Superficially she seems to rule him through her own servility. The
sight of her complete degradation impressed an eye satiated
with the glories of this world. I tried to discover in her some
alluring quality, some trace of lost or ruined beauty, some
charm, however humble or even perverse. I hoped to discover her secret by seeming to agree with her and appreciate
the situation. I watched for some sign of a change in her
soul, some symptom of expiation or conversion. I found instead
a crude, stained, stubborn, bestial, lumpish, unformed creature.

" I shuddered. All too near was the time when it had taken
all my passionate energy to save myself from the slime; too
deeply had I suffered among those from whom the Lord averts
His countenance; too many midnights lay behind me in which
my soul hovered over the abyss; too long had I been ground
between the millstones of sin; too accursed was this woman in
my eyes, far too accursed for me to see her glide calmly and
sinuously to a point of sloth where she could rest from past
evil and prepare herself for more. I felt impelled to flee. It
was no spectacle for me. My spirit threatened to become
poisoned again and also my heart—that writhing thing that
made me a burden to myself and to mankind. I told Wahnschaffe that he could have my rooms; but he urged me to
stay, saying that he felt uncomfortable in the house and would
leave it. Aha, I thought, he is lusting after palaces; this is
too humble for him. But to every one's astonishment he sought
far humbler quarters, stayed but a week, sought others that
were still meaner, and thus changed his abode twice more
until he moved with the woman to the reeking and buzzing
tenement house in the north end of the city where he is now.

" If I did not know the facts and were told them, I should
laugh incredulously. The widow Engelschall, Karen's mother,
was furious when she heard of it. I have met her too, and I
cannot describe her without physical nausea. Karen's brother,
a rogue and an outcast, questioned Wahnschaffe and threatened

him. He is surrounded by the offscourings of the earth. Yet there he studies, sleeps in a dark hole on a shabby sofa of leather—he the spoiled darling, the expectancy and rose of his own class, the epicure and the allurer, the Adonis and Crœsus! Does my voice seem to pierce your ears even from the pallor of this written sheet? Is your inmost mind petrified? Then pray come here and be a witness to this experiment in monasticism, this modern hermitage, this sombre farce. Come, for perhaps we need you as one of the hearts that once glowed for him. Perhaps eyes from the world of his old delights will be the mirrors in which he will see himself, and find and recover himself once more.

" Do I seem to triumph in his downfall? I should not wish to do so; yet there may be a touch of grimness in my soul. For it is I who prepared the way, I whom dreams of sin like a leprosy of the soul condemn to this very day to an accursed disquietude. He throws away what he has. Millions that breed new millions lie in the bank, and he does not regard them. He lives without luxury or diversion or agreeable company, without plays or cars or games or love or flirtation, without being honoured or admired or spoiled. I await the hour in which he will laugh and declare the period of forgetfulness to be over. So long as the millions breed millions, and his father and mother guard their strong-boxes for him in the background, there is no room for serious fear. His clothes and linen, his cravats and jewels and toilet articles are largely still here where I live alone. He drops in at times to bathe and change his garments. His appearance is what it always was; he looks as though he were going to a luncheon with a minister of state or to a rendezvous with a duchess. He is not melancholy or thoughtful or hollow-eyed. He is as arrogant, as dry of soul, as insignificant, as princely as ever. But there is a new lightness in his actions, a new decisiveness in his speech. And he laughs oftener.

" Once he did not laugh, on that day in his castle when I

told him of darkness and of terror, before he went to meet the dancer. He listened, listened day and night, and asked and listened again. But was it compassion that stirred in his soul? By no means. He is not even a Christian; no heavenly spark enlightens his soul; he knows nothing of God, and is of those to whom the passage in Corinthians applies: The natural man receiveth not the things of the Spirit of God, for they are foolishness unto him; neither can he know them, because they are spiritually discerned. I had desired to awaken him. I spoke as with tongues of flame out of the nethermost depths. But he was the stronger: he lured me to his Saturnalia and drove me into crime, and I forgot my eternal weal for the sake of the lusts of this earth. He was like a shadow to me; now I am myself like a shadow, and he insults the holy thing he mocks. What knows he of the axe and the ring? I know of both. What knows he of the signs and symbols that become torches in the darkness of the soul? To him all things are concrete and finite;—the nail and the board, the bell and the candle, the stone and the root, the trowel and the hammer are but dead things to him, but not to me. Rome and Galilee rise and battle. Torment proceeds from him; a torment drives me to him. It is as though we were brothers and linked in the flesh and had crept out of the same womb, and yet neither can find or understand the other.

"Why does he live close to that woman? What does he expect of her? He speaks of her in a tone of strange suspense. It is an uncanny, rash, and insatiable curiosity that is in him. Once he lusted after palaces, now he lusts after sties; once he desired counts and artists, cavaliers and cocottes with ropes of pearls, now he seeks drunkards and paupers, pimps and prostitutes. It is a lust that is in him, and neither pilgrimage nor aspiration nor prayer—lust after the nail and stone, the bell and candle, the stone and root, the trowel and hammer, and all things wherein there is power and from which proceed both suffering and knowledge. I

have seen his eyes gleam when I spoke of the death of an outcast, or of a deaf-mute's drowning himself, who was my own
brother and died through his fault; and likewise when I spoke
of the self-inflicted death of another which I caused in my
downtrodden youth. I watched him well amid his jewels
and paintings and silver plate, and the flowers and costly
books of his houses, when these things began to satiate him,
and when he began to listen greedily for the wailing that comes
from prison houses, and when a sleep full of fear came over
him. And now he plays with the poor and the things of the
poor, and wanders by and collects these things and takes delight in them; he reaches out after one and then after another,
and desires to know what is in each and what that signifies,
and yet remains the man he was. There is no salvation in this,
for it is written: Eye hath not seen, nor ear heard, neither
have entered into the heart of man, the things which God hath
prepared for them that love him.

"But why does the woman follow him? Why does she
refuse the monstrous sums which his family has offered her
to leave him? Why does she calmly return with him to her
own underworld, when she must be panting after his gold, his
jewels, his houses and gardens, his power and his freedom?
What holds her? Why does she tarry? What devil's work
is being done? It happened recently that I walked home with
him during a violent snow-storm. He had given me a letter
of his friend Crammon to read. It was a long and foolish
whine, such as one would rather expect from an elderly blue-
stocking than from a man of sense. We argued about the
letter, that is to say, he would not take it seriously, while I
talked myself into a rage over it.

"Then he told me that a certain Baron von Thüngen,
one of his former boon-companions, had visited him on
the previous day. You may remember him; he was one
of those who danced attendance on Eva Sorel—a reddish-
blond, affected dandy. This man, Wahnschaffe told me, had

hunted for him long and had sat talking with him a whole day. He had said that he was dissatisfied with his life and longed for another way of living; that he did not know what to do, but had become a prey to unbearable melancholy; that he had always felt a deep sympathy for Wahnschaffe, but had not ventured to approach him; and that all he asked now was the privilege of sometimes spending an hour in his company. All this Wahnschaffe told me half diffidently, half in surprise. But the matter was not clear to me, and I said that Thüngen was probably merely one of those half-crazy idlers who had lost his appetite, and whose palate lusts for more sharply seasoned food. He did not take my rudeness amiss, and only said that such a judgment was rash.

"When we had reached our goal I went upstairs with him to Karen Engelschall's rooms. I did not wish to leave him. I was angry because he had again gotten the better of me by his icy sobriety. When we had passed through the narrow hallway, we heard Karen's screeching voice from the kitchen as well as the sound of wood chopping. We opened the kitchen door. The pregnant woman was kneeling by the hearth and splitting kindling wood. On a chair near the wall Isolde Schirmacher, the young girl that waits on her, leaned back with a yellowish pale face and closed eyes. An indisposition had overtaken her; it seemed epileptic in character, for her limbs were rigid and her head bent over backwards. She had evidently been at this task before, and Karen had taken her place. The girl's condition seemed to have caused her no concern. She split the wood with her hatchet, and, unconscious of our presence on the threshold, talked bitterly and blasphemously concerning her pregnancy: she didn't want another brat; she had a horror of it; it ought to be throttled at its first breath. Her talk was pure filth—impossible to report. Then Wahnschaffe entered the room, and lifted Isolde Schirmacher from her chair, and carried her, as though she were no burden at all, into the next room, and laid her on the bed. Then he came back, and said to the woman: 'Let that be, Karen,' and took the hatchet from her hand and heaped up the wood that had been cut. The woman was frightened. She obeyed him, and was silent, as though speech had died within her. This thing I saw with my own eyes, and from this picture you can see the nature of the woman and the relations of Wahn-schaffe and herself.

"No peace is left in me. From an invisible wound in the world's body the blood keeps flowing. I cry out for a vessel to receive it, but no one brings me such a vessel. Or are the sickness and the wound within myself? Is there such a thing as the yearning of the shadow for its body? Is it conceivable that the unimaginable has come to pass, and yet that he who yearned and sobbed and struggled and prayed for it to come to pass cannot recognize it now? There is some strange fatality in it all. I have learned now to tell fruit from rottenness, the bitter from the sweet, the fragrant from the stinking, the hurtful from the harmless. And I have also learned how limbs swing from their sockets, how vertebra joins vertebra, how muscle is intertwined with muscle, how ligament grows on ligament, how the veins pulse and how the brain is stratified. I can open the magic clockwork and put my hand into the mechanism that is forever rigid. There are compensations; but always at the sombre gates of existence must I pay my entrance fee to brighter regions. The other day I had a vision: You stood with me beside the corpse of a young person, and asked me to cut out the heart which had survived by a little the death of its body and twitched under my knife.

"That one more thing I wanted to tell you. With it I close."

Johanna sat over that letter all night until morning. A storm of March swept about the house. Her virginal room, with its hangings of white silk and the white enamelled furniture, seemed already bare and rifled to her. For on the morrow she was to leave it forever.

VII

Dead and wounded men lay on the red velvet sofas of the restaurant. They had been carried here hurriedly, and people were trying to help the living. Through the open doors there blew in an icy blast mixed with snow. Random shots were still fired in the streets, soldiers galloped up and down, an infantry squad appeared and disappeared. Guests hovered at the windows. A German waiter said: " They have mounted cannons on the Neva." A gentleman in a fur-coat entered hastily and said: " Kronstadt is in flames."

In one of the halls which were used for exclusive banquets, there was a brilliant company invited by Count Tutchkoff, one of the friends of the Grand Duke Cyril. There were Lord and Lady Elmster, the Earl of Somerset, Count and Countess Finkenrode, gentlemen belonging to the German and Austrian embassies, the Marquis du Caille, and the Princes Tolstoi, Trubetzkoi, Szilaghin, and their ladies.

The Grand Duke and Eva Sorel had come late. The dinner was over, and the general conversation had ceased. The couples whispered. The Duke, sitting between Lady Elmster and the Princess Trubetzkoi, had fallen asleep. However animated the company, this would happen from time to time; every one knew it, and had become accustomed to it.

Though he slept, his pose remained erect and careful. From time to time his lids twitched; the furrow on his forehead deepened so that it seemed black; his colourless beard was like a fern on the bark of a tree. One might have suspected that he feigned sleep in order to listen; but there was a slackness in his features that showed the uncontrolled muscles of sleep, and lent his face the appearance of a lemur. On his excessively long, lean hand, which rested on the cloth, and, like his lids, twitched at times, gleamed a solitaire diamond, the size of a hazelnut.

A restlessness had stolen over the company. When the

rifles outside began to rattle again, the young Countess Finkenrode arose and turned frightened glances toward the door. Szilaghin approached her, and calmed her with a smile. An officer of the guards entered, and whispered a report to Tutchkoff.

Eva and Wiguniewski sat a little aside, in front of a tall mirror that reflected a pallid image of them and of a part of the room.

Wiguniewski said to her: " Unhappily the report is vouched for. No one thought of such a thing."

" I was told he was in Petrograd," Eva answered. " In a German newspaper, moreover, I read a report that he was arrested in Moscow. And where are your proofs? To condemn Ivan Becker on hearsay is almost as terrible as the crime of which he is accused."

Wiguniewski took a letter from his pocket, looked about him carefully, unfolded it, and said: " From Nice he wrote this to a friend of his who is also my friend. I am afraid it puts an end to all doubt." Painfully, and with many hesitations, he translated the Russian words into French. " I am no longer what I was. Your suppositions are not groundless, and the rumours have not lied. Announce and confirm it to all who have set their hopes on me and given me their trust on definite conditions. A terrible time lies behind me. I could not go farther on my old and chosen path. You have been deceived in me, even as a phantom has misled me. In a case like mine it requires greater courage and strength to confess sincerely, and to wound those who had put their faith and trust in me, than to mount the scaffold and give up one's life. Gladly would I have suffered death for the ideas to which all my thoughts and feelings have been devoted hitherto. All of you know that. For I had already sacrificed to them my possessions, my peace, my youth, my liberty. But now when I have come to recognize these ideas as destructive errors, I must not serve them for another hour. I fear neither your accusations nor your contempt. I follow my inner light and the God that is within. There are three truths that have guided me in that searching of my soul which led to my conversion: It is a sin to resist; it is a sin to persuade others to resistance; it is a sin to shed the blood of man. I know all that threatens me; I know the isolation that will be mine. I am prepared for all persecutions. Do what you must, even as I do what I must."

After a long silence Eva said: "That is he. That is his voice; that is the bell whose chime none can resist. I believe him and I believe in him." She threw a sombre glance at the face of that sleeper beside the radiant board.

Wiguniewski crushed the letter, and thrust forward his chin with a bitter gesture. "His three truths," he replied, "will be as effective against our cause as three army divisions of Cossacks. They will suffice to fill the dungeons on both sides of the Urals, to unman our youth, to bury our hopes. Each one is a whip that will smite unto the earth an hundred thousand awakened spirits. Crime? It is worse; it is the tragedy of all this land. Three truths! " He laughed through his compressed teeth. "Three truths, and a blood-bath will begin that will make those of Bethlehem and St. Bartholomew seem jests. You may look at me. I do not weep; I laugh. Why should I weep? I shall go home, summon the popes, and give them this rag; and let them made amulets of it to distribute among those who wait for salvation. Perhaps that will suffice them."

Eva's face grew hard. An evil fascination still drew her eyes toward that sleeper's face. Upon the edges of her lips hovered a morbid smile; the skin of her cheek glimmered like an opal. "Why should he not follow the command of his soul? " she asked, and for a moment turned her diademed brow toward the prince. "Is it not better that a man should express and embody himself completely than that many hundreds of thousands be helped in the dreary mediocrity of their rigid lives? He has said it in his own beautiful way: 'I follow the inner light and the God that is within.' How many can do that? How many dare? And now I understand something he once said "—more penetratingly she looked into that sleeper's face—" ' one must bow down before that! ' So that was in his mind. Strange ploughs are passing over this earth of yours, prince. In its lacerated body there streams a darkness into which one would like to plunge in order to be born again. A primitive breath is there, and chaos; there the elements thunder and the most terrible dream becomes reality, an epic reality of immemorial ages. Of such life I once had no perception, except in some great marble in which a nameless woe had become rigid and eternal. I feel as though I were looking back on this scene from the height of centuries to come or from a star, and as though everything were vision." All this she said in a trembling voice and with an impassioned melancholy.

Wiguniewski, who had been a constant witness of her inner transformations for months past, was not surprised at her speech. His eyes, too, sought the sleeper's face. With a deep breath he said, " Yesterday a student of nineteen, Semyon Markovitch, heard of Ivan Becker's recanting and shot himself in his room. I went there and saw the body. If you had seen that dead boy, Eva, you would speak differently. A little differently, at all events. Did you ever see a lad lie in his coffin with a little black wound in his temple? He was charming and innocent as a girl, and yet he could experience this unspeakable woe and entertain this determined despair at a loss beyond measure."

A shiver passed over Eva's shoulders, and she smiled with a glittering feverishness that made her seem strangely possessed and heartless. The Prince continued in a matter-of-fact tone. " No doubt there's a good deal that is alluring about this letter. Why shouldn't a man like Ivan Becker render his breach of faith less repulsive by some plausible psychological excuses?

I am ready to grant you that he acted neither in conscious hypocrisy nor from any self-seeking motive. But he wouldn't be the genuine Russian that he is—emotional, turbid, fanatical, self-tormenting—if his transformation were not to entail all the fatal consequences of a systematic and deliberate treachery. He thinks that what he calls his awakening will serve mankind. In the meantime, out of blindness and weakness, confusion and mistaken moral fervour, he rushes into the claws of the beast that waits mercilessly in every corner and nook of Europe seeking to destroy and annihilate. And what I am doing now is passing a most charitable judgment. We happen to know that he has opened negotiations with the Holy Synod and is corresponding eagerly with the secret cabinet. Here in Moscow, as well as in Kiev and Odessa, arrests have been made in rapid succession which must be attributed to him. As things are, he alone could have furnished the information without which the authorities would not have ventured on these steps. These are facts that speak for themselves."

Eva pressed her right hand against her bosom, and stared, as though fascinated, into the air where she saw a vision that caused her to feel a rapidly alternating horror and ecstasy. Her lips moved as though to put a question, but she restrained herself.

With large and earnest eyes she looked at Wiguniewski, and whispered: " I suddenly have a longing that burns my heart, but I do not know after what. I should like to climb a mountain far beyond the snowline; or fare on a ship out into uncharted seas; or fly above the earth in an aeroplane. No, it is none of these things. I should like to go into a forest, to a lonely chapel, and cast myself down and pray. Will you go on such a pilgrimage with me? To some far monastery in the steppes? "

Wiguniewski was puzzled. Passion and sadness were in her words, but also a challenge that wounded him. Before he could formulate an answer, the Marquis du Caille and Prince Szilaghin approached them.

The sleeper opened his eyes and showed their slothful stare.

VIII

The costumer and the wig-maker had arrived in Edgar Lorm's study. He was going to try on his costume for the rôle of Petrucchio. " The Taming of the Shrew " was soon to be given with new scenery and a new cast, and he looked forward to playing the impetuous and serene tamer.

Judith, sitting on a low stool in her over-dainty sitting-room, her arms folded on her knees, heard his resonant voice, although three closed doors separated them. He was quarrelling; tradesmen and assistants always enraged him. He was difficult to satisfy, for what he demanded of himself he also required of others—the tensest exertion and the most conscientious toil.

Judith was bored. She opened a drawer filled with ribands, turned over the contents, tried the effect of different ribands in her hair, and looked at herself in the glass with a frown. That occupation tired her too. She left the drawer open and the many-coloured silks scattered about.

She went through the rooms, knocked at Lorm's door and entered. She was surprised at his appearance In the lace-trimmed, velvet doublet, the pied hose, the broad-brimmed hat with its adventurous feather, the brown locks of the wig that fell to his shoulders, he looked a victor, handsome, bold, fascinating. And his very way of standing there was art and interpretation; the whole world was his stage.

Like soldiers at attention, the costumer and wig-maker stood before him and smiled admiringly.

Judith smiled too. She had not expected to find him in a new transformation, and she was grateful for the experience.

She came to him, and touched his cheeks with her fingers. His eyes, still lit by the ardour of the poet's creation, asked after her desire. He was accustomed to have her express some wish whenever she condescended to a caress. With her arm she drew his head down a little and whispered: "I want you to make me a present, Edgar."

He laughed, embarrassed and amused. The good-natured observation of the two strangers was painful to him. He drew her arm through his and led her to the library. "What shall I give you, child?" The bold fervour of Petrucchio which, with the donning of the costume, had passed into him, faded from his face.

"Anything you please," Judith answered, "but something remarkable that will delight me and something that you are fond of."

He smacked his lips, looked merry and yielding, glanced about him, took up one object after another, pushed his chin forward and reflected, mimicked a whole scale of emotions from puzzled helplessness to anxious serviceableness, and finally struck his forehead with a roguish and graceful gesture. "I have it," he cried. He opened a little cabinet, and with a bow gave Judith a watch of very old Nürnberger make. Its case was of exquisite old gold filigree work.

"How charming," said Judith, and balanced the watch on the palm of her hand.

Lorm said: "Now amuse yourself admiring it. I must go and send those fellows away." With a swift, resilient tread he left the room.

Judith sat down at the great oak table, looked at the engraved ornamentation on the watch, pressed a little spring, and, when the oval sides of the case flew open, gazed into the ancient, lifeless works. "I shall take it all apart," she determined. "But not now; to-night. I want to see what's inside." And she looked forward with a glow to the evening hour when she would take the watch apart.

But the present, charming as it was, did not suffice her. When Lorm returned in modern dress, a clean-shaven gentleman and husband, she held out the watch-case from which she had slipped the works, and begged or rather commanded him, who was now the man of common clay: " Fill it with gold pieces, Edgar. That's what I want."

She was all voracity, avidity, desire.

Lorm lowered his head in vicarious shame. In a drawer of his desk he had a little roll of gold-pieces. He filled the watch-case and gave it to her. Then he said, "While you were out driving to-day, your brother Wolfgang called. He stayed about an hour. He seems to have a rather sterile nature. It amused me—the difficulty he had in placing me in some social category whose ways he understood. He's a born bureaucrat."

" What did he want? " Judith asked.

" He wanted to consult you about Christian. He's coming again to do so."

Judith arose. Her face was pale and her eyes glittered. Her knowledge of Christian's changed way of life was derived from a talk she had had with Crammon during his visit to Berlin, from the letters of a former friend, and from messages that had come to her directly from her parents. The first news had awakened a rage in her that gnawed at her soul. Sometimes when she was alone and thought of it she gritted her teeth and stamped her feet. Further details she heard made the very thought of him fill her to the brim with bitterness. If she had not possessed the gift of forcing herself to forgetfulness, of commanding it so successfully as to annihilate the things she desired not to be, her inner conflicts over this matter would have made her ill and morose. Every enforced recollection awakened that rage in her, and recoiled against him who caused it.

Lorm knew and feared this fact. His instinct told him, moreover, that what Judith feared in Christian's actions was an evil caricature of her own fate; for she did not conceal the fact from him that she considered herself as one who had voluntarily fallen from her original station. But he thought too modestly of himself to resent this attitude of hers. To tremble at the opinions of people had become a part of her innermost nature. Although she was no longer upheld by the elements that had once nourished her aristocratic consciousness, her being was still rooted in them, and she felt herself degraded in her new life.

But even this could not explain the wild fury to which she yielded at any mention of Christian's name.

Her attitude was that of a cat at bay. " I don't want him to come back," she hissed. " I don't want to hear anything about that man. I've told you that a hundred times. But you're always so flabby, and go in for everything. Couldn't you have told him that I won't listen? Get a car and drive to him at once. Forbid him absolutely to enter my house or to write me. But no! You're such a coward. I'll write to him myself. I'll tell him that his visits will always be a pleasure to me, although his sudden fondness is queer enough, but that I will not, under any circumstances, listen to a word about that man."

Lorm did not dare to contradict her. With gentle superiority he said: " I don't understand your extreme bitterness. No one considers your brother Christian to have done anything criminal. He is very eccentric, at the worst. He harms no one. What injury has he done you? Weren't you and he very fond of each other? You used always to speak of him with an affectionate and proud emphasis. I don't understand."

She became livid and drunk with rage. " Of course," she jeered, " you! Does anything touch you? Have you any sense left for anything but grease-paint and old rags? Have you any conception of what those words stood for—Christian Wahnschaffe? What they meant? You in your world of lies and hollowness—what should you understand? "

Lorm came a step nearer to her. He looked at her compassionately. She drew back with a gesture of aversion.

She was beating, beating the fish.

IX

Karen Engelschall said: " You don't have to worry; there's no chance of his getting back before night. If he does, I'll tell him you're an acquaintance of mine."

She gave Girke a slow and watchful look. She sat by the window, resting her body with the broad satisfaction of those women of the people to whom sitting still is an achievement and a luxury. She was sewing a baby's shift.

" Anyhow we don't have much to talk about," she continued with a malicious enjoyment. " You've said your say. They offer me sixty thousand if I go and disappear. That's all right enough. But if I wait they'll go a good bit higher. I'm somebody now. I'll think it over; you can come back next week."

" You should think very seriously," Girke replied in his official manner. " Think of your future. This may be the highest offer. Six months ago you didn't dream of such a thing. It's very pleasant to live on one's own income; it's every one's ideal. It is very foolish of you to lose such an opportunity."

With her malicious smile she bent lower over her work. An undefined well-being made her press her knees together and close her eyes. Then she looked up, swept her tousled, yellow hair from her forehead, and said: " I'd have to be a bigger fool than I am to be taken in. D'you think I don't know how rich he is? If he wanted to buy me off he'd make your offer look like dirt. Why shouldn't I make a good bargain? No, I'm no fool. This here, as you say, is my great chance, but not the way you think. I'm going to wait and see. If I'm wrong, well, I done it to myself."

Girke shifted his position uncomfortably. He looked at his watch, and then with his prying eyes regarded the room with its common wall-paper, furniture, and carpet.

"I can tell you one thing that'll please you, and I don't mind because it don't change nothing," Karen Engelschall said. "His people are all wrong if they think it's on my account that he's acting the way he does, and that he'd have stayed with them except for me. 'Course, I could make fools of you all and pretend he'd changed his life on my account. What good would that do? A new-born child could see that there's something queer and crazy about it. So why should I go and play-act in front of you, when I myself just sit here and wonder and wonder! "

"That's very true," said Girke, amazed at her frankness. "I understand, and what you say interests me immensely. I have always said that we could count on the most valuable assistance from you. Now you would do me a very real service if you would answer a few questions. I should not, of course, forget your assistance but show my appreciation very practically."

Karen giggled quietly. "I believe you," she answered. "You'd like to spy around a bit and then go and report. No, I'm not fond of that sort o' thing. There're other places where you can hear a lot. There're people what can tell you all you want to know. There's that friend of his, that Voss: Go to him! " The name brought rage to her eyes. "He acts as if there wasn't nothing he didn't know in the world, and treats a person so mean and low that you'd like to punch his dirty nose for him. Ask him who gets the money. I don't, but Voss ought to be able to tell you."

"I'm afraid you overestimate that," said Girke, with his most expert air. "There is no doubt that the man in question is at the bottom of all the trouble. But things being as they are, even ten times the amount that satisfies his greed would be inconsiderable. I can give you that very definite assurance. There must be other and quite unaccounted drains on his purse."

" I don't understand a word of what you're saying there," Karen answered, and showed her small, yellow, evil teeth. " Maybe you'd like to search my wardrobe or my mattress here, eh? Maybe you think this place is too fine or that I got expensive clothes and jewels? And did you ever see that hole over at Gisevius's where the elegant gentleman himself sleeps? We're living in luxury, we are! Why, the very mice starve here. I found one dead in a corner over there the other day. Most people hate mice, but they don't bother him. And it's pitiful for a man that's lived like he has. According to what people say, he must have been just like the emperor. He had castles and game-preserves and motor cars and the handsomest women, and they just threw themselves at his head. And never no trouble and no worry, more of everything than he could use, and money and clothes and eating and drinking and friends and servants and everything. And now he's at Gisevius's, where the mice die of hunger."

Her burning eyes were fixed on Girke, but in reality she saw him no longer. She was no longer speaking to this un-known man, whose professional curiosity left her quite un-moved. She was relieving herself by breaking the convulsive silence of her lonely days. Her hands lay on her lap like empty shells, and the child's garment had slipped to the floor. Her tongue was unleashed. The words poured forth—words born of her brooding, words familiar to her through many days and nights of strangeness and amazement. In her voice there was something metallic, and in her face the slack muscles grew taut.

Girke listened tensely and took mental notes. He noticed that he need ask no questions now. The machine, fed by a secret fire, had started itself.

Karen went on: " He comes here and sits down and looks around. He sits down and opens a book and studies. Then he puts the book away and looks around again. Then he notices me sudden like, as if I'd just been blown in. If only he don't begin asking questions again, I says to myself. Then I say to him: ' There was a big noise in the street to-day,' Or I say: ' Isolde's hands are swollen; we got to have some ointment. My mother was here,' I says maybe, ' and told me of a place on Alexander Square where you can buy linen cheap.' He just nods. Then I put on the water for the coffee, and he tells me how a mangy dog followed him for a long time and how he fed it, and that he'd been to a working-men's meeting in Moabit and had talked to some people. But he don't tell me much, and acts kind of ashamed. I'm satisfied so long as he don't ask questions. But his eyes get that expression in 'em, and then he asks if my time wasn't coming soon,"—brutally she pointed to her distended body—" and if I wasn't glad, and how it was the other times, and if I was glad then, and if I'd like to have this or that. And he brings me apples and cake and chocolate and a shawl and a fur-piece for my neck. ' Look, Karen,' he says, ' what I've brought you,' and he kisses my hand. Kisses my hand, I tell you, 'sif I was God knows what, and he didn't know about me. Did you ever hear of anybody kissing the hand of a woman like me? "

She was pale as she asked the question; her features were distorted, and the helmet of her yellow hair seemed to rise. Girke's eyes became blank and stony. " Very remarkable," he murmured; " most interesting."

Karen paid no attention to him. " ' How are you, Karen? ' " she mocked Christian's voice. " ' Do you want for anything? ' What should I be wanting? So I get desperate and I says: ' A runner for the floor or cretonne curtains for the bedroom. Red cretonne,' I says, ' because it pops into my mind. Sometimes we go out together to Humboldthain or the Oranienburger Gate. He thinks to himself and smiles and says nothing. The people stare and I get a goose-flesh. I'd like to scream out at 'em: ' Yes, there he is, the great man, that's him walking with me. And this is me—a woman of the streets that's going to have a baby. A fine couple, eh? Mighty fine! We're a grand couple, we are! ' Sometimes that Voss comes and they talk in the other room; or anyhow Voss talks. He knows how to, too; better'n any preacher. And once there was a baron here, a young blond fellow. That was a funny business. He took to crying, and cried and cried like a child. Christian said nothing, but just sat down by him. You never know what he's thinking. Sometimes he walks up and down the room, and other times he'll stand and look out of the window. I don't know where he goes, and I don't know where he comes from. Mother says I'm a fool. She says she's going to find out what's what. If she smells money she sticks like a burr. Only I wish she hadn't sicked Niels Heinrich on to me. He gets more shameless all the time. I get scared when I hear him on the stairs. He begins to cut up rough in the hall. Last Monday he was here and wanted money. ' I got none,' I says, ' you go to work.' He's learned bricklaying and can earn good money, but doing nothing suits him better. He told me to shut my trap or he'd lay me out. Just then Christian came in. Niels Heinrich glares at him. My legs was shaking, and I draws Christian aside and says: ' He wants brass.' Christian didn't know what I meant. So I says: ' Money.' And he gave him money, gave him a cool hundred, and turned and went out. Niels Heinrich followed him; I thought there'd be a fight. Nothing happened; but it was a nasty business. I can't get the scare out of my bones."

She stopped and panted for breath.

Girke thought it his duty to interpolate: " We have accumulated sufficient evidence to prove that Niels Heinrich pursues him with demands for money."

Karen scarcely listened. Her face grew darker and darker. She put her hands against her breast, arose clumsily, and looked around in the room. Her feet were turned inward and

her abdomen protruded. " He comes and he goes, he comes
and he goes," she complained, in a voice that gradually became
almost a scream. " That's the way it is, day out and day in.
If only he wouldn't ask questions. It makes me feel hot and
cold. It's like being searched by a matron. D'you know
how that is? Everything's turned inside out and everything's
handled. Awful! And I ought to try to be comfortable here;
there's nothing better in the world. When you've been kicked
around like some stinking animal, you ought to thank God to
have a chance to breathe easy. But to sit and wait and tell
how things was at this place and at that, and how this thing
happened and the other—no, I can't stand it no more! It's
too much! It's like splitting a person's head open! " She
struck her fist against her temple. She seemed an animal,
an animal with all the ugliness of a human soul dead or distorted, a wicked savage awakened now and untamable.

Girke was confounded. He got up, and pushed the chair,
both as a protection and a weapon, between the woman and
himself. He said: " I won't take up more of your time. I
beg you to consider my proposition carefully. I shall drop
in again some time." He went with a sensation as of danger
at his back.

Karen hardly observed that she was alone in the room. She
brooded. Her thinking processes were primitive. Two uncer-
tainties tormented her to the point of morbidness and rage:
What impelled Christian to search her soul and past, again
and again, with the same patience, kindliness, and curiosity?
And what inexplicable force made her answer, explain, relate,
and give an accounting of her life?

Every time he began she struggled, but she always yielded to
that force. She always began by turning her face in horror
from her own past. But soon she was forced by an implacable power to embrace that vision, and everything that she had
experienced, everything that had vanished, all that was desolate, turbid, dark, and dangerous reappeared with an incom-

parable vividness. It was her own life, and yet seemed another's, who was herself and yet some one else. It seemed to her that all those desolate, turbid, dark, dangerous things began over again, doubly terrible, with a foreknowledge of each day's disconsolate end.

Forgotten things and places plagued her and emerged terribly from her consciousness: rooms and beds and walls, cities and streets and street-corners and public houses and dark halls that led to police courts; human beings and words, and certain hours and days and tears and cries; and all terrors and degradations and crimes, all mockery and wild laughter— all this came back to her, and the past arose and lacerated her mind.

It was like being in an inconceivably long shaft through which one had already passed. And now one was commanded to retrace one's steps and fetch something that one had forgotten. One resisted desperately and struggled against the command, but in vain. One had to turn back to search for that forgotten thing without knowing what it was. And as one wandered along, a figure met one from the opposite direction, and that other figure was one's very self. One was inclined to believe in a mirror and its image. But that other self was lacerated; its breast was torn open, and within it one saw the crimson gleaming of a naked heart.

What was it? What did it all mean?

She fell back on the chair with a deep moan, and covered her face with her hands. Oh, he should be made to pay dearly for it—that tormentor of hers.

The darkness crept in and blotted out her form.

X

Amadeus Voss said to Christian: " I'll tell you exactly how you feel. You are like a man who wants to harden himself to bear cold, and suddenly strips off his garments; or like one who

has never drunk whiskey nor even smelt it, and suddenly pours
down a bottle of the vilest sort. But you are freezing in the
cold, and reeling from the liquor. And that is not the worst.
The worst is that you feel a secret horror. And how could
it be otherwise? The elements of which you are made are in
bitter conflict with your will. You are full of horror and will
not confess it to yourself. Your hands are touching a hundred
things, dirty and common and ugly, that once did not so much
as enter the circle of your life. Now you sit and look at your
nails that are still well manicured. You look at them with
disgust, and you cannot bring yourself to touch the glass that
greasy lips have touched and calloused hands have held. Yes,
you are sorriest of all for your hands. And of what avail is
the whole experiment so long as you feel sorry for your
hands? Do you think you really lie on that bed and rest on
that sofa? "

" I believe I do, Amadeus."

" You are wrong. When the nights are cold, is it really you
who stir the fire in that stove? "

" Who else? I've even learned how to do it."

" And is it you who light the kerosene lamp, you whose
light pressure made the lustres in palaces to radiate? No, it
is not your real self. Think of that smoky ceiling. How
restless you must be, and how shaken by aversion! Can
you really sleep there? And is not your awakening ghastly?
You go about among the poor, but your clothes are handsome;
any one can see that a good tailor made them, and that they
were pressed recently. It makes those people grin and feel
cheated, for in their eyes the greatest cheat is a rich man
who apes the poor. They will not take you seriously, though
you were to throw your whole fortune into the river or were
to wander among them in rags. You only embitter them, and
they take your mood for a deception and a morbid whim. You
don't know them. You do not know the utter raggedness of
their souls; you do not know what they have lacked and have

been forced to lack for generations, nor how they hate you
for the bitterness of that necessity. You do not know their
interests, nor their thought, nor their speech. And they will
never, never comprehend that a man can renounce that which
is the very blood of all their hopes and wishes, the essence of
their dreams, their envy and their rancour. They toil for
ten, twenty, thirty years, to have breath and food in their
belly. And you expect them to believe that all you ask is
a little breath and food—you, to whom they were hitherto
but nameless beasts of burden, you for whom they sent
their sons into mines and their daughters into the streets
and hospitals, for whom their lungs were corroded by the
fumes of mercury and the shavings of steel, for whom hundreds
of thousands were sacrificed in the dumb heat of those daily
battles which the proletarian fights with capital, sacrificed
as stokers and masons, weavers and smiths, glass-blowers and
machine-hands, all wage-slaves of your own? What do you
hope to accomplish? With what powers of the spirit are you
reckoning? What space of time do you give yourself? You are
but a gamester, nothing but a gamester; and so far you are
but playing with counters, without knowing whether you will
ever be able to redeem them."

" All that you say is true," Christian replied.

" Well, then? "

" I cannot do otherwise than I am doing."

" Not a week ago such a horror of that place seized you
that you fled to the Hotel Westminster to spend the night
there."

" It is true, Amadeus. How do you know it? "

" Never mind that. Do you want to smother your very
soul in horror? See to it that you leave a way of escape for
yourself. These Engelschalls, mother and son, will make
your life a veritable hell. If you fall into their snares, you'll
be worse off than some poor devil in the hands of usurers.
Surely you're not deceived in regard to the character of that

crowd? A child would know what they are after. I warn
you. They and others like them—the longer you live with
them, the nearer will they bring you to despair."

" I am not afraid, Amadeus," Christian said. " One thing
I don't understand," he added gently, " and it is that you of all
people would deter me from doing what I feel to be right and
necessary."

Voss answered with intense passion. " You threw me a
plank so that I might save myself and reach the shore. Will
you thrust me back into the abyss before I feel the firm
earth beneath my feet? Be what you really are! Don't
turn into a shadow before my very eyes! If you withdraw the
plank, I cannot tell what will become of either of us."

His face was horribly distorted, and his clenched hands
shook.

XI

In his increasing oppression and confusion of mind, surrounded by hostility, mockery, and unbelief, the face of Ivan
Becker appeared to Christian like a beautiful vision. Suddenly
he knew that in some sense he had been waiting for Becker and
counting on him.

He was heavily burdened, and it seemed to him that Becker
was the one human being who could ease that burden. At
times he was near despair. But whenever he thought of the
words and the voice of Becker and those hours of the beginning
of his present path—hours between darkness and dawn—his
faith would return.

To him Becker's word was the word of man, and Becker's
eye the eye of the race; and the man himself one upon whom
one could cast all one's own burdens and fetters and obstacles.

That vision grew clearer and clearer. Becker became a
figure with an abyss in his breast, an inverted heaven, in
which the tormenting and the heavy things of the world could
be cast, and in which they became invisible.

He sent a telegram to Prince Wiguniewski requesting Becker's present address. The reply informed him that, in all likelihood, Becker was in Geneva.

Christian made all preparations to go to Switzerland.

XII

Karen gave birth to a boy.

At six o'clock in the morning she called Isolde Schirmacher and bade her go for the midwife. When she was alone she screamed so piercingly that a young girl from a neighbouring flat hastened in to ask what ailed her. This girl was the daughter of a Jewish salesman who went about the city taking orders for a thread mill. Her name was Ruth Hofmann. She was about sixteen. She had dark grey eyes and ash-blond hair that fell loose to her shoulders, where it was evenly clipped and made little attempts to curl.

Isolde in her haste had left the hall-door open, and Ruth Hofmann had been able to enter. Her pale face grew a shade paler when she caught sight of the screaming and writhing woman. She had never yet seen a woman in labour. Yet she grasped Karen's hands and held them firmly in her own, and spoke to the suffering woman in a sweet and soothing voice until the midwife came.

When Christian arrived, a cradle stood by Karen's bed, and on its pillows lay an unspeakably ugly little creature. Karen nursed the child herself; but no maternal happiness was to be seen in her. A sombre contempt lay in the very way in which she handled the infant. If it cried, she gave it to Isolde Schirmacher. The odour of diapers filled the room.

On the second day Karen was up and about again. When Christian came that evening, he found the widow Engelschall and Ruth Hofmann. The widow Engelschall said that she would take the child into her care. Karen cast an uncertain glance at Christian. The woman said in a loud tone:

" Five thousand marks for the care of it, and everything's settled. What you need is rest, and then you'll have it."

" Far's I'm concerned you can do what you please," said Karen peevishly.

"What do you think, Herr Wahnschaffe?" The widow Engelschall turned to Christian.

He replied: " It seems to me that a child should stay with its mother."

Karen gave a dry laugh, in which her mother joined. Ruth Hofmann arose. Christian asked her courteously whether she had any request to make. She shook her head so that her hair moved a little. Suddenly she gave him her hand, and it seemed to Christian as though he had long known her.

He had already told Karen that he was leaving the city for a time; but he postponed his departure a whole week.

XIII

The house was slowly turning in for the night. Heavy trucks rattled on the street. Boys whistled piercingly. The outer door was closed thunderously. The walls shook with the tread of a hundred feet. In the yard some one was driving nails into a box. Somewhere a discordant voice was singing. Tumult arose from the public houses at the corners. A bestial laugh sounded from above.

Christian opened the window. It was warm. Groups of workingmen came from Malmöer Street and scattered. At one corner there was a green-grocer's shop. In front of it stood an old woman with a lidless basket, in which there were dirty vegetables and a dead chicken with a bloody neck. Christian could see these things, because the light of the street lamp fell on them.

" She'll take the child for four thousand," said Karen.

Surreptitiously Christian glanced at the cradle. The infant

both repelled and attracted him. "You had better keep it," he said.

Hollow tones could be heard from the adjoining flat. Hofmann had come home. He was talking, and a clear boyish treble answered him.

The clock ticked. Gradually the confused noises of the house blended into a hum.

Karen sat down at the table and strung glass beads. Her hair had recently become even yellower and more touselled; but her features had a firmer modelling. Her face, no longer swollen and puffed from drinking, was slimmer and showed purer tints.

She looked at Christian, and, for a moment, she had an almost mad feeling; she yearned to know some yearning. It was like the glowing of a last spark in an extinguished charcoal stove.

The spark crimsoned and died.

"You were going to tell me about Hilde Karstens and your foster-father, Karen," Christian said persuasively. "You made a promise."

"For God's sake, leave me alone! It's so long ago I can't remember about it!" She almost whined the words. She held her head between her hands and rested her elbows on her knees. Her sitting posture always had a boastful lasciviousness. Thus women sit in low public houses.

Minutes passed. Christian sat down at the table facing her. "I want to give the brat away," she said defiantly. "I can't stand looking at it. Come across with the four thousand—do! I can't, I just can't bear looking at it!"

"But strangers will let the child sicken and perhaps die," said Christian.

A grin, half coarse and half sombre, flitted across her face. Then she grew pale. Again she saw that mirrored image of herself: it came from afar, from the very end of the shaft. She shivered, and Christian thought she was cold. He went for a shawl and covered her shoulders. His gestures, as he did so, had something exquisitely chivalrous about them. Karen asked for a cigarette. She smoked as one accustomed to it, and the way she held the cigarette and let the smoke roll out of her mouth or curl out from between pointed lips was also subtly lascivious.

Again some minutes passed. She was evidently struggling against the confession. Her nervous fingers crushed one of the glass beads.

Then suddenly she spoke: " There's many that isn't born at all. Maybe we'd love them. Maybe only the bad ones are born because we're too low to deserve the good ones. When I was a little girl I saw a boy carry seven kittens in a sack to the pool to drown 'em. I was right there when he spilled them into the water. They struggled like anything and came up again and tried to get to land. But as soon as one of the little heads came up, the boy whacked at it with a stick. Six of 'em drowned, and only the ugliest of 'em managed to get into a bush and get away. The others that was drowned— they was pretty and dainty."

" You're bleeding," said Christian. The broken bead had cut her hand. Christian wiped the blood with his handkerchief. She let him do it quietly, while her gaze was fixed on old visions that approached and receded. The tension was such that Christian dared scarcely breathe. Upon his lips hovered that strange, equivocal smile that always deceived men concerning his sympathies.

He said softly: " You have something definite in mind now, Karen."

" Yes, I have," she said, and she turned terribly pale. " You wanted to know how it was with Hilde Karstens and with the cabinet-maker. He was the man with whom my mother was living at that time. Hilde was fifteen and I was thirteen. She and I was good friends, together all the time, even on the dunes one night when the spring-tide came. The men were wild after her. Lord, she was pretty and sweet. But she laughed at 'em. She said: 'When I'm eighteen I'm going to marry a man—a real man that can do things; till then, just don't bother me.' I didn't go to the dance at the 'Jug of Hösing'; I had to stay home and help mother pickle fish. That's when it all happened. I could never find out how Hilde Karstens got to the mounds on the heath alone. Maybe she went willingly with the pilot's mate. It was a pilot's mate; that's all we ever knew about him. He was at the 'Jug' for the first time that night, and, of course, he wasn't never seen again. It was by the mounds that he must have attacked her and done her the mischief, 'cause otherwise she wouldn't have walked out into the sea. I knew Hilde Karstens; she was desperate. That evening the waves washed her body ashore. I was there. I threw myself down and grasped her wet, dead hair. They separated me from her, but I threw myself down again. It took three men to get me back home. Mother locked me up and told me to sift lentils, but I jumped out of the window and ran to Hilde's house. They said she'd been buried. I ran to the church yard and looked for her grave. The grave-digger showed it to me far off in a corner. They looked for me all night and found me by the grave and dragged me home. Half the village turned out to see. Because I'd run away from the lentils my mother beat me with a spade handle so that my skin peeled from my flesh. And while I lay there and couldn't stir, she went to the schoolmaster, and they wrote a letter to the squire asking if he wouldn't take me to work on the estate. The house was empty, and the cabinet-maker came into the kitchen where I was lying. He was drunk as a lord. He saw me stretched out there by the hearth, and stared and stared. Then he picked me up and carried me into the bedroom."

She stopped and looked about as though she were in a strange place and as though Christian were a menacing stranger.

" He tore off my clothes, my skirts and my bodice and my shirt and everything, and his hands shook. In his eyes there was a sparkling like burning alcohol. And when I lay naked before him he stroked me with his trembling hands over and over again. I felt as if I'd have to scratch the brain out of his skull; but I couldn't do nothing. I just felt paralyzed, and my head as heavy as iron. If I get to be as old as a tree, I'll never forget that man's face over me that time. A person can't forget things like that—never in this world. And as soon as ever I could stir again, he reeled in a corner and fell down flat, and it was all dark in the room." She gave a deep sigh. " That was the way of it. That's how it started."

Christian did not turn his eyes from her for the shadow of a moment.

" After that," she went on, " people began to say, ' Lass, your eyes are too bold.' Well, they was. I couldn't tell everybody why. The vicar drivelled about some secret shame and turning my soul to God. He made me laugh. When I went into service on the estate, they grudged me the food I ate. I had to wait on the children, fetch water, polish boots, clean rooms, run errands for the Madame. There was an overseer that was after me—a fellow with rheumy eyes and a hare-lip. Once at night when I got to my little room, there he was and grabbed me. I took a stone jug and broke it across his head. He roared like a steer, and everybody came hurrying in—the servants and the master and the mistress. They all screamed and howled, and the overseer tells them a whacking lie about me, and the master says: ' Out with you, you baggage! ' Well, why not, I thought. And that very night I tied up my few rags, and off I was. But next night I slunk back, 'cause I'd found no shelter anywhere. I crept all around the house, not because I was tired or hungry, but to pay them out for what they'd done to me. I wanted to set the house on fire and burn it down and have my revenge. But I didn't dare, and I wandered about the countryside for three days, and always at night came back to the house. I just couldn't sleep and I'd keep seeing the fire that I ought to have lit, and the house and stables flaring up and the cattle burning and the hay flying and the beams smoking and the singed dogs tugging at their chains. And I could almost hear them whine—the dogs and the children who'd tormented me so, and the mistress who'd stood under the Christmas tree in a silk dress and given presents to everybody except to me. Oh, yes, I did get three apples and a handful o' nuts, and then she told me to hurry and wash the stockings for Anne-Marie. But at last my strength gave out, wandering about that way and looking for a chance. The rural policeman picked me up and wanted to question me. But I fainted, and he couldn't find out nothing. If only I'd set fire to that house, everything would have been different, and I wouldn't have had to go with the captain when my mother got me in her claws again. I let him talk me into going for a blue velvet dress and a pair of cheap patent leather shoes. And I never heard till later about the bargain that mother'd struck with him."

With her whole weight she shoved the chair she sat on farther from the table, and bent over and rested her forehead on the table's edge. " O gee," she said, absorbed by the horror of her fate, " O gee, if I'd set fire to that house, I wouldn't have had to let everybody wipe their boots on me. If only I'd done it! It would have been a good thing! "

Silently Christian looked down upon her. He covered his eyes with his hand, and the pallor of his face and hand was one.

XIV

On the train between Basel and Geneva Christian learned from some fellow travellers that an attempt to assassinate Ivan Michailovitch Becker had been made in Lausanne. A student named Sonya Granoffska had fired at him.

Christian knew nothing of the events that explained the

deed. He neither read newspapers nor took any interest in public events. He now asked some questions, and was told what all the world was talking about.

The *Matin* of Paris had printed a series of articles that had caused intense excitement all over Europe, and had been widely reprinted and commented on. They were signed by a certain Jegor Ulitch, and consisted of revelations concerning the Russian revolution, its foreign committee, and the activities of the terrorists. They dragged evidence with so wide a net that they materially strengthened the case of the Russian state against the workingmen's delegate Trotzky, who was then being tried at Petrograd, and thus contributed to his condemnation.

Jegor Ulitch remained in the background. The initiated asserted that there was no such person, and that the name was the mask assumed by a traitor to the revolution. The *Gaulois* and the Geneva *Journal* published vitriolic attacks on the unknown writer. Ulitch did not hesitate to reply. To justify himself he published letters and secret documents that vitally incriminated several leaders of the revolutionary party.

With increasing definiteness the authorship of the *Matin* articles was being assigned to Becker. The newspapers openly voiced this suspicion, and had daily reports of his supposed activities. During a strike of the dock-hands of Marseilles, he was said to have appeared at a strikers' meeting in the garb of a Russian pope; a report had it that he had addressed a humble letter to the Czarina, another that he had become an outcast fleeing from land to land, a third that he had succeeded in mediating between the Russian police and his exiled countrymen, and that hence the Western Powers, who were slavishly supine before Czarism, had somewhat relaxed their cruel vigilance.

Yet Becker's very face remained a mystery and a source of confusion, and the knowledge of his mere existence spread a wide restlessness

And Christian sought him. He sought him in Geneva, Lausanne, Nice, Marseilles. Finally he followed a hint that led him to Zürich. There he happened to meet the Russian Councillor of State Koch, who introduced him to several of his compatriots. These finally gave him Becker's address.

XV

" I've never lost sight of you," said Becker. " Alexander Wiguniewski wrote me about you, and told me that you had altered the conditions of your life. But his hints were equivocal; so I commissioned friends in Berlin to inquire, and their information was more exact."

They sat in a wine room in an obscure quarter. They were the only guests. From the smoky ceiling hung the great antlers of a stag, to which the electric bulbs had been fastened with an effect of picturesqueness.

Becker wore a dark litevka buttoned to his chin. He looked poor and ill; his bearing had a touch of the subtly fugitive. Sometimes a sad quietude overspread his features, like the quietude of waves where a ship has gone down. In moments of silence his face seemed to become larger, and his gaze to be fixed upon an outer emptiness and an inner flame.

" Are you still in communication with Wiguniewski and the—others? " Christian asked; and his eyes seemed to express a delicate deprecation of the level impersonality of his own demeanour.

Becker shook his head. " My old friends have all turned against me," he replied. " Inwardly I am still deeply at one with them; but I no longer share their views."

" Must one absolutely share the views of one's friends? " Christian asked.

" Yes, in so far as those views express one's central aim in life. The answer depends also on the degree of affection that exists among people. I've tried to win them over, but my

strength failed me. They simply don't understand. Now I no
longer feel the urge to shake men and awaken them, unless
some one flings his folly at me in the form of a polemic, or
unless I feel so close to one that any dissonance between us
robs me of peace or weighs upon my heart."

Christian paid less attention to the meaning of the words
than to Becker's enchanting intonation, the gentleness of his
voice, the wandering yet penetrating glance, the morbid, mar-
tyred face. And he thought: "All that they say of him is
false." A great trust filled him.

XVI

One night, as they were walking together, Becker spoke of
Eva Sorel. "She has attained an extraordinary position," he
said. "I've heard people say that she is the real ruler of
Russia and is having a decisive influence on European diplomacy. She lives in incomparable luxury. The Grand Duke
presented to her the famous palace of Duke Biron of unblessed
memory. She receives ministers of state and foreign am-
bassadors like a crowned sovereign. Paris and London reckon
with her, bargain with her, consult her. She will be heard of
more and more. Her ambition is inconceivable."

"It was to be foreseen that she would rise high," Christian
remarked softly. He wanted more and more to talk to Becker
about his own affairs and explain the errand on which he had
come. But he did not find the right word.

Becker continued: "Her soul was bound to lose the harmony
that rules her body so severely. It is a natural process of
compensation. She desires power, insight, knowledge of the
obscure and intricate. She plays with the fate of men and
nations. Once she said to me, ' The whole world is but a single
heart.' Well, one can destroy that single heart, which is all
humanity, in one's own bosom. Ambition is but another form
of despair; it will carry her to the outermost boundary of life.

There she will meet me and many others who have come to the same spot from another direction, and we shall clasp hands once more."

They had reached the shores of the lake. Becker buttoned his coat and turned up the collar. His voice sank almost to a whisper. " I saw her in Paris once crossing the floor in an old house. In either hand she bore a candelabrum, and in each candelabrum burned two candles. A brownish smoke came from the flames, a white veil flowed from her shoulders; an undreamed-of lightness took possession of me. Once when she was still appearing at the Sapajou, I saw her lying on the floor behind the stage, watching with the intensest scrutiny a spider that was spinning its web in a crack between two boards. She raised her arm and bade me stand still, and lay there and observed the spider. I saw her learning of the spider, and I knew then the power of utter absorption that she had. I scarcely knew it, but she drew me into the burning circle of her being. Her unquenchable thirst for form and creation and unveiling and new vision taught me whom she called her master. Yes, the whole world is but a single heart, and we all serve but a single God. He and I together are my doom."

Christian thought restlessly: " How can I speak to him? " But the right word did not come.

" The other day," Becker said, " I stood in a chapel, lost in the contemplation of a miracle-working image of the Mother of God, and thinking about the simple faith of the people. A few sick men and women and old men were kneeling there and crossing themselves and bowing to the earth. I lost myself in the features of the image, and gradually the secret of its power became clear to me. It was not just a painted piece of wood. For centuries the image had absorbed the streams of passionate prayer and adoration that had come to it from the hearts of the weary and the heavy-laden, and it became filled with a power that seemed to proceed from it to the faithful and that was mirrored in itself again. It became a

living organism, a meeting place between man and God. Filled
with this thought, I looked again upon the old men and the
women and the children there, and I saw the features of the
image stirred by compassion, and I also kneeled down in the
dust and prayed."

Christian made no comment. It was not given him to share
such feelings. But Becker's speech and ecstatic expression and
the great glow of his eyes cast a spell upon him; and in the
exaltation which he now felt, his purpose seemed more possible to realize.

Walking restlessly up and down in the inhospitable room of
his hotel, he was surprised to find himself in an imaginary
conversation with Becker, which drew from him an eloquence
that was denied him in the presence of men.

" Hear me. Perhaps you can understand. I possess fourteen
millions, but that is not all. More money pours in on me
daily and hourly, and I can do nothing to dam the torrent.
Not only is the money a vain thing to me, but an actual
hindrance. Wherever I turn, it is in my way. Everything
I undertake appears in a false light on account of it. It is
not like something that belongs to me, but like something that
I owe; and every human being with whom I speak explains
in some way how and why I owe it to him or to another or to
all. Do you understand that? "

Christian had the feeling that he was addressing the Ivan
Becker of his imagination in a friendly, natural, and convincing
tone; and it seemed to him that Ivan Becker understood and
approved. He opened the window, and caught sight of some
stars.

" If I distribute it I cause mischief," he continued, and
walked up and down again without articulating a sound.
" That has been proved. The fault is probably in me; I
haven't the art of doing good or useful things with money.
And it's unpleasant to have people remind me wherever I go:
' You've got your millions behind you; whenever you have

enough of this, you can quit and go home.' This is the reason
why everything glides from my grasp and no ground is secure
under my feet; this is the reason why I cannot live as I would
live, nor find any pleasantness within myself. Therefore relieve me of my millions, Ivan Michailovitch. Do with them
whatever you wish. If necessary we can go to a notary and
make out a deed of gift. Distribute the money, if you desire,
feed the hungry, and relieve the suffering. I can't do it; it
repels me. I want to be rid of my burden. Have books
printed or build refuges or bury it or waste it; only take the
burden from me. I can only use it to fill maws that afterwards
show me their teeth."

And as he spoke those words within himself, a serenity overspread his features. His smooth forehead, his deep blue eyes,
his large and rather pallid cheeks, his healthy red lips, and
the clean-shaven skin about them were all bathed in that new
serenity.

It seemed to him that on the next day, when he would see
Becker, he might be able to speak to him quite as he had
spoken to-night, or at least nearly so.

XVII

One passed through a little hall-way into a poorly furnished
room. There were several young men in this hall. One of
these exchanged a few words with Becker, and then went
away.

" It's my bodyguard," Becker explained, with a faint smile.
" But like all the others they distrust me. They've been ordered not to lose sight of me. Didn't you notice that we
were constantly shadowed out of doors? "

Christian shook his head.

" When that unhappy woman pointed her revolver at me in
Lausanne," Becker went on, shivering, " her lips flung the word
' traitor ' at me. I looked into the black muzzle and awaited

death. She missed me, but since that moment I have been afraid of death. That evening many of my friends came to me, and besought me to clear and justify myself. I replied to them and said: 'If I am to be a traitor in your eyes, I shall not avoid any of the horror, any of the frightfulness of that position.' They did not understand me. But a summons has come to me to destroy, to extinguish and destroy myself. I am to build the pyre on which I am to be consumed. I am to spread my suffering until it infects all who come near me. I am to forget what I have done and abandon hope, and be lowly and loathed and an outcast, and deny principles and break fetters and bow down before the spirit of evil, and bear pain and cause pain, and tear up and plough the earth, even though beautiful harvests be destroyed. Traitor—how little that means! I wander about and hunger after myself. I flee from myself, and yet cry out after myself, and am the sacrificer and the sacrifice. And that has caused an unparalleled increase of pain in the world. The souls of men descend to the source of things in order to become brothers to the damned."

He pressed his hands together and looked like a madman. " My body seeks the earth, the depths, pollution, and the night," he said. " My innermost being gapes like a wound; I feel the thongs and weight of doom and the terror of time; I pray for prayers; I am a shadowy figure in the ghostly procession of created things in travail; the grief that fills the air of the world grinds me to dust; *mea culpa, mea maxima culpa!* "

The feeling of pained embarrassment grew in Christian. He simply looked at Becker.

Suddenly a repeated knocking sounded at the outer door. Becker started and listened. The knocking increased in loudness and speed.

" It has come after all," Becker murmured in consternation. " I must leave. Forgive me, I must leave. A car is waiting for me. Stay a few minutes longer, I beg of you." He took a valise that lay on the bed, looked about vaguely, pressed his mutilated hand to his coat, and murmured hastily, " Lend me five hundred francs. I spent my last money at noon. Don't be angry with me; I'm in a fearful hurry."

Mechanically Christian took out his wallet and gave Becker five bank-notes. The latter stammered a word of thanks and farewell, and was gone.

Christian left the house fifteen minutes later in a bewildered condition. For hours he wandered in the valleys and on the hills around the city. He took the night train back to Berlin.

During the many hours of the journey he felt very wretched in body and soul.

XVIII

In his flat he found many begging letters, one from his former valet, one from a Society for Succouring the Shelterless, one from a musician whom he had met casually in Frankfort. There was also a letter from the bank, requesting his signature on an enclosed document.

Next day Amadeus Voss asked for six thousand marks; the widow Engelschall, loudly lamenting that her furniture would be sold unless she met a promissory note, asked for three thousand.

He gave and gave, and the act of giving disgusted him. In the lecture halls of the university they came to him—the merest strangers, the most indifferent persons. Wherever he appeared, even in an eating-house, people came to him and told him of their troubles, and were diffident or brazen, and begged or demanded.

He gave and gave, and saw no end to it and no salvation in it, and felt a leaden heaviness steal over him. And he gave and gave.

He saw greed and expectation in every eye. He dressed himself more plainly, he cut down his expenditures to the barest necessities; the gold towered up behind him like rolling lava, and burned everything he touched. He gave and gave, and people asked and asked.

And so he wrote to his father: " Take my money from me! " He was aware of the strangeness and the unheard-of nature of what he asked, so he accompanied his request with elaborate reasons and persuasive phrases. " Assume that I have emigrated and have been lost sight of, or that I live far away under a false name, or that through your fault or mine there had been a definite breach between us, that you had therefore reduced my allowance to a minimum, but that my pride forbade my accepting even that, since I desire to stand on my own feet and live by the work of my hands. Or else imagine that I had wasted my means, and hopelessly mortgaged the capital and interest still due me. Or, finally, imagine that you yourself had become impoverished, and were forced to withdraw all assistance from me. At all events, I want to live without independent means. I have lost all pleasure in living with them. It is hard, I know, to explain that to any one who has money and has never been without it. Do me this favour! First of all, dispose of the sums that are banked in my name; next stop the income that has hitherto been paid out to me. The money is all yours, indisputably so. During our conversation last year you gave me very clearly and justly to understand that I have always lived on the fruit of your labour."

Lastly he made the proposal to which he had referred in his imaginary conversation with Ivan Becker. " If it wounds your sensibilities to make a personal or practical use of the money which I am returning to you who gave it—use it to build orphanages, homes for foundlings, hospitals, institutions for the disabled, or libraries. There is so much misery in the world, and so much suffering that needs to be alleviated. I cannot do these things. They do not attract me; indeed, the very thought of them is disagreeable. I do not deny that this specific inability argues a weakness in my character; so if you determine to expend the money upon charities, don't do it in my name."

He ended thus: " I do not know whether it even interests you to have me say that I think of you affectionately. Perhaps in your heart you have already cast me off and separated yourself from me wholly. If any bond is to continue to exist between us, it can only be, however, if you do not refuse me your help in this matter, which is, from one point of view, so difficult, and from another, so perfectly simple."

The letter remained unanswered. But several days after it had been sent, a friend of the Wahnschaffe family, Pastor Werner, called on Christian. He came both on a mission from the Privy Councillor and of his own impulse. Christian had known him since childhood.

XIX

Very attentively the clergyman examined the room, the shabby, ugly furniture, the window shades bordered by sentimental pictures, the dirty, white-washed walls, the dim, little lamp, the split boards of the flooring, the imitation leather of the sofa, the chest of drawers which was broken and which bore a cheap plaster of Paris bust. A dumb yet fiery amazement appeared on his face.

" I am asked to inform you," Pastor Werner said, " that your father is of course ready to comply with your request. What else, after all, can he do? But I need not conceal from you the fact that his anxiety about you is very grave, and that he finds your actions wholly incomprehensible."

Christian answered a little impatiently. " I told him months ago that there wasn't the slightest ground for anxiety."

" You must admit," Werner objected gently, " that your latest plan does involve the question of your very existence. Have you taken up any occupation that secures you from need? "

Christian replied that, as his father was aware, he was definitely preparing himself for a profession. The measure of his talent and success was, of course, still in question.

"And until that profession begins to pay, what will you live on? " the pastor asked " Let me repeat to you the words which your father cried out at our last interview: ' Does he intend to beg? Or to accept gifts from the charitable? Or starve? Or trust to chance and false friends? Or take refuge in shady and dishonourable things, and yet be forced at last, a remorseful fool, to ask for that which he now casts aside? ' I have never in all these many years seen your father in such a state of mind, or heard him express such grief and such passion."

" My father may calm himself," Christian replied. " Nothing of what he fears is likely to happen; nor what, perhaps, he hopes, namely, that I shall ask my patrimony back again. It is as inconceivable as that the bird should return to the egg or the burning log to the tree whence it came."

" Then you did not intend to renounce all pecuniary assistance at once? " the pastor asked, feeling his way carefully.

" No." Christian hesitated. " I suppose not. I'm not equal to that; not yet. One has to learn that. It is a difficult thing and must be learned: and life in a great city would involve fatal and disturbing elements. Then, too, I have assumed certain obligations; there are several people who have definitely been counting on my help. I don't know whether they could follow my own course. I haven't in fact, any programme at all. What good would it do me? My great aim just now is to get into a situation that is clear and reasonable, and get rid of all sorts of stupid torments. I want to drop the burden of the superfluous; and everything is superfluous except what I and those few people absolutely need on the most stringent estimate. But every supposed need, I think, can be reduced, until such gradual renunciation produces a profit."

" If I understand you correctly." the pastor said, " it is

your intention to retain such a portion of your fortune as will secure you against actual need."

Christian sat down at the table and rested his head on his hand. "Yes," he said softly. "Yes. But there the great difficulty arises. I cannot fix the boundary between necessity and superfluity in terms of money. Unhappily I was brought up amid conditions that make it hard for me to have a practical opinion on this net basis. I lack a norm of what is necessary and what is dispensable, and I lack it especially where others are concerned. You've understood me quite rightly. I want to retain a part, but only a very small part; and I hate to bargain with myself over the exact amount. The whole question of money is so absurd and trivial; it is only dragged in the wake of the really important things. One thing I couldn't endure; and that would be to invest a capital, however modest, and use the interest. Then I'd be a capitalist again, and back in the world of the protected. But what other way is there? You're an experienced man. Advise me."

The clergyman considered. From time to time he looked searchingly at Christian; then he lowered his eyes and reflected again. "I am rather confounded by your words," he confessed at last. "Much that you say surprises me—no, everything—yet it also seems to give me a certain insight. Very well then; you ask my advice." Again he thought, and again observed Christian. "You renounce your personal fortune as well as the income which the firm and family have paid you. So far, so good. This renunciation will be officially acknowledged. I am also willing to believe that you will never ask back what you now renounce. The manner in which you bind yourself impresses me more than many solemn oaths would do. You are through with your past. That, too, will be respected on the other side. I understand the spiritual pain caused you by the question as to what leeway you should permit yourself in the matter of your personal and bodily needs during the period on which you are entering, and which will be bitter and full of necessities for self-conquest. I understand that. The problem is one of inner delicacy, of spiritual modesty. To consider it runs counter to your feelings and attitude. Yes, I understand that."

Christian nodded, and the pastor continued in a raised voice. "Then listen to me. What I shall propose is subtle and difficult. It is almost like a game or a trick. You may remember that I am chaplain of the prison at Hanau. I try to help the souls of the lost and the outcast. I study these people. I know their inmost motives, the darkness of their hearts, their frozen yearnings. I dare to assert that there is not one of them who cannot, in the higher sense, be saved, nor one whose heart will not be reached by simple words earnestly realized in action. That awakens the divine spark, and the vision of such an awakening is beautiful. I serve my cause with all my strength, and the improvement and transformation of some of my flock has been so complete, that they have returned into society as new men, and bravely resisted all temptations. I admit that success often depends on my ability to save them from immediate need. Here is my problem. Kindly people help; the state, too, though in its frugal manner, contributes. But it is not enough. How would it be if from the fortune which you are returning to your father a capital were to be deducted the interest of which is to be used for my discharged convicts? Don't draw back, but hear me out. This capital would be in good securities and would amount, let us say, to three hundred thousand marks. The interest would be in the neighbourhood of fifteen thousand marks. That would suffice. A great deal of good could be done with it. To touch or sell the securities would be a privilege reserved to you alone. From the capital itself you take in monthly or quarterly installments such sum or sums as you need to live on. To draw and expend the interest should be a privilege reserved to me and my successors. All these conditions must be secured by legal means. The purpose, as you see, is a double one. First, the plan will effect a great and needed good; secondly, it furnishes an inherent norm and aim for you. Every superfluous or thoughtless expenditure of yours jeopardizes a human soul; every frugality you practise is at once translated into concrete human weal. That gives you a point of orientation, a line of moral action. It is, if I may call it so, an automatic moral mechanism. I judge that the independence you desire will be achieved in two or three years. Within that time you can hardly use up even one-tenth of the capital according to your present standard of life. Of course, even this plan involves a problem for you, but it is a problem that would, I think, attract you. You don't have to think of my humanitarian aims. I know that in your letter to your father you expressed your dislike of such aims, a dislike which I have no means of understanding. But I could tell you things and relate circumstances that would show you how the subtlest fibres of humanity are poisoned, and what a sacred duty it is to plough up the spiritual soil in my particular little field. If you could once see face to face some of these men restored to freedom and hope, your heart would be won for my cause. It is such visible evidence that instructs and converts."

" You have too high an opinion of me," Christian said, with his old, equivocal smile. " It's always the same. Everybody overestimates me in this respect and judges me wrongly. But don't bother about that, and don't ask about it. It doesn't matter."

" And what answer do you make to my proposal? "

Christian lowered his head, and said: " It's a nice little trap that you are setting for me. Let me consider it a moment. I am to feed, one might say, on my own charity. What a horrible word that is—charity. And by feeding on it myself I, of course, diminish it. And that, you think, will constitute a sort of moral gymnastic for me, and make it easier to realize my purpose——? "

"Yes, that was what, since you have chosen this path, I had in mind."

"Well, if I disappoint you, you will have nothing to regret but your own modesty," Christian continued, with a peculiarly mocking expression. "You could ask twice or even three times the sum you named, and I would probably or, rather, assuredly not refuse. For into whose pockets the millions go that I refuse, is a matter I care little about. Why don't you do that and thus decrease your own risk?"

"Is your question inspired by distrust of the cause I represent?"

"I don't know. Answer it, if you don't mind."

"I've explained the situation to you. The circumstances themselves are the guide to what I can and ought to ask for. On the one hand there is an urgent need. On the other hand there are definite considerations that not only set a natural limit, but forbid my using this opportunity in such a way as to give a handle to the malicious and quarrelsome."

Christian continued his purely argumentative resistance. "Do you think it means anything to me or attracts me to know that you will give some discharged criminal, whose moral nature you think you have saved, one or two hundred marks to start life anew? That doesn't mean a thing to me. I don't know those men. I don't know how they look or act or talk or smell, or what they'll do with the money, or whether it will really be of service to them. And since I don't know that, the arrangement has no meaning to me."

Pastor Werner was taken aback. "To be sure," he replied. "But I do know them, you see."

Christian smiled again. "We're very differently constituted; we neither think nor act alike." Suddenly he looked up. "But I'm not making these objections to create difficulties. Quite the contrary. You personally ask me for assistance and I personally render it. In return you do me the service of acting as my paymaster and showing me how to solve my problem. I hope you will have no reason to complain."

" Then you do consent and I may proceed to make definite arrangements? " the clergyman asked, half delighted and half doubtful still.

Christian nodded. " Go ahead," he said. " Make what arrangements seem best to you. It's all too trivial to bother about."

" What do you mean by that exactly? " Werner asked, just as Eva had once, between laughter and amazement, asked his meaning. " A while ago you also said that what was really important was dragged down by these matters of money. What is the truly important thing to you? "

" I can't explain that to you. But I feel the triviality of all this. All I am doing is the merest beginning, and everyone overestimates it absurdly and makes a mountain of this molehill. I haven't reached the real difficulty yet. And that will consist in earning back all one has given away—earning it back in another manner, and so, above all, that one does not feel one's loss."

" Strange," murmured the pastor. " It is strange. To hear you talk, one would think you were discussing a sporting event or a matter of barter."

Christian laughed.

The pastor came up to him and laid a hand on his shoulder. His eyes were serious as he asked: " Where is the woman whom you . . . have taken in? "

Christian's reply was a gesture in the direction of Karen's flat.

A thought that was strange and new seemed to flash into the clergyman's mind. " Then you don't live with her? " His voice sank to a whisper. " You are not living together? "

" No," Christian answered with a frown. " Certainly not."

The pastor's arm dropped. There came a long silence. Then he spoke again: " Your father is stricken to the heart by a feeling as though several people whom he loves had succumbed to the same disease. He tries to hide his emotion, but he doesn't succeed. Before he had any reason to be anxious about you, he once spoke to me of your sister Judith. He used the expression, 'self-degradation.' He described her as afflicted by a perverse impulse toward self-degradation."

Christian swept the matter aside with a vivid gesture. " Oh, yes, Judith! She flings a trivial challenge at the world. That's no self-degradation. She's curious as to how far she dare go, how far others will go for her, and what the upshot will be. She confessed as much to me. She'll plunge into water and be affronted because it's wet; she'll go through fire in the hope that it won't burn her. After her experiment she'll hate both fire and water. No, I have nothing in common with that."

" You speak very harshly for a brother," the pastor said with gentle reproachfulness. " However that may be, this new trouble has wounded your father to the very core. He feels that all his life's effort is being negated from within, and that the fruit of all his toil is rotting in his hands. He stood on the very peaks of success. What does it mean to him now? His own flesh and blood rises up against him. His hand seemed blessed; he feels it withering now. His wealth carried him to a very great height. Now he is lonely there, and the son who, above all others, should rejoice in that station, turns from him, and fills him with a feeling for which he knows no name but shame and disgrace."

Christian did not answer. He seemed quite indifferent. Werner continued: " I ask you to consider the social structure of mankind. Cruelty and force may seem to cling to it, yet there is something infinitely delicate and venerable within. You might liken it to a tree, deep-rooted in the earth, expanding in the air with many branches and twigs, buds and blossoms. It has come to be through some action of God, and no one should contemn it."

"Why do you tell me that?" Christian asked, with a subtle withdrawal of himself.

"Because your father suffers. Go to him, and explain yourself and your ways. You are his son; it is your duty."

Christian shook his head. "No," he answered. "I cannot."

"And your mother? Do I have to remind you of her too? I did not think I should have to admonish you in her name. She waits. All her days are one long waiting."

Once more Christian shook his head. "No," he said, "I cannot."

The pastor buried his chin in his hollow hand and looked dully at the floor. He left with divided feelings.

XX

Crammon desired a friend. The one who was lost could never be replaced. The hope of winning him back still smouldered within, but the empty space in his bosom was desolate and chill. To install a lodger there seemed wise and would be stimulating.

Franz Lothar von Westernach had the first claim upon the place. They had agreed by letter to meet at Franz Lothar's country house in Styria, so at the beginning of spring Crammon left Vienna. At Nürnberg he left in the lurch a certain handsome Miss Herkinson in whose car he had travelled from Spa.

To an acquaintance whom, by a mere chance, he met in the dining-car, he said, "I can no longer bear the noise that young people always make. The subdued and clarified attracts me now. The fifth decade of our lives demands milder ways."

Crammon found Franz Lothar in the thick of a mental struggle. His sister Clementine wanted him to get married. Laughing and yet helpless, he confided the state of affairs to Crammon. His sister had picked out a girl of excellent family, and was sure that the alliance would have a wholesome influence on her brother's career, as well as on his uncertain and idle way of life. All preliminaries had been arranged, and the parents of the young lady had intimated their full approval.

Crammon said: "Don't let them take you in, my son. The affair can have none but a disgraceful outcome. I do not know the girl in question personally. But she is a vampire. Her ancestors were among the most infamous robber knights of the Middle Ages. Later they came into conflict with the empire on account of cruelty to their serfs. You can imagine what your future would be."

Franz Lothar was highly amused. Crammon's rage at the thought of being robbed of this friend too, in the same old stupid way, was positively rabid and passed all the bounds of decency. He treated Clementine with embittered silence. If any dispute arose, he barked at her like an angry dog.

Franz Lothar's own indecision and fear of change saved Crammon from further conflicts. He simply informed his disappointed sister one day that he was thoroughly unprepared for so important a step, and begged her to break off the negotiations.

This turn of affairs satisfied Crammon, but brought him no definite peace of mind. He wanted to prevent the possibility of a similar assault on his contentment. The best thing seemed to be to marry off Clementine herself. It would not be easy. She was no longer in her first youth; she had had her experiences and knew her world; she possessed a clear vision and a sharp understanding. Great care would have to be taken. He looked about in his mind for a candidate, and his choice fell on a man of considerable wealth, distinguished ancestry, and spotless reputation, the Cavaliere Morini. He had made his acquaintance years ago through friends in Trieste.

He took to cultivating Clementine's society. Fragrant little anecdotes of married bliss and unstilled longing and cosy households flowed from his lips. He found her very receptive. He dropped, as though casually, intimations of his friendship with an uncommonly distinguished and able Italian gentleman. He built up the character with an artist's care, and turned the excellent cavaliere into a striking figure. Next he wrote to Morini, feigned deep concern for his well-being, recalled the memory of hours they had passed together, pretended a great longing and a desire to see him again, and inquired after his plans. So soon as the correspondence flourished it was not difficult to mention Clementine and praise her admirable qualities.

Morini nibbled at the bait. He wrote that he would be in Vienna in May, and would be charmed to meet Crammon there. He added that he dared scarcely hope to meet the Baroness von Westernach at the same time. Crammon thought, " The old idiot! " but he persuaded Franz Lothar and Clementine to promise to join him in Vienna. The plan succeeded; Morini and Clementine liked each other at once. Crammon said to her: " You have charmed him wholly." And to him: " You have made an ineffaceable impression on her." Two weeks later the betrothal took place. Clementine seemed to revive and was full of gratitude toward Crammon. What he had planned, hardly with the purest intentions, became an unalloyed blessing to her.

Crammon bestowed upon himself the recognition he held to be his due. His action was as useful as any other. He said: " Be fruitful and multiply! I shall be the godfather of your first-born. It goes without saying that I shall celebrate that event with a solemn feast."

Furthermore he said: " In the records of history I shall be known as Bernard the Founder. Perhaps I am myself the remote ancestor of a race destined to fame—a race of kings. Who can tell? In that case my far descendants, whom God protect, will have every reason to regard me with veneration."

But all this was but the deceptive flash of a fleeting mood. The worm of doubt burrowed in his mind. The future seemed

black to him. He prophesied war and revolution. He took
no joy in himself or in his deeds. When he lay in bed and
the lights were out, he felt surrounded by troops of evils;
and these evils fought with one another for the chance to
lacerate him first. Then he would close his eyes, and sigh
deeply.

Fräulein Aglaia became aware of his depression, and admonished him to pray more industriously. He thanked her
for her counsel, and promised to follow it.

XXI

The sweetishly luring waltz arose. Amadeus Voss ordered
champagne. "Drink, Lucile," he said, "drink, Ingeborg! Life
is short, and the flesh demands its delight; and what comes
after is the horror of hell."

He leaned back in his chair and compressed his lips. The
two ladies, dressed with the typical extravagance of the Berlin
cocotte, giggled. "The dear little doctor is as crazy as they're
made," one of the two said. "What's that rot he's talking
again? Is it meant to be indecent or gruesome? You never
can tell."

The other lady remarked deprecatingly: "He's had a wonderful dinner, he's smoking a Henry Clay, he's in charming
company, and he talks about the horror of hell. You don't
need us nor the Esplanade for that! I don't like such expressions. Why don't you pull yourself together, and try to
be normal and good-natured and to have a little spirit, eh?"

They both laughed. Voss blinked his eyes in a bored way.
The sweetishly luring waltz ended with an unexpected crash.
The naked arms and shoulders, the withering faces of young
men, the wrinkled corruption of faces more aged—all blended
in the tobacco fumes into a glimmer as of mother of pearl.
Visitors to the city came in from the street. They stared into
the dazzling room half greedily and half perplexed. Last of

all a young girl entered and remained standing at the door.
Amadeus Voss jumped up. He had recognized Johanna
Schöntag.

He went up to her and bowed. Taken by surprise she
smiled with an eagerness that she at once regretted. He asked
her questions. She gave a start, as though something were
snapping within her, and turned cold eyes upon him. She
shuddered at him in memory of her old shudders. Her face
was more unbeautiful than ever, but the charm of her whole
personality more compelling.

She told him that she had arrived two days ago. At present
she was in a hotel, but on the morrow she would move to
the house of a cousin near the Tiergarten.

"So you have rich relations?" Voss said tactlessly. He
smiled patronizingly, and asked her how long she intended
to stay in this nerve-racking city.

Probably throughout the autumn and winter, she told him.
She added that she didn't feel Berlin to be nerve-racking, only
tiresome and trivial.

He asked her whether he would have the pleasure of seeing
her soon, and remarked that if Wahnschaffe knew she was
here, he would assuredly look her up.

He talked with an insistent courtesy and worldly coolness
that had apparently been recently acquired. Johanna's soul
shrank from him. When he named Christian's name she grew
pale, and looked toward the stairs as though seeking help. In
her trouble the little nursery rhyme came to her which was often
her refuge in times of trouble: "If only some one kind and
strong, would come this way and take me along." Then she
smiled. "Yes, I want to see Christian," she said suddenly;
"that is why I have come."

"And I?" Voss asked. "What are you going to do with
me? Am I to be discarded? Can't I be of assistance to you
in any way? Couldn't we take a little walk together? There's
a good deal to be discussed."

" Nothing that I know of," Johanna replied. She wrinkled her forehead like one who was helpless and at bay. To get rid of the burden of his insistence courteously, she promised to write him; but she had scarcely uttered the words when they made her very unhappy. A promise had something very binding to her. It made her feel a victim; and the uncanny tension which this man caused her to feel paralyzed her will, and yet had a morbid attraction for her.

Voss drove home in a motor car. His mind was filled by one gnawing, flaring thought: Had she been Christian's mistress or not? From the moment he had seen Johanna again, this question had assumed an overwhelming importance in his mind. It involved possession and renunciation, ultimate veracity and deceit; it involved inferences that inflamed his senses, and possibilities that threatened to be decisive in his life. He fixed his thoughts upon the image of Johanna's face, and studied it like a cabalistic document. He argued and analysed and shredded motives and actions like a pettifogger. For his darkened life had again been entered by one who caused strange entanglements and enchainments and focused all decisions in one point. He felt the presage of storms such as he had not ever known.

Next morning, when he came from his bath and was about to sit down to breakfast, his housekeeper said to him: " Fräulein Engelschall is here to see you. She's in the sitting-room."

He swallowed his chocolate hastily and went in. Karen sat at a round table, and looked at photographs that were lying on it. They all belonged to Christian and were pictures of friends, of landscapes and houses, of dogs and horses.

Karen wore a very simple suit of blue. Her yellow hair was hidden by a grey felt hat adorned by a silk riband. Her face was thin, her skin pale, her expression sombre.

She disdained to use any introductory turns of speech and said: " I've come to ask you if you know about things. He

might have told you first; he didn't tell me till yesterday.
So you don't know? Well, you couldn't have done nothing
about it either. He's given away all his money. All the money
he had, he's given to his father. The rest too, that came in
by the year, I don't know how many hundred thousands—
he's refused that too. He kept his claim to just a little,—not
much more than to keep from starving, and, by what he told
me, he can't use that the way he wants to. And you know
how he is; he won't change. It's just like when the sexton's
through ringing the church bell; you can't get back the sound
of the chiming. It makes me feel like screaming, like just lying
down and screaming. I says to him: ' My God, what've you
gone and done? ' And he made a face, as if he was surprised
to see any one get excited over a little thing like that. And
now I ask you: Can he do that? Is it possible? Does the
law allow it? "

Amadeus was quite silent. His face was ashen. Yellow
sparks leaped behind his lenses. Twice he passed his hand
over his mouth.

Karen got up and walked up and down. " That's the way
things are," she muttered, and with grim satisfaction her eyes
wandered about the elegant room. " First on the box and
then in the dirt. That's the way it is. Far's I'm concerned
I could make my bargain now—if only it's not too late. Maybe it is, maybe I've waited too long. We'll see. Anyhow,
what good's the money to me? Maybe I'd better wait a
while longer." She stepped to the other side of the table, and
caught sight of a photograph which she had not yet seen. It
was a picture of Frau Wahnschaffe, and showed her in full
evening dress, wearing her famous rope of pearls which, though
slung twice, hung down over her bosom.

Karen grasped the picture, and regarded it with raised brows.
" Who's this? Looks like him. His mother, I suppose. Is it
his mother? " Voss's only answer was a nod. In greedy astonishment she went on: " Look at those pearls! Can they be

real? Is it possible? Why, they must be the size of a baby's
fist! " In her pale eyes there was a hot glow; her wicked
little nether teeth gnawed at her lip: " Can I keep this? " she
asked. Voss did not answer. She looked about hastily,
wrapped the photograph in a piece of newspaper and slid it
under her jacket. " Good Lord, man, why don't you say
something? " She flung the question at Voss brutally. " You
look like hell. But don't you think I feel it too? More than
you perhaps. You got legs of your own to stand on like the
rest of us! " She gave a cynical laugh, glanced once more
at Voss and at the room, and then she went.

For a while Voss sat without moving. Again and again he
passed his hand over his mouth; then he jumped up and hurried
into the bedroom. He went to the dressing-table on which lay
the precious toilet articles that Christian had left behind him—
gold-backed brushes and combs, gold-topped flasks, gold cases
and boxes for salves and shaving powder. With feverish haste
Voss swept these things into a heap, and threw them into a
leather hand-bag which he locked and secured in a closet.
Then he went back to the sitting-room, and paced up and
down with folded arms. His face shrunk more and more like
the faces of the dead.

Then he stood still, made the sign of the cross, and said:
" Lead us not into temptation, but deliver us from evil."

XXII

An old-fashioned phaeton was waiting at the station.
Botho von Thüngen got into it. He wrapped his feet in the
carriage robes, for the evening was cool and the drive to the
manor house long. The road passed straight across the flat
Brandenburg plain.

Botho sat rigidly erect in the carriage and thought over the
coming interview with the baron, his grandfather, who had
summoned him. Herr von Grunow-Reckenhausen of Recken-

hausen was the head of the family, final judge in all con-
troversies and court of last appeal. His sentences and commands were no more to be disputed than those of the king.
His sons, his sons-in-law, and his grandsons trembled before
him.

The ramifications of the family spread far and wide. Its
members were in the government and in the Reichstag; they
were general officers in the army, landed proprietors, industrial
magnates, superior deaconesses of the state church, governors
of provinces, and judges in the higher courts. On the occasion of Bismarck's death, the old baron had retired from
public life.

Black and verging upon ruin, the manor house arose in its
neglected park. Two great Danes growled as they emerged
from the entrance hall, which was illuminated by candles. The
rather desolate hall in which Botho faced his grandfather at
supper was also lit by candles. Everything about the house
had a ghastly air—the shabby wall-hangings, the cracked and
dusty stucco of the ceilings, the withered flowers on the table,
the eighteenth century china, the two dogs who lay at the
baron's feet, and not least the old baron himself, whose small
head and oblong, lean, malicious face bore a resemblance to
the later pictures of Frederick the Great.

They remained in the hall. The baron sat down in an
armchair by the fire. A silent, white-haired servitor threw logs
into the fireplace, cleared the table, and withdrew.

"On the first you are going to Stockholm," the old gentleman declared, and with a moan wrapped his plaid shawl tighter
about him. "I've written to our ambassador there; his father
was an old friend and fraternity brother of mine, and he
will be sure to befriend you. So soon as you return to Berlin,
be sure to call on the secretary of state. Give him my regards.
He knows me well; we were in the field together in the year
'seventy."

Botho cleared his throat. But the old baron neither desired

nor expected an interruption. He continued: "Your mother and I have agreed that your engagement is to be officially announced within a few days. Things have dragged on long enough. Next winter you two are to marry. You are in luck, my boy. Not only has Sophie Aurore a princely estate and a million in cash, but she's a beauty of the first order, and a racy one to boot. By Gad, sir, you hardly deserve that, and you seem hardly to appreciate it."

"I feel very close to Sophie Aurore, and love her very dearly," Botho replied diffidently.

"You say that, and you look as nervous as a cat when it thunders." The old gentleman was irate. "That sort of effeminate and sentimental twaddle is sickening. We weren't debating whether you loved her or not, and I didn't ask you. It would be much more pertinent to ask you about your recent conduct. And if I did, the best thing you could do would be to observe silence in seven languages, as the late lamented Schleiermacher used to say. You ran after a dancing woman, wasted a fortune, and almost missed the proper moment for entering upon your career. Well, I understand that. Madness, of course. But I was young once. Wild oats. But that, as I am told, you consort with filthy proletarians, spend your nights in God knows what dens, and frequent meetings of the Salvation Army—that surpasses both belief and decency. I thought I'd let those things be, but you have a trick of rousing one's gall. What I wanted to do was this: to give you definite directions and get a definite answer."

"Very well. My answer is that I can neither go to Stockholm nor marry Sophie Aurore."

The old baron almost flew out of his chair. "What——? You——? I don't——!" He grew inarticulate.

"I am already married."

"You are already . . . already . . . what! " The old man, greenish pale, stared at his grandson, and collapsed in his chair.

"I have married a girl whom I seduced three years ago. She was the daughter of my landlady. You know what life is like. After a night of revelry I came back to my rooms rather drunk and morally insensitive. The girl was a seam‑stress in a fashionable tailoring establishment. It was early morning and she was on her way to work. I drew her into my room. When she gave birth to my child, I was far away, and had long forgotten the incident. Her parents disowned her; the child was boarded out and died; the girl herself sank lower and lower. It's a common enough story. Through an unescapable dispensation of fate I met her again two months ago, and learned of all the wretchedness she had gone through. In the meantime my views of life had undergone a radical change, chiefly through my meeting a . . . peculiar per‑sonality. I did my duty. I know that I have lost everything— my future, my happiness, the love of my mother and my betrothed, the advantages of my birth, the respect of my equals. But I could not do differently."

The young man's firm and quiet words seemed to have turned the baron to stone. The bushy eyebrows almost hid the eyes beneath; the bitter mouth was but a cavern between chin and nose. "Is that so?" he said after a while in the wheezing pipe of age. "Is that so? You come to me with a *fait accompli* and with one of a particularly loathsome sort. Well, well. I haven't any desire to bandy words with a God damned fool. The necessary steps will be taken. All support will be withdrawn from you, and you will be put under lock and key where you belong. Fortunately there are madhouses in Prussia, and I am not quite without influence. It would be a nice spectacle, would it not, a Botho Thüngen publicly wallow‑ing in the gutter? A new triumph for the Jewish press! Yes, no doubt. I needn't stop to remark that we are strangers from this day on. You need expect no consideration under any circumstances. Unfortunately I must endure your presence in the house to-night. The horses are too tired to drive back to the station."

Botho had arisen. He passed his hands several times over his reddish blond hair. His freckled face had a sickish pallor. "I can go on foot," he said. But he listened and heard the downpour of rain, and the thought of the long tramp frightened him. Then he said: "Are you so sure of your own righteousness? Do you feel so utterly sure of all you have and do and say? I don't deny that your threats frighten me. I know that you will try to carry them out. But my conviction cannot be changed by that fact."

The baron's only answer was a commanding gesture toward the door.

In the room which had been prepared for him, Botho sat down at a table, and by the light of a candle wrote with feverish intensity:

"Dear Wahnschaffe:—My difficult task is accomplished. My grandfather sat before me strong as a cliff; I received his verdict like a shaking coward. The fieriest emotions turn into lies before these inexorable souls, whose prejudices are their laws and whose caste is their fate. Ah, their courage in living themselves out! Their iron souls and foreheads! And I, on the other hand, I am the *reductio ad absurdum* of my race; I am a prodigal son from top to toe. Somewhere I read about a man who overcame God through the strength of his utter weakness. This sombre landscape, this rigid northern world—what could it produce as an adversary of that old Torquemada of high lineage but an hysterical revolutionary like myself?

"My childhood, my boyhood, my youth, these are but paragraphs in a heartless tract on the art of seeming what one is not, of striving for what is without worth. I knew as little about myself as the nut's kernel knows of the nut. I idled and drank and gambled, and made a prostitute of time itself, which had to please me or en-

dure my hate. We were all blind and deaf and unfeeling.
But it is a crime to gain sight and hearing and a heart. I met
Sophie Aurore and loved her. But I loved her imperfectly,
for I was a man with crippled senses. One is supposed to
sow one's wild oats, as you know; and one is supposed to do
that before uniting one's life with a being whose image and
memory should be too sacred to be dragged through vice and
dirt. But some fate in this mad world brought me under the
influence of Eva Sorel. For the first time I learned what a
woman truly is and what her significance may be. It helped
me to understand Sophie and to feel what I must be to her.

"And then I saw you, Christian. Do you recall the day
when you read those French verses to Eva and the others?
The way you did it forced me to think of you for days and days.
And do you remember how in Hamburg you broke the silver
handle of the whip with which Eva had struck your friend's
face? The scales dropped from my eyes. I remained on your
track; I sought every opportunity of being near you. You did
not know it. When you disappeared I looked for you. They
told me you were in Berlin, and I sought and at last found
you, and under what conditions? My soul was so terribly full
that neither then nor later could I explain to you the inexplicable mystery and strange magnetism that drew me to you.
To-day I had to speak out to you, and the words that I address
to you give me strength.

"I need consolation. I love Sophie Aurore and I shall
love her till I die. The letter of parting which I had
to write her was the bitterest thing in all my useless
and mistaken life. She has not answered it. I have
broken her life and trodden on her heart, but I have saved
another life and kept another heart from despair. Have I done
right? When people used to talk of sacrificing oneself for a
cause or for another human being, it always seemed empty
verbiage to me. Since I have known you, the thought has acquired a deeply serious significance. All this may sound

strange to you and even discordant. You do not brood nor take yourself spiritually to task; and that is the incomprehensible thing about you. Yet I know none but you whom I would make the arbiter of my conscience and whom I would ask: Have I done right? "

XXIII

The latch must have been left open. Isolde Schirmacher had been the last to go out. Twilight had just fallen when the door of the room opened, and Niels Heinrich entered.

Karen did not get up. She looked over at him. She wanted to speak, but the words seemed to perish in the drouth of her throat.

His face had its usual expression of impudent disgust. His flat, eternally sniffing, and inquisitive nose had a yellow tinge. He wore a blue cap, baggy trowsers, and a yellow shawl slung around his neck.

Wrinkling his nose like a dog he looked about him. Then he closed his left eye and spat.

At last Karen murmured: " What do you want? "

He shrugged his shoulders, and showed his neglected teeth. In one, near the corner of his mouth, he had a large gold-filling which was evidently new.

" Well, what is it? " Karen asked again. There was the fear in her voice that she felt so often now.

Again he showed his decayed front-teeth. It might have been a smile. He went up to the chest of drawers and pulled out one of the drawers. Deliberately he rummaged among its contents. He took out under garments, neck-wear, stockings, corsets, and threw them on the floor. He went on to the second drawer, then to the third, and littered the floor with what he found. Then he approached the wardrobe, but it was locked. He stretched out his hand toward her with a speaking gesture of command. Karen saw the destruction and confusion he had caused, and did not respond at once. An hallucination as of renewed impoverishment flamed up in her blunted soul. Niels Heinrich seemed its messenger. She was so in fear of him that she wanted to cry out. He made a grimace and gently swung his hand about on the pivot of his wrist. Karen acknowledged the compulsion of that gesture; she put her hand into her pocket, and gave him the key.

He wrenched open the door of the wardrobe, peered in, hauled out card-board boxes, which he calmly overturned, threw garments on the floor as he had thrown the linen, finally discovered a wooden box, and pried off the cover with his knife. He found a golden brooch, the old brooch with the motto, " Ricordo di Venezia," and a little silver chain. He slipped these three objects into his pocket. Then he went into the adjoining room, where Karen heard him moving about. There was no expression in her staring eyes. He came back at the end of a few minutes. It had grown dark, and in the inner room a candle which he had lit was left burning. In passing he threw a contemptuous glance at the cradle. He did not take the trouble to close the outer door behind him.

In the dim light that shone in from the inner room, Karen surveyed her scattered possessions. Suddenly she put her hand into her bosom, drew forth the photograph of Frau Wahnschaffe, and lost herself in an absorbed and sombre contemplation of it.

She saw the pearls, only the pearls.

XXIV

At the foot of the stairs by the street door, Niels Heinrich saw the figure of Ruth Hofmann. She was waiting for her brother, who had gone across the street to buy bread. The lad limped a little, and Ruth had never been able to fight off the fear that he would be run over.

She looked at the pavement, glittering under the street

lamps, at the light of other lamps in the many windows, and finally higher, where she was accustomed to see the stars, but where now there was only the confused and reddish glow of clouds.

Niels Heinrich stopped. Ruth looked up at him with her large grey eyes. He took in all details of the little figure—the thick hair with its curling ends, the shabby flannel dress, the soiled, worn shoes, and last of all the clear, pale face flooded with an alien spiritual life. His glance clung savagely to her, and ripped the garments from her body. The girl, shuddering as she had never done before, chilled to the marrow by an unknown force, turned away toward the stairs, and hesitantly began to mount them.

Niels Heinrich looked after her. " Jew wench! " he murmured from clenched teeth. A greeting from the home-coming Gisevius awakened him from his thoughts. He lit a cigar, pushed the blue cap down toward the nape of his neck, and slouched down the street.

xxv

Toward the end of May Letitia gave birth to twins—both girls. Stephen had the feeling that this was rather excessive; nevertheless festivities were arranged. The house and garden were hung with gay lanterns, the neighbours were invited, and the common people fed. There was music and dancing and shouting. His brothers got drunk and brawled, and there were wild goings-on.

Letitia lay in her handsome bed under the sky-blue canopy. From time to time she asked to see the twins. Each was presented appetizingly reposing on a pillow. They were mysteriously alike. The nurse, who bore the mellifluous name Eleutheria, brought them in—one on her right arm, one on her left. One had a red riband fastened to its shoulder, the other a green; this was for identification. The red-ribanded baby was to be christened Georgette, the other Christina. Such was Letitia's wish. Stephen desired each child to have in addition a string of richer and more gorgeous names. Tirelessly he turned the pages of all the novels and chronicles within reach, and finally brought a florilegium of names to his wife: Honorata, Friedegunda, Reinilda, Roswitha, Portiuncula, Symphorosa, Sigolina, Amalberga. Letitia laughed until she cried. She pointed to the ugly nurse and said: " None has so beautiful a sound as Eleutheria. I insist on Georgette and Christina." And already she knew that Christina was going to be her favourite.

She looked so charming as she lay there that people came to admire her as one admires a painting. These people were all uneducated and stupid, and Letitia was bored. Sometimes she played chess with Esmeralda, and the girl, drunk with curiosity, asked her a thousand questions. When Letitia was in labour, the girl had lain huddled on the verandah, and her crude and sensual imagination was filled with images that both allured and horrified her. Letitia felt that and said: " Go away! I don't like you to-day."

She seemed to herself beloved of God and blessed by His angels. She was proud of being what she was—an unusual being chosen for an unusual fate. She seemed new to herself in every way. She loved herself, but there was no raw selfishness nor idle admiration in this love. It was something akin to the gratitude and joy of one who had been found worthy of great gifts.

The fact that she possessed two children, two real children with little hands and feet, who could struggle and cry, who could be dressed and undressed, who could be fed and caressed —no, it was not this fact that filled her so full of happiness. It was the expectation that grew out of the children, the mystery of these unknown personalities whose being and becoming proceeded from her own. And so she lay there, lovely, dainty, serene, given over to her dreams.

In the meantime Stephen and old Gunderam renewed their old fight over the Escurial. " The contract's a scrap of paper," the old man jeered. " Two girls don't make one boy. I'm not looking out for quantity. Two hens don't make a rooster." Stephen shouted that he was not going to be cheated of his rightful inheritance, that he would take the matter into court, and make a public scandal of it. The old man, his hands at his hips, had no reply but an evil chuckle. So the quarrelling went on, morning, noon, and night. The old man locked his door, and had the boxes that had stood packed for twenty years gotten into final readiness. Stephen smashed plates and glasses, threw chairs about, cursed and threatened, rode horses half to death, was himself seized with convulsions, sent for a doctor, and had morphine injections prescribed to quiet him.

Partisanship rose high. The old man gained the support of his wife, Stephen that of his brothers. The latter made the servants rebellious, and Doña Barbara shrieked and cursed them. The brawls increased in violence; night was full of ghastly rumours. Once the report of a pistol rang out, and every one rushed into the open. Stephen was missing. He lay abed with a smoking revolver and moaned. He had aimed at his heart and hit a medicine bottle. Its fragments swam in a yellow liquid on the floor. The old man said: " I'm not surprised that a man who's such a fool as a lawyer can't shoot straight. But it takes a damned lot of malice to aim as badly as that." Whereupon Doña Barbara could not help observing: " Only a Gunderam could say anything so vile! " And so the two old people quarrelled until dawn.

Stephen succumbed more and more to the use of morphine. When he was not under its influence he tormented man and beast. His brothers finally rebelled against the insults which he heaped upon them. They laid a plot, and fell upon him and beat him so that he roared like a buffalo. Letitia rushed to help him, and summoned men servants. A regular battle ensued. " Don't leave me," Stephen whined, and she had to sit down by him, and offer him consolation from the depths of her contempt. He asked her to read him poetry, and she consented. She did not read poems of her own choice, but easy, sentimental verses by second-rate writers. Among the fifteen or sixteen volumes which formed the family library, there was a greasy copy of an old-fashioned anthology of German verse. She read from it, and Stephen said: " What wonderful words! " And he wept.

But at other times he treated her with coldness and contempt; for, in the last analysis, she seemed to him to bear the guilt of all his failures and troubles. Letitia was quite indifferent; her mind was made up. Strength was given her will by the very horror with which the house and its inhabitants, the family and its life, the land and its whole atmosphere filled her. Whenever Stephen wanted to kiss her, she grew very pale, and looked at him as though he had lost his senses. Then he would rage, and threaten her with the cowhide whip. But she had learned to smile in a way that tamed him and robbed him of inner assurance.

For six weeks Friedrich Pestel had now been in Buenos Ayres. She corresponded with him secretly. The Indian boy who had once accompanied her to the observatory was her faithful and discreet messenger. She promised to take him along to Europe, for this was his great wish. Eleutheria desired the same, and swore eternal devotion when Letitia carefully and gradually gave her her confidence. All details of the flight were discussed with Friedrich Pestel. Letitia was to be in Buenos Ayres on the day of the sailing of the Portuguese steamer *Dom Pedro*. An intricate intrigue was needed to convey the twins to the city. Letitia thought out a clever plan; it was like the plot of a detective novel.

There lived in the capital city an aged and childless couple, Señor and Señora Herzales. The old man was a brother of Doña Barbara, and his wealth would, upon his death, fall to the Gunderam children. But since both he and his wife

were misers of the filthiest kind, there was always the fear
lest by some whim or in some rage they should make a will
to the disadvantage of their kinsmen. They had not written
to the Gunderams in years. There were no personal contacts
except visits of state, which Stephen and his brothers occasionally paid them. Letitia was, of course, aware of all this.
She forged a letter, supposedly from Señora Herzales, in which
the old woman expressed the desire to see the young wife of
Stephen and her children, and, in order that the uncle and
aunt might get the better acquainted with her, the letter demanded that Letitia come alone, although there was no objection to Stephen's coming to fetch her home at the end of
a week.

This letter, cleverly written by Letitia in a handwriting unlike her own, arrived with the proper postmark from Buenos
Ayres and caused a great stir in the Gunderam clan. A solemn
family council was held; greed and fear conquered all hesitation. Doña Barbara dictated to Letitia a humble and grateful
letter of acceptance, in which she was permitted to announce
her arrival on a day set by herself. This letter Letitia succeeded in intercepting.

On the fateful morning her heart beat like an alarm clock.
The rickety coach drew up; Eleutheria got in; the slumbering
twins were handed to her. Stephen examined the carriage,
tested the harness, and graciously patted the horses. The
Indian boy brought the hand luggage, stowed it away properly,
and calmly mounted the box. Don Gottfried, Doña Barbara,
Esmeralda and her brothers solemnly awaited Letitia. Five
minutes passed, and ten and twenty, and still Letitia did not
come. Stephen grumbled, Don Gottfried laughed a jeering
laugh, Doña Barbara glanced furiously up at Letitia's windows.
At last she appeared.

At the last moment she had mislaid the little bag that held
her jewels. They were her one possession. She had no money
at all.

With a radiant smile she gave her hand to each in turn, permitted her husband to kiss the tip of her chin, and cried out in a slightly husky and long-drawn-out and lamenting voice: " Don't forget me, and remember me to Father Theodore! " The latter was a Capuchin monk, who occasionally came to the farm to beg. It was a sheer, joyous whim that made her mention him at this moment.

The wintry sun disappeared in the fog. Letitia thought: " Where I am going now it is summer."

Twenty-four hours later she stood with Friedrich Pestel on the deck of the *Dom Pedro*, and looked back with happy eyes upon the disappearing shore.

XXVI

The driver roared, but it was too late. An edge of the rattling wagon laden with steel rails caught the limping boy and knocked him down. A crowd gathered, and a helmeted policeman made his way through it.

Christian had just turned the corner when he saw the boy lying there. He approached, and some women made room for him. As he bent over the boy, he saw that the latter had only been stunned; he was stirring and opened his eyes. Nor did he seem to be hurt. He peered anxiously about, and asked after the money that he had had in his hand before he had fallen. It had consisted of twenty or thirty nickel coins, which were now scattered in the mud.

Christian helped the boy get up, and wiped the spattered face with his white handkerchief. But to the boy the recovering of his money was of greater importance, although he could not bend over and could hardly stand. " Have patience until the wagon is gone," Christian said to him, and motioned the driver to proceed. The latter had become involved in a violent altercation with the policeman. But when the policeman saw that no great damage had been done, he also told the driver to go ahead, and merely took down the man's name as well as the boy's. The boy was Michael Hofmann, Ruth's brother.

Christian bent over, and gathered the coins out of the mire. The spectators were amazed that a well-dressed gentleman should bend over in the street to gather nickel coins. Some recognized him. They said: "He's the one that lives back there with Gisevius."

Now at last Ruth came hurrying. She had been frightened from her post by Niels Heinrich Engelschall. She had waited on the stairs until he had disappeared. Then she had come down and heard the hubbub in the street, and had thought that it must be connected with the fellow who had stared at her with such savage impudence. She had hesitated again until a foreboding drove her forth.

She did not make much ado and hid her fright. She questioned her brother in a cheerful voice. Her German was very pure and perfect, and she spoke very swiftly, with a bird-like twitter in her throat.

When he had gathered the coins, Christian said: "Now let us count them to be sure that they are all here." Taking the boy by the arm, he led him across the street and into the house. Ruth had taken her brother's other arm, and thus they mounted the stairs. They entered a room which looked empty on account of its size, although it held two beds, a table, and a wardrobe. It was the only room of that dwelling. A kitchen adjoined it.

Michael sat down on the bed, still slightly stunned by his fall. He was about fourteen, but his tense features and his passionate eyes had a maturity far beyond his years.

Christian laid the coins on the table. They made no sound, so encrusted were they with mud. Ruth looked at Christian, shook her head compassionately, and hurried into the kitchen for a wet cloth with which to clean his spattered garments. She kneeled down before him. He drew back, but she did not perceive his motive and followed him on her knees.

So he resisted no longer, and felt a little foolish as she eagerly and skilfully brushed his trousers.

Suddenly she raised her face to him. His glance had been resting on the table, which was covered with many books. " Are those your books? " he asked.

She answered: " To be sure they are." And she looked at him with eyes that were astonishingly bright with a frank spiritual recognition of their inner kinship. The old arrogant expression with which he had been wont to shield his soul melted from his face. But even as it did he became aware of something that made him angry with himself, that seemed unnatural and absurd to him, and filled him with the fear of something evil and ghastly in his own eyes. For it seemed to him that he had seen a bloody mark on the girl's forehead.

In his fright he turned his eyes away, and resisted the impulse to look again. But when he had regained his self-control and looked upon her, there was nothing to be seen. He sighed with relief, but frowned angrily at himself.

XXVII

When the *Dom Pedro* had been on the high seas not more than a week, Letitia was forced to the sorrowful conclusion that Friedrich Pestel was not the right man for her.

She desired a man of imaginative ardour and impassioned soul. In face of the unending sea and the starry vault of heaven, a fadeless yearning had reawakened in her, and she told Pestel frankly and honestly that she could not be happy with him. Pestel was overwhelmed with amazement. He did not answer, and became melancholy.

Among the passengers there was an Austrian engineer who had been building railroads in Peru and was on his way home. His boldly romantic appearance and happy faculty of anecdote delighted Letitia. She could not let him perceive it on account of the other passengers who took her to be Pestel's wife. But

the engineer, who was something of an adventurer and courageous, had his own thoughts.

In spite of his genuine pain and disappointment, Pestel reproached himself for having bought the expensive first-cabin
tickets for Letitia, the nurse, and the twins, and a second-cabin
passage for the Indian boy, out of his own pocket. In addition he had, just before their departure and in all haste,
bought several frocks and some linen for the woman whom
he had saved from captivity, and to whom, as he thought, he
was about to be united for life.

The Indian boy was sea-sick and also home-sick, and Letitia
promised to send him back to the Argentine from Genoa.

Among the other passengers who regarded Letitia with a
vivid eye was an American journalist who had spent several
months in Brazil. He was witty, wrote clever verses, organized
parties and dances, and soon seemed as charming to Letitia
as the Austrian engineer. Between these two little skirmishes
of jealousy took place, and each felt the other to be an obstacle.

One night they were the last guests at the bar; neither
wanted to turn in, and they agreed to throw dice for a bottle
of claret.

The Austrian lost.

The bottle arrived. The American filled the glasses; they
drank, leaned back and smoked, looked searchingly at each
other from time to time, and said nothing.

Suddenly the Yankee, still holding his pipe between his
teeth, said: " Nice woman."

" Charming," the Austrian agreed.

" Has a strong sense of humour for a German."

The engineer thoughtfully blew rings of smoke. " She is
altogether delightful," he said.

They fell silent again. Then the American said: " Isn't it
rather absurd of us to spoil each other's chances? Let us
throw dice, and abide by that! "

" Very well, let us do so," the engineer agreed. He took

the dice-box, shook it, and emptied it. The little cubes rattled down on the marble. "Eighteen," the engineer announced, astonished at his own good fortune.

The other gathered up the dice, also shook the box, let the dice glide on the table-top, and calmly announced "Eighteen!" He was equally unable—with more reason of course—to hide his astonishment.

The two men felt rather helpless. They were careful not to repeat their question to fate. They finished their wine, and separated with all due courtesy.

Letitia lay abed with wide-open eyes and listened to the throb of the engines, the soft crashing of the walls of the ship, and the humming of Eleutheria, who was soothing the twins in the adjoining stateroom. She thought of Genoa, the fast approaching goal of her voyage; and her imagination showed her gorgeously clad grandees and romantic conspirators in the style of Fiesco of Genoa, and torch-lit alleys and adventures of love and passion. Life seemed to her aglow with colour, and the future a gate of gold.

XXVIII

The child had disappeared.

Christian asked after its whereabouts. Karen shrugged her shoulders stubbornly. So Christian went to the dwelling of the widow Engelschall, who informed him with harsh brevity: "I put the child in good hands. You've got no right to worry. Why do you? It ain't yours!"

Christian said: "You have no reason not to tell me where it is."

The woman answered insolently: "Not on yer life! I ain't got no call to do it. The kid's well off where he is, and you ain't going to refuse to pay a bit to his foster-mother, are you? It's your dooty, and you can't get out of it."

Silently Christian regarded the fat moon-like face on its

triple chin, from which the voice rumbled like that of an old salt. Then he became aware of the fact that that sweaty mass of flesh was contorting itself to an expression of friendliness. Pointing to the glass door, which separated the hexagonal room in which they were from the other rooms, she asked in sweetish High German whether he wouldn't come in and partake of a little coffee. Coffee and fine pastry, she said, who would refuse that? She explained that she was expecting a baroness, who was coming from Küstrin especially to see her in order to get advice on important family matters. He could see that she wasn't born yesterday either, had nice friends of her own, and knew how to treat people of rank. Again she asked him to stay.

In this dim room there were several tables covered with well-thumbed copies of periodicals and comic papers. It looked like a dentist's reception room. The woman's fat fingers were covered with rings that had brightly coloured stones. She wore a bodice of red silk and a black skirt, the girdle of which was held by a silver buckle as massive as a door knob.

When Christian came in to see Karen that evening, she sat by the oven resting her head on her hand. Christian had brought her some oranges, and he laid the fruit on her lap. She did not stir; she did not thank him. He thought that perhaps she was longing for her child, and did not break her long silence.

Suddenly she said: " It's seven years ago to-day that Adam Larsen died."

" I have never heard of Adam Larsen," Christian said. Since she made no remark, he repeated: " I've never heard of Adam Larsen. Won't you tell me about him? "

She shook her head. She seemed to crouch as for a leap at the wall under his look. Christian carried a chair close up to Karen. He sat down beside her, and urged her to speak: " What about Adam Larsen? "

She took in a deep breath. " It was the only good time

in my life, the time I had with him, the only beautiful time—
five months and a half."

She delved deep, deep into her consciousness. Things there
yearned for the light. " It was the time I was expecting my
second child," she said. " We were on the way from Memel to
Königsberg, myself and Mathilde Sorge and her intended.
Oh, well, intended is what they call it. On the way I noticed
that I was going to get into a mess pretty soon. They advised
me to leave the train. One station before we got to Königsberg
I did get out. Mathilde stayed with me, though she scolded;
her intended went on to the city. It was a March evening,
cold and wet. There was an inn near the station where they
knew Mathilde. She thought we could get lodging there, and
there was no time to lose; but they were having a fair in that
place, and every room was taken. We begged for a garret
or anything; but the innkeeper looked at me, and saw what was
the matter. I was leaning against the wall and shaking. He
roared, and told us to go to the devil; he didn't want to have
anything to do with such things. I lay down on a low wagon
in the yard. I couldn't have gone on, not if they'd set the
dogs on me. The farmer that owned the wagon came, and
he wasn't pleased; but Mathilde, she talked to him a while, and
so he drove on slowly toward the city. Mathilde walked beside the wagon. I felt I don't know how; I thought if I
could just be dead—quite dead! The wheels bumped on the
stones, and I screamed and shrieked. The farmer said he'd had
enough of that. We were in the suburbs by this time, so they
tugged me out of the wagon, and held me up. There was a
young man who had seen us, and he helped too. The rain
fell by the bucket, and I was clean done for. I asked them
for God's sake to get me in anywhere, if it was only a hole
or a cellar. At the corner there was a cheap music-hall for
working people. They dragged me through the door into a
little room, and pushed two benches together, and laid me on
them. The room was full of the gay dresses of the lady per-

formers; on one side of the room was the bar, on the other side the auditorium. You could hear the music and the applause and the roars of laughter. Some women, got up in dirty silks and spangles, came in and stood around me, and quarrelled and screamed for one thing or another. Well, there's no use going on with that part. The child was born there, and it was dead. They'd sent for a policeman and for a doctor too; but it was the young man we had met on the street who was really kind and wouldn't leave me in my trouble. And that was Adam Larsen."

"And he continued to help you? And you stayed with him?" Christian asked tensely.

Karen went on: "He was a painter, a real one, an artist. His home was in Jutland; he was lean and very fair. In those days my hair was just the colour of his. He had an aunt living in Königsberg, and he was glad to stay with her a while, because he was hard up. But when I was lying in the charity home to which they'd removed me, he got the news from Copenhagen that he'd been given a stipend by the state of two thousand talers for two years. He asked me if I wouldn't like to go with him. He meant to go to Belgium to a famous painter who was living somewhere on the French frontier. He wanted to study with him, like others who were already there. Well, he said he was fond of me, and I said that was all very nice, and asked him if he knew the sort of woman I was. He said he didn't want to know anything, and all I'd have to do was to have confidence in him. So I thought to myself, 'Here's one that's got a heart,' and I grew to be fond of him too. I'd never cared for any man yet; he was the first, and he was the last too. And so I went away with him. The great painter lived in a French village, and we moved to a little town called Wassigny not far from there. Larsen rented a little house. Every morning he'd ride over to the village on his bicycle; if the weather was bad he walked. It was half an hour's walk. In the evening he'd come back, and we'd have a nice little dinner and tea and chat. And he'd get real enthusiastic, and tell me how he loved painting here— the trees and the fields and the peasants and the miners and the river and the sky, and I don't know what all. I didn't understand that, of course; but what I understood was that I felt as I'd never felt before in life. I couldn't believe it when I woke up in the morning; I couldn't believe it when the neighbours smiled at me. Near the village there was a pool with water lilies, and I used to go often and often and look at it. I'd never seen anything like that before, and I couldn't rightly believe in it. I knew that couldn't last; it wasn't possible that it could last long. And sure enough, in August, Adam took to his bed one day. He had a fever, and it got worse and worse; and in six days he was dead. That was the end of everything. That was the end of everything."

Her hands kept clutching her hair, and for the third time she said: " That was the end of everything."

" And then? " Christian whispered.

She looked at him, and every muscle in her face quivered: " Then? Oh, the things that happened then . . . then . . . ! "

" Couldn't you somehow find a way of life without . . . without . . ." Christian stammered, frightened by the blind, white rage in her face. She clenched her fists and cried so loud that her words re-echoed from the walls: " Oh, then! The things that happened then! "

Her whole body quivered. " Don't touch me," she said with a nervous start.

Christian had not touched her at all.

" Go on now," she said. " I'm tired. I've got to sleep." She got up.

He stood at one door, Karen at the opposite one. She lowered her head, and said in a toneless voice: " It's crazy— me talking to you this way—so familiar and all." And her face showed both hatred and fear.

When she was alone beside her bed, she lost herself in the contemplation of the picture of the woman with the pearls. Once she turned around, and looked wildly into the other room, to the spot where Christian had stood.

And Christian could not forget her words and the way she had said: "Oh, then . . . ."

XXIX

Weikhardt had been working at his Descent from the Cross for two years, yet he could not finish the picture. No effort, no absorption, no lonely contemplation, no spiritual seeking would bring him the expression on the face of Christ.

He could not create that expression—the compassion and the pain.

He had scratched the face from the canvas a hundred times; he had tried many models; he had spent hours and days studying the old masters; he had made hundreds and hundreds of sketches; he had tried and tried. It was all in vain; he could not create it.

In the spring he had married Helen Falkenhaus, the girl of whom he had once spoken to Imhof. Their married life was a quiet one. Their means were small, and they had to be content with very little. Helen bore every privation with great sweetness. Her piety, which often had a touch of expectant passion, helped her to ease her husband of the consciousness of his burdens and responsibilities.

She had an understanding of art, a high and fine perception of its qualities. He showed her his sketches, and she thought many of them very beautiful. At times he seemed to her to have come near the vision of which she too had a glimpse; but she was forced to admit that he never quite embodied it. He attained compassion and pain, but not the compassion and the pain of Christ.

Just then there arrived in Munich the Polish countess for

whom he had copied the cycle of Luini. One evening she gave an entertainment to which Weikhardt was invited, and among the crowd he caught sight of Sybil Scharnitzer. He had seen her years ago in the studio of a fashionable painter. She had been surrounded by admirers and flatterers, and he had carried away only a general impression of her beauty.

This time she inspired him with a strange and magical excitement. He knew at once that he needed her, that between her and his work there was some mystic bond. He approached her and held her by his vivid eloquence. Carefully he revealed his purpose. Absorbing her mien, her gesture, that look of hers that went to the very soul, he saw clearly what he expected of her and what she could give him. In this eye, when it was wide open, he saw that more than mortal look which had hitherto been but dim in his mind. He begged her to sit for him. She thought a little and consented.

She came. He asked her to bare her neck and shoulders, and to swathe her bust in a black shawl of Venetian lace. He stood at his easel, and for ten minutes he gazed at her steadily. Scarcely did his lids stir. Then he took a piece of charcoal, and drew the outlines of the head of Christ. Sybil was astonished. At the end of an hour he thanked her, and that was the first time he had spoken. He begged her to come again. Quite as amazed as she had been at first, she pointed at the canvas. But he smiled secretively, told her that his technical approach was a roundabout one, and asked her to have patience.

When she left, Helen came in. He had told her of his plan, and his confidence had prevailed over her doubts. She knew the history of Sybil Scharnitzer, and had observed her that evening at the countess's with the cold scrutiny which one woman gives another. She looked at the charcoal sketch, and was silent for many minutes. At last, under his questioning look, casting down her own eyes, she asked: " Did any model ever appear so disguised? "

Weikhardt had recovered his usual, phlegmatic temper. "Very few people will understand my excursion behind the scenes—painters least of all. I can see them crossing themselves and making venomous comments."

"That doesn't matter," said Helen. "But what do you mean by an excursion behind the scenes?"

"I mean the scenes set by God."

Helen thought this over, but his words hurt her. She said: "I could understand that perfectly if Sybil's face were genuine; but you yourself have told me who and what she is. You know that it is a beautiful screen, with emptiness behind it. And in this vain deception you think you will find what is deepest in the world—the Saviour, your vision of the Saviour? Isn't it as though you had delivered yourself into the power of falseness itself?"

"No," Weikhardt answered, "it is not. You don't see far enough. Things cohere together far more closely than you think. One body, one element, one stream—each is more interwoven with all things than you realize. The soulless emptiness in Sybil Scharnitzer's breast is the reflection of some light, and to me personally it is a concrete thing. If a form deceives me, I am still grateful to it, for it forces me to create its content from within myself; and the creative dream is the greater thing. Can a blade of grass be a lie? Or a shell by the shore? And if I were strong enough and guiltless enough and devout enough, it would be given me to find in every blade and shell the compassion and the pain of Christ. There is an element of chance in these things, or else some dispensation."

Helen did not contradict him.

xxx

That word of Karen's, that desperate "then!" gave Christian no rest.

He had worked hard all day. He had not left the Physiological Institute until seven o'clock. Then he had eaten a frugal evening meal, and had gone home on foot. Thoroughly tired, he had thrown himself on the sofa, and fallen asleep.

When he woke up it was dark night. The house was quite silent. He lit a light, and looked at his watch; it pointed to half-past eleven. He considered for a little, and then determined to go across the courtyard to see Karen. He was sure to find her awake; sometimes she kept her lamp burning until two o'clock. For some time she had been doing embroidery work; she said she wanted to earn some money. So far she had not succeeded, but she had taken no great pains to sell her work.

He crossed the dark court, and mounted the dark stairs. He stopped at the open hall window of the third floor. The night was sultry. On one side, through a canyon between the black and lifeless brick walls of two houses, he saw smoke stacks project into the darkness. They came from the earth itself and overtopped the roofs. They were tipped with lightning-rods, and from some of them came thick fumes shot with the quiver of flames. Below was blackness, empty land hedged in by wooden fences, rough beams piled in heaps, low isolated huts, sand-pits and mortar-pits, and darkness and silence over all.

To the left of the stairs was the door to the Hofmanns' flat. When he was letting himself into Karen's rooms, he still gazed back at that door. He thought he was being called thither, but it was a delusion.

Karen was in bed. "Why, what do you want so late?" she grumbled. "I'd like a little quiet sometime."

"I beg your pardon," he said courteously. "I didn't mean to disturb you. I thought we might chat for a little while."

"I'd like to know the good of all this talking, day and night." She was annoyed, and even her laugh showed it.

He sat down on the edge of the bed. "You must tell me

what happened to you after Adam Larsen's death," he said. " I can't get rid of the impression of your words: the things that happened then . . . Of course, I can imagine in a general way. I have insight enough into life now to make a guess . . ."

She interrupted him with a note of contempt in her voice. " No, you can't guess nothing and you can't imagine nothing, I'd bet my last rag on that."

" That's all the more reason why I'd like you to tell me about it," he urged her. " You have never done so."

There was an hostility in her silence, and it suddenly became clear to him that some stubborn instinct in her refused to initiate him wholly into her world. All that he had done for her had not sufficed to conquer the distrust of him and his kind that was bred into her very bone. The realization of this fact made him feel sad and helpless.

" I went to bed at seven to-day," she said, blinking her eyes. " I wasn't feeling a bit well. I believe I'm going to be sick."

Christian looked at her, and he could not keep the disquietude and urgency out of his eyes.

Karen closed her lids. " Nothing but torment, torment, torment," she moaned.

Christian was frightened. " No, no. Forgive me. I'll go."

" You might as well stay." She laid her cheek on her folded hands, and drew up her limbs under the covers. A common but not disagreeable odour came from her hair and skin.

Wearily and idly she talked into the pillow. " It's the common, ordinary thing, always the same. Women that tell you something else are liars. Of course, a good many will invent long romances to seem interesting, but I can't do that. What do I care about it? No, it's always the same story, common and horrible and filthy from A to Z. Oh, yes, you might as well stay now and sit down. I'll tell you what I can. If you've just got to know, I might as well tell you, but it's hard.

I don't know where to begin. There is no beginning. There's nothing definite,—no romance nor nothing."

Christian sat down again. " When Adam Larsen died," he said, " was there no path for you? Was there no one among his friends or relatives who paid any attention to you or helped you? "

She laughed a sarcastic laugh. " Hell! You're all off there. His friends didn't hardly know about me. His brother came to the funeral, but I didn't dare so much as speak to him. He was one of the righteous kind, with a golden watch-chain and a tip of five sous for the servants. And I was in a strange country, and didn't know the language, and had to see about getting away. I had thirty francs in cash, and the question was: where could I go? I tried to get work once or twice. But what sort of work was I to do? I hadn't learned nothing. Was I to go as a servant, and black boots and scrub floors? No, thank you! I was used to something different now, and I thought I could get along somehow. Anyhow I didn't give a damn what became of me; I didn't matter so much. In Aachen I took a job as a waitress. Nice occupation! I can't give you an idea of that—the tiredness in your legs, the abuse you got to take! For food they give you the scraps; the bed ain't fit for a dog. What they expect of you makes you crazy mad.

" Well, when you live that way you're open to all sorts of swindling talk. I went into a house; stayed there four months, and then went into another. I had debts, too. Suddenly you're in debt, you can't figure out why. Board and lodging and clothes—they charge you three times over for everything: you got to pay for the air you breathe. All you think of is how to get out, or something awful will happen. Well, then maybe some fellow comes along in high feather, throws money out of the windows, pays for you, and gets you out. You go with him, and on the third morning somebody knocks at the door. Who's there? Police! Your man's a thief, and you

have the devil's own time clearing yourself of complicity.
What now? You have to have a roof and a bed, and some one
to talk to; you want a warm bite and a cool drink. You've got
the mark of the trade on you, and no one trusts you. You're
shoved and you're pulled, and you go down and down, day by
day, step by step. You hardly notice it, and suddenly you're
at the bottom."

She curled herself up more compactly under the covers, and
continued in a blunter tone. "It's easy to say that—at the
bottom; but really there's no such thing. There's a lower
depth under every depth; and there ain't no words to tell
you how it is down there. No one can imagine it who hasn't
been there. No seeing from the outside and no knowing
will make people realize it. You live in a place for which they
charge you five times as much as is fair and decent. You're
common property, and everybody gets out of you all he can.
You don't care if the place is elegant or like a pigsty. It gives
you the horrors to open the door of it. It ain't yours; it's
everybody's. It's the place where everybody sort of sheds
his filth, and you know them all and remember them all. It
does you no good to go to bed and try to sleep. Another day
is bound to come. There are the same greasy public houses
and the same faces, always the same crowd. And then there's
the street—what you call your territory. That's where you
go by night. You know every window and crossing and
lantern: you stare and turn and ogle and grin, and open your
umbrella if it rains, and walk and stand around and keep a
sharp eye on the police, and make up to any man if he's got
torn shoes or sports a fur ulster. And then you promise him
God knows what; and all the time you'd like to scratch his
heart out if he walks off, or spit in his face if he condescends
to you. There it is! That's the main thing. Pain and worry
—Lord, all people have them. But what you get to find out
about men there—oh, I tell you!"

Her last words were a cry again, a great cry, such as that

other cry which Christian had not been able to forget. He sat very straight, and looked past the lamp to a certain spot on the wall.

Karen seemed, as she went on, to be addressing the floor. " Then there's the lodging-house keeper, who steals and cheats. There's the owner of the house, who acts by daylight as if he wanted to kick you, and comes slinking to your door at twilight. There's the shop-keeper, who overcharges you, and acts as if he was doing you a favour by giving you rotten stuff for your good money. There's the policeman that grudges you every step you take. If you don't slip him a bribe, he pulls you in and you go to jail. There's the innkeeper; maybe you owe him a bit. He torments you if you got no brass, and wheedles and flatters when you have a little. I don't mention your own man; but you got to have one if you want to or not, otherwise you've got no protection. When he's sent to the penitentiary, you got to get another. They're all handy with their knives, but Mesecke was the worst of the lot. But I tell you what's hell—hell like nothing else in the whole, wide world—that's your business and your customers. It don't matter if they're elegant or common, young or old, skinflints or spendthrifts—when they get to you they're no better than carrion on a dung-heap. There you see what hypocrisy is and rascality; there you see the dirty souls as they are, with their terror and their lies and their lusts. Everything comes out. It comes out, I tell you, because they ain't ashamed to let it. They don't have to be. You get to see human beings without shame, and what you see is the miserable, hideous flesh. Would you like to know how it is? Drink of a cess-pool and you'll know! It don't matter if it's a man that beats his wife when she's with child, or lets his children starve, or a student or an officer that's gone to the dogs, or a frightened parson, or a merchant with a huge belly—it's the same, the same—man without shame and the hideous flesh."

She laughed with tormented scorn, and went on: " I met

Mesecke when I was discharged from the hospital. I had no
one then. Before that I'd been in jail three weeks on account
of a scamp named Max. He was bad enough, but he was a
sweet innocent compared to Mesecke. A young man happened
to turn up in the café, a college student or something like
that. He treated us to one bottle of champagne after another,
day in and day out. You knew right away that there was
something rotten about it. And he always wanted me, just
me, and he made the money fly. So one day Mesecke took
him aside, and said to him right out: ' That money comes out
of your father's safe. You stole it.' The boy owned right
up, and his knees just shook. So Mesecke got his claws
into him, and showed him how to get more. And he and a
skunk named Woldemar promised to take him to an opium
den that was, they told him, just like heaven on earth. That
night, when the boy was with me, he began to cry and whine
like everything. I felt sorry for him, 'cause I knew he'd come
to a bad end; and I told him so, and told him straight and
rough. Then he emptied his pockets, and I'd never seen that
much money in my life; and it was all stolen money. I got
kind of dizzy, and told him to take it and put it back; but
he wanted me to have it and buy myself something for it.
I trembled all over, and told him for God's sake to take it
home; but he cried and fell on his knees and hugged me, and
suddenly Mesecke was in the room. He'd been hidden and
heard everything, and I hadn't had an idea. But the boy's
face turned as grey as a piece of pumice stone; he looked at
me and at Mesecke, and of course he thought it was a plot.
I was glad when Mesecke crashed his fist into my temple, so
that the air seemed to be full of fire and blood, and then
kicked me into a corner. That must have made the boy see
I was innocent. Then Mesecke took hold of Adalbert—that
was his name—and went off with him. Adalbert said nothing,
and just followed. He didn't turn up the next day nor the
next nor the day after that, so I asked Mesecke: ' What did

you do to Adalbert?' And he said: 'I put him on board a ship that was going overseas.' Yes, I thought to myself, that's a likely story. So I asked him again; and this time he said if I didn't hold my tongue he'd scatter my bones for me. Well, I kept still. Maybe Adalbert did take passage on a ship; it's possible. We didn't ever hear no more about him. And I didn't care so much, for there was something else every day. I had to be careful of my own skin, and get through the night somehow, and through the day. And it was always the same, always the same."

She sat up, and took hold of Christian's arm with an iron grip. Her eyes sparkled, and she hissed out through clenched teeth: "But I didn't really know it. When you're in the thick of it you don't know. You don't feel that it's no life for a human being; and you don't want to see, and you don't dare to know that you're damned and in a burning hell! Why did you take me out of it? Why did things have to happen this way?"

Christian did not answer. He heard the air roar past his ears.

After a while she let his arm go, or, rather, she thrust it from her, and he arose. She flung herself back on her pillows. Christian thought: "It has been in vain." The dread that he had felt turned to despair. In vain! He heard the words in the air about him: "In vain, in vain, in vain!"

Then, in a clear voice that he had never heard her use before, Karen said: "I'd like to have your mother's rope of pearls."

"What?" Christian said. It seemed to him that he must have misunderstood her.

And in the same, almost childlike voice, Karen repeated: "Your mother's pearls—that's what I'd like." She was talking nonsense, and she knew it. Not for a moment did she think it conceivable that her desire could be fulfilled.

Christian approached the bed. "What made you think of

that? " he whispered. " What do you mean by that? What? "

" I've never wished for anything so much," Karen said in the same clear voice. She was lying very still now. " Never, never. At least, I'd love to see them once—see how things like that look. I'd like to hold them, touch them, just once. They don't seem real. Go to her and ask for them. Go and say: ' Karen wants so much to see your pearls.' Maybe she'll lend them to you." She laughed half madly. " Maybe she'd let you have them for a while. It seems to me that then "— she opened her eyes wide, and there was a new flame in them— " that then things might be different between us."

" Who told you of them? " Christian asked as though in a dream. " Who spoke to you of my mother's pearls? "

She opened the drawer of the little table beside her bed, and took out the photograph. Christian reached out for it eagerly, although she was going to give it to him. " Voss gave it to me," she said.

Christian looked at the picture and quietly put it away.

" Yes, that's what I'd like," Karen said again; and there was a wildness in her face, and a childlikeness and a pathos and a greed, and a certain defiance which was also like a child's. And her smile was wild, and her laughter. " Oh, there's nothing else I'd want then. I would taste the pearls with my tongue and bury them in my flesh; and I'd let no one know and show them to no one. Yes, that's what I want, only that—your mother's pearls, even if it's for just a little while."

Nothing could so have pierced the soul of Christian as this wild stammering and this wild begging. He stood by the window, gazing into the night, and said slowly and reflectively: " Very well, you shall have them."

Karen did not answer. She stretched herself out and closed her eyes. She didn't take his words seriously. When he left her, there was a silent mockery in her mind—of him, of her-self.

But the next morning Christian took the underground railway to the Anhalter Station, and bought a third-class ticket to Frankfort. In his hand he carried a small travelling bag.

XXXI

" Come on then, let's see what you know! " Niels Heinrich said to his mother, the fortune-teller Engelschall.

They were in her inner sanctum. Attached to the ceiling by a black cord hung a stuffed bat with outstretched wings. Dark, glowing glass-beads had been set in its head. On the table, which was covered with cards, lay a death's head.

It was Sunday night, and Niels Heinrich came from his favourite pub. He only stopped here on his way to a suburban dancing-hall. He wore a black suit and a blue and white linen waistcoat. He had pushed his derby hat so far to the back of his head that one saw the whole parting of his hair. In his left arm-pit he held a thin, little stick. He see-sawed on the chair on which he had slouched himself down.

" Come on now, trot out your tricks," and he flung a five-mark piece on the table. In his dissipated eyes there was a shimmer as of some mineral and an indeterminate lustfulness.

The widow Engelschall was always afraid of him. She shuffled her cards. " You seem to be well fixed, my lad," she fawned on him. " That's right. Cut! And now let's see what you let yourself in for."

Niels Heinrich see-sawed on his chair. For many days his throat had been on fire. He was sick of his very teeth and hands. He wanted to grasp something, and hold it and crush it in his fist—something smooth and warm, something that had life and begged for life. He hated all things else, all hours, all ways.

" A ten and a ace o' diamonds," he heard his mother say, " the king o' clubs and the jack o' spades—that don't mean nothing good. Then another ten and a grey woman "—consternation was on her face—" you ain't going to do nothing awful, boy? "

" Aw, don't get crazy, ol' woman," Niels Heinrich snarled at her. " You'd make a dog laugh." He frowned, and said with assumed indifference, " Look and see if the cards say something about a Jew wench."

The widow Engelschall shook her head in astonishment. " No, my boy, nothing like that." She turned the cards again. " No. Another ten and a queen o' hearts—that might mean a money order. Lord love us—three more queens. You always was a great one for the women. And that reminds me that red Hetty asked after you to-day. She wanted to know if you'd come to the Pit to-night.

Niels Heinrich answered: " Gee, I just kicked her out a day or two ago. Her memory must be frozen. Gee! " He leaned back and see-sawed again. " Aw, well, if you can't tell me nothing pleasant, I'll take back my fiver."

" It's coming, my boy, it's coming," the old woman said soothingly. She shuffled the cards again. " Have patience. We'll get that business with the Jew wench yet."

Niels Heinrich stared into emptiness. Wherever he looked he had seen the same thing for days and days—a young, smooth neck, two young, smooth shoulders, two young, smooth breasts; and all these were strange, of a strange race, and filled with a strange sweet blood. And he felt that if he could not grasp these, grasp them and smell and taste, he would die the death of a dog. He got up and forced himself to a careless gesture. " You can stop," he said. " It's all a damn' swindle. You can keep the tip too. I don't give a damn." He passed his stick across the cards, jumbled them together, and went out.

The widow Engelschall, left alone, shook her head. The ambition of her calling stirred in her. She shuffled and laid down the cards anew. " We'll get it yet," she murmured, " we'll get it yet .   .   ."

RUTH AND JOHANNA

I

It was in the Hotel Fratazza in San Martino di Castrozza that, at the end of years, Crammon and the Countess Brainitz met again.

The countess sat on the balcony of her room, embroidering a Slavonic peasant scarf, and searching with her satisfied eyes the craggy mountains and the wooded slopes and paths. As she did so, a dust-covered motor car stopped at the entrance below, and from it stepped two ladies and two gentlemen in the fashionable swathings of motoring. The gentlemen took off their goggles, and made arrangements with the manager of the hotel.

" Look down, Stöhr," the countess turned to her companion. " Look at that stoutish man with a face like an actor. He seems familiar to——" At that moment Crammon looked up and bowed. The countess uttered a little cry.

That evening, in the dining-hall, Crammon could not avoid going to the countess' table and asking after her health, the length of her stay here, and similar matters. The countess rudely interrupted his courteous phrases. " Herr von Crammon, there's something I have to say to you privately. I'm glad to have this opportunity. I have been waiting for it very long."

" I am entirely at your service, countess," said Crammon, with ill-concealed vexation. " I shall take the liberty of calling on you to-morrow at eleven."

At ten minutes past eleven on the next day he had himself announced. In spite of the energetic way in which she had demanded this interview, he felt neither curiosity nor anxiety.

The countess pointed to a chair, sat down opposite her guest, and assumed the expression of a judge. " My dear sister, whom you, Herr von Crammon, cannot fail to remember, passed from this world to a better one after a long illness eighteen months ago. I was permitted to be with her to the end, and in her last hours she made a confession to me."

The sympathy which Crammon exhibited was of such obvious superficiality that the countess added with knife-like sharpness of tone: " It was my sister Else, Herr von Crammon, the mother of Letitia. Haven't you anything to say? "

Crammon nodded dreamily. " So she too is gone," he sighed, " dear woman! And all that was twenty years ago! It was a glorious time, countess. Youth, youth—ah, all the meaning in that word! Don't remind me, dear countess, don't remind me!

> "'Even the beautiful dies, though it conquer men and immortals,
> Zeus of the iron breast feels no compassion within.'"

" Spare me your poetical quotations," the countess replied angrily. " You shan't get the better of me as you did once upon a time. In those days the mask of discretion was the most convenient and comfortable for you to assume; and I don't deny that you assumed it with the utmost skill. But let me add this at once: One may be as discreet as a mummy, yet there are situations in life in which one is forced to follow the call of one's heart, that is, if one is provided with such a thing. A momentary hoarseness, a quiver of the lips, a moisture of the eye—that would have sufficed. I observed nothing of the kind in you. Instead you stood by quite calmly, while that poor girl, your daughter, your own flesh and blood, was sold to a filthy maniac, a tiger in human form."

Crammon's answer was temperate and dignified. " Perhaps you will have the kindness, dear countess, to recall my sincere and insistent warning. I came to you late at night, tormented by conscience, and made the most weighty and solemn representations to you."

"Warning! Fudge! You told me wild stories. You cheated me right and left."

"Those are strong expressions, countess."

"I mean them to be!"

"Too bad! Ah, well! The dewy moisture of the eye, countess, is the sort of thing you mustn't expect of me; I haven't the required gift. I found the little girl sympathetic, very sympathetic, but merely as a human being. You mustn't expect paternal emotions of me. Frankly and honestly, countess, I consider those emotions vastly overestimated by sentimental people. A mother—ah, there the voice of nature speaks. But a father is a more or less unlucky accident. Suppose you had planned to overwhelm me with an effective scene. Let us picture it. Yonder door opens, and there appears a young gentleman or a young lady armed with all necessary documents or proofs. Such proper documents and proofs could be gathered against any normal man of forty-three like the sands of the sea. And so this young man or young lady approaches me with the claims of a son or a daughter. Well, do you really believe that I would be deeply moved, and that the feelings of a father would gush from my heart like waters from a fountain? On the contrary, I would say: 'My dear young man, or my dear young lady, I am charmed to make your acquaintance,' but that exhausts the entire present possibilities of the situation. And wouldn't it, by the way, be most damnably uncomfortable, if one had to live in the constant expectation of meeting one's unpaid bills of twenty years ago in human form? Where would that lead to? The offspring in question, whether male or female, if possessed of any tact, would thoroughly consider such a step, and pause before using an ill-timed intrusion to burden a man who is busy stirring the dregs in the cup of life for some palatable remnants. The conception of our charming Letitia, my dear lady, was woven into so peculiar a mesh of circumstance, and so evidently due to the interposition of higher powers, that my own service in the matter shrinks into insignificance. When I met the dear girl, I had the feeling of a wanderer who once thoughtlessly buried a cherry kernel by the roadside. Years later he passes the same spot, and is surprised by a cherry tree. Delightful but quite natural. But do you expect the man to raise a cry of triumph? Is he to haunt the neighbourhood, and say: ' Look at my cherry-tree! Am I not a remarkable fellow? ' Or would you expect him to go to the owner of the land and demand the tree and uproot it, or even steal it by night in order to transplant it he knows not where? Such a man would be a fool, countess, or a maniac."

" I didn't suspect you of having much spirituality, Herr von Crammon," the countess replied bitterly, " but I thought a little might be found. I confess that I'm dumbfounded. Pray tell me this: Do all men share your views, or are you unique in this respect? It would console me to believe the latter, for otherwise humanity would seem to cut too sorry a figure."

" God forbid, dearest countess, that I should be guilty of disturbing the admirable equilibrium of your mind and soul," Crammon returned eagerly. " God forbid! By all means consider me an exception. Most of the people I know are quite proud of their productions, whether the latter take the form of verse, or a new fashion in waistcoats, or a quite original way of preparing the livers of geese. They are insatiable for the fame of authorship. When you see them from afar, you feel yourself forced to invent compliments; and there is no lie that they do not swallow with a greed that makes you ashamed for them. And no chef, no poet, and no tailor is so puffed up with creative vanity as your common bourgeois progenitor. Compared to him the rhinoceros is a delicate and sensitive creature. My dislike of the institution of the family was heightened by an incident that illustrates my point. I once

asked a man, who was a notorious cuckold, how his two
boys happened to be so extraordinarily fair, since both he
and his wife were very dark. He replied with the utmost
impudence that his ancestors had been Norman knights. Norman knights, of all things in the world! And the man was
a Jew from Prague. Norman knights! "

The countess shook her head. " You're telling me anecdotes again," she said, " and I'm not fond of them, least of
all of yours. So you repudiate all responsibility? You consider Letitia a stranger, and deny the darling child? Is that,
in a word, the meaning of all your discourse? "

" Not at all, countess. I am ready for any amicable rap-
prochement; only I refuse to be nailed down, and have a
sentimental moral responsibility foisted on me. Were that
attempted, I should be apt to flee, although I am by nature
calm and deliberate. But let us not waste the time discussing
theories. Tell me the precise nature of little Letitia's misfortunes."

Mastering the horror with which Crammon filled her, the
countess related how she had received a telegram from
Genoa a month ago. The message had been: " Send money or
come immediately." She had hastened to Genoa, and found
the poor child in a pitiful condition. Letitia had so little
money that she had to pawn her jewels to pay her hotel bills;
she was tyrannized and cheated by the Argentinian nurse whom
she had brought over; one of the twins had a touch of intestinal catarrh, the other of inflammation of the eyes——"

" Twins? Did you say twins? " Crammon interrupted her
in consternation.

" Twins. Precisely what I said. You are the grandfather
of twins." The countess's reply reeked with malicious satisfaction.

" The ways of Providence are indeed wonderful," Crammon
murmured, and his eyes dulled a little, " grandfather of twins
. . . Extraordinary, I confess. I must say that the affair

doesn't look humorous. Why did she leave her husband? Why didn't you stay with her?"

"You shall hear all. The man maltreated her—actually and physically. She fell into the hands of drunkards, robbers, poisoners, horse-thieves, forgers, and slanderers. She was a prisoner in the house; she suffered hunger; they tormented her body and soul, and made cruel threats; she was in fear of her life; they trained wild animals to terrorize her, and hired escaped convicts to watch her. Fear and horror brought her to the brink of the grave. It was unspeakable. Without the interposition and noble-hearted assistance of a German captain, who offered her passage to Europe, she would have perished miserably. Unhappily I could not even thank her unselfish friend; he had left Genoa when I arrived. But Letitia gave me his address, and I shall write him."

"It's all very regrettable," said Crammon, "and yet it is what I expected. I had a foreboding, and thence my prophecy. I thought this Stephen Gunderam odious from the start. He was like a cheap showman blowing a tin trumpet. I wouldn't have trusted him with an old umbrella, not to speak of a young girl whose exquisite qualities were patent to all the world. Nevertheless I disapprove of her flight. If the conditions were demonstrably insufferable, she should have sought her freedom through the appropriate legal methods. Marriage is a sacrament. First she jumps at it, as though it were a well-warranted seventh heaven. Next, having experienced the discomforts which a very imbecile would have expected under the circumstances, she takes French leave, and steams off to Europe with two helpless and unsheltered babes. That is neither consistent nor prudent, and I must distinctly withhold my approval."

The countess was indignant. "It's your opinion that the poor child should rather have let them torment her to death?"

"I beg your pardon. I merely point out her unfortunate

way of seeking redress; beyond that I do not presume to judge. I consider it a wrong step to break the union sanctified by the Church, and desert both hearth and country. It is a godless thing, and leads to destruction. And what happened while you were with her? What did she determine on? Where is she now? "

" In Paris."

" In Paris! Is that so? And the purpose of her visit? "

" She wants to recuperate. I don't grudge her the chance. She needs it."

" I don't question it, countess. But Paris seems an unusual place for such a purpose. And did she directly refuse the pleasure of your society, or do you merely fail to share her taste for recuperating in Paris? "

The countess was visibly embarrassed. She wrinkled her brow, and her little red cheeks glowed. " In the hotel she made the acquaintance of a Vicomte Seignan-Castreul, who was staying there with his sister," she said hesitantly. " They invited Letitia to be their guest in Paris and afterwards at their château in Brittany. The child wept, and said to me: ' Auntie, I'd love to go, but I can't because I haven't a cent.' It cut me to the heart, and I scraped together what I could— five thousand francs in all. The darling thanked me from the heart, and then left with the vicomte and vicomtesse, and promised to meet me in Baden-Baden in October."

" And where are the twins in the meanwhile? "

" She took them with her, of course—the twins, and their Argentinian nurse, an English maid, and her own maid."

" I honour your generosity, countess, but I don't somehow like either your vicomte or your vicomtesse."

The countess suddenly gave a loud sob. " I don't either! " she cried, and pressed her hands to her face. " I don't either. If only the dear child does not meet with new misfortunes! But what was I to do? Can one resist her pleading? I was so happy to have her back; I felt as though she'd risen from the grave. No, the vicomte is not sympathetic to me at all. He has a dæmoniac character."

"People with dæmoniac characters are always swindlers, countess," Crammon said drily. "A decent man is never that. It's a swindle in itself, that word."

"Herr von Crammon," the countess announced with decision, "I expect of you now that you show character in the other and beautiful sense of the word, I expect you to come to Baden-Baden when Letitia has arrived, to interest yourself in her who is closer to you than any one else on earth, and to make up for your wrong and your neglect."

"For the love of all the saints, not that!" Crammon cried in terror. "Recognition, deep emotion, father and daughter fall into each other's arms, remorse and damp handkerchiefs! No! Anything you want, but not that."

"No excuses, Herr von Crammon, it is your duty!" The countess had arisen, and her eyes were majestic. Crammon writhed and begged and besought her. It did no good. The countess would not let him go until he had pledged her his word of honour to be in Baden-Baden by the end of October or, at latest, the beginning of November.

When the countess was alone, she walked up and down for a little, still hot and gasping. Then she called her companion. "Send me the waiter, Stöhr," she moaned, "I'm weak with hunger."

Fräulein Stöhr did as she was bidden.

II

Frau Wahnschaffe was on one of her rare outings. She was driving in her electric car toward Schwanheim, when she caught sight of a group of young men at the entrance to the polo-grounds. Among them was one who reminded her strongly of Christian. His slenderness and noble grace of gesture

gave her so strong an illusion of Christian's presence that she
bade her chauffeur halt, and requested her companion to walk
to the gate and inquire after the young man's identity.

The companion obeyed, and Frau Wahnschaffe, still watching the group, waited very quietly. The companion had no
difficulty in getting the information, and reported that the
young man was an Englishman named Anthony Potter.

"Ah, yes, yes." That was all Frau Wahnschaffe said, and
her interest was extinguished.

That very evening a special delivery letter was brought her.
She recognized Christian's handwriting, and everything danced
before her eyes. The first thing she was able to see was the
name of a small, third-rate Frankfort hotel. Gradually her
sight grew steadier, and she read the letter: "Dear Mother:
I beg you to grant me an interview in the course of the forenoon to-morrow. It is too late for me to come to you to-day;
I have travelled all day and am tired. If I do not hear from
you to the contrary, I shall be with you at ten o'clock. I am
confident that you will be so good as to see me alone."

Her only thought was: "At last!" And she said the words
out loud to herself: "At last!"

She looked at her watch. It was ten o'clock. That meant
twelve hours. How was she to pass those twelve hours? All
her long life seemed shorter to her than this coming space
of time.

She went downstairs through the dark and empty rooms,
through the marble hall with its great columns, through the
gigantic, mirrored dining-hall, in which the last, faint light of
the long summer evening was dying. She went into the park,
and heard the plaint of a nightingale. Stars glittered, a fountain plashed, and distant music met her ear. She returned,
and found that only fifty minutes had passed. An expression
of rage contorted her cold and rigid face. She considered
whether she should drive to the city to that shabby little hostelry. She dismissed that plan at once. He was asleep; he

was weary with travel. But why is he in such a place, she asked herself, in a humble house, among strange and lowly people?

She sat down in an armchair, and entered upon her bitter duel with the slothfulness of time, from eleven to midnight, from midnight to the first grey glint of dawn, from that first glint to the early flush of the young morning, thence to full sunrise, and on to the appointed hour.

III

Wherever Johanna Schöntag went she was treated with loving-kindness. Even her relatives with whom she lived treated her with tender considerateness. This tended to lower rather than to raise her in her own self-esteem. She considered subtly: "If I please these, what can I possibly amount to?"

She said: "It is ever so funny that I should be living in this city of egoists. I am the direct antithesis of such brave persons."

Nothing seemed worth doing to her, not even what her heart demanded loudly—the setting out to find Christian. She waited for some compulsion, but none came. She lost herself in trivial fancies. She would sit in a corner, and watch things and people with her clever eyes. "If that bearded man," she thought, "had the nose of his bald neighbour he might look quite human." Or: "Why are there six stucco roses above the door? Why not five or seven?" She tormented herself with these things. The wrongly placed nose and the perverse number of the stucco roses incited her to plan the world's improvement. Suddenly she would laugh, and then blush if people looked her way.

Every night, before she fell asleep, she thought, in spite of herself, of Amadeus Voss and of her promise to write him. Then she would take flight in sleep and forget the morrow. His long letter weighed on her memory as the

most painful experience of her life. Words that made her
restless emerged from it in her consciousness—the saying, for
instance, concerning the shadow's yearning for its body. The
words' mystery lured her on. All voices in the outer world
warned her. Their warning but heightened the sting of allurement. She enjoyed her fear and let it grow. The reflection
of mirrored things in other mirrors of the mind confused her.
At last she wrote; an arrow flew from the taut string.

They met on Kurfürsten Square, and walked up the avenue
of chestnut trees toward Charlottenburg. In order to limit the
interview, Johanna announced that she must be home at the
end of an hour. But the path they chose robbed her of the
hope of a quite brief interview. She yielded. To hide her
embarrassment, she remarked jestingly on the trees, houses,
monuments, beasts, and men. Voss preserved a dry seriousness. She turned to him impatiently. "Well, teacher, aren't
you going to talk a bit to the well-behaved little pupil with
whom you're taking a walk?"

But Voss had no understanding of the nervous humour of
her gentle rebuke. He said: "I am an easy prey; you have
but to mock, and I am without defence. I must accustom
myself to such lightness and smoothness. It is a bad tone
for us to use. You keep looking at me searchingly, as though
my sleeve might be torn or my collar stained. I had determined to speak to you as to a comrade. It cannot be done.
You are a young lady, and I am hopelessly spoiled for your
kind."

Johanna answered sarcastically that at all events it calmed
her to see her person and presence extorting a consideration
from him which she had not always enjoyed. Voss started.
Her contemptuous expression revealed her meaning to him.
He lowered his head, and for a while said nothing. Then
bitterness gathered on his features. Johanna, gazing straight
ahead, felt the danger to herself; she could have averted it;
she knew that a courteous phrase would have robbed him of

courage. But she disdained the way out. She wanted to defy
him, and said frankly that she was not in the least hurt by
his disappointment in her, since it was scarcely her ambition
to impress him. Voss endured this in silence, too, but seemed
to crouch as for an attack. Johanna asked with an innocent air whether he was still in Christian Wahnschaffe's
apartment, and still had charge of his friend's private correspondence.

Voss's answer was dry and objective. He said that he had
moved, since his means did not permit him such luxury. The
mocking smile on Johanna's lips showed him that she was
acquainted with the situation. He added that he had better
say that the source of his income had given out. He was
living, he told her, in quarters befitting a student in Ansbacher
Street, and had made the acquaintance of poverty again. He
was not yet so poor, however, that he had to deny himself the
pleasure of a guest; so he asked her whether she would take
tea with him some day. He did not understand her laughter.
Ah, yes, she was a young lady; he had forgotten. Well, perhaps she would condescend to the shop of a confiseur.

His talk aroused her scorn and her impatience.

It was Sunday, and the weather was gloomy. Night was
falling. Music resounded from the pavilions in the public
gardens. They met many soldiers, each with his girl. Johanna
opened her umbrella and walked wearily. "It isn't raining,"
said Voss. She answered: "I do it so as not to have to think
of the rain." The real reason was that the umbrella widened
the distance between them. "When do you see Christian?"
she suddenly asked in a high-pitched voice, and looked away
from him to the other side. "Do you see him often?" She
regretted her question at once. It bared her heart to these
ambushed eyes.

But Voss had not even heard her. "You still resent the
matter of your letter. You can't forgive me for having spied
upon your secret. You have no notion of what I gave you

in return. You waste no thought on the fact that I revealed
my whole soul to you. Perhaps it wasn't even clear to you
that all I wrote you in regard to Wahnschaffe was a confession
such as one human being rarely makes to another. It was
done by implication, and you, evidently, do not understand
that method. I probably overestimated both your understanding and your good will."

" Probably," Johanna replied; " and likewise my good nature, for here you've been as rude as possible again. You
would be quite right in what you said, if you didn't leave
out one very important thing: there must first be a basic
sympathy between two people before you can expect such demands to be honoured."

"Sympathy!" Voss jeered. "A phrase—a conventional
formula! What you call sympathy is the Philistine's first
resort—tepid, flat, colourless. True sympathy requires such
delicate insight of the soul that he who feels it scorns to use
the shop-worn, vulgar word. I did not reckon on sympathy.
A cleft, such as the cleft between you and me, cannot be
bridged by cheap trappings. Do you think I had no instinctive knowledge of your coldness, your aloofness, your
irony? Do you take me for the type of pachydermatous animal
that leaps into a hedge of roses, because it knows the thorns
cannot wound him? Oh, no! Every thorn penetrates my
skin. I tell you this in order that you may know henceforth
just what you are doing. Each thorn pierces me till I bleed.
That was clear to me from the beginning, and yet I took the
risk. I have staked all that I am on this game; I have
gathered my whole self together and cast it at your feet,
careless of the result. Once I desired to deliver myself utterly
into the hands of fate."

" I must turn back," Johanna said, and shut her umbrella.
" I must take a cab. Where are we? "

" I live on Ansbacher Street, corner of Augsburger, in the
third story of the third house. Come to me for one hour; let

it be as a sign that I am an equal in your eyes. You cannot imagine what depends on it for me. It is a wretched and desolate hole. If ever you cross its threshold, it will be a place in which I can breathe. I am not in the habit of begging, but I beg you for this favour. The suspicion which I see in your eyes is fully justified. I have planned to beg you for this, to bring it about. But this plan of mine did not originate to-day or yesterday. It is weeks old; it is older than I know. But that is all. Any other distrust you feel is unjustified."

He stammered these words and gasped them. Johanna looked helplessly away. She was too weak to withstand the passionate eloquence of the man, repulsive and fear-inspiring as he was. Also there was a fearful lure in the daring, in the presence of a flame, in fanning it, in danger, and in watching what would happen. Her life was empty. She needed something to expect and court and fear. She needed the brink of some abyss, some bitter fume, some transcendence of common boundaries. But for the moment she needed to gain time. "Not to-day," she said, with a veiled expression, "some other time. Next week. No, don't urge me. But perhaps toward the end of the week; perhaps Friday. I don't see your purpose, but if you wish it, I'll come Friday."

"It is agreed then. Friday at the same hour." He held out his hand. Hesitatingly she put hers into it. She felt imprisoned in her own aversion, but her glance was firm and almost challenging.

IV

When Christian entered, Frau Wahnschaffe stood massively in the middle of the room. Her arms were lightly folded below her bosom. A wave of pallor passed over her, and she felt chilled. Christian approached. She turned her face, and looked at him out of the corners of her eyes. She sought to speak, but her lips twitched nervously. Christian suddenly lost the simple assurance born of his swift and unreflective action. He suddenly realized the monstrousness of his errand, and stood quite silent.

"Will you stay with us for some time?" Frau Wahnschaffe asked hoarsely. "Surely you will. I have had your room made ready; you will find everything in order. It was unnecessarily considerate of you to spend the night at an hotel. Do you not know your mother well enough to take it for granted that the house is always ready to receive you?"

"I am sorry, mother," answered Christian, "but I can stay only a few hours. I must not and dare not delay. I have to return to Berlin on the five o'clock train. I am sorry."

Frau Wahnschaffe now turned her full face upon Christian so slowly that the motion had the air of a marionette's. "You are sorry," she murmured. "Ah, yes. I scarcely expected even that much. But everything is ready for you, Christian, your bed and your wardrobes. You have not been here for very long, and it is very long since I have seen you. Let me think: it must be eighteen months. Pastor Werner told me some things about you; they were not pleasant to hear. He was here several times. I seemed unable to grasp his report except in small doses. It seemed to me the man must have had hallucinations, yet he expressed himself very carefully. I said to him: 'Nonsense, my dear pastor, people don't do such things.' You know, Christian, that I find matters of a certain sort difficult to understand. . . . But you look strange, Christian. . . . You look changed, my son. You're dressed differently. Do you no longer dress as you used to? It is strange. Do you not frequent good society? And these fancies of the pastor concerning voluntary poverty and renunciations that you desire to suffer . . . and I hardly recall what—tell me: is there any foundation of truth to all that? For I do not understand."

Christian said: "Won't you sit down beside me for a little, mother? We can't talk comfortably while you stand there."

" Gladly, Christian, let us sit down and talk. It is nice of you to say it in that way."

They sat down side by side on the sofa, and Christian said: " I know I have been guilty of neglect toward you, mother. I should not have waited to let strangers inform you of my decisions and actions. I see now that it makes a mutual understanding harder; only it is so unpleasant and so troublesome to talk about oneself. Yet I suppose it must be done, for what other people report is usually thoroughly wrong. I sometimes planned to write to you, but I couldn't; even while I thought the words, they became misleading and false. Yet I felt no impulse to come to you without any other motive than to give you an explanation. It seemed to me that there should be enough confidence in me in your heart to make a detailed self-justification unnecessary. And I thought it better to risk a breach and estrangement caused by silence, than to indulge in ill-timed talk, and yet avoid neither because I had not been understood."

" You speak of breach and estrangement," Frau Wahnschaffe replied, " as though it were only now threatening us. And you speak as calmly as though it were a punishment for children, and you were quite reconciled to it. Very well, Christian, the breach and the estrangement may come. You will find me too proud to struggle against your mind and your decision. I am not a mother who wants her son's devotion as an alms, nor a woman who would interfere in your world, nor one who will stoop to strive for a right that is denied her. Nothing that breaks my heart need stop your course. But give me, at least, one word to which I can cling in my lonely days of brooding and questioning. The air gives me no answer to my questions, nor my own mind, nor any other's. Explain to me what you are really doing, and why you are doing it. At last, at last you are here; I can see you and hear you. Speak! "

Her words, spoken in a monotonous and hollow voice, stirred

Christian deeply, less through their meaning than through his mother's attitude and gesture—her stern, lost glance, the grief she felt, and the coldness that she feigned. She had found the way to his innermost being, and his great silence was broken. He said: " It isn't easy to explain the life one lives or the events whose necessity is rooted uncertainly in the past. If I search my own past, I cannot tell where these things had their beginning, nor when, nor how. But let me put it this way: He whom a great glare blinds, desires darkness; he who is satiated finds food distasteful; he who has never lost himself in some cause feels shame and the desire to prove himself. Yet even that does not explain what seems to me the essential thing. You see, mother, the world as I gradually got to know it, the institutions of men, harbours a wrong that is very great and that is inaccessible to our ordinary thinking. I cannot tell you exactly in what this great wrong consists. No man can tell us yet, neither the happy man nor the wretched, neither the learned nor the unlettered one. But it exists, and it meets you at every turn. It does no good to reflect about it. But like the swimmer who strips before he leaps, one must dive to the very bottom of life to find the root and origin of that great wrong. And one can be seized by a yearning for that search, which sweeps away all other interests and ambitions, and masters one utterly. It is a feeling that I could not describe to you, mother, not if I were to talk from now until night. It pierces one through, all one's soul and all one's life; and if one strives to withdraw from it, it only becomes keener."

He rose under the impression of the unwonted excitement that he felt, and continued speaking more swiftly. " That wrong does not consist in the mere contrast between poor and rich, between arbitrary licence on the one hand and enforced endurance on the other. No, no. Look, we've all grown up with the view that crime meets its expiation, guilt its punishment, that every human deed bears its reward within itself, and that, in a word, a justice rules which compensates, orders, avenges, if not before our eyes, then in some higher region. But that is not true. I believe in no such justice; it does not exist. Nor is it possible that such a justice exists in the universe, for if it did, the lives men lead could not be as they are. And if this superhuman justice of which men speak and on which they rely does not exist, then the source of that great wrong that is in the world must be within the life of man itself, and we must find that source and know its nature. But you cannot find it by observing life from without; you must be within it, within it to the lowest depths. That is it, mother, that is it. Perhaps you understand now."

A measureless astonishment spread over Frau Wahnschaffe's features. She had never heard such things, she had never prepared her mind to hear them, and least of all to hear them from him, the beautiful, the ever festive, the inviolable by any ugliness. For it was that vision of him which she still nursed within. She meant to answer, she almost thought the words had escaped her: " That search is not your function in the world, yours less than any other's! " The desperate words had already shadowed her face, when she looked upon him, and saw that he was rapt not from the sphere she hated, avoided, and feared for him, but from herself, her world, his world and former self. She beheld one almost unknown in a ghostly shimmer, and a presage stirred in her frozen soul; and in that presage was the yearning of which he had spoken, although its very name was strange to her. Also the fear of losing his love utterly let all the years behind her seem but wasted years, and she said shyly: " You indicated, did you not, that a particular purpose had brought you here? What is it? "

Christian sat down again. " It is a very difficult and delicate matter," he answered. " I came without realizing its exact nature, of which I seem but now to become aware. The woman whom I am taking care of, Karen Engelschall—you have heard of her, mother—desires your pearls; and I, I promised to bring them to her. Her desire is as strange as my request. The whole thing, put bluntly, sounds like madness." He smiled, he even laughed, yet his face had grown very pale.

Frau Wahnschaffe merely pronounced his name: "Christian." That was all. She spoke the word in a toneless, lingering voice, almost hissing the s.

Christian went on: "I said I was taking care of that woman . . . that isn't the right expression. It was a critical moment in my life when I found her. Many people were astonished that I didn't surround her with splendour and luxury, when that was still in my power. But that would have availed nothing. I would have missed my aim utterly by such a method; and she herself did not dream of demanding it. If it weren't for her relatives, who constantly urge her to rebellion and desire, she would be quite contented. People chatter to her too much. She, of course, doesn't understand my purpose; often she regards me as an enemy. But is that strange after such a life as hers? Mother, you may believe me when I assure you that all the pearls in the world can not bring a soul forgetfulness of such a life."

He spoke disconnectedly and nervously. His fingers twitched, his brow was wrinkled and smooth in turn. The words he spoke and must yet speak pained him; the monstrousness of his demand, which he had but now fully realized, and the possibility that his request might be refused—these things drove the blood to his heart. His mother neither stirred nor spoke. Within a few minutes her features seemed to have shrunk into the crumpled mask of extreme old age.

Christian's fright stung him to further speech. "She is an outcast, one of the despised and rejected. That is true; or rather, that is what she was. But it is not permitted us to pass judgment. An accident placed a photograph of you, wearing your pearls, in her possession; and perhaps she felt as though you stood before her in person, and there came over her a sud-

den sense of what it means to be an outcast and despised. You
and she—perhaps the world should hold no such contrasts; and
the pearls became to her confused and half-mad vision a symbol
of compensation, of moral equilibrium. She will not keep the
pearls, by the way, nor would I permit her to do so. I pledge
myself that they shall be returned, if you will accept my mere
word as a pledge. I shall return the pearls, and you yourself
may set the date. Only please don't disappoint me in my
quandary."

Frau Wahnschaffe took a deep breath, and her tone was
harsh: "You foolish boy."

Christian lowered his eyes.

"You foolish boy," Frau Wahnschaffe repeated, and her
lips trembled.

"Why do you say that?" Christian asked softly.

She arose, and beckoned him with a weary gesture. He
followed her into her bed-chamber. She took a key out of a
leather-case, and unlocked the steel door of the safe built into
the wall. There were her jewels—diadems and clasps, bracelets, brooches, pins, rings and lavallières studded with precious
stones. She grasped the rope of pearls, and, as she took it
out, its end trailed on the floor. The pearls were almost equal
in magnificence and of uncommon size. Frau Wahnschaffe
said: "These pearls, Christian, have meant more to me than
such things usually do to a woman. Your father gave them
to me when you were born. I always wore them in a spirit
of thankfulness to God for the gift of you. I am not ashamed
to confess that. They seemed, I thought, to form a circle
within which you and I alone had being. I have neither
touched them nor looked at them since you started on your
strange wanderings, and I believe that the pearls themselves
have sickened. They are so yellow, and some have lost their
lustre. Did you seriously think I could deny you anything,
no matter what it is? It is true that your ways are too strange
for me now. My brain seems befogged when I try to grasp

all that, and I feel blind and lame. Yet to-day some voice has spoken for you, and I would not lose that voice. So far I have heard only vain lamentations. My whole soul shudders, but I begin to see you again, and whatever you ask I must give you. You are to know that, and indeed, you must have known that or you would not have come. Take them! " She turned aside to hide the pain upon her face, and with outstretched arm held out to him the rope of pearls. " But your father must never know," she murmured. " If you desire to return the pearls, bring them yourself if possible. I would not know for whom they are. Do with them as though they were your property."

Property! Christian listened to the word, but it did not penetrate his consciousness. It fell and disappeared like a stone in water; for him it had lost all meaning. And he looked upon the pearls with surprise and indifference, as though they were a toy, and it were strange to talk and trouble so much about them. Their preciousness, the value which amounted to millions, was no longer a living fact of consciousness to him, but like a dim memory of something heard long ago. Therefore he did not feel the burden of his mother's trust and his possession. The way in which he tucked the pearls into a case his mother had found, had something so carelessly business-like, and his word of thanks so obvious a formality, that it was clear he had forgotten the obstacles to his errand which he had felt so keenly a little while before.

He remained with his mother for another hour. But he spoke little, and the environment, the splendour of the room, the air of the house, the solemnity and sloth, the emptiness and aloofness, all this seemed to disquiet him. Frau Wahn-schaffe was unconscious of that. She talked and became silent, and in her eyes flickered the fear over the passing of her hour. When Christian arose to bid her farewell, her face became ashen, and she controlled herself with extreme difficulty. But when she was alone she reeled a little, and grasped for support one of the carven columns of her bed and gave a cry. Then suddenly she smiled.

Perhaps it was a delusion that caused her to smile; perhaps it was a flash of insight like lightning in a dark sky.

V

After his return from Africa, Felix Imhof was practically a ruined man. Unfortunate mining speculations had swallowed up the greater part of his fortune. But his attitude and behaviour were unchanged.

Exposure to the sun and air had almost blackened his skin, and his bohemian friends called him the Abyssinian prince. He was leaner than ever, his eyes protruded more greedily, his laughter and speech were noisier, and the tempo of his life was more accelerated. If any one asked after his well-being, he answered: " There's two years' fuel left in this machine. After that—exit! "

He had one dwelling in Munich and another in Berlin, but his numerous and complicated undertakings drove him to a different city every week.

Some political friends persuaded him to join in the founding of a great daily representing the left wing of liberalism, and he consented. A new catchword arose, a People's Theatre; and it was his ambition to be named among those who furthered the new panacea. He caused the publishing house that he had financed to issue a new edition of the classics, distinguished by tasteful editing and exquisite bookmaking. He received twenty to thirty telegrams daily, and sent between forty and fifty; he kept three typists busy, and suffered from the lack of a telephone while he was in motor cars or on express trains. He discovered the value of a half-forgotten painter of the Quattrocento for modern connoisseurs, and by means of literary advertisements caused fabulous prices to be offered for the painter's few and faded works. He gambled on the American stock exchange, and made four hundred thousand marks; next week he lost double the amount in a deal in Roumanian timber.

Sitting in his steam-bath, he sketched the plan of a mock-heroic poem; between three and five at night he dictated in alternation a translation of a novel by Lesage and an essay in economics; he carried on an elaborate correspondence with the chief of a theosophical society; drank like an aristocratic fraternity student, spent money like water, subsidized young artists, was constantly on the trail of new inventions, and fairly pursued promising engineers, chemists, and experts in aeronautics. One of his boldest plans was the founding of a stock company for the exploitation of the hidden coal-fields of the Antarctic regions. He assured all doubters that the profits would run to billions and that the difficulties were trifling.

One day he made the acquaintance of a technical expert named Schlehdorn. The man hardly inspired confidence, but Imhof overlooked that as well as his shabbiness. As though by the way Schlehdorn mentioned the difficulty caused the German marine by the fact that all glass for ships' port-holes had to be imported from Belgium and France. The secret of its manufacture was stringently guarded by certain factories in those countries. Whoever succeeded in unearthing it was a made man. Imhof swallowed the bait. He let the man inform him in regard to possible plans, agreed with him upon a special telegraphic code, and financed him generously. The telegrams he received sounded hopeful. Schlehdorn, to be sure, demanded larger and larger sums. He explained that he had had to bribe influential persons. Imhof deliberately silenced his suspicions; he was curious what the end would be.

One day he received a telegram from Schlehdorn demanding that he come at once to Andenne with fifty thousand francs. The matter was as good as settled. Imhof took fifty thousand francs as well as his revolver, and followed the summons. Schlehdorn was waiting for him, and conducted him through the darkness to a suspicious looking inn. He was led to a room at the end of a long hall, and the moment he had entered it, Imhof recognized the situation for what it was. He had hardly looked about when two elegantly dressed gentlemen appeared. The company took seats about a round table. Schlehdorn spread out some documents in front of him, and looked significantly at one of his accomplices. At that moment Imhof leaped up, backed against the wall, drew his revolver, and said calmly: " You needn't take any further trouble, gentlemen. The fifty thousand francs are deposited in my bank in Brussels. The trick was too obvious and this place too suspicious. If any one stirs, he'll have to have his tailor mend small, round holes in his suit to-morrow." His cool determination saved him. The three men were intimidated, and let him take his travelling bag and slip out. They themselves, of course, escaped as swiftly as possible after that.

But this experience, though he gave a humorous description of it, had a paralysing effect on Imhof. Considering the causes of his inner tension, this incident was trivial, yet it somehow brought into relief symptoms of weariness and satiety that multiplied and became noticeable. His cynicism would rise to the point of savagery, and then break down into sentimentality. " Give me a little garden, two little rooms, a dog and a cow, and I won't look at the scarlet woman of the world's Babylon again," he perorated insincerely. A violent illness seized upon him. Theatrically he made his final dispositions, and summoned his friends to hear his last words. When he recovered, he gave a feast that was the talk of all Munich for three weeks and cost him sixty thousand marks.

On this occasion he met Sybil Scharnitzer and fell in love with her. It was like an inner explosion. He acted like a madman; he declared himself capable of any crime for this woman's sake. Sybil was asked how she liked him. Her answer was quite laconic: " I don't like niggers."

Her words were reported to him by three different witnesses. The sting of them went deep. He stood in front of his mirror in the night, laughed bitterly, and smashed the glass with his fist so that the blood flowed.

The image of Sybil pursued him. He went wherever he was likely to meet her. In the girl's presence he became a boy again. He found no words, blushed and stammered, and became the laughing stock of those who knew him. One evening he ventured most shyly to speak to her of his feelings. She looked at him coldly, and her eyes said: "I don't like niggers." They were hard, selfish, stubborn eyes.

"I don't like niggers." The words became furies that pursued him. A month later business took him to Paris, and in a cabaret he saw a young Negro woman dancing a snake dance. An impulse of revenge urged him to make advances to the girl. The revenge was directed less against the unfeeling woman who had repulsed him so pitilessly than against himself. It was the defiant rage of his own desires. He boasted of his relations with the Negro woman, and appeared with her in public. What drove him thereafter from dissipation to dissipation was the terror of emptiness, the excess at the edge of life, where nature itself demands the final fulfilment of human fate.

And his fate was fulfilled.

VI

"Oh, you're lying to me!" Karen screamed, as Christian handed her the jewel-box. He had not even spoken, but his gesture had promised her the incredible; and she screamed to guard herself against the ravage of a premature delight.

The greed with which she opened the little lock and lifted the top of the box was indescribable. Her blood fled from beneath her skin. She felt throttled. There lay the lustrous pearls, with their faint tints of pink and lilac. "Latch the door! " she hissed, and raced to do it, since he seemed too slow. She shot the bolt and turned the key. For a moment she stood still and pressed her hands to her head. Then she went back to the jewels.

She touched the pearls with timid finger-tips. She had two fears: the pearls seemed as warm as living flesh; her own touch, though so gentle, might have been too rough. The glance she turned upon Christian faltered like a wounded bird. Suddenly she grasped his left hand brutally with both of hers, bowed deep down, and pressed her mouth to it.

"Don't, Karen, don't," Christian stammered, but he sought in vain to draw his hand from her furious clasp. More than a minute she crouched there on her knees, over his hand, and he saw the flesh of her back quiver under the cloth of her garment. " Be sensible, Karen," he begged her, and tried to persuade himself that he neither felt a profound stirring of the soul nor gazed into the depth of another. "What are you doing, Karen? Please don't! "

She released him, and he left her. Behind him she locked the door again. It was a curious circumstance that she took off her shoes and thus approached the treasure. When she was not beholding it, she still doubted its presence. With disconnected gestures, full of fear, she finally lifted the pearls from their case. At every soft clink she sighed and looked around. The unexpected length and weight of the chain amazed her utterly. Gently she let it glide upon the floor, then followed it first on her knees, then with her whole body, until she had brought her lips, her breath, her eyes as near as possible to that gleaming splendour. She counted the pearls, and counted them again. She made an error. Once she counted one hundred and thirty-three, and another time one hundred and thirty-seven. Then she counted no more, but looked at single pearls and breathed upon them, or moistened her finger and touched them.

She started at a rustling in the outer hall; then she again

sunk her whole self into the act of seeing. She dreamed herself
into rooms which had known the glow of these marvels, into
the bodies of women whom they had adorned, into coils of
events in which they had played a part. Shivers ran over her
body. She fought with the desire to place the pearls about her
own neck. First it seemed blasphemous rashness; then it
seemed conceivable after all. She arose softly, held the neck-
lace in her hand, and slipped it over her head. On tip-toe she
walked to the mirror, and peered at her image from half-closed
lids. It was here, here with her, and she wore it like that
woman in the picture. The pearls were on her body—the
pearls!

Evening came upon her, then night, but it brought no sleep.
The pearls were in bed with her, close to her breast, warm by
her skin. She felt them to assure herself of their presence;
she listened to vague noises in the house, which were like
threats of robbery to her. Then she lit a lamp and gazed at
the pearls, and already she knew some of them. They turned
faces upon her, and whispered to her, and were distinguishable
through a warmer glow or a more pallid tint. Some of these
were familiar and some quite strange, but they were all here
—a shimmering wonder and a new life.

Thus too she passed the day that came and the night that
followed the day. She knew that disease was burrowing in
her body. She had expected it to show; but when it came,
it was not with sudden violence but with treacherous sloth.
One part of her after another was affected, and at last she
could move freely no longer. She knew, too, that it was no
ordinary indisposition from which one recovers within a few
days. She felt it to be a process as of ripening which brings
a fruit to its fall, as a concentration of the hostile forces that
had before been scattered in effectiveness and in time. The
life she had lived demanded a reckoning. The physician in
the Hamburg hospital had foretold it all months before; now
the time had come. She was very undemonstrative about her

condition. She lay quietly in bed. She suffered no pain, and had but little fever.

Lying still there did not make her impatient. She was glad of the necessity; there was no better way of guarding the pearls. People might come and go. She had her treasure next her body, beside her very breast. She was sure of it at every moment and with every movement, and no one was the wiser. She pictured to herself what they would say and do, if she were to show them her secret treasure, if she were to call in one of those who all unconsciously passed her door or climbed the rickety stairs, or some one from the street or the tavern or the grog-shop—a poor fellow who had slaved all week, or a woman who sold her body for three marks, or another who had seven children to feed. In concentrated triumph she looked through the window at the rows of windows across the street. There lived the others whom misery throttled and in whom suffering whined. Like ants they crept about in the tall houses from cellar to garret, and had no suspicion of Karen's pearls. Karen's pearls! How that sounded and sang and glowed and glimmered—Karen's pearls. . . .

At last the secrecy became a burden. She did not enjoy her great possession as she would have done, had but one other shared the knowledge of it. She needed at least one other pair of eyes. She thought of Isolde Schirmacher, but the girl was too talkative and too stupid. She thought of the wife of Gisevius, of a seamstress on the fourth floor, of the huckstress in the street, of Amadeus Voss.

At last she hit upon Ruth Hofmann. The girl seemed the least harmful of all, and she determined to show her the pearls.

Under the pretext of asking the girl to fetch her something from the apothecary's, she sent a message to the Hofmanns, and Ruth came in. Karen waited until Isolde had left the room; then she sat up and asked the girl to lock the door.

Then she said: "Come here!" She turned the coverlet aside, and there lay the great heap of pearls upon the linen. "Look at that," she said. "Those are real pearls, and they're mine. But if you mention it to anybody, God help you, or my name ain't Karen Engelschall."

Ruth was amazed. Yet she looked on the pearls not with womanish desirousness, but like an imaginative soul beholding a marvel of the natural world. There was tension in her face, but it was wholly pleasurable. "Where did you get them?" she asked naïvely. "How wonderful they are. I've never seen anything like them. Are they all yours? They remind me of the Arabian Nights." She kneeled down beside the bed, and surrounded the heap of pearls with her hands and smiled. The hanging lamp burned, and in the dim light of the room the pearls had an almost purple glow, and seemed animated by some dusky blood that pulsed within them.

Karen was annoyed by Ruth's question, and yet she was almost as happy as she thought she would be in the surprise of another beholder. "Stupid! 'Course they belong to me. D'you think I'd steal them? They're his mother's pearls," she added mysteriously, and bowed her head to Ruth's ear. She was startled for a moment as she did so by the fragrance as of grass or the moist earth of February that emanated from the girl. "They're his mother's pearls," she repeated, "and he brought them to me." She did not know in what a deeply moved and reverential tone she spoke of Christian. Ruth listened to that tone, and doubts and guesses of her own were hushed.

"What ails you?" she asked, as she arose from her knees.

"I don't know," Karen answered, covering the pearls again. "Maybe nothing. I like to rest; sometimes it does a person good."

"Is any one with you at night? It might happen that you need something. Have you no one?"

"Lord, I don't need anything," Karen answered with as

much indifference as possible. " And if I do, I can get out o' bed and fetch it. I'm not that bad yet." The coarseness vanished from her face, and yielded to an expression of helpless wonder as she went on hurriedly: " He offered to stay up here at night. He wanted to sleep on the sofa, so I could wake him up if I felt bad. He said he wouldn't mind and it'd be a pleasure. He spends his whole evenings here now, and sits at the table studying in his books. Why does he study so much? Does a man like him have to do that? But what do you think of him wanting to sleep there and watch me? It's foolish! "

" Foolish? " Ruth answered. " No, I don't think so at all. I was going to suggest doing the same thing. He and I could take turns. I can work while I watch too. I mean, of course, if it is necessary. But it won't do to leave any one who is sick alone at night." She shook her head, and her ash-blond hair moved gently.

" What funny people you are," Karen said, and thrust her disordered hair almost to her eyes. " Real funny people." She feigned to be looking for something on the bed, and her eyes that refused to look at Ruth seemed to flee.

Ruth determined to consult Christian concerning the night-watches.

VII

She spoke to Christian, but he said that her services as a night nurse were not necessary. He could not bring himself to assign such a task to her. She amazed him by her inner clarity and ripeness of character, yet he saw the child in her that should be spared all the more because she was not willing to spare herself.

She herself had thought a great deal about him, and had arrived at definite conclusions which were not very far from the truth. To be sure, she had heard gossip in the house, both from Karen Engelschall and from others, but her own vision and instinct had taught her best. What seemed mysterious to all others revealed itself as simple and necessary to her. It was never the rare and beautiful that astonished her in life; it was always the common and the mean.

At first she had been badly frightened of Karen. The poverty in which her family had always lived had brought her into familiar contact with the ugly things beneath the surface of society, yet she had never met a woman like Karen —so degraded and so sunk in savagery. To approach her had cost her each time a pang and a struggle.

But she had helped when Karen's child was born; and on the following morning she had been there when Christian was in the room too. She had seen him bring the woman a glass of wine on an earthenware plate. He had smiled awkwardly, and his gestures had been uncertain; and in a flash she had comprehended everything. She knew whence he came and whence the woman came, and what had brought them to-gether, and why they were living as they were. The truth which came to her seemed so beautiful a one to her that she flushed and hurried from the room; for she was afraid of laughing out in her joy, and seeming frivolous and foolish.

From that day on she no longer regarded Karen shyly or with aversion, but with a sisterly feeling that was quite natu-ral, at least, to her.

Then came the incident of the pearls. She suspected their value only from Karen's feverish ecstasy, her infinitely careful touch, the morbid glitter of her eyes. But what impressed her most was not the pearls, nor Karen, nor Karen's horrible happiness, but what she guessed of Christian's action and its motives.

One Saturday night, when Isolde Schirmacher had gone out with one of her father's journeymen, Christian rang the bell of the Hofmann flat, and begged Ruth to go to a nearby public telephone and summon a physician. Karen was evidently worse. She complained of no pain, but she was approaching a state of exhaustion. Ruth hastened to a certain Doctor Voltolini in Gleim Street who was known to her, and brought him back with her. The physician examined Karen. He was frank concerning his uncertainty with regard to her symptoms, and gave some general advice. Afterward Ruth and Christian sat together beside the bed. Karen stared at the ceiling. Her expression changed continually; her breathing was regular but rapid. At times she sighed; at times her glance sought Christian, but flitted past him. Once or twice she gazed searchingly at Ruth.

Next day Christian came to see Ruth. She was alone; she was usually alone. When she unlatched the door which gave immediately upon the public hall she held a pen-holder in her hand. Her eyes still held the absorption of the occupation from which she had come. But when Christian asked whether he was interrupting her, she answered " No " with quieting assurance.

He held out his hand. With a gently rhythmic gesture she put her smooth, young hand into his.

She was voluble. Everything about her was touched with swiftness—her walk and glance, her speech and decisions and actions.

" I must see the place where you live," she announced to him, and on the next forenoon she visited his room. She was a little breathless, because, according to her custom, she had run down the stairs. She looked about her very frankly, and hid her seriousness under a cheerful vividness of behaviour. With boyish innocence of movement she sat down on the edge of the table, took an apple from her pocket, and began to nibble at it. She said she had mentioned Karen to an assistant whom she knew at the Polyclinic, and the lady had promised to come and examine Karen.

Christian thanked her. " I don't believe that medical help can do much for her," he said.

" Why not? "

"I can't tell you the reason. But where Karen is concerned, nature pursues a quite logical method."

"Perhaps you are right," Ruth answered. "But that sounds as though you had little confidence in science. Am I right? Why, then, are you studying medicine?"

"It's the merest accident. Some one happened to call my attention to it as one of a hundred possible doors into the open. It seemed to me that it might lead to a very early usefulness. It offers a definite aim, and it is concerned with people—with human beings!" More pertinent reasons that stirred within him, and that he might have given her, were not yet ripe for speech, so he clung to a banality.

"Yes, people," said Ruth, and looked at him searchingly. After a while she added: "You must know a great deal; there must be a great deal in you."

"What do you mean by that?"

She was the first human being in whose presence he felt wholly free of the compulsion to feign and to guard himself. In her there was a pure element that was frank and enthusiastic, that lived and vibrated with the souls of others. Her instincts had freedom and sureness, and her whole inner life radiated an irresistible intensity. The very stones gave up their souls to her. She was the seeing friend of inanimate things. She forgot neither words nor images, and her impatience to communicate what she had felt and the courage she had to acknowledge and follow her own heart surrounded her with an atmosphere as definite as the strong, sanative fragrance of plants in spring.

Life and its law seemed simple to her. The stars ruled one's fate; that fate expressed itself through the passions of our blood; the mind formed, illuminated, cleansed the process.

She told Christian about her father.

David Hofmann was a typical Jew of the lower middle-classes from the eastern part of the country. He had been a merchant, but his business had failed, and he had left home

to begin life over again. By indomitable toil he had saved
up a few thousand marks; but a sharper had done him out
of his savings, and in poverty and debt he had renewed the
struggle for a third time. His industry was tireless, his
patience magnificent. From Breslau he had moved to Posen,
from Posen to Stettin, thence to Lodz, and from Lodz to
Königsberg. All winter he had tramped the country roads
from village to village and from manor-house to manor-house.
He had seen his wife and his youngest child sicken and die,
and had finally set his last hope on the life and opportunities
of the metropolis. Eighteen months ago he had come to
Berlin with Ruth and Michael, and here too he was on his
feet day and night. With mind exhausted and enfeebled body,
he still dreamed of some reward and success to ease his approaching latter years. But failure was his portion, and in
hours of reflection he would yield to despair.

She told Christian about her brother.

Michael was taciturn. He never laughed; he had no
friend, sought no diversions, and avoided the society of men.
He suffered from his Jewishness, shrank nervously from the
hatred that he suspected everywhere, repelled every advance,
and felt all activity to be futile. During the forenoon he
would lie on his bed for hours with his hands behind his head
and smoke cigarettes; then he strolled to the little restaurant
where he met his father for their midday meal. When he
returned he would loiter in the yard and the alleys and at
the factory gates, beside fences or public-houses. With hat
pulled down and hunched shoulders, he observed life. Then
he returned home and sat around, brooding and smoking. He
tried to avoid being seen in the evening, when Ruth sat down
to her work or their father sighed with weariness.

His eyes, which seemed to lift their gaze from a great
depth, were of a golden brown, and their irises, like Ruth's,
contrasted strongly with the brilliant whiteness of the eye-ball.

Ruth said: " The other day I happened to come up when

half a dozen street Arabs were following him and crying:
'Sheeny!' He slunk along with bowed back and lowered
head. His face was terribly white; he twitched every time
he heard the word. I took him by the hand, but he thrust
me back. That evening father complained that business had
been poor. Michael suddenly leaped up, and said: 'What
does it matter? Why do you try to do anything in such a
world as this? It is too loathsome to touch. Let's starve to
death and be done with it. Why torment ourselves? " Father
was horrified, and did not answer. He thinks that Michael
hates him because he has not been able to keep us from
poverty and want. I do my best to talk him out of it, but
he feels himself guilty, guilty toward us, his children; and
that is hard, harder than penury."

She felt it to be her duty to try to sustain the poor man,
who tormented himself with reproaches, and to renew his
hope. She consoled him with her lovely serenity. It was
her pleasure to clear difficulties from his path, and then to
declare that they had been negligible.

When she had been a little girl of seven she had nursed her
mother through her last illness. She had done the work of
a servant, and cooked at the great stove, when she could
hardly reach the lids of the pots. She had watched over
her brother, gone errands, put off creditors, and gained respite
from sheriffs. She had collected money that was due; and at
each change of dwelling she had created order in the house,
and won the good-will of those on whom her family would
be dependent. She had mended linen and brushed clothes,
driven care away, caused insults to be forgotten, and brought
some cheer into the darkest hours. She had found some
sweetness in life, even when bitterness rose to the very brim.

Christian asked her what she was working at. She answered
that she was preparing herself to take her degree. She had
been relieved of all fees at the gymnasium. To help her
father, whose earnings decreased steadily, she gave private

lessons. To prolong her efforts far into the night cost her no struggle; five hours of sleep refreshed her and renewed her strength. In the morning she would get breakfast, set the room and kitchen to rights, and then start upon her path of work and duty with an air and mien as though it were a pleasure trip. She carried her dinner in her pocket. If it was too frugal, she would run to an automatic restaurant late in the afternoon.

One evening she returned from a charity kitchen, where twice a week she helped for half an hour to serve the meals. She told Christian about the people whom she was accustomed to see there—those whom the great city had conquered. She imitated gestures and expressions, and reported fragments of overheard speech. She communicated to him the greed, disgust, contempt, and shame that she had seen. Her observation was of a marvellous precision. Christian accompanied her on the next occasion, and saw little, almost nothing. He was aware of people in torn and shabby garments, who devoured a stingy meal without pleasure, dipped the crusts of bread into soup, and surreptitiously licked the spoon that had conveyed their last mouthful. There were hollow faces and dim eyes, foreheads that seemed to have been flattened by hydraulic pressure, and over it all a lifelessness as of scrapped machinery. Christian was teased as by a letter in an unknown tongue, and he began to understand how little he had learned to feel and see.

Although he had tried in no way to call attention to his presence, and had seemed at first glance but another wanderer from the street, a strange movement had passed through the hall. It had lasted no longer than three seconds, but Ruth, too, had felt the vibration. She was just filling one hundred and twenty plates, set in a fourfold circle, with vegetables from a huge cauldron. She looked up in surprise. She caught sight of the distinguished, almost absurdly courteous face of Christian, and she was startled. With mystical clarity she perceived the radiation of a power that wandered through the air without aim and lay buried in a soul. She bent her head over the steaming cauldron, so that her hair fell forward over her cheeks, and went on ladling out the vegetables. But she thought of the many unhappy creatures who waited for her on some hour of some day—suffering, confused, broken men and women—whom she desired so passionately to help, but to whom she could never be or give the miracle which had suddenly been revealed in that all but momentary vibration.

In a wild enthusiasm that was foreign to her nature she thought: "One must kneel and gather up all one's soul. . . ."

The one hundred and twenty tin plates were filled.

She thought of her poor. There was a young girl in a home for the blind, to whom she read on Sunday evenings. There was an asylum for the shelterless in Acker Street. She would look over the inmates and then ask help for them from charitable men and women who had come to expect her on this errand. In Moabit she had by chance come upon a woman with a baby at her breast; both were near starvation. She had saved them, had procured work and shelter for the woman, and taken the child to a home for infants. But these external things did not suffice her. She sought the establishment of human relations and the gift of confidence. She wrote letters for people, mediated between those whom life was threatening to divide, and thus, by giving her very self, she had also earned the fanatical devotion of that young mother.

She knew the names of many who were in great danger, and she knew many houses in which want was bitter. Once her interest had been excited by some children cowering in a corner during a socialistic women's meeting. Another time chance had led her into the home of a striker. She had been present when a poor woman had been dragged from the canal, and hastened to the suicide's family. On her way from giving a lesson to an errand of charity in a hospital, she had met an expelled student named Jacoby at the greasy table of a coffee-house, where he had begged her to meet him. Bad company and want threatened him with destruction. She had argued with him concerning his beliefs and principles and friends, and persuaded him into new courage and another attempt.

In the street that ran parallel to her own, there lived a machinist by the name of Heinzen with his family. An accident in a factory had robbed the man of both his legs, and the frightful nervous shock had reduced him to a paralytic condition. He usually lay in a state of convulsive rigour. One day a neighbour who was plagued with rheumatism had visited him; and this man had become aware of the fact that if Heinzen touched any part of his body the pain there was alleviated at once. The rumour had spread like fire. People talked of the miracle of magnetic healing, and a great many sick men and women came to Heinzen to be cured. He would take no money from them; but those who believed—and their numbers increased daily—brought his wife food and other gifts.

Ruth had heard of this. She had been in Heinzen's flat. She was filled by what she had seen, and gave Christian a vivid account of her impressions.

Christian looked at her wonderingly. "Ruth," he said, "little Ruth, those are such difficult matters. If you once begin to be absorbed by them, life itself is too short. I always thought that if one succeeded in quite exhausting but a single human soul, one would know a great deal and could well be content. But life is like the sea. Don't you have to think of it every minute? And how is it that you are always so full of brightness? I don't understand that."

With radiant eyes Ruth looked into space. Then she arose, and from her single shelf of books she took down a narrow yellow volume, turned to a familiar page, and read out with childlike emphasis: "Concerning the joy of the fishes.

Chuang-tse and Hui-tse stood on a bridge that spans the Hao. Chuang-tse said: ' Look how the fishes dart. It is the joy of the fishes.' ' Thou art no fish,' said Hui-tse, ' how canst thou know wherein the joy of the fishes consists? ' And he continued: ' I am not like thee and know thee not, but this I know, that thou art no fish and canst know naught of the fishes.' Chuang-tse answered: ' Let us return to thy question, which was: How can I know wherein the joy of the fishes consists? In truth thou didst know that I knew and yet thou askedst. It matters not. I know from my own delight in the water.' "

Christian pondered the parable.

" Don't you know it, you of all people, from your delight in the water? " asked Ruth, and bent her head forward to catch his look.

Christian smiled an uncertain smile.

" Won't you go with me to Heinzen's house to-morrow? "

He nodded and smiled again. He understood suddenly what manner of human being sat beside him.

VIII

It was two o'clock at night when Christian got up from the table in Karen's room and closed his books. He went to the sofa to lie down as he was. Toward evening Karen had been seized by a violent fever. The woman physician to whom Ruth had appealed had been there at noon, and had spoken of tuberculosis of the bones.

Curled up in a wooden chair by the oven lay a small, white cat. She had run in a few days before, and had made herself at home since no one drove her out. Christian had always disliked cats intensely. He stopped a moment and considered whether he shouldn't drive the cat out. Observing the animal he reconsidered.

Ruth, little Ruth. . . . The words ran through his head.

Karen slept heavily. On her dim face the muscles were taut. A dream raged behind her forehead. In her throat a fearful cry was gathering.

A dream! She stood in front of a barn which had a little window in its slanting roof. A man and a woman had just disappeared through that window. She knew their purpose at once. In the darkness, half-invisible, stood two lads, and it enraged the dreamer that the lads were eagerly listening. She herself was tormented by the sensual envy and hatred that arises in people when they see others in the throes of passion. Her blood tingled and her heart throbbed. Suddenly the barn seemed to have swung around, or she to have insensibly changed her station. The barn was open; one whole wall had disappeared. But the couple were not above, where they had entered; they were down in the depths. The man was fully clothed, but nothing was visible of the woman except her black stockings in the straw. From them both streamed forth something unspeakably disgustful—a heated, sweetish air. The two lads, as though seized by St. Vitus' dance, hurled themselves at each other. Then Karen felt her bodily personality dissolve. She was no longer Karen; she was that sensual miasma, she was the woman with the man. She lost herself in the straw, in its reddish-brown light, in those black stockings; and as she lay there, her body swelled and expanded and became a gelatinous, greyish-yellow ball, and reached even to the roof of the barn. Then the ball became transparent, and she saw within it lizards and toads and tiny, scarlet horses, on which tiny horsemen were riding, and soldiers and spiders and worms, a loathsome swarm. The horrible passions that penetrated everything turned into a throttling torment. The ball burst. A corpse fluttered about like charred paper. A white shadow expanded. Karen gave a shriek, and started from her sleep.

Her first gesture was to grasp the pearls.

Christian went up to the bed.

She murmured wildly: " Are you still here? What are you doing? "

He gave her water to drink. " I've been dreaming," she said, and touched the glass with trembling lips. The elements of her dream were already dissolving in her mind and escaping a formulation in speech. But the sense of that dream's frightfulness increased; in the depth of her consciousness flickered the terror of death.

" I've been dreaming," she repeated and shook. After a while she asked: " Why are you up so late? What did you do all day that you've got to work till late at night? Why do you work so hard? Tell me! "

He shook his head and the words, " Ruth, little Ruth," passed through his head. " Didn't your mother visit you to-day? " he asked, and smoothed her pillows.

" Tell me what you've been doing all day! " she persisted. " In the forenoon I went to lectures." " And then? " " Then I went to see Botho Thüngen, who was very anxious to talk something over with me." " And then? " " Then I went to court with Lamprecht and Jacoby. A servant girl in Kurfürsten Street gave birth to a child and strangled it to death immediately after birth." " Did they send her up? " " She was condemned to five years in the penitentiary. Her counsel took us to her, and Lamprecht talked to her. She was half-clad, and kept staring at me." " And where were you then? " " I went to meet Amadeus Voss. He wrote me." " Did he ask you for money? " " No, he begged me to come and meet Johanna Schöntag in his room." " Who is she? " " An old friend." " What does she want of you? " " I don't know." " And then? " " Then I came back by way of Moabit and Plötzensee." " On foot? All that distance? And then? " " Then I came here." " But you didn't stay! " " I went over to see Ruth." " Why do you always go to see the Jewess? " Karen murmured, and her face was sombre. " Give me your hand," she suddenly said roughly, and stretched out her right hand, while her left clawed itself into the pearls under the coverlet. She had hurt her left hand. When the widow Engelschall had been there she had dug her nails into her own palm, so convulsively had she grasped her treasure.

The widow Engelschall had written a blackmailing letter to Privy Councillor Wahnschaffe, and had read it to Karen. Niels Heinrich had stolen two thousand marks; the money had to be found or he would be apprehended. In the letter she had shamelessly demanded ten thousand. Karen had tried to prevent her mother from sending the letter, and the old woman had raised a terrible outcry.

Karen thought it was almost pleasant to be ill. But why did he not give her his hand?

The little cat had jumped from the chair. With tail erect she stood in front of Christian, and blinked her eyes and mewed very softly. She seemed undecided, then suddenly took heart and jumped on his knee. For a moment he struggled with his old aversion. Then the soft white fur and the grace of the little body tempted him. Timidly he touched the little animal's head and back, and bent over it and smiled. The kitten pleased him.

" What've you done with my child? " Karen had asked her mother. The answer had been a rowdy laugh. If he knew that she had asked after her child, perhaps he would look at her more kindly. But she could not tell him; and the memory of the old woman's laughter had left a dread.

For a while she held out her hand dumbly. Then she let it fall, and folded back the covers and crept out of bed. She whimpered strangely. Sitting on the edge of the bed opposite Christian, she had an icy stare and went on whimpering. One could scarcely hear her words. " He don't touch a person's hand," she whispered. Barefoot, in her long night-dress, with bowed back she crawled to the oven, crouched down beside it, hid her head in her hands and howled.

With increasing astonishment Christian had observed her

behaviour. The kitten had snuggled into his hands and purred and thrust her rosy little nozzle against his breast. This awakened a sense of pleasure in him such as he had not felt for long, and he wished secretly that he could be alone with the little beast and play with it. But Karen's doings horrified him. He got up, carrying the kitten with him, and went to Karen and kneeled down beside her. He asked her what ailed her, and begged her to return to bed. She paid no attention to his words, but writhed there on the floor and howled.

And it was chaos that was howling there.

IX

Among the boon companions of Niels Heinrich Engelschall was Joachim Heinzen, the son of the crippled machinist. The fellow was a simpleton. His indiscriminate pursuit of every woman subjected him to malicious practical jokes. Since, on account of his absurdity, no woman wanted to be seen with him, he was gradually obsessed by a silent rage which made him really dangerous, although his original nature had been kindly enough.

Among other women, the one called Red Hetty had attracted him. He followed her in the dark streets; in public houses he sat near her and stared. She mocked at his attempts to become friendly with her. Moreover, so long as she was the mistress of Niels Heinrich, he dared to undertake nothing further, and his interest seemed gradually to subside. When Niels Heinrich, however, had cast the woman off, Heinzen began to pursue her again, but his efforts were fruitless.

But Niels Heinrich himself came to his aid, and promised to help him for a certain sum. Joachim Heinzen hesitated to risk so much. At last they agreed that half of the price was to be paid at once, the other half later and in instalments. Red Hetty, badly frightened by Niels Heinrich, became friendlier with Joachim; but after her breach with her former lover she got drunk daily, and made fearful and disgusting scenes. Joachim declared that Niels had cheated him, refused to pay the instalments, and demanded the return of his original fifty marks. Thus a quarrel arose.

Niels Heinrich did not fear the simpleton, and it would have been easy for him to rid himself of the fellow. But since he had unbounded influence over Joachim and had found him a useful tool on many occasions, he did not want a definite breach, and sought ways and means of soothing him. He flattered him by his attentions, permitted him to be his neighbour in public places, and took his part in quarrels and fights. Something loathsome and frightful was gathering gradually in his brain. Dark plans employed his mind, though they had taken yet no definite shape or form. He chose his creature, though he knew not yet what for. But he did know that Joachim could be used for all things, no matter how infamous, and had nevertheless a degree of inner innocence. Perhaps a plan, with which his thoughts played only cynically and indefinitely, gained form and certainty from the simpleton's slavish devotion. Perhaps it fired him, gave him courage, and stung his imagination to enter the abyss of the unspeakable.

He assured Joachim that Red Hetty didn't amount to much, that she was a withered drab and a stinking carrion. He might have others, if he would only open his eyes. There were some that made a fellow's mouth water; a count would be glad of 'em. In such and such places there were some—ah, that was different. The poor fool asked where and who. Then Niels Heinrich gave an evil chuckle, and said he was thinking of a Jewess. You had to see her, that was all! Like a peeled egg. Firm on her legs. Not too fat, not too lean. Eyes like the Irishwoman's in the pub. Hair like the tail of a race-horse. Ready to bite. Ah! "Hold on now," Joachim Heinzen answered, taken aback. "Hold on!"

It gave Niels Heinrich a bitter pleasure to tell the fellow of the girl over and over again. He filled him with the

image and goaded his senses. He directed all the idiot's desires upon a being he had not even seen. But also he described her for his own benefit, and heightened and stung
his own appetites, and made himself impatient and jeered at
himself in order to test the possibility of their realization by
his rage over the apparently unattainable products of his
fancy. He took Joachim with him to Stolpische Street, and
they lay in wait for Ruth's home-coming. Then he showed
her to him, and they followed her up the stairs. Ruth felt
nervous and frightened.

It so happened that at this time a fellow student called her
attention to the curious healings accomplished by old Heinzen.
When she went there she did not know, of course, that it was
Joachim Heinzen who had followed her, nor did she recognize
him when she saw him in the room. But his stupid, steady
glare disquieted her.

In great excitement Joachim announced to his patron that
he had seen the Jewess, whom he already regarded as his
property, in his father's flat. "That's rot," said Niels Heinrich coldly. He had before this jeered venomously at the
cures old Heinzen performed. He repeated that jeer now, and
added that if the Jewess had gone to the old man's, there was
no doubt but that she had done so because she had taken a
liking to Joachim. The fellow grinned. In the drinking den
where they spent many of their nights, Niels Heinrich had
craftily arranged that the prospective affair of Joachim and
the Jewess should be frequently discussed and commented.
Joachim did not know that he and his affair were a joke. He
took Niels Heinrich aside, and asked how he could get at the
girl most quickly. Niels Heinrich looked at him mockingly,
and told him he had better put off all attempts for a while
yet; this was a matter in which one had to proceed cleverly;
the Jewess was distrustful, and was furthermore one of those
new-fangled student wenches. You couldn't go at her with
a club; you had to be elegant and considerate. But the

simpleton was not to be persuaded. He said he wanted to
go to her and invite her to a ball on the following Sunday.
Niels Heinrich laughed uproariously. " I guess you're crazy,"
he said. " Your head must've gone addled." He paled and
laughed anew, and said: " You got to wait and see. I'll lay
ten to one the girl will turn up at your old man's pretty soon.
I'll have some one watching, and you stay home so you don't
miss her."

He slapped Joachim's shoulder. He stood there like a pole
—lean, dry, pointed. In the embankment on the road to
Weissensee the wheels of an express train thundered on the
rails.

x

Ruth and Christian entered a dim, stuffy room. The door
to the little hall was open, as well as the door to the adjoining
room. There were a good many people in the flat. Careless
of all these strangers, Mother Heinzen sat at her table and
pared potatoes. The table was covered with innumerable
things—files, boxes, ink-bottles, even a pair of shoes. In the
background, at a second table which was as narrow as a carpenter's bench, Joachim and an apprentice were making metal
stoppers with a hand machine. Old Heinzen leaned in a
wicker chair. A shabby black cloth hid the lower part of
his body and concealed its mutilation. His lean and almost
rigid face, with its thick, inflamed lids, its yellowish beard, and
its sharp, straight nose, expressed no inner participation in
what went on around him.

A few whispering women stood nearest to him. A little beyond there was a group consisting of a sergeant, a journeyman butcher with a blood-stained apron and naked arms, a
salvation army lass with blue spectacles, and the porter of a
business house in a fancy uniform. Behind Christian and
Ruth appeared a man whose head was swathed in bandages,
another who looked frightened as he leaned on his crutches,

and a woman whose face was a mass of repulsive sores. Other figures emerged gradually into that narrow circle.

While no one dared yet to approach the miracle worker, a woman rushed panting and moaning into the room. In her arms she carried a child between three and four years old. The child's face was like lead, its eyes were convulsively turned outward, and its neck and limbs were unnaturally contorted. The woman was trembling all over, and seemed not to know where to turn, so Ruth took the child from her and carried it to old Heinzen. The people willingly made way for her. On her face was a radiance of sweet serviceableness.

Joachim Heinzen got up. The apprentice poured a mass of finished stoppers into a basket filled with saw-dust, and shook the stoppers down. Joachim, his arms akimbo, approached his father's chair, and devoured Ruth with his eyes. His mouth was open, his head craned forward, his whole person quivered with excitement. Ruth held the child out toward old Heinzen, and spoke words that could not be heard for the rattle of the metal stoppers. Joachim made a threatening gesture toward the apprentice, who stopped the noise.

Old Heinzen opened his eyes and raised his right arm. This was his miraculous gesture, and a silence fell upon the room. Christian watched the devotion, the utter loving-kindness with which Ruth held out the epileptic child to the stricken man. Her grace pierced him, and he asked himself with amazement: " Does she believe in it? Is it possible to believe in such things? " But even as his amazement increased, there seemed to arise in him the presentiment of something unknown and incomprehensible; and as often before in moments of extraordinary feeling, he had to fight down a secret desire to laugh.

Suddenly Heinzen dropped the raised arm. He seemed confused. He moved his head and shoulders, and said wearily: " I can do nothing to-day. There's somebody here who takes my power from me. I can do nothing."

His words made a deep impression, and all eyes sought the disturber. They glided from one to another. Heads turned and pupils shifted. Before a minute had passed the eyes of all the people in the room were fixed on Christian. Even Mother Heinzen had stopped paring the potatoes and had arisen and was staring at him.

Christian had heard Heinzen's words. What did those glances demand of him? What was their meaning? What did they desire? Were they angry? Was there something in him or about him that affronted or disturbed them? Yet they seemed timid and wondering rather than hostile. That old seal of his silence, his equivocal little smile, hovered about his lips. He looked up as though asking for help, and his eyes met Ruth's; and in her eyes he saw that radiant understanding, that silvery, spiritual love that animated her wholly and at all times.

The mother of the child uttered a cry. " How do you mean —takes your power? Pull yourself together, old man, for God's sake! "

" I can't say nothing different," murmured Heinzen. " There's somebody here that takes my power away."

" And has he got the power? " the Salvationist cried shrilly.

" I don't know," Heinzen answered, in an oppressed manner. " Maybe, but I don't know."

Slowly Christian went up to Ruth, who was still holding the child in her arms, and bent over and gazed at the apparently lifeless form. At once the epileptic rigour relaxed, flecks of foam appeared on the child's lips, and it began to weep softly.

The emotion that passed through the room was like a great sigh.

But noises from without broke in upon the silence here. Laughter and curses had been heard a while before. Now the sounds came nearer, and Niels Heinrich and Red Hetty appeared in the doorway.

He tugged the woman into the room. She reeled drunkenly, waved her arms, and laughed shrilly. Pushed forward by Niels Heinrich, she stretched out her fingers for some support; but the people whom she touched drew back in vexation. Niels Heinrich caught her by the shoulders, and shoved her at Joachim Heinzen. He chuckled as he did so, and the noise he made was like the clucking of a hen. Joachim was scared, and gazed stupidly and angrily at the wild looking creature. She wound her arms about his neck and clung to him and babbled drunkenly. Her black, wide-brimmed hat, with its huge green feather, slipped grotesquely to the back of her head. Joachim tried to shake her off, fixing his half-crazed eyes on Ruth. But as the woman clung the more tenaciously, he struck her a blow full in the breast, so that she fell to the floor with a moan and lay there in an absurd posture.

People hurried to and fro protesting. A few bent over the drunken woman, who at once began to hiccough and babble again. Others threatened Joachim with their fists. Mother Heinzen tried to calm the tumult, Ruth sought refuge near Christian and took his hand. Then an uncanny thing happened. Joachim Heinzen grasped her arm, and pulled her roughly toward him. Perhaps it was a weak-minded jealousy that impelled him, or else a brutal and stupid attempt to convince her that he cared nothing for Red Hetty and was guiltless of the incident. With glassy eyes he stared at Ruth; a vicious grin was on his face. Ruth gave a soft cry, held up her hand to shield herself, and struggled gently. Her lids were lowered. Her attitude went to Christian's heart. He went up to the fellow, and said very quietly: " Let her go." Joachim hesitated. " Let her go," Christian repeated, without raising his voice. Joachim obeyed and snorted.

Niels Heinrich seemed to be immensely entertained by it all. He urged those about him to watch what was going on, laughed his clucking laugh, and sought to encourage the simpleton. " Go ahead, Joachim," he cried. " You got to take what you want! " But while he laughed and goaded Joachim on, his brows remained knit, and the upper part of his face seemed rigid with some horror. He had recently grown a little, pointed, goat-like beard which had a reddish colour. When he spoke or laughed it moved stiffly up and down, and gave his head the appearance of a marionette's.

When he saw that Christian had restrained Joachim's impudent roughness, he came and stood before him, and said in an insolent, knife-like voice: " Mornin'. I should think you'd know me."

" I do," Christian answered courteously.

" An' I said good mornin' to you! " Niels Heinrich said, with an unconcealed jeer. His little beard twitched. The horror seemed to spread over his whole face.

" Good evening," said Christian courteously.

Niels Heinrich gritted his teeth. " Mornin'! " he yelled, livid with rage. All those present gave a start and became silent.

Christian looked at him quietly. Then he turned quite deliberately to Ruth, and said: " Let us go, little Ruth." With the bow of a man of the world he let her precede him. He also bowed courteously to those about him. He might have been leaving a drawing-room.

Niels Heinrich, bent far forward, stared after him. He clenched his fist, and went through the pantomime of pulling a cork-screw out of a bottle.

XI

" Were you frightened? " Christian asked, when they were in the street.

" A little," Ruth answered. She smiled, but she was still trembling.

They did not turn homeward. They walked in the opposite direction and passed through many streets. Christian walked swiftly, and Ruth had difficulty in keeping up with him. A sharp wind blew, and her shabby little cloak fluttered.

"Are you cold?" Christian asked. She said "No." A cloud of yellow leaves whirled up in front of them; and Christian strode on and on.

"The stars are coming out," he said, and looked fleetingly at the sky.

They came to a wide, desolate street. A line of arc-lamps seemed to stretch into infinity, but the houses looked empty.

They walked on and on.

"Say something," Ruth begged. "Tell me something about yourself. Just this once. Just to-day."

"There's little good to be told about myself," he said into the wind.

"Whether it's good or not, I'd like to know it."

"But what?"

"Anything."

"I must think. I have a poor memory for my own experiences." But even as he spoke there emerged the memory of a night which he had thought quite faded. What had happened then seemed menacing now, and seemed in some mysterious way related to Ruth; and the need of confession came upon him like hunger.

"Don't search in your mind," said Ruth. "Tell what happens to occur to you."

He walked more slowly. Poor in words as he was, he strove first to gather the bare facts in his mind.

Ruth smiled and urged him. "Just start. The first word is the hardest."

"Yes, that is true," he agreed.

"Did the thing you're thinking of happen long ago?"

"You are right," he said. "I am thinking of something definite. You have clear perceptions." He was surprised. "It's four years ago. I was motoring with two friends in the south of Italy." He hesitated. The words were so lame. But the lovely compulsion of Ruth's glances drew them from their hiding-places, and they gradually came forth more willingly.

On a beautiful day of May he and his friends had reached the city of Acquapendente in the Abruzzi. They had really intended to proceed to Viterbo, but the little mountain town pleased his friends, and they persuaded him to stay. He stopped in his story. "I seemed always to want to race from one spot to another," he said. His friends kept on urging him, but when they stopped in front of the inn, it seemed so dirty that he hated to think of passing the night there. At that moment there came down the steps of the near-by church a girl of such majestic loveliness as he had never seen before; and that vision determined him to stay. The innkeeper, when he was asked who the girl was, pronounced her name full of respect. She was the daughter of a stone-mason named Pratti. Christian bade the innkeeper get ready a supper and invite Angiolina Pratti to it. The innkeeper refused. Thereupon Christian bade him invite the girl's father, and this the man agreed to do. His friends sought to dissuade Christian, telling him that the women of this land were shy and proud, and that their favours were not easily won. He would, at least, have to go about the business more delicately than he was doing. Christian laughed at them. They reasoned and argued, so that finally he grew stubborn, and declared to them that he would bring about what they held to be quite impossible—that he would accomplish it without artfulness or adroitness or exertion, but simply through his knowledge of the character of these people.

The girl's father came to wait upon the foreign gentlemen. He had white hair and a white beard and a noble demeanour. Christian approached and addressed him. He said that it would give him and his friends pleasure if the Signorina Pratti would sup with them. Pratti wrinkled his forehead and

expressed his astonishment. He had not, he said, the honour
of the gentlemen's acquaintance. Christian looked sharply into
his eyes, and asked for how much money he would, that
evening at eight, conduct his daughter Angiolina naked into
their room and to their table. Pratti stepped back and gasped.
His eyes rolled in his head, and Christian's friends were
frightened. Christian said to the old man: " We are perfectly
decent. You may depend on our discretion. We desire merely
to admire the girl's beauty." With wildly raised arms Pratti
started to rush at him. But he was prepared for that, and
said: " Will five thousand suffice? " The Italian stopped.
" Or ten thousand? " And he took ten bank notes of a thousand lire each out of his wallet. The Italian grew pale and
tottered. " Twelve thousand? " Christian asked. He saw that
the sum represented an inconceivable treasure to the old man;
in a long life of toil he had never had so much. The perception increased Christian's madness, and he offered fifteen
thousand. Pratti opened his lips, and sighed: " Oh, Signore."
The sound should have touched him, Christian said to Ruth.
But nothing touched him in those days; all that he cared for
was to have his will. The man took the money, and went
away falteringly.

That evening the young men took their places at the
charmingly arranged table in some suspense. The innkeeper
had brought forth old silver vessels and cut-glass goblets.
Roses were placed in vases of copper, and thick candles had
been lit. The room was like one in a castle. Eight o'clock
came, and then a quarter past eight. The conversation lagged;
they gazed at the door. Christian had commanded the innkeeper not to appear until he was summoned, so that the
promised discretion should be observed. At last, at half-past
eight, old Pratti appeared carrying his daughter in his arms.
He had wrapped her in a cloak. He beckoned the young men
to close the doors. When they had done so, he pulled the
cloak away and they beheld the naked body of the beautiful

girl. Her hands and feet were fettered. Her father placed her on the empty chair beside Christian. Her eyes were closed; she was asleep. But it was no natural sleep; she had been drugged, probably with the juice of poppies. Pratti bowed and left.

The three friends looked at that lovely form, the gently inclined head, the rosy face, the streaming hair. But their triumph and arrogant delight had died within them. One went into the bed-room, fetched a coverlet, and covered the girl with it; and Christian was grateful to him for the action. Hastily they ate a few bites; the wine remained untouched. Then they went down, paid their reckoning, summoned their chauffeur, and drove through the night along the road to Rome. No one spoke during the drive; none of them ever mentioned Angiolina Pratti later. But Christian found it difficult to escape the picture in his mind—the fettered, drugged girl alone in the room with the roses and the yellow candle-light. But at last he forgot, for so many other images crowded the old one out. "But just now," he said, "as we left the house, that image was as clear to me as it was that day in Acquapendente. I had to keep thinking of it, I don't know why."

"How strange," Ruth whispered.

They walked on and on.

"Where are we going?" Ruth asked.

Christian looked at her. "What is so strange? That I told you about it? It really seemed superfluous, quite as though you knew it without being told."

"Yes," she admitted shyly. "I often seem to stand within your soul as within a flame."

"It is brave of you to say a thing like that." He disliked swelling words, but this thing moved him.

"You must not be so ashamed," she whispered.

He answered: "If I could talk like other people, much would be spared me."

"Spared you? Would you be a niggard of yourself? Then it would no longer be you. That's not the question. One should be a spendthrift of oneself—give oneself without stint or measure."

"Where have you learned to make such judgments, Ruth? To see and feel and know, and to have the courage of your vision?"

"I'd like to tell you about something too," said Ruth.

"Yes, tell me something about yourself."

"About myself? I don't think I can do that. But I will tell you about some one to whom I felt very close. It was a sister; no bodily sister, for I haven't one. The reason I said 'strange' just now was because this Angiolina Pratti seemed like a sister to me too. Suddenly there seemed to be three sisters: Angiolina and I and the one I shall tell you about. It is a rather sad story. At least, it is at first. Afterwards it is no longer quite so sad. Oh, life is so wonderful and so deeply moving and so rich and so full of power!"

"Ruth, little Ruth," said Christian.

Then she told her story. "There was a little girl, a child. She lived with her parents at Slonsk, far in the eastern part of the country. Five years have gone since it all happened. Her father was very poor; he was assistant bookkeeper in a cotton mill, but he was so poorly paid that he could hardly scrape together the rent of their wretched dwelling. His wife had been ailing for long. Sorrow over their failure and suffering had robbed her of strength, and in the winter she died. These people were the only Jews in Slonsk, and in order to bury the body they had to take it to the nearest Jewish cemetery at Inowraztlaw. Since no railroad connects the towns, they had to use a wagon. So at seven o'clock in the morning—it was toward the end of December—the wagon came, and the coffin with the mother's body was lifted on it. The father and the brother and the little girl followed on foot. The girl was eleven years old and the boy eight and a half. Thick flakes of snow fell, and soon the road had disappeared, and you could tell it only from the line of trees on either hand.

" It was still dark when they started, and even when day came there was only a murky twilight. The girl was unbearably sad, and her sadness increased at every step. When day had fully come, a dim, misty day, the crows flew thither from all directions. It may be that the body in the coffin brought them. But the girl had never seen so many; they seemed to pour from the sky. On great black wings they flew back and forth, and croaked uncannily through the icy, murky silence. And the girl's sadness became so great that she wished to die. She lagged behind a little, and neither her father nor her brother noticed it in the snow-flurries, nor yet the man who led the horses. So she crossed a field to a wood, and there she sat down and made up her mind to die. Soon her senses were numbed.

" But an old peasant, who had been gathering wood, came from among the trees, and when he saw her and perceived that she did not move and was asleep, he first looked at her a while, and then he started to strip her body of all she had, her cloak, her shoes, her dress, her stockings, and even her shift; for the peasants are very poor thereabouts. She could not resist. She felt what was happening only as from the depth of a dream. So the peasant made a little bundle of her things, and left her naked body there as dead and limped away. He marched along for a while, and came upon the wagon with the coffin and the two men and the boy. The wagon had stopped, for the child had been missed. On the edge of the road a crucifix had been set up, and that was the first thing that gave the peasant pause. It did not seem to him to be chance that Christ was standing there beside the wagon with the coffin. He confessed that later. Also he saw the hundreds of crows that croaked wildly and hungrily, and he was frightened. Then he saw how desperate the father was, and that he was preparing to turn back and gazed in all directions and tried to halloo through the mist.

" The peasant's conscience began to burn. He fell on his knees before the cross and prayed. The father asked him whether he had seen the child. He pointed and wanted to run away, and he did run across the fields. But something within him forced him to run to the very spot where he had robbed and abandoned the girl. He lifted her in his arms, wrapped his coat about her, and held her to his breast. The father had followed and received the child, and did not ask why she was naked and bare. They rubbed her skin so long with snow till she was warm and opened her eyes. Then the peasant kissed her forehead, and made the sign of the cross over the Jewish child. The father rebuked him for that, but the peasant said: ' Forgive me, brother,' and he kissed his hand. From that time on no sadness of the old kind ever came to the girl again. She had only a very faint recollection of the moment when the peasant wrapped her in his coat and held her to his breast. But I believe that she was born again in that moment, born better and stronger than she had been before."

" Ruth, little Ruth," said Christian.

" And perhaps Angiolina, that other sister of mine, also awakened to a happier life from that hour of dimness and of death."

Christian did not answer. He felt as though a light were walking by his side.

At a corner of that desolate street they came upon a very brilliant show-window. They went up to it and stopped as by a common impulse. The shop had long been closed, but in the window was draped a magnificent coat of Russian sable, a symbol of wealth and warmth and adornment. Christian turned to Ruth, and saw the threadbare little cloak in which she shivered. And he saw that she was poor. Then it came into his mind that he too was poor, poor like her, and irrevocably so. He smiled, for the fact seemed significant to him, and he felt a joy that was secret and almost ecstatic.

XII

Johanna Schöntag's first visit to Voss passed off in a very commonplace manner. Trying to let him forget that she was a young lady made her more and more conventional. To hide her embarrassment, she was half capricious and half critical in mood. It amused her that there was a rocking-chair in the room. " It reminds one of one's grandmother," she said, " and gives one an anachronistic and homelike feeling." Then she sat down in it and rocked, took candied fruits from her little beaded bag and crushed them on her tongue, which gave her a comical and pouting expression.

On the table there was a tea-urn, two cups, and plates with pastry. Voss's demeanour seemed to say that narrow means did not prevent one from entertaining properly. It amused Johanna. She thought to herself: " If he brings out a photograph album with pictures of himself as a child, I shall giggle right into his face." And at the same time her heart throbbed with quite other fears.

Voss spoke of his loneliness. He alluded to experiences of his own that had made him shy. There were people, he said, who seemed fated to suffer shipwreck in all matters where their hearts were involved. They had to grow calluses of the soul. He was busy doing that. He had never had a friend, though the illusion of friendship often enough. To realize the futility of some great longing was bitterer than to discover the insufficiency of a human being.

Johanna's secret fears grew as she heard him wax sentimental. She said: " This rocking-chair is the nicest thing I've come across for long. It gives me a queer, pleasant little seasickness. Are you sure the people under you won't believe that you've become a father and are rocking your offspring

to sleep? " She laughed and left the chair. Then she drank
tea and nibbled at a piece of pastry, and quite suddenly said
good-bye and left him.

Voss gritted his teeth. His hand was as empty as before.
He took a piece of soft cake, formed it into the rude image
of a girl, and pierced it with the pin that Christian had given
him. The room still held the faint aroma of a woman's body
and garments and clothes and hair. He rocked the empty
chair, and talked to an invisible person who was leaning back
in it and coquettishly withdrew from his glance. For a while
he worked. Then his work wearied him, and his thoughts were
busy laying snares.

All he did and thought showed the sincerity of his feeling
of loneliness. His soul exuded poisonous fumes.

He opened a drawer of his desk, and took out the letters of
the unknown lady who had signed herself F. He read them
through, and then took pen and paper and began to copy
them. He copied them word for word, but whenever Christian's name occurred he substituted dots for it. There were
twenty-three of these letters, and when he had finished dawn
was rising.

He slept a few hours, and then wrote to Johanna as follows: " I propose this riddle to you: Who is F. and who
is the thief and robber who took French leave with such
a treasure of enthusiasm and devotion? Perhaps it is only
a product of my fancy or a by-product of my morbid imagination. I leave you to guess. Has there been an attempt
here to substitute a magnificent invention for the unromantic
sobriety of real life, or did this rare and miraculous thing
really form a part of human experience? It seems to me
that something in the modulation and tone-colour, something
subtle but unmistakable, points to the latter conclusion.
Where is the man who could invent such pain and such delight?
Who would have the courage to represent the life of the senses
as so blended of shamelessness and of a primal innocence?

Compared to such an one our most vaunted poets would be the merest tyros. I have, of course, never admired poets inordinately. They falsify appearances, and, in the last analysis, they are but rationalists in whose hands our dreams become transparent and two-dimensional. There is a verbal veraciousness which is as penetrating as the glow of living flesh. Here is an example of it. It is a miracle to be adored, a thing of envy to all hungry souls. It is life itself, and since it is life, where are the living two that begot it? She, the marvellous author of the letters, is probably dead—consumed in the glow of her own soul. Her very shadow bears the stigmata of doom. But her ecstatic pen paints the picture of him whom she loved. I know him, we both know him. He stands at the gate of the penitents, and offers for old debts a payment that no one wants. To love as she loved is like worship; to be so loved and not to value it, to let its evidence rot in the dust of a library—that is a sin which nothing can wipe out. If one whom God himself pampered spews the food of angels out of his mouth, nothing but carrion remains for the step-children of fate. And yet we know: not wholly hopeless is the cry of the blood's need. Come to me soon; I have much to ask you and to say to you. I was like stone yesterday; the happiness of your presence drugged me. I shall be waiting for you. Each day I shall be at home at five o'clock and wait for you for three hours. Is there not some compulsion in that? When would you like to see Wahnschaffe? I shall tell him and arrange the meeting."

Johanna felt the same consternation this time that she had felt months before when Voss had written her in Christian's stead. First she thought he had perpetrated a hoax. But when she read the letters she was convinced of their authenticity and deeply moved. Voss's indications left no doubt as to their origin; again he had stolen another's secret in order to make use of it. His motives seemed inexplicable to her. But she promised herself not to see him again, whatever happened. The very thought of him made her freeze. The morbid and heated hatred of Christian which he always manifested made her reconsider. At moments she nursed the flattering delusion that she might be the means of saving Christian from a great danger. And yet, somehow, the man himself exerted the stronger lure. There was a will in him! A strange temptation—to feel the compulsion of an alien will! Whither would it lead?

Thus when, against her determination and her better instinct, she entered the house on Ansbacher Street once more, she said to herself: "O Rumpelstiltzkin, I'm afraid you're rushing into destruction. But run on and be destroyed. Then, at least, something will have happened."

She carried the letters back to him. She asked coldly what had been his intention in sending them. She feigned not to hear his answer that his letter had explained his intention. She refused to sit down. Voss tried to find a subject of conversation; he walked up and down before her like a sentinel. In her mind she passed caustic comments on him; she observed the negligence of his clothes, and thought his way of swinging on his heel and suddenly rubbing his hands absurd. Everything about him seemed silly and comical to her. She mocked at him to herself: "A schoolmaster who has gone a little crazy."

He told her he had made up his mind to move to Zehlendorf. Out there he had found a peaceful attic room in a villa. He felt the need of trees and fields, at least of their odour. In the morning he would ride in to attend lectures and in the afternoon return. Even if this plan could not be carried out daily, yet he would have the consolation of knowing that he had a refuge beyond this stony pandemonium which tasted of maltreated minds and of ink. He would move in two weeks.

"All the better." The words slipped out before Johanna was aware.

"What do you mean by that?" he asked, with a cattish

look. Then he laughed, and his laughter sounded like the clashing of shards. " Ah," he said, and stopped, " do you really think the distance will make any difference? You will come to me, I assure you; and you will come not only when I summon you, but of your own impulse. So please don't cling to a delusive hope."

Johanna had no answer ready. His insolence shook her self-control. Voss laughed again, and took no notice of the impression made by his words. He spoke of the progress of his studies: he had worked for two semesters, and was as far advanced as others at the end of six. The professors were saying excellent things of him. He considered all that part of medical knowledge that could be directly acquired mere child's play. No man of normal mind and decent industry should need more than eighteen months to master it. After that, to be sure, the paths divided. On one were artisans, dilettanti, mere professionals, and charlatans; on the other were great brains and spirits, pioneers and illustrious discoverers. At first surgery had attracted him, but that attraction had been brief. It was the merest butchery. He would refuse to depend wholly on knife and saw, and at all crucial moments of practice to submit to the dictates of a professional diagnostician, with nothing left him but whether the butcher would turn out to be an executioner or not. What attracted him inordinately was psychiatry. In it mystery was heaped on mystery. Unexplored and undiscovered countries stretched out there—great epidemics of the soul, illnesses of the sexes, deep-rooted maladies of whole nations, a ghostly chase between heaven and earth, new proofs of psychical bonds that stretched from millennium to millennium as well as from man to man, the discovery of whose nature would make the whole structure of science totter.

Johanna was repelled. One couldn't go much further in the way of boasting. His voice, which constantly passed from falsetto to bass, like a young bird thudding awkwardly between two walls, gave her a physical pain. She murmured a polite formula of agreement, and gave him her hand in farewell. Even this she hated to do.

" Stay! " he said commandingly.

She threw back her head and looked at him in astonishment.

Now he begged. " Do stay! You always leave in such a mood that the minute you are outside I'm tempted to hang myself."

Johanna changed colour and wrinkled her childlike forehead. " Will you kindly tell me what you want of me? "

" That is a question of remarkably—shall we call it innocent frankness? What I want would seem to be sufficiently clear. Or can you accuse me of a lack of plain speaking? Am I a very deft and crafty wooer? I should rather expect you to reprove me for my impetuousness; that would be reasonable. But I cannot play at games; I have no skill in sinuous approaches. I cannot symbolize my feelings through flowers, nor have I learned to set springes of words or feign a bait upon the waters or make sweetish speeches. If I could do these things I might be more certain of reaching my goal. But I have no time; my time is limited, Fräulein Johanna. My life is crystallizing to a catastrophic point. Its great decision is at hand! "

" Your frankness leaves nothing to be desired," Johanna replied, and looked coolly and firmly into his eyes. She waited for a few seconds; then she asked, with a forced smile, concealing both her dread and her curiosity: " And why am I the arbiter in that great decision? What qualities have attracted your attention toward me? To what virtue or to what vice do I owe such an honour? " Awaiting his reply, she all but closed her eyes; and that gave her face a melting charm. She knew the danger of such coquettishness, but the abysses lured her.

But to Amadeus Voss she was exactly what she seemed to

be. He gazed ecstatically at her face, and asked: " May I be frank? "

" You frighten me. Can one be more so than you have already been? "

" You see—it is your race. It is, I do not deny it, the same race which I have always . . . Well, it's speaking mildly to say that I've always hated the Jews. Merely to scent a Jew was always to me like having an explosive stuck into my nerves. An immemorial crime is symbolized there, an ancient guilt; the Crucified One sighs across lands and ages to my ear. My blood rebels against the noblest of your race. It may be that I am the tool of an age-long lie; it may be that he who lacks the love that makes a priest acquires the stupidity and intolerance that mark the parson; it may be that our apparent enemies shall prove at last to be our brothers, and that Cain and Abel will clasp hands on Judgment Day. But it is part of my very being to nourish hatred when the roots of my life under the earth beyond my reach are crippled by the insolent growth of alien seedlings. And when one proposes to be my comrade and my neighbour, and yet meets me with the reserve of an alien soul—am I not to feel it and not to pay him back in the same coin? That is the way I've always felt. I never before knew a Jewish woman; and I cannot say that my feeling has undergone any essential change. Had it done so, I should suffer less. Oh, you are quite right to despise me on account of what I am saying; and, indeed, I am prepared to hear your contempt often. That is a part of my suffering. The first time I saw you I thought at once of Jephtha's daughter. She was, you remember, sacrificed by her father, because she happened to be the first to welcome him on his return home; for he had made a vow, and his daughter came to meet him with cymbals and with dancing. It is a profound notion—that notion of sacrificing the first one who comes to bid you welcome. And she must have been sweet and dainty—the daughter of Jephtha. She is to-day—experienced in dreams; rash where it is a matter of mere dreams; spoiled, incapable of any deed, submerging all enthusiasm and initiative in an exquisite yearning. The long wealth gathered by her ancestors has made her faint-hearted. She loves music and all that flatters the senses—delicate textures and beautiful words. She loves also the things that arouse and sting, but they must neither burden nor bind her. She loves the shiver of fear and of small intoxications; she loves to be tempted, to challenge fate, to put her little hand into the tiger's cage. But everything within her is delicate and in transition toward something—blossoming or decay. She is sensitive, without resistance, weary, and so full of subtle knowledge and various gropings that each desire in her negates another. Inbreeding has curdled her blood, and even when she laughs her face is touched with pain. And one day her father Jephtha, Judge in Israel, returns home and sacrifices her. Oh, I am sure he went mad after that."

Johanna's face was as pale as death. "That, I suppose, was a lesson in your admired science of psychiatry?" She forced herself to mockery.

Voss did not answer.

"Good-bye, you learned man." She walked to the door.

Voss followed her. "When are you coming again?" he asked softly.

She shook her head.

"When are you coming again?"

"Don't torment me."

"Wahnschaffe will be here the day after to-morrow. Will you come?"

"I don't know."

"Johanna, will you come?" He stood before her with uplifted hands, and the muscles of his cheeks and temples twitched.

"I don't know." She went out.

But he knew that she would come.

XIII

Between the acts of a dress rehearsal Lorm and Emanuel Herbst walked up and down in the foyer, discussing Lorm's rôle. " Hold yourself a little more in reserve." Herbst talked slightly through his nose. " And at the climax of the second act I expected a somewhat stronger emphasis. There's nothing else to criticize."

" Very well," said Lorm drily. " I'll stick on a little more grease-paint."

Many of the invited guests also walked through the curved passage way. Admiring glances followed Lorm. A girl approached him determinedly. She had evidently struggled with herself. She handed him a bunch of carnations, and silently withdrew, frightened by her own temerity.

" How nice of you! " Lorm exclaimed with kindliness, and stuck his nose into the flowers.

" Well, you old reveller, do the broken hearts taste as well as ever? " Herbst asked mockingly. " One is served at breakfast, too, isn't it? Or more than one? It makes an old codger like me feel sad."

" You can get too much of a good thing," said Lorm. " The poor dears go to excesses. Yes, early in the morning one will be trying to bribe the house attendants. When my chauffeur appears they flutter about him. Many of them know how I've planned my day and turn up at unexpected places—in an art dealer's shop, at my photographer's studio. I've been told of one poor girl who spent nights promenading in front of the house. When I was on tour there was one who followed me from town to town. And then there are all those unhappy letters. The amount of feeling that goes to waste, the confessions that are made, the intricate problems that are presented—you would be astonished. And all make the same naïve presumptions. I shouldn't care very greatly if this whole business didn't have its serious aspect. All these young creatures put their capital into an undertaking doomed to failure. It's bound to revenge itself. Clever people say that it doesn't matter what the young are enthusiastic about, if only they're enthusiastic about something. It isn't true. Decent young people shouldn't rave about an actor. Don't misunderstand me. I don't mean to belittle our profession; it has its definite merits. I don't want to display any false modesty about myself either. I know precisely what I am. The point is that those young people do not. They want me to be what I only represent. That is the height of absurdity. No, decent young people shouldn't adore an actor who is only a caricature of a hero."

" Well, well, well," said Emanuel Herbst, in a tone of soothing irony. " You're too severe and too pessimistic. I know a few rather authoritative persons who sincerely assign to you quite a high position among mortals. I'll not mention immortals in deference to your mood. And in your really lucid moments you're proud of your position, which is quite as it should be. What attitude does your wife take to your attacks of hypochondria? Doesn't she scold you? "

" It seems to me," Lorm said impassively, " that Judith has arrived on the other shore of her disillusion. In this dispute she would hardly take your side. My convictions have fallen on fertile ground in her case."

Emanuel Herbst rocked his head from side to side and protruded his nether lip. Lorm's tone made him anxious. " How is she anyhow? " he asked. " I haven't seen her for a long time. I heard she was ill."

" It's hard to say how she is," Lorm answered. " Ill? No, she wasn't ill, although she did spend a great deal of time in bed. There are a few middle-class women who've formed a kind of court about her. They give her all their time, and she's trained them marvellously. She says she's losing her slenderness, so she got a fashionable physician to prescribe a hunger cure. She follows the directions religiously.

But my house is in splendid condition. Tip-top. Why shouldn't it be? It's cleaned to the last corner twice a week. The cuisine is excellent, and I've got some rather nice things in my cellar. You must come and try them."

" All right, old man, you can count on me," said Emanuel Herbst. But his anxiety for his friend had grown with each word that Lorm had uttered. He knew that coldness which hid the most quivering sensitiveness, that princely smoothness beneath which great wounds were bleeding, that indeterminate element which was half spiritual malady, half an ascetic impulse. He was afraid of the destruction wrought by a worm in a noble fruit.

The signal sounded. A new act began. From the stage that voice of steel exerted its compelling resonance once more.

XIV

Johanna did come.

She had waited until it was quite late, in order to avoid waiting for Christian alone with Voss. When, after all, she found only Voss, she could not conceal her contempt. Her vexation made her face look old and peaked.

The weather was cold and wet. She sat down near the oven and put her hands against the tiles. She did not take off her coat. It was an ample, fur-trimmed garment with large buttons. She looked in it like a thin and hiding child. Nor did she raise her veil, which extended rather tautly from her wide-brimmed hat to her chin and accentuated the whiteness of her skin.

" You lied to me," she said harshly. " It was mere bait. You knew he wouldn't be here."

Voss answered: " What you have just said relegates me pretty clearly to a mere means to an end. What do you expect of a meeting with him anyhow? What is it to serve? Is it to revive memories or give the opportunity for an explanation? No, I know you're not fond of explanations. You like tension, provided your way of escape is ready for you. Very clever. I am to be at once the opportunity and the way of escape. Very clever. But why don't you simply go to him? Because, of course, you don't want to assume the psychical obligation implied in such a step. It might look as though you meant something; you are not sure how it would be interpreted. Your cowardice is almost funny. When it's convenient, you're a sensitive plant; when it's not, you're quite capable of putting your heel on some defenceless neck."

"This is intolerable," Johanna cried, and arose. "Don't you know that my being here compromises me more, especially in my own eyes, than anything else I could do?"

Voss was frightened. "Calm yourself," he said, and touched her arm. Recoiling from his touch she sank back into her chair. "Calm yourself," Voss repeated. "He promised definitely to be here; but he has many errands nowadays and has to meet many people and is constantly on the way from one place to another."

Johanna tormented herself. She was an experienced expert at it. She was glad when things went ill with her, when her hopes failed, when she was insulted or misunderstood. She was glad when the silk stocking into which she slipped her foot tore, when ink dropped on her paper, when she missed a train or found something for which she had paid generously prove worthless. It was a bitter, mischievous gladness, such as one feels at the absurd downfall of a hated rival.

It was this feeling that made her smile now. "I'm a charming creature, am I not?" she said, with a bizarre look and gesture.

Voss was disconcerted.

"Tell me about him," she said, half-defiantly, half-resignedly, and again pressed her hands against the tiles.

Amadeus looked upon her hands, which were bluish with cold. "You are cold," he murmured. "You are always cold."

"Yes, I'm always cold. There's not enough sunshine for me."

"People say that foundlings never get really warm; but you are no foundling. I imagine, on the contrary, that your childhood was a hotbed of carefulness. Undoubtedly the rooms were overheated, and hot-water bottles were put into your bed at night, and tonics were prescribed. Yet your soul froze all the more as the attempt was made to reach it through material things. You are no foundling in the body; your bourgeois descent is clear. But your soul is probably a foundling soul. There are such souls. They flutter yearningly up and down in space between heaven and hell, and their fate depends on whether an angel or a demon assigns them their earthly tabernacle. Most of them get into the wrong bodies. They are so anxious for a mortal form that they usually fall into the hands of a demon to whom they are tributary all their lives. Such are the foundling souls."

"Fantastic nonsense!" Johanna said. "You had better tell me something about him."

"About him? As I told you before, he is concerned in many different things. The woman Karen is ill, and will probably not get better. It is her rightful reward; vice demands the payment of its debt. You can find the sword foretold for such in Scripture. Well, he nurses her; he watches with her at night. Then there is a Jewish girl who lives in the house. He goes about with her to all sorts of people—a kind of suburban saint. Only he doesn't preach; preaching is not among his gifts. He is dumb, and that is a blessing. I have never sat so near to a woman," he went on in precisely the same tone, so as to prevent her interrupting him, "never at least to one who makes me feel that her very existence is a good. And one is so damnably in need of something pure, so filled with terrible longing for a human eye—to know none other regards you as she does. Almighty God, to lose for once the curse of my isolation! What is it that I ask? It is so little! Only not to sicken of my rage and famish of my thirst; once to lay my head into a woman's lap and feel nothing but the beloved night; and when the silence falls, to feel a hand in my hair and hear a word, a breath, and so to be redeemed! " His voice had grown softer and softer, and at last sank to a whisper.

"Don't . . . don't . . . don't," Johanna implored him, almost as softly. " Tell me about him," she went on hastily. " Does he really live in complete poverty? One hears so many things. Last week I was invited by some people, and the company talked of nothing else. Impudent and stupid as these parvenus of yesterday always are, they fairly outdid themselves. They joked about him and pitied his family, or even suggested that the whole thing was an imposture. My gorge rose. But I ask you this one thing: Why haven't I heard from you a single cordial word about him? Why nothing but venom and slander? You must know him. It is unthinkable that you really entertain the opinion of him by which you try to add to your self-importance in my eyes, and no doubt in the eyes of others. I assure you that there isn't the remotest chance of our really becoming friends, unless you're candid with me on this point."

For a long time Voss was silent. First he passed his handkerchief across his damp forehead. Then, bending far forward, he leaned his chin upon his folded hands, and looked upward through his glasses as though he were listening. " Friendship," he murmured in a sarcastic tone. " Friendship. I call that pouring water into the wine before the grapes have gone to the winepress." After a pause he spoke again. " I am not called to be his judge. At the beginning of our acquaintance it was given me to behold him with astonishment upon his pedestal. I kneeled in the mud and lifted my eyes as to a demigod. Then I kindled a little fire, and there was considerable smoke. But I would be a liar to assert that he did not stir me to the innermost soul. At times he so mastered

my evil and common instincts that when I was left alone I
cast myself down and wept. But love surrounded him and
hate surrounded me. Wherever he appeared love burst into
bloom; whatever I touched turned upon me in hatred. Light
and beauty and open hearts were about him; blackness and
humiliation and blocked paths were my portion. All good
spirits guarded him; I was fighting Satan, and out of my
darkness crying to God, who cast me off. Ay, cast me off and
rejected me, and set a mark of shame upon me, and pursued
me ever more cruelly, as my self-humiliation deepened and my
penitence grew tenser and my roots emerged more energetically
from the earth. Then it came to pass that he recognized a
brother in me. We passed an unforgettable night, and unforgettable words were exchanged between us. But love remained about him, and about me hate. He took my flame
from me, and carried it to men; and love was about him, and
about me was hate. He made a beggar of me, and gave me
hundreds of thousands; and love was about him, and about
me was hate. Do you think me so dull that I cannot measure
his deeds or their heavy weight and cost? The consciousness
of them steals into my sleep, and makes it terrible as an open
wound, so that I lie as among stinging nettles without heaven
or aspiration. Who would be so accursed a traitor to himself
that he would neither hear nor see the truth when it roars
like a flame of fire? But how about that brother in the dust?
The contrast was easier to bear while he dwelt amid the
splendours of the world. Now he goes and renounces, lives
amid want and stench, nurses a woman of the streets and
mingles with outcasts; and what is the result? Love grows
about him like a mountain. It is necessary to have experienced
and to have seen it. He comes into rooms out there, and all
glances cling to him and touch him tenderly; and each creature
seems fairer and better to itself while he is there. Is it magic?
But that mountain of love crushes me where I lie."

Again he dried his forehead. Johanna observed him attentively; at last an insight into his nature dawned in her.

"It is they who take the last step who are the chosen," Amadeus Voss continued. "Those like myself stop at the step before the last, and that is our purgatory. Perhaps Judas Iscariot could have done what the Master did, but the Master preceded him, and that doomed him to crime. He was alone. That is the solution of his mystery: he was alone. Just now, before you came, I was reading in a book the story of the marriage of Saint Francis to the Lady Poverty. Do you know it? 'Woe to him who is alone,' it says there. 'When he falls, he has no one to lift him up.'"

The book lay on the table. He took it up, and said: "Saint Francis had left the city, and met two old men. He asked them whether they could tell him the abode of Lady Poverty. Let me read you what the two old men answered."

He read aloud: "We have been here for a long time, and we have often seen her passing along this road. Sometimes she was accompanied by many, and often she returned alone without any companions, naked, devoid of dress and adornment, and surrounded only by a little cloud. And she wept very bitterly, and said: 'The sons of my mother have fought against me.' And we made answer: 'Have patience, for those who are good love thee.' And now we say to thee: Climb that high mountain among the holy hills which God has given her as a dwelling-place because He loves it more than all the dwelling-places of Jacob. The giants cannot approach its paths nor the eagles reach its peak. If thou wouldst go to her, strip off thy costly garments, and lay down every burden and every occasion of sin. For if thou art not stripped of these things, thou wilt never rise to her who dwells upon so great a height. But since she is kind of heart, they who love her see her without trouble, and they who seek her find her with ease. Think of her, brother, for they who yield themselves to her are safe. But take with thee faithful companions, with whom thou mayest take counsel when thou climbest the mountain, and who may be thy helpers. For woe to him who is alone. When he falls he has no one to lift him up."

His manner of reading tormented Johanna. There was a fanaticism in it from which her soul, attuned to semitones, shrank.

"Woe to him who is alone," said Voss. He kneeled down before Johanna. All his limbs trembled. "Johanna," he implored her, "give me your hand, only your hand, and have pity on me."

Her will failed her. More in consternation than obedience, she gave him her hand, which he kissed with a devouring passion. What he did seemed blasphemous and desperate after his words and his reading; but she dared not withdraw her hand.

Her watchful ear caught a noise. "Some one is coming," she whispered faintly. Voss arose. There was a knock at the door, and Christian entered.

He greeted them in a friendly way. His calm contrasted almost resonantly with Amadeus's wild distraction, for Voss could not control himself wholly. While Christian sat down at the table with the lamplight full upon his face, and looked now at Johanna, now at Voss, the latter walked excitedly up and down, and said: "We have been talking about Saint Francis, Fräulein Johanna and I."

Christian looked his surprise.

"I know nothing of him," he said. "All I remember is that once in Paris, at Eva Sorel's, some verses about him were read. Every one was delighted, but I didn't like the poem. I have forgotten why, but I recall that Eva was very angry." He smiled. "Why did you two talk about Saint Francis?"

"We were talking of his poverty," replied Voss, "and of his marriage to the Lady Poverty, as the legend has it. And we agreed that such things must not be translated into actual life, for the result would be falshood and misunderstanding. . . ."

"We agreed about nothing," Johanna interrupted him drily. "I am no support for any one's opinions."

"Never mind," said Voss, somewhat depressed. "It is a vision, a vision born of the sufferings of religious souls. That poverty, that sacred poverty is unthinkable except upon a Christian foundation. Whoever would dare to attempt it, and to turn backward the overwhelming stream of life in a distorted world, amid distorted conditions, where poverty means dirt and crime and degradation—such an one would only create evil and challenge humanity itself."

"That may be correct," said Christian. "But one must do what one considers right."

"It's cheap enough to take refuge in the purely personal when general questions are discussed," Voss said rancorously.

Johanna rose to say good-bye, and Christian prepared himself to follow her, since it was on her account that he had come. Voss said he would walk with them as far as Nollendorf Square. There he left them.

"It is hard for us to talk," said Christian. "There is much for which I should ask you to forgive me, dear Johanna."

"Oh," said Johanna, "it doesn't matter about me. I've conquered that. Unless I probe too deeply, even the pain is gone."

"And how do you live?"

"As best I can."

"You don't mind my calling you Johanna still, do you? Won't you come to see me some day? I'm usually at home in the evening. Then we could sit together and talk."

"Yes, I'll come," said Johanna, who felt her own embarrassment yielding before Christian's frank and simple tone.

While she was walking beside him and hearing and answering his direct and simple questions, all that had happened in the past seemed a matter of course, and the present seemed harmonious enough. But when she was alone again she was as vexed with herself as ever; the nearest goal seemed as irrational as the farthest, and the world and life shut in by dreariness.

Two days later she went to Christian's dwelling. The wife of the night watchman Gisevius ushered her into Christian's room. Shivering and oppressed by the room, in which she could not imagine him, she waited for over an hour. Frau Gisevius advised her to look in at Karen Engelschall's or the Hofmanns' flat. To this she could not make up her mind. " I'll come again," she said.

When she stepped out into the street she saw Amadeus Voss. He greeted her without words, and his expression seemed to take it for granted that they had agreed to meet here. He walked on at her side.

" I love you, Johanna," he said.

She did not answer, nor turn her eyes toward him. She walked more swiftly, then more slowly, then more swiftly again.

" I love you, Johanna," said Amadeus Voss, and his teeth rattled.

XV

On the alabaster mantelshelf candles were burning in the silver Renaissance candlesticks. The more salient light of the burning logs reached only far enough to envelop the figures of Eva and of Cornelius Ermelang in its glow. It did not penetrate as far as the porphyry columns or the gold of the ceiling. A dim, red flicker danced in the tall mirrors, and the purple damask curtains before the huge windows, which shut in the room more solemnly than the great doors, absorbed the remnants of light without reflection.

The tea-gown of white lace which the dancer wore—experts declared each square inch of it to have the value of a provincial governor's annual pay—was vivid as a fantastic pastel on the side turned to the fire.

"You have been very kind to me," said Eva. "After you had been here so many times in vain, I was afraid you would leave without having seen me. But Susan probably told you how my days are spent. Men and happenings whirl through them so that I find it hard to retain a consciousness of my own self. Thus friends become estranged, and the faces about me change and I hardly notice it. A mad life!"

"Yet you summoned me in spite of that," Ermelang whispered, "and I have the happiness of being with you at last. Now I have attained everything that my stay in Russia promised. How shall I thank you? I have only my poor words." He looked at her with emotion, with a kind of ecstasy in his watery blue eyes. He had a habit of repeating the formula concerning his poor words; but despite the artifices of his speech, his feeling was genuine. Indeed, there was always a trifle too much feeling, too much soulfulness in his speech. Sometimes the impression arose that he was in reality not quite so deeply stirred, and that, if necessary, he could well limit his emotional expansion.

"What would one not do to please a poet?" Eva said with a courteous gesture. "It is pure selfishness too. I would have the image of me made perpetual in your mind. Both ancient and modern tyrants assure us that the only man whom they strove to please is the poet."

Ermelang said: "A being like you exists in so elemental a fashion that any image is as negligible in comparison as the shadow of a thing when the sun is at its zenith."

"You are subtle. Yet images persist. I have so great a faith in your vision that I should like you to tell me whether I am really so changed as those friends assert who knew me in my Parisian days. I laugh at them; but in my laughter there is a little rebellion of my vanity and a little fear of withering and fading. Don't say anything; a contradiction would be trivial. Tell me, above all, how you came to be travelling in Russia, and what you have seen and heard and experienced."

" I have experienced very little. The total impression has been so unforgettable that details have faded into insignificance. Various difficulties made Paris unpleasant to me, and the Princess Valuyeff offered me a refuge on her estate near Petrograd. Now I must return to the West—to Europe, as the Russians mockingly say. And they are right. For I must leave my spiritual home-land, and people who were close to me, although I did not know them, and a loneliness full of melody and presage, and return to senseless noise and confusion and isolation. I have spoken to Tolstoi and to Pobiedonostzev; I have been to the fair at Nijni-Novgorod, and been driven across the steppe in a troika. And about all— the people and the landscape—there is a breath of innocence and of the times to come, of mystery and of power."

Eva had not listened very attentively. The hymns to Russia, intoned by wayfaring literary men and observers, began seriously to bore her. She made a faintly wry mouth. " Yes," she said, " it's a world all its own," and held out her lovely hands toward the warmth of the fire.

It seemed to Ermelang that she had never, in the old days, let some one to whom she was talking thus drift out of the circle of her mind. He felt that his words had had no friendly reception. He became diffident and silent. Guardedly he observed her with his inner eye, which was truly austere. He saw the change of which she had spoken, and recorded the image as she had demanded.

The oval of her face had acquired a line hardened as by the will. Nothing was left of goodness in it, little of serenity. An almost harsh determination was about her mouth. There were losses, too. Shadows lay on her temples and under her lids. Her body still betrayed her lordship over it, precisely in its flowing ease, its expansion and repose, such as one sees in wildcats. Ermelang had heard that she toiled unceasingly, spending six to seven hours a day in practice, as in the years of her apprenticeship. The result was evident in the satiation with rhythm and grace which her limbs and joints showed and her perfect control of them.

Yet nothing gracious, nothing of freedom came from her. Ermelang thought of the rumours that accused her of an unquenchable lust after power, of dangerous political plotting, fatal conspiracies, and a definite influence upon certain secret treaties that threatened to disquiet the nations, and of not being guiltless of journalistic campaigns that in their blended brutality and subtlety menaced the peace of Europe. It had seemed as though great coal deposits in the depth of the earth were on fire; but the men above still lived and breathed without suspicion.

Those who distrusted her declared her to be a secret agent of Germany, yet she enjoyed the friendship of French and British diplomatists. Her defenders asserted that she was used without her knowledge to cover the plans and guile of the Grand Duke Cyril. Those who believed in her wholly declared that she really crossed his plans and only feigned to be his tool. The nobility disliked her; the court feared her; the common people, goaded by priests and sectaries, saw in her the embodied misfortune of their country. At a rebellion in Ivanova she had been publicly proclaimed a witch, and her name had been pronounced accursed with solemn rites. Not later than the day before, a deputation of peasants from Mohilev, whom he had met in the fish market, had told him that they had seen the Tsar at Tsarskoye Selo, and in their complaints concerning the famine in their province had, in their stubborn superstition, pointed out the wicked splendour of the foreign dancer's life. It had become proverbial among them. The Tsar, they said, had been unable to give an answer, and had gazed at the floor.

All these things were incontrovertible parts of her life and fate. He looked upon her lovely hands, rosy in the glow of the flames, and felt a dread for her.

" Is it true," he asked, with a shy smile, " that you entered the forbidden fortress thrice in succession? "

" It is true. Has it been taken amiss? "

" It has certainly aroused amazement. No stranger has ever before crossed that threshold, nor any Russian unless he entered as a prisoner. No one seems able to fathom your impulse. Many suppose that you merely wanted to see Dmitri Sheltov, who fired at the Grand Duke. Tell me your motive; I should like to have a reply to the gossips."

" They need no reply," Eva said. " I do not fear them, and need no defence. I don't know why I went. Perhaps I did want to see Sheltov. He had insulted me; he even took the trouble to publish a broadside against me. Five of his friends were sent to Siberia for that—boys of sixteen and seventeen. The mother of one of the boys wrote me a letter imploring me to save him. I tried but failed. Perhaps I really wanted to see Dmitri Sheltov. They say that he has vowed to kill Ivan Becker."

" Sheltov is one of the purest characters in the world," Ermelang said very softly. " To force a confession from him, they beat him with whips."

Eva was silent.

" With whips," Ermelang repeated. " This man! And men still dare to laugh and speak, and the sun to shine."

" Perhaps I wanted to see a man writhing under the blows of the knout," Eva said. " Perhaps it meant much to me as a stimulus. I must be nourished somehow, and the uncommon is my nourishment. A strange twitching, an original posture in crouching—such things satisfy my imagination. But as a matter of fact "—her voice grew sombre, and she stared fixedly at a spot on the wall—" I did not see him at all. But I saw others who have spent ten, twelve, fifteen years in dark cells of stone. Once they moved about in the great world and busied their minds with noble things; now they cower in their rags, and blink at the light of a little lantern. They have forgotten how to look, to walk, to speak. An odour of decomposition was about them, and all their gestures were full of a gentle madness. But it was not for their sake either that I went. I went for the sake of the imprisoned women, who, on account of an intellectual conviction, have been torn from love and life and motherhood and devotion, and condemned to death by slow torture. Many of them had never been condemned by any tribunal. They had merely been forgotten—simply forgotten; and if their friends were to demand a trial, the same fate would threaten them. I saw one who had been brought in when she was a girl; now she was an aged woman and near her death. I saw Natalie Elkan, who was violated by a colonel of gendarmes at Kiev, and killed the monster with his own sword. I saw Sophie Fleming, who put out her own eyes with a piece of steel wire, because they had hanged her brother in her presence. Do you know what she said when I entered her cell? She lifted her blind face, and said: ‘That's the way a lady smells.’ Ah, that taught me something concerning women. I put my arms about her and kissed her, and whispered in her ear, asking whether I should smuggle some poison to her; but she refused.”

Eva arose and walked up and down. “Yes,” she said, “and still men speak and laugh, and still the sun shines. This room is filled with precious things. Lackeys stand on the stairs. Fifty feet from here is the bed of state in which I sleep. It is all mine. What I touch is mine, what I glance at is mine. They would give me the round earth itself if they had it to give and I asked it. And I would cast it like a billiard-ball into a noisome puddle, so that it might no longer defile the home of stars with its filth and its torments. I am so full of hate! I no longer know where to hide it or how to be redeemed from it! I no longer believe in anything—neither in art, nor in poets, nor in myself. I only hate and destroy. I am a lost soul! "

Ermelang folded his hands. " Wonderful as you are, you should remember all you have given and to how many."

Eva stood still. " I am a lost soul. I feel it."

" Why lost? You are playing a sad game with yourself."

She shook her head and whispered the verses of the *Inferno:*

> " O Simon mago, o miseri seguaci,
> Che le cose di Dio, che di bontate
> Deono essere spose, e voi rapaci
> Per oro e per argento adulterate." [1]

Thoughtfully Ermelang added:

> " Fatto v'avete Dio d'oro e d'argento;
> E che altro è da voi all'idolatre,
> Se non ch'egli uno, e voi n'orate cento? " [2]

" What is that I hear? " Eva asked, and listened. Raucous and angry voices were heard from the street, and yells and hisses. Ermelang listened too. Then he went to the window, pushed the draperies aside, and looked out.

On the snow-covered street in front of the palace fifty or sixty mujiks had assembled. One could clearly distinguish their sheepskin caps and their long coats. They stood there silently and gazed up at the windows. They had attracted a great crowd of people, men and women, and these gesticulated, full of hatred, and seemed to urge the mujiks on.

" I believe those are the Mohilev peasants," Ermelang said nervously. " I saw them march through the city yesterday."

Eva joined him for a moment at the window, and glanced

---

[1] " O Simon Magus, O forlorn disciples,
Ye who the things of God, which ought to be
The brides of holiness, rapaciously
For silver and for gold do prostitute."

[2] " Ye have made yourselves a god of gold and silver;
And from the idolater how differ ye,
Save that he one, and ye a hundred worship? "

out; then she returned to the middle of the room. Her smile was contemptuous. At that moment Susan Rappard came in, badly frightened. " There are people downstairs. Pierre went out to ask them what they wanted. They want to talk to you; they beg humbly to be admitted to your presence. What are we to answer such riffraff? I've telephoned police headquarters. Good heavens, what a country, what an abominable country! "

Eva lowered her eyes. " They are very poor people, Susan," she said. " Give them money. Give them all the money that is in the house."

" Nonsense! " Susan cried, horrified. " Then the next time they'll break down the door and rob us."

" Do as I tell you," Eva replied. " Go to M. Labourdemont and tell him to let you have all available cash. Then go out and take it to them. No, you had better send some one who can speak to them, and let him say that I have gone to bed and cannot receive them. And telephone the police at once and assure them that we have no need of protection. Do you understand? "

". Yes," said Susan and went out.

The crowd had increased, the noise grew, and drunken men yelled. Only the peasants remained silent. The oldest of them had come to the edge of the sidewalk. A little white lump of snow lay on his cap, and to his beard clung snow and ice. Pierre, the doorkeeper, in his livery set with silver tresses, was facing him arrogantly. The old peasant bowed low while the lackey spoke.

Eva turned to Ermelang. " Good-bye, dear friend. I am tired. Guard this hour in your memory, but forget it when you speak of me to others. The innermost things are revealed to but one. Good night."

When Ermelang reached the door of the palace, he saw a troop of mounted police appear at the other end of the street. The crowd melted away with an agility that showed long

experience. It took but a minute. Only the peasants remained.
Ermelang did not know whether money had been given them
as Eva had commanded. He did not care to witness the play of
crude force that was sure to occur on the arrival of the armed
men.

XVI

Ruth hurried home. Every Sunday afternoon her father
was accustomed to spend a few hours with her. She was
surprised not to find him in the flat. A letter lay on the
table addressed: "To my children."

The letter read: "Dear daughter and dear son: I must
leave you, and only Almighty God knows when I shall see
you again. I have hesitated, and I have fought against my
decision, but it is made at last. I am no longer equal to the
struggle of existence under the circumstances which obtain.
To get ahead in Berlin a man needs iron fists and an iron
forehead. I am no longer young enough to push all obstacles
brutally out of the way, so utter destitution threatens us.
Instead of being your protector and provider, I am faced by
the terrible possibility of becoming a burden to you, Ruth,
and your exertions are even now superhuman. I have often
been attracted by the thought of putting an end to my life;
but my religion as well as my concern for my children's
memory of me has kept me alive. I have found a friend, a
fellow Jew, who has persuaded me to emigrate to America.
He is advancing me the money for the voyage, and is hopeful
of our success. Perhaps fate will relent to me at last. Perhaps
my terrible sacrifice in leaving you two in uncertainty and
want will move it to pity. I see no other way of saving
myself from certain destruction. Only because I know your
strength of soul, dear Ruth, only because I have the firm
faith that some kind angel watches over you, do I venture
upon this difficult and bitter step. I must not and dare not
think. You are so young, both of you, and without pro-

tection or friends or kinsmen. Perhaps God will forgive me and protect you. I could bear no farewell but this. If I have anything good to report I shall write. Then you, too, must let me hear. I am inclosing fifty marks for your immediate needs; I cannot spare more. The rent for November is paid. Six marks and fifty pfennigs are due to the shoemaker Rösicke. With all my heart I embrace you both. Your unhappy Father."

Ruth wept.

She had been sitting still for a whole hour, when she heard a knocking at the door. She thought it was Michael. She was a little afraid of his coming, and in her need of a confidant she hoped deeply that it was Christian Wahnschaffe.

It was neither. She opened the door, and saw a ragged girl accompanied by a dog, a butcher's dog, big as a calf, with a horribly smooth, gleaming, black and white skin.

Ruth kept her hand on the door-knob while she asked the girl, who might have been anything from twelve to twenty, what she wanted. The dog had an evil glare.

The girl quietly handed her a piece of paper. It was greasy and covered with the writing of some illiterate. Ruth was frightened, and thought: " All bad news comes in writing to-day." She had not yet read the writing on the paper, but she felt that it boded some evil.

For a moment she looked out through the hall window that framed a group of black chimneys. The uncanny dog growled.

The writing on the paper was difficult to decipher. She read: " You must plese come rite away to somebody what is terrible bad of. He has took poisen it is killing him and he has got to tel you something before he dis. He is in the back room of Adeles Rest a wine room Prenzlaur Alley 112 in the yard to the left. Plese come rite away with the girl and god wil reward you. Plese for gods sake do come."

" What is the matter? What can I do? " Ruth whispered.

The girl shrugged her shoulders. As though she were dumb, she pointed to the piece of paper.

She was full of foreboding and of an inner warning, full of pain over the letter and the flight of her father, and full of horror of the butcher's dog. She was undecided, looked at the paper, and stammered: " I don't know . . . I ought to wait for Michael . . . Who is it . . . He should have given his name."

The girl shrugged her shoulders.

It seemed to Ruth that it would be wrong to disregard this cry for help. The bloodshot eyes of the dog were fixed upon her. Never had she seen an animal that seemed so naked. She put her hand over her forehead and tried to gather her troubled thoughts. She went back into the room and looked about. It seemed very lonely and bare. She slipped into her little coat and put on her hat. A faint smile gleamed for a moment on her face, as though she were glad to have come to a decision. She ran her eyes over the writing once more. " Plese for gods sake do come." One's duty seemed quite clear.

For a little she held her father's letter uncertainly in her hand. Then she folded it again, and laid it on the table beside her slightly disordered books and writing utensils. She closed the books that were open, and made a little pile of them. The dog had noiselessly followed her into the room. It followed her as she left. On the door there hung by a string a little slate and a slate pencil. Ruth wrote: " I'll be back soon. Have gone to Prenzlauer Alley. Wait for me. I must talk to you about something important." She locked the door and hid the key under the door-mat of straw.

The strange girl preserved her sleepy indifference.

On the stairs Ruth bethought herself, and knocked at Karen's door. If Christian were there, she could say a few words to him; but no one opened. She thought that Karen was asleep, and did not ring. As she descended the stairs behind the girl and the naked dog the new responsibilities and problems of her life came into her mind. But in Ruth's young and intrepid heart, confusions grew clear and difficult things lost their terror.

In the lower hall she hesitated for a last time. She wanted to stop at Gisevius's to see if Christian were there. But two old women were reviling each other loudly and filthily in the yard, and she went on.

It was raining. It was Sunday afternoon, a time of ghastly dreariness in Stolpische Street. There was quiet under the grey November sky, save for a hum from the public houses. The pale street-lamps flickered in the twilight.

" Let us go, then," Ruth said to the girl.

The naked dog trotted between them on the wet pavement.

XVII

Crammon had written as follows to the Countess Brainitz: " Since I have pledged my word, of course I shall come. But I beg you to have the kindness to prepare Letitia in some appropriate way. As the fatal moment approaches I feel more and more uncomfortable. It is a very difficult act of expiation that you demand of me. I would rather make a pilgrimage to Mount Ararat and become a hermit there for a few years and seek for the remains of Noah's ark. I grant you that I have always enjoyed the delights that came to me without scruple; but it does not seem to me that I have deserved this. It is too much."

The countess replied that she would do her utmost to mitigate the painfulness of the meeting. She had no objection to the dear child's weeping on her bosom, before facing a father who admitted his fatherhood with so many hesitations and fears. "And so, Herr von Crammon," she wrote at the end of her letter, " we are expecting you. Letitia has returned from Paris more enchanting than ever. All the world is at her feet. I trust you will not be an exception."

" The devil take her! " Crammon growled, as he packed his bags.

When he arrived at the countess's country-house, which was called the Villa Ophelia, he was told that the ladies had gone to the theatre. He was taken to the room that had been prepared for him. He washed, dressed for dinner, strolled back to the drawing-room, stuck his hands deep into his pockets like a shivering tramp, and dropped morosely into an easy chair. He heard the rain plash, and from another room the crying of an infant. " Aha," he thought, in his vexation, " that is my grandchild, one of the twins. How do I know that some misguided creature won't put it on my knee, and ask me to admire and pet and even kiss it? Who, I say, will protect me from a bourgeois idyl of that sort? You might expect anything of a woman like the countess. These sentimental actresses who refuse to grow old are capable of anything. Is there anything more annoying in the world than a baby? It is neither a human being nor an animal; it smells of cow-udders and scented powder, and makes an insufferable and repulsive noise. It pokes its limbs into the faces of older persons; and if there are two of them, and all these horrors assail one doubly, one is apt to be quite defence-less, and may fairly inquire: ' What have you, Bernard Cram-mon, whose interest in the propagation of the race has always been strictly negative—what have you to do with such things? ' "

Crammon ended his reflections with a smile of self-mockery. At that moment he heard cheerful voices, and Letitia and the countess entered.

He arose with exquisite chivalry. He was most friendly and most polished.

He did not conceal his astonishment over Letitia's appear-ance. His Austrian delight in feminine charm and his im-pulse to do homage to it scattered the fog of his egotistical vexation. Either, he thought, his memory was playing him false, or else Letitia had undergone a marvellous development since the days at Wahnschaffe Castle. Crude young girls had never, to be sure, attracted him. The women whom he admired and courted had to be rich in knowledge and responsible, for that eased his own responsibility.

After the first greetings the countess spoke. " Dear people," she said, with her North German readiness to meet all occasions, " I must leave you for half an hour now. A theatre is a grimy place. I must wash my hands. Everything about it is grimy—the seats, the spectators, the actors, and the play. It always gives me a yearning for soap and water. You can use the time to chat a bit. Afterwards we'll have supper."

She rustled out, not without having cast a severe glance at Crammon.

Crammon asked thoughtfully: " I wonder why she called this building the Villa Ophelia. There are many inexplicable things in life. This is one of them."

Letitia laughed. She regarded him with a mixture of irony and shyness. But as she stood before him in her frock of soft, pale yellow silk, her neck and bosom radiating an ivory shimmer, Crammon found it difficult to sustain his self-pity. Letitia approached him, and said archly yet with feeling: " So you are my papa. Who would have thought it? It must have been quite unpleasant for you to have an old, forgotten sin suddenly transformed into a great girl."

Crammon chuckled, although a shadow still lay on his face. He took her hand into both of his and pressed it warmly. " I see that we understand each other," he said, " and that consoles me. What I feared was an outburst and tears and the emotional display that is considered fitting. It is so nice of you to be sensible. But let us sacrifice something to the ceremonial tradition of the emotions. I shall imprint a paternal kiss upon your brow."

Letitia inclined her head, and he kissed her. She said: " We share a delightful secret now. How shall I call you in company —Uncle, or Uncle Crammon, or Uncle Bernard, or simply Bernard? "

" Simply Bernard, I'm sure," Crammon replied. " I need not remind you, of course, that you are legally the daughter of the late Herr von Febronius and of his late wife. Our situation demands of us both the most delicate tactfulness."

" Certainly," Letitia agreed, and sat down. " But just fancy the dangers that lurk in this world. Suppose I hadn't known anything and had fallen in love with you. How horrible! And I must tell you at once that I don't seem to revere you a bit. My feeling is rather sisterly, and I'm sure that I like you very, very much. Will you be satisfied with that, or is it terribly unfilial? "

" It quite suffices," said Crammon. " I can't indeed impress on you too strongly the wisdom of emotional frugality. Most people carry their feelings about the way the Ashanti women do their glass beads. They rattle them in public, and never realize what very ordinary stuff they are. But that is by the way. For our relations we must have a very special programme. This is important in order to ward off the intrusion of outsiders. I am—it goes without saying—at your service at any time and in any way. You may rely wholly upon my friendship, upon my . . . let us use the odious word—paternal friendship."

Letitia was immensely amused at his grave and anxious zeal to gain what easements the situation permitted. She was quite worthy of him in the capacity for a certain hypocrisy. Beneath her charming expression and her innocent appearance of pliability, she hid a good deal of mockery and not a little self-will. She answered: " There's no reason why we should limit each other's freedom. We shall not stand in each other's way, nor become unduly indebted to each other. Each has the right to assume the other's confidence, and thus to preserve his freedom of action. I hope that that suits you."

"You are a very determined little person, and I took you to be foolishly enthusiastic and fanciful. Did the cattle drivers in the land of fire sharpen your wits? Yes, it suits me; it suits me admirably."

"There is so much ahead of me," Letitia continued, and her eyes glowed with desires and dreams, "I hardly know how I shall get through it all—people, countries, cities, works of art. I've lost so much time and I'm nearly twenty-one. Auntie wants me to stay with her, but that's impossible. I'm expected in Munich on the first of December and in Meran on the tenth. In Paris it was divine. The people were perfectly charming to me. Every one wanted me at once."

"I quite believe it, quite," said Crammon, and rubbed his chin. "But tell me, how did that adventure with the vicomte end that the countess told me about?"

"Oh, did she tell you about it?" Letitia blushed. "That wasn't very discreet." For a moment her face showed an expression of sorrow and of embarrassment. But unhappy experiences, even when they made their way into her consciousness, could not really darken it. In a moment her eyes were again full of laughter. All dark memories had fled. "Take me on a motor drive to-morrow, won't you, Bernard," she urged him, and stretched out her hands impulsively. "And you must invite the little Baron Rehmer who lives in the Grand Hotel. He's Stanislaus Rehmer, the Polish sculptor. He's going to model me and teach me Polish. He's a charming person."

Crammon interrupted her: "Explain one thing to me! Tell me what is happening in the Argentine. Hasn't that blue-skinned bandit in whom you once saw the essence of all manly virtues taken any steps against you? You don't imagine, do you, that he will simply stand by while you take French leave with his double offspring? As for me, I wouldn't have shared

the same board with him, far less the same bed. But that
was not your opinion, and the law doesn't consider fluctuations
of taste."

"He's brought a suit for divorce against me, and I've entered a countersuit," Letitia said. "I've seen mountains of
documents. The children are mine, since he forced me to flight
by his extreme cruelty. I'm not worried about it a bit."

"Does he pay you an income?"

"Not a penny so far."

"Then how do you live? You're obviously not retrenching.
Where does the money come from? Who pays for all these
luxuries? Or is it all a sham with a background of debts?"

Letitia shrugged her shoulders. "I hardly know," she answered, with some embarrassment. "Sometimes I have money
and sometimes I haven't any. Poor auntie sold a few old
Dutch pictures that she had. One can't spend one's life reckoning like a shopkeeper. Why do you talk of such horrid
things?" There was such sincere pain and reproachfulness in
her voice that Crammon felt like a sinner. He looked aside.
Held by her charm, he lost the courage to burden her farther
with coarse realities. And now, too, the countess appeared in
the room. She had put on gloves of gleaming white, and her
face glowed like freshly scrubbed porcelain. In her arms she
carried Puck, the little Pekingese, who had grown old and slept
much.

"My dears, supper is served," she cried, with the slightly
stagy cheeriness of her youth.

XVIII

Karen believed that, in his own mind, Christian expected
her to pay some attention to her child. She had secretly written
to her mother, but no answer had come.

Christian had never mentioned the child. He did not expect
to find any softening in Karen. Her behaviour gave no sign
of any.

But brooding in her bed she wondered both what Christian expected of her and what had become of her child. Occasionally a glassy clinking could be heard. It came from the pearls. She would reach for them to assure herself of their presence. When she felt them, a smile of mysterious well-being appeared on her face.

For three days Christian had not been out of his clothes. He fell asleep in a corner of the sofa. Since morning a formless disquietude had possessed him.

Isolde Schirmacher, noisily bringing in Karen's soup, wakened him. He put the chairs in their places, cleared the table of his books, put the checked cover on it, and opened the window. "It's Sunday," he said.

"I don't want soup," Karen grumbled.

"And I went and made it for you extry," Isolde whined, "and a pork fricassee and all. You never want nothing."

"Eat the stuff yourself," Karen said spitefully.

Isolde carried the soup out again.

"Can't you close the window?" Karen whined. "Why do you always have to open it? A person can freeze to death."

Christian closed the window.

"I'd like to know why she carried the soup out again," Karen said after a while. "That'd suit her, to gorge herself on what's meant for me. I'm hungry."

Christian went to the kitchen and brought in the soup. He sat down beside her bed, and held the plate in both hands while she laboriously ate the soup. "It's hot," she moaned, and pressed her head against the pillows. "Open the window so's I can get a bit of air."

He opened the window. Karen looked at him with a dull wonder in her eyes. His patience was unfathomable to her. She wanted to get him to the point of scolding and showing her her place.

During the night she would make twenty demands and then reverse them with embittered impatience. His kindliness remained uniform. It enraged her; she wanted to scream. She cried out to him: "What kind of a man are you, for God's sake?" She shook her fists.

Christian did not know what to answer.

At two o'clock Dr. Voltolini arrived. The clinical assistant who had examined Karen at Ruth's request had no time to make regular visits, so Ruth had suggested that Voltolini, whom she knew, be permitted to continue the treatment.

Karen refused to answer nearly all his questions. Her hatred of physicians dated from her experiences on the streets.

"I hardly know what attitude to take," Dr. Voltolini said to Christian, who accompanied him to the stairs. "There's an incomprehensible stubbornness in her. If I didn't want to accommodate you, I would have given up the case long ago." He had been deeply charmed by Christian, and often observed him tensely. Christian did not notice this.

He reproached Karen for her behaviour.

"Never mind," she said curtly. "These doctors are swindlers and thieves. They speculate on people's foolishness. I don't want him to lay his hand on me. I don't want him to listen to my heart so I can smell his bald head, or tap me all over and look like an executioner. I don't need him if I'm going to live, and less if I've got to die."

Christian did not answer.

Karen crouched in her bed. She suffered from pain to-day. A saw seemed to be drawn up and down between her ribs. She went on: "I'd like to know why you bother to study medicine. Tell me that. I've never asked you anything, but I'd like to know. What attracts you about being a saw-bones? What good will you get out of it?"

Christian was surprised at her insistent tone and at the glitter in her eyes. He tried to tell her, arguing clumsily. He talked to her as to an equal, with respect and courtesy. She did not wholly understand the sense of his words, but she thrust her head far forward, and listened breathlessly.

Christian said that it was not the study itself that had attracted him, but the constant contact with human beings into which it brought you. Then, too, there was the natural temptation to choose a study the length of which could be shortened by bits of knowledge that he already had. When he first determined to take it up, he had also thought of its practical usefulness to him. That thought he had now abandoned. He had believed that he might earn his livelihood by practising medicine; but he had been forced to the conclusion that he was morally incapable of earning money by any means. He had reached this conclusion not long since. He had gone to visit the student Jacoby and found him out. Just then a child of the landlady had fallen from a ladder and become unconscious. He had carried the child into the room, rubbed it with alcohol, listened to its heart, and stayed with it a while. When the child had quite recovered and he himself had been ready to go, the mother had pressed a two-mark piece into his hand. He had had the impulse to laugh into the woman's face. He hadn't been able to realize the cause of his shame, but the sense of it had been so strong as to make him dizzy. And that incident had taught him the impossibility of his taking money for services.

Even while he was speaking, it came to him that this was the first time he had ever talked to Karen about himself. It seemed quite easy to do so, because of the solemn attention with which she listened and which changed her whole expression. It seemed to rejuvenate him. A sense of well-being surged through him, a peculiar joy that seemed to affect his very skin. He had never known a joy like that. It was a new feeling.

And so he continued more freely—quite frankly and without reserve. Science, he told her, was rather indifferent to him in itself. He valued it as a means to an end. He didn't know whither it would lead him. The future had grown less rather than more clear to him recently. At first, as he had told her, he thought that he might enter a profession and practise it like most young men. In that hope he had been disappointed. Nevertheless he knew that he was fundamentally on the right track. It was a time of preparation for him, and every day was enriching him. He got a great deal closer to people now, and saw them without pretence and falseness. In a hospital dormitory, in the waiting-room of a clinic, in the operating room, in the presence of hundreds of sufferers—in such scenes all hypocrisy died; there truth gripped one, and one understood what one had never understood before, and one could read the open book of life. Tubercular children, scrofulous children, large-eyed children beholding death—whoever had not seen that had not yet truly lived. And he knew whence they came and whither they went and what they said to one another, these fathers and mothers and strange crowds, and how each human creature was supremely interesting and important to itself. No horror frightened him any more, no wound, no terrible operative incision; he could see such things quite coldly now; he had even thought of volunteering for service in the lepers' colony in East Prussia. But his urge was toward deeper and ever deeper abysses of life. He was never satisfied. He wanted to steep himself in humanity. There were always new horrors behind the old, other torment beyond any he had seen; and unless he could absorb all that into himself, he had no peace. Later he hoped to find still other ways. He was only practising upon sick bodies; later he would sink himself into sick souls. But it was only when he had unveiled something secret and hidden that his heart felt free and light.

Resting her arms on the edge of the bed and bending over far, Karen watched him with avid wonder. She understood and yet did not understand. At times she caught the drift, at times the sense of the words themselves. She nodded and brooded, contorted her mouth and laughed silently and a little wildly; she held her breath, and had a dim vision of him at last, of this noble and strange and beautiful being who had been utterly mysterious to her to this very hour. She saw him as he was, and it seemed to her as though she were in the midst of a flaming fire. It made her desperate that she had to be so silent, that she was so like stone within, that she had no words at her command, not one, that she could not even say: " Come to me, brother." For he was of flesh like her own; and that made her feel alive. She felt gratitude as she had before felt despair and weariness, disgrace and hatred. Her gratitude was like a flame cleansing her wilderness, and it was also a great urge and a woeful joy, and at last again despair. For she felt that she was dumb.

Christian left in strange haste. Karen called in Isolde Schirmacher, and told the girl she was free for the evening. She got up and dressed slowly and painfully. She could hardly stand, and the room whirled around with her. The table seemed to cling to the ceiling and the oven to be upside down. But at each step she trod more firmly. She hid the pearls in her bosom. She faltered down the stairs, and strange colours flickered before her eyes. But she wanted to do something for him. That thought drove her onward. She wanted to drag herself to a cab and drive to her mother and ask: " Where is the child? Where did you take it? " And if the old woman was impudent, she meant to clutch her and strangle her till she told the truth.

To do something for him! To prove to him that there was a Karen whom he did not know.

She crept along the walls of the houses.

Christian was just coming back when a policeman and a working man, followed by an idle crowd, half led, half carried her home. He was confounded. She was white as chalk. They laid her on the bed. Since Isolde was not there, Christian knocked at the door of the Hofmann flat to ask Ruth to help him with Karen. But he caught sight of the little slate, and read the message that Ruth had left for her brother.

The chaotic unrest that he had felt all day rose more power-fully within his soul.

XIX

And now things had gone so far with Johanna that she had given herself to him whom she despised. At last she had the valid proof of her own feebleness of soul. She needed no longer to fear an inner voice that would defend her, nor any hope that might counsel her to guard herself. It was superfluous now to spare her body, and no longer necessary to keep up the little self-deceptions that bolstered up her brittle pride. She was unmasked in her own eyes, and, in a sense so different from the ordinary moral one, dishonoured . . . dis-honoured for all time and all eternity . . . branded. . . . She had become what she had always suspected herself capable of becoming. Things were settled.

From the moment that he had waited for her in the street that day, Amadeus Voss had not left her side. From time to time he had repeated with mad monotony: "I love you, Johanna." She had made no reply. With compressed lips and lowered eyes she had walked on and on, for more than an hour. The fear of human glances and human presences had kept her from fleeing by tram. Furthermore it was he who chose their path by a silent command. At last he had stopped in front of a little coffee-house. He neither asked her nor invited her in. He took it for granted that she would follow, and she did.

In a dim corner they sat facing each other. He took out a pencil and drew mystic symbols on the marble top of the table. This oppressive state of silence had lasted nearly half an hour. At last he had spoken: "To utter the word 'love' is to become guilty of an enormous triviality. It has been flattened out and savours of cheap fiction. Speak it and you become secondhand. The feeling is unique, incomparable, strange, and wondrous—an unheard-of adventure, a dream of

dreams. The word is a base sound taken from a tattered
reader. But how shall one communicate with another when the
feeling strangles and shakes you, and your days are the days
of a madman? I came to the age of twenty-six without
knowing this magic and this wonder. No hand was stretched
out toward me, no eye sought me out, and so I looked with
hatred upon all who were in the grip of what seemed to be
a blasphemous passion. Among the playmates of my childhood little erotic friendships were common. Every boy had
his little sweetheart with whom he flirted instinctively and
yet innocently. I excluded myself from all that and hated. On
Sunday afternoon they would stroll out beyond the village.
I would follow some couple, and if the boy and girl sat down
somewhere to chat, I would observe them from some ambush
with rage and bitterness. You have a keen enough insight to
realize how I felt then and later and until this very day.
Longing—yes, well, that's another of those pale, drained con-
cepts. Occasionally I stretched out my hand in my confusion
and my cowardly desire, and trembled when a woman's sleeve
brushed mine. I became the fool of one who sought to trap
me, and I let the accursed dancer poison my blood. Sometimes I flung myself into the gutter, and became defiled merely
to silence the pitiless voice of nature, which is a heritage of the
Evil One and the work of Satan."

She had not raised her eyes from the table, and the
hieroglyphs covered half of its top. "I won't make any
promises in the name of my so-called love," he continued,
and his bowed face became a mask of pain. "I don't know
whither it will lead either me or her who elects to be mine.
To be mine—that has a sound of horror, hasn't it? All I
can say is that that woman will contribute to my salvation
and redeem me from torment. You may reply: 'What have
I to do with your salvation or with the torments of a lost
soul?' Very well. Let us not bring that in. But consider
whether in all the world there is another man whom you can

win wholly, utterly, body and soul? Every step and every breath of yours is infinitely precious to me; there is an equal life and loveliness to me in the lashes of your eyes and the hem of your garment. I am within your very body, and throb in the pulsing of your heart. There is a fear that one feels of one's own heart-beats; and there is one that is felt of another's. Shall I use more words? These are enough. All words are unholy, and creep on the fringe of experience."

The woman in Johanna had succumbed. A terrible curiosity had enslaved her. Because all that she was and did seemed unnatural and distorted to her, and because she was weary and sore, she let herself glide into those desperately out-stretched arms.

She seemed to fall into a depth where heat and glow corroded what they touched. Shattering ecstasy and crushing weariness alternated. Scenes pallid and terrible flitted by as on the screen of a cinematograph, and the hours raced to their hideous death.

She wrote to her sister in Bucharest: " You're so very near the Orient, and I've always been told that it is full of mighty wizards. Couldn't you, please, use your well-tried charms to get the better of one of them, and steal from him some magic formula by virtue of which one can lose the consciousness of one's self? Mine, you see, is quite ragged and tattered. And if I could exchange it for a nice, new, fashionable one, I'd be helped so much! I could marry a nice Jewish manufacturer and have babies and eat chocolates and flirt with the *jeunesse dorée* and realize similar ideals. I beseech you, Clarisse, find me a wizard—young or old, it doesn't matter. But I must have a wizard to be saved."

XX

At eight o'clock in the evening Christian knocked at Ruth's door again. No one answered. He was surprised.

He knew that the key was put under the door-mat when no one was at home. He raised the mat and saw the key. Then he went back to Karen's rooms.

She seemed to be sleeping. Her face was like a piece of chalk. Her strawy hair, like a flaming helmet, contrasted in ghastly fashion with that pallor. After she had lain rigid for a while, she had undressed herself and crept back into bed.

Christian listened at the wall again and again, trying to catch some voice, some sign of life from the Hofmann flat. Silence. When two hours had passed, he took a lighted candle and stepped out into the hall. The key was still under the mat.

He thought he heard a sound of lamentation in the air. He did not think he had the right to unlock the door and enter the flat. And yet, after he had stood there for some time in indecision, he slipped the key into the keyhole and opened the door.

A breath of melancholy came from the empty room. He put the candle on the table and caught sight of Hofmann's letter of farewell. He hesitated to read it. He thought he heard steps and stopped to listen. The feeling that the letter would explain Ruth's absence finally decided him to read it.

The letter seemed to him to remove all doubt. She had probably thought her father still in the city, and set out to find him and dissuade him from his plan. The acquaintance with whom she had hoped to find him probably lived in Prenzlauer Alley, and Michael, when he had read her message, had probably hurried on to the same place.

Although this reasoning seemed plausible enough, his imagination was unsatisfied. He looked questioningly at the furniture and the walls, and touched with tenderness the books on the table that Ruth had so recently had in her hands. He left the room, locked the door, hid the key under the mat, and returned to Karen's rooms.

He blew out the light and lay down on the sofa. These

nights of brief and light slumber were exhausting him. His cheeks were thin, his profile peaked, his lids inflamed, and his brain morbidly tense.

The house, sunk into the treacherous immobility of its nights, appeared to him in the guise of a monstrous skeleton, consisting of countless walls and beds and doors steeped in malodorous darkness. Yet he loved it—loved the shabby stairs, the weather-beaten walls and posts, the fires in its many hearths that he had seen in passing, the emaciated woman who, in some room, scolded her wailing babe to sleep. He loved the manifold disconsolateness of these tangled lives; he loved the withered, sooty little flowerpots by the court windows, the yellow apples on the shelves, the scraps of paper in the halls, the very refuse that dishevelled women carried in troughs into the street.

But still his inner vision clung to the door-mat of straw and to the key under it, to Hofmann's letter, the books and papers on the table, the little cotton frock on a nail, the loaf of bread on the side table. And from all these things there emerged in his consciousness the figure of Ruth, as though it were rising from the elements of which it was made.

He remembered accompanying her to one of the great shops, where she bought a pair of cheap gloves. With the crowd they had drifted through the show-rooms and he recalled the very still delight upon her face with which she had regarded the mountains of snowy lingerie and of brilliantly hued silks— the laces and hats and girdles and costumes and all things that enchant and lure a young girl. But she had been content with that strange, still delight that seemed to say: how well it is that such things are! She had had no desire, no reaching out of her own, only a pleasure in the lovely qualities of things that were.

And thus too, without desire and without reaching out, she passed among men, and perceived the festive glitter of the great shops, the radiant wealth of palaces, and the fever of pleasure-seeking that throbbed in the streets when the great city strove to forget its toil. With that same gesture and that still content, she withdrew herself from sharp allurements and the anodynes of a thousand temptations, from all that transcended true measure and her own power; she threw the mantle of her youth over the world and stood in its midst, deeply moved, and yet aloof.

He had been present one day when she was arguing with the student Lamprecht, whose ideas were those of a demagogue. She had a charming lightness of speech, although her opinions were decided enough. Action and sacrifice had been mentioned, and Ruth said that she could not see the difference, that often they were closely akin or even identical. And finally she said: " It is the mind alone that conquers obstacles, and in it action and sacrifice are one." When her opponent replied that the mind must somehow communicate itself to the world and that this was, in itself, action, she had replied with burning cheeks: " Must one really proclaim and communicate the mind to the world? Then it ceases to be itself. The service of the heart is better than the service of lips or hands."

Although Christian had listened with the superior smile of one who never engages in argument, he had seen then that this voice had become necessary to his very life, and also this radiant eye and this glowing heart, and this vibrant soul that was so profoundly experienced and yet so incomparably young. She gave him to himself. She was his sister and his friend. He was revealed to himself through her pure humanity. And he could find no sleep, for her shadow appeared to him constantly and yet did not find the courage to address him. Now and then he started suddenly and his heart beat quickly. Once he beheld her in bodily form, and seemed to hear an imploring whisper; and a cold shudder ran over him. He arose and lit the candle again. Karen moaned.

He stepped up to her bed. " Water," she murmured.

He brought her water, and while she drank he bent affectionately over her. Her eyes were large and looked at him with a great sadness. There were tears in them.

XXI

Amadeus Voss lived in Zehlendorf, near the race track, in the gabled attic of a new house. He had a view of meadows stretching toward a rim of pine-woods. On the green plain projected a huge advertising sign with gigantic letters: Zehlendorf-Grunewald Development Company, Ltd.

"They put that up within the last week so as to keep my soul within proper bounds," Voss said. "It's a clever memento, isn't it? I'm told the company plans to build a church here. Magnificent! In the neighbourhood there is also a bell-foundry."

Johanna sat at the opposite window, through which the sunlight that she sought shone in. Her little face had grown thin. Her beautifully curved mouth with its sweet sadness lost its charm on account of her homely nose. "You might get employment as a lay reader," she said impudently, and dangled her legs like a schoolgirl. "Or do you think it's a Protestant business? Of course, every one is Protestant here. Why don't you convert the unbelievers? You let your most solid talents go to waste."

Voss made a grimace. With dragging steps he went through the large studio-like room. "To your kind of free thought all faith is an object of barter," he said bitterly. "Why do you mock even at yourself? See to it lest the light that is in you be not darkness! That is the monition of the Gospel. But what does that word 'Gospel' mean to you? A cultured phrase, or something to buy and sell."

Johanna, supporting her head on her hand, whispered inaudibly, "No one knows how it came that Rumpelstilzkin is my name." Aloud she said: "I'm getting a bad report, I see.

I'm resuming my seat, teacher. I know that my laziness is obvious even from your exalted seat."

Amadeus stopped in front of her. "Have you never believed? Has the inscrutable never touched your heart? Have you never trembled before Him? Have you no reverence? What kind of a world do you come from? "

She answered with biting sarcasm. "We spent our days dancing around the golden calf—all of us, great-grandmother, grandmother, mother and child. Fancy that! It's dizzying."

Impervious to the mockery through which she expressed the fragile charm of her clever mind, Voss fixed on her a look of sombre passion. "Do you at least believe in me? " he asked, and grasped her shoulders.

She resisted and withdrew herself. She thrust her hands against his chest and bent back her head. "I believe in nothing, nothing." Her whole body throbbed and shook. "Not in myself nor you nor God nor anything. You are quite right. I don't." Her brows contracted with pain. Yet she melted, as always, before his glow. It was her ultimate of earth and life, her last anodyne, her weakness yearning for destruction. Her lips grew soft and her lids closed.

With savage strength Amadeus lifted her in his arms. "Neither in yourself nor God nor me," he murmured. "But in him! Or perhaps you do not believe in him either? Tell me! "

She opened her eyes again. "In whom? " she asked astonished.

"In him! " His utterance was tormented. She understood him, and with an infinitely sinuous movement glided from his arms.

"What do you want of me? " she asked, and rearranged her abundant brown hair with nervous gestures.

"I want to know," he answered, "to know at last. I cannot bear this any longer. What happened between you two? How do you explain the intimate tone of your letter to him, and your questions whether he had already forgotten you, whether you dared even ask? No doubt you played the well-known game—the dangerous, lecherous game of moths in the lamplight. I am not so stupid as not to have guessed that. But how far did you venture toward the lamp—as far as the chimney or as far as the flame? And when he left you, what demands had you the right to make? What was he to you? What is he?"

It was the first time that Voss had spoken out. The question had been strangling him. He had set little traps for Johanna and searched her expression, resented her evasions and yet respected her delicacy. And all that had heightened his impatience and suspicion. The fingers of one hand clenched under his chin, he stood there lean and rocking strangely to and fro.

Johanna said nothing. A smile, half mocking, half of suffering, hovered about her lips. She wished that she were far away.

Voss gritted his teeth and went on: " Don't think it's jealousy. And if it is—perhaps there is no other word—yet I do not mean what you were taught to think it in the poisoned gardens in which you grew up. Why have you not been frank with me? Am I not worthy of so much? Did you not feel my dumb beseeching? I need not tell you what is at stake. If you did not suspect it, you would not fear to speak. From my childhood on I have lived in outer servitude and inner obedience. I have been taught the lofty and sacred ideal of chastity of our faith. Only despair over the unreachable farness of that ideal plunged me into the sinks of the earth's iniquity. And so I place on innocence and spotless purity quite another value than the sleek little gentlemen, the trained animals, of your world. I who stand before you am sin and the sense of sin, with all its misery and uncleanness; and you can save me by a word. I have confessed to you all the cries of my own breast. Have I not said enough? Yet even what

I have said seems shameless beside the vanity of your reserve. Can I do nothing but sting your senses, you heathen girl, and never reach your vitals or your soul? Confess, or I will tear the truth from you with red-hot pincers. Shall I have waited and renounced, to be fed on the leavings of another's satiety? Did you live with him? Speak! Did he cheat me of your purity—he who has cheated me of everything? Speak! "

Johanna, aflame with indignation, took her hat and coat and left him. He did not move. Scarcely had she closed the door behind her, scarcely did he hear the sound of her retreating steps, when he raced after her. With equal speed he returned for his hat. When she was leaving the house he was beside her. " Hear me," he stammered. " Don't judge me harshly." She quickened her pace to escape him. He would not fall behind. " My words were rough, Johanna, even brutal. But they were inspired by the very humbleness of love." She turned into the street to the railway station. He blocked her path; he threatened to use force if she persisted. Passers-by turned and looked at them. To avoid a public scandal she had to go back with him. " At least," she pleaded, " let us not return to the house. I can't stay in the room. We can talk while we are out. But don't come so near. People are laughing at us."

" People, people! The world is full of people. They know nothing of us nor we of them. Say that you forgive me, and I'll be as calm as though I had come from a card party." He was pale to his forehead.

They walked in the wet, snowy air and over the soaking earth. The street ran into a field-path. Above the setting sun the sky was full of shredded clouds—red, yellow, green, blue. An express train thundered past them. Electric signals trilled. It was tiring to walk over the slippery leaves, but the damp wind cooled their faces.

Amadeus wore himself out in explanations. In the defence of himself, the rejected and humiliated one, the tormented member of a caste and race of the rejected and humiliated, he found expressions of such power that they oppressed Johanna and bent her will. He spoke of his love for her, of this terrible storm in his blood, from which he had hoped purification and strength and liberation, but which was wasting and crushing him instead. And so his doubt of her was like a doubt of God. If a youth doubts God the world breaks down and sinks into pure agony. And such was his case in the nights in which he panted for alleviation, and the darkness became an abyss filled with a thousand purple tongues of flame.

And like a blinded man turning in a circle, he began again to ask his question, first carefully and slyly, then impetuously and with passion. He pointed out incriminating details and circumstances that poisoned his imagination. He appealed to her pity, her sense of honesty, to some not wholly buried spark of piety within her. And again he painted the state of his soul, besought her with uplifted hands, then became silent, and with his sombre eyes looked helplessly about.

Johanna had been astonished from the beginning that the nature of her brief contact with Christian, which shone to her from the past like a bit of dawn, had not been obvious to him. If he had understood and taken what had happened as a matter of course, she would probably have admitted it quite naïvely. But his savagery and his avidity aroused her defiance and her fear more and more. Every new attack of his made her feel more unapproachable, and she suddenly felt that she had a secret to guard from him, a deep and proud secret, which no assurances and no persecutions would make her yield up. It was a possession that all good spirits bade her keep, that she should never give up to him who would regard it as a shameful thing and into whose unblessed power she had fallen. So she built defences, and was ready to fight and to lie, to endure all that was ugly and repulsive, reproof and degradation.

And these, indeed, she came to endure. All his obsessions

concentrated themselves on this one point.   His glances searched and his words probed her; behind every tenderness and every touch there lurked a question.   If she evaded him, he became enraged.   If she soothed him, he cast himself down and kissed her feet.   She took pity on him, and for the space of a few ecstatic hours deceived him with the liberally invented details of a platonic relationship.   He seemed to believe her and begged her forgiveness, promising more gentleness and silence and consideration.   But hardly had a day passed before the old mischief sprang up anew.   His eye was sharpened as by acid.   Christian Wahnschaffe was the enemy, the thief, the adversary.   What happened at such and such a time? What did she say to him on such an occasion?   What had he answered?   Whence had he come?   Whither was he going? Did he ask her to yield herself?   Did she kiss him?   Once? Many times?   Had she desired his kisses?   When was she ever alone with him?   How did the room look?   What sort of a dress had she worn?   It was hopeless.   It was like a drill that turns and eats into wood.   Johanna repulsed him violently; she jeered and sighed and hid her face.   She wept and she laughed, but she did not yield by the breadth of a hair.

Next came utter exhaustion.   She was often so worn out that she lay on a sofa all day, pale and still.   She let her relatives take her to theatres, concerts, picture galleries.   With dull eyes and freezing indifference she endured these demands. The sympathy of people was a burden to her.   What could they do to soften her cruel self-contempt?   This killing contempt she transformed into a weapon, the two-edged sword of her wit, and this she turned against her own breast.   Her sayings became famous in large circles of society.   She described how she had once been bathing by a lake and how a sudden gust of wind had blown away her bath-chair.   "And there," she closed, "I stood as naked as God had created me in His wrath."

Her aversion from him who was her lover rose to such a

point that a cold fever shook her if she thought of him, that she secretly mocked his gestures, his tones, his clerical speech, his voracious glance. She made appointments with him which she did not keep. He sent telegrams and special delivery letters and messengers. He lay in wait at her door and questioned the servants until, beside herself, she went to him, and in her indignation said icy and unspeakably cruel things. Then he would become humble and rueful, and sincerely so. And the terror of losing her would wring words from him that were mad and diabolical.

She wasted away. She scarcely ate and slept. Again and again she determined to make an end of everything and leave the city. But there was the element of perverse desire. Her over-refined body, her over-subtle soul, her morbidly sensitive organism melted into a yearning for the cruel, for mysterious voluptuousness, for slavery and degradation, for every extremity of suffering and delight.

One evening she was crouching, half dressed, in a chair. Her long hair flowed beautifully over her slender shoulders. She held her head between her hands and looked like a disconsolate little harlequin, very pale and still. Amadeus Voss sat at the table with folded arms, and stared into the lamp. This isolation of two beings, without friends or dignity or happiness, seemed to Johanna like the inexorable fate of galley-slaves tied to the same oar. Suddenly she arose and gathered up her hair with a graceful gesture, and said with a scurrilous dryness: " Come in, ladies and gentlemen. This is the great modern show. The latest. Up to the minute. Sensation guaranteed. Magnificent suspense interest. Revelation of all the secrets of modern woman and modern man. Gorgeous finale. Don't miss it! "

She went up to the mirror, gazed at her image as though she did not know it, and made a comical bow.

Amadeus lowered his head in silence.

XXII

The poor imbecile Heinzen said he heard a whispering always in his ears. He shook like a leaf and his face was green.

Niels Heinrich kicked him under the table.

Whenever the door was opened the laughter and the screeching of women leapt out into the fog. Also one could see the building lots at the edge of which this drinking shanty had been erected. A new quarter was springing up here. Beams and scaffoldings and cranes presented a confusion like a forest struck by a tornado. Walled foundations, pits, construction huts, trenches, bridges, hills of bricks and sand, carts—everything was dimly lit by the arc-lamps, which seemed to be hidden in grey wadding.

When the door was closed one was in a cave.

There was a whispering in his ears, Joachim Heinzen insisted. Without understanding he listened to the filthy witticisms with which an old stone-mason regaled the company. Niels Heinrich threw a dark glance at Joachim and forbade the publican to fill his glass. The fellow, he said, was crazy enough now.

Gradually the room grew empty. One o'clock was approaching. Three steady topers still stood by the bar. The nightwatchman had just looked in on his rounds and drunk a nip of kümmel. The innkeeper regarded his late guests morosely, sat down, and nodded.

Niels Heinrich said to the simpleton that he would give him five talers to clear out. " If you don't fade away you'll catch hell, my boy," he said. His reddish beard rose and fell. About his neck he had wound a yellow shawl so many times that his head seemed to be resting on a cushion. His sallow, freckled face seemed a mere mass of bone.

Joachim's limbs trembled. Ontside the women of the streets were passing by, and their laughter sounded like the clatter of

crockery. "Five talers," said the imbecile and grinned.
"That's all right." But he was still trembling. He had
trembled just so the whole day, and the day before, and the
day before that. "I'd like to buy a black-haired wench," he
murmured.

"For money you can see the very devil dance," Niels
Heinrich replied.

Now even those at the bar got ready to leave. "Closing
time, gentlemen," the innkeeper called out. He repeated his
warning three times. A clock rattled.

"I'll get what I want," said the simpleton. "I want one
like a merry-go-round. Merry. Around and around."

"All right, boy! Go ahead! But don't you let no balloon
run you down," Niels Heinrich jeered, and stared at his own
fingers as though they had spoken to him. "Go ahead! "

"And I want one like a parrot," said the simpleton, "all
dressed up and fine." And in a broken voice he sang a stave
of a vulgar song.

Niels Heinrich's silence was grim.

"And I want one that's like what a lady is, elegant and
handsome," Joachim continued, and emptied the lees in his
glass. "That's what! Give me the five talers. Give 'em to
me." But suddenly he shuddered, his eyes seemed to protrude
from their hollows, and he uttered a sound that had a strange
and horrible kinship with a whine.

Niels Heinrich arose, and jerked his companion upward by
the collar. He threw the money to pay his reckoning on the
table, and pulled the simpleton out into the street. He grasped
his arm, and drew the reeling, horribly whimpering creature
along with him. He did not speak. He had pulled his blue
cap over his eyes. His face was full of brooding thoughts.
He paid no attention to snow or mud.

The fog swallowed up the two figures.

XXIII

David Hofmann had written a last message of farewell to his children from Bremerhaven. The postman had stuck the card halfway under the door, and Christian read it.

So Ruth could not be with her father. Here was a certainty that terrified him. Where was she then? And where was Michael?

He informed the house agent of the disappearance of the two, and the police were notified.

Christian knew the names of some of the families where she had given lessons. He visited these people, but no one could give him a hint. He went to the institutions that she had attended and to friends with whom she had associated. Everywhere there was the same surprise and helplessness. He was sent on wild errands and to other people. Some one would think he or she had last seen Ruth at such a place. The track was always lost. He would follow chance traces from morning until night, but they always faded from sight. In his anxiety and his anxious inquiries he finally found himself going in a futile circle.

He had entrusted Isolde Schirmacher and the widow Spindler with the care of Karen.

At the end of the fifth day he came home wearily. Botho Thüngen and the student Lamprecht had helped him in his search. It had all been in vain. If a faint hope arose, it was extinguished the next moment.

And where was Michael?

Christian climbed the stairs. The gas jet in the hall hissed. Near the balustrade cowered the white kitten and mewed. Christian bent over and gathered it up in his hands. It began to purr with infinite content, and snuggled against his coat. He stroked the silken fur, and a sense of the animal's well-being passed into his nerves.

By agreement with the agent he had taken the key of the

Hofmann flat into his keeping. He was to deliver it up next morning to a police detective who would come to investigate.

He unlocked the door and entered the dark room. The air was stuffy. Every breath of Ruth's presence had faded. Ruth, little Ruth! As his emotion gathered in him, the darkness ceased to be unnatural and disturbing.

He sat down beside the table. The dim light that came in from the hall fell on the books and papers of his little friend. He got up and closed the door. Only now was he able to summon up the image of Ruth as vividly as he had been able to do during the first night after her disappearance. Not only did she emerge from the darkness as she had done then; she even spoke to him.

She fixed on him her exquisitely laughing eyes, and in a tone whose seriousness belied that expression utterly, she said: " No, never, nevermore."

What did the words mean? What was their significance?

The fog gathered more thickly against the window panes. The kitten snuggled deeper into his arms. Its white fur shimmered indistinctly in the darkness. This breathing, living creature, warm and affectionate, prevented him from yielding to a grief that threatened to drag him into unknown depths.

Suddenly he had a vision. A landscape appeared before him. There was a path bordered by tall poplars in autumnal foliage, a path of mud, of black morass. On either side of it the heath stretched to infinity. There were the black, triangular silhouettes of a few huts, with windows red from the hearth-fires within. Here and there were puddles of dirty, yellow water, which reflected the grey sky and in which tree-trunks rotted. Over the whole scene was a whitish twilight, and in the distance emerged the rude form of a shepherd; and in that distance was a mass of egg-shaped bodies, half of wool, half of slime, that jostled one another. It was the herd of sheep. With gloom and difficulty they crept along the muddy path to a farmstead—a few mossy roofs of straw and turf amid the poplars. There was the dark sheepfold. Its open door showed a cavernous blackness; but through chinks in the back wall of the sheepfold flickered faint glints of the twilight. The caravan of wool and slime disappeared in the cavern. The shepherd and a woman with a lantern closed the door.

How was it that the invisible-visible presence of Ruth evoked this landscape in his soul? He had never, so far as he knew, seen such a landscape. How did it happen that this landscape exhaled something calming and shattering at once, yearning and fear—that it had power over him as scarcely any human fate or form or face? And how did it come to pass that Ruth's " no, never, nevermore," seemed the mysterious meaning of this landscape, the symbol of this vision?

Ruth, little Ruth!

Grief and sadness entered into Christian's very marrow.

XXIV

Crammon had determined to stay only one week at the Villa Ophelia. In the first place he did not like to prolong the family idyl beyond decent and appropriate limits. In the second place his programme, which he was not in the habit of changing except for catastrophes, demanded his departure for England. But the one week merged into a second, and the second into a third. At the end of the third week he was still unable to come to a decision.

He was rancorous against his surroundings and against himself, and as whimsical as a woman. He blamed himself, accused himself of senile indecision, and was full of bitter dissatisfaction with the slovenliness of the countess's establishment. The cuisine was, in his view, too greasy, and threatened to upset his sensitive digestion; the servants were not properly respectful, because their wages were too often in arrears. The constant stream of guests was generally lacking in nothing so much as in distinction. There were second-rate musicians

and poets and painters, and women of the same calibre.
Futhermore there were aristocrats of doubtful reputation. In
brief, a gathering of parasites, the thriftless, the unprofit-
able.

Among them Crammon had the appearance of a relic of an
exalted and hieratic age.

One day the two nephews of the countess, Ottomar and
Reinhold Stojenthin, appeared. They had succeeded in getting
leave of absence for two months. Leave of absence from what?
Crammon inquired with raised brows. They wanted to accompany Letitia to Munich. " They are splendid chaps, Herr von
Crammon," said the countess. " Do take them under your
protection." Crammon was vexed. " I've always lived in
perfect dread of some one's discovering my hidden talent for
the rôle of a governess. The achievement was reserved for
you, countess."

His relations to Puck, the Pekingese, were strained. The
little animal enraged him inexplicably. Whenever he saw it
his eyes grew round and his face scarlet with anger. Perhaps
it was the dog's deep tawny coat; perhaps it was its sleepiness;
perhaps he suspected it of maliciously feigning a delicate state
of health so that it could sprawl on silken couches and have
tidbits stuck into its mouth. The anxious care that Letitia
gave the creature annoyed him. Once the little dog had
gotten up from the carpet and, wheezing asthmatically, had
slipped out through the door. " Where is Puck? " Letitia asked
after a while from the depth of her armchair. Puck wasn't
to be seen. " Do whistle to him, Bernard," she begged in
her flute-like voice. " You can do that yourself," said Crammon quite rudely. Letitia, calmly pathetic, dreamily preoccupied, said: " Please do it for me. I can't whistle when
I'm excited."

So Crammon whistled to the hateful beast.

Still, a decision had to be arrived at. " Are you going to
Munich with me? " the siren Letitia cooed, and laughed at

his anger. To her aunt she said: "He's still raging, but he'll go with us in the end."

Crammon nursed an ethical intention. He would influence Letitia to her own advantage. He could open her eyes to the dangerous downward slope of the path which she pursued with such unfortunate cheerfulness. She could be helped and supported and given a timely warning. Her extravagance could be checked, and her complete lack of judgment could be corrected. She was utterly inexperienced and thoughtless. She believed every liar, and gave her confidence to every chatterer. She was enthusiastic over any charlatan, held all flattery to be sincere, and provided every fool who paid court to her with a halo of wisdom and of pain. She needed to be brought to reason.

Crammon was quite right. Yet a mere smile of Letitia would silence him. She blunted the point of the most pertinent maxims and of the soundest moralizing by holding her head a little on one side, looking at him soulfully and saying in a sweetly and archly penitential tone: "You see, dear Bernard, I'm made this way. What's the use of trying to be different? Would you want me to be different? If I were, I'd only have other faults. Do let me be as I am." And she would slip one hand through his arm, and with the other tickle his almost double chin. And he would hold still and sigh.

The following persons started on the journey to Munich: Letitia, her personal maid, the nurse Eleutheria, the twins, the countess, Fräulein Stöhr, Ottomar and Reinhold, Crammon, the Pole Stanislaus Rehmer. Also the following animals: Puck, the Pekingese, a bullfinch in one cage and a tame squirrel in another. The luggage consisted of fourteen large trunks, sixteen hand-bags, seven hat-boxes, one perambulator, three luncheon baskets, and innumerable smaller packages wrapped in paper, leather, or sack-cloth, not to mention coats, umbrellas, sticks, and flowers. In the train the countess wrung her hands, Puck barked and whined pathetically, Letitia made a long list of things that had been forgotten at the last moment, the maid quarreled with the conductor, the twins screamed, Eleutheria offended the other passengers by baring her voluminous breasts, Fräulein Stöhr had her devout and patient heavenward glance, Ottomar and Reinhold debated some literary matter, the Pole spent his time gazing at Letitia, Crammon sat in sombre mood with legs crossed and twiddled his thumbs.

With the exception of the Stojenthin brothers, who went to a more modest hostelry, the whole company took rooms in the Hotel Continental. The bill which was presented to the countess at the end of each day was rarely for less than three hundred marks. " Stöhr," she said, " we must find new sources of help. The child suspects nothing, of course. It would break her heart if she had an inkling of my pecuniary anxieties." Fräulein Stöhr, without abandoning her air of virtue, succeeded in implying her doubt of that.

A lawyer of the highest reputation was entrusted with the suit against the Gunderams. The representative of the defendants had been instructed to refuse all demands. There were endless conferences, during which the countess flamed with noble indignation, while Letitia exhibited an elegiac amazement, as though these things did not concern her and had faded from her memory. Her statements as to what she had said and done, concerning agreements and events, were never twice the same. When these contradictions were brought to her attention, she answered, ashamed and dreamy and angry at once: " You're frightfully pedantic. How am I to remember it all? I suppose things were as you've said they were in your documents. What are the documents for? "

The old litigation concerning the forest of Heiligenkreuz was also to be accelerated. The countess's hopes in this matter were justified in no respect. Nevertheless she felt that she was a wealthy landowner, and sought capitalists to finance her on the security of this dusty and hopeless claim.

She failed, yet her faith was unshaken. She even prevailed upon herself to enter places that she considered unhygienic, and chaffer with persons who were not immaculate. " Don't worry, my angel," she said to Letitia. " Everything will turn out well. By Easter we shall be rolling in money."

Letitia did not, indeed, worry. She enjoyed herself and was radiant. Every day was so full of delight and pleasure that it seemed rank ingratitude to think of the morrow except under the same aspect. Life clung to her as pliantly and adorningly as a charming frock. Since her inner life was unshadowed and all men smiled upon her, she believed the world at large to be in a lasting condition of content. Rumours of pain and misfortune, she thought, must somewhere have their ground in reality. But by the time that a knowledge of them reached her, they were transformed into the likeness of beauty and legend.

She read the books of poets, listened to music, danced at balls, chatted and walked, and everything was to her a mirror of her loveliness and a free, playful activity. She was quite free, for she never felt the impulse toward restraint. She had time for every one, for the moment was her master. And so she was most disarmingly unpunctual, and so innocent in her faithlessness that those whom she betrayed always ended by consoling her. Her affairs were quickly going from bad to worse. She knew nothing of it. She created an unparalleled confusion among men, but she was quite unconscious of it. Whoever spoke to her of love received love. She was sorry for them. Why not share one's overflowing wealth? Six or eight passionate wooers could always simultaneously boast of weighty evidences of her favour. If any one reproached her, she was astonished and not seldom on the verge of tears, like some one whose pure intentions had been incomprehensibly misunderstood.

One of the twins fell ill, and a physician was summoned. He delayed coming, and she sent for another. Next morning she had forgotten both, and sent for a third, simply because his name in the telephone directory had pleased her. The consequence was confusion. It happened too that she would fall in love with one of the physicians for a few hours. Then the confusion was heightened.

She accepted three separate invitations for Christmas week, and promised to go at the same time to Meran, Salzburg, and Baireuth. When the time came she had forgotten all three, and went nowhere.

Her maid was discovered to be a thief. A dozen girls presented themselves for the vacant position. She took a liking to the last, and forgot that she had already taken a liking to the first and had hired her.

She was invited to luncheon and appeared at tea. A sum had been scraped up to pay pressing bills. She loaned it to Rehmer, who was poor as a church mouse and needed new clothes. The confusion grew and grew.

But it did not touch her. Her mood was exalted and festive, her gait a little careless, her head charmingly bent a little to one side. Her soft, deer-like eyes were full of expectation and delight and just a shade of cunning.

Crammon could not possibly approve this state of affairs. It was a topsyturvy world, in which all rules were trodden under foot. A very dainty, very pretty foot, no doubt, but the result was enough to frighten any one. He growled his complaints like Burbero in Goldoni's play. He said things would come to a bad end. He had never known such slovenliness in all things not to come to a bad end. His horror was that of a bourgeois who sees his pet virtues outraged. Fascinated and frightened by the spectacle of Letitia's gambols on the edge of an abyss, he denied his own past, forgot his follies, his adventures, his freebooting days, his greed and varied lusts, and the remnants of them that accompanied him even now. He forgot all that. He complained.

One evening he was dining alone with the countess. Letitia

had gone to a concert. The countess had something on her heart, and his suspicions were vigilant. Her ways were mild and she served him the best of everything. She spoke of the change of domicile that had been planned, and said that she and Letitia had not yet been able to agree whether it were better to spend the coming months in Wiesbaden or Berlin. She asked Crammon's advice. He begged her to permit him not to interfere in the controversy. He had other plans of his own, and no desire to witness a noisy débâcle.

At that the countess began to lament her pecuniary embarrassment and complain of the impatience of her creditors. For the dear child's sake she had determined to ask him for a considerable loan. She would give him any security he desired, provided her name and person and reputation did not suffice. Nothing, of course, could greatly mitigate the painfulness of having to make such a request. Yet the sense of asking the father of her darling did console her for her suffering.

Her red round cheeks did, in fact, become a shade less rosy, and in her forget-me-not blue eyes shimmered a tear or two.

Crammon laid down his knife and fork. "You misjudge me, countess," he said with the melancholy of a Tartuffe. "You misjudge me gravely. Never in my life have I loaned out money—neither at interest nor out of friendship. Nothing could move me to change my principle. You probably fancy me well off. That is a most astonishing error, countess. I may give that impression, but you must not draw false inferences. I have had the art of thrift and frugality, that is all. I have been careful in the choice of my associates—men as well as women. If ever I had two invitations, one from the East and one from the West, and the Eastern invitation was issued by an unquestionably wealthier source, my decision was immediate and unhesitating. Thus I was guarded from scruples and regrets. All that I call my own is a little farm in Moravia that yields a most modest revenue—a little grain, a little fruit, and an old ramshackle house in Vienna with a few sticks of worm-eaten furniture, which is guarded for me by two rare pearls of the female sex. No one, countess, I assure you, has ever before made the quaint mistake of asking me for money. No one."

Sadly the countess leaned her head upon her hand.

" But my conscience would forbid my acquiescence in this case even had I the ability," Crammon continued morosely. "I would never forgive myself for having been the banker of the follies that are perpetrated here, or the financier of mad extravagance. No, no, countess. Let us talk of more cheerful things."

He was still up when, at midnight, he heard a tapping at his door. Letitia entered. She sat down beside him, and said to him with a wide-eyed gentle look: " It wasn't nice of you, Bernard, to treat auntie so cruelly. Neither you nor I can let a thing like that go. Are you stingy? For heaven's sake, Bernard, don't tell me that you're stingy! Look me in the eyes, and tell me if such a thing is possible. My dear, I'd have to disown you! "

She laughed and put her arms about his neck, pulled his hair and kissed the tip of his nose, and was, in a word, so arch and so irresistible that Crammon's cast-iron principles were fatally shattered. He revoked his refusal and promised to pay Letitia's debts.

Once again the breath and speech of a woman had power over him. But it was late, and the sweetness was shot with pain. For he was no more the robber but the victim. Ah, it was time to practise modesty and renunciation. No longer did one bite into a juicy pear. No longer did one eat; one was eaten.

Letitia determined to go to Berlin. After some vain refusals, Crammon consented to accompany her.

XXV

In spite of the warmth of the room Johanna sat wrapped in her cloak.

Amadeus Voss told her a story: " I know of a holy priest who lived in France in the seventeenth century and whose name was Louis Gaufridy. In those days the people still believed in magic and witchcraft, and that was well, since it served as an antidote to godless desires. To-day a few chosen spirits believe in magic again, and thus exorcize the evil spirit which is called science. Louis Gaufridy was considered the most devout man of his age. Not even his enemies denied that. In a convent which he served as father confessor, there was a nun who was called Madeleine de la Palud. This woman's imagination had embraced the Saviour under the aspect of the flesh, and the chronicles say that she had fed her evil desires upon His picture. This fact was written in her troubled looks, and the priest Gaufridy saw the truth and desired to liberate her through the grace of confession. But the demons sealed her lips and hardened her heart. They took possession of her, and the devils Asmodeus and Leviathan spoke through her. She who had hitherto been chaste had unchaste hallucinations, and accused the priest of having bewitched and misused her. Gaufridy was arrested and examined under torture and confronted with Madeleine. He swore by God and all His saints that he was being falsely accused. But the nun, misled by her hallucinations, swore that he was the prince of magicians, that he had misused her during confession, and had poisoned her soul. Before the judges the priest implored Madeleine to give up her delusion and confess the truth; but she was incapable of truth. Beside herself, she cried out that he had pledged himself to the devil in his own blood and that he had forced her to do the same. Thereupon he was cruelly tortured once more, and publicly burned on the Dominican's Square at Aix."

Johanna smiled a tormented smile.

"That is the story of Madeleine de la Palud," said Voss, "the profound story concerning the heavenly and the earthly Eros and the Fata Morgana of the senses. Who was the guilty one? Madeleine, who had blasphemed and defiled the image of the Saviour with fleshly desires, or Gaufridy, who had plunged her into a consciousness of sin by creating in her the division between spirit and flesh? For that he had to suffer, as every one has to suffer. But what I feel, and what our sources indeed hint at, is that he was seized by a mysterious and terrible love for Madeleine de la Palud even when she was thrusting him into the torture chamber, and that this love mitigated for him even the horrors of his fiery death. In every human breast love arises but once and for but one being. All else is misunderstanding, and a sterile attempt to resuscitate what is dead. It leads to falsehood and to torture."

Johanna smiled a tormented smile.

"I walked with a harlot yesterday," Voss said suddenly, and stared into space.

Johanna did not stir.

"It is an old horror that draws me toward harlots," he said in a hollow voice. "Sometimes when I walked the streets penniless, sick with longing, utterly deserted, I gazed after them and envied the men who could go with them. It is an old feeling and springs from a deep source. I cannot get rid of it, least of all now that I err in the darkness and the ground is melting under my feet."

"You talk and talk," said Johanna, and arose. "If I had learned to speak I could tell you what you . . . do!"

"I suffer in the flesh," he answered, and his glance burned her.

Twice she walked up and down the room. She hated her own tread, her own perceptions, and her own thoughts. She had so deep a longing for some human touch, some friendly, handsome, kindly word, that she would not admit even to herself how far it might lead her. She only had a dim vision of herself sitting in that rear room in Stolpische Street, waiting for Christian many hours, whole nights, it mattered not how long, but just to wait and to be there at his coming, to smile with her lips though her heart were weeping—she knew that condition so well—without explanation or confessions or complaints, as is the custom among well-bred people who settle their inner difficulties in silence and alone. Just to be there and nothing else, in order that the temperature of her heart might rise by a few degrees.

But to plan or undertake or hope for anything from any source was so criminal, it seemed, and so stupid. An empty thing—like a hungry bird picking at painted grains of wheat.

" You told me the other day that you weren't able to pay your rent. Permit me to help you out." She spoke in her frugal, pointed way, and with an angular gesture placed some money on the table. " Do not speak. Just this once, please do not speak."

He looked at her devouringly, and laughed with a jeer. She stood very cold and still. He kissed her.

She endured it like one to whose throat a knife is put.

XXVI

When she arrived in Stolpische Street it was seven o'clock in the evening. Christian was not at home, and she waited.

She lit the lamp, sat down beside the table, and did not move. After a while, since the chill of the unheated room penetrated through her cloak and even her frock, she got up and walked up and down. Sometimes she lightly touched the objects on the table—a notebook, or a dusty ink-well. She let down the shades, and saw the silly pictures with which they were adorned.

As on that other occasion she heard the house. It was full of rumours and whispers, and oppressed her fatefully.

Swift, violent knocks at the door resounded. She started and then hastened to open it. A boy stood before her. His condition made her shudder. His clothes were spattered over and over with mud. Here and there, about his knees and on his chest, the mud had caked and formed a thick crust. His head was bare. His coal-black hair, which was also muddy, hung down. His face had an utter bleached whiteness, such as Johanna had never seen upon a human face. No drop of blood seemed left beneath his skin.

Limping a little, he passed by Johanna and entered the room. His movements were mechanical and trance-like. The volitional impulse always far antedated the action it produced.

"I am Michael Hofmann," he said, and his teeth chattered.

Johanna did not know him and had not heard of him. She thought she must be dealing with a madman. In her fear she did not leave the door. She expected him to attack her at any moment, and listened for some chance step in the hall or yard. She wanted to flee, but she was afraid to move. When the boy came into the circle of the lamplight, a sigh which ended in a broken cry escaped her, so terrible was the expression in his eyes.

He stopped, and looked about him. He was obviously seeking Christian Wahnschaffe; but in the act of gazing he forgot to look, and his glance became a stare. He grasped the back of a chair. Exhaustion seemed to overtake him. When he was about to sit down, he reeled and half-whirled about, and would have fallen but for the support of the back of the chair. Now Johanna saw clearly that he was neither mad nor drunk. He was a human being who had been robbed of strength and speech and almost vision and consciousness by an experience of the supremest horror. Not only his shaking limbs, not only the whiteness of his face betrayed the fact, but the atmosphere that surrounded him.

Gently she closed the door. Hesitatingly she approached the chair upon which he seemed now wedged fast. She dared to ask no question. Gnawing her lip, she suppressed a feeling that welled up hotly within her. She felt herself shrink and become thin and shadowy. She seemed suddenly to have lost the very right to breathe.

Every passing second heightened her unspeakable consternation. Her limbs trembled. She sat down on the other side of the room. The lad had his back turned to her, and she observed that his body began to twitch. She saw it by the creases in his coat and his arms, which were hanging down. It was like an endless convulsion. The helplessness which she felt in the face of this unknown tragedy caused her an almost physical pain, and inspired her with self-disgust and self-contempt. Her soul seemed steeped in blackness, shredded and crushed. While she suffered so, a desire came over her, a defiant and struggling desire, as for something ultimate to lay hold upon in life. It was the desire to see how Christian would take the terrible thing in which he was, to all appearances, implicated. Would he let it slide from him with his old elegant smoothness? Would he let it be shattered against that impenetrability against which all her life and fate had been shattered? Or would he be that other who was frank and changed and had wrought a miracle upon himself and upon all others except herself—who was incapable of faith out of shame and despair and desolation and an inner hurt? But if he was that other and changed man, if he approved himself in this supreme instance, then she need torment herself so cruelly no more. For in that case, what did her little sorrows matter? Then she must be humble, and wait for her summons, though she did not know what it would be.

And she waited, stretching out her slim throat like a thirsty deer.

XXVII

That "no, never, nevermore," had driven Christian about without another thought. On this day he forgot that Karen was sick unto death.

As he was coming home that night it was raining. Nevertheless there were groups of people in front of the houses. Some uncommon event had brought them out of their rooms.

He had had no umbrella, and was wet to the skin. In the doorway, too, stood people who lived in the house. They whispered excitedly. When they saw him they became silent, stepped aside, and let him pass.

Their faces frightened him. He looked at them. They were silent. Terror fell on his chest like a lump of ice.

He went on. He was about to go up to Karen's flat, but reconsidered and went toward the court. He wanted to be alone in his room for a while. Several people followed him. Among them was the wife of Gisevius and her son, a young man whose behaviour was marked by the well-defined class-consciousness of the organized worker.

Christian did not even observe that the window of his room was lit. He walked close to the wall; he was so wet. Opening the door, he saw Johanna and the boy. He did not at once recognize Michael, who sat turned aside. He nodded to Johanna in surprise. The tense and glittering look which she turned upon him made him start. He reached the table and recognized Michael Hofmann. He grew pale, and had to hold on to the table's edge.

The door was still open, and in the dim light of the hall were crowded the five or six people who had followed him. It was not insolence that brought them to the threshold. They had been disquieted by rumours, and thought that he could give them some information.

Christian put his hand in the lad's shoulder, and asked:

"Where have you been, Michael? Where have you come from?"

The boy continued rigid and silent.

"Where is Ruth?" Christian asked, as by a supreme effort.

Michael arose. His eyes were unnaturally wide open. With both arms he made a large, obscure gesture. Horror shook him so that a gurgling sound which arose in his throat was throttled before it reached his lips. Suddenly he swayed and reeled and fell like a log. He lay on the floor.

Christian kneeled down and put his arms about him. He lifted him a little, and gathered the muddy, trembling boy close to him. He bent down his face, and learned an unheard-of thing from the beseeching, horror-stricken glance that sought him as from fathomless depths. Passionately he pressed Michael's body against his own, which was so wet but no longer aware of its wetness. He pressed the boy to his heart, as though he would open to him his breast as a shelter, and the boy, too, clung to Christian with all his might. The convulsive rigidity relaxed, and from that unbelievably emaciated body there broke forth a sobbing like the moan of a wind of doom.

The boy knew. No one could be so shattered but one who knew.

Then Christian kissed the stony, dirty, tear-stained face.

Johanna saw it, and the timid people at the door saw it also.

INQUISITION

EDGAR LORM was accustomed to taking his meals without Judith, so he was not surprised at her absence to-day and sat down alone.

The meal was served: a lobster, breast of veal with salad and three kinds of vegetables, a pheasant with compote, a large boule de Berlin, pineapple and cheese. He drank two glasses of red Bordeaux and a pint of champagne.

He ate this excessively rich meal daily with the appetite of a giant and the philosophical delight of a gourmet. As he was lighting his heavy Havana cigar over his coffee, he heard Judith's voice. She burst in, perturbed to the utmost.

" What has happened, dear child? " he asked.

" Something frightful," she gasped, and sank into a chair.

Lorm arose. " But what has happened, my dear? "

She panted. " I haven't been feeling at all well for several days. I got the doctor to look me over, and he says I'm pregnant."

A sudden light came into Lorm's eyes. " I don't think that's such a terrible misfortune." He had difficulty in concealing his surprised delight. " On the contrary, I think it's a blessed thing. I hardly dared hope for it. Indeed, my dear wife, I don't know what I wouldn't give to have it true."

Judith's eyes glittered as she replied: " It shall never be— never, never! I shall not remind you of our agreement; I shall not lay the blame on you if this terrible thing has really happened. I can't believe it yet. It would make me feel be- witched. But you are mistaken if you count on any yielding on my part, any womanly weakness, or any awakening of certain so-called instincts. Never, never! My body shall remain as it is—mine, all mine. I won't have it lacerated and I won't share it. It's the only thing I still call my own. I won't have a strange creature take possession of it, and I refuse to age by nine years in nine months. And I don't want some mocking image of you or me to appear. Never, never! The horror of it! Be careful! If you take delight in something I detest so, the horror will extend itself to you! "

Lorm stretched himself a little, and regarded her with amazement. There was nothing for him to say.

She went into her bedroom and locked the door. Lorm gave orders that no visitors were to be admitted. Then he went into the library, and spent the time until eight reading a treatise on the motions of the fixed stars. But often he raised his eyes from the book, for he was preoccupied not so much with the secrets of the heavens as with very mundane and very depressing things. He got up and went to the door of Judith's room. He listened and knocked, but Judith did not answer. At the end of half an hour he returned and knocked again. She knew his humble way of seeking admission, but she did not answer. The door remained locked.

At the end of each half hour, which he spent in reading about the stars, he returned to the door and knocked. He called her name. He begged her to have some confidence in him and hear what he had to say. He spoke in muffled tones, so as not to arouse the attention of the servants. He asked her not to blame him for his premature delight. He saw his error and deplored it. Only let her listen to him. He promised her gifts—an antique candlestick, a set of Dresden china, a frock made by Worth. In vain. She did not answer.

Three days passed. An oppressive atmosphere rested on the household. Lorm slunk through the rooms like an intimidated guest. He humiliated himself so far as to send Judith a letter by the housekeeper, who took in her meals and who alone had access to her. At night he returned to the door again and again, placed his lips against it, and implored her. There was no stirring of anger in him, no impulse to clench his fist and break down the door. Judith knew that. She was beating her fish.

She knew that she could go any length.

This man had been the idol of a whole nation. He had been spoiled by fame, by the friendship of distinguished people, by the kindness of fate and all the amenities of life. His very whims had been feared; a frown of his had swept all opposition aside. Now he not only endured the maltreatment of this woman whom he had married after long solitariness and hesitation; he accepted insult and humiliation like the just rewards of some guilt. Weary of fame, appreciation, friendship, success, and domination, he seemed to lust after mortification, the reversal of all things, and the very voluptuousness of pain.

Quite late on the third evening he was summoned to the telephone by Wolfgang Wahnschaffe. The breach between Wolfgang and Judith that had followed his first visit forbade his visiting the house.

He begged Lorm for an interview on neutral ground. The occasion, he said, was most pressing. Lorm asked for details. The bitter and excited answer was that the question concerned Christian. Some common proceeding against him, some decision and plan, some protective measures were absolutely necessary. The family must be saved from both danger and inconceivable disgrace.

At this point Lorm interrupted him. "I feel rather sure that my wife will prove quite unapproachable in the matter. And what could I do more than the merest stranger?" Urged anew, he finally promised to meet Wolfgang at luncheon in a restaurant on Potsdamer Street.

He had scarcely hung up the receiver when Judith entered. She had on a négligée of dark-green velvet trimmed with fur.

The garment had a long train. Her hair was carefully dressed, a cheerful smile was on her lips, and she stretched out both hands to Lorm.

He was happy, and took her hands and kissed them.

She put her arms about his neck and her lips close to his ear: " Everything is all right. The doctor is a donkey. I did you wrong. Everything is nice now, so be nice! "

" If only you are satisfied," said Lorm, " nothing else matters."

She nestled closer to him, and coaxed with eyes and mouth and hands: " How about the antique candlestick, darling, and the frock by Worth? Are you going to get them for me? And am I not to have my set of Dresden china? "

Lorm laughed. " Since you admit that you wronged me, the price of reconciliation is a trifle high," he mocked. " But don't worry. You shall have everything."

He breathed a kiss upon her forehead. That disembodied tenderness was the symbol of the ultimate paralysis of his energy before her and men and the world. And from day to day this paralysis grew more noticeable, and bore all the physical symptoms of an affection of the heart.

II

An identical account in all newspapers gave the first public notification that a murder had been committed:

"At six o'clock yesterday a foreman and a workman from Brenner's factory found the headless body of a girl in a shed on Bornholmer Street. The body was held by ropes in an unnatural position, and was so tightly wedged in among beams, boards, ladders, barrows, and refuse, that the police officers who were immediately summoned had the greatest difficulty in disentangling their gruesome find. The news spread rapidly through the neighbourhood, and a rumour that increased in definiteness pointed to the body of the murdered girl as that of the sixteen-year-old Ruth Hofmann residing in Stolpische Street. A notification of her disappearance had been lodged at police headquarters several days ago. The theory that it was she who was the victim of a murder of unparalleled bestiality became a certainty some hours later. A mason's wife found in the mortar-pit of a building lot on Beller-mann Street the severed head, which proved to belong to the body and was identified by several inhabitants of the house on Stolpische Street as that of Ruth Hofmann. Except for stockings and shoes, the body was entirely naked, and its mutilations indicated felonious assault. There is at present no trace of the murderer. But the investigations are being present with all possible care and energy, and it is warmly to be desired that the inhuman brute may soon be turned over to the ministers of justice."

III

In the little rear room he had now been sleeping for fourteen hours. The widow Engelschall determined to go to him.

She passed through the half-dark passage-way in which the supplies were stored. Hams and smoked sausages dangled from the ceiling. On the floor stood kegs with sardines, herrings, and pickled gherkins. There were shelves filled with glasses of preserved fruit. The place smelled like a shop.

She stopped, took a little gherkin out of an open keg, and swallowed it without chewing.

The bell of the front-door rang. A sluttish creature, broom in hand, became visible at the end of the passage, and called out to the widow Engelschall that Isolde Schirmacher had come with an important message. "Let her wait," the widow Engelschall growled. Softly she went into the small room in which Niels Heinrich was sleeping.

He lay on a mattress. A bluish flannel coverlet was over him. His hairy chest was bare; his naked feet protruded. The room was so small that not even a chest of drawers could have been squeezed in. Heaps of malodorous, soiled linen lay in the corners. Tools were scattered about the floor—a plane, a hammer, a saw. Old newspapers increased the litter, and on nails in the wall hung dirty clothes, ties, and a couple of overcoats. On the walls red splotches showed where bedbugs had been killed. On the table stood a candlestick with a piece of candle, an empty beer bottle, and a half empty whiskey bottle.

He lay on his back. The muscles of his face had snapped under an inhuman tension. Between his reddish eyebrows vibrated three dark furrows. His skin was the tint of cheese. On his neck and forehead were beads of sweat. His lids looked like two black holes. The slim, red little beard on his chin moved as he breathed—moved like a separate and living thing, a watchful, hairy insect.

He snored loudly. A bubble of saliva rose now and then from the horrible opening of his lips that showed his decayed teeth.

The widow Engelschall had had plans which had seemed easy to execute outside. Now she dared do nothing. Last night she had stood above him as she stood now. He had begun to murmur in his sleep, and she had hurried out in terror.

It buzzed in her head: What had he done with the two thousand marks which he had embezzled from the builder? She distrusted his assertion that he had spent it all on the cashier of the Metropolitan Moving Picture Theatre. To make up a part of the money and prevent his arrest, she had had to pawn all her linen, two chests of drawers, the furnishings of her waiting-room, and also to mortgage a life insurance policy. Her letter to Privy Councillor Wahnschaffe had not even been answered.

She didn't believe that he had wasted so much good money on that slut. He must have a few hundreds lying about somewhere. The thought gave her no rest. It was dangerous to let him notice her suspicion; but she could risk entering the room while he slept, burrowing in his clothes, and slipping her hand under his pillow.

But she stood perfectly still. In his presence she was always prepared for the unexpected. If he but opened his mouth, she trembled within. If people came to speak of him, she grew cold all over. If she stopped to think, she knew that it had always been so.

When the village schoolmaster had caught the ten-year-old boy in disgusting practices with a girl of eight, he had said: "He'll end on the gallows." When he was an apprentice, he had quarrelled over wages with his employer and threatened to strike him. The man had said: "He'll end on the gallows." When he had stolen a silver chain from the desk of the minister's wife at Friesoythe, and his mother had gone to return it, the lady had said: "He'll end on the gallows."

The memories came thick and fast. He had beaten his first mistress, fat Lola who lived in Köpnicker Street, with barbarous cruelty, because at a dance in Halensee she had winked at a postal clerk. When the girl had writhed whining on the floor, and shrieked out in her pain: "There ain't such another devil in the world!" the widow Engelschall had appealed to the enraged fellow's conscience, and had said to him: "Go easy, my boy, go easy;" but her advice had been futile. When his second mistress was pregnant, he forced her to go for treatment to an evil woman with whom he was also intimate, and the girl died of the operation. He jeered at the swinish dullness of women who couldn't do the least things right—couldn't bear and couldn't kill a brat properly. No one, fortunately, had heard this remark but the widow Engelschall. Again she had besought him: "Boy, go it a bit easier, do!"

At bottom she admired his qualities. You couldn't fool with him. He knew how to take care of himself; he could get around anybody. If only he hadn't always vented his childish rage on harmless things. The expense of it! If the fire didn't burn properly, he'd tear the oven door from its hinges; if his watch was fast or slow, he'd sling it on the floor so that it was smashed; if meat was not done to his liking, he broke plates with his knife; if a cravat balked in the tying, he'd tear it to shreds, and often his shirt too. Then he laughed his goatlike laugh, and one had to pretend to share his amusement. If he noticed that one was annoyed, he became rabid, spared nothing, and destroyed whatever he could reach.

She wondered what he lived on in ordinary times, when he had had no special piece of good luck. For he seemed always in the midst of plenty, with pockets full of money, and no hesitation to spend and treat. Sometimes he worked—four days a week or five. And he could always get work. He knew his trade, and accomplished in one day more than other workmen did in three. But usually he extended blue Monday until Saturday, and passed his time in unspeakable dives with rogues and loose women.

The widow Engelschall knew a good deal about him. But there was a great deal that she did not know. His ways were mysterious. To ask him and to receive an answer was to be none the wiser. He was always planning something, brewing something. All this commanded the widow Engelschall's profound respect. He was flesh of her flesh and spirit of her spirit. Yet her anxiety was great; and recently the cards had foretold evil with great pertinacity.

And so she hesitated, full of fear. The palish, yellow skull on the coarse, fustian pillow paralysed her. The slack flesh of her fat neck drooped and shook, as she finally bent and reached down after his coat and waistcoat, which were lying under the chair. She turned away a little so as to conceal her motions. Suddenly she felt a hand on her shoulder and shrieked.

Niels Heinrich had risen noiselessly. He stood there in his shirt, and pierced her with the yellowish flare of his glance. "What're you doing there, you old slut?" he asked with calm rage. She let the garments fall and retreated toward the door trembling. He stretched forth his arm: "Out!"

His appearance was fear-inspiring. Words died on her lips. With reeling steps she went out.

Isolde Schirmacher was still waiting in the hall. She began to weep when she gave her message: the widow Engelschall was to come to Stolpische Street without delay. Karen was very sick, was dying.

The widow Engelschall seemed incredulous. "Dying? Ah,

it ain't so easy to die. Give her my love, and say I'm coming.
I'll be there in an hour."

IV

A further account appeared in the papers:

"The mystery which surrounds the murder of young Ruth
Hofmann is beginning to clear up. The public will be glad to learn
that the efforts of the police have brought about the apprehension
of her probable slayer. The latter is Joachim Heinzen of Czerni-
kauer Street, twenty years old, of evil reputation and apparently of
not altogether responsible mind. Even before the discovery of the
crime his behaviour attracted attention. Within the last few days
the evidence against him has increased to the extent of justifying
his arrest. When the police frankly accused him of the crime, he
first broke down, but immediately thereafter resisted arrest with the
utmost violence. Lodged in jail, he made a full and comprehensive
confession. When asked to sign the protocol, however, he retracted
his entire statement, and denied his guilt with extreme stubbornness. In his demeanour brutish stupidity alternated with remorse
and terror. There can hardly be any doubt but that he is the
criminal. The first formal examination by the investigating judge
entrusted with the case will take place to-day. All the inhabitants
of the house in Stolpische Street have been examined, among them
a personality whose presence in that locality throws a curious side-
light on a widely discussed affair, in which one of the most respected families among our captains of industry is involved."

V

The hint in the last sentence caused endless talk. The name,
which had considerately been left unmentioned, passed from
mouth to mouth, no one knew how. The rumour reached
Wolfgang Wahnschaffe. Colleagues asked him with cool amazement what his brother had to do with the murder of a Jewish
girl in the slums. Even the chief of his chancellery in the
Ministry of Foreign Affairs summoned him, and questioned
him with an expression that made him blanch with shame.

He wrote to his father: " I am in the position of a peaceful
pedestrian who is in constant danger of a madman attacking
him from behind. You are aware, dear father, that in the
career I have chosen an unblemished repute is the first
requisite. If my reputation and my name are to be constantly

at the public mercy of an insane eccentric, who unhappily bears that name only to stain it, the time has come to use every means, no matter how drastic, to protect oneself. We have had patience. I was for far too long a flickering little flame beside the dazzling but, as is clear now, quite deceptive radiance of Christian. Now that my whole life's happiness is at stake, as well as the honour of myself and my house, it would be the merest weakness on my part if I were to regard passively all that is happening and still likely to happen. This is likewise the opinion of my friends and of every right thinking person. Some energetic action is necessary if I am to sustain myself in the station which I have achieved, not to mention any other unpleasantness in which we may become involved. Until I hear from you, I shall try to get in touch with Judith, and take counsel with her. Although she ceased from all association with myself, in the most insulting manner and for reasons still dark to me, I believe that she will realize the seriousness of the situation."

The Privy Councillor received this letter immediately on the heels of a conference with a delegation of strikers. It was some time before the pained amazement it automatically aroused in him really penetrated his consciousness. In any other circumstances the letter's unfilial, almost impudent tone would have angered him. To-day he gave it no further thought. Swiftly he wrote a telegram in cipher to Girke and Graurock.

The reply which came by special delivery reached him the next evening at his house in Würzburg. Willibald Girke wrote:

" My dear Privy Councillor:—Although it is some time since we have had the pleasure of working under direct orders from you, yet in the hope of renewed relations between us, we have been forward-looking enough to continue our investigations, and to keep up to date in all matters concerning Herr Christian Wahnschaffe at our own risk and expense. Thanks to this efficient farsightedness which we have made our rule, we are able to answer your question with the celerity and precision which the situation calls for.

"We proceed at once to the root of the matter, the murder of the young Jewess. We can give you the consoling assurance that there is no other connection between your son and the foul crime in question than through the warm and much discussed friendship which your son entertained for the murdered girl. Hence he is implicated as a witness, and as such will have to appear in court in due time. This painful necessity is unhappily unavoidable. Who touches pitch is defiled. His close association with proletarians necessarily involved him in such matters and in a knowledge of their affairs. It has been proved and admitted that he once visited the dwelling of the murderer Heinzen. He did so in the company of Ruth Hofmann, and on that occasion a scandalous scene is said to have taken place which was provoked by Niels Heinrich, the brother of Karen Engelschall. This Niels Heinrich is a close friend of Joachim Heinzen, has been kept under close surveillance by the police and examined, and his evidence is said to have been very serious for the accused. It is this connection with Engelschall, casual and innocent as it may be, that will be held against your son, and its disagreeable results cannot yet be absolutely estimated.

"Ruth Hofmann was seen almost daily in your son's society. Her father's flat was immediately opposite Karen Engelschall's, a circumstance which facilitated their friendship. A new party has already moved in, a certain Stübbe with his wife and three children. This Stübbe is a drunkard of the most degraded sort. He is noisy every evening, and treats his family with such cruelty that your son has already found it necessary to interfere on several occasions. We touch upon this fact to illustrate the ease with which, in these dwelling-places, comradeships are established and annoyances incurred. The former tenant, David Hofmann, was indeed peaceful and well-behaved. But he must have been in the utmost difficul-

ties, since he left for America only a few days before the
murder. Although telegrams were sent after him at once, he
has not been heard from. It is supposed that, for reasons
of his own, he emigrated under an assumed name, since the
passenger lists of all ships that have sailed within the past
two weeks have been searched for his own name in vain. It is
possible, moreover, that he sailed from a Dutch or British
port. The authorities are investigating.

" Ruth's young brother had also disappeared for six days,
and did not show up until the very evening on which the
murder was discovered, when he was found in your son's room.
He has remained there ever since. His state of mind is
inexplicable. No urging, neither requests nor commands, could
extract from him the slightest hint as to where he had passed
the crucial days between Sunday and Thursday. As his silence
is prolonged, it assumes a more and more mysterious aspect,
and every effort is made to break it in the belief that it may
be connected with the murder and may conceal important
bits of evidence.

" It has not failed to be observed that your son not only
gives no assistance to those who desire to question young
Hofmann, but frustrates their purpose whenever he can. Since
he is absent from his room during the greater part of the day,
a certain Fräulein Schöntag has undertaken to watch over the
boy. Recently, however, the necessity for such constant
watchfulness seems to have decreased. In the absence of
Fräulein Schöntag the boy Hofmann is now often left alone
for hours, and only the wife of Gisevius occasionally looks
in to see that he is still safely there. Nevertheless a plain
clothes detective is keeping the house under close and constant observation.

" From all this it is obvious that, in assuming the care of
this enfeebled boy, your son has taken upon himself a new
burden, which, in view of his other responsibilities and restricted pecuniary means, will be not a little difficult to bear.

We take the liberty of making this observation, in spite of the fact that a real understanding of your son's intentions and purposes is still lacking to us as to every one.

" This concludes our report. In the hope that our thoroughness and exactness corresponds to your hopes and wishes, and in the expectation of such further directions as you may be pleased to give us, We beg to remain, Most respectfully yours, Girke and Graurock. Per W. Girke."

Albrecht Wahnschaffe wandered through the rooms of the old house, followed by the dog Freya. To avoid the most crushing of his thoughts, he summoned up the face of the workingman who had been the spokesman of yesterday's deputation. He recalled with great exactness the brutal features—the protruding chin, the thin lips, the black moustache brushed upward, the cold, sharp glance, the determined expression. And in this face he saw no longer the visage of this particular man who had come to him on this particular and accidental errand, but of a whole world, mysterious, inevitable, terrible, full of menace and coldness and determination.

The energy and circumspection which he had shown in his conference with the delegates seemed to him monstrously futile. The power of no individual would avail in the conflict with that world.

He did not want to think—not of the letter of the private detective agency, nor of its horrible revelations, which seemed dim and turbid scenes of an immeasurably alien life, and yet the life of his son whom he had loved and whom he still loved. Ah, no, he did not want to think of the innumerable lowly and ugly and horrible events which whirled past his mind in a ghostly panorama—the rooms, the courts, the houses full of groaning, wretched bodies. To prevent himself from thinking of these, he turned the pages of a book, hunted through a drawer filled with old letters, and wandered tirelessly from room to room, followed by the dog Freya.

Fleeing from these images, he encountered others that concerned the realm of his work, in which the hopes of all his life were rooted and had ripened, in which the very wheels of his existence had been set in motion. He saw the great shops desolate, the furnaces extinguished, the trip-hammers still, and from a thousand doors and windows arms in gestures of command stretched out toward him who had thought himself the master of them all. It was not the first time that a strike had interfered with the intricate organization of the works. But it was the first time that the feeling came to him that struggle was useless and the end imminent.

And the question rose to his lips: "Why have you done this to me?" And this question he addressed to Christian, as though Christian were guilty of the demands of those who had once been willing slaves, of the empty halls, the extinguished furnaces, the silent hammers—guilty, somehow, because of his presence in those rooms amid harlots and murderers, mad and sick men, and in all those haunts of human vermin. Rage quivered up in him, one of those rare attacks that all but robbed him of consciousness. His eyes seemed filled with blood; he sought a sacrifice and a creature to make atonement, and observed the dog gnawing at a rug. He took a bamboo stick, and beat the animal so that it whined piteously—beat it for minutes, until his arm fell exhausted.

Calm came, and he felt remorse and shame. But the core of his anger remained in his heart, and he carried it about with him like a hidden poison. The gnawing and burning did not cease, and he knew that it would not cease until he had had a reckoning with Christian, until Christian had given some accounting of himself as man to man, son to father, criminal to judge.

The rage corroded his soul. Yet what was the way out? How could he reach Christian? How summon him to an accounting? No active step but would betray his dignity. Was he doomed merely to wait? For weeks and months? The silent rage gnawed at his very life.

VI

Johanna's absence made Amadeus Voss more and more anxious. Using the methods of a spy, he had discovered that she had left the house of her relatives quite suddenly. On the day after her last visit to Zehlendorf, she had come home silent and sorrowful. Her absence had caused worry, since every one was now thinking of murders and mysterious disappearances. She had refused to tell where she had passed the night, and had simply declared that she was going away altogether. She had resisted all questions and arguments in silence and had quickly packed her possessions. Then a motor car, which she had ordered, had appeared, and with formal words of thanks she had said good-bye. She had told her cousin, with whom she was more intimate than with the rest, that she needed a period of concentration and loneliness, and was moving into a furnished room. She begged that no one try to seek her out. It would be useless and only drive her farther. Indeed, she had threatened more desperate things if she were not left in peace. Nevertheless her frightened kinsmen had followed her track, and had discovered that she had rented a room in Kommandanten Street. But since she was lodging with a respectable woman and seemed guilty of nothing exciting or dangerous, her desire was finally respected, and all vain speculation as to her incomprehensible action abandoned.

These details had been recounted to Voss by a maid whom he had bribed with five marks. With tense face and inflamed heart he went home to consider what he should do. He found a letter from Johanna, who wrote: " I do not know how things will be between us in the future. At this moment I am incapable of any decision. I am not in the least interested either in myself or in my fate, and I have weighty reason for that feeling. Don't seek me out. I am in Stolpische Street almost all day long, but don't seek me out if you have any interest in me or if you want me to have the least interest

in you in the future. I don't want to see you; I can't bear
to listen to you at present. The experience I have had has
been too dreadful and too unexpected. You would find me
changed in a way that you would not like at all. Johanna."

Pale with rage, he immediately rode into the city as far as
the station on Schönhauser Avenue. When he reached Stolpische Street it was nine o'clock in the evening. Frau Gisevius
told him that Fräulein Schöntag had left half an hour ago.
He looked into Christian's room, and saw an unknown boy
sitting at the table. He drew the woman aside, and asked
her who it was. She was amazed that he didn't know, and
told him that it was the brother of the murdered girl. She
added that Wahnschaffe was quite unlike himself since the
tragedy. He walked about like a lost soul. If you talked
to him he either didn't answer at all or answered at random.
He didn't touch his breakfast which she brought him every
morning. Often he would stand for half an hour on the same
spot with lowered head. She was afraid he was losing his
mind. A couple of days ago she had met him in Rhinower
Street, and there, in bright daylight, he had been talking out
loud to himself so that the passers-by had laughed. Yesterday
he had left without a hat, and her little girl had run after
him with it. He had stared at the child for a while as if he
didn't understand. Shortly after that he had returned home
with several of his friends. Suddenly she had heard him cry
out and had rushed into his room. She had found him on
his knees before the others, sobbing like a little child. Then
he had struck the floor in his despair and had cried out that
this thing could not be and dared not be true, that it wasn't
possible and he couldn't endure it. Fräulein Schöntag had
been there too. But she had been silent and so had the others.
They had just sat there and trembled. This attack had been
caused by some young men imprudently telling him that this
was the day set for the official examination and autopsy of
Ruth's body. He had wanted to hasten to the court. They

had restrained him with difficulty, and finally had to assure him that he would be too late, that everything would be over. All night long he had walked up and down in his room, while Michael had been lying on the leather sofa. The two hadn't exchanged one word all night. She had slipped out of her room and listened repeatedly—not a syllable. At five o'clock in the morning Fräulein Schöntag had come; at seven Lamprecht and another student. They had persuaded him to go out to Treptow with them to spend the day. He had neither consented nor refused, and they had just dragged him along. Friends of Ruth Hofmann had come too and staid till noon— a woman and a young man. They sometimes came in the evening too, after Fräulein Schöntag had gone, so that Michael need not be alone. No one knew what was going to be done with the boy. His condition hadn't changed in the least. He hadn't even undressed, and if Fräulein Schöntag hadn't known just how to get around him, he would not even have let anybody brush the mud from his clothes or wash his hands and face. Sometimes a red-haired gentleman would come to see the boy. She had heard that he was a baron and a friend of Wahnschaffe. This gentleman had brought a chessboard day before yesterday, because some one had said that Michael knew how to play chess and had often played with his sister. But when the chessmen had been set up, Michael had only shuddered and had not touched them. The board was still there on the table. Herr Voss could go and see for himself.

The woman would have gossipped on and on. But Voss left her with a silent nod. He had grown thoughtful. What he had heard of Christian had made him thoughtful. Careless of his direction, he turned toward Exerzier Square. He brooded and doubted. His imagination refused to see Christian as the woman had pictured him. It seemed an absolute contradiction of the possible, a mockery of all experience. Grief, such grief— and Christian? Despair, such despair—and Christian? The world was rocking on its foundations. Some mystery must

be behind it all. Under the pressure of huge forces the very
elements may change their character, but it was inconceivable
to him that blood should issue from a stone, or a heart be
born where none had been.

Forced back against his will, he returned to Stolpische
Street. Suddenly he saw Johanna immediately in front of him.
He called out to her; she stopped and nodded, and showed
no surprise. But his hasty, whispered questions left her silent.
Her face was of a transparent pallor. At the door of the
house she stopped and considered. Then she walked back into
the court to the window of Christian's room. She wanted to
look in, but a hanging had been drawn. She hurried into the
hall, rang the bell, and exchanged some words with Frau
Gisevius. Then she came back. "I must go upstairs," she
said, "I must see how Karen is." She did not indicate that
Voss was to wait. He waited with all the more determination.
From the dwellings about he heard music, laughter, the crying
of children, the dull whirr of a sewing-machine. At last
Johanna came back and returned to the street at his side.
She said in a helpless tone: "The poor woman will hardly
outlive the night, and Christian isn't at home. What is to
be done?"

He did not answer.

"You must understand what is happening to me," Johanna
said, softly and insistently.

"I understand nothing," Voss replied dully. "Nothing—
except that I suffer, suffer beyond endurance."

Johanna said harshly: "You don't count."

They were near the Humboldt Grove. It was cold, but
Johanna sat down on a bench. She seemed wearied; exertions
hurt her delicate body like wounds. Shyly Voss took her hand,
and asked: "What is it, then?"

"Don't," she breathed, and withdrew her hand. After a
long silence she said: "People always thought him insensitive.
Some even said that that was the reason for his success with

all who came near him. It was a nice theory. I myself
never believed it. Most theories are wrong; why should this
one have been right? There is so much vain talk about people;
it is all painful and futile, both when it asserts and when it
denies. His society wasn't, I grant you, spiritually edifying.
If one was deeply moved by something, one somehow, instinctively, hid it from him and felt a sense of embarrassment.
And now—this! You can't imagine it. And how am I to
describe it? All the time, that first evening while he was
taking care of Michael, he hadn't yet been told anything.
At nine or half-past he went up to Karen's, intending to come
back in an hour, but he came earlier. There were people
loitering in the yard, and they told him. Then he came into
the room, quite softly. He came in and . . ." She took
out a handkerchief, pressed it to her eyes, and wept very
gently.

Voss let her cry for a little while. Then he asked very
tensely: "He came in and——? And what? "

Johanna kept her eyes covered, and went on: "You had
the feeling: This is the end for him, the end of all content, of
smiles and laughter—the end. In fifteen minutes his face had
aged by twenty years. I looked at it for just a moment; then
my courage failed me. You may think it fantastic, but I tell
you the whole room was one pain, the air was pain and so
was the light. It's the truth. Everything hurt; everything
one thought or saw hurt. But he was absolutely silent, and
his expression was like that of one who was straining his eyes
to read some illegible script. And that was the most painful
thing of all."

She fell silent and Voss did not break this silence. Enviously
and rancorously he reflected: "We shall have to convince ourselves that blood can issue from a stone; we must see and
hear and test." Deliberately he fortified his will to doubt.
The explanations which he gave in his own mind were of an
unworthy character. Not to provoke Johanna he feigned to

share her faith; and yet there was something about her story that stirred his vitals and made him afraid.

Johanna needed some support. She froze in her new freedom; she distrusted her strength to bear it. With a touch of dread and longing she wondered that no one dragged her back by force into the comfort of a sheltered, care-free, secure life.

She was not sorry to have Amadeus walking at her side. Ah, it was inconsistent and weak and faithless to one's own self, but there was such a horror in being alone. Yet her gesture of farewell seemed utterly final when they reached the house in Kommandanten Street where she lived. Amadeus Voss, suspecting her weakness and her melancholy, accompanied her to the dark stairs, and there grasped her with such violence as though he meant to devour her. She merely sighed.

At that moment an irresistible desire for motherhood welled up in her. She did not care through whose agency, nor whether his kiss inspired disgust or delight. She wanted to become a mother—to give birth to something, to create something, not to be so empty and cold and alone, but to cling to something and seem more worthy to herself and indispensable to another being. Had not this very man who held her like a beast of prey spoken of the yearning of the shadow for its body? Suddenly she understood that saying.

Sombre and searching and strong was the look she gave him when they stepped out upon the street again. Then she went with him.

VII

Karen was still alive in the morning. Death had a hard struggle with her. Late at night she had once more fought herself free of its embrace; now she lay there, exhausted by the effort. Her arms, her hands, her breasts were covered with sores filled with pus. Many had broken open.

Three women rustled through the room—Isolde Schirmacher, the widow Spindler, and the wife of a bookbinder who lived in the rear. They whispered, fetched things back and forth, waited for the physician and for the end.

Karen heard their whispers and their tread with hatred. She could not speak; she could scarcely make herself understood; but she could still hate. She heard the screeching and rumbling in the flat that had been the Hofmanns' and was now the Stübbes'. The drunkard's rising in the morning was as baleful to his wife and children as his going to bed at night. All the misery that he caused penetrated the wall, and aroused in Karen memories of equal horrors in dim and distant years.

Yet for her there was really but one pain and one misery— Christian's absence. For days he had paid her only short visits; during the last twenty-four hours, none at all. Dimly she knew of the murder of the Jewish girl, and dimly felt that Christian was changed since then; but she felt so terribly desolate without him that she tried not to think of that. His absence was like a fire in which her still living body was turned to cinders. It cried out at her. In the midst of the moaning of her agony she admonished herself to be patient, raised her head and peered, let it drop back upon the pillows, and choked in the extremity of her woe.

The door opened and she gave a start. It was Dr. Voltolini, and her face contorted itself.

There was little that the physician could do. The complications that had appeared and had affected the lungs destroyed every vestige of hope. Nothing was left to do but ease her pain by increasing the doses of morphine. " And why save such a life," Dr. Voltolini was forced to reflect, as he saw the terrible aspect of the woman still fighting death, " a life so complete and superfluous and unclean? "

It was the third occasion on which he had not found Christian here, yet he felt the old need of some familiar talk with him. He himself was a reserved man. To initiate a stranger into the secrets of his fate had been to him, hereto-

fore, an unfamiliar temptation. But in Christian's presence
that temptation assailed him strongly and he suffered from
it; and this was especially true since he had witnessed an
apparently meaningless scene.

A journeyman of her father of whom she was fond had given
Isolde Schirmacher a ring with an imitation ruby. Near the
kitchen door she had shown Christian the ring in her delight.
Dr. Voltolini was just coming out of the sick room. She
took the ring from her finger, let the worthless stone sparkle
in the light, and asked Christian whether it wasn't wonderful.
And Christian had smiled in his peculiar way and had answered: " Yes, it is very beautiful." The widow Spindler, who
stood in the kitchen door, had laughed a loud laugh. But
an expression of such gratitude had irradiated the girl's face
that, for a moment, it had seemed almost lovely.

On the stairs the widow Engelschall met Dr. Voltolini. She
stopped him and asked him his opinion of Karen's condition.
He shrugged his shoulders and told her there was no hope. It
was a question of hours.

The widow Engelschall had long had her suspicions of
Karen. Whenever she entered the room Karen grew restless,
avoided her glance, and pulled the covers up to her chin. The
widow knew what it was to have a bad conscience. She
scented a mystery and determined to fathom it. There was
no time to lose. If she hesitated now she might be too late
and regret it forever after. Undoubtedly the secret was that
Wahnschaffe had given her money, which, according to an
old habit, she kept concealed about her person in an old
stocking or chemise or even sewn up in the mattress. All the
money that man had couldn't have just vanished. He had
probably put aside a few dozen thousand-mark notes or some
securities. And who else should have them but Karen? If
one put two and two together, considered his craziness and
her behaviour, the matter seemed pretty clear, and the thing
to do now was to prevent mischief. For if she didn't happen

to be present at the moment of Karen's death, all sorts of people would be about, and the treasure would slip into the pocket of God knows who. You couldn't read the theft in the thief's face. These were the things that presented themselves very strongly to the widow Engelschall on her way to Stolpische Street.

Karen had her own presentiment regarding her mother's thoughts. As her illness progressed her fear for the pearls rose and rose. They no longer seemed safe upon her body. She might lose consciousness and people might handle her and discover them. These fears disturbed her sleep. She often awakened with a start, stared wildly, and smothered a scream in her throat. She had accustomed herself to keep her hands under the covers, and her grasp of the pearls became mechanically convulsive whenever her senses sank into sleep or swoon. A frightful nightmare which she had, presented to her all the possibilities of danger. People came. Whoever wanted to, simply stepped into her room. She couldn't prevent it; she could not get up and latch the door. She guarded herself most carefully from the doctor. She trembled before his eye, and the very pores of her body seemed to cling from below to the coverlet lest he turn it suddenly back.

She let the pearls wander about—now under her pillow, now under the sheet, sometimes upon her naked breast where they touched the open wounds. Becoming aware of this contact, she addressed herself with the cruel mockery of sombre pain: "What's left of you? What are you now? A leprous carrion—ruined and done for and disgusted with yourself."

Gradually she had become indifferent to the pecuniary value of the pearls, even though, during a sleepless night, in answer to her ceaseless questions, Christian had given her an insight into it which surpassed her wildest guesses. The figures were mere empty numbers to her. She shuddered, shook her head, and let the matter slide. The jewels had quite another effect on her now, and this increased in power as the old glamour of their mere value faded. At first the pearls had been a symbol and a lamentation over her fate; their lustre glimmered to her from that other shore of life from which no breath or message had ever before floated to her. But now they no longer stirred her to envy and wrath as they had once done, but only to regret over that all of life which she had wasted and flung aside. And she had wasted her life and flung it aside, because she had known nothing of beauty or loveliness or joy or adornment or, she could truly say, of earth and heaven. She could not re-live her ruined life; there was no other, and this one was gone.

But it seemed to her, as she lay there and brooded and let her flesh disintegrate, as though her lost earth and lost heaven were given back to her in every single pearl and in the whole string. Everything was in the pearls—the children she had conceived and born and lost in hatred, the poverty-stricken, all but unfulfilled dreams, the longing she had faintly felt for some human being, the wizened love, the jaded light, the petty hopes, the small delight. Everything crystallized in the pearls and became a soul. All that she had missed and gambled or thrown away or never reached, all that had been darkened for her or driven from her by want and sorrow— all this became a soul. And to this soul she was immeasurably devoted as she lay there and brooded and let her flesh disintegrate. For this soul was the soul of Christian. His soul was in the rope of pearls. It was this that she grasped and clung to, and wanted to possess even in her grave. Her blue eyes, under the narrow forehead and the strawy dishevelled hair, had the fetish-worshipper's glow.

VIII

The widow Engelschall's first concern was to get the women out of Karen's room. To succeed she had to make her command abundantly clear. She hissed at the Schirmacher girl:

"Would you mind taking your snub-nose out of this here place?" Isolde went, but she felt sure that the old woman had evil intentions.

When the widow Engelschall approached the bed, she saw that there was but just time for her to use the last glimmer of her daughter's consciousness. If she had miscalculated—well, no harm was done, and she would be the first one, at all events, to have access to the dead woman's body. Only there must be no shilly-shallying.

She began to talk. She sat down on a chair, bent far over toward Karen, and spoke in a raised voice so that no word should escape the dying woman. She said that she had meant to bring along some pastry, but the pastry-cook's shop had been closed. In the evening, however, she intended to boil a chicken in rice or make a Styrian pudding with apple-sauce. That refreshed the stomach and improved the digestion. Sick people needed strengthening food, and one mustn't be stingy with them. Stinginess, she declared, had never been a fault of hers, anyhow. No one could say that. And she had always been ready to do the right thing by her children. It had been toil and trouble enough, and she hadn't counted on gratitude. You didn't get that in this world anyhow, no more from your children than from Tom, Dick, or Harry.

Beset by death as she was, Karen heard only the tone of this hypocritical speech. She moved her arms. An instinct told her that her mother wanted something; a last effort at reflection told her what that was, and a last impulse warned her not to betray herself. She forced herself to lie still and not to let an eyelid quiver. But the widow Engelschall knew that she was on the right track. She herself, she continued, had never striven after riches. If ever a little superfluity had come to her, she had shared it with others. You couldn't take anything into the grave with you anyhow, and though you clung to what you had like iron, it didn't do you no good in the end. So it was more sensible and nobler too to give it up, and live to share the pleasure of the people you gave it to, and listen to their praises. Didn't Karen remember, she asked, how when that old hag of a Kränich woman had died and eighty-seven pieces of gold had been found in her straw-mattress—didn't she remember how, amid the joy, people had railed at the stingy beast? No one had shed a tear over her. They had consigned her to hell where she belonged.

Having said this, the widow Engelschall stretched out her hand, and with apparent carelessness began to feel about the pillow. The rope of pearls lay under it. She had not yet reached it; but Karen thought she had grasped it, and with feeble hands fought off the hands of her mother. Breathing stertorously, she raised herself a little, and threw herself across the pillow. The widow Engelschall murmured: "Aha, there we have it!" She was sure now. Swiftly she thrust her hand farther and pulled out an end of the rope of pearls. She uttered a dull cry. Her fat face oozed sweat and turned crimson, for she recognized at once the fabulous value of what she held. Her eyes started from their sockets, saliva dripped from her mouth. She grasped what she held more and more firmly, as Karen rested the whole weight of her body upon the pillow, stretched out her hands, dug her nails into her mother's wrists, and whined a long, piteous whine. But in spite of her ghastly display of strength she succumbed in that unequal struggle. Already the widow Engelschall, uttering a low howl, had torn the pearls from their hiding-place; she was about to flee from Karen's inarticulate screeching and blind rage and fierce moans and chattering teeth, when the door opened and Christian entered.

The women in the hall had noticed that something strange and fearful was taking place in Karen's room. The struggle between mother and daughter had not lasted long enough to give them a chance to make a decision or fight down their fear of the old woman. But they received Christian with frightened faces and pointed toward the door. They wanted to follow him into the room; but since he paid no attention to them and closed the door behind him, they remained where they were and listened. But they heard no sound.

Christian approached Karen's bed. He had taken in what was happening. Silently he took the pearls from the old woman's hands. Wrought up and inflamed by greed as she was, she did not dare make a gesture of resistance. On his face there was an expression which beat down her boiling rage at his interference. It was a strange expression—a lordly mournfulness was in it, a proud absorption, a smile that was remote, a something estranged and penetrating and inviolable. He laid the pearls upon Karen's breast, and took both of her hands into his. She looked up to him—relieved, redeemed. Her body quivered in convulsions, but was eased as he held her hands. Freezing and icy under the touch of death, she thrust herself nearer to him, babbling, moaning, trembling in every limb, and with a hot moisture in her eyes. And he did not recoil. He did not feel any repulsion at the malodorousness of the dripping sores. That smile still on his face, he embraced her and gave her a last warmth against his breast, as though she were a little bird whom the storm had blown hither. At last she lay very quiet, without motion or sound. And thus she died in his arms.

IX

Broken by his wild dissipations, Felix Imhof had to halt at last. His strength was at an end.

He summoned physicians, and with a smile begged for the truth. The last whom he consulted, a famous specialist, bade him be prepared for the worst, since his spinal marrow was affected. "Tubercular?" Imhof asked objectively. "Yes, exactly," was the answer.

"All right, old boy! Fifth act, last scene," he said to himself. Since fever ensued, and exhaustion alternated with violent pain, he took to his bed, had the windows darkened and the mirrors covered, and stared into space through the long hours with the expression of a frightened child.

He had never been able to get along without people. As far back as his memory went, his life had been as crowded as a fair. He had been hail-fellow-well-met with every one; they had all clung to him, and he had taken great pains to mean something to them all and to meet their wishes. And who was left to him now? No one. Whom did he desire? No one. Who would mourn for him? No man and no woman.

" I wonder what they'll say about me when I'm gone? " he kept wondering. " Oh, yes, Imhof, they'll say, don't you recall him? Good fellow, pleasant companion, nothing slack about him, always in good spirits, always on the lookout for something new—a little touched, maybe. You must remember him. Why, he looked so and so and so. He talked like an Italian priest, wasted his money like an idiot, and drank like a fish."

And in spite of such reminders many would not remember, but shrug their shoulders and begin to talk about something else.

He had neither father nor mother, sister nor brother, no relative and, in reality, no friends. His very birth was obscure. Its mystery would never be unveiled now. Perhaps he came of the dregs of mankind, perhaps of noble blood. But this mystery had, so far as he was concerned, neither romance nor charm. Only fate, for the sake of clearness, had stamped his being thus as that of a solitary, alienated, and self-dependent creature.

He had neither root nor connection nor bond. He was himself; nothing else. A personality fashioned by its moment in time—unique and complete in itself.

There was not even a servant who was faithful to him through personal devotion or through attachment to his house. No soul belonged to him—only things for which he had paid.

He had given much unselfish devotion to artists and works of art. A beautiful poem, an excellent picture had given his mind the elasticity and his mood the serenity which had conpensated him for all the weariness and flatness of his environment. But seeking now to recall the impressions that had seemed unforgettable to him, he faced emptiness. The bubbling spring was choked with stone and sand. Did art, which he had loved so truly, sustain the spirit no better than some fleeting roadside adventure? What did it lack?

From the wreck of his fortune a few treasures had remained —a painting by Mantegna, the Three Kings from the East, an early Greek statue of Dionysos, a statue by Rodin, and a still-life by Von Gogh. He had these exquisite things and several others brought into his room, and sought to lose himself in the contemplation of them. But the old happy ecstasy would not return. The colours seemed dull and the marble without warmth or life. What had passed from these things? What change had come over them?

On the table beside his bed stood an hour-glass. He watched the reddish sand, fluid and swift as water, flicker through an eye from the upper bulb into the lower. It took twelve minutes. Leaning on his arms he watched it and reversed the bulbs whenever the upper one was empty. And again his eyes had the expression of a frightened child's.

One day, as he was watching the running of the sand in the hour-glass, he said aloud to himself: " Death? What's the meaning of that? It's nonsense."

It was an absurd word and idea, and he could not grasp it or penetrate it. Scarcely had he begun to gain the slightest conception of dying when he found that that very conception started from the idea of life. One had always been in space and was to leave it now. Yet wherever one passed to, there must be space also. And one could not think the concept space without also thinking oneself. Well, then . . .

A shiver passed over him. Then he smiled avidly. He

thought of the delights that had been his—the fullness and
wealth of pleasure and expectation, of ecstasy and triumph;
of the feasts and revels and journeys and enterprises and
games; of all the merry, multicoloured, changeful conflict.
How delightful it had been to rise in the morning with one's
straight limbs; how delightful that wheels whirred and news-
boys shrilled and bells clanged and dogs barked; and how
exquisite it had been when a young woman, ready for love,
loosened her hair and dropped her garments and her white
flesh gleamed like the flesh of a fruit. Ah, and the pleasant
comrades and the splendid horses, and the homecomings at
night, just a little drunk. In the hall one longed for the first
step of the stairs; it seemed so comfortable, logical, inviting.
Upstairs the windows were open, and in one of them was a
bunch of flowers. At all times and in all places one felt:
" I am here, in the midst of it, lord of the foam and music
of life. I command and life obeys, and there will be a to-
morrow and a day after to-morrow, and endless days like
slender trees along an avenue." And at such moments he had
felt tender toward himself and flattered by his own breath, and
had fed on air and light and clouds and men and songs. And
everything had been goodly to his taste—even the ugly things
and the rain and the very puddles in the street. For he was
alive . . . alive. . . .

He reversed the hour-glass and fell back among the pillows.
His eyes became aware of a small, grey spider that crept up
the purple silk of the wall-hangings. It frightened him.
Suddenly the thought struck him: " It is possible, even likely,
that the spider will still exist when I am gone." This reflection frightened him beyond expression, and he watched the
spider's slow progress with breathless suspense.

" Is it conceivable," he thought, " that the horrible and
trivial spider will be in a world from which I am gone? It is
maddening. I have never believed in it and cannot believe in
it—in unconsciousness and darkness, and the damp and the

earth and the worms. And the spider is to live and I am not?
Not I who filled all space with my being and my vitality? Is
there any philosophy or religion or conviction that is not
smashed to bits against this one fact?   Supposing there
were someone who had the power to let me go on living as a
street-sweeper, a beggar, a jail-bird, despised, deformed, absurd, impotent. It almost seems to me that I would accept life
even at that price. Good God, where do such thoughts lead
one? What shameful ideas are these for a man who has
always insisted on cleanliness and honour! Have I ever slunk
away before an affront or failed to uphold my dignity? And
yet I know that I would choose life at any price. The pains
of the soul? Much I care about them! I would welcome grief,
disappointment, bitterness, hatred, and loss—so I could but
live . . . but live. . . ."

An hour later Weikhardt was announced. Imhof considered
whether he should see him. He had denied himself to all
callers during the past few days, but he could not make up
his mind to refuse to see the painter, whom he had always
liked uncommonly well.

"Is it Eliphaz, Bildad, or Zophar who comes to comfort
Job? " he addressed Weikhardt. "You remember the incident, don't you? 'They lifted up their eyes afar off, and
knew him not, they lifted up their voice and wept; and they
rent every one his mantle, and sprinkled dust upon their heads
toward heaven.' "

Weikhardt smiled. But when his eyes had become accustomed to the semi-darkness of the room and he saw the
emaciated face, his mocking impulse fled.

For a while their talk was superficial. Weikhardt told about
his marriage, his work, his vain efforts after economic security,
and finally gossiped a little. Imhof listened with wavering attention. Suddenly he asked with apparent equanimity: " How
is that marvellous female salamander? "

"What salamander? Whom do you mean? "

"Whom should I mean? Sybil, of course! Wasn't it the maddest and wildest thing that the trivial word of a soulless creature should have brought swift decision into the slow process of my fate? Was it Providence? Was it so written in the stars?"

"I don't understand," Weikhardt murmured.

"Don't you? Didn't you know that the horrible little wooden fay called me a 'nigger,' and that I revenged myself in my characteristic way by playing a trump that lost me the whole game? I went and sought the company to which her icy scorn had sent me. I slept with a Negro woman to shame the white girl and break her vanity, at least in my imagination. Wasn't it sublime? And you didn't know it?"

"I knew of nothing," Weikhardt murmured in astonishment. A long silence followed.

Imhof continued in a changed voice. "The things that followed weren't so different from former experiences. But the central nerve was sick and the source of life poisoned. Sometimes I'm tempted to hasten the disgustingly slow execution by a clean bullet. It's too undignified to have death glide about you as an overfed cat circles around a trapped mouse. Or else one could do the Sardanapalus act—light fireworks and burn the house down, and make one's exit with a grandiose gesture."

"It would be cheap and meretricious," Weikhardt said, "you'd never forgive another for it."

"I'm not capable of it in reality. I cling desperately to the depressing rag of life that's left. Ah, to live at all—what that means!" He bit into his pillow, and moaned: "I don't want to die! I don't want to die! I don't want to die!"

Weikhardt arose to approach the bed. But Imhof beckoned him passionately away. "Thus do I expiate," he moaned. "Thus is the great devourer being devoured. Thus Time hurls me from its bosom. Look upon me writhing here and crying for pardon, and go out and tell the others about it. Give them my love! And give my love to all dear boys and girls! Good-bye, my friend, good-bye! "

Weikhardt took his leave without a word.

X

Karen's body had been given back to the earth. Many of the people from the house had accompanied it to the grave. Christian thought he had also observed Johanna and Voss.

On the way home Dr. Voltolini walked beside him. For a while they did not speak. Then Christian with the perception of something unpleasant at his back, suddenly turned around. Ten paces behind he saw Niels Heinrich Engelschall. As Christian stopped, the other stopped too, and pretended to look at a shop window.

In the cemetery Christian had escaped from the friends who had accompanied him. Now, too, he would have preferred loneliness; but he did not want to wound the physician.

Continuing a conversation which they had started before the funeral, Dr. Voltolini said: " Stübbe ought to be separated from his family and placed in an institution. At any time delirium tremens might break out and he might kill the whole crowd. And even as it is, the poor woman can't endure his cruelty much longer. She's at the end of her strength."

" I've interfered several times during the past few days," Christian answered softly. " Other neighbours helped too. A man like that is worse than a wolf. The children stand around and tremble."

" And it's so difficult," said Dr. Voltolini, " to get the authorities to take any preventive measures. The law is unreasonably severe. Once a misfortune has taken place, it enters more mercilessly than is necessary; but it can never be moved to prevent anything."

Again Christian turned around. Niels Heinrich was still

following. Again he stopped, looked about him indifferently, and spat on the sidewalk.

"It is never a question of what one knows or desires, but always of what one does," Christian said, walking on again.

"And even what one has done, though it be inspired by the purest motives and the strictest sense of duty, is spattered with mud, and one must suffer for it as for a crime," Dr. Voltolini said bitterly.

"Has that been your experience?" Christian asked, with apparently conventional sympathy, but with his aware and listening glance.

"I don't like to talk about it," Dr. Voltolini said, with a saddened mien. "I haven't done so to any one here so far. You're the first and only one who have made me want to talk. I felt that way so soon as I had met you. It isn't as though you could advise or help me; it's far too late for either. My misfortune has done its worst and has receded into the past. But constant silence gnaws at me, and I can escape a period of paralysis if I can tell you the story of what happened to me."

Christian shook his head very slightly in his astonishment. Many people had already said similar words to him, and he did not understand their motive.

Dr. Voltolini continued: "Until two years ago I practised at Riedberg, near Freiwaldau, in Austrian Silesia. The town is several miles from the frontier of Prussia. Quite near it medicinal springs were discovered. It became a health resort of increasing popularity, and I and my family gradually attained a modest prosperity. But in the beginning of the summer of 1905 it happened that the wife of a cottager was attacked by typhoid fever, and I, according to my sworn duty, reported the case to the health authorities. Several citizens wanted to prevent my action. Even the commission on sanitation, whose chairman was mayor of the town, raised objections, and represented to me how the guests would be scared away

for a long time and the town get a bad name. I told them
I was acting in the interests of every one and could not be
deterred by merely material considerations. First they besought and finally threatened me, but I remained firm.

" The first consequence was that a regiment, which had
been ordered to Riedberg, and whose being stationed there
would have been profitable to the town, was sent elsewhere.
The panic that had been feared among the guests in the hotels
did break out, and most of them fled. And now a wretched
stream of abuse was poured out over me, and every one raged
against me in the filthiest terms. The men did not respond
to my greeting on the street. The butcher and baker and
dairyman refused to sell their goods to my wife. Daily I
received anonymous letters; you can imagine their character.
My windows were smashed; no one came to my consultation
hours, no patient dared to summon me. The fees that people
owed me were not paid, and suspicions and slanders arose,
ranging from silly talk to the vilest insinuations.

" Finally I was discharged from my office of district
physician. I appealed to the National Medical Association,
which in its turn appealed to the highest authorities. The
town council and the sanitary commission were both dissolved by the governor of the province, the mayor was removed from office, my own dismissal revoked, and an escort
of gendarmes despatched to the town to protect me and mine
from violence. The trouble was that my situation was as
bad as ever. The government could protect me from bodily
hurt, but it could neither give me back my practice nor force
my old patients to pay what they owed me. I was ruined. In
the course of five months I brought twenty-one suits of slander
and won every case. But I was more discouraged each time.
It became clear that I could not stay at Riedberg. But where
was I to go—a country doctor without private means, with a
wife and children and a feeble, aged mother to support?
How was I to silence the slanderers, wash off the stain, and

heal the inner hurt? I had no friend there who could lend me support; from the consolations of my wife there came to me only the voice of her own despair.

" I broke down completely. For eleven months I lay in a hospital. With unexampled energy my wife was busy during this period founding a new home for us and finding a new field of activity for me. I received permission to practise in Germany, and began life anew. Although I had lost faith both in my own powers and in mankind, my soul gradually grew calm again. Our circumstances are the most modest; but in this great city it is possible to be alone and to prevent the interference of strangers. For a long time I could practise my profession only if I forgot that my patients were human. I had to regard them as mechanisms that were to be repaired. Their pain and sorrow I passed over, and I hated to notice either. Do you understand that? Do you understand my coldness and contempt? "

" After all your experiences I can well understand it," Christian answered. " But I believe your standpoint is no longer the same. Am I right? It seems to me that a change has taken place in you."

" Yes, a change has taken place," Dr. Voltolini admitted. " And it began——" He stopped and cast an unobtrusive glance at his companion. After a pause he said timidly: " Why did you smile that day when the Schirmacher girl showed you her ring? Do you remember? You may, of course, reply: it was natural to smile, for the stone which delighted her so was quite worthless, and yet to disillusion her would have been cruel. And yet your smile didn't express that. It expressed something else."

Christian said: " I really don't remember precisely. I do remember the ring and the girl's pleasure in it, but I can't tell you to-day just why ı smiled. It would have been better, by the way, if the girl had been less happy. A few days later she lost the ring, and the poor thing cried for hours. It would have been better if I had said to her: 'Neither the ring nor the stone is worth anything.' I should have told her to throw it away. On such occasions it is almost always better to say to people, 'Throw it away.' Perhaps I smiled because that is what I wanted to say and didn't have the courage."

"That's how it looked," Dr. Voltolini said quickly and with a touch of excitement. "That's the impression I had."

"Why speak of it?" Christian said.

They had reached the house on Stolpische Street. Niels Heinrich, who had followed them, disappeared among the vehicles on the street.

Dr. Voltolini looked at the pavement, and said with embarrassment and hesitation: "You could do a great deal for me in the sense you suggested, if I might call on you every now and then. It sounds strange and like a confession of weakness, coming from a man of my years to one of yours. I can't justify my request, but I know I should be helped. I would get on and be more reconciled to my fate and work harder at the re-establishment of my life." His eyes were turned tensely to Christian's face.

Christian lowered his head, and after some reflection answered: "Your request is very flattering. I should be glad to serve you; I hope I may. But in order not to put you off with empty phrases, I should tell you that I shall be deeply preoccupied in the immediate future—not only inwardly, I am always that, but outwardly too. I am confronted with a difficult task—a terribly difficult task."

Struck by Christian's terrible seriousness Dr. Voltolini said: "I don't mean to be inquisitive. But may I ask what that task is?"

"To find the man who murdered Ruth Hofmann."

"How?" The physician was utterly astonished. "But I thought that the . . . murderer had been arrested."

Christian shook his head. "It is not the right man," he said, softly but with assurance. "I saw him. I saw him when he appeared before the investigating judge. I knew him before the crime too. He is not the murderer."

"That sounds strange," said Dr. Voltolini. "Is that merely your personal opinion, or do the authorities also——? "

"It's not an opinion," Christian said meditatively. "Perhaps it's more, perhaps it's less—quite as one chooses. I don't know what the authorities suspect. Undoubtedly they consider Joachim Heinzen the murderer. He has confessed, but I consider his confession false."

"Did you express that opinion before the judge? "

"No. How could I have done that? I haven't even a legitimate suspicion. Only I know that the man who is now held is not the murderer."

"But how do you expect to find the real criminal, if you haven't even a suspicion? "

"I don't know, but I must do it."

"You . . . you must? What does that mean? "

Christian did not answer. He raised his eyes and held out a friendly hand to Dr. Voltolini. "And so, if you should come and not find me, don't be angry at me. We shall meet again."

The doctor clasped his hand firmly and silently.

Christian went into the house and up to Karen's rooms. Fifteen minutes later Niels Heinrich mounted the same stairs.

XI

A fleck of sunlight trembled on the opposite wall of the courtyard. Its reflection lighted up the mirror over the leather sofa. A feeble fire was burning in the oven. Before going to the funeral Johanna Schöntag had thrown in a few small shovelfuls of coal. The fire crackled a little, but the room was growing cold.

Michael Hofmann sat in front of the chessboard. The student Lamprecht had set him a problem, and Michael stared at the board and the chessmen. Occasionally his thoughts converged in a will to find a solution, then they went wandering again. He had now succeeded in turning his mind toward outward things sufficiently to remember the chessmen and their positions. Even in the darkness of the night, during which he slept but rarely, he saw the figures of the two kings.

The fleck of sunshine sank lower on the wall, and the snow on the pavement glittered. Michael looked out through the window, and the gleaming of the snow caused his eyes to move. The whiteness—why did it torment him? He wanted to wipe it out or blow it away or cover it. Whiteness was a lie.

He got up and walked through the room. The glitter of the sunlight came insolently from the whiteness, and the room was filled with its lying shimmer. He hated it.

He stopped and listened and his eyelids twitched. Something floated before his mind, knocked at its door—not so much a forgotten thing as one suppressed and throttled. From his trousers pocket he drew forth a round, tightly rolled, blackish-brown object. He looked at it and began to shudder. For a moment his eyes had the same brooding look as when he regarded the chessmen. Then his fingers grew restless, and, growing paler and paler, he sought to unroll the object in his hand. It was a cloth, a handkerchief. Once it had been white, now it was drenched in blood.

It had been white, but now it was black with blood; and the blood had congealed so that the cloth had the toughness of leather and was hard to unfold. At last the surface appeared, and in one corner of it the embroided initials, R. H.

"Whiteness is evil and redness is evil," Michael whispered to himself, with the look of a beaten dog. He was struggling with a temptation, hunting for a way out, and all his being spoke of despair. He looked about him, hurried to the oven, opened the little iron door, and threw in the blood-drenched handkerchief. When the swift flame flared up he sighed with relief, and stood still and quivering.

XII

No one was in the rooms. The bed in which Karen had died had been taken away.

Christian walked up and down for a while. Then he sat down beside the table and rested his head on his hand. He thought: " Ruth has summoned Karen, as she will summon many more. What is the world without Ruth? For Ruth was the kernel and the soul of all things. And what is it that happened to Ruth, what really happened? Something unspeakably horrible, immeasurably depraved, but also impenetrably mysterious. To fathom it, one must subordinate every other feeling and occupation, all delight, all pain, all plans, and even eating and sleeping and seeing."

He reflected over the confusion that Karen's death had created within him. There was so much empty space about him since she was gone. The empty space cried out after her and was not to be silenced. No mournfulness arose that was not reluctant. Her existence had been as violent and garish as a burning mountain. The earth had swallowed the mountain, and in its place stretched a great waste.

Steps resounded, the door opened, and Niels Heinrich came in.

He nodded contemptuously toward the table at which Christian sat. He had pushed his bowler hat far back and kept it on his head. He looked about like some one examining quarters that had been advertised to be let. He walked into the second room, came back, stood impudently in front of Christian, and made a grimace.

" What do you want? " Christian asked.

He had come for Karen's things, Niels Heinrich announced. The widow had sent him. He always called his mother that. His falsetto voice penetrated to every corner of the room. Everything of Karen's would have to be handed over to him, he said, and counted and taken away.

Very calmly Christian said: "I shall not hinder you. Do as you please."

Niels Heinrich whistled softly through his teeth. He turned around and saw Karen's wooden box standing in a corner. He pulled it into the middle of the room. It was locked. First he struck it with his fist, then with his heel. Christian said it was not necessary to use force; Isolde Schirmacher had the key. Rudely Niels Heinrich swung around, and asked whether the pearls were in it. As Christian was silent in his surprise, the other added with growing irritation that the widow had told him a long story about a rope of pearls the size of pigeon's eggs. He wanted to know who'd inherit those? Undoubtedly they'd belonged to Karen, had been given to her, in fact. Who'd inherit them, he'd like to know! Surely the family who were the rightful heirs. He hoped there'd be no damned nonsense on that point.

"You are mistaken," Christian said coldly. "The pearls did not belong to Karen. They belong to my mother, and I am bound by a promise to return them. At the first opportunity I shall send them to Frankfort."

Niels Heinrich stood quite still for a while, and a green rage seethed in his eyes. "Is that so?" he said finally. The gentleman wanted to liquidate the firm now, did he? First take a poor, stupid wench and trick her out and make a fool of her year in and year out, and then, when she was gone, not even put up something decent for her mourning family. Well, the gentleman needn't think he'd get off so cheaply as long as he, Niels Heinrich, was on deck. And if the gentleman didn't come across with a good pile of shekels, he'd live to see something that'd surprise him; he'd find out, so sure's his name was Niels Heinrich Engelschall. He laughed a short harsh laugh and spread out his legs.

"I know who you are, and I'm not afraid of you," said Christian, with an almost cheerful expression.

Niels Heinrich was taken aback. His glance, which had

grown unsteady, fell upon Christian's delicate, narrow, cultivated hands. Suddenly he looked at his own hands, holding them out and spreading the fingers apart. This gesture interested Christian immensely, though he could not account for the source of his interest. The whole man fascinated him suddenly from a point of view which he had never before assumed; and it was solely due to this curious gesture. Niels Heinrich observed this and was startled anew.

Was that all, he asked, that the gentleman had to say? His mood was menacing now. The gentleman could speak fine High German, he went on, that was sure. But if necessary, he, Niels Heinrich, could do as much. Why not? But if a man was a man of family, and especially of a family where they breed millions the way common folks breed rabbits— well, it was shabby to try to sneak off like a cheat in an inn. He wasn't going to insist on the pearls, although he didn't like to decide how much of a pretence and a hypocrisy this story of lending them was. No gentleman would do such things. But some compensation—he did demand that, he'd insist on it, he owed that to his own honour; and his late sister, if the truth were known, would have expected that much.

Again he regarded his hands.

Christian looked at him attentively, and replied: " You are mistaken in this too. I have no money at my disposal. My liberty of action, so far as money is concerned, is more restricted than your own, more so than that of any one who earns his bread by his own work." He interrupted himself as he observed Niels Heinrich's incredulously jeering smile. The spiritual vulgarity in that smile was overwhelming.

He could take no stock in those stories, Niels Heinrich answered; no, not if he was to be hanged, drawn, and quartered. If the gentleman would tell him what was behind it all, maybe he'd believe it. To do a thing like that a man must have bran in his head. If the gentleman would tell him the real facts,

maybe he'd be able to see light. He'd gladly believe that there
was something behind it all. Nobody could tell, of course,
what sort of things the gentleman had on his conscience; so
his Papa and Mama wouldn't budge with the brass, and he
told elegant stories. But one might make things pretty lively
for the gentleman. There were a good many people, not only
in Stolpische Street but elsewhere, who didn't think the gentleman's love affair with the murdered Jewess all straight and
aboveboard. He, Niels Heinrich, knew a thing or two; other
people knew other things, the gentleman himself knew a damned
lot more than he showed, and he'd have to own up if things
got serious. All one'd have to do was to give a hint to the
right people, and the gentleman would find himself more
clearly described in the newspapers than he had so far. His
name'd be coupled with the name of that bloodhound Joachim
Heinzen. Then the fat would be in the fire, or, to use the
gentleman's manner of speech, he'd be irretrievably com-
promised.

In Christian's expression there did not appear the faintest
trace of indignation or disgust. He sat there with lowered
eyes, as though reflecting how he could answer most per-
tinently and objectively. Then he said: " Your hidden threats
frighten me no more than your open ones. I do not care
in the least where my name is mentioned or under what
circumstances, whether it be spoken or written or printed.
No one's opinion or attitude has any influence on me, not
even theirs who were once closest to me. So that is the third
error which you have made. There is no basis in reality to
anything you have said, least of all in your references to my
friendship with Ruth Hofmann. No one knows anything about
it, and I have spoken to no one; nor did Ruth do so, I am
sure. By what right do you pass a judgment on it, and so
shameful a one too? You have no suspicion how infinitely
far from the truth it is. And yet it surprises me that you
expect it to be effective. that you expect so false and empty an

accusation to wound or frighten me. But won't you sit down? You're standing there in such a hostile attitude. There's no occasion for enmity between us; I meant to tell you that long ago. If there's anything concerning your late sister or myself that you want to know, I shall be glad to inform you. In return, I'd like to ask you to answer me a few questions too. Do sit down." He pointed courteously to a chair.

These words, with their calm and their courtesy, amazed Niels Heinrich to the utmost. He had been prepared for tempestuous anger, a proud and irate repulse, for the customary counter-threat that veiled attempts at blackmail are wont to receive, for consternation, possibly for fear. But he was not prepared for this courtesy. It was so fundamentally different from anything that he had met with among men, that his eyes stared in stupid astonishment for a while, as though they saw an irresponsible moron whose behaviour was half absurd and half suspicious. He grasped the chair and sat down on it—half-crouching, ready for an attack or any mischief.

" The gentleman talks like a lawyer," he jeered. " You could make a success at the bar. What do you want to ask me anyhow? Fire away! Don't you have no fear. And seeing as how you talk so educated, I can polish my rough snout too. I ain't without education myself. I don't have to take nothing from no one. I even had a spell at a gymnasium once. The widow had ambitions in her day."

Suddenly his mockery sounded pained and forced. He bit on the iron of his chain.

" You mentioned Joachim Heinzen a moment ago," Christian said. " You called him a bloodhound. Is that your real opinion of him? You and he were very constant companions, and you must have a fairly accurate knowledge of his character. Do you really think he was capable of having committed the murder? Please consider your answer carefully for a moment; a great deal depends on it. Why do you look at me like that?

What is it? " Involuntarily Christian arose, for the look that Niels Heinrich fixed on him was literally frightful.

Niels Heinrich arose at the same moment and almost shrieked. Why ask him such fool questions? What in hell did he mean by 'em? A cardboard box lay on the table; he picked it up and hurled it down on the floor. Becoming aware of the imprudence of his outburst and regretting it, he laughed his goat-like laugh. Then stealthily, with colourless, furtive eyes he went on. Why shouldn't Heinzen be capable of the crime? He said he'd done it and he ought to know. How did the gentleman come to stick his nose into such affairs? Maybe he was a police spy or something? He tried to steady his lightless, furtive eyes in vain. But the slack muscles of his face began to grow taut again as he continued: " I know the feller. Sure, I know him. But you never know what any one is capable of till he does it. I didn't have no notion that he carried about a plan like that. The devil must've gotten into him; he must've swallowed poison. But I told him often enough: ' You ain't going to come to no good end.' " He stuck his fists in his trousers pockets, took a few steps, and leaned boastfully against the oven.

Christian approached him. " It is my impression that Heinzen lies," he said calmly. " He lied to the judge, he lied to himself. He doesn't realize the nature of what he says or does or accuses himself of. Don't you share the opinion that his mind is wholly confused? Assuredly he is but the tool of some one else. Some frightful pressure must have been exerted on him, and under its weight he made statements so incriminating that he became hopelessly enmeshed. Unless a miracle happens or the real criminal is discovered, he is lost."

Niels Heinrich's neck seemed thin as a stalk. His Adam's apple slid strangely up and down. His skin was white; only his ears were red as raw beef. " Would you be so kind as to tell me, my dear fellow, in what way this whole matter concerns you? " he asked, in his brittle falsetto and with an unexpected abandonment of his gutter jargon, of which he retained only the sharp, staccato rhythm. " What conclusions are you trying to draw? What are you aiming at? And how the devil does it all concern me? Perhaps you'll have the kindness to explain."

" It concerns you," Christian answered, breathing deeply, " because you associated constantly with Joachim Heinzen, and so you ought to be in a position to give me a hint. You must have some definite thoughts of your own on the matter; in one way or another it must touch you. It is my unalterable conviction that Heinzen is not and cannot be the murderer, but I am equally convinced that he has acted under the influence of the real culprit, so the latter must be among those with whom Heinzen associated. Now I cannot imagine that this individual failed to concentrate upon himself the attention of all his acquaintances, for he must be a man who is essentially different from the others. It only confirms my opinion of him that he has so far escaped the arm of justice. But he must be known; a man who was capable of that deed could not be overlooked. And that is why I turn to you. If you had not come to me, I would have gone to you."

Niels Heinrich grinned. " Awf'ly good of you," he said, with contorted lips. " I'd've been tickled to death." Oppression and rending excitement betrayed themselves in his convulsively raised brows. He tried to control himself, and yet stammered as he continued: " Is that so? So that's your conviction—unalterable conviction, eh? And where do you get that conviction, I'd like to ask, eh? Why shouldn't he have killed her, seeing as how he confessed in court? Why not, eh? Nobody made him say it. This is all dam' nonsense; you just simply dreamed this business or you was drunk. What made you think of it? "

" I shall tell you that," said Christian, with an expression that had grown more meditative from minute to minute. " A human being like this Joachim Heinzen was not capable of killing Ruth. Think what it means to kill a human being. And when that human being is Ruth! Oh, no, it's quite out of the question. The poor fellow is actually weak-minded. Many believe him guilty for that very reason; but no weak-minded man could have killed Ruth. Even if we suppose that he obeyed his animal instincts utterly, and that in his bestial rage he lost all self-control and all human semblance, yet he could never have gone to the ultimate length, to murder. Not this lad; it is out of the question. I have looked at his hands—at his hands and at his eyes. It is out of the question."

He paused. Niels Heinrich leaned against the oven, holding his hands carefully between his back and the tiles.

Christian continued, in a voice that was gentle and yet extraordinarily clear and penetrating: "It is out of the question, because he does not possess the necessary qualifications for the deed. I have tried to sink myself as profoundly as possible into his psychical life. I have succeeded in excluding from my consciousness all other thoughts and images, in order to arrive at a vision of his character as well as of the rôle which he played in connection with the crime. And when I have imagined him in his most bestial unrestraint, in all the rage of his lechery, I am still convinced that at the last moment he would have succumbed to Ruth. If Ruth had looked at him as he raised his arm, being what he is and as I know him, he would have weakened. He would have fallen whimpering on his knees, and rather killed himself than done her any hurt. And if she had inspired him with but one spark of thought or feeling, she would have won him over entirely. You may reply that these are mere hypotheses and suppositions; but that is not the case when one considers what Ruth was. Did you know her? Had you ever met her?"

This innocent and harmless question brought a ghastly pallor into the face of Niels Heinrich. He murmured something, and shrugged his shoulders.

" You may also make this objection: the same pressure which drove him to his confession may also have driven him to the deed itself. What will not a human being do in the darkness of mania, especially one so degraded and brutal and spiritually infirm. I consider his confessions quite valueless; it is clear that he has been influenced and commanded to make them. He contradicts himself constantly, and denies to-day what he affirmed yesterday. He sticks only to the one point of his guilt. But in this stubborn self-accusation there is more than mere persistence; there is despair and utter horror. And these are not manifested as they would be by a guilty soul in the torments of conscience, but as they would be manifested by a child who has spent a long night in a dark room, where monstrous and ghastly horrors shook the very foundations of its soul. His conscience should have been eased by confession, but the contrary is true. How is that to be explained?

" Furthermore, he is supposed to have lured Ruth to a hidden place. Certainly it must have been obscure and hidden, for the deed was not done in woods or lonely fields. But in spite of the most rigid search, no such spot has been discovered, and at no hearing has it been possible to persuade Heinzen to point it out. He is being questioned on this point continually, but he is resolutely silent or answers nonsense. Two explanations have been proposed. One is that he desires to save an accomplice who might be tracked from the scene of the crime. The other is that he suffers from one of those disturbances or even complete interruptions of the memory, such as are familiar to psychiatrists in their study of abnormal types. I accept neither the one explanation nor the other. It is my opinion that he doesn't know the place. He was not perhaps even present when the murder was committed. It is possible that he was drugged or drunk, and awakened from his stupor only to see the body. And it is possible that the sight of the body produced in him a fearful self-deception, or that he was tricked and driven into believing himself the murderer. . . ."

Niels Heinrich advanced a single step. His jaw shook. He felt as though a rain of burning stones were falling on him. A dark astonishment and horror were revealed in his face. He wanted to be silent, to jeer, to go; he wanted to seem cold and unconscious of any knowledge or understanding. For danger was upon him, the ultimate danger of vengeance, of the sword, the rope, the axe. He saw them all. Yet he was not capable of self-control; something within was stronger than he. "Man alive . . ." The words came clucking from his throat on fire. "Man alive . . ." Then came a wild terror of increasing the danger by his behaviour. He couldn't stand that; it was too much for his nerves. What had that man to do with it? And again he fell silent before Christian's slightly blinking glance, and became tense with staring and waiting. He'd have to watch this man now; the business was getting bad; it was necessary now to guard his life. God, what wouldn't that accursed mouth utter?

Christian walked to the window and returned. He walked around the table and returned. He had become aware of the stirring in Niels Heinrich; and he had the impression of having witnessed the bursting of some taut vessel and felt the flick of flying slime. But this impression was not tangible at once. Only he had the curious feeling of having received a confirmation of thoughts and visions of which he was himself still faintly doubtful; and these he wanted to develop and fortify. He said: " To lure Ruth to the spot where she was killed needed a certain cunning. Careful preparations were necessary, and guarded plans; and these were skilfully made, as their success illustrates. But all witnesses who know Heinzen agree that he is incapable of such activities. He is described as so stupid that he cannot remember names or numbers; and then it is assumed that he could have committed the murder with the brutal, merciless violence of a degraded debauchee.

The experts in criminology assert that precisely this mixture of the cunning and the brutal is characteristic of such types and such crimes. That may be true; but it proves nothing in this case, which was not so simple. Ruth went another path from that to Joachim Heinzen."

"Another, eh? What one, eh? Well, well," Niels Heinrich croaked. "Ain't it enough to give you a belly-ache? Ain't it enough to——" He took his hat, which he had hung up at the beginning of the conversation, put it on at a dashing angle, and prepared to go. But Christian knew that Niels Heinrich would not go, and followed him with a passionately inquiring glance. He was terribly moved.

Niels Heinrich got as far as the door. There he turned around, and with a peering, repressed look drew from his pocket, with apparent indifference, a little revolver. He held it in one hand. With the other hand he played, still indifferently and as though to amuse himself, with the trigger and the barrel.

Christian paid no attention to this perfidious gesture. He scarcely saw it. He stood in the middle of the room, and, in the irresistible excitement which had mastered him, pressed his right hand over his eyes. He said: " Perhaps I only dreamed that she determined of her own free will to die. Oh, it was murder, none the less. But she consented to it. And those last hours of hers! They must have been unheard of— verging on the ultimate which no feeling can reach. Step by step! And then at last she begged for the end. Perhaps I have only dreamed it, but it seems to me as though I had seen . . ."

He stopped, for a sharp, whip-like report resounded. A shot had been fired. One of the chairs beside the table trembled; the bullet was buried in its leg. But it had also grazed the back of Niels Heinrich's hand, and from the wound, which was like a cut, the blood trickled. He cursed and shook himself.

"You've hurt yourself," Christian said, sympathetically, and went up to him. Yet both were listening—like accomplices. The entrance of another seemed equally undesirable to both. Although the detonation had been moderate, it had been heard in the adjoining flats. One heard doors opening and questioning, scolding, frightened voices. After a few minutes the silence fell again. The people in the house were used to sudden alarms, and quickly quieted down.

Niels Heinrich wrapped his rather soiled handkerchief about his wounded hand. But Christian hurried into the next room, and returned with a jug of water and a clean cloth. He washed the wound and bandaged it expertly. He did so with a tenderness and care that made Niels Heinrich regard him with tensely wrinkled forehead and sombre shyness. He had never seen any one, no man at least, act thus. He was passive. He was contemptuous, yet could not hold his contempt. He could not but let Christian finish.

"It might have had dangerous consequences," Christian murmured.

Niels Heinrich did not answer, and so there ensued a long and rather strange silence.

Niels Heinrich became aware of the terrible meaning of this silence, and words came from him raspingly: "Well, what's wanted?"

Christian leaned with both hands upon the back of the chair, and looked at Niels Heinrich. He was pale, and struggled for expression. "It would be important to determine where Michael was hidden in the time during which he was gone," he began. He spoke differently now—more gropingly and searchingly, quiveringly and uncertainly, as though, during his very speaking, he were constantly addressing questions to himself. "It would be extremely important. Michael is Ruth's brother. Perhaps you have heard that for six days he could not be found anywhere. Whenever the commissary of police or the investigating judge try to question him, he has an

attack of hysterics. So they have determined to let him be
for a while, merely keeping a strict watch over him; but he
will not move from the room, and utters no sound. The
medical experts shake their heads and are at a loss. And
everything depends on his being persuaded to speak at last.
Surely it would throw some light on the mystery. But much
would be gained if only we discovered where he was hidden."

Niels Heinrich stared in dark consternation. This man grew
more and more terrible. The thought of flight quivered in
his eyes. "How d'you expect me to know? " he grunted.
"What the bloody hell do I care? How should I know?
I told you before—what the——" He lapsed back into his
Berlinese jargon, as though it were a refuge.

"I merely thought that rumours might have come your
way, that perhaps people who live near the Heinzens noticed
or heard something. Do you recall any such thing? "

The question was so earnest, so full of monition and almost
of beseeching, that Niels Heinrich, instead of yielding to an
impulse of anger, listened, listened to that voice, and had the
appearance of one who was bound in fetters. And gradually
he really recalled a rumour of that kind which had come to
him. There was among his acquaintances a woman of the
streets called Molly Gutkind. On account of her plump body
and white skin she was known as the Little Maggot. She
was quite young, barely seventeen. A few days ago he had
been told that the Little Maggot had given shelter to a boy
for quite a while, that she had carefully hidden him from
everyone, and that, since then, a complete change had come
over her. Before that, she had been cheerful and careless;
now she was melancholy, and haunted the streets no more.

He had been told this as he was told all the news of the
lower world, but he had paid no attention to the anecdote,
and it had slipped from his memory. Now it emerged in his
mind and fitted the case in question. An instinct told him
that it fitted; but that very perception increased his feeling

of defencelessness before this man who seemed now to be gazing into him and tearing from him things silent and hidden and even forgotten. He must follow up the rumour, and very secretively get to the bottom of it and test it. In order to say something and tear himself away at last, he murmured that he'd see what could be done, but the gentleman mustn't count on him, because spying was not his kind of business. He dragged himself shiftily to the door with a wavering, withered expression. He rubbed his moist fingers together and lit a cigarette, shivered in the coolness that met him from the outer hall, and turned up the collar of his yellow overcoat.

Christian courteously accompanied him to the door, and said softly: " I hope to see you soon. I shall expect you."

On the landing of the second storey Niels Heinrich stopped and laughed his goat-like laugh senselessly into the void.

XIII

Prince Wiguniewski wrote to Cornelius Ermelang at Vaucluse in the South of France:

" In your Petrarchan solitude you seem to have lost all touch with the world, since you inquire so insistently after our diva. I thought you were still in Paris and that you had seen Eva Sorel. For she returned from there only a few weeks ago—returned like a general after a victorious campaign of three weeks, full of fame and booty. Didn't you learn from the newspapers at least of the feverish enthusiasm which she has recently created in international society?

" In your inquiry there is an undertone of anxiety. I understand the reason for it, even though you are reserved on that point. Brief as your visit to her during your stay in Petrograd may have been, your eyes, which are so practised in reading the souls of men, must have perceived the change that has come over her. I hesitate to call that change one that should cause us anxiety, for doubtless it conforms somehow to the law of her being. Yet to behold it means pain to us who witnessed her beginnings and her rise—to those ten or twelve people in Europe, the fairest experience of whose youth was her sweetness and radiance and starry freedom from earth's heaviness. She was timeless; she was at each moment that very moment's gift. I need not describe to you what she was; you knew her. But is it for us to quarrel or mourn because a given development does not correspond to our expectations? However we may strive and cry, that which has become and now is unquestionably holds the wiser and the deeper sense of life. We always want too much, and so end by seeing and understanding too little. We need more humility.

" It is a fact that she employs and stirs public opinion in our country as scarcely any other human being does. Every one knows at all times who is in her favour and who has fallen from grace. The luxury that surrounds her generates the wildest fables, and does, indeed, surpass anything ever known. Her monthly income runs into the hundreds of thousands, and her fortune is estimated at between twenty and thirty millions of rubles. Twice a week she receives a carload of flowers from the Riviera, and twice from the Crimea.

" Concerning the castle which she is building at Yalta on the sea, details are told that remind one of the Arabian Nights. It is to be finished in a month, and magnificent festivities are planned for the house-warming. I am among the guests invited. Every one is talking about this castle. The park is said to cover an area of five square miles. Only by a most extravagant expenditure of money and labour could the whole thing have been completed within a year. I am told that the central building has a tower from which one has a magnificent view of the sea, and that this tower is a copy of the tower of the Signoria at Florence. A gilded spiral staircase with a balustrade of costly enamel leads upward within, and each window affords a carefully selected view of the southern landscape.

To adorn the walls of one of her great rooms she desired the remaining paintings which the British had still left in El Hira, the celebrated ruin in the Arabian desert. To obtain them, extensive commercial and diplomatic negotiations were necessary. Further large sums were spent and difficulties surmounted to fit out an expedition which was in the desert for three months and has but just returned. Its task was as dangerous as it was romantic, and seven of its members lost their lives. When Eva was told of this, she seemed to be frightened and to regret the boldness of her desires. But then she saw the pictures, and was so entranced that her smile seemed almost to express a satisfaction at the sacrifices they had cost.

"There is no exaggeration in this account. Such is her nature now. Those inconceivably beautiful hands treat the world as though it were possessed by slaves and meant and destined for her alone. I myself beheld her one day crouching before the paintings of a strange, far age, and I was shaken by the expression with which she regarded the gestures of those archaic figures. It was an expression of estrangedness and cruelty.

"It is quite by chance that I drifted to the subject of the ancient paintings and how they were procured. But I see now that I could have chosen no shorter path to the kernel of what I should like to tell you. The events of the past few days actually start from that incident. Few men, of course, can raise the veil that hides these events to-day and will probably always hide them. Any one who has not, like myself, gained some insight through a series of lucky accidents, is simply groping in the dark. I must beg you, too, to observe the strictest secrecy. This letter, which is being sent with especial precautions and which as courier of the embassy is taking across the frontier, may serve as a document entrusted to your care. By its help a later age will be able to track the genesis of certain happenings to their most distant roots.

" Scarcely had the paintings of El Hira arrived, than re-clamations on the ground of violated property rights were made by France. The arrangements with England were as-serted to have omitted all consideration of the legal rights of a Parisian stock-company, and the French government overwhelmed our ministry with notes and protests. The leader of the expedition, a courageous and witty scholar named Andrei Gabrilovitch Yaminsky, was accused of open robbery. The whole matter was unpleasant and the consternation great, and the noise intimidated even the old foxes of diplomacy. They feared that they had committed a bad blunder, and thus promenaded into the trap set for them. Since this affair, amusingly enough, actually threatened to darken the political sky, the important thing, above all, was to keep it from the knowledge of the Grand Duke Cyril, who holds the threads of foreign affairs in his hands like a spider in the midst of its web, and who feels the gentlest vibration. All efforts were directed to this end. Terror of the Grand Duke's rage created the most grotesque situations in the responsible ministerial offices.

" The minister in person went to Eva Sorel. She declared proudly that she would assume full responsibility and guard everyone concerned from unpleasant consequences. But there were grave doubts as to that. Similar cases were recalled, in which later on a malicious punishment had, after all, been the portion of the subordinates. So Eva was earnestly begged to give up the mural paintings. She resisted steadily, asserted her right to them, and grew defiant. When the officials were foolish enough to have Andrei Yaminsky, to whom she had taken a great liking, arrested, she threatened to inform the Grand Duke, who happened to be staying at Tsarskoye Selo. Thus terror rose to its utmost height. And now the original instigators of the whole intrigue held their fit time to have come. Suddenly there was calm and the storm had passed. But what had been the hidden and ultimate occasion of it all?

"The initiated whispered of an unholy bargain; but their knowledge, it seems to me, reaches no farther than mine. I sit near enough to the loom to see the shuttles flying to and fro. But I can assert that it is weaving an evil web. In what age have not the arts of a courtesan served to drag nations into slaughter? Perhaps you think the twentieth century too advanced for cabals in the style of Mazarin? I am not so sure of it. And perhaps you also think that the great catastrophes and revolutions use the wills and the actions of trivial mortals only in appearance, and that both accusation and guilt lose their validity when we become aware of the impersonal march of fate? But we do not grasp that march. We are human and we must judge, even as we must suffer, just because we must suffer.

"The unholy bargain involved in this instance concerns the building of fortresses on our Polish and Volhynian frontiers. For unknown reasons the Grand Duke opposed this plan until now. But during the past few days there has been talk of a new government loan. Well, there is one human being and only one capable of having inclined his rigid will toward this project. Why say more? One shudders at the thought of a connection between mural paintings five thousand years old and the springs of modern diplomatic trickery; between the bought complaisance of that incomparable body, that true adornment of the world, and the erection of fortress walls and casemates. The comedy rends one's heart.

"But that is not all my story. Connected with these events is the death of Andrei Gabrilovitch Yaminsky. I have indicated the fact that Eva was markedly attracted toward him. The courage and energy he had shown in that expedition to the desert, his mind, and not least of all his physical advantages dazzled her. She distinguished him in every way. Since she admits the existence of no barriers and gives her impulses complete expression in action, she did not hesitate in this instance, and Yaminsky was granted a happiness of which he had not dared to dream, and which seems to have robbed him of all moral equilibrium. It filled him to overflowing; it crazed him. Among his friends one evening, over the wine, of course, he began to chatter and boasted of his conquest. He realized his frightful error too late. What would have been contemptible weakness in any instance was sheer crime here. Too late he besought his witnesses to forget his words, to be silent, to consider him a liar and a boaster. Nor did it help him to seek them out singly and persuade them to secrecy. The rumour was started. A discreet and suspected affair would not have caused more than silent or whispered curiosity. The thing openly acknowledged became a topic of general talk. Punishment did not delay long, and Fyodor Szilaghin was the executioner.

"It is not easy to define the rôle which Szilaghin plays in Eva's present life. Now he seems to be her warder, now her seducer. No one knows whether he desires to please and win her, or whether he is but the servant and Argus of his sombre lord and friend. I believe that Eva herself is in the dark on this point. His enigmatic character, his masterly subtlety and impenetrable faithlessness seemed to me like the visible symbols of the darkening and disquietude of Eva's soul. There is no doubt that he acted with her knowledge and consent when he undertook to punish Yaminsky. But I dare not decide whether they ever actually spoke of the matter, whether it was done at his or her demand, whether her disappointment made her yield to him or her anger made her revengeful for herself, whether he acted in defence of her honour or that of his master. At all events, the punishment was accomplished.

"The deed itself is hidden in mystery and twilight, and is described with rather repulsive details. Last Wednesday evening Yaminsky was dining with friends in a side room at Cubat's on the great Morskaia. Shortly before midnight the door was torn open, and four young men, muffled in furs to their eyes, made their way in. Three of them surrounded

Yaminsky, and one turned out the lights. Immediately a shot resounded, and before Yaminsky's friends had recovered from their amazement, the strangers were gone. Yaminsky lay on the floor, soaking in his blood. Szilaghin was definitely recognized as one of the four.

" The boldest stroke came later. In the tumult that arose among the guests of the restaurant, the body of the murdered man had been forgotten. People called for the police and ran and shoved and asked questions. In the meantime a cab stopped at the door. Two men made their way through the crowd to where the dead man lay, and carried him past the staring bystanders into the cab. No one prevented them. The cab raced down the Nevski to the Palace Bridge and stopped. The two dragged the body to the shore, and flung it down among the ice floes of the wintry Neva.

" That same evening I was at Eva's, together with Caille, Lord Elmster, and some Russian artists. She was entrancing, and of a sparkling gaiety that made one feel loth to lose a breath of it. I no longer remember how the conversation happened to turn to sidereal phenomena and solar systems. For a while in the usual light way, the question was considered whether other planets might not be inhabited by men or man-like beings. And Eva said: ' I have read, and wise men have told me, that Saturn has ten moons and also a ring of glowing fire that surrounds the great star with purple and violet flame. The planet itself, I am told, is still composed of red-hot lava. But on the ten moons there might be life and creatures like ourselves. Imagine the night in those regions—the dark glow of the great mother star, the purple rainbow forever spanning the whole firmament, and the ten moons circling beside and above one another, so near perhaps that those beings can speak and communicate from world to world. What possibilities! What visions of happiness and beauty! ' Such, or nearly such were her words. One of us replied that it was quite as easy to conceive of moon at war with moon, even as here land wars

with land, despite the glory of the heavens, and that experience made us fear that nowhere in the universe would the
wonders of a sky save restless creatures like ourselves from
robbery and violence. But she said: 'Do not destroy my
faith; leave me my Saturnian Paradise.'

"And she knew, she could not but have known, that in
that very hour Yaminsky, whom she had loved, was dying an
ugly and a murderous death.

"It is difficult to have humility."

XIV

Christian shared his meals with Michael, and cared for
him in brotherly fashion. At night he spread a couch for
him with his own hands. He knew how to accustom the boy
to his presence; his gift of unobtrusiveness stood him in good
stead. In his presence Michael lost the convulsive rigour
which not even Johanna's affectionate considerateness had been
able to break. At times he would follow Christian with his
eyes. "Why do you look at me?" Christian asked. The
boy was silent.

"I should like to know what you are thinking," Christian
said.

The boy was silent. Again and again he followed Christian
with his eyes, and seemed torn between two feelings.

On a certain evening he spoke for the first time. "What
will happen to me?" he whispered, in a scarcely audible
voice.

"You should have a little confidence in me," Christian said,
winningly.

Michael stared in front of him. "I am afraid," he said
at last.

"What are you afraid of?"

"Of everything. Of everything in the world. Of people
and animals and darkness and light and of myself."

" Have you felt that way long? "

" You think it is only since . . . No. It has always been so. The fear is in my body like my lungs or my brain. When I was a child I lay abed at night trembling with fear. I was afraid if I heard a noise. I was afraid of the house and the wall and the window. I was afraid of a dream which I had not yet dreamed. I thought: ' Now I shall hear a scream,' or: ' Now there will be a fire.' If father was out in the country I thought: ' He will never come back; there are many who never come back; why should he? ' If he was at home I thought: ' He has had a dreadful experience, but no one must know it.' But it was worse when Ruth was away. I never hated any one as I hated Ruth in those days, and it was only because she was away so much. It was my fear."

" And you went about with that fear in your heart and spoke of it to no one? "

" To whom could I have spoken? It all seemed so stupid. I would have been laughed at."

" But as you grew older the fear must have left? "

" On the contrary." Michael shook his head and looked undecided. He seemed to waver. Should he say more? " On the contrary," he repeated. " Such fear grows up with one. Thoughts have no power over it. If once you have it, all that you dread comes true. One should know less; to know less is to suffer less fear."

" I don't understand that," said Christian, although the boy's words moved him. " The fear of childhood—that I understand. But it passes with childhood."

Again Michael shook his head.

" Explain it to me," Christian continued. " You probably see danger everywhere, and fear illnesses and misfortunes and meetings with people."

" No," Michael answered swiftly, and wrinkled his forehead. " It's not so simple. That happens too, but it can't harm one

much. It isn't reality. Reality is like a deep well; a deep,
black, bottomless hole. Reality is . . . Wait a moment:
Suppose I take up the chessboard. Suddenly it's not a chessboard at all. It's something strange. I know what it is, but
I can't remember. Its name gives me no clue to what it is.
But the name causes me to be satisfied for a while. Do you
understand? "

"Not at all. It's quite incomprehensible."

"Well, yes," Michael said, morosely. "I suppose it is
foolishness."

"Couldn't you take some other example? "

"Another? Wait a moment. It's so hard for me to find
the right expressions. Wait . . . A couple of weeks ago
father had gone to Fürstenwalde. He went one evening, and
he was to be back the next morning. I was alone at home.
Ruth was with friends, in Schmargendorf, I think. She had
told me she would be home late, and as it grew later I grew
more and more restless. Not because I feared that something
might have happened to Ruth; I didn't even think of that. It
was the empty room and the evening and the flight of time.
Time runs on so, with such terrible swiftness and with such
terrible relentlessness. It runs like water in which one must
drown. If Ruth had come, there would have been a barrier
to that awful flowing; time would have had to start anew.
But Ruth did not come. There was a clock on the wall of
that room. You must have seen it often—a round clock
with a blue dial and a pendulum of brass. It ticked and ticked,
and its ticking was like hammer blows. At last I went and
held the pendulum, and the ticking stopped. Then the fear
stopped too, and I could go to sleep. Time was no more, and
my fear was no more."

"It is very strange," Christian murmured.

"Years ago, when we were taught to be religious, it was
better. One could pray. Of course, the prayers too were
pure fear, but they eased one."

" I am surprised," said Christian, " that you never confided in your sister."

Michael gave a start. Then he answered very shyly, and so softly that Christian had to move his chair nearer to hear at all. " My sister . . . no, that was impossible. Ruth had so much to bear as it was; but it would have been impossible anyhow. Among Jews, brothers and sisters are not as close as among Christians; I mean Jews who don't live among Christians. We're from the country, you know, and so we were farther removed from other people than here. A brother can't confide in his sister. From the very beginning the sister is a woman; you feel that, even when she's a little girl. And the whole misery comes from just that . . ."

" How is that? What particular misery? " Christian asked, in a whisper.

" It is frightfully hard to tell," Michael continued, dreamily. " I don't believe I can express it; it might sound so ugly. But it goes on and on, and one detail arises from another. Brother and sister—it sound so innocent. But each of the two has a body and a soul. The soul is clean, but the body is unclean. Sister—she is sacred. But it's a woman, too, that one sees. Day and night it steals into your brooding— woman . . . woman. And woman is terror, because woman is the body, and the body is fear. Without the body one could understand the world; without woman one could understand God. And until one understands God, the fear is upon one. Always the nearness of that other body that you are forced to think about. Where we lived last we all had to sleep in one room. Every evening I hid my head under the covering and held my thoughts in check. Don't misunderstand me, please! It wasn't anything ugly; my thoughts weren't ugly thoughts. But there was that terrible, nameless fear . . . Oh, how can I explain it? The fear of . . . No, I can't put it into words. There was Ruth, so tender and delicate. Everything about her was in direct contradiction to the idea of woman; and yet I trembled with aversion because she was one. Man as he is made and as he shows himself—ah, those are two different things. I must tell you about a dream I had—not once, but twenty times, always alike. I dreamed that a fire had broken out, and that Ruth and I had to flee quite naked down the stairs and out of the house. Ruth had to drag me along by force, or I would have rushed back right into the fire, so terrible was my shame. And I thought: ' Ruth, that isn't you, that mustn't be you.' I didn't, in that dream, ever see her, but I knew and felt that she was naked. And she—she acted quite naturally and even smiled. ' Dear God,' I thought, ' how can she smile? ' And then by day I didn't dare look at her, and every kind glance of hers reminded me of my sin. But why do I tell you all that—why? It makes me feel so defiled, so unspeakably defiled."

" No, Michael, go on," Christian said, gently and calmly. " Don't be afraid. Tell me everything. I shall understand, or, at all events, I shall do my best to understand."

Michael looked searchingly up at Christian. His precocious features were furrowed with spiritual pain. " I sought a woman whom I might approach," he began, after a pause. " It seemed to me that I had soiled Ruth in my mind, and that I must cleanse that soilure. I was guilty before her, and must be liberated from that guilt."

" It was a fatal delusion in which you were caught," Christian said. " You weren't guilty. You had painfully constructed that guilt." He waited, but Michael said nothing. " Guilty," Christian repeated, as though he were weighing the word in his hand. " Guilty . . ." His face expressed absolute doubt.

" Guilty or not," the boy persisted, " it was as I have told you. If I feel a sense of guilt, who can redeem me from it? One can only do that oneself."

" Believe me," said Christian, " it is a delusion."

"But they were all Ruth," Michael continued, and his voice was full of dread. "They were all Ruth—the most depraved and degraded. I had so much reverence for them, and at the same time I felt a great disgust. The unclean thing always grew more powerful in my thoughts. While I sought and sought, my life became one pain. I cursed my blood. Whatever I touched became slimy and unclean."

"You should have confessed to Ruth, just to her, she was the best refuge you had," said Christian.

"I couldn't," Michael assured him. "I couldn't. Rather I should have done, I don't know what . . . I couldn't."

For a while he lost himself in brooding. Then he spoke quickly and hastily. "On the Saturday before the Sunday on which Ruth was at home for the last time, father sent me to the coal-dealer to pay the bill in person. There was no one in the shop, so I went into the room behind the shop, and there lay the coal-dealer with a woman in his arms. They did not notice me, and I fled; I don't remember how I got out, but until evening I ran about senselessly in the streets. The terror had never been so great. Next afternoon—it was that very Sunday—between four and five I was walking on Lichener Street. Suddenly a rainstorm came up, and a girl took me under her umbrella. It was Molly Gutkind. I saw at once the sort of girl she was. She asked me to come home with her. I didn't answer, but she kept on walking beside me. She said if I didn't want to come now, she'd wait for me that evening, that she lived on Prenzlauer Alley, opposite the gas-tank near the freight station, over a public house called 'Adele's Rest.' She took my hand and coaxed me: 'You come, little boy, you look so sad. I like your dark eyes; you're an innocent little creature.' When I reached home I saw what Ruth had written on the slate. Prenzlauer Alley—how strange that was! It might so easily have been some other neighbourhood. It was very strange. I felt desolate, and sat down on the stairs. Then I went up to the room and read father's letter, and it seemed to me as though I had known everything beforehand. I felt so lonely that I went down again, and walked and walked until I stood in front of that house in Prenzlauer Alley."

"And so, of course, you went up to the girl's room?" Christian asked, with a strangely cheerful expression that hid his suspense.

Michael nodded. He said he had hesitated a long time. In the public-house he had heard the playing of a harmonica. It was an exceedingly dirty house standing back from the street, an old house with splotches of moisture on the wall and a wooden fence, and a pile of bricks and refuse in front of it. At the door a dog had stood. "I didn't dare go past that dog," said Michael, and mechanically folded his hands. "He was so big and stared at me so treacherously. But Molly Gutkind had seen me from the window (the house has only two storeys); she beckoned to me, and the dog trotted out into the street. I went into the house, and there was Molly on the stairs. She laughed and drew me into her room. She served me with food, ham sandwiches and pastry. To-day, she said, she'd be my hostess; next time I'd have to be her host. She said she knew I was a Jew and she was glad; she always liked Jews. If I'd be just a little bit nice to her, I'd never regret it. It was all so peculiar. What was I to her? What could I be to her? I said I'd go now, but she wouldn't let me, and said I must stay with her. And then . . . !"

"My dear boy," Christian said, softly.

The tender words made the boy shudder all the more. He was silent for many minutes. When he spoke again his voice sounded changed. He said dully: "Three times I begged her to blow out the lamp, and at last she did so. But something happened to the girl that I hadn't expected. She said she wouldn't sin against me; she saw that she was a bad girl, and I must forgive her. As she said this she wept, and she added that she longed for her home with all her heart, and had a horror of her present life. I seemed to be stricken dumb, but I was sorry for her with all my heart. My body trembled and my teeth chattered, and I let her speak and lament. When I saw that she had fallen asleep, I thought about myself as deeply and severely as I could. It was dark and silent; I heard nothing but the breathing of the girl. No guests were left in the public-house below. It was uncannily silent; and with every moment's silence my old fear grew within me. Every moment it seemed to me that that terrible silence must be broken. I watched the very seconds pass. And suddenly I heard a cry. A sudden cry. How shall I describe it? It came from deep, deep below, from under the earth, from behind walls. It was not very loud or shrill, but it was a cry to make the heart stop beating. It was like a ray, do you understand, a hot, thin, piercing ray. I can compare it to nothing else. I thought—Ruth! My single thought was—Ruth! Do you understand that? It was as though some one had plunged an icy blade into my back. O God, it was terrible! "

"And what did you do? " asked Christian, white as the wall.

And Michael stammered that he had lain there and lain there, and listened and listened.

"Is it possible that you didn't jump up and rush out? That you didn't——? Is it possible? "

How could he have believed, Michael said, that it was really Ruth? The thought had shot into his brain only like a little, flickering flame of terror. He stared wide-eyed into nothingness, and suddenly sobbed. "And now listen," he said, and reached for Christian's hand, " listen! "

And this is what he told. His face was veiled, tear-stained, pale as death. He hadn't been able to forget that cry. He didn't know how much time had passed, when finally he arose from the girl's side. He had left the room on tiptoe. The darkness had been solid; outside he had seen and heard nothing. He had stood on the stairs for perhaps fifteen minutes. Then he had heard steps, steps and gasps as of some one carrying a heavy burden. He hadn't moved. Then he had seen a light, the beam of a bull's-eye lantern; and he had seen a man, not his face, only his back. This man had carried a large bale on his back and a bundle in his hand. The man's feet had been bare, and the feet had been red— with blood. He had gone in front of the house and set down the bale; then he had gone back into the cellar and come back with another man. He had shoved this man in front of him as one shoves a keg. One could tell that from the sound, but nothing could be seen, because the lantern had now been darkened. The second man had uttered sounds as though he had a gag in his mouth. Then they had gone away, after closing the door of the house, and all had been silent again. " I had been at the head of the stairs the whole time," Michael said, and took a deep breath.

Christian said nothing. He seemed turned to stone.

" It was very quiet and I went down," Michael continued his account. " Something drew me on. I groped my way to the cellar stairs step by step. There I stood a long time. Dawn was rising; I could see it from the narrow window above the door. I stood at the head of the cellar stairs. Steps of stone lead downwards. I saw first one, then two, then three, then four. The lighter it grew, the more steps I saw, but the light could not get beyond the sixth step."

It was harder and harder for him to speak. Sweat stood on his forehead. He leaned back and seemed about to fall over. Christian supported him. He got up and bent over the boy. In his attitude and gesture there was something wonderfully winning. Everything depended now on discovering the last, most fearful truth. His whole being concentrated itself in his will, and the boy yielded to this silent power. What he confessed now sounded at first confused and dim as the story of ghostly visions or the dreams of fever. One could hardly tell from the words what was reality and what the compulsive imaginings of fear. One grisly fact stood out— the finding of the blood-soaked handkerchief. Thrice Christian asked whether he had found it on the stairs or in the cellar. Each time the boy's answer was different. He quivered like a rope in the wind when Christian begged him to be exact and to think carefully. He said he didn't remember. Yes, he did, too; it had been down below. He described a partition, wooden railings, and a small, barred cellar window, through which the yellowish pale light of morning had now come in. But he hadn't really been master of his senses, and couldn't remember whether he had really entered the room. And at that he gave a loud sob.

Christian stood beside him, laying both hands on the boy's shoulders. The boy quivered as though an electric current were passing through him. " I beseech you," said Christian, " Michael, I beseech you! " and he felt his own strength ebbing. Then Michael whispered that he had recognized Ruth's initials on the handkerchief at once. But from that moment his brain seemed to have been hacked to pieces, and he begged Christian to plague him no more. He wouldn't go on; he'd rather drop down dead. But Christian grasped the boy's wrists. And Michael whispered: the house had betrayed the fact to him that something nameless had happened to Ruth, and the air had roared it to him. The walls seemed to have piled themselves on him and he had had a vision of everything, everything, and had whined and moaned and lacerated his neck with his own nails. " Here and here and here," he sobbed and pointed to his neck, which was indeed covered with the scars of recent scratches. Then he had run to the door of the house and rattled the knob, and then back again and had counted the cellar steps, just out of sheer despair. Then he had run up the stairs, and suddenly, at a door, he had seen a man; in the twilight he had seen a fat man with a white apron and a white cap, such as are worn by bakers, and a kerchief around his neck with stiff, white, protruding ends. The man had stood on the threshold, white and fat and sleepy. He might have been a shadow or an apparition. But he had said in a low, sleepy, surly voice: "Now they've gone and killed her, lad." After that he had vanished, simply vanished; and he, Michael, had rushed breathlessly into Molly Gutkind's room. She had waked up, and he had lain down on the bed and besought her with all the passion of his stricken soul to be silent and to keep him hidden, even if he were to fall ill, to tell no one but to keep him there and be silent. Why he had asked that, why it had seemed so necessary to him that the girl should say nothing— even now he didn't understand that. But he felt just the same this minute, and he would be utterly devoted to Christian all his life if he, too, would never betray what he had just confessed to him.

"Will you? Will you?" he asked, solemnly, and with a dark glow in his tormented eyes.

"I shall keep silent," Christian replied.

"Then perhaps I can go on living," the boy said.

Christian looked at him, and their eyes met in a strange harmony and understanding.

"And how long did you stay with the girl after that?" Christian asked.

"I don't know. But one morning she said she couldn't keep me any longer and I'd have to go. All the previous time my consciousness hadn't been clear. I must have talked as in delirium. The girl did all she could for me; my condition went to her heart. She sat at the bedside for hours and held my hands. After I left her I wandered about in the suburbs and in the woods, I don't know where. At last I came here. I don't know why I came to you, except that it seemed as though Ruth were sending me to you. You seemed to be the only human being that existed for me in all the world. But what am I to do now? What is going to happen?"

Christian reflected for several seconds before he answered with a strange smile: " We must wait for him."

" For him?   For whom? "

" For him."

And again their eyes met.

It was late at night, but they did not think of sleeping.

xv

In addition to the room which his mother gave him, Niels Heinrich had another lodging at a tinsmith's in Rheinsberger Street on the fourth floor.   On the day after his conversation with Christian he moved away from there.   He did it because too many people knew that he lodged here.   Also he couldn't sleep there any more.   He slept half an hour, at most; then he lay awake smoking cigarettes, tossing from side to side.   From time to time he laughed a dry, rattling laugh, whenever the recollection of something which that man Wahnschaffe had said became particularly vivid.

Who was that man, anyhow?   You could think till your brain cracked.   That man!

Curiosity was like a conflagration in Niels Heinrich.

He took a room in Demminer Street with a grocer named Kahle.   The room was immediately over the shop.   The big sign saying " Eggs, Butter, Cheese " almost covered the low window; consequently there was little light in that hole.   In addition the flooring and the walls were so thin that one could hear the ringing of the shop bell, the talk of the cus-tomers, and all other sounds.   There he lay again and smoked cigarettes and thought of that man.

That man and he—there was no place in the world for them both.   That was the upshot of his reflections.

Kahle demanded his rent money in advance.   Niels Heinrich said that that demand offended his honour; he always paid on the last of the month.   Kahle answered that that might be so, but that it was his custom to get rent in advance. Kahle's wife—lean as a nail and with tall hair-dressing—screamed and became vulgar at once. Niels Heinrich contented himself with a few dry insults and promised to pay on the third.

He tried to work in a factory. But hammer and drill seemed to offer a conscious resistance to him; the wheels and flying belts seemed to whirl through his body, and the regular working-hours to smother him. After the noon-rest it was found that one of the machines was out of order. A screw was loose, and only the vigilance of the machinist had prevented a disaster. He declared to both the foreman and the engineer that the trouble was due to the deliberate act of a rogue; but investigation proved fruitless.

He had been ruined, so far as work was concerned, Niels Heinrich said to himself; and since he needed money he went to the widow. She said that all her available money consisted of sixteen marks. She offered him six. It wasn't enough. " Boy, you look a sight! " she cried, frightened. He told her roughly not to put on airs, and added that she certainly couldn't expect him to be satisfied with a few dirty pennies. She whined and explained that business was wretchedly slack; it hardly paid to tell people's fortunes any more. She seemed to have nothing but ill-luck and to have lost her skill. Niels Heinrich answered darkly that he'd go to the colonies; he'd sail next week, and then she'd be rid of him. The widow was moved, and produced three small gold coins.

One he gave to Kahle.

Then he went to Griebenow's gin shop, next to a dancing hall, finally to a notorious dive in a cellar.

He was a changed man—everybody said that, and he stared at them in an evil way. Nothing had any savour to him. Everything was disjointed; the world seemed to be coming apart. His fingers itched to jerk the lamps from their hooks. If he saw two people whispering together, it made him feel like raving; he wanted to pick up a chair, and bring it crashing down on their skulls. A woman made advances to him; he caught her so roughly by the neck that she screamed with terror. Her sweetheart called him to account, and drew his knife; the eyes of both blazed with hatred. The keeper of the dive, and several others in whose interest it was to have the peace kept, effected a partial reconciliation. The fellow's mien was still menacing, but Niels Heinrich laughed his goat-like laugh. What could that fellow do to him? What could any of them do to him? Swine! All men, all—swine! What did they matter?

But there were four little words that he couldn't get away from. " I shall expect you." And these words sounded into the jabbering and slavering of the curs about him. " I shall expect you." And how that man had stood up in front of him! Niels Heinrich drew in his lips with his teeth; and his own flesh disgusted him.

" ' I shall expect you.' All right, old boy! You can go on expecting till you're blue in the face.

" ' I shall expect you.' Aw, can't a man get no rest? Keep still or I'll knock your teeth down your throat.

" ' I shall expect you.' Yes, and you'll meet me some day— in hell.

" ' I shall expect you.' "

New witnesses had appeared. In both Wisbyer and Stol-pische Streets there were people who had last seen Ruth Hofmann in the company of a girl and of a huge butcher's dog. All suspicious houses in Prenzlauer Alley had been searched. There were dives in plenty, but the place called " Adele's Rest " attracted particular attention. In it was found a dog like the one described—a masterless dog, to be sure. Some said the dog had belonged to a Negro who worked in a circus; others that it had come from the stock-yards.

In the cellar traces of the murder were discovered. A worm-eaten board found behind a partition was black with blood. When the deed was done it must have rested on two wooden frames that still remained in the cellar. When the masterless dog was taken into the cellar, he howled. Between fifteen and twenty persons, including the innkeeper, the barmaid, frequenters of the inn, and dwellers in the house, were subjected to rigorous cross-questioning. Among the latter Molly Gutkind appeared highly suspicious by reason of her confused answers and perturbed demeanour. She was arrested and held as a witness.

Niels Heinrich had been to see her the night before. His private inquiries had confirmed the rumours that had previously come to him. It was undoubtedly she who had given refuge to the unknown boy. He determined to put on the thumbscrews. He was an expert at that.

His general impression was that she could hardly become a source of direct danger to him, but that she had gained a general notion of what must have happened. And when he recalled what Wahnschaffe had told him concerning Ruth's brother, the connection was quite clear. If only he could have laid his hands on the boy, he would have seen to it that the latter didn't wag his damned tongue for a while at least. It was the rottenest luck that took just him to the Little Maggot's house. Now he'd have to make the wench harmless some way. Although he couldn't extract three coherent words from her, and though she trembled like a straw beneath his gaze, yet she betrayed the knowledge she had gained from the boy's delirious talk and had completed from what had transpired later. She wept copiously and confessed that she hadn't left the house since then in her terror of meeting any one. Niels Heinrich told her icily that if she had any interest in her own life and didn't want to ruin the boy into the bargain, she'd better not behave as much like a fool and an idiot as she had toward him. He knew a certain person who, if he got wind of her chatter, would wring her neck in five minutes. She'd better take the train and fade away quickly. Where was her home—in Pasewalk or Itzehoe? And if she didn't fade

away in double-quick time, he'd help her along! At that she
sobbed and said she couldn't go home. Her father had
threatened to kill her; her mother had cursed her for the
disgrace she had brought on them. He said if he came back
to-morrow and still found her here, she'd have to dance to a
less agreeable tune.

Next day she was arrested. On the day following Niels
Heinrich was told that the Little Maggot, unwatched by her
fellow-prisoners, had hanged herself by night on the window-
bars of her cell.

He gave an appreciative nod.

But security in this one direction meant little to him. The
net was being drawn tighter. There was whispering everywhere. Furtive glances followed him. Often he swung around
wildly as though he would grasp some pursuer. Money was
harder and harder to get. All that Karen had left brought
him scarcely fifty talers. And everything that had once given
him pleasure now filled him with loathing. It wasn't an evil
conscience; that conception was wholly unknown to him. It
was contempt of life. He could hardly force himself to get
up in the morning. The day was like melting, rancid cheese.
Now and then he thought of flight. He was clever enough;
he could make a fool of spies and detectives without much
exertion. He'd find a place where they wouldn't follow; he
had planned it all out: first he'd leave on foot, then take a
train, next a ship—if necessary as a stowaway in the coal-
bunkers. It had been done before and done successfully. But
what was the use? First of all he'd have to clear things up
between himself and—that man! First he'd have to find out
what that man knew and make him eat humble-pie. He
couldn't have that danger at his back. The man expected him.
Very well. He'd go.

Though this reasoning may but have disguised an impulse
stronger than hatred and sinister curiosity, the impulse itself
was of driving and compelling force. He set out on that

errand several times. At first he would be calm and determined, but whenever he saw the street and the house he would
turn back. His restlessness turned into choking rage, until
at last the suspense became insufferable. It was Friday; he
delayed one more day. On Saturday he delayed until evening;
then he went. He wandered about the house for a little, loitered
in the doorway and in the yard. Then he saw a light in
Christian's room and entered.

XVI

Letitia with the countess and her whole train moved into
a magnificently furnished apartment on Prince Bismarck
Street near the Reichstag. Crammon took rooms in the Hotel
de Rome. He didn't like the modern Berlin hotels, with their
deceptive veneer of luxury. He didn't, indeed, like the city,
and his stay in it gave him a daily sense of discomfort. Even
when he strolled Unter den Linden or in the Tiergarten he
was an image of joylessness. The collar of his fur-coat was
turned up, and of his face nothing was visible but his morose
eyes and his small but rather ignobly shaped nose.

The solitary walks increased his hypochondria more and
more.

"Child, you are ruining me," he said to Letitia one Sunday
morning, as she outlined to him her programme for the week's
diversions.

She looked at him in astonishment. "But auntie gets
twenty thousand a year from the head of the house of Brainitz,"
she cried. "You've heard her say so herself."

"I've heard," Crammon replied. "But I've seen nothing.
Money is something that one has to see in order to have faith
in it."

"Oh, what a prosaic person you are!" Letitia said. "Do
you think auntie is lying?"

"Not exactly. But her personal relations to arithmetic

may be called rather idealistic. From her point of view a cipher more or less matters no more than a pea more or less in a bag of peas. But a cipher is something gigantic, my dear, something demonic. It is the great belly of the world; it is mightier than the brains of an Aristotle or the armies of an empire. Reverence it, I beseech you."

"How wise you are, how wise," Letitia said, sadly. "By the way," she added in a livelier tone, "auntie is ill. She has heart trouble. The doctor saw her and wrote her a prescription; a new remedy that he's going to try on her— a mixture of bromine and calcium."

"Why precisely bromine and calcium?" Crammon asked irritably.

"Oh, well, bromine is calming and calcium is stimulating," Letitia chattered, quite at random, hesitated, stopped, and broke into her charming laughter. Crammon, like a school-teacher, tried for a while to preserve his dignity, but finally joined in her laughter. He threw himself into a deep arm-chair, drew up a little table on which was a bowl of fruit and little golden knives, and began to peel an apple. Letitia, sitting opposite him with a closed book in her hand, watched him with delicate and cunning attention. His graceful gestures pleased her. The contrast he afforded between plumpness and grace of movement always delighted her.

"I am told that you're flirting with Count Egon Rochlitz," Crammon said, while he ate his apple with massive zest. "I should like to sound a warning. The man is a notorious and indiscriminate Don Juan; all he requires is hips and a bosom. Furthermore, he is up to the eyes in debt; the only hope of his creditors is that he makes a rich marriage. Finally, he is a widower and the father of three small girls. Now you are informed."

"It's awfully nice and kind of you to tell me," Letitia replied. "But if I like the man, why should your moral scruples keep me from continuing to like him? Nearly all men chase after women; all men have debts; very few have three little daughters, and I think that's charming. He is clever, cultivated, and distinguished, and has the nicest voice. A man who has an agreeable voice can't be quite bad. But I'm not proposing to marry him. Surely you're not such a bad, stubborn old stepfather that you think I mean to marry every man who . . . who, well, who has an agreeable voice? Or are you afraid, you wicked miser, that I'll try to extract a dowry from you? I'm sure that's the cause of your very bad humour. Come, Bernard, confess! Isn't it so? "

Smiling she stood in front of him with a jesting motion of command. She touched his forehead with the index-finger of one hand; the other she raised half threateningly, half solemnly.

Crammon said: " Child, you are once more omitting the respect due me. Consider my whitening locks, my years and experience. Be humble and learn of me, and don't mock at your venerable progenitor. My humour? Well, it isn't the best in the world, I admit. Ah, it was better once. You seem not to know that somewhere in this city, far beyond our haunts, in its slums and morasses, there lives one who was dear to me above all men—Christian Wahnschaffe. You too, in some hoary antiquity, threw out your line after him. Do you remember? Ah, how long ago that is! That would have been a catch. And I, ass that I was, opposed that charming, little intrigue. Perhaps everything might have turned out differently. But complaint is futile. Everything is over between us. There is no path for me to where he is; and yet my soul is driven and goaded toward him, and while I sit here in decent comfort, I feel as though I were committing a scoundrelly action."

Letitia had opened her eyes very wide while he spoke. It was the first time since the days at Wahnschaffe Castle that any one had spoken to her of Christian. His image arose, and she felt within her breast the faint beating of the wings of dread. There was a sweetness in that feeling and a poignancy . . . One had to be as capable of forgetting as she was, in order to be able to recapture for a moment, in the deep chiming of a memoried hour, the keen emotion of a long ago.

She questioned him. At first he answered reluctantly, sentence by sentence; then, urged on by her impatience, his narrative flowed on. The utter astonishment of Letitia flattered him; he painted his picture in violent colours. Her delicate face mirrored the fleeting emotions of her soul. In her responsive imagination and vibrant heart everything assumed concreteness and immediate vividness. She needed no interpretations; they were all within her. She gazed into that unknown darkness full of presage and full of understanding. In truth, it all seemed familiar to her, familiar like a poem, as though she had lived with Christian all that time, and she knew more than Crammon could tell her, infinitely more, for she grasped the whole, its idea and form, its fatefulness and pain. She glowed and cried: "I must go to him." But picturing that meeting, she grew frightened, and imagined a rapt look she would use, and Crammon's lack of intensity annoyed her, and his whine of complaint seemed senseless to her.

"I always felt," she said, with gleaming eyes, "that there was a hidden power in him. Whenever I had wicked little thoughts and he looked at me, I grew ashamed. He could read thoughts even then, but he did not know it."

"I have heard you say cleverer things than you are doing now," Crammon said, mockingly. But her enthusiasm moved him, and there welled up in him a jealousy of all the men who stretched out their hands after her.

"I shall go to him," she said, smiling, "and ease my heart in his presence."

"You were wiser in those days when you played at ball

in that beautiful room while the lightning flashed," Crammon murmured, lost in memories. "Has madness overtaken you, little girl, that you would act the part of a Magdalene?"

"I'd like, just once, to live for a month in utter loneliness," Letitia said, yearningly.

"And then?"

"Then perhaps I should understand the world. Ah, everything is so mysterious and so sad."

"Youth! Youth! Thy words are fume and folly!" Crammon sighed, and reached for a second apple.

At this point the dressmaker arrived with a new evening gown for Letitia. She withdrew to her room, and after a little while she reappeared, excited by her frock, and demanding that Crammon admire her, since she felt worthy of admiration. Yet a patina of melancholy shimmered on her, and even while she imagined the admiring looks that would soon be fixed on her—for Crammon's did not suffice her—she dreamed with a sense of luxury of renunciation and of turning from the world.

And while she went to her aunt to collect the tribute of that lady's noisier admiration, she still dreamed of renunciation and of turning from the world.

A bunch of roses was brought her. But even while she gave herself up to their beauty and fragrance with a characteristic completeness, she grew pale and thought of Christian's hard and sombre life; and she determined to go to him. Only that night there was a ball at the house of Prince Radziwill.

There she met Wolfgang Wahnschaffe, but avoided him with an instinctive timidity. She was a great success. Her nature and fate had reached a peak of life and exercised an assured magic from which, in innocent cunning, she wrung all possible advantages.

On the way home in the motor she asked Crammon: "Tell me, Bernard, doesn't Judith live in Berlin too? Do you ever

hear from her? Is she happy with her actor? Why don't
we call on her? "

"No one will prevent you from calling on her," answered
Crammon. The snow was falling thickly. "She lives in
Matthäikirch Street. I cannot tell you whether she is happy;
it doesn't interest me. One would have a lot to do if one
insisted on finding out whether the women who drag our friends
to the nuptial couch discover the game to have been worth
the candle or not. One thing is certain—Lorm is no longer
what he was, the incomparable and unique. I once called him
the last prince in a world doomed to hopeless vulgarization.
That is all over. He is going downhill, and therefore I avoid
him. There is nothing sadder on earth than a man who
deteriorates and an artist who loses himself. And it is the
woman's fault. Ah, yes, you may laugh—it is her fault."

"How cruel you are, and how malevolent," said Letitia,
and sleepily leaned her cheek against his shoulder.

She determined to visit Judith. It seemed to her like a
preparation for that other and more difficult visit, which she
might thus delay for a little while, and to which her courage
was not yet equal. It lured her when she thought of it as an
adventure; but a voice within her told her that she must not
let it be one.

XVII

Every time Christian saw Johanna Schöntag she seemed
more emaciated and more worn. Beneath his observant glance
she smiled, and that glance was meant to deceive him. She
thought herself well hidden under her wit and her little
harlequin-like grimaces.

She usually appeared toward evening to sit with Michael
for an hour or two. She felt it to be her duty. She pretended to be utterly frivolous; yet when she had assumed a
task she was pedantically faithful in its execution. On the
day when she observed that the boy's improvement had reached

a point which made her service unnecessary, so vivid a look betokening her sense of futility stole into her face that Michael gazed at her and conceived a definite idea of her character. Checked though it still was by his old terror of human beings, gratitude for her sacrifices shone in his eyes. She began to employ his thoughts; her ways were so alien and yet so familiar. He could not rise to the point of frank communication, but when she rose to go he begged her to stay a little longer. Then the habitual silence fell between them, and Johanna, not really reading, let her tormented eyes glide over the page of some French or English novel that she had brought with her. But this time he put a question to her, and after a while another, and then another; and thus arose conversations in which they sought and explored each other. Johanna was by turns superior or mocking or motherly or elusive. She had weapons and veils in plenty. What he said was didactic or shy, or sudden and heated. Her sayings were often double-edged, and confused him; then she would laugh her sharp laughter, and he would be disillusioned and hurt.

He asked her to tell him whence she came, who she was, what she was doing, and she told him of her girlhood and her parents' house. To him who was familiar with poverty alone it sounded like a fairy-tale. He said: " You are beautiful," and she really seemed so to him, and his naïve homage made her blush and gave her a little inner courage. But her hands, he added, were not the hands of a rich girl. She seemed surprised, and answered with an expression of self-hatred that her hands, like a cripple's hump or the devil's splay foot, were the symbol of what she really was.

Michael shook his head; but he now understood her poor, chilled soul with its infinite yearning and its infinite disappointment. When he asked her what was her aim in life and what her occupation, she looked at him with disturbed surprise. What aim or occupation was there for a creature like herself? On another occasion, driven by the desire for self-torment, she revealed to him the complete emptiness of her life. It was a bad joke that fate was playing on her, a medicine one had to swallow in order to be healed; and healing was where life is not.

She chatted in this strain, but told him not to be bitter. It wasn't worth while; the world was too trivial, grey, and wretched. "If only there weren't so many people in it," she sighed, and wrinkled her forehead in her comic way. Yet she was ashamed before the lad too, and became conscious of the fact that her words were blasphemous. Her feeling was a torment to herself, and she did not perceive that it communicated warmth to another. Timidly she tried to measure the young lad's power of comprehension by his terrible experience, of which she knew no details, or by the sombre earnestness of his mind that made him seem maturer than his years. And she sank even lower in her own esteem when she saw him thoughtful and moved.

But precisely the secret wound of her weakness, which she revealed to him, and the lacerating conflict which she carried on with herself—these brought an awakening to him and stirred his will to life. He said: "You should have known Ruth." A strange shadow and yet a living contradiction of Ruth came to him from Johanna. He said again and again: "You should have known Ruth." To her question why, he had no answer but a sudden radiance in his glance in which Ruth seemed hitherto but to have slumbered. But now her image was a flame of fire that guided him.

Johanna said to Christian: "I don't believe your protégé needs me any longer. You certainly don't. So I'm superfluous, and had better get out of the way."

"I want very much to talk to you," said Christian. "I have wanted to beg you for long to talk to me. Will you come at the same hour to-morrow, or shall I come to you? I shall be glad to do whatever you like."

She grew pale, and said she would come.

XVIII

She arrived at five o'clock. The darkness had fallen. They went into Karen's old rooms, since Michael was in Christian's. To the latter's surprise the boy had suddenly expressed the desire for instruction and for a teacher to-day. He had also asked how his life was to be arranged in future, where he had better go and to whom, and from whom he might hope for help, since he was unwilling to be a burden to Christian any longer. His words and demeanour showed a determination which he had never yet displayed. Christian had not been able to answer his questions satisfactorily at once. The change caused him, first of all, astonishment; and while he preceded Johanna to light the lamp, he reflected on the difficult decision ahead.

The door to the room in which Karen had died was locked. A feeble fire of wood that Isolde Schirmacher had lit at Christian's bidding burned in the oven. She came in now, put on another log, and tripped out again.

Johanna sat on the sofa and looked about her expectantly. She trembled at the thought of the first word she would hear and the first she would speak. She had not taken off her cloak. Her neck and chin were buried in its collar of fur.

"It's a little uncanny here," she said softly at last, since Christian's silence was so prolonged.

Christian sat down beside and took her hand. "You look so full of suffering, Johanna," he said. "What is the cause of your suffering? Would it ease you to speak out? Tell me about it. You will reply that I cannot help you. And that is true; one can never really help another. Yet once you communicate yourself to a friend, the troubles within no longer rot in dull stagnation. Don't you think so?"

"You come to me so late," Johanna whispered, with a shudder, and drew up her shoulders, "so very, very late."

"Too late?"

" Too late."

Christian reflected sadly for a little. He grasped her hand more firmly, and asked timidly: " Does he torment you? What is there between him and you? "

She started and stared at him, and then collapsed again. She smiled morbidly and said: " I'd be grateful to anyone who took an axe and killed me. It's all I'm worth."

" Why, Johanna? "

" Because I threw myself away to roll in filth where it's thickest and most horrible," she cried out, in a cutting voice that was full of lamentation too, while her lips quivered, and she looked up.

" You see both yourself and others falsely," said Christian. " Everything within you is distorted. All that you say torments you, and all that you hide chokes you. Have a little pity on yourself."

" On myself? " She laughed a mirthless laugh. " On a thing like myself? It would be waste. Nothing is needed but the axe, the axe." Her words changed to a wild sob. Then came an icy silence.

" What did you do, Johanna, to make you so desperate? Or what was done to you? "

" You come too late. Oh, if you had asked me before, just asked, just once. It is too late. There was too much empty time. The time was the ruin of me. I've wasted my heart."

" Tell me how."

" Once there was one who opened the dark and heavy portal just a tiny bit. Then I thought: it will be beautiful now. But he slammed the door shut in my face. And the crash— I still feel it in my bones. It was rash and foolish in me. I should not have had that glimpse of the lovely things beyond the gate."

" You are right, Johanna; I deserve it. But tell me how it is with you now? Why are you so torn and perturbed? "

She did not answer for a while. Then she said: " Do you know the old fairy-tale of the goose-girl who creeps into the iron oven to complain of her woe? ' O Falada, as thou hangest, O Princess, as thou goest, if thy mother knew of thy fate, the heart in her bosom would be broken.' I haven't taken a vow of silence, and I haven't a burning oven for refuge, but I can't look at anyone or let him look at me. Go over by the window and take your eyes from me, and I'll tell you of my woes."

With serious promptness Christian obeyed. He sat down by the window and looked out.

With a high, almost singing voice Johanna began. " You know that I got caught in the snares of that man who was once your friend. You see there was too much time in the world and the time was too empty. He acted as though he would die if he didn't have me. He put me to sleep with his words and broke my will, my little rudimentary will, and took me as one takes a lost thing by the roadside that no one wants or claims. And when he had me in his grip the misery began. Day and night he tortured me with questions, day and night, as though I'd been his thing from my mother's womb. No peace was left in me, and I was like one blinded by his own shame. And one day I ran away and came here, and it was just the day on which Michael came in after the terrible thing had happened to him, and of course you had no eyes for me and I—I saw more clearly than before how low I had fallen and what I had made of my life."

She stared down emptily for a moment; then she shut her eyes and continued. There had been an evening on which she had felt so desolate and deserted that she had envied each paving stone because it lay beside another. And so she had suddenly, with all the strength of all the yearning in her, wished for a child. She couldn't explain just how it had come over her—that insane yearning after a child, after something of flesh and blood that she might love. Just as that day in

Christian's room she had turned his behaviour into an envious experiment and test, and had wondered in suspense how he would take and withstand the utter misery of Michael; so, on that other day, she had put her own life to the test, and had made everything dependent on whether she would have a child or not. And when Amadeus had come, she had thrown herself at him—coldly and calculatingly. She wondered whether such things often happened in the world or had, indeed, ever happened before. But as time passed it became clear that her wish was not to be fulfilled and she was not even capable of what any woman of the people can accomplish. She wasn't good enough for even that.

But in the meantime fate had played its direst trick on her. She had begun to love the man. It could not have come about differently, for he seemed so like herself—so full of envy, so avoided of men, so enmeshed and helpless within. The likeness in his soul had conquered her. To be sure, she could not tell whether it was really love, or something strange and terrible that is written of in no book and has no name. But if it was love to cling to some last contact while waiting for the end, to be extinguished and set on fire again, so that between fire and fire no breath was one's own, and one wore an alien face and spoke alien words; if it was love to be ashamed and remorseful and flee from one's own consciousness and drag oneself about in terror of the senses and of the spirit and own no thing on earth, no friend or sister or flower or dream—if such were love, well, it had been hers. But it hadn't lasted long. Amadeus had shown signs of coldness and satiety. He had been paralysed. When he had devoured everything within her that could be devoured, he had been tired and had given her to understand that she was in the way. A cold horror had struck her, and she had gone. But the horror was still in her heart and everything in her was old and cold. She could never forget the man's coarse face in that last hour—his scorn and satisfaction. Now she could neither laugh nor cry any more; she was ashamed. She would like to lie down very gently and wait for death. She was so frightfully tired, and disgust of life filled her to the brim.

She stopped, and Christian did not move. Long minutes passed. Then Johanna arose and went over to him. Without stirring she gazed with him out into the darkness, and then laid a ghostly hand upon his shoulder. " If my mother knew of my fate, the heart in her bosom would be broken," she whispered.

He understood that touch, which sought a refuge, and her silent beseeching. Resting his chin upon his hand, he said: " O men, men, what are these things you do! "

" We despair," she answered, drily, and with sardonic lips.

Christian arose, took her head between his two hands, and said: " You must be on your guard, Johanna, against yourself."

" The devil has fetched me," she answered; but at the same moment she became aware of the power of his touch. She became pale and reeled and pulled herself together. She looked into his eyes, first waveringly, then firmly. She tried to smile, and her smile was full of pain. Then it became less full of herself, and lastly, after a deep breath, showed a shimmer of joy.

He took his hands away. He wanted to say something more, but he felt the insufficiency and poverty of all words.

She went from him with lowered head. But on her lips there was still that smile of many meanings which she had won.

XIX

It happened that Christian, sleeping in the rooms upstairs, was awakened by the piercing cries of the Stübbe children. He slipped into his clothes and went over.

On the table stood a smoking kerosene lamp; next to it lay a baby huddled in greasy rags. From a sack of straw two children had risen up. They were clad in ragged shirts, and, clinging despairingly to each other, uttered their shrieks of terror. A fourth child, a boy of five, indescribably ragged and neglected, bent over a heap of broken plates and glasses. He hid his face in his hands and howled. The fifth child, a girl of eight or nine, stood by her mother, who lay quite still on the floor, and lifted her thin, beseeching arms and folded hands toward the monster who was her father, and who struck the woman blow after vicious blow in the beastliness of his rage. He used the leg of a chair, and under the mad fury of his blows terrible wounds appeared on the body of the woman, who uttered no sound. Only now and then she twitched. Her face was of a greyish blue. The bodice and the red petticoat she wore were shredded, and from every rent dripped her blood.

Stübbe's madness increased with every blow. In his eyes there was a ghastly glitter; slime and foam flecked his beard; his hair stood on end and was stiff with sweat, and his swollen face was a dark violet hue. Sounds, half laughter, half gurgling, then again moans and curses and stertorous breathing and whistling came from his gullet. One blow fell on the beseeching child. She dropped on her face and moaned.

Christian grasped the man. With both hands he strangled him; with tenfold strength he fought him down. He felt an unspeakable horror of the flesh his fingers touched; in his horror it seemed to him that the wretched room became a conical vault in the emptiness of which he and this beast swayed to and fro. He smelt the whiskey fumes that rose from the beast's open gullet, and his horror assumed odour and savour and burned his eyes. And as he struggled on—the claws of the man, who despite his drunkenness had a bear's strength, against his throat, that belly against his, those knees close to his own—this moment seemed to stretch and stretch to an hour, a month, a year, and fate seemed to force him into a fatal hole. All nearness seemed to become closer and turn into touch. Man, the world, the sky—all were upon him, close as his own skin. And this became the meaning of it to him—deeper, deeper, closer, closer into the horrible and menacing.

A thin, little voice sounded: " Please don't hurt father! Please, please don't." It was the voice of the little girl. She got up and approached Christian and clung to his arm.

Stübbe, gasping for air, collapsed. Christian stood there, pale as death. He smelt and felt that there was blood on him. People came in; the noise had roused them from their beds. A woman took the little children and sought to soothe them. One man kneeled by the murdered woman; another went for water. There were some who cried out and were excited; others looked on calmly. After a while a policeman appeared. Stübbe lay in a corner and snored; the lamp still smoked and stank. A second policeman drifted in, and took counsel with the first whether Stübbe was to be left here till morning or removed at once.

Christian still stood there, pale as death. Suddenly every eye was turned upon him. A dull silence fell on the room. One of the policemen cleared his throat. The child looked up at him breathlessly. It had a colourless, stern old face. Its unnaturally large, blue-rimmed eyes were filled with the immeasurable misery of the life it had lived. Christian's look seemed to charm the child. The little figure seemed to grow and twine itself about that look like a sapling, and to lose its cold and suffering and sickness and fear.

Christian recognized the heroic soul of the little creature, its innocence and guiltlessness and rich, undying heart.

" Come with me, I have a bed for you," he said to the child, and led it past the people and out of the room.

The little girl went with him willingly. In his room he touched her and raised her up. He could hardly believe such delicate limbs and joints capable of motion. So soon as she lay on his bed and was covered she fell into deep slumber.

He sat beside her and gazed into the colourless, stern, old face.

XX

And again, while he sat there, a landscape seemed to be about him.

On either side of a marshy path bare trees were standing, and their limbs protruded confusedly and crookedly into the air. The light was dim, as though it were a very early autumn morning. Heavy clouds hung down, mirroring their ragged masses in pools and puddles. Here and there were structures of brick, all half finished. One had no roof and another no windows. Everywhere were mortar-pits full of white mortar, and tools lay on the ground—trowels and spirit-levels and shovels and spades; also barrows and beams. No human being was in sight. The loneliness was damp and mouldy and ugly, and seemed to be waiting for man. All objects shared that tense and menacing mood of expectancy—the thin light falling from the ragged clouds, the marshy fluid in the ruts, the trees which were like dead, gigantic insects thrown on their backs, the unfinished brick structures, the mortar-pits and tools.

The only living creature was a crow sitting by the roadside, and observing Christian with a spiteful glance. Each time he approached the bird, it fluttered silently up and settled down a little distance ahead on a bare tree; and there it waited until he approached again. In the round eyes that glimmered brown as polished beans, there was a devilish jeering, and Christian grew tired of the pursuit. The moisture penetrated his garments, the mud filled his shoes, which stuck in the ooze at every step; the uncanny twilight obliterated all outlines, and deceived him in regard to the distances of objects. Exhausted, he leaned against a low tree-trunk, and waited in his turn. The crow hopped and flew, now farther, now nearer; it seemed vexed at his waiting and finally alighted on the roadside, and the polished bean-like eyes lost their treacherous expression and were slowly extinguished.

A prophetic shiver passed through space. The breath of the landscape was Ruth's name; it strained to proclaim her fate.

And Christian waited.

XXI

Niels Heinrich hesitated a few minutes before he entered the room.

It happened to be empty, so that he was alone for a little while. In this short time he succeeded in getting possession of the string of pearls.

When Niels Heinrich arrived, Christian was just about to accompany the student Lamprecht for a walk. He desired to engage him as Michael's teacher, and he could not speak quite openly to him in the boy's presence. He was startled and found it difficult to control himself. To leave at this moment seemed hazardous. Niels Heinrich, who was moody and irresponsible, might not await his return, nor was it advisable to leave him alone with Michael. On the other hand, Christian had waited with electrically charged nerves for this important interview. He had waited from day to day, and he desired to gather his inner forces and subdue the excitement which Niels Heinrich's silent entering had caused him. That would take time, and his indecision and embarrassment increased while he addressed Niels Heinrich courteously and asked him to be seated. At that moment the door opened again, and Johanna Schöntag came in. Christian received her eagerly, and in over-hasty words begged her to stay with Michael until his return; then he would go to the other flat with Herr Engelschall, with whom he had matters to discuss. Johanna was surprised at his impetuousness, and also looked in surprise at Niels Heinrich. Her expression showed very clearly that she didn't know who

the man was, and so Christian was obliged to introduce the
two to each other. That seemed to him so absurd a proceeding
that he only murmured the names hesitantly. Niels Heinrich
grinned; and when Christian begged to be excused for a little
while, he shrugged his shoulders.

The echo of Christian's and Lamprecht's steps had hardly
died away in the courtyard when Johanna turned to Michael
and said: " I was coming in to ask you to go with me to
the Memorial Church in Charlottenburg. Cantatas of Bach
will be sung. Do come; you have probably never heard
anything like it. This gentleman will be so kind as to tell
Herr Wahnschaffe where we have gone." She looked at Niels
Heinrich, but lowered her eyes at once. He gave her a feeling
of profound discomfort. She had felt that discomfort the
moment she had entered, and after Christian had gone, it
had become so violent that she had made her proposal to
Michael solely in order to avoid this hateful presence at any
cost. She had had a vague intention earlier of attending
the concert, but had dropped it again. The thought of taking
the boy along had occurred to her but now.

" Charlottenburg, Memorial Church—all right, I'll tell him,"
Niels Heinrich said, and crossed his legs. He had been gazing
at Michael uninterruptedly, and his gaze had been growing
more and more sombre.

Michael had been conscious of a feeling quite akin to
Johanna's, but he endured bravely the yellow heat of those
eyes. His fingers played nervously with a piece of paper on
the table; his mind was seeking a hint, an image, a lost thread;
he nodded at Johanna without looking at her, and followed her
silently when she touched his arm. She had taken his hat and
coat from the hook, and so they went.

Issuing from the house they saw Christian at the nearest
corner, standing with Lamprecht under a lantern. Hastily
they walked in the opposite direction.

Niels Heinrich got up. He lit a cigarette, and strode up

and down with clicking steps. He stopped in front of a chest of drawers and tried each drawer. He did that mechanically, without curiosity and without definite expectation. The chest had a little top made of small, carved columns; this, too, contained a drawer. He pulled it open, and started violently as though he had been stung. Before his eyes lay a heap of enormous pearls.

Christian had almost forgotten them in the unlocked little drawer. Several days after Karen's death Botho von Thüngen had told him that he was going to Frankfort. Members of his family were gathering there and a conference was to be held. Christian thought of taking advantage of this opportunity to send the pearls to his mother. A dreamy memory of their high value made him hesitate to entrust them to the mails. Thüngen had declared himself most willing to undertake the commission; but he never went to Frankfort. His relatives cast him off mercilessly; they were trying to get the courts to declare him irresponsible; their hue and cry robbed him of all repose, of every home, of all work. He was stripped of all means, and he had not been able to hold the woman whom he had married. She had fallen into deeper degradation than that from which he had sought to save her. In this utter distress of his, Christian had become his sole refuge and support.

Thus, in his anxiety over his friend, Christian had scarcely thought of the pearls for days. Though he had that faint memory of their value, no authentic impulse bade him secure them more carefully than in that open drawer, where Niels Heinrich's furtive instinct had discovered them.

A long, slow, astonished whistle; a quivering of the emaciated cheeks; a look of hunger and one of criminal determination. Then a hesitation, as though even this marvellous treasure were of no import any more; and then again a burning in his eyes. The pearls promised unheard-of delights. And then again disgust: what for? He must fight

out his conflict with this man. Behind him was a ravenous
pack: witnesses, spies, hints, accomplices, and also the dog,
the cellar, the blood, the body, the head, the Little Maggot
hanged by the cord of her petticoat. And face to face with
him was this man. We'll see; we'll measure our strength.

He reflected for some moments; then he flung out both
hands, and the pearls were in his possession. There was a
soft clinking, a gathering up, a shoving, and they disappeared
in his trousers pocket. The pocket stuck out, but his coat
hid the fact. If the man looked into the drawer and raised
an alarm, why, one could fling the stuff back at him.

When Christian returned, Niels Heinrich was sitting on a
chair and smoking.

XXII

" Forgive me," said Christian. " It was an urgent appointment. . . ." He interrupted himself, as he observed that
Niels Heinrich was in the room alone.

" The young lady wants you to know that she took the
boy and went to Charlottenburg to go to church," Niels
Heinrich said.

Christian was amazed. He answered: " So much the better.
That leaves us undisturbed, and we can stay here."

" That's right. We're undisturbed." Next came a pause,
and they looked at each other. Christian went to the threshold
of the little bedroom to make sure that no one was within,
then to the door that led to the hall. He turned the key.

" Why do you lock the door? " Niels Heinrich asked, with
raised brows.

" It is necessary," said Christian, " because all the people
who come to see me are accustomed to finding the door open."

" Then maybe you'd better blow out the lamp too," Niels
Heinrich jeered; " that'd be the sensible thing to do, eh?
Dark's a good place for secrets. And we're going to fish for
secrets, eh? "

Christian sat down on a chair at the opposite end of the table. He purposely disregarded the other's cynical remark; but his silence and his tense expression aroused Niels Heinrich's rage. Challengingly he leaned back in his chair and spat elaborately on the floor. They sat facing each other as though neither dared lose sight of the other for a second. Yet Christian continued to show his obliging and friendly attitude. Only a quivering of the muscles of his forehead and the peering intensity of his gaze revealed something of what was passing within him.

"Have you discovered anything new?" he finally asked, in his courteous way.

Niels Heinrich lit another cigarette. "Aw, something," he said, and went on to tell that he had in the meantime discovered the woman who had hidden the Jew boy. It had been Molly Gutkind, known as the Little Maggot, and living at "Adele's Rest." He had followed the matter up and got the girl to confess. But on that very day, as the devil would have it, persons had come from the court and questioned her. The poor fool had probably talked more than was good for her. Anyhow, she'd fallen under suspicion and had been put in jail. There she'd evidently lost what little brains she ever had and had hanged herself. She was dead as a door-nail. That's what he wanted to report, since the gentleman seemed to be interested. Now the gentleman knew, and had an idea of his, Niels Heinrich's, willingness to oblige.

He blew clouds of smoke, and twirled his little beard with the fingers of his left hand.

"I knew that," said Christian. "I knew where Michael had been; he confessed it himself. The girl's death was reported to me this morning. Nevertheless I thank you for the trouble you have taken."

No trouble at all; didn't amount to nothing. He was still at the gentleman's service. It seemed to him that the gentleman was given to detective work. Maybe he meant to take it up professionally later. Maybe the gentleman knew something more? He, Niels Heinrich, was quite willing to be questioned. This was his expansive day. If there was anything the gentleman wanted to know he was not to hesitate but fire away.

He blinked and stared watchfully at Christian's lips.

Christian reflected and lowered his eyes. " Since you're so willing to give information," he answered softly, " tell me why you removed the screw from the machine at Pohl and Pacheke's works? You must remember. . . ."

Niels Heinrich's mouth opened like a trap. The stark horror simply caused his lower jaw to drop.

" You are surprised that I know of the incident," Christian ·continued. He did not want the other to think that he would try to make him pliant by dealing in mysteries and surprises. " But it's quite natural that I should. The son of Gisevius is a foreman at Pohl and Pacheke's. He told me that you worked there for two days and that the accident happened on one of them. He didn't connect the two acts at all; he simply happened to relate both to me. He had no suspicion; it was clear to no one but myself that you must have done it. I can't tell you the reason, but I had an unmistakable vision of you fumbling at the machine and loosening the screw. I was forced to think of it constantly and to see it constantly. If I am wrong, you must forgive me."

" Don't understand. . . ." The words came heavy with fear and in gasps from Niels Heinrich's lips. " Don't understand that. . . ."

" I had the feeling that the machine seemed to you a living and organized being and therefore an enemy, and aroused in you a desire to murder. Yes, quite clearly and irrefutably, I got the feeling of murder from you. Am I mistaken? "

Niels Heinrich uttered no sound. He could not move. Roots seemed to grow from the floor and entwine themselves about the chair on which he sat, to creep about his legs, and hold him in an iron grip.

Christian arose. "All that is useless," he said, taking a deep breath.

"What? What is useless?" Niels Heinrich murmured. "What? What then?" The blood in his body grew chill.

His arms pressed to his side, his hands joining below, Christian stood there, and whispered: "Speak! Tell me!"

What was he to speak of? What was he to tell? The neck of Niels Heinrich was like an emptied tube, slack and quivering.

Their eyes met. Words died. The air roared.

Suddenly Christian blew out the lamp. The sudden darkness was like the thud of an explosion. "You were right," he said. "The light would betray us to any passerby. Now we are quite secure, from any outside thing, at all events. What happens here now concerns no one but ourselves. You can do as you choose. You can draw your revolver as you did the other day and fire. I am prepared for that. And since I shall not move from where I sit, you cannot fail to hit me. But perhaps you will wait until you have told me what is to be told and what I must know."

Silence.

"You murdered Ruth."

Silence.

"It was you who lured her into that house and into that cellar, and killed her there."

Silence.

"And you made an accomplice of that poor simpleton, Joachim Heinzen, and by a well-devised plan filled him so full of fear and anguish that he deemed himself alone to be the murderer, and did not venture even to utter your name. How did that come about?"

Silence.

"And how did it come about that Ruth found no mercy in your soul? Ruth! Of all creatures! And that the knife

. . . that the knife in your hand obeyed you . . . and that thereafter you could go and speak and drink, and decide on actions and go from one house to another. With that image and with that deed within you? How is that possible?"

Silence.

Christian's voice had nothing of its old coolness and reserve. It was hoarse and passionate and naked. "What did you want of her? What was your ultimate desire? Why did Ruth have to die? Why? What could she give you by her death? What did you gain through murdering her?"

Suddenly Niels Heinrich's voice uttered a scream and a roar: "Her virginity, man!"

And now it was Christian's turn to be silent.

XXIII

Neither could see the other in the darkness. The heavy shades at the window created a blackness so impenetrable that not even the outlines of things were visible. Neither could see the movements of the other, but they had the sharpest awareness of each other, a horrible and physical awareness, as though they were chained and imprisoned together, forehead to forehead, breath to breath. They lacked no light, for they needed none.

The darkness gave Niels Heinrich a sense of freedom. It gave him an impulse of defiance and boastfulness and shameless self-revealment. It was chaos, massive and terrible. He did not refuse its demand that he should give an accounting of himself. It split and shattered his inward being, and liberated speech. He dared not jeer; he dropped all defences.

The darkness was a maw that spewed forth his deed. He could himself now hear what had happened. Many things seemed new to him as they were uttered. The thought that yonder a man was listening and dragging your vitals out as though you were a dead animal—there was a certain strange stimulation in the thought. He would turn his mind inside out; then at least that man would trouble him no more. There was time enough later to take proper precautions.

As he was saying, then, it was her virginity. There wasn't no use denying that. Every one knew how a boy like him grew up, with what sort of creatures. Sometimes they were one kind, sometimes another—red or black, sentimental or jolly, a little better, a little lower, but sluttish creatures all. Well, not exactly prostitutes, but mighty near it; on the edge of it—elegant or dirty, fifteen or thirty, every one had a rotten spot. And even if they hadn't exactly the rotten spot yet, they'd turn rotten under one's very hands. And what you got, you couldn't have faith in, and once you had your claws in 'em, it was all over. So that's the way life went— Male on Monday and Lottie on Tuesday and Trine on Wednesday; but the difference wasn't as much as you could put on the tip of a knife. Finally, of course, you got to be like an animal that feeds on everything—wheat and tares, clover and thistles. If it burns—all right; if it tastes good— all right.

Virgins? Sure, you met virgins too. But it was all shoddy and pawed over and second-hand. They'd talk of not staying out late and being afraid of the landlady, and of marrying and buying furniture; and on the third Sunday you had 'em as well trained as poodle dogs. And anyhow, you never knew who'd stirred your soup before you. It was all doubtful, and you had no proper belief in it. Even if sometimes you met a better sort, it wasn't never the best. They'd be coy and kittenish, and there was no naturalness and no honesty. First you had to lie to 'em and make 'em tame, and then when they got scared about being in trouble, they chilled and disgusted you so, you'd like to kill them.

Sailors who had been on long voyages had told him that

they got so sick of the salt-meat and the pickled meat that when they landed and happened to meet a lamb or a rabbit, they felt as if they could tear the living animal limb from limb and devour the warm, fresh flesh. That's what could happen to a man with women; that's what had happened to him when he'd seen the Jewess. The sight of her had gone through and through him. It had pierced him as a red-hot iron will slide through ice. It had whirled him around; all his life he hadn't had no such sensation—as if the lightning had struck him or he'd been bewitched or had drunk a gallon of alcohol. From that moment he had had a twitching in his fingers as though velvet was passing over them; he had felt a terrible avidity to touch something that moves and trembles and is warm, an avidity for the terror of those eyes and her wonderful struggles, as the depth of her soul made moan, and she wept and begged. How she walked in her in- violateness and pride, as in a haze! One wanted to lie down and have her step on one's chest, and look up at her as at a slender column. Jesus and all the Saints! That had done for him and been the end of him! He knew he'd have to have her, if it cost him his eternal weal, which nobody gives a damn for anyhow.

He knew from the start, of course, that a being like that wasn't for the like of him. She was like the sacrament that no one could touch but the priest. He had known that; but there was more to it than that from the start. From the start it had been a matter of life and death. There'd been no doubt about that in him at any time: she'd have to die for him—him! He had lain in wait for her, and she had fled like a deer. It had made him laugh. "You'll come into my net," he had said, and had fixed his eyes and thoughts on her day and night, so that she didn't know no more what to do. She had appeared to him in vision, yes, appeared to him whenever he'd commanded her, and begged him to let her off. And he'd told her that was impossible, that she must

come to him, that her body and blood must become his, and
that he must make an end of her. Unless he did, there wasn't
no peace on earth for him nor for her either.

So he had thought out his plan. He had persuaded the
besotted fool that he was crazy about the Jewess and that
she was gone on him too. That had made him quite crazy
and he hadn't had an idea left in his skull, and had been
soft as mush and had taken every trick and swindle as reality.
So they had taken counsel and worked out their plan. They
had sent the Jewess a note and had hired out the wench who
carried it right afterward to an old acquaintance in Pankow.
In the note they'd written to the Jewess that some one wanted
her on his bed of death and that his salvation depended on
her coming. Sure enough, she had come. The idiot had
led her into the cellar. It had been dark there. They had
locked the cellar door. Then he had persuaded the idiot to
go behind the partition and had given him a bottle of rum,
and told him if he so much as made a sound he might as well
order his coffin, but if he'd wait, the affair with the Jewess
would be fixed up for him. Thereupon he himself had returned to the cellar, and there the Jewess had stood. . . .

He interrupted himself, and felt how the whole being of his
invisible neighbour had become a breathless listening, a rapt
absorption of every syllable he spoke. It gave him but a scant
satisfaction, yet it urged him on. And as he burrowed in his
mind and represented what he found there, the events assumed
an unnatural size and seemed steeped in an atmosphere fiery-
red and violet. He did not so much speak of them as let
them speak to him, and thus build themselves up in a guise in
which he had never yet seen them. And as he continued, his
voice changed. It took on a sharper edge and became hollower,
and betrayed for the first time a stirring within, a wildly
gathering primordial pain.

She had stood there, he went on, and that had removed
his last doubt.

"How?" Christian's voice came, scarcely audible, out of the blackness. "How?"

He said he couldn't describe it. She had looked about with a proud astonishment and yet a twitching of fear about her mouth. She had asked where the person was who had sent for her. On the moon, he had answered. Then what was wanted of her? Why was the iron door locked? Good reasons! Couldn't she be told the reasons? What a voice she had had, like a little silver bell ringing in her throat. The ear drank it in like a wonderful liquor. There weren't many reasons, he had said; there was just one. She didn't understand. He'd try to make it plain. She had said she couldn't think. Then he had taken her by the arm and put his arm about her shoulder and her neck. She had cried out and begun to tremble, run into a corner, and put out her hands to guard herself. The candle-light had fallen straight into her face, which had been like a white rose in the light of a flame. He had rushed toward her, and she had taken refuge behind the table. She had cried for mercy. He had laughed, laughed, utterly beside himself at the little silver bell in her throat. What a woman! God, what a woman! A child still, pure in every fibre, and a woman. It pierced him; it went into his marrow. A man couldn't let such a woman escape him if his next hour were to be spent in hell-fire.

He had soothed her a bit and made pretty speeches and said she should listen to him. She had been willing, and he had spoken. The table with the candle had been between them—he in front of it, she behind it against the wall. He had said there was a terrible necessity; no way out—not for her and not for him. He was like one damned, and she must redeem him. He was panting for her and withering away for her—for her body and soul, blood and breath, and it had been predetermined thus since the world began. He must be close to her and within her, or the whole world would go mad and life burst with poison. He must have her, whether she

was willing or not, through kindness or force. God couldn't
help her. There was a law that compelled them both, and the
hour had come. She might better yield herself, and give him
the heaven he was bound to have.

Thereupon she had whispered with a rigid expression: " No,
never, nevermore."

He had gazed at her a long time.

From time to time, with a moist glance upward, she had
whispered: " No, never, nevermore."

He had warned her to put away all hope. If she resisted, it
would only be the more fearful. And he had laid the knife
on the table.

Christian moaned in his supreme pain as he heard this.

Niels Heinrich continued with his fatalistic outer calm.
Ruth had tried to make him relent. He would never forget
her words, but he could not repeat them. She had spoken
feverishly, with glowing eyes, her hair falling over her cheeks;
she had lifted her hands in beseeching and leaned across the
table, and in her sweet, bell-like voice had spoken of people
who needed her, of work and duty, of difficult tasks ahead,
and also of the pleasant things in the world. And she had
asked him whether nothing in the world was pleasant to him,
whether his own life meant nothing to him at all, and he was
willing to take up the burden of this crime before man and
God. This is what she had said, only her words had been
finer and firmer and exacter. At that a rancorous rage had
flamed up in his brain, and he had roared at her to stop her
crazy jabbering, damned Jewess that she was, and listen to him,
listen to what he had to say in reply.

In silence and with a drawn expression, she had listened.
Crime, he had said, crime and such talk—there wasn't no
sense in that; he didn't know what it meant. It had all been
thought out by the people who pay the soldiers and the courts
to do their bidding, but who, if it served their purposes, committed the same crimes in the name of the State or the Church

or Progress or Liberty. If a man was strong enough and cunning enough, he didn't give a damn for all their laws. Laws were for fools and cowards. If the individual has got to submit to force, he's got the right to use force too. If he was willing to risk the vengeance and punishment of society, he had a right to satisfy his desires. The only question was whether he was willing to take up the burden of crime, and couldn't be made to stop by the hocus-pocus invented by teachers and parsons. If he, Niels Heinrich, could work his will, there wouldn't be one stone left standing on another, all rules would be wiped out, all order destroyed, all cities blown up sky-high, all wells choked, all bridges broken, all books burned, all roads torn up, and destruction would be preached, and war—war of each against all, all against each, all against all. Mankind wasn't worthy of nothing better.

He could truthfully say that because he had studied people and had seen through them. He had seen nothing but liars and thieves, wretched fools, misers, and the meanly ambitious. He had seen the dogs cringe and creep when they wanted to rise, cringe before those above, snap at those below. He knew the rich with their full bellies and their rotten phrases, and the poor with their contemptible patience. He knew the bribe-takers and the stiff-necked ones, the braggarts and the slinkers, the thieves and forgers, ladies' men and cowards, the harlots and their pro-curers, the respectable women with their hypocrisy and envy, their pretence and masquerade and play-acting; he knew it all, and it couldn't impress him no more. And there were no real things in the world except stench and misery and avarice and greed and treachery and malevolence and lust. The world was a loathsome thing and had to be destroyed. And any one who had come to see that, must take the last step, the very last, to the place where despair and contempt are self-throttled, where you could go no further, where you heard the Angel of the Last Day beating at the dull walls of the flesh, whither

neither the light penetrated nor the darkness, but where one
was alone with one's rage and could feel oneself utterly, and
heighten that self and take something sacred and smash it
into bits. That was it, that! To take something holy, something pure, and become master of it and grind it to the earth
and stamp it out.

Christian had never heard anything more dreadful. He
gazed into a broken universe. Even in its pale representation,
the fury of hatred burst forth like seething lava, and turned
the blossoms of the earth to ashes. Horror had reached its
supreme point. The fate of the immemorial race of man was
sealed. And yet—the fact that this man had come hither,
had had the impulse to reveal himself, that he sat there in
the darkness and writhed and spoke of monstrous things and
plunged into the great deeps that he had opened—in this very
fact Christian perceived a shimmer of most mysterious hope,
and a first faint ray of dawn upon a hitherto unknown, uncertain path.

Niels Heinrich continued. Slowly the Jewess had understood and looked at him with her great child's eyes. She had
put a question to him, but he couldn't remember what it was.
Then she had said that she saw there was no hope for her, and
that it was her fate to be his victim. He had answered that
her insight did credit to her understanding. Then she asked
whether he knew that he was destroying himself; and he had
said that he believed in no expiation, and the rest was his
business. Anyhow, there had been enough talk; time was
pressing, and the end must come. She had asked what she
should do, and this question had confounded him, and he had
had no answer to it. She had repeated the question, and
he had said that the candle was burning down. Then she
had asked him whether he could give her the assurance of
death. Yes, he could give her that. Wouldn't he let her die
before he attacked her? No. She had grasped the knife, but
he had wrung it from her. The touch of her hand had

driven him utterly mad. The walls seemed to crunch and the house to thunder. She had begged him to let her die by her own will. He could not do that, he had answered; he must get to her living heart or there was no help for him.

She begged him to grant her a little quarter of an hour; then she would be ready to die. To this he had consented, and gone out and looked after the idiot, who had lain there helpless and drunk as a swine. That had pleased him; now he could put the fellow to what uses he would. This had been proved later when he had dragged him into the cellar; and the swine still thought he could be gotten out of jail if only to the last gasp he didn't mention the name of Niels Heinrich.

When he had returned to the Jewess, he had found her leaning against the wall with closed eyes. Her face had been very pale, but she had smiled from time to time. He had asked her why she was smiling and she had not answered, but looked at him most strangely, as though she were trying to remember something. He had gone to her behind the table and she had not stirred, and so he had grasped her shoulders. She had lifted her hands, and then he had seen that, while he was outside, she had severed the veins of both her wrists, and the thick blood was dripping down. She must have done it with a shard of glass that stuck between the bricks of the wall. He had been swept into a storm of madness, as though some one were upon him to rob him of her, and he had caught her by the hair and hurled her on the floor.

And she had uttered one cry, one single, long cry. That cry he still heard, always . . . always. . . .

She had become his. He felt no remorse; he would feel none. But that cry—he heard it always and forever.

Silence came upon him. The stillness in that dark chamber was so great that it seemed to gather in the corners and threaten to burst the walls asunder.

XXIV

More than half an hour had passed in this complete stillness when Christian arose to light the lamp. The base and the chimney tinkled in his trembling hands. He feared the very functioning of his senses—sight, hearing, smell. Every perception was like a wound in consciousness and dripped like poison into the core of life. Slowly the turbid outlines re-formed an image of reality.

Both from within and from without everything drove and pressed toward a decision.

Convulsively bent over, leaning back in the chair, he saw that man whose face had no colour for which there is a name. The eyes were closed, the mouth half-open. The decayed teeth and the limp droop of the beard gave him an expression of bestiality. The sharp-fingered hands with the blue, swollen veins stirred like reptiles. The forehead was covered all over with sweat. Like drops from the cover of an overheated vessel filled with liquid, thus the sweat oozed out and stood in thick beads on that forehead.

His aspect was so frightful that Christian took his handkerchief, and with a careful gesture wiped that forehead and those temples. And as he did so he felt his own brow become moist. He hesitated to use the same cloth for himself. But at that moment Niels Heinrich opened his eyes and looked at him—sombre, deep, cold. He conquered his aversion, and wiped his own brow with the same cloth.

There came a knocking at the door. Niels Heinrich started as though a heavy blow had struck him, and stared wildly with pale and empty eyes.

Christian opened the door. It was Michael and Johanna who were returning.

Reeling, Niels Heinrich sought his cap with his eyes. Christian gave it to him with all his impenetrable courtesy of demeanour, and prepared himself to accompany Niels Heinrich. The latter had an expression of dullness and of being utterly puzzled. Then he pulled up his shoulders and, followed by Christian, walked first falteringly, then with increasing firmness, toward the threshold.

XXV

The interview with Wolfgang Wahnschaffe made a thoroughly unpleasant impression on Lorm. He had the vexatious feeling that this well-bred young gentleman harboured the very naïve opinion that in the presence of a mere actor he could exhibit his complete ruthlessness and brutal self-seeking. Because what did an actor matter? One need take no trouble and could magnificently show one's cards.

On that very evening Lorm felt the approaching symptoms of serious illness. He was laconic; what he said was brief and sharp.

It was proposed to him to take part in a conspiracy. The plan was to imprison Christian in a sanatorium by the unanimous decision of the family.

" I can quite imagine what you mean by a sanatorium," said Lorm, " but what do you gain by it? "

" A clear road," was the answer, " the immediate setting aside of his troublesome rights and claims as the firstborn. The shame and disgrace that he spreads pass all belief."

He explained that certain individuals, including physicians, were willing to serve as witnesses and to co-operate. Yet actual internment was an extreme measure. If it should fail or the parental consent to carry it out should be unobtainable, there was another plan which was being prepared with equal care. The ground would be dug away from under his feet; he must be brought to leave the city and, preferably, the country. It was possible to have Christian boycotted at the university, though he rarely appeared there now. Another promising plan was to prejudice against him the people of the quarter where he lived; a beginning in that direction had already been

made. But there wasn't much time; the evil was infectious,
and the shameful rumours grew more troublesome daily. It
would not do to wait until the murder case with its fatal
publicity came to trial; he must be made to disappear before
that. There would be good prospects in Judith going to him
in a friendly way and persuading him with sisterly kindness
to disappear and not compel his relatives to use the force which
the law would readily place in their hands. If Judith failed
and he refused, everything must be done to send their father
on the same errand. He had written to his father; if no
decisive measures were taken within a week, he would telegraph.
Furthermore, friends had gone to the Privy Councillor to plead
for swift action.

There Wolfgang sat, pale with rage, balked in his mean
worldliness.

" So far as Judith is concerned, she's unapproachable in
the matter," Lorm said coldly. " I'll speak to her once more,
but I fear it will be useless. I myself would consider it desirable for her to go to Christian, though my reasons are
not yours; but Judith cannot be persuaded. The fate of
others, even of her own brother, are mere phantoms to her.
A year ago she was still capable of refusing passionately any
participation in such a plan; to-day she has probably simply
forgotten Christian. She plays and dreams her life away.
I am sorry that I do not know Christian myself. But people
have come to seek me out for so many years that I have lost
the impulse and ability to go to them. I must resign myself
to that, though it is an evil, no doubt."

Wolfgang was surprised at these words and grew quite icy.
He asked Lorm whether Judith would receive him, Wolfgang,
pleasantly. Lorm thought that she would. Therewith the
interview came to an end. They shook hands with conventional indifference.

Lorm did not dare tell Judith of his meeting with Wolfgang.
He was afraid of her questions, of her feeling his sympathy

with Christian, of clouding the puppet-show of her life. Yet she was gradually draining all the light out of his own existence. Her niggardliness in the household became so extreme that the servants complained of hunger. The baker and the butcher could obtain settlement of their bills only when they threatened to bring suit. Judith intercepted the dunning letters they addressed to Lorm. She sorted the mail every morning. He knew it; one of the maids, whom she had discharged after an ugly quarrel, had flung the information at him. He did not reproach Judith. She began to cut down the expenses for his personal needs too, and he had to eke out his diet in restaurants and wine-rooms. But the sums that she wasted for frocks, coats, hats, and antiquities increased to the point of madness. She bought old cases and chests which she promptly sent to the attic; Chinese vases, Renaissance embroideries, ivory boxes, cut-glass goblets, candelabra of chased metal work. Her purchases were without discrimination, and served only the whim of the moment. The things stood or lay about as in a shop; they served neither use nor adornment. Now and then she had a generous impulse, and presented some object to one of the women who flattered her and whose society had therefore become indispensable to her. Afterwards she would regret her generosity, and abuse its recipient as though a trick had been played on her. In spite of the great number of things about her, she would observe the absence or displacement of any object at once, accuse every one who had entered the room of theft, and know no rest until the lost thing had been found. In her dressing-room there hung dozens of garments and hats and shawls that had never touched her body except when she had tried them on on the day of their purchase. It satisfied her to possess them. They might go out of fashion or be full of moths; to possess them was enough.

Lorm knew this, but he bore her no resentment. He made no objection; he let her do as she desired. He did not or would not see the obvious consequences of his boundless ac-

quiescence—her degeneration and degradation and heartless-
ness. She was to him still the woman who had sacrificed everything in order to enter his lonely and joyless life. He had
condemned his achingly modest soul to permanent gratitude,
and had no conviction of any right of protest. He who had
thrust so many from him, and had been cold toward so many,
and had contemned so much genuine and active love, whose
gentlest gesture had not only commanded but entranced thousands of watchers and listeners, this same man endured humiliation and neglect as though to expiate his sins, and was
silent and steadfast in undeviating fidelity.

During this period his colleagues in the theatre trembled
at his outbursts of irritability; even Emanuel Herbst's
philosophical calm had little power over him. He went to
fill engagements in Breslau, Leipzig, and Stuttgart. He
impressed people more profoundly than any actor had done
for decades. One felt in him the turning-point of an epoch
and the ultimate perfect moment of an artist. The public,
wrought upon by his spirit to the height of rare perceptions,
had a presentiment of the finality of his appearances, and
was shaken in the passion of its applause as by the tragic,
scarlet glow of a sunset that betokens doom.

He returned home, and took to his bed. After a thorough
examination his physician's face grew serious. He demanded
a trained nurse. Judith was at a concert; the housekeeper
promised to report to her mistress. When Judith returned,
she sat down at his bedside. She was astonished and pouted
a little, and talked to Lorm as though he were a parrot who
refuses to chatter his accustomed words. It was the housekeeper who received the trained nurse.

" Well, Puggie dear," Judith said next morning, " aren't you
well yet? Shall I have them cook you a little soup? I suppose
the Suabians gave you too many goodies? "

" Puggie " smiled, reached for his wife's hand, and kissed
it.

Judith withdrew her hand in terror. " Oh, you wicked boy," she cried, " you mustn't do that! Do you want to infect your sweetheart? Think of it! Puggie mustn't do that till we know what ails him and that it isn't dangerous. Understand that? "

Letitia had announced her visit for that afternoon. She came, accompanied by Crammon. Judith's cordial reception was largely the result of consuming curiosity. The two women, who had not seen each other since their girlhood, regarded each other. Where have you been stranded? And you? Thus their eyes asked, while their lips flowed with flattery. Crammon seemed to curdle of his own sourness.

Fifteen minutes later the maid appeared and announced that Count Rochlitz's chauffeur was at the door. The count was waiting in the car. " Ask him to come up," Letitia commanded. " You don't mind, do you? " She turned to Judith. " An old friend of mine."

The count obeyed and came up. He was charming and told racing anecdotes.

At the end of another fifteen minutes came the Countess Brainitz with Ottomar and Reinhold. It had been agreed that they were to call for Letitia. They all filled Judith's drawing-room, and there was a hubbub of talk.

Crammon said to Ottomar, whom his condescension at times permitted to learn his opinions and feelings: " Once when I was in Tunis I was awakened by violent voices in the morning. I thought the native population had risen in revolt and rushed from my bed. But there were only two elderly, dark-brown ladies carrying on a friendly conversation under my window. It is characteristic of women to produce a maximum of din with a minimum of motive. They are constantly saving the Capitol. I am inclined to believe that the Romans, a nation of braggarts and sabre-rattlers, infused a rather ungallant implication into the pleasant fable of the geese. Usually their judgment of female nature was blithely sophomoric. As proof I adduce the story of Tarquin and Lucretia. Monstrous nonsense, penny-dreadful stuff! In my parental house we had a calendar on which the story was related in verse and bodied forth in pictures. This cataract of chastity gave me an utterly perverse notion of certain fundamental facts of human nature. It took years to penetrate the character of the deception."

Ottomar said: "I grant you what you say of all women except of Letitia. Observe how she moves, how she carries her head. She is an exquisite exception. Her presence makes every occasion festive; she is the symbol of lovely moments. She will never age, and all her actions are actions in a dream. They have no consequences, they have no objective reality, and she expects them to have neither."

"Very deep and very finely observed," said Crammon, with a sigh. "But heaven guard you from trying to establish a practical household with such a fairy creature."

"One shouldn't, one mustn't," the young man replied, with conviction.

Crammon arose, and went over to Judith. "Isn't Edgar at home, Frau Lorm?" he asked. "Can one get to him? We have not seen each other for long."

"Edgar is ill," Judith answered, with a frown, as though she had reason to feel affronted by the fact.

A silence fell on the room. All felt a sense of discomfort. And Crammon saw, as in a new and sudden vision, Judith's projecting cheek-bones, her skin injured by cosmetics, her morbidly compressed mouth with its lines of bitterness, her fluttering glance, and her restless hands. There was something of decay in her and about her, something that came of over-intensity and the fever of gambling, of a slackening and rotting of tissues. Her cheerfulness arose from rancour, her vivacity was that of a marionette with creaking joints.

Letitia had forgotten to mention Christian. Not until they reached the street did she recall the purpose of her visit. She reproached Crammon for not having reminded her. "It doesn't matter," Crammon said. "I'm going back to-morrow and you can come with me. I want to see Lorm. I have a presentiment of evil; misfortune is brewing."

"O Bernard," Letitia said, plaintively, "you croak enough to make the sun lose its brightness and roses their fragrance."

"No. Only I happen to know that a change is coming over the face of the earth; and you poor, lost souls do not see it," answered Crammon, with forefinger admonishingly raised.

And he departed and went to Borchardt, where he intended to dine exquisitely. Each time he dined there, he called it the murderer's last meal.

XXVI

When Michael left the church at Johanna's side he felt profoundly stirred by the experience of the past hour.

They rode as far as Schönhauser Avenue, and from there on they went on foot. The flurries of snow and the drifts on the ground made walking doubly difficult for the limping boy.

During their long ride he had been silent, although his face showed the pathetic eagerness of his thoughts and feelings. He had but recently learned to express himself; formerly he had had to choke everything down. And since he had learned to speak out he seized every opportunity. His words were fresh, and his gestures expressive and extreme. His tone belied his youth. With shrill accents he deadened attacks of timidity. Afraid of not being taken as seriously as seemed to befit him and his confusions and insights and experiences, he would often defend daring assertions stubbornly, while his own conviction of their truth was already wavering. On the way out he had repeatedly begun to talk of Christian. His soul was filled by Christian. His worship, half timid, half full of wild enthusiasm, expressed itself in various ways. His mind had lacked an ideal and the spiritual centres and intoxications of youth;

now he gave himself up to these the more gladly. Yet, in conformity to his brooding nature, he tricked out Christian's simpleness in various mysteries and problems, and on this point Johanna could not set him right. She evaded his remarks. The boy seemed to her too impetuous, too absolute, too eager. He affronted the modesty of her feelings; he was too fond of rending veils. Yet he fascinated her, and kept her in a state of restlessness and gentle pain; and she needed both. She could fancy that she was protecting him, and through this duty she was better protected against herself.

He said it hadn't been the music that had overwhelmed him. Music of that kind was an expression through difficult forms, and one should not, it seemed to him, let pleasure in the sounds deceive one in regard to one's ignorance. One must know and learn.

"What was it then? What did impress you?" Johanna asked. But her question showed only a superficial curiosity. The way and the day had wearied her beyond the desire of speech.

"It was the church," said Michael. "It was the song in praise of Christ. It was the devout multitude." He stopped, and his head fell. In his childhood and until quite recently, he told her in his hoarse and slightly broken boyish voice, he had not been able to think of Jesus Christ without hatred. A religiously brought up Jewish child out in the country, who had suffered the jeers and abuse of Gentiles, felt that hatred in his very bones. To such a child Christ was the enemy who had deserted and traduced his people, the renegade and source of all that people's suffering. "I remember how I used to slink past all churches," Michael said; "I remember with what fear and rage. Ruth never felt so. Ruth had no sense for the reality of bitter things; to her everything was sweet and clear. She left the vulgar far below her. It ate into me, and I had no one to talk to."

But one evening, a few days before her disappearance, Ruth without his asking her and without any preliminary speech, but simply as though she wanted to get closer to him and release him from his oppressed state, had read him a passage from the Gospel of the Christians. It was the passage in which the risen Lord asks Peter: "Lovest thou me more than these? He saith unto him, Yea, Lord; thou knowest that I love thee. He said unto him, Feed my lambs. He saith to him again the second time, Simon, lovest thou me? He saith unto him, Yea, Lord; thou knowest that I love thee. He saith unto him, Feed my sheep. He saith unto him the third time, Lovest thou me? Peter was grieved that he said unto him the third time, Lovest thou me? And he said unto him, Lord, thou knowest all things; thou knowest that I love thee. Jesus saith unto him, Feed my sheep." And later on he said: "Follow me."

He told how he had torn the book from his sister's hand and had turned its pages and had not desired to be led astray by it. But one sentence had held his attention, and he had dwelt upon it. It was this: "And he needed not to have knowledge of a man, for he knew what was in man." At that the hatred of Christ had vanished from his soul. Yet he had not been able to believe in him or to turn to him. He didn't mean in the way of piety and prayer; he meant the idea which gave men assurance and help to their minds. He had grasped that to-day, during the soaring song, and as he watched the thousand eyes that seemed first extinguished and then lit by a solemn flame. "Lovest thou me, Simon?" He had grasped that utterly, and also the saying: "Follow me." And his consciousness of being a Jew and having been cast out had been transformed from pain and shame into wealth and pride through the assurance of a certain service and a peculiar power. "It was wonderful, wonderful," he assured her. "I don't quite understand it yet. I am like a lamp that has been lit."

Johanna was frightened at the outburst of a passion so strange and incomprehensible to her.

"Feed my sheep," Michael almost sang the words out into the snow. "Feed my sheep."

"It is an awakening," Johanna thought, with faint horror and envy. "He has been awakened."

The boy's impassioned attachment to Christian became ever clearer to her. When they waited at the locked door in Stolpische Street and Christian came out with Niels Heinrich and passed the two without noticing them, without glance or greeting, and went off with that shaking, shuffling, distorted creature, Michael limped behind him for a few paces, stared into the dark yard filled with the whirl of snow, and then returned to Johanna and said beseechingly: "He mustn't go with that man. Do run after him and call him back. He mustn't, for God's sake, go with him."

Johanna, although she was herself perturbed, soothed the overwrought boy. She remained for half an hour, forced herself to a natural cheerfulness, chatted pleasantly as she made tea and laid the cloth for a cold supper. Then she went home. At eight o'clock the next morning Michael rang the bell at her dwelling. She had scarcely finished dressing. She met him in the hall. He was pale, sleepless, struggling for words. "Wahnschaffe hasn't come home yet," he murmured. "What shall we do?"

Fighting down her first consternation, Johanna smiled. She took Michael's hand and said: "Don't be afraid. Nothing will happen to him."

"Are you so sure of that?"

"Quite sure!"

"Why are you?"

"I don't know. But it would never occur to me to be afraid for him. That would be a sheer waste of emotional energy."

Her calm and assurance impressed Michael; yet he asked her to come with him and stay with him if she could. After a moment's reflection she consented. On the way back they entered a bookshop and bought the volumes that Lamprecht had suggested. Christian had given Michael money for the purchase. He wanted to begin his studies alone and at once, but he could not collect his thoughts. He sat at the table, turned the leaves of books, arranged paper, lifted his head and listened, pressed his hands together or jumped up and walked to and fro in the room, looked out into the yard, gazed searchingly at Johanna, who was working at a piece of embroidery and sat shivering and worn in a corner of the sofa, gnawing at her lip with her small white teeth.

Thus that day passed and another night, and yet Christian did not return. The impatience and anxiety of the boy became unrestrainable. "We must bestir ourselves," he said. "It is stupid to sit here and wait." Johanna, who was also beginning to grow anxious, prepared to go either to Botho von Thüngen or to Dr. Voltolini. While she was putting on her hat Lamprecht came in. When he had been told of the situation he said: "You're doing Wahnschaffe no favour by raising an alarm. If he doesn't come, it is for reasons of his own. Your fear is childish and unworthy of him. We'd better start at something useful, my boy."

His firmer intellect shared in an even higher degree Johanna's instinctive assurance. Michael submitted once more, and for two hours he was an obedient pupil. Toward noon, when Johanna and Lamprecht had left, a teamster presented himself with an unpaid bill. He said he hadn't received payment yet for the horses furnished for the funeral of the late Fräulein Engelschall. Michael assured the man that he would receive his money on the morrow, since Wahnschaffe had of course merely forgotten the matter. The man grumbled and went out; but in the yard he was joined by several other people, and Michael heard the sound of hostile talk and of Christian's name. He went into the hall and to the outer door. The venomous words and references in the vilest jargon drove the blood into his cheeks. He felt at once that the feeling against Christian had been deliberately instigated by some one. A red-haired fellow, a painter who lived on the fourth floor, was especially scurrilous. He called the attention of the others to Michael; a coarse remark was made; the crowd roared. When the courage of his indignation drove Michael out into the yard, he was met by menacing glances.

"What have you to say against Wahnschaffe?" he asked in a loud voice, yet with an instinctive shrinking of his body.

Again they roared. Laughing, the red-haired fellow turned up his sleeves. A woman at a window above reached into the room and poured a pailful of dirty water into the yard. The water spattered Michael, and there was thunderous laughter. The teamster Scholz put his hands to his hips, and discoursed of idlers who set fleas into the ears of the working-people with dam' fool talk and hypocrisy. And suddenly other words hissed into Michael's face: "Get out o' here, Jew!" He became pale, and touched the wall behind him with his hands.

At that moment Botho von Thüngen and Johanna came in through the doorway. They stopped and silently regarded the group of people in the snow and also Michael. They understood. Johanna drew Michael into the house. He gave a breathless report; he was so ardent, so nobly indignant, that his features took on a kind of beauty.

After a while someone knocked at the door, and Amadeus Voss entered. His courtesy was exaggerated, but he seemed in no wise astonished to find Johanna here, nor did it seem to annoy him. He said he wanted to talk to Christian Wahnschaffe. Thüngen replied that no one knew when Christian would return or whether he would return on that day at all.

Voss said drily that he had time and could wait.

Johanna felt paralysed. She could not will to go away. All she wanted to avoid was any demonstration, any scene. Like an animal that slinks to a hiding-place, she cowered in the corner of the sofa, and gnawed her lip with her little teeth.

Suddenly the thought flashed into her mind—" death, death, that's the only thing."

XXVII

The festivities were over; the guests had departed; Eva and Susan remained alone in the castle.

The fullness of spring had come thus early to that southern coast. The festivals had been festivals of spring amid a tropical wealth of flowers and in that heroic landscape. The flight from the winter of the North had been so swift that no dignity could withstand its effects. It had intoxicated every soul. They had given themselves up to the mere delight of breathing, to the astonishment of the senses. Some had felt like carousers and gluttons merely, others like liberated prisoners, and all had been conscious of the brevity of their respite; and this consciousness breathed a breath of melancholy over all delight.

The atmosphere still echoed the thrill of impassioned words and the tread and laughter of women; the sounds had not yet quite died away, and in the night the darkness of the silent park still yearned for the glow of lights which the stars above could not cause it to forget.

But they were all gone.

The Grand Duke had accepted the invitation of an Austrian Archduke to shoot on his estates. In April Eva was to meet him in Vienna and accompany him to Florence. She had asked none of her friends to stay longer, no woman, no artist, and no paladin. It had become a very hunger of her soul to be alone once more. She had not been alone for four years.

She felt even Susan to be in the way. When the woman crept about her in foolish anxiety, she sent her out of the room. She desired not to be addressed nor to be beheld; she wanted to escape into a crystalline structure of loneliness. She had built it, and wanted the full experience of it; and suddenly she became aware of the fact that it estranged her from herself. Something had happened to make the blood of her heart cool and sick.

She could not read nor write letters nor consider plans. No hour seemed to grow out of another living hour. All day she walked alone by the sea or sat amid flowers in the garden. The greater part of the night she lay on an open terrace, in front of which the sky hung down like a curtain of dark-blue velvet. Often the dawn had arisen before she went to bed. She had a sensation within herself as of loosened organization and rhythms dissolved. At times she felt a sting of dread. Noon glowed on her like steel; evening was a gate into the unknown.

She had forbidden all messages. Letters that laid claim to any urgency were answered by Susan or Monsieur Labourde-mont. Yet casting a chance and inattentive look at the letter of a friend she saw something about Ivan Becker. What she read took possession of her mind. It was like a presage and a touch of danger. When she lay at night on her terrace, there was a pallid flashing behind the azure curtain of the sky, and the silence breathed treachery.

At the head of fifteen thousand workingmen, all loyal to the Tsar, Ivan Becker had appeared in front of the Winter Palace, in order to effect a direct explanation and reconciliation between the Tsar and his people. Regiments of Cossacks had surrounded the peaceful demonstration, and it had ended in a shambles. Again the people had gathered, and Ivan Becker on a tribunal had stretched out his arms to heaven and cursed the Tsar. He was a fugitive in the land, hiding in monasteries and in peasants' huts. Next the mutineers of the " Panteleymon " and the " Potemkin " sent him a message, bidding him join them. The crews of the two dreadnoughts had refused obedience to their officers in the harbour of Sebas-topol. They had murdered their captains and other officers, and cast their bodies into the sea or into the ships' fires. They had taken possession of the ships, elected their own officers, and had steamed out to sea. It was not known whether Ivan Becker had followed the summons of the mutineers; all trace of him had been lost. But many people asserted with assurance that he had sought security from the pursuit of the political police on board of the rebellious ships, and had acquired a remarkable influence over the savage seamen.

It was his third appearance in the midst of revolt and blood.

Rumours were brought and spread by gardeners, fishermen, and peasants. It was said that the mutineers had turned pirates, that they captured merchantmen and bombarded cities. During many nights rockets flared up in the sky, and the thunder of artillery was heard. Wherever they needed not to fear the attack of superior forces, it was said, they landed and looted towns and villages, killed all who resisted, and filled the province far inland with terror.

Eva was warned. She was warned by the elder of a village that lay on the confines of her park; she was warned by messengers sent by the naval commander at Nicolayev, who informed her that the mutinous sailors planned to attack all imperial estates in the Crimea, especially those of the Grand Duke; she was finally warned by an anonymous telegram from Moscow.

She did not heed these warnings. She had a feeling that she should not and must not fear this thing of all others—not this menace of degradation and ugliness. So she remained; but her stay was one long waiting. A conviction of a thing ineluctable had come over her. It proceeded not from the mutineers or their reign of crime, but from her own mind and from the profound logic of things.

One evening she mounted the golden stairs to the tower. Gazing from the platform across the dark tree-tops and over land and sea, she saw along the northern horizon a seam of scarlet. Wrapped in a filmy veil, she thoughtfully watched the spreading of that glow without anxiety or curiosity as to its cause. She had a penetrant feeling of the presence of fate, and bowed to it in fatalistic resignation.

Susan was waiting in the room with the Arabic frescoes. Walking up and down with the stride of a dervish, she fought against her darkening fears. The flame was burning low. How was it with Lucas Anselmo? Her deep awareness of him, her sense of living for him, had not grown feebler during these years of radiance and fulfilment. The dancer who was his work, into whom he had breathed the breath of life and art, had been to her, now as before, the assurance of his being and the message of his soul. And what was happening now? Darkness was creeping on; the shadow-creature of his making drooped in its lovely motions. Was the hand that had formed and commanded it stricken and cold? Had that lofty spirit grown weary, and lost the strength to project itself afar? Had the end come?

Eva entered. She was startled by Susan's appearance, and sat down on a couch, at whose head stood glowing hortensias that were renewed each morning. The sea wind had chilled her. The eyes in their carven hollows were stern. " What do you want? " she asked.

" I think we ought to leave," Susan answered. " It is foolish to delay. The small military escort that is on the way from Yalta could not protect us if the castle were to be attacked."

" What are you afraid of? " Eva asked again. " Of men? "

" Yes, I am afraid of men; and it is a very reasonable fear. Use your imagination, and think of their bodies and voices. We ought to leave."

" It is foolish to be afraid of men," Eva insisted, leaning her arm on the pillows and her head upon her hand.

Susan said: " But you too are afraid. Or what is it? What is happening to you? Is it fear? What are you afraid of? "

" Afraid . . . yes, I am afraid," Eva murmured. " Of what? I don't know. Of shadows and dreams. Some thing has gone from me; my guardian deity has fled. That makes me afraid."

Susan trembled at these confirmatory words. "Shall we order our boxes packed?" she asked humbly.

Overhearing her question Eva continued: "Fear grows from guilt. Look you, I wander about here, and am guilty. I open my garment because it binds me, and feel my guilt. I stretch out my hand after one of those blue blossoms, and know my guilt. I think and think, and brood and brood, and cannot fathom the reason. The innermost, ultimate reason—I cannot find it."

"Guilt?" Susan stammered in her consternation. "Guilty? You? Child, what are you saying? You are ill! Dearest, sweetest, you are ill!" She kneeled at Eva's feet, embraced her delicate body, and looked up at her with swimming eyes. "Let us flee, dear heart, let us flee to our friends. I knew this land would kill you. Yesterday's wilderness which your enchantment transformed into an unreal paradise still guards the old malevolence of its remote and accursed earth. Arise and smile, dear one. I shall sit down at the piano and play Schumann, whom you love. I shall bring you a mirror, that you may behold yourself and see how beautiful you still are. Who that is so beautiful can be guilty?"

Sadly Eva shook her head. "Beauty?" she asked. "Beauty? You would cheat me of my deep perceptions with your talk of beauty. I know nothing of beauty. If it be indeed a real thing, it is without blessing. No, do not speak of beauty. I have reached out after too much in too short a time, robbed too much, used too much, wasted too much— men and souls and given pledges. I could not hold it all nor bear it. All my wishes were fulfilled. The more measureless they became, the swifter was the fulfilment. I had fame and love and wealth and power, the service of slaves and adoration—everything, everything! So much that I could burrow in it as in a heap of precious stones. I desired to

rise—from what depths you know, and wings were given me.
I desired to break obstacles; they melted at my glance. I
wanted to devote myself to a great cause, and its servants
had faith in me before I had begun to master its meaning.
They proclaimed it in my name while I still needed to be
taught it. All things came too soon and too fully. Millions
sacrifice what is dearest to them, tremblingly and devoutly,
not to be swept away from the cliff to which they are clinging;
I was like Aladdin, to whom the genii bow the knee before
his command is uttered. And I thrust from me and misprized
the only one whose heart ever resisted me—though he himself
knew not why. Every step has been a step toward guilt, every
yearning has been guilt, and every stirring of gratitude.
Every hour of delight has been guilt, every enjoyment an
impoverishment, and every rise a fall."

"Blasphemer," Susan murmured. "Pride and satiety cause
you to sin against yourself and your fate."

"How you torment me," Eva answered. "How all of you
torment me—men and women. How sterile I become through
you. How your voices torture me, and your eyes and words
and thoughts. You lie so frivolously; you would not listen,
and truth is hateful to you. Who are you? Who are
you, Susan? You have a name; but I do not know you.
You are another self; and you torment me out of that other
selfhood. Go! Have I asked you to be with me? I want
to enter my own soul, and you would keep me without? I
tell you I shall stay, though they burn the house down over
my head."

She spoke these words with a repressed passionateness, and
arose. She withdrew herself from her sobbing companion
and entered her bedchamber.

An hour later Susan burst in, pale and with dishevelled
hair. She called out to her mistress, who was still awake
and meditating by the light of a shaded lamp: "They are
upon us. They are approaching the castle! Labourdemont

has telephoned to Yalta. We are advised to flee at once. During the past fifteen minutes the wires have been cut. I've just left the garage; the motor will drive up in twenty minutes. Quickly, quickly, while there is still time."

Calmly Eva said: " There is no occasion for alarm or outcry; control yourself. Experience in similar cases seems to show that flight only goads the people on to plundering and destruction. If they have the temerity to enter here, I shall face their leaders and deal with them. That is the right and natural thing. I shall stay; but I shall force no one to stay with me."

Susan was quite calm at once, and her tone was dry: " You are very much in error, if you think I tremble for myself. If you stay, it goes without saying that I stay too. Let us not waste another word." And she gave her mistress the garment which a gesture had demanded.

Then were heard hurrying steps and cries, the whir of the motor, and the barking of dogs. Monsieur Labourdemont strode wildly up and down in the ante-room. The sergeant of gendarmes addressed his men from the stairs. With equanimity Eva sat down at her toilet table, and let Susan arrange her hair. The roar of the sea came through the open window. The heavy dragging noise was suddenly interrupted by the rattle of rifle fire.

A brief silence ensued. Labourdemont knocked at the door of the sleeping chamber. There wasn't another minute to be lost, he called out, with a lump of terror in his throat. " Tell him what is needful," Eva commanded. Susan went out, and returned shortly with a sombre smile on her lips. Eva's glance questioned her. " Panic," Susan said, and shrugged her shoulders. " Naturally. They don't know what to do."

Again cries were heard; they were frightened and confused. A light flickered; muffled commands followed. Loud cries burst into the silence, then the howling of hundreds. Next came a sudden crash, as though a wooden door had been broken down. Crackling of flames swallowed the barking of the dogs, and was itself silenced by piercing cries, hisses, roars. A pillar of fire arose without; the chamber was crimson in the glow. Susan stood crimson in its midst; her eyes were glassy, and her face a rigid mask.

Eva went to the window. Trees and bushes were steeped in glow. The centre of the fire was not to be seen. The space in front of the castle was deserted. The guards had vanished; seeing the hopelessness of facing the superior forces of the mutineers, they had fled; nor was a single one of Eva's servants to be seen. Uncertain shadows rolled forward, hissing in the glow and the darkness. Shots sounded from all directions. The clash of shards resounded; they were stoning the hothouses. Suddenly from the right and from the left, surging about the house, masses of men burst out of the fiery twilight, that was momently transformed into yellow brilliancy. It was a wild throng of arms and rumps and heads, a raging mass, impetuously driving forward, whose roaring and growling and whistling shook the very air.

" Leave the window! " Susan murmured, in rough beseeching.

Eva did not stir. Faces looked up and saw her. An incomprehensible word flashed through the whirling mass. Many remained standing; but while they stared upward, they were thrust aside by others behind them. The human surge broke against the castle steps and ebbed away a little. A wavering came upon it, then a silence.

" Leave the window! " Susan begged, with uplifted hands.

Masses of scarlet-tinged faces turned toward Eva. Close-packed, they filled the semicircle in front of the castle; and still the mass increased, like a dark fluid in a vessel that is slowly filled to the brim. Those farthest behind stamped on the sward and flower-beds, uprooted bushes, hurled statues to the ground. Most of them wore the uniform of marines; but among them was also the mob of cities, human offscourings eager for booty and blood—the men of the Black Hundreds.

They were armed with rifles, sabres, clubs, revolvers, iron bars, and axes. A great number were drunk.

That incomprehensible word clanged once more above the serried heads. The whirling forward rush started again. Fists worked their way upward. A shot resounded. Susan uttered a throttled cry, as the hanging lamp over the bed fell shattered. Eva stepped back from the window. She shivered. Absent-mindedly she took a few steps, and lifted an apple from a bowl. It slipped from her hand and rolled along the floor.

They entered the house. Blows of the axe were heard, the shuffle of feet, the opening of doors. They were seeking.

" We are doomed," Susan whispered, and clung to Eva's arm with both hands, as though someone were thrusting her into water.

" Let me be," Eva repulsed her. " I shall try to speak to them. It will suffice to show them courage."

" Don't go! For God's sake, don't! " Susan besought her.

" Let me go, I tell you. I see no other way. Hide, and let me go! "

Her step was the step of a queen. Perhaps she knew the sentence that had been pronounced. Upon the threshold an icy feeling of ultimate decision came over her. Her eyes were veiled. The way seemed far to her and moved her to impatience. From the reflection of fire and the twilit greyness, men bounded toward her and receded, surrounded her and melted back. The nobility of her figure still had power over them; but behind them venomous demons raged and made a path toward her. She spoke some Russian words. The flaring whirl of heads and shoulders surged fantastically up and down. She saw necks, beards, teeth, fists, ears, eyes, foreheads, veins, nails. Features dislimned; the faces melted into a glow of flame. Fire crackled in her gymnasium; hatchets crashed against costly things; smoke filled the corridors; maniacal cries tore the air. Eva turned.

It was too late. No magic of look or gesture availed. The depths were unleashed.

She fled with the lightness of a gazelle. Loutish steps followed her, and the wheezing of loud lungs. She reached the stairs of the quadrangular tower, the structure of her whim. She ran up the stairs. High up the gilded steps sparkled in the first glint of dawn. Her hand glided without friction over the balustrade. The painted enamel, another creation of her whims, was cool and calming to her palms. Her pursuers grunted like wolves. But the light seemed to lift her upward. She burst into the silvery morning, and beheld the burning buildings swaying in the wind and the wide sea. Her pursuers surged after her like a great heap of limbs, a polypus with hair and noses and cruel teeth.

She leaped upon the parapet. Arms reached out after her. Higher! Ah, if there were a higher height! Clouds covered the sky. Once upon a time it had been different. Stars had comforted her—the lordly reaches of the firmament. The memory lasted but a second. Hands grasped her; claws were at her very breast. Four, six, eight pairs of arms were stretched out toward her. A last reflection, a last struggle, a last sigh. The air divided with a whir. She plunged. . . .

On slabs of marble lay her body. That marvellous body was a mass of bloody pulp. The broken eyes were open— empty, void of depth or knowledge or consciousness. Over the parapet the human wolves howled in their disappointed rage. Below others fell upon her dead. They tore the garments from her body, and stuck shreds of them, like flags, on poles and branches.

Slain on the threshold of her mistress' bedchamber lay Susan Rappard.

When the work of plundering and destruction had been completed, the wild horde withdrew. A man of mercy and shame had finally thrown a horse-blanket over the dancer's soiled and naked body.

As evening came, one man still wandered about amid the ruins, a lonely man in lonely travail of spirit. He wore the garb of a priest, and on his features was the stamp of a fate fulfilled. Those who came at a late hour to seek and accompany him, greeted him with reverence, for he was accounted by them a saint of the people and a prophet of the kingdom to come.

He spoke to them: "I have lied to you; I am but a weak creature like the rest."

They rocked their heads and one answered: "Little Father Ivan Michailovitch, do not destroy our hope or cease leading us in our weakness."

Thereupon this saint of his people gazed at the body that lay under a horse-blanket amid the trampled flowers and the charred ruins, and said: "Let us proceed then even unto the end."

XXVIII

Thrice on the street Niels Heinrich stopped and stared into Christian's face. Then he went on, stumping his feet against the asphalt and hunching his back. At first he dragged himself painfully along; gradually his tread grew steadier.

At Kahle's shop he asked with toneless jeer whether the gentleman was employed by the police. In that case the gentleman needn't delay or worry. He knew the way to headquarters himself.

"I did not go with you from such a motive."

"Well, what for then?" The gentleman was talking crazy again. He had a way of trying to make people drunk with talk.

"Do you live in this house?" Christian asked.

Yes, he lived there. Maybe the gentleman would like to look at the stinking hole? Right ahead then. He himself wouldn't stay upstairs long. He just wanted to fix himself up a little more neatly and then go to Gottlieb's Inn. That was a better class café with girlies and champagne. He was going to treat to fifteen or twenty bottles to-day. Why not—since he had the brass? But first he'd have to go to Grün-busch's to pawn something. Maybe all that'd bore the gentleman; and maybe not, eh?

These words he snarled out in his rage on the dark stairs; but beneath his rage seethed a hell of terror.

The light of a street-lamp close by his window threw a pale, greenish light into the room, and saved Niels Heinrich the trouble of lighting a lamp. He pointed to it and remarked with a snicker that to have one's lighting at public expense was pure gain. He could read his paper in bed and didn't even have to blow out the lamp before going to bed. That showed you how a man had to live who wasn't without brains and might have gotten ahead in the world. It was a lousy, stinking hole. But now things would change; he was going to move to the Hotel Adlon and have a room with a private bath, and buy his linen at the Nürnberger Bazaar.

He put his hand in his pocket, and a clinking could be heard. Christian took his words for incoherent babble and did not answer.

Niels Heinrich tore off his crumpled collar, and threw his coat and waistcoat on the bed. He opened a drawer and then a wardrobe, and with astonishing dexterity put on a clean collar, so tall that it seemed to enclose his neck in a white tube, tied a cravat of yellow silk, and slipped into a striped waist-coat and a morning coat. These things looked new, and con-trasted absurdly with the stained, checked trousers which, for some reason, he did not change for others. The cuffs of his shirt were also soiled.

"Well, then why? " Suddenly he asked again, and his eyes flickered rabidly in the greenish light. "Why in hell do you stick to me like a leech? "

"I need you," answered Christian, who had remained near the door.

"You need me? What for? Don't understand. Talk plain, man, talk plain!"

"It serves no purpose to talk in that manner," Christian said. "You misunderstand my being here and my . . . how shall I put it?—my interest in you. No, not interest. That's not the right word. But the word doesn't matter. You probably think it was my purpose to have you surrender to the authorities and to repeat in court the confession you have made to me. But I assure you that that does not seem important to me or, rather, important only in so far as it is desirable for the sake of Joachim Heinzen, who is innocent and whom his position and inner confusion must make very wretched. He must be in a terrible state. I have felt that constantly, and felt the pain of it especially since your confession. I can almost see him. I have a vision of him trying to climb up the stony prison wall and wounding his hands and knees. He doesn't understand; he doesn't understand how a wall can be so steep and stony; he doesn't understand what has happened to him. The world must seem sick to him at its core. You have evidently succeeded in hypnotizing him so effectively and lastingly, that under this terrible influence he has lost all control of his own actions. There is something in you that makes the exertion of such power quite credible. I am quite sure that your very name has faded from his memory. If some one went to him and whispered that name, Niels Heinrich Engelschall, into his ear, he would probably collapse as under a paralytic stroke. Of course, as I have thought it out, it is an exaggeration. But try to imagine him. One must try to grasp men and things imaginatively. Very few people do it; they cheat themselves. I see him as robbed of his very soul, as so poverty-stricken that the thought is scarcely bearable. You will reply: he is an idiot, irresponsible, with an undeveloped sensorium—more animal than human. Even science uses that argument; but it it a false argument. The premises are false and therefore the conclusion. My opinion is that all human beings have equally deep perceptions. There is no difference in sensitiveness to pain; there is only a difference in the consciousness of that sensitiveness. There is, one may say, no difference in the method of bookkeeping, only in the accounting."

With lowered head he went a pace nearer to Niels Heinrich, who remained quite still, and continued, while a veiled smile hovered over his lips: " Don't misunderstand me. I don't desire to exert the slightest influence on your decisions. What you do or fail to do is your own affair. Whether one may desire to free that poor devil from his terrible situation, or not, is a problem of decency and humanity. So far as I am concerned, there is nothing I care about so little as to persuade you to an action which does not arise from your own conviction. I don't regard myself as a representative of public authority; it is not for me to see to it that the laws are obeyed and people informed in regard to a crime that has troubled them. What would be the use of that? Would it avail to make things better? I neither want to ensnare you nor get the better of you. Your going to court, confessing your crime, expiating in the world's sight, being punished— what have I to do with all that? Not to bring that about am I here."

Niels Heinrich felt as though his very brain were turning in his skull with a creaking noise. He grasped the edge of the table for support. In his face was a boundless astonishment. His jaw dropped; he listened open-mouthed.

" Punishment? What does that mean? And is it my office or within my power to drag you to punishment? Shall I use cunning or force to make you suffer punishment? It does not even become me to say to you: You are guilty. I do not know whether you are guilty. I know that guilt exists; but whether you are guilty or in what relation to guilt you stand— that I cannot tell. The knowledge of that is yours alone; you and you alone possess the standard by which to judge

what you have done, and not those who will be your judges.
Neither do I possess it, and so I do not judge. I ask myself:
Who dares to be a judge? I see no one, no one. In order that
men may live together, it is perhaps necessary that judgments
be passed; but the individual gains nothing by such judgments, either for his soul or for his knowledge."

It was a bottomless silence into which Niels Heinrich had
sunk. He suddenly remembered the moment in which the
impulse to murder the machine had come upon him. With
utter clearness he saw again the steel parts with their film of
oil, the swiftly whirling wheels, the whole accurately functioning structure that had, somehow, seemed hostile and destructive to him. Why that image of all others came to him
now, and why he remembered his vengeful impulse with an
access of shame now—he did not understand.

Christian was speaking again: " So all that does not concern
me at all. You need have no fear. What I want has nothing
to do with it. I want—" he stopped, hesitated, and struggled
for the word, " I want you. I need you. . . ."

" Need me? Need me? " Niels Heinrich murmured, without understanding. " How? What for? "

" I can't explain it, I can't possibly explain it," said
Christian.

Whereupon Niels Heinrich laughed—a toneless, broken
laugh. He walked around the whole table; then he repeated
that same repressed, half-mad laugh.

" You have removed a being from this earth," said Christian, softly; " you have destroyed a being so precious, so irreplaceable, that centuries, perhaps many centuries, will pass
till one can arise comparable to it or like it. Don't you know
that? Every living creature is like a screw in a most marvellously built machine. . . ."

Niels Heinrich began to tremble so violently that Christian noticed it. " What ails you? " he asked. " Are you
ill? "

Niels Heinrich took his felt hat, that hung on a nail, and began to stroke it nervously. "Man alive," he said, "you make a fellow crazy, crazy." His tone was hollow.

"Please listen," Christian continued insistently, "—in a most marvellously built machine. Now there are important screws and less important ones; and this being was one of the most important of all. So important indeed that I am convinced that the machine is hurt forever, because it has ceased to function. No one can ever again provide a part of such delicacy and exquisite exactness, and even though a substitute be found, the machine will never be what it once was. But aside from the machine and my comparison, you have inflicted a loss on me for which there are no words. Pain, grief, sadness—these words do not reach far or deep enough. You have robbed me of something utterly precious, forever irreplaceable, and you must give me something in return. You must give me something in return! Do you hear that? That is why I am standing here; that is why I am following you. You must give me something in return. I don't know what. But unless you do, I shall be desperate, and become a murderer myself."

He buried his face in his hands, and burst into hoarse, wild, passionate weeping.

With quivering lips, in a small voice like a naughty child's, Niels Heinrich stammered: "Saviour above, what can I give you in return?"

Christian wept and did not answer.

XXIX

Thereupon they went from that room together, without having exchanged another word.

The pawnbroker Grünbusch had already closed his shop. Niels Heinrich sought another whom he knew to be reliable. He left Christian in the street while he slipped into a dirty vault.　He had torn one pearl from the string, just one, to serve as a sample for the present.　After the old rascal who kept the shop had tested and weighed the pearl exactly, he gave Niels Heinrich fifteen hundred marks.　The money was partly in bank-notes and partly in gold.　He scarcely counted it.　He stuffed the coins into one pocket; the notes crackled as he crushed them into another.

"Give him?　What does he think I can give him?" He brooded.　"Maybe he smells a rat, and suspects that I stole the pearls.　Does he mean that?　Does he want me to give them to him?"

When he reached the street again, and saw that Christian had waited patiently and without suspicion, he merely made a wry face; and he continued silently by the other's side. Dumbfounded, he bore the heavy weight of Christian's continued presence; he could not imagine what would come of it.

But the man's weeping was still in his ears and in his limbs. A cold, clear stillness filled the air of night, yet everywhere rustled the sound of that weeping.　The streets through which they passed were nearly empty, yet in them was that weeping embodied in the whitish mist.　In the walls and balconies of the houses to the right and to the left, it lifted up its treacherous voice—this weeping of a man.

He dared not think.　Beside him went one who knew his thoughts.　A rope was about him, and he could move only so far as that other permitted.　Who is he?　The question went through and through him.　He tried to remember his name, but the name had slipped from his mind.　And all that this man, this suddenly nameless man, had said to him, whirled up within him like sparks of fire.

They had reached their goal at the end of half an hour. Gottlieb's Inn was a drinking place for workingmen and small shopkeepers.　It contained quite a number of rooms.　First one entered the restaurant proper, which was filled with guests all night.　Its chief attraction consisted in a dozen pretty

waitresses, as well as twenty to thirty other ladies, who smiled
and smoked and lounged in their provocative costumes on the
green plush sofas, waiting for victims. Adjoining the restaurant there were a number of cell-like private dining-rooms
for couples. Beyond these was a longish, narrow hall, which
was rented out for parties or to clubs, or in which gambling
took place. The decoration of the rooms corresponded to the
quarter and its taste. Everything was gilt; everywhere were
pretentious sculptures of stucco. There were tall pillars that
were hollow and supported nothing, but blocked one's path.
The walls were covered with paintings that had been the latest
thing the day before yesterday. Everything was new, and
everything was dirty and touched with decay.

Niels Heinrich went in through the swinging door, looked
about dazzled by the light, lurched past the tables, went into
the passage that led to the little private rooms, came back,
stared into the painted faces of the girls, called the head-waiter,
and said he wanted to go into the long hall at the rear, wanted
the hall for the whole evening, in fact, no matter what it cost.
Twenty quarts of Mumm's Extra Dry were to be put on ice.
He drew forth three one hundred mark bank-notes, and tossed
them contemptuously to the head-waiter. That cleared the
situation. The functionary in question had a mien at once
official and ingratiating. Two minutes later the hall was
festively lit.

The women appeared, and young men who were parasites
by trade, corrupt boys who looked like consumptive lackeys,
clerks out of a berth in loud, checked clothes—doubtful lives
with a dark past and a darker future. At Gottlieb's Inn
there was never any lack of such. Cordially they insisted
on their long friendship for the giver of the feast. He
remembered not one, but turned no one away.

He sat at the centre of the long table. He had pushed his
hat far back on his head and crossed his legs and gritted his
teeth. His face was as white as the cloth on the table. Im-

pudent songs were sung; they crowed and cried and screeched
and giggled and joked and guzzled and wallowed and smacked
each other; foul stories were told and boastful experiences;
they mounted on chairs and smashed glasses. In half an hour
the bacchanal destroyed all sobriety and reserve. It wasn't
often that a man dropped in, as from the clouds, fairly dripping
with money.

Niels Heinrich presided icily. From time to time he called
out his commands: " Six bottles! A chocolate cake! Nine
bottles Veuve Cliquot! A tray of pastry! " The commands
were swiftly obeyed, and the company yelled and cheered. A
black-haired woman put an arm about his shoulder. Brutally
he thrust her back, but she made no complaint. A fat woman,
excessively rouged and décolletée, held a goblet to his lips.
Rancorously he spat into it, and the applause rattled about
him.

He did not drink. On the wall immediately opposite him
was a gigantic mirror. In it he saw the table and the roisterers.
He also saw the red drapery that covered the wall behind him.
He also saw several little tables that stood against the drapery.
They were unoccupied, save that Christian sat at one. So
through the mirror Niels Heinrich gazed across and shyly
observed that alienated guest, whose silent presence had at
first been noticed, but had now been long forgotten.

At Niels Heinrich's left four men played at cards. They
attracted a public and sympathizers. From time to time Niels
Heinrich threw a couple of gold pieces on the table. He lost
every stake; but always at the same moment he threw down
more gold.

He looked into the mirror and saw himself—colourless, lean,
withered.

He threw down a hundred mark note. " Small stakes, big
winnings! " he boasted. A few of the spectators got between
him and the mirror. " Out of the way! " he roared. " I want
to see that! " Obediently they slunk aside.

He looked into the mirror and beheld Christian, who sat there straight and slender, stirless and tense.

He threw down two more bank notes. " They'll bring back others," he murmured.

And when he looked into the mirror again, he saw a vision in it. It was a human trunk, a virginal body, radiant with an earthly and also with another, with an immortal purity. The scarcely curving breasts with their rosy blossoms had a sweet loveliness of form that filled him with dread and with pain. It was only the trunk: there was no head; there were no limbs. Where the neck ended there was a ring of curdled blood; the dark triangle revealed its mystery below.

Niels Heinrich got up. The chair behind him clattered to the floor. All were silent. " Out with you! " he roared. " Out! Out! " With swinging arms he indicated the door.

The company rose frightened. A few lingered; others thronged toward the door. Beside himself, Niels Heinrich grasped the chair, lifted it far above his head, and stormed toward the loiterers. They scattered; the women screamed and the men growled. Only the gamblers had remained seated, as if the whole incident did not concern them. Niels Heinrich swept with his hand across the tablecloth, and the cards flew in all directions. The gamblers jumped up, determined to resist; but at the sight of their adversary they backed away from him, and one by one strolled from the hall. Immediately thereafter the head-waiter, with a look of well-bred astonishment, came in and presented his bill. Niels Heinrich had sat down on the edge of the table with his back toward the mirror. A thin foam clung to his lips.

He paid the reckoning. The amount of his tip assuaged the deprecation and surprise of the head-waiter. He asked whether the gentleman had any further commands. Niels Heinrich answered that he wanted to drink alone now. He ordered a bottle of the best and some caviare. One of the doll-like waitresses hastened in with the bottle and opened it.

Niels Heinrich emptied a glassful greedily. At the food he shuddered. He ordered the superfluous lights to be turned out; he didn't need so much light. All but a few of the incandescent lamps were darkened, and the hall grew dim. The door was to be closed, he commanded further, and no one was to enter unless he rang. Again he threw gold on the table. He was obeyed in everything.

Suddenly it grew still.

Niels Heinrich still sat on the edge of the table.

Christian said: " That took a long time."

XXX

Niels Heinrich slid from the edge of the table, and began to pace up and down the entire length of the hall. Christian's eyes followed him uninterruptedly.

He had once read in a book, Niels Heinrich said, the story of a French count, who had killed an innocent peasant girl, and had cut the heart out of her breast and cooked and eaten it. And that had given him the power of becoming invisible. Did Christian believe that there was any truth to that story?

Christian answered that he did not.

He, for his part, didn't believe it either, Niels Heinrich said. But it was not to be denied that there was a certain magic in the innocence of virgins. Perhaps they had hidden powers which they communicated to one. It seemed to him this way, that in the guilty there was an instinct that drew them to the guiltless. The thought, then, that underlay the story would be, wouldn't it, that virginity did communicate some hidden powers? Was the gentleman prepared to deny that?

Christian, whose whole attention was given to these questions, answered that he did not deny it.

But the gentleman had asserted that there were none who are guilty? How did these things go together? If there were none who are guilty, then none are guiltless either.

"It is not to be understood in that fashion," Christian answered, conscious of the difficulty, and conscious in every nerve of the strangeness of the place, the hour, and the circumstances. "Guilt and guiltlessness do not sustain the relation of effect and cause. One is not derived from the other. Guilt cannot become innocence nor innocence guilt. Light is light and darkness is darkness, but neither can be transformed into the other, neither can be created by the other. Light issues from some body—fire or the sun or a constellation. Whence does darkness issue? It exists. It has no source; none other than the absence of light."

Niels Heinrich seemed to reflect. Still walking up and down, he flung his words into the air. Every one was made a fool of—every one from his childhood on. There had always been palavering about sin and wrong, and everything had been aimed at giving one an evil conscience. If once you had an evil conscience, no confession or penitence, no parson and no absolution did you any good. And at bottom one was but a wretched creature—a doomed creature, and condemned to damnation from the start. That had convinced him, what the gentleman had said—without looking at Christian, he stretched out his arm and index-finger toward him—oh, that had convinced him, that no one had the right to judge another. That was true. He hadn't ever seen anyone either to whom one could say: you shall pass judgment. Every one bore the mark of shame and of theft and of blood, and was condemned to the same damnation from the beginning. But if there was to be no more judging, that meant the end of bourgeois society and the capitalistic order. For that was founded on courts and on the necessity of finding men to assume its guilt, and judges who were ignorant of mercy.

Christian said: "Won't you stop walking up and down? Won't you come and sit by me? Come here; sit by me."

No, he said, he didn't want to sit by him. He wanted all these matters explained just once. He didn't want to be submissive with his mind like a boy at school. The gentleman was incomprehensible, and was making a fool of him with phrases. Let him give to him, Niels Heinrich, something certain, something by which he could be guided.

"What do you mean by that—something certain?" Christian asked, deeply moved. "I am a man like yourself; I know no more than yourself; like yourself I have sinned and am helpless and puzzled. What is it I shall give you—I?"

"But I?" Niels Heinrich was beside himself. "What shall I give? And you wanted me to give you something! What is it? What can I give you?"

"Don't you feel it?" Christian asked. "Don't you know it yet—not yet?"

Silently they looked into each other's eyes, for Niels Heinrich had stopped walking. A shiver, an almost visible shiver ran down his limbs. His face seemed as though singed by the desire of one who rattles at an iron gate and would be free.

"Listen," he said, suddenly, with a desperate and convulsive calmness, "I stole those pearls in your house. I simply put them into my pocket. One of them I pawned, and made those swine drunk with the money. You can have them back if you want them. Those I can give you. If that's what you want, I can give it to you."

Christian seemed surprised; but the passionate tensity of his face did not relax at all.

Niels Heinrich put his hand into his trousers pocket. The string had been broken, so that his hand was full of the loose pearls. He held it out toward Christian; but Christian did not stir, and made no move to receive the pearls. This seemed to embitter Niels Heinrich strangely. He stretched out his hand until it was flat, and let the pearls roll on the floor. White and shimmering, they rolled on the parquetry. And as Christian still did not stir, Niels Heinrich's rage seemed to increase. He turned his pocket inside out, so that all the rest of the pearls fell on the floor.

"Why do you do that?" Christian asked, more in astonishment than in blame.

"Well, maybe the gentleman wanted a little exercise," was the impudent answer. And again that thin foam, like the white of an egg, clung to his lips.

Christian lowered his eyes. Then this thing happened: he arose and drew a deep breath, smiled, leaned over, dropped on his knees, and began to gather up the pearls. He picked up each one singly, so as not to soil his hands unnecessarily; on his knees he slid over the floor, picking up pearl after pearl. He reached under the table and under the stairs, where spilt wine lay in little puddles, and out of these nauseating little puddles he scratched the pearls. With his right hand he gathered them; and always, when his left hand was half full, he slipped its contents into his pocket.

Niels Heinrich looked down at him. Then his eyes fled from that sight, wandered through the room, found the mirror and fled from it, sought it anew and fled again. For the mirror had become a glow to him. He no longer saw his image in it; the mirror had ceased to reflect images. And again he looked toward the floor where Christian crept, and something monstrous happened in his soul. A stertorous moan issued from his breast. Christian stopped in his occupation, and looked up at him.

He saw and understood. At last! At last! A trembling hand moved forward to meet his own. He took it; it had no life. He had never yet so deeply grasped it all—the body, the spirit, time, eternity. The hand had no warmth: it was the hand of the deed, the hand of crime, the hand of guilt. But when he touched it, for the first time, it began to live and grow warm; a glow streamed into it—glow of the mirror, of service, of insight, of renewal.

It was that touch, that touch alone.

Niels Heinrich, drawn forward, sank upon his knees. In this matter of Joachim Heinzen, he stammered in a barely audible voice, why, one might discuss it, you know. His eyes seemed broken and his features extinguished. And they kneeled—each before the other.

Saved and freed from himself by that touch, the murderer cast his guilt upon the man who judged and did not condemn him.

He was free. And Christian was likewise free.

The hall had a side-exit by which one could leave the house. There they said farewell to each other. Christian knew well where Niels Heinrich was going. He himself returned to Stolpische Street, mounted the stairs to Karen's rooms, locked himself in, lay down as he was, and slept for three and thirty hours.

A vigorous ringing of the bell aroused him.

XXXI

Lorm was sick unto death. He lay in a sanatorium. An intestinal operation had been performed, and there was slight hope of his recovery.

Friends visited him. Emanuel Herbst, most faithful of them all, concealed his pain and fear beneath a changeless mask of fatalistic calm. Since the first day on which he had seen on the face of his beloved friend the first traces of fate's destructive work, the shadow-world of the theatre with all its activities had nauseated him. With the dying of its central fire, he had a presentiment of the approaching end of many things.

Crammon also came often. He loved to talk to Lorm of past days, and Lorm was glad to remember and to smile. He also smiled when he was told how numerous were the inquiries after him; that telegrams came uninterruptedly from all the cities of the land, and showed how profoundly his image and character had affected the heart of the nation. He did not believe it; in his innermost soul he did not believe it. He despised men too deeply.

There was but one human being in whose love he believed. That was Judith. Unswervingly he believed in her love, though each hour might have offered proof of his delusion, each hour of the day in which he expressed the desire to see her, each hour of the night when he controlled his moans of pain not to annoy the ears of paid, strange women.

For Judith came at most for half an hour in the forenoon or for half an hour in the afternoon, tried to conceal her impatient annoyance by overtenderness and artificial eagerness, and said: " Puggie, aren't you going to be well soon? " or " Aren't you ashamed to be so lazy and lie here, while poor Judith longs for you at home? " She filled the sick-room with noise and with futile advice, scolded the nurse, showed the doctor his place, flirted with the consultant physician, chattered of a hundred trivialities—a trip to a health resort, the last cook's latest pilfering, and never lacked reasons with which to palliate the shortness of her stay.

Lorm would confirm these reasons. He had no doubt of any of them; he gave her opportunities to produce them. He was remarkably inventive in making excuses for her when he saw in others' faces astonishment or disapproval of her behaviour. He said: " Don't bother her. She is an airy creature. She has her own way of showing devotion, and her own way of feeling grief. You must not apply ordinary standards."

Crammon said to Letitia: " I didn't know that this Judith was one of those soulless creatures of porcelain. It was always my opinion that the phrases concerning the superior tenderness of the female soul—that's the official expression, isn't it?— constituted one of those myths by which men, the truly more delicate and noble organs of creation, were to be deceived into undue indulgence. But such spiritual coarseness as hers would make a cowboy blush. Go to her and try to stir her conscience. A great artist is leaving us, and his last sigh will be given to a popinjay, who bears his name as a fool might wear the robes of a king. Let her at least appear to do her duty, else she is worthy of being stoned. One should follow the ancient Hindoo custom, and burn her on her husband's pyre. What a pity that these pleasant laws have gone out of use."

When Letitia next saw Judith she reproached her gently. Judith seemed overwhelmed by remorse. " You are quite right, dear child," she answered. " But you see I can't, I just can't bear to be around sick people. They always seem to wear a mask; they don't seem to be the same people at all; and there's such a terrible odour. They remind one of the most frightful thing in the world—of death. You'll reply, of course, that he's my husband, my own husband. That makes it all the worse. It creates a tragic conflict for me. One should rather have pity on me than accuse me of things. He hasn't the right to demand that I do violence to my nature, and as a matter of fact, he doesn't. He's far too subtle and too magnanimous. It's only other people who do. Well, what do they know about us? What do they know of our married life? What do they know of my sacrifices? What do they know of a woman's heart? And furthermore "—she went on hastily, becoming aware of Letitia's inner estrangement from her—" so many things are happening just now, so many horrid things. My father has just arrived. I haven't seen him since my marriage to Imhof. Do you know, by the way, that Imhof is dying? They say, too, that he's utterly ruined. I have been spared a great deal; but wouldn't it make you think that it is unlucky to love me? Why do you suppose that is? My life is as harmless as the playing of a little girl, and yet. . . . Why do you suppose it is? " She wrinkled her forehead and shivered. " Well, my father is here. There will be an interview—he, Wolfgang, and I. And oh, my dear, it's such a hideous affair that has to be discussed."

" It concerns Christian, doesn't it? " Letitia asked, and it was the first time that she had uttered his name in Judith's presence. She had forgotten again and again; she had aban-

doned her purpose over and over. She had felt Judith's
mysterious spite and hate against her brother, and had not had
the courage to face it. Always something more important and
more amusing had seemed to appear on the gay stage of life.
Now she repeated hesitantly: " It concerns Christian, doesn't
it? "

Judith lapsed into sombre silence.

But from that hour Letitia was tormented by a secret
curiosity, and this curiosity forbade forgetfulness. She had
lost her way. Oh, she had lost her way long ago, and daily
she stumbled farther into the pathless wild. Lost, confused,
entangled,—thus did she seem to herself, and she had many
minutes of a fleeting melancholy. All the things that happened
in her life became too much for her, and yet all the trivialities
of the day disappeared as water does in sand, leaving no form,
no echo, no purpose. And in these moments of her sadness,
she had the illusion of a new beginning, and yearned for a
hand to lead her forth from these thickets of her life. She
remembered that far night when her full heart had been rejected, and nursed the ecstatic dream that now, when it was
used up and a little weary, it might find acceptance.

But she delayed and played with the vision in her mind.
And then she had a dream. She dreamed that she was in the
lobby of a magnificent hotel among many people; but she
was clothed only in her shift, and could scarcely move for
shame. No one appeared to observe this. She wanted to flee,
but saw no door at all. While she looked about her in her
misery, the lift suddenly came down from the upper storeys.
She rushed into it and the door closed and the lift rose. But
her dread did not leave her, and she had a sense of approaching
disaster. Voices from without came to her: " There is some
one dead—dead in the house." To stop the lift, she groped for
the electric button, but she could not find it. The lift rose
higher and higher, and the voices died away. Without knowing
how she had come there, she stood in a long corridor along

which were the doors of many rooms. In one of the rooms lay a crucifix about two yards long; it was of bronze covered with a patina. She went in, and men moved respectfully aside. Now suddenly she was clothed in a garment of white satin. She kneeled down beside the crucifix. Someone said: " It is one o'clock, we must go to luncheon." Her heart was like a wound with compassion and yearning. She pressed her lips against the forehead of the image of Christ. The metal body stirred and grew and grew, and assumed the stature of life; and she, more and more tenderly giving herself, infused blood into the image, and gave its skin the colour of life, so that even the wounds of the nails flushed red. Her feeling rose to an ardent pitch of gratitude and adoration. She encircled the body and the feet of the rising Christ, who lifted her as he rose. But one of the gentlemen said: " The gong is sounding for the last call to table." And at that she awoke.

Next morning she went to Crammon, and persuaded him to drive with her to Stolpische Street.

XXXII

When Christian opened the door, his father stood before him. It was he who had rung the bell.

The emotion which this unexpected sight aroused in him was so restrained in its expression that the Privy Councillor's eyes lost their brief brightness and grew dark again.

" May one enter? " he asked, and crossed the threshold.

He walked to the middle of the room, placed his hat on the table, and looked about him with astonishment held in check. It was better than he had imagined and also worse. It was cleaner, more respectable, more habitable; it was also more lonely and desolate. " So this is where you live," he said.

" Yes, this is where I live," Christian repeated, with some embarrassment. " Here and in a room across the court I have lived until now. These were Karen's rooms."

" Why do you say until now? Are you planning to move again? "

Since Christian hesitated to answer, the Privy Councillor, not without embarrassment in his turn, went on: " You must forgive me for coming upon you so suddenly. I could not know whether you would consent to such an explanation as has become necessary, and so I made no announcement of my coming. You will understand that this step was not an easy one to take."

Christian nodded. " Won't you sit down? " he asked, courteously.

" Not yet, if you don't mind. There are things that cannot be discussed while one is sitting still. They have not been thought out in that posture either." The Privy Councillor opened his fur-coat. His attitude was one of superiority and dignity. His silvery, carefully trimmed beard contrasted picturesquely with the silky blackness of his fur.

There was an oppressive pause. " Is mother well? " Christian asked.

The Privy Councillor's face twitched. The conventional tone of the question made it seem frivolous to him.

Worn out for a moment by this dumb summons to laws of life that had lost their content and their meaning for him, Christian said: " Will you permit me to withdraw for five minutes? I had been sleeping when you rang. I think it was a sleep of many hours, and in my clothes, too, so I must wash. And I want also to beg you to take along a little package for mother. It contains an object that she values. I'm sorry that I haven't the right to explain more fully. Perhaps, if you desire, she will give you the explanation herself, since the whole matter now belongs to the past. So pardon me for a few minutes; I shall be at your service almost immediately."

He went into the adjoining room. The Privy Councillor looked after him with consternation in his large, blue eyes.

While he was alone, he did not stir nor move a muscle of his body.

Christian re-entered. He had bathed his face and combed his hair. He gave the Privy Councillor a little package tied with a cord. On the white paper wrapping he had written: " For my mother. Gratefully returned on the day of final parting. One piece is lacking through the force of unavoidable circumstances; its value has been made up to me a thousandfold. Greeting and farewell. Christian."

The Privy Councillor read the words. " More riddles? " he asked, coldly. " Why riddles on a placard? Have you not time to write a letter? Your ways were more courtly once."

" Mother will understand," Christian replied.

" And have you no other message for her? "

" None."

" May I ask the meaning of these words: ' on the day of final parting ' ? You referred once before to departure. . . ."

" It would be more practical, perhaps, if you first told me the purpose of your visit."

" You have still your old technique of evasion."

" You are mistaken," said Christian. " I am not trying to evade at all. You come to me like an enemy and you speak like one. I suspect you have come to try to arrange something in the nature of a pact between us. Wouldn't it be simpler if you were frankly to state your proposals? It may be that our intentions coincide. You want all to be rid of me, I suppose. I believe that I can remove myself from your path."

" It is so indeed," the Privy Councillor said, with a rigid and aimless glance. " The situation will brook no further delay. Your brother feels himself trammelled and menaced in his vital interests. You are a source of offence and anger to your sister. Although she has herself left the appointed way, she feels your eccentricity like a deformity of her flesh. Kinsmen of every degree declare the name and honour of the family defiled and demand action. I shall not speak of your mother, nor should I speak of myself. You cannot be ignorant of the fact that you have struck at me where I was most vulnerable. I have been urged to use force, but I have resisted. Force is painful and futile, and merely recoils against him who uses it. Your plan of simply disappearing—I do not know who mentioned it first—has many advantages. Other continents offer a more grateful soil for ideas so obviously abstruse as your own. It would be easy for you to change the mere scene of your activities, and it would free us from a constant nightmare."

"To disappear—that is precisely my intention," Christian said. "I used that very word to myself. If you had come yesterday, I should probably not have been able to give you as complete satisfaction as I can do to-day. Events have so shaped themselves, however, that we find ourselves at the same point at the same time."

"Since I do not know what events you mean, I cannot, to my regret, follow you," the Privy Councillor said, icily.

Without regarding the interruption, Christian continued, with his vision lost in space. "It is, however, rather difficult to disappear. In our world it is a difficult task. It means to renounce one's very personality, one's home, one's friends, and last of all one's very name. That is the hardest thing of all, but I shall try to do it."

Roused to suspicion by his easy victory, the Privy Councillor asked: "And is that what you meant by your final parting?"

"It was."

"And whither have you determined to go?"

"It is not clear to me yet. It is better for you not to know."

"And you will go without means, in shameful dependence and poverty?"

"Without means and in poverty. Not in dependence."

"Folly!"

" What can hard words avail to-day, father? "

" And is this an irrevocable necessity? "

" Yes, irrevocable."

" And also the parting between ourselves and you? "

" It is you who desire it; it has become a necessity to me."

The Privy Councillor fell silent. Only a gentle swaying of his trunk gave evidence that inwardly he was a broken man. Up to this moment he had nursed a hope; he had not believed in the inevitable. He had followed a faint beam of light, which had now vanished and left him in the darkness. His heart crumbled in a vain love for the son who had faced him with an inevitability which he could not comprehend. And all that he had conquered in this world—power, wealth, honours, a golden station in a realm of splendour—suddenly became to him frightfully meaningless and desolate.

Once more he heard Christian's clear and gentle voice. " You wanted to fetter me through my inheritance; you sought to buy me with it. I came to see that one must escape that snare. One must break even with the love of those who proclaim: ' You are ours, our property, and must continue what we have begun.' I could not be your heir; I could not continue what you had begun, so I was in a snare. All whom I knew lived in delight and all lived in guilt; yet though there was so much guilt, no one was guilty. There was, in fact, a fundamental mistake in the whole structure of life. I said to myself: the guilt that arises from what men do is small and scarcely comparable to the guilt that arises from what they fail to do. For what kinds of men are those, after all, who become guilty through their deeds? Poor, wretched, driven, desperate, half-mad creatures, who lift themselves up and bite the foot that treads them under. Yet they are made responsible and held guilty and punished with endless torments. But those who are guilty through failure in action are spared and are always secure, and have ready and reasonable subterfuges and excuses; yet they are, so far as I can see, the true criminals. All evil comes from them. That was the snare I had to escape."

The Privy Councillor struggled for an expression of his confused and painful feelings. It was all so different from anything he had expected. A human being spoke to him— a man. Words came to him to which he had to reconcile himself. They held the memory of recent and unhealed wounds that had been dealt him. Arguments refused to come to him. It was false and it was true. It depended on one's attitude— on one's measure of imagination and willingness to see, on one's insight or fear, on one's stubbornness or one's courage to render an accounting to oneself. The ground which had long been swaying under his feet seemed suddenly to show huge cracks and fissures. The pride of his caste still tried in that last moment to raise barricades and search for weapons, but its power was spent.

Without hope of a favourable answer, he asked: " And do not the bonds of blood exist for you any longer? "

" When you stand before me and I see you, I feel that they exist," was the answer. " When you speak and act, I feel them no longer."

" Can there be such a thing as an accounting between father and son? "

" Why not? If sincerity and truth are to prevail, why not? Father and son must begin anew, it seems to me, and as equals. They must cease to depend on what has been, on what has been formulated and is prescribed by use. Every mature consciousness is worthy of respect. The relation must become a more delicate one than any other, since it is more vulnerable; but because nature created it, men believe that it will bear boundless burdens without breaking. It was necessary for me to ease it of some burdens, and you regarded that action as a sin. It is only worldly ideas that have chilled and blinded you to me."

" Am I chilled and blinded? " The Privy Councillor's voice was very low. " Does it seem so to you? "

" Yes, since I renounced your wealth, it has been so. You have constantly been tempted to use all the force you control against me. You face me now with the demands of an affronted authority; and all that, simply because I dared to break with the views of property and acquisition current in the class in which I grew up. On the one hand, you did not venture to violate my freedom, because in addition to social and external considerations, you were conscious of a relation between your heart and mine. I am afraid that prejudice and custom had more to do with sustaining that relation than insight and sympathy; but it exists, and I respect it. On the other hand, you were unable to escape the influences of your surroundings and your worldly station, and so you assumed that I was guilty of ugly and foolish and aimless things. What are these ugly and foolish and aimless things that you think me concerned with? And how do they hinder you and disturb you, even granting their ugliness and folly and futility? Wherein do they disturb Judith or Wolfgang, except in a few empty notions and fancied advantages? And yet if it were more than that— would that little more count? No, it would not count. No annoyance that they might suffer through me would really count. And how have I wounded you, as you say, and affronted your authority? I am your son and you are my father; does that mean serf and lord? I am no longer of your world; your world has made me its adversary. Son and adversary—only that combination will ever change your world. Obedience without conviction—what is it? The root of all evil. You do not truly see me; the father no longer sees the son. The world of the sons must rise up against the world of the fathers, if any change is to be wrought."

He had sat down at the table and rested his head upon his hands. He had suddenly abandoned the uses of society and his own conventional courtesy. His words had risen from sobriety to passion; his face was pale, and his eyes had a fevered glow. The Privy Councillor, who had believed him incapable of such outbursts and such transformations, gazed down at him rigidly. " These assertions are difficult to refute," he murmured, as he buttoned his fur-coat with trembling fingers. " And what shall a debate avail us at this hour? You spoke of those who fail through not doing. What will you do? It would mean much to me to hear that from you. What will you do, and what have you done hitherto? "

" Until now it was all a mere preparation," Christian said more calmly. " Closely looked upon, it was nothing; it was something only as measured by my powers and ability. I still cling too much to the surface. My character has been against me; I do not succeed in breaking the crust that separates me from the depth. The depth—ah, what is that really? It is impossible to discuss it; every word is forwardness and falsehood. I wish to perform no works, to accomplish nothing good or useful or great. I want to sink, to steep, to hide, to bury myself in the life of man. I care nothing for myself, I would know nothing of myself. But I would know everything about human beings, for they, you see, they are the mystery and the terror, and all that torments and affrights and causes suffering. . . . To go to one, always to a single one, then to the next, and to the third, and know and learn and reveal and take his suffering from him, as one takes out the vitals of a fowl. . . . But it is impossible to talk about it; it is too terrrible. The great thing is to guard against weariness of the heart. The heart must not grow weary—that is the supreme matter. And what I shall do first of all you know," he ended with a winning, boyish smile, " I shall vanish."

" It would be a kind of death," said the Privy Councillor.

" Or another kind of life," Christian replied. " Yes, that is quite the right name for it and also its purpose—to create another kind of life. For this," he arose, and his eyes burned, " this way of life is unendurable. Yours is unendurable."

The Privy Councillor came closer. " And surely, surely you will go on living? That anxiety need not torment me too, need it? "

" Oh," Christian said, vividly and serenely, " I must. What are you thinking of? I must live! "

" You speak of it with a cheerfulness, and I . . . and we . . . Christian! " the Privy Councillor cried in his despair. " I had none but you! Do you not know it? Did you not? I have no one but you. What is to happen now, and what is to be done? "

Christian stretched out his hand toward his father, who took it with the gesture of a broken man. With a mighty effort he controlled himself. " If it be inevitable, let us not drag it out," he said. " God guard you, Christian. In reality I never knew you; I do not now. It is hard to be forced to say: ' I had a firstborn son; he lives and has died to me.' But I shall submit. I see that there is something in you to which one must submit. But perhaps the day will come when that something within you will not utterly suffice; perhaps you will demand something more. Well, I am sixty-two; it would avail me little. God guard you, Christian."

Restrained, erect, he turned to go.

XXXIII

Amadeus Voss said: " He will not enter upon the conflict. He has been placed before the final choice. You think: ' Oh, it is only his family that would make him submit and conform.' But the family is to-day the decisive factor of power in the state. It is the cornerstone and keystone of millennial stratifications and crystallizations. He who defies it is outlawed; he has nowhere to lay his head. He is placed in a perpetual position of criminality, and that wears down the strongest."

" His people seem to have made a considerable impression on you," Lamprecht remarked.

" I discuss a principle and you speak of persons," Voss replied, irritably. " Refute me on my own ground, if you don't mind. As a matter of fact, I saw no one face to face except Wahnschaffe's brother, Wolfgang. He invited me, ostensibly to obtain information, but in fact to test me. A remarkable chap; representative to the last degree. He is penetrated by the unshakable seriousness of those who have counted every rung of the social ladder and measured all social distances to a millimetre. Ready for anything; venal through and through; stopping at nothing; cruel by nature, and consistent through lack of mind. I don't deny the impressiveness of such an extraordinarily pure type. You can't image a better object lesson of all that constitutes the society of the period."

" And, of course, you took Christian's part, and declared that you were unapproachable and unbribable for diplomatic services? " Johanna asked, in a tone of subtle carelessness. " Or didn't you? " She walked up and down in order to lay the board for Christian, whom she yearned for with a deep impatience.

Michael did not take his eyes from the face of Amadeus Voss.

" I never dreamed of such folly," Amadeus answered. " My occupation is research, not moralizing. I have ceased sacrificing myself to phantoms. I no longer believe in ideas or in the victory of ideas. So far as I am concerned, the battle has been decided, and peace has been made. Why should I not admit it frankly? I have made a pact with things as they are. Do not call it cynicism; it is an honest confession of my sincere self. It is the fruit of the insight I have gained into the useful, the effective, into all that helps man actually and tangibly. There was no necessity in the wide world for me to become a martyr. Martyrs confuse the world; they tear open the hell of our agonies, and do so quite in vain. When or where has pain ever been assuaged or healed through pain? Once upon a time I went the way of sighs and the way of the cross; I know what it means to suffer for dreams and spill one's blood for the unattainable; breast to breast have I wrestled with Satan till at last it became clear to me: you can strip him off only if you give yourself to the world wholly and without chaffering. Nor must you look back, or, like Lot's wife, you will be turned into a pillar of salt. Thus I overcame the devil, or, if you prefer, myself."

"It was, to say the least, a very weighty and significant transformation," said Johanna, cutting the buns in half and buttering them. Her gestures were of an exquisitely calculated ease and charm.

"And what did you finally say to Wolfgang Wahnschaffe?" asked Botho von Thüngen. He sat beside the window, and from time to time looked out into the yard, for in him too there was a deep desire for Christian's presence. In each of them was a dark feeling of his nearness.

"I told him just about what I think," Voss answered. "I said: 'The best thing you can do is to let everything take its natural course. He will be entangled in his own snares. Resistance offers support, persecution creates aureoles. Why should you want to crown him with an aureole? A structure of paradoxes must be permitted to fall of its own weight. All the visions of Saint Anthony have not the converting power of one instant of real knowledge. There must be no wall about him and no bridge for his feet; then he will want to erect walls and build bridges. Have patience,' I said, 'have patience. I who was the midwife of his soul on the road of conversion may take it upon myself to prophesy; and I prophesy that the day is not far off when he will lust after a woman's lips.' For this, I confess, was the thing that mainly gave me pause—this life without Eros. And it was not satiety, no, it was not, but a true and entire renunciation. But let Eros once awaken, and he will find his way back. Nor is the day far off." His face had a look of fanatical certitude.

"It will be another Eros, not him you name," said Thüngen.

Then Michael arose, looked upon Voss with burning eyes, and cried out to him: " Betrayer! ".

Amadeus Voss gave a start. " Eh, little worm, what's gotten into you? " he murmured, contemptuously.

" Betrayer! " Michael said.

Voss approached him with a threatening gesture.

" Michael! Amadeus! " Johanna admonished, beseechingly, and laid her hand on Voss's arm.

And while she did so, the door was opened softly, and the little Stübbe girl slipped silently into the room. She was neatly dressed as always. Her two blond braids were wound about her head and made her pain-touched child's face seem even older and more madonna-like. She looked about her, and when she caught sight of Michael, she went up to him and handed him a letter. Thereupon she left the room again.

Michael unfolded the letter and read it, and all the colour left his face. It slipped from his hand. Lamprecht picked it up. " Does it concern us too? " he asked, with a clear presentiment. " Is it from him? "

Michael nodded and Lamprecht read the letter aloud: " Dear Michael:—I take this way of saying farewell to you, and beg you to greet our friends. I must go away from here now, and you will not receive any news of me. Let no one try to seek me out. It seemed simpler and more useful to me to depart in this way than to put off and confuse the unavoidable by explanations and questions. I have taken with me the few things of mine that were in Karen's rooms. They all went into a little travelling bag. What remains you can pack into the box in the other room; there are a few necessities— some linen and a suit of clothes. Perhaps I shall find it possible to have these sent after me, but it is uncertain. For you, Michael, I am sending one thousand marks to Lamprecht, in order that your instruction may be continued for a time; it may also serve in time of need. Johanna will find in the house-agent's care to-morrow, when I shall send it, an envelope

containing two hundred and fifty marks. Perhaps she will
be kind enough to use this money to satisfy a few obligations
that I leave behind. Once more: Greet our friends. Cling
to them. Farewell. Be brave. Think of Ruth. Your
Christian Wahnschaffe."

They had all arisen and grouped themselves about Lamprecht. Shaken to the soul, Lamprecht spoke: "I am his,
now and in future, in heart and mind."

"What is the meaning of it, and what the reason?" Thüngen
asked, in the shy stillness.

"Exactly like Wahnschaffe," Voss's voice was heard. "Flat
and wooden as a police regulation."

"Be silent," Johanna breathed at him, in her soul's pain.
"Be silent, Judas!"

No other word was said. They all stood about the table, but
the place that had been laid for Christian remained empty.
Twilight was beginning to fall, and one after another they
went away. Amadeus Voss approached Johanna, and said:
"That word you spoke to me, following the boy's example,
will burn your soul yet, I promise you."

Michael, rapt from the things about him, looked upward
with visionary, gleaming eyes.

In weary melancholy Johanna said to herself: "How runs
the stage-direction in the old comedies? Exit. Yes, exit.
Short and sweet. Exit Johanna. Go your ways." She threw
a last look around the dim room, and, lean and shadowy, was
the last to slip through the door.

XXXIV

When, two days later, Letitia and Crammon arrived in
Stolpische Street, they were told that Christian Wahnschaffe
was no longer there. Both flats had been cleared of furniture
and were announced as to let. Nor could any one give them
any light on whither he had gone or where he was. The

house-agent said he had told his acquaintances that he was leaving the city. To Crammon's discomfort, a little crowd of people gathered around the motor car, and jeering remarks were heard.

" Too late," Letitia said. " I shall never forgive myself."

" Oh, yes, you will, my child, you will," Crammon assured her; and they returned to the realms of pleasure.

Letitia forgave herself that very evening. And what could she have done with so questionable a burden on her conscience? It was but a venial sin. The first tinkle of a glass, the first twang of a violin, the first fragrance of a flower obliterated it.

But at Crammon that neglect and lateness gnawed more and more and not less. In his naïve ignorance he imagined that he could have prevented that extreme step, had he but come two days earlier. Now his loss was sealed and final. He fancied that he might have laid his hand on Christian's shoulder and given him an earnest and admonishing look, and that Christian, put to shame, might have spoken: " Yes, Bernard, you are right. It was all a mistake. Let us send for a bottle of wine, and consider how we may spend the future most amusingly."

Whenever, like a collector who examines his enviously guarded treasures, Crammon turned over his memories of life, it was always the figure of Christian that arose before him in a kind of apotheosis. It was the Christian of the early days, and he only—amid the dogs in the park, in the moonlit nights under the plantain, in the exquisite halls of the dancer, Christian laughing, laughing more beautifully than the muleteer of Cordova, Christian the seductive, the extravagant, the lord of life—Eidolon.

Thus he saw him. Thus he carried his image through time.

And rumours came to him which he did not believe. People appeared who had heard it said that Christian Wahnschaffe had been seen during the great catastrophe in the mines of Hamm. He had gone down into the shafts and helped bring up the bodies of men. Others came who asserted that he was living in the East End of London, in the companionship of the lowest and most depraved; and again others pretended to know that he had been seen in the Chinese quarter of New York.

Crammon said: "Nonsense, it isn't Christian. It's his double."

He was afraid of the grey years that drew nearer like fogs over the face of the waters.

"What would you say to a little house in some valley of the Carinthian Alps?" he asked Letitia one day. "A quaint and modest little house. You plant your vegetables and grow your roses and read your favourite books, in a word, you are secure and at peace."

"Charming," answered Letitia, "I'd love to visit you now and then."

"Why now and then? Why not make it your abiding place?"

"But would you take in the twins, too, and the servants and auntie?"

"I'm afraid that would require a special wing. Impossible."

"And furthermore . . .   I must confess to you that Egon Rochlitz and I have come to an agreement. We're going to be married. That would be one more person."

Crammon was silent for a while. Then he said irritably: "I give you my curse. You offer me no alternative."

With a smile Letitia offered him her cheek.

He kissed her with paternal reserve, and said: "Your skin is as velvety as the skin of an apricot."

LEGEND

IN ancient times there lived a king named Saldschal who had a very ill-favoured daughter. Her skin was rough and hard as that of a tiger, and the hair of her head like the mane of a horse. This vexed the king's spirit sorely, and he caused her to be educated in the innermost chambers of the palace, hidden from the eyes of men. When she had grown up, and her marriage had to be thought of, the king said to his minister: " Seek out and bring to me a poor, wandering noble-man." The minister sought and found such a nobleman. Him the king led to a lonely place, and spoke: " I have a repulsively ill-favoured daughter. Will you take her for your wife, because she is the daughter of a king? " The youth kneeled and made answer: " I shall obey my lord." So those two were made man and wife, and the king gave them a house and closed it with sevenfold doors, and said to his son-in-law: " Whenever you leave the house, lock the doors and carry the key upon your person." And in this the youth was also obedient.

Now one day he and other nobles were bidden to a feast. The other guests came in the company of their wives. But the king's son-in-law came alone, and the people marvelled greatly. " Either," they said one to another, " the wife of this man is so comely and delightful that he hides her from jealousy, or she is so ill-favoured that he fears to show her." To resolve their doubts, they determined to make their way into the house of the man. They caused him to be drunken and robbed him of his keys, and when he lay in a stupor they set out toward his dwelling.

While these things happened, the woman had grievous

thoughts in her lonely captivity. "Of what sin can I be guilty," she asked herself, "that my husband despises me and lets me dwell woefully in this place, where I see neither the sun nor the moon?" And furthermore she thought: "The Victorious and Perfect is present in His world. He is the refuge and redeemer of all who suffer pain and grief. I shall bow down from afar before the Victorious and Perfect. Think of me in thy mercy," she prayed, "and appear visibly before me, and, if so it be possible, in this hour." The Victorious and Perfect, who knew that the thoughts of the king's daughter were pure and filled with the deepest reverence, raised her into His dwelling and showed her His head, which has the hue of lapis lazuli. And when the king's daughter beheld the head of the Victorious and Perfect, she was filled with a very great joy, and her mind was wholly cleansed. And in her purified estate it came to pass that her hair grew soft and became the colour of lapis lazuli. Thereupon the Victorious and Perfect showed her His face entire and unconcealed. At that the joy of the king's daughter grew so great that her own face became comely and delightful, and every trace of ugliness and coarseness vanished. But when at last the Victorious and Perfect showed her the golden radiance of His majestic body, the devout ecstasy felt by the king's daughter caused her own body to be changed to a perfection so divine that nothing comparable to it could be found in all the world. In all His splendour the Victorious and Perfect appeared before her; her joyous faith reached its utmost height, and her inner-most being became like to the soul of an angel.

And then came the men who desired to see her, and opened the doors and entered in, and beheld a miracle of beauty. And they said, one to another: "He did not bring the woman with him, because she is so beautiful." They returned to the feast, and made fast the key to the man's girdle. When he awakened from his drunkenness, and went to his house and beheld his wife, and saw that she was incomparable for beauty

among women, he marvelled and asked: " How has it happened
that you, who were so ill-favoured, have become comely and
delightful? " She answered: " I became thus after I had seen
the Victorious and Perfect. Go and relate this thing to my
father." The man went and told this matter to the king. But
the king replied: " Speak to me not of such things. Hasten
to your house, and close it fast so that she may not escape."
The son-in-law said: " She is like a goddess." Whereupon
the king said: " If it be so in truth, lead her to me." And
greatly marvelling, he received the beautiful one in the inner
chambers of his palace. Then he betook him to the place
where is the seat of the Victorious and Perfect, and bowed
down before Him and worshipped Him.

THE END